Leonore's Suite

A Novel

Mary Beth Klee

Copyright © 2019 by Mary Beth Klee

All rights reserved
Printed in the United States of America
Revised Edition 2020

Book Design by Eileen Klee Sweeney

Hardcover ISBN: 978-1-7340920-0-4
Softcover ISBN: 978-1-7340920-1-1

Clio Publishing, Hanover, New Hampshire 03755

To my mother, Leonore Agnes Iserson Klee
(1928-1996)
Internee and Inspiration

and to

Mary Louella Cleland Hedrick
The best friend a girl ever had

Table of Contents

Preface

Part One	Mañana Came (Jan 1942-Sep 25, 1943)	1
Chapter 1	IJA	3
Chapter 2	First Night	13
Chapter 3	The Gate	25
Chapter 4	Side-By-Side	41
Chapter 5	Leonore's Suite	57
Chapter 6	Lulu	69
Chapter 7	Operation Arigato	79
Chapter 8	Super Girl	93
Chapter 9	Southern Cross	103
Chapter 10	Halo-Halo	121
Chapter 11	O Holy Night	129
Chapter 12	Spread Your Wings	139
Chapter 13	Purple Smudge on the Pearl	149
Chapter 14	Return to Oz	163
Chapter 15	Starlight Arena	177
Chapter 16	Lessons from Ovid	191
Chapter 17	The Locust Rule	203
Chapter 18	Going to Goa	215
Part Two	Our Daily Bread (Sep 26, 1943-Feb 3, 1945)	229
Chapter 19	Bread of Life	231
Chapter 20	Shall We Dance?	243
Chapter 21	The Tempest	253
Chapter 22	Undanced Dance	265
Chapter 23	Comfort Kids	273
Chapter 24	Prison Camp Number One	287
Chapter 25	Curve Ball	295
Chapter 26	Advantageous to Our Growth	307

Chapter 27 Unusual Skills	319
Chapter 28 Abiko	327
Chapter 29 Mass at the Museum	337
Chapter 30 Wings	349
Chapter 31 Hope Returned	363
Chapter 32 Spot Search	377
Chapter 33 Christmas Concert	389
Chapter 34 Roll Out the Barrel	403
Part 3 This is More Like It! (Feb 3, 1945-April 1945)	413
Chapter 35 Too Damn Big	415
Chapter 36 A Fine Fellow	423
Chapter 37 Get Strong	433
Chapter 38 Smoke on the Waters	441
Chapter 39 The Second Coming	449
Chapter 40 Choose Life	461
Chapter 41 Birdseye View	467
Chapter 42 Keepsakes	477
Chapter 43 Victory Rolls	489
Chapter 44 Not Before Lunch	499
Chapter 45 Call Me Al	507
Chapter 46 The Road Less Traveled	521
Chapter 47 Roar Like a Lion	533
Chapter 48 Man Overboard	547
Chapter 49 The Golden Gate	559
Epilogue	569
Author's Note	577
Acknowledgments	583
Chapter Notes	589
Bibliography	645

Preface

Leonore's Suite is a work of historical fiction inspired, but not constrained, by true events. This novel, the fruit of a decade of research, is intended primarily for the descendants and friends of Leonore Iserson Klee. I tried to walk with young Lee through her thirty-seven months of captivity in the Philippines, asking how the pampered young ex-pat (thirteen-and-a-half at the time of capture) became the strong and driven woman that she was. Lee saw Santo Tomas Internment Camp as the crucible of her life—so much so that even her headstone bears her POW medal.

In these pages I may have given the reader more detail than he or she wishes to know. Much of it is quotidian, but the day-to-day experience of Santo Tomas is so counter-intuitive and so quickly fading from our grasp, that I have assumed Lee's children, grandchildren, and great-grandchildren might like to understand more, rather than less, about this rich tapestry.

The Author's Note at the end clarifies key elements of truth and fiction in the novel, and the Chapter Notes do so in detail, but Lee Iserson and her best friend, Mary Louella Cleland—along with many other characters in these pages—were real Americans interned by the Japanese in Manila's Santo Tomas Internment Camp between 1942 and 1945. As teens, they came of age under adverse and very unusual circumstances. As adults, they never ceased to marvel at how profoundly their experience had shaped them.

* * *

A note on the historical circumstances framing their capture: In December 1941, the Philippine Islands were American territory. This western Pacific archipelago of more than seven thousand islands had been colonized by Spain in the sixteenth century, but when U.S. Commodore George Dewey sailed his squadron into Manila Bay during the Spanish-American War, that era ended. Dewey destroyed the colonial fleet and in 1898, Spain ceded the Philippines to the United States.

Newly installed Governor-General William Howard Taft made sure the seaside capital got a face lift. Manila's spectacular setting, along with new bridges, roads, parks, and waterways earned the city its nickname, "Pearl of the Orient." Formidable U.S. military bases were erected as well. By 1941, as many as ten-thousand American expats lived and did business in the Philippines under the protection of the U.S. government. Douglas MacArthur, commander of U.S. Army Forces in the Far East, worked closely with Filipino President, Manuel Quezon to ensure the islands' safety, and an eventual transition to an independent future.

As tensions mounted with Japan in the fall of 1941, General MacArthur scrambled to plot Philippine defense. He was taken by surprise on December 8, 1941, when nine hours after the attack on Pearl Harbor, the Japanese trained their might on American military bases in the Philippines. These were the U.S. outposts closest to Japan. Rising Sun bombers pummeled American planes at Manila's Clark Air Base and Nichols Field, forced the evacuation of the U.S. Navy's Asiatic Fleet at Cavite and Subic Bay, then mounted an unexpected land invasion from Lingayen Gulf in the north.

By Christmas 1941, General Douglas MacArthur's outnumbered forces decided to evacuate Manila, declaring it an "Open City." MacArthur wanted to spare the city's residents a blood-bath by allowing the Japanese to simply take the city, while he fought for Philippine liberation from the island of Corregidor and the peninsula of Bataan. On December 26, thousands of American civilians trapped in Manila watched their own forces march out, and—on January 2, 1942—they watched the Japanese march in.

Leonore's Suite

Part One
MAÑANA CAME

October 28, 1941
690 Taft Ave.
Manila, P.I.

Dear Francis,

It is almost one year since I was honored with a letter from you so I thought I would try again and maybe have a little better success.

Since the last time I wrote (without answer) a lot of things have happened. We have had four blackouts. The time has increased for each one, from the first blackout of 50 minutes to the last of two hours. In each, the sirens blew, the street lights went out, traffic was stopped, cigarettes put out, and house lights went off. We have had air raid drills too. During air raid drills the siren rings about noon and every place with 75 or more people in it stirs. People file in orderly lines to basement cellars, or in some cases, bomb shelters. In school, all classes are disturbed and everyone goes to the first floor.

Daddy says these safety drills are necessary, but late, because in the Philippines people put off worry and planning until tomorrow. "Mañana," we say. We will do the work, but tomorrow. Disaster won't come today, perhaps mañana. But, Francis: what if mañana came?

Please write soon, and if possible, send snapshots. Hopefully yours.

Your loving cousin,
Lee I.

Chapter 1
I. J. A.

Manila, January 6, 1942

I went off to prison in a Cadillac.

When I saw that shiny, black limo pull up outside our Taft Avenue apartment building, an electric jolt shot through me. Was this our jailor's pick-up truck? Just weeks before, that gleaming Caddie probably sped Americans in evening gowns and dinner jackets to Christmas parties at the Manila Hotel. Now here it was again, curbside in the red haze of a beastly hot morning. Its toothy, chrome grille smiled at me, and its fenders bulged like black angel wings. But would it speed us to our doom? My heart hammered and for a second, my chest tightened painfully.

"Let's go, Lee." My mother's no-nonsense tone jerked me into the present.

Well, at least the waiting was over: at thirteen-and-a half, I specialized in impatience. I was first out the door and onto the sidewalk, straw suitcase in hand.

"Put here! Put here!" a Japanese officer barked, slashing his curved sword from my suitcase to the rounded trunk of the Caddie. The tip of his saber just missed my leg. I almost barked right back at him, but Mommy darted forward and whisked the little *maleta* from my hands and into the trunk.

Another soldier with round glasses gestured and shouted something I took to mean: "In, in, in!" Mohair scratched the backs of my thighs as I slid across the seat. Whose limo was this, anyway? My mother and eleven-year-old sister Betty slid in next to me, Betty clutching her small stuffed bear.

If I hadn't been so terrified, the whole situation would have seemed funny. No open convoy truck or soot-covered bus for the American Family Iserson. Instead, a seven-passenger limo—Cadillac's 1942 model with rounded headlamps, white-walled tires, and posh mohair seats. We were going off to prison in style.

Kay and Harry Hodges, our neighbors, squeezed onto the bench seat alongside us. Then came a British family of four, the unshaven dad smelling of gin. Our captors tossed in six suitcases that didn't fit in the trunk. Finally, the three Japanese soldiers crammed into the front seat, completing our sardine arrangement. Where were they taking us?

"Snug for twelve, isn't it?" Kay drawled. Her southern accent and attempt at humor soothed despite our circumstances.

"Let's hope we don't have far to go." My mother placed her chin close to my ear and spoke with forced lightness. "Daddy will be sorry to have missed this part."

A knot loosened in my stomach. Daddy loved Cadillacs, but he was a thousand miles away in the tiny town of Zamboanga on the southernmost island of Mindanao. He'd been gone for almost two months. I knew his job—building an airstrip down there—was important, but I missed him every single day, and worried that the Japanese would conquer Mindanao too. *All of these islands are American territory and will be targets*, I'd heard him tell my mother the day before he left. *We'll defend from Mindanao.* But that hadn't worked very well. The knot in my stomach tightened again.

A glass partition separated us from our captors, but we saw the soldier behind the wheel hesitate. Then he floored the gas pedal, rocketing us forward. Betty's bear, Cuddles, hit the floor, and she clasped our mother's arm in a death grip.

"Runty little bastards can't even drive," the grizzled Brit across from us muttered in a deep voice that carried all too well.

Mommy's green eyes darted toward the window partition, then back to the loose-lipped Englishman.

"Two wheels or four legs—if it ain't got those, they can't manage it," he groused. "Never saw such a pathetic excuse for a conquering army in all my life." His voice was rising now, and the smell of gin wafted from his breath.

Harry Hodges leaned toward the Brit. "Let's talk history later, shall we old chap?"

"Please, Aubrey," the man's wife fixed him with a pleading stare.

The Aubrey Man was right though—about the pathetic conquering army. We sped past four soldiers of the Imperial Japanese Army cycling with all their might down Taft Avenue, one of Manila's main boulevards. They looked like something right out of a Keystone Cops movie.

Mommy, Betty and I had watched the Army parade into Manila four days before, from behind the slatted shutters of our apartment. Dozens of soldiers came pedaling in—on bicycles, for gosh sake—with Rising Sun pennants flying from the handlebars. Then a few trucks lumbered by, then soldiers on horseback with sabers trailing the beasts' bellies.

We couldn't believe it. Our invincible American army had abandoned us to these puny warriors on bicycles and horses?

Well, that explained why our conquerors were hijacking every nice car they could find. Some of our friends typed up receipts for the Japanese to sign before they took their cars. And some of their officers were so polite they actually signed them. "One Packard Limousine requisitioned from Mr. Milton Greenfield on January 3, 1942." Uncle Milton showed me his receipt. He had a few choice words to say about General Douglas MacArthur when he did.

MacArthur is an ass. I'd heard Daddy say that a million times.

General MacArthur, Commander of U.S. Armed Forces in the Far East, sure wasn't the most popular guy in the PI right now. *Ego size of the Titanic,* my father complained. MacArthur had been a hot-shot military celebrity, living in a fancy penthouse suite on the top floor of the Manila Hotel, eyes trained west "on the turquoise waters of Manila Bay and the Jap menace," he said. That was before the Japanese bombed Pearl Harbor and outfoxed him by invading from the north. Now MacArthur was holed up on the island fortress of Corregidor in Manila Bay, vowing "to rout the invaders" from that position of strength. But could he do it?

"Mommy!" Betty shrieked as our Caddie bucked to an abrupt halt, catapulting all of us forward.

The boney rear end of a carabao—a plodding, horned ox—practically mounted the hood of our Caddie. Carabao were accustomed to sharing crowded roads with cars, trolleys, and horses. But they sped up for no man. We Americans, in our Studebakers, Packards, and Caddies, were used to jockeying for position with Manila's oxen and horse-drawn taxis, but that experience—as well as driving itself—seemed brand new to the Japanese. Welcome to Manila, Mr. Rising Sun.

My mother scooped pop-eyed Betty on to her lap to comfort her, while the soldiers squabbled over how to restart the car. The guard with round glasses rifled through the glove box and unearthed a treasure that he waved proudly before his fellow captors. I craned my neck above the glass partition to see "Operating Hints for the 1942 Cadillac." Mommy saw it too and rolled her eyes.

* * *

As we waited for the car to start, the temperature in the sedan rose, and the mohair—supposed to feel luxurious on a cool evening—itched my bare and sweaty legs.

"It's going to be all right, pet. Don't worry." Mommy tried to calm Betty, but I saw a tear roll down her cheek.

"Phh… It'll be all right if they don't rape every single one of you," the Aubrey Man muttered back. "You ask those Nanking women and girls if they're all right."

"Zip it!" Harry hissed. "You're scaring women and children."

Was the Aubrey Man right? Would they rape us like they did those

Chinese women? I thought about how our mother had nixed us wearing short-shorts on this simmering morning and my stomach tensed. I was not going to think about rape or China. I tugged my longish skirt over my knees, leaned back in the seat.

It had to be a hundred degrees in here. I cranked down the window, but Betty coughed almost immediately.

"Lee, we don't need any more smoke," my mother snapped, and I rolled it right back up.

"Why is there so much of it?" Betty rasped.

We were so tired of tasting smoke. For almost a month, choking clouds had been everywhere.

"Why a Black New Year?" Tipsy Aubrey Man sounded like a melodramatic radio broadcaster, but no one stopped him. "Following the dastardly sneak attack on Pearl Harbor," he slurred, "Japanese bombers pounded Manila's airfields, destroying American planes and sending funnels of soot into the pristine skies."

We just stared at him and hoped he was finished, but he wasn't. "By Christmas, General MacArthur deemed it imperative to evacuate the troops. But his soldiers must destroy the city's oil reserves before their withdrawal!" His fingers mimicked an explosion, and Aubrey's son shifted uneasily. "Then, the conquering forces of the Rising Sun bombed the harbor, sinking straggling American ships and spewing ever-more ash." He seemed to be gathering steam. "So, for over a week now, ladies and gentlemen, deafening blasts have rocked the city and flames licked the sky. An oily grime hangs in the once golden air." Then Aubrey Man just stopped and stared out the window.

So did I. We'd called it *Black New Year's*. Smoke still scorched my throat and stung my eyes. Manila, once famous for its turquoise bay and technicolor sunsets, had gone grey. It broke my heart.

When the limo jerked back to life, my mind coughed up images of the last week and I latched on to them like lifeboats. If I thought about those, I wouldn't think about my darkest fears.

and clothing for three days. We were already packed. I didn't feel protected though—especially with Daddy far away in Zamboanga.

* * *

The limo lurched to a halt in front of the University of the Philippines. Wildly gesticulating Japanese soldiers pointed us toward Villamor Hall, the university's impressive School of Music.

"Out here! Out here!"

Frightened, I followed my mother toward the building's massive, scroll-top columns. Were they Doric? No. We'd just studied ancient Greece before Christmas, and I liked the architecture part. Scroll-tops … definitely Ionic. (The "Dorics" are unadorned—that's how I'd remembered it for the test.)

"Lee, get up here!" Mommy snapped. I raced to the top of the red tile stairs, embarrassed. My mother said said my daydreaming was a bad habit.

When I reached the landing, I glanced back at the Caddie, and wondered if it would ever speed cocky Americans to the polo club and dinner dances again. Maybe. Everyone said we'd be liberated in a matter of weeks. But what about now? Would they beat us?

"Inside, Lee. Let's go," said my determined mother, holding a suitcase in one hand and Betty's hand in the other.

Hundreds of bedraggled men and women filed past us and a locker room stench followed. Didn't these people use showers? And why did they all look like they had measles? Two lines snaked ahead: one for women and one for men. Betty and I stuck close to Mommy, and the good news was that we could. Kay and Harry had to separate, even though they were married. The Aubrey Man and his son drifted off to the Boys Only line too. Good riddance. I lost track of Mrs. Aubrey.

Within an hour, our little family was seated on one of the many hard student benches with Mommy filling out lengthy forms. Most of the questions were not surprising. Fill in your name, citizenship, passport number, number of family members, addresses in the PI and United States, location of family members in PI not resident in Manila, health at time of internment, assets in property, assets in cash, bank accounts in PI, numbers of bank accounts in PI.... It went on and on. Did Mommy know the numbers of our bank accounts? Would she tell them the truth if she did?

Japanese soldiers strutted through the rows, keeping watch. There were so many forms that I kept a neat starting pile, and handed my mother one at a time. Betty collected the finished forms. It gave us something to do. I pushed my unruly brown curls from my forehead and looked around. A tall Japanese guard with a broad forehead and wide eyes smiled slightly and dipped his head toward me, and I turned quickly. I wasn't sure if he was being friendly or leering.

A group of puffy-faced Americans trudged by me, and one disheveled woman with a familiar bearing nodded at me as if to say, "We're all in this together now." Her face was covered with red welts. Did they beat her? A prickle of fear ran down my spine. I smiled back at her feebly, as the group filed out. Did I know her? Two seconds later, it struck me.

"Mrs. Gewald! Mommy, that was Mrs. Gewald! What did they do to her?"

Mrs. Gewald was my seventh-grade English teacher and had always been smartly dressed, gracious, and dignified. She loved her students. Everything I knew about Rudyard Kipling or Ogden Nash, I'd learned from her. Her lessons on rhyme scheme and meter had kept our twelve-year-old feet tapping. Despite the heat, the hair on my arms lifted thinking of what they'd done to her. What were they going to do to us?

My mother looked up from her papers, and said in a low voice, "She was in the first pickup, honey. She's probably been here for three days with no shower or bedding. They've been eating out of cans and sleeping on the floor."

"Are we going to look like that in three days?" I asked.

"Maybe. But if we do, we will still be in God's hands," she replied a little too matter-of-factly. If that was supposed to inspire me, it did not. Mrs. Gewald looked like she had been trampled by a carabao. She was in Jap hands, more than God's hands, if you asked me.

Mommy worked her way through the papers quickly and methodically, her secretarial training coming in handy. My mother had not let her skills go "a-moldering," as she would say. When our family embroidery business went belly up two years ago, Mommy sacrificed her high society life of leisure and became a "working gal," as she liked to call herself. She'd been Secretary to the Vice President of the Philippine Long Distance Telephone Company for the last year, and that was why she moved through these forms at such a brisk clip.

I stared at the final question: "Who do you believe will win the War? Imperial Japanese Army or US and Allies?" Then a big, empty, fill-in-the-blank line.

We were in trouble now. Daddy was with the U.S. army in Mindanao, helping to build an airstrip. My mother was so proud of him. They'd come to Manila to run his family business and ended up living in luxury in America's "Pearl of the Orient." Fifteen years of life in Manila had only made my mother more of a feisty fan of Uncle Sam. It was crazy, but here in the PI, she and Daddy had come to live the American dream.

Mommy's hand had slowed. She wagged the pen tip back and forth with uncharacteristic hesitation. Then she dashed IJA on the form, and passed it to Betty with brisk finality.

I.J.A! My mother, the patriotic Agnes Hanagan Iserson, had voted for the Imperial Japanese Army? Well, maybe that would keep us safe, but I couldn't believe it and was kind of disappointed in her.

A short Japanese soldier with scraggly mustache collected the papers, looked at the last answer, and nodded his approval with smug satisfaction.

He herded us out the door. The army convoy trucks were lined up outside. No more limos for us. The Aubrey Man and his family were a few feet ahead of us. Mommy smoothed a stray curl under my headband, and held my hand. I couldn't help challenging her.

"You put IJA," I hissed, close to tears, as we edged closer to the door and the truck.

"Yes, I did, honey," she replied in the low silken voice that had sung me to sleep so many nights. "Yes, I did."

"Imperial Japanese Army…." I muttered, already feeling defeated.

"Oh, no, pet," she corrected and lowered her lips to my ear as we were herded into the back of a truck. "I.J.A. is Intrepid Jumbo-sized Americans."

Chapter 2
FIRST NIGHT

January 6, 1942 (continued)

"Fried egg." The Aubrey Man angled his chin to the Japanese flag, which soared high above the sprawling legislative building.

I struggled to keep my footing in the lurching truck, but for one second the shock of seeing the Rising Sun up there rooted me to my spot. Only American and Philippine flags belonged up there! Gosh, the whole darn building—with its triangular temple front and colossal columns—could have been imported directly from Washington D.C. *Which flag doesn't belong?* as if it were a page from one of Betty's children's magazines. *X that out!* my mind screamed at the Rising Sun.

Mommy, Betty, and I braced against the side rail as the army transport lumbered along familiar thoroughfares. There had to be thirty sweaty people jockeying for standing room in the little truck, so I was glad to be near the rail—looking out to the city I so loved and hated. The suffocating heat and the spider I'd just plucked from my arm reminded me why I hated Manila: the city was too hot, too humid, and had way too many spiders and bugs. But I'd grown up here, lived my whole life here, and as we rode off to prison, I thought of all the things about the city I just loved. Sunset on Dewey Boulevard. Movies at the air-cooled Metropolitan Theater. Ice Cream at the Rendezvous Café. Honey Bee Cake at the Astoria.

Seeing Manila now from the back of a truck was both scary and thrilling. Another *X-It-Out* Rising Sun waved over the new post office with its socko Ionic arcade and half-moon wings. A welcome breeze lifted damp curls from my sticky neck as we crossed the Quezon Bridge that we were so proud of: four lanes wide, enormous concrete girders, and a big graceful arch. When it opened just two years ago, it had been had named after Filipino President Manuel Quezon. Where was President Quezon now? Was he in Corregidor with MacArthur? Or was he here negotiating with the Japanese? The Philippines was a Commonwealth "under American protection." Well, I guess we botched that job—the protection part.

"Where are we going?" Betty asked, her voice wobbly.

"I think it'll be Santo Tomas." Harry Hodges answered from behind.

There had been rumors that the University of Santo Tomas, owned by Spanish Dominican priests, would be our jail for the next three days. We could see the university's tall cross tower in the distance—the highest point in the city.

Mommy put her arm around Betty. "There are worse places," she said in a low, firm voice. "It's big. It's open. They'll have more than one bathroom."

"Main Building's earthquake-proof, too," said Harry. "I remember reading about it when it went up in the twenties. The priest who designed it went to Tokyo to study quake-proof building after Japan's big one in '23. It's built in separate sections with rebar imported straight from Japan."

"How appropriate." My mother's voice had an acid edge. "We'll be imprisoned behind their own rebars."

I tried not to think about our three days in prison. I stared down at the Pasig River, which separated the old city from the newer business district. Even with all the smoke and chaos, I could see hard-working Filipinos poling their *cascos* along the shallow waterways. These water gypsies lived and worked on their flat-bottomed boats with curved thatched roofs. On any given day, they'd sell hand-woven baskets or straw hats or fresh-caught fish on the docks, right from their cascos. Usually, if I called out to them from the bridge, some friendly vendor would shout back and wave. But I didn't call out today, and nobody shouted up to us. They kept their broad-brimmed hats down and concentrated on the oily water.

Our truck finally turned on España Street, heading for the front gate of Santo Tomas. A hushed crowd of Filipinos lined the sidewalks, many of them weeping.

"Lee! Betty!" I heard a familiar, high-pitched voice and spotted Rosalina, our pretty house girl, waving her handkerchief.

For just a second, I shot her a big smile and waved. She was always so cheerful and lively, but now tears streamed down her face. Then I realized there was nothing to smile about— for her or for me—so I snatched my arm back inside the truck, but I kept my eyes on hers. She looked so afraid. Be brave, Rosalina. I silently mouthed to our loyal friend. Be brave, Little Lee, I knew she was silently willing me.

The spiked iron gates of the university—twelve foot high, wrought iron spears tipped with gold—swung open for us. Our truck turned down a looping drive that opened onto a broad lawn dotted with palms and acacias. The cross tower shot high above. Betty and I gripped the truck rails with one hand and Mommy's waist with the other. When the iron gate clanged shut behind us and we lurched forward, I felt the warmth of my mother's strong hand on my shoulder.

No sooner had the truck halted in front of the Main Building than a Japanese guard with bayoneted rifle waved us out.

"Daddy will want both of you to be very strong and courageous girls." Mommy's voice soothed me.

Betty clung to her small stuffed bear. Even at eleven, Betty never went anywhere without Cuddles, whereas I had left my enormous stuffed panda, Max—my twelfth birthday present from Daddy—in the apartment. Mommy thought he was too big to bring and that I was old enough to be without him. I suppose she was right, but I sure missed having something of Daddy's close to me.

"OK, quickly, girls," Mommy whispered, as we climbed out of the truck.

Hundreds of confused people milled about on the lawn or sat on the woven grass mats we called *petates*. Betty and I scrambled for our luggage, which had been tossed to the ground. A blue-eyed man with rimless glasses and slicked-back hair approached our group. He was a Clark Kent look-alike, and seemed to be in charge.

"Earl Carroll." He introduced himself in a clipped manner.

American, for sure. Why was an American working for the Japs? Mr. Carroll toted a clipboard and sported a red armband with Japanese characters on it. He raised his voice just loud enough to be heard.

"Ladies, find whatever space you can here in the Main Building." He pointed to the long, grey four-story building before us. "Gentlemen, to the gymnasium. You can help your wives settle in first. Roll call at 7 PM sharp. Let's not give the Japs any reason to get angry at us," he cautioned.

"Who put you in charge?" the Aubrey Man challenged.

"Unfortunately, they did." Mr. Carroll nodded his head in the direction of a Japanese guard. "It wouldn't have been my first choice for an overseas posting. I'm in insurance—from San Francisco. Got into Manila just before Pearl."

I liked Mr. Carroll right away. He had the bum luck to arrive from the US just before the Japs took the Philippines, but he wasn't spending any time feeling sorry for himself. He seemed to telegraph "we'll get through this" to the rest of us.

"What's your Nip band say?" The Aubrey Man pointed at the Japanese characters on the red armband.

"Man with a big belly." Carroll smiled. "Their shorthand for 'American.' The red means I'm supposed to tell you what to do. Go get settled now."

I glanced at the clock on the base of the tall cross tower. It was noon. Thousands of people were milling about, and we were lucky that it was January, the mildest month in the Philippines. The heat and humidity still soaked you by day, but the evening air was cooler, and with all these people packed together, we would need that.

"Grab your bags, girls," my mother said.

We pushed through the crowd, and scaled the steps to the Main Building, its double-door entry shaded by an enormous limestone portico. A bronze plaque at the doors proclaimed the University of Santo Tomas, founded in 1611, the oldest university under the American flag. Except now it wasn't—under the American flag, that is. And it wasn't a university any more either. It was our prison camp.

My gaze flew to another sign, handwritten in crabbed, child-like letters and taped to the front door: "Internees in this camp shall be responsible for feeding themselves."

My blood ran cold. We'd brought canned food, but how much? I showed the sign to my mother, who was a step behind me. "Three days, Mommy?" I just wanted to be sure.

She paused and furrowed her brow. "Three days. Let's go, Lee."

* * *

I hardly had to move my legs: the sea of women and children surged forward and bore us through the front doors into an enormous foyer. White stone walls rose on every side, and opened right and left into soaring halls framed by clipped arches. I spotted a crucifix above the arch. Bodies jostled against me, but my instinct was to look up and take it all in. How tall were these ceilings? Fifteen feet? *Stop daydreaming, Lee.*

A double-width stairwell led to a broad landing, then up again to a mezzanine, and then reversed direction, and shot up another two flights to a second floor. Heavy mahogany railings flanked each side of the enormous staircase. Somebody really thought about this. What a building. Women pushed behind me and swarmed the stairs like ants.

"Third and second are full. Find your spot on the first floor, new" woman shouted from the mezzanine.

Armed Japanese guards stood in the halls, but looked dazen nothing.

"Lee!" My mother grabbed my arm, and hustled us dow

Betty held Mommy's hand, and we edged ahead of the crowd. The first three rooms looked full, so we continued. Mommy stopped before the closed door of a classroom. "ROOM 4." She opened the door cautiously and a thick cloud of dust, spiders, and beetles whipped through the empty lecture hall. Cobwebs festooned the ceiling and corners. Mommy held her hand to her face and moved in to claim a spot. She decided on a space in the back, away from the door, but near a row of windows.

"Doesn't this school have maids?" Betty was incredulous at the thick covering of dust.

"Silly, they're closed. It's Christmas vacation," I reminded her.

Some vacation. The University of Santo Tomas had closed its doors on December eighth, just after Pearl Harbor and the attack on the Philippines. It was now January sixth, and no one had taken a mop or dust cloth to these rooms in nearly a month.

"Kay, over here!" I heard my mother call.

Our lively neighbor from the apartment building elbowed her way through the crowd with husband Harry in tow. With his six-foot three, athletic frame, he looked hopelessly out of place in this room of hens.

"Oh, Agnes, thank God! Just like old times," she drawled. Kay was from North Carolina. "Neighbors. Let's camp here."

Harry positioned Kay's bags near ours, and glanced around. "No cots? Nothing?"

My mother shook her head.

Cots? A shiver ran through me. Sleep here? On the concrete floor? With the armies of creepy-crawlies all around us? Sleep here?

My mother, Kay, and Harry were spreading out suitcases to claim a space s large as they could for the four of us. (Harry would have to sleep in the m.) "Mommy, did we bring mosquito netting?" I asked.

veryone froze. "Damn," Harry blurted. He looked at me a little arrassed, and Mommy took a deep breath.

Jo, pumpkin. They said food and clothing for three days. That's all."

"But the guards might bring the nets, don't you think, Mommy?" Betty thought all people were as good and caring as she was.

My mother hesitated. "Actually, I think we're going to have something of an adventure tonight, honey. Just like *Swallows and Amazons*." She knew we loved the story of the enterprising English children who set off to camp on Wild Cat Island, far, far from all the comforts of home. They fought off pirates, savages, and of course, wild cats.

"Do we have pemmican and grog?" I asked in my best wise-guy tone. In *Swallows and Amazons* the children were always well supplied with a concentrate of dried beef called pemmican and a thermos of ginger beer they called "grog."

"Dahlin," Kay chimed in, "we have Spam. And we have Karo Syrup, from which I am sure we can whip up some delicious grog for our picnic."

My mother smiled but seemed distracted and continued to scan the room. More and more women pushed through the door looking for a place to sleep. It was getting harder to hold our space. I saw a long wooden student bench close to the wall, and drew it over to our section. It formed a sort of fence.

Harry went off to check out the men's digs, and said he would meet us in the front plaza for "dinner." He and Kay decided on a spot under a large acacia out front. My mother asked Kay to stay with Betty and me for a minute.

"I think I see a janitor's closet," she said. "I'm going to get us a mop, and see if we can clean this spot up before night."

I marveled that my mother always seemed to be one step ahead of the game. "Pluck and luck are two things that get you through in life," she always told Betty and me. "You can't control the luck, but you better have the pluck." Agnes Hanagan Iserson certainly did.

She'd told Betty and me that she'd left her Utica farm girl life behind as soon as she could. Mommy was proud of having trained as a stenographer and left "Nowheresville" for New York City. There she'd met our Big Apple Daddy—her boss. They got married and set out to the Far East, where until a few months ago she'd had servants, and more long gowns in her closet than street clothes.

But I also knew my mother could pivot on a dime: she could reverse-spin faster than my skating idol Sonja Henie. I'd seen it a hundred times since our father's embroidery business went bankrupt three years ago. Mommy just put her nose to the grindstone and planned the next step—whether it was going back to work herself or moving from our villa in the beautiful Manila suburb of San Francisco del Monte to a three-room apartment downtown on Taft Avenue.

"All set." My mother returned with cleaning supplies, and put us all to work. Betty and I had learned to clean bathrooms at home even though we had maids. We only did it once a month, but Mommy thought it was good training. And fortunately, there was a sink in this room. (Had it been an art classroom? Or domestic science?) Other women—who probably couldn't identify a mop—glanced at our cleaning crew with a mixture of ridicule and disdain. When we'd done the best we could with our spot, we passed the tools along to some ladies next to us, who had begun to see the wisdom of a clean floor space.

The room seemed full to bursting, and women on all sides bickered over exactly where their space began and ended.

"This ain't the MacArthur Suite, honey child. Move those bags over!" A stocky middle-aged American matron shoved two precisely spaced suitcases to one side.

"The cheek!" Their prim English owner re-positioned her barricades defiantly. "I'll have you know that the MacArthurs are personal friends of ours," she said, pulling rank.

"Well, just ducky that he helped you get away," the matron responded. And with a decisive punt, she knocked two of three bags to one side, and plunked her own straw suitcase where the British pair had been.

Women were turning to watch. "Easy does it, ladies. We're all in this together. We're Allies, remember?" I heard the gravel-throated female voice from the opposite corner say.

"No more! No more in here!" A staccato bark rang out from an armed, bewhiskered Japanese guard at the door.

Every voice fell silent. All eyes locked on the angry man with the bayoneted rifle. Then a saber-wielding guard came alongside him. Their eyes swept the room and took in the spectacle of lightly clad, disheveled women. Some of the women stared back defiantly, others just looked at the ground. I looked away from them and the rifle with its sharp bayonet. The smell of our sweating bodies and the smell of fear rose around me.

Every woman in that room knew about China. "Worst mass rape in history," Don Bell, the voice of Philippine radio, branded the Nanking conquest. Forty, maybe sixty-thousand women and girls raped. Pregnant women bayoneted. I tried not to show any fear at all, but I was glad to be far from the door.

The guards glared at us, while my mother and Kay quietly positioned themselves in front of Betty and me. Then the saber-wielding intruder bellowed, "Room 4 full! No more in here!" And the two stormed out.

A long silence and then quiet murmuring among the ladies turned to smiles and giggles.

"Well, thank God for that, honey! No more in here!" The gravel voice on the other side of the room called out, and she lit a cigarette. Laughter erupted.

* * *

Later that night after our picnic dinner (of Spam, crackers, and "Grog") and lights out, all fifty-six of us struggled to sleep on the cold concrete floor. No pillows. No blankets. No curtains on the windows. I should've brought Max, I thought as the grim reality hit me. We could wad clothes under our heads for pillows, but it didn't take long to figure out that any garments we had were better used for cover. A welcome breeze blew through the open window, but with it came hordes of hungry mosquitoes. I had learned in school that hundreds of species of mosquitoes lived in the PI, and I was sure most of them were here tonight. We were under siege from below as well.

"Damn!" I heard Kay mutter.

She turned it into two-syllable word, and when I craned my neck off the floor to peek, I saw her pull a six-inch huntsman spider off her bare leg. From all around the room came sounds of women swatting and quietly swearing, as we waged war against spiders. Betty could sleep through anything. But when a hairy jumping spider crawled up my arm, and two other eight-legged friends climbed on my left leg, I bolted upright and leapt to my feet.

"Lee, get down. You're in front of the window!" I heard my mother whisper urgently. Guards patrolled outside.

Tears were welling up inside me but I fought them back. I would not, I just would not sleep on this creepy-crawly floor. I spotted the student bench I had drawn to our space earlier that afternoon. The wooden seat had five places separated by looped iron arm rails. What if I wedged myself through the rails? I wriggled through each, seeking the security of a fully raised platform. Yes. A blissful moment of relief. Then seconds later, my whole back seemed aflame, alive with tunneling creatures and a burning itch. Ani! Bedbugs! These tiny white termites usually fed on the slats of wood, but now feasted on a real treat: me.

I yelped, scurried off the bench, and quickly returned to the floor, resigned now to my spider and mosquito-bitten fate. Lying on the cold cement, I stared out the window and heard the thud of artillery shells far away. I felt a tear trickle down my face but wiped it away. I didn't want my mother to see her biggest girl cry. Still, this was the most horrible night of my life. Where was Daddy? Was he safe? I felt my mother's cool fingers comb through my curls.

"D'you think we'll get out of here?" I asked my voice nearly breaking.

She didn't answer right away. She just squeezed my hand, and I thought she might be crying. A deep ache welled inside me. Then I heard her breathe, "Yes. Yes, I do."

I tried to be as strong as she was, and blinked back tears. Through the window, I could see stars gleaming on this moonless night, and a familiar constellation came into focus: the Southern Cross. For a moment, I was transported to the vast garden outside our villa.

I was eight-years-old, and Daddy was showing me that constellation for the very first time. "You can't see it in most of the States," he'd told me. "It's like a special present for living near the equator. And it's like our family—four stars: you, Betty, your mom, and me." "Which one am I?" I'd asked, squinting at the kite-shaped beacon. "The bottom one, sweetheart," he responded without a moment's hesitation. "The brightest one of all." "No, that's you, Daddy. I'll be the second brightest off to the left," I pointed to the cross-bar section. "Well OK, honey. But remember I'm shining for you."

Now the vibrant star at the foot of the cross pulsed and streamed its blue-white light right at me. I stared at it and everything inside me suddenly quieted. I said an *Our Father*, and fell asleep.

Chapter 3
THE GATE

January 7, 1942

Oh no—Betty has measles! In the gray, early morning light I squinted at my little sister asleep beside me. Red welts ravaged her angular face and erupted from her arms. Cuddles still rested secure in Betty's grasp, but the horrid pock marks surged from every exposed part of her body. Poor Boops, she'll be so upset and uncomfortable. She looks just like Mrs. Gewald yesterday. My heart stopped. Mrs. Gewald. The image of my "measle-ridden" teacher skittered before me, and the echo of my mother's words: *she's been here for three days with no bedding.* I rolled over on the concrete floor, and realized with a start that Mommy looked like Mrs. Gewald too. And, oh my gosh, Kay too! A horrible thought dawned on me.

I sat up, raised a hand to my cheek and skimmed my own face. A lumpy mass greeted my touch, and my cheeks now itched furiously. Oh no. The army of Philippine bugs and creepy crawlies had feasted on us all night, and won. They'd beaten every single one of us.

"Mommy." I jostled my mother. She opened her eyes slowly and shot into wakefulness.

"Oh, Lee. I'll get you calamine lotion! Oh, pet..."

"I don't think calamine lotion can fix us," I said, trying not to wake my sister or anyone else. But all the emotion I'd kept inside me the night before poured into the gray dawn, and I felt a flood of tears well up. "It can't fix us," I repeated in a whisper, shook my head, and stretched out my cratered arms for her to see. I just wept.

"Oh, honey." She sat upright to take me in her arms.

I was too big to be in my mother's arms, but she rocked me back and forth anyway, stroking my hair as I sobbed. Other women stirred and a baby near the door bawled. But through my tears and the rising din, I heard Mommy humming a low, melancholy version of "You Are My Sunshine."

At home, Daddy used to play that song on the piano, and Mommy stood next to him, singing in a deep velvet voice that broke your heart. Especially when she got to the part about how she lay dreaming that her love was in her arms only to wake and find him gone. "I just hung my head and I cried," the second verse wailed. Hot tears streamed down my face and flooded my mother's nightgown. Where was Daddy? I knew Mommy had to be missing my father even more than I was, but here she was—humming and rocking, not crying. *You are my sunshine...*

Room 4 stirred to life, and fifty-six itchy women and cranky children awoke to protest the new day. A rising chorus of shrieks pierced the air as women took stock of their pock-marked bodies. "No, Joey, don't scratch, honey you'll make it worse," one overwhelmed mother ordered her little boy, who kept whining "I itchy, Mommy. I itchy all ower." As weary, perspiring women stood to stretch, it was hard to tell which was more wrinkled—our clothing or our faces.

Boxes and suitcases spewed garments in all directions. Out of the corner of my eye, I saw the heavy-set American matron who'd kicked the British suitcases aside. She tripped over the handle of a *maleta* as she made her way to the washroom. "Oh for Christ's sake!" she swore.

And here was my mother, still holding me and intoning her love song. Something about my mother's rich alto steadied me. Mommy had run out of luck, but she still had the pluck. I closed my eyes and remembered bedraggled

Mrs. Gewald, who'd nodded meaningfully to me back at Villamor Hall. She hadn't given up either. *Now Daddy will want you to be very strong and courageous girls*, I could hear my mother's voice less than 24 hours earlier. I sniffed mightily and dug deep inside me. I sure didn't feel like anybody's "sunshine" this morning, but I wasn't going to add one more tear to this grim dawn. I wiped my cheek and freed myself from my mother's embrace. "I'm OK, Mommy."

January 10, 1942

"We have to be ready for the long haul," I overheard Mr. Carroll telling Harry Hodges on the fifth day of our internment.

Our "three days" of protective custody had come and gone, and now everyone treated the original call-up as a cruel joke. The Japanese showed no signs of willingness to release us. But on the other hand, they hadn't beaten us...or worse. Japanese guards barked at us, and they insisted that we bow to them—in fact, they had given us two much-resented bowing lessons. But so far they were all bark and no bite.

"We may be here a month or two, maybe longer. So we have to dig in," said Mr. Carroll.

Harry nodded grimly, but I felt like I had been punched in the stomach. More than two months on the floor with the bugs and creepy-crawlies? More than two months before being reunited with Daddy? Would it take MacArthur that long?

I looked back at the stone mass of the Main Building with its endlessly ticking clock and boxy cross tower. Narrow rectangular windows lined its ashen front, framed by columns that weren't even there, just hollowed into the building. Recessed columns, Harry called them. Cheater columns, I called them. Why didn't we get one decent Ionic or Corinthian column in this place? Those capitals were bound sheaves of wheat hacked off at the top and flattened, a harvest lopped off in its prime, then quashed. That was us.

But men really were "digging in." You never saw so many trenches being dug and pipes being laid in your entire life. The Japanese had stuffed more than three thousand of us into Santo Tomas now. Every classroom housed thirty to fifty internees. We stood in half-hour lines for the toilets, and longer lines still for the showers, which we had to share: two or three ladies under a single head. "If you want privacy, close your eyes, honey," Kay had quipped.

The whole darn camp had "measles." And here was the kicker: the Japanese still refused to feed us. They'd allowed the Philippine Red Cross in to set up a little canteen serving coffee and rolls for breakfast in the morning, and stew in the late afternoon. But mostly we still ate out of the cans and boxes we'd brought with us. Our Spam, peanut butter, crackers, tinned fish, Karo Syrup, and Cream of Wheat were disappearing fast. Ooh, what I wouldn't give for some mango ice cream! Maybe there'd be something for us Isersons at the gate today.

"Harry, dahlin', I'd like you to make tripling the size of those first floor ladies bathrooms a priority," Kay smiled and batted her eyelashes at her husband like some Betty Boop cartoon character.

"Yes, Ma'am!" he saluted and turned on his heel, throwing us a look of mock despair. Harry was part of the construction committee that was rigging more toilets and showers, while another group worked on expanding the kitchen.

I'd learned in these first few days in camp that Americans and Brits are born organizers. If you stuff hordes of us together in a small space with no rules, we'll get a million committees up and running in no time flat. We already had a Central or "Internee Committee" that set the rules and tried to get us food (that was headed by Mr. Carroll), a sanitation committee that regulated water use, a health committee that had made a hospital out of a tent and got all the doctors and nurses to give us cholera and typhoid shots, and of course, Harry's construction committee.

The Japanese encouraged all this organizing, Mr. Carroll said, because they'd arrested us before they were ready to deal with us. They seemed just as confused about this new prison life as we did.

"Agnes, why don't you and Betty head over to the Red Cross chow line, and Lee and I will check the Gate," Kay offered.

My heart leapt. Kay knew full well that my mother didn't do anything in the morning without her coffee, but she and I both wanted to see if our friends had brought desperately needed supplies to the chaotic Gate.

"Oh, that's merciful of you, Kay. Coffee before craziness. Lee, can you go without me?"

"Sure—I'm looking for Rosalina." I reminded her. "I saw her in the crowd the day they brought us in, and I keep thinking she'll be there. We just haven't found her yet."

My mother had had the same thought apparently. "Here." She handed me an envelope. "We need to pay her for her work. I wanted to give this to her myself, but if you find her first, make sure she takes it. And tell her not to worry about us or the apartment. She has to get out of Manila as soon as she can. She's young and pretty. She's not safe here."

I puzzled over what being young and pretty had to do with her not being safe here, while I peeked inside the envelope. Twelve pesos. "Mommy! Where'd you get this?" I hissed. "I thought the Japs took all our money when we came in."

Mommy shook her head. "No. We just had to list funds. They didn't take our money, and even if they'd tried, your mother is not without imagination," she replied in a low voice.

"That money could do something for you here in camp, Agnes." Kay reminded her, brow knit.

My mother shook her head. "Rosalina has more than earned it, Kay, and she'll need it. Now scoot, you two. I need some coffee."

* * *

As we neared the España Street entry, my spirits soared just looking at those crowds pressing at the University's massive wrought iron gate. Hundreds of Filipinos had thronged its bars each day, clamoring to know what we needed. For the first three days, pandemonium had reigned, as Filipino friends and former servants tossed mattresses, cots, food, clothing, and all manner of supplies over the twelve-foot-high spears.

Now we had a new system: large items had to be checked in at a package line, just inside the gate. A long line of Filipinos waited to deliver supplies, while Japanese guards patrolled the line and shouted at them.

"You'd think the Japs would be grateful, wouldn't you, Kay? With the Filipinos bringing us food, they don't have to feed us. Don't captors usually have to feed their prisoners?"

"Dahlin, this whole scene mortifies them." Kay lowered her voice. "Here they are, trying to convince our Filipino friends that their Asian brothers," her voice dripped with sarcasm, "have freed them from the yoke of us evil Yankee Imperialists. And the freed Filipinos keep trying to help us evil Yankee Imperialists."

My heart swelled with love for them. As we approached the free-for-all, I squinted at the placards behind the iron bars. "Message for Mrs. George Miller. Where is Mrs. Miller?" a large sign flashed. Someone was looking for Hope, the gravel-throated New Hampshire school teacher in our room. I would have to tell her. Then another sign: "Laundry washed—5 centavos. Ask Marina Fuentes." Wow, people were actually paying to have their clothes washed on the outside. How'd they get them out? Then, I saw a large sign with big block letters, "I am Iserson House Girl. Where are Isersons?"

"Rosa!" I shrieked and dashed for the fence. She didn't hear me right away, but with Kay by my side, we pushed to the front, jumped up and down, and I waved my yellow handkerchief until I caught Rosalina's eye. She pushed forward through the crowd and reached the iron bars, eyes bright with relief, delighted that her sign had worked.

"I come every day for three days, Lee! Only now I find you! *Kamusta*?" The words poured out of her mouth in a single stream. 'Kamusta' meant 'how are you?' in the Filipino language of Tagalog. Just then she saw all the welts on our puffy faces. Her eyes widened. "Do they beat you?"

"No, it's the bugs. Spiders: Four. Humans: Zero in the latest inning," I joked, pretending our four nights on the cement floor meant nothing to me. "Did you bring mosquito nets?" I tried to mask my desperation.

"Yes! Telephone Company send cots and blankets and more food, too."

Kay came along side me. "It's a good thing your Mama is a working gal, Lee. She's got connections." Mommy's job as secretary to the Vice President of the Philippine Telephone Company was paying off: It looked like the company's executives would watch out for us if they could. "And Rosa, you are an absolute angel come to our little corner of hell. Thank you, dahlin'."

"Yes, thank you, Rosa!" I had never been so grateful to see anyone in my life.

Rosalina spoke quickly. "Felix and Warlito deliver all over there in Iserson name." She pointed to the folding tables now mobbed with internees, and the snaking package lines. Felix, our houseboy, and Warlito, our driver, must have done some heavy lifting. "I hope you get all things," she said, as she eyed the rifle-toting Japanese guards. One of them leered at her before being called away. "And look inside melon." She lowered her voice, and tried to put her mouth to my ear through the iron bars. "We make slit. Money inside melon."

Kay sized up the lines, and immediately sped off to claim a spot for us, while I risked a little more time at the gate with Rosa. The Japanese didn't want us to talk to the Filipinos directly, but the crowds standing in line for the packages hid us from the nearest guard.

"Rosa, is Daddy safe? Did he call?"

"We hear nothing from him."

My chest tightened. Daddy should've called. If he were safe, he would've called.

Rosa's brown eyes filled with compassion. "All phone lines still down. We know that Japanese march on Mindanao, but they do not capture Zamboanga yet."

OK, maybe that was it: Daddy could be fine if the phone lines were down. And the good news was that Zamboanga was on the southernmost tip of the island of Mindanao.

"Singapore is still strong—in British hands, and Corregidor ours. Bataan too," Rosalina said. "Maybe our Americans will figure surprise victory plan."

I nodded, hoping she was right. I liked that she said "our Americans."

"Did you bring Max?" I asked eagerly. I missed my large stuffed panda from Daddy more than I could say. Max tied me to the love of my faraway father. If nothing else, I could lay my head on his bulging tummy at night, and keep my face off the ground.

Rosa looked taken aback. "No, Lee, I bring food and bedding."

"Rosa! I sleep with Max every night! How could you forget Max?" Rosalina was at least ten years older than me, but servants were servants and sometimes they were just careless and stupid. I fell into my old habit of bossing her, just like at home. For the first time ever, I saw anger flash in her amber eyes.

"Time for childish things over now, Lee." Her voice was stern and her jaw tight. "Not easy for me to bring you what I brought today."

Our eyes locked in a showdown of wills, and suddenly, I was ashamed of myself and looked away. Rosalina had risked a lot: she had no family in this camp. She didn't need to spend three days at the gate trying to bring us food and bedding. I remembered my mother's remark about her being young and pretty, and maybe in danger on the streets—now that Japanese troops roamed the city as new lords of the land. And here I was, almost fourteen, going on about my stuffed animal.

"I'm sorry, Rosa. I shouldn't have yelled at you. Here you are helping us… It's just that… well, I miss Max." Through the gate, she still leveled a hard stare at me, and I looked at the ground, before looking back at her. "I can sure be awful mean and bossy sometimes, huh?"

She nodded in agreement.

"And selfish too," I added. She nodded again, but this time she smiled a little. "Are you safe?" I asked.

"So far, okeydokey," but she looked at me with new urgency. "Today we leave for Baguio—Warlito, Felix, and me. We have family in hills and know where to hide. Grandma Naylor will help you. She say she bring food and whatever else she can."

"Grandma Naylor" was an elderly American widow with lots of spunk and a knack for baking. When she offered to be our "grandma" in Manila years ago, Betty and I accepted on the spot—thrilled because all our real family was back in the States. We'd met our own grandparents only once, and envied our neighbor friends, Buddy and Billy Naylor, who had a perfect, cookie-baking grandmother living with them. Mrs. Naylor said she had enough love for four grandchildren, so Betty and I got adopted, and we loved her like a real grandmother. Fortunately, Grandma wasn't interned because her late husband was a Filipino and she had honorary Filipino citizenship.

"Grandma has all precious treasures from your apartment. She will hide them and sell others for you, and buy you food." Rosalina tried to reassure me.

There sure weren't many "precious treasures" that I knew about. Daddy's fortunes had been going downhill for the last three years, and we'd been moving into smaller and smaller homes. I just hoped Grandma got the photo albums. Suddenly, I remembered the twelve pesos in my skirt pocket. I gripped one of Rosalina's small hands in mine through the iron bars and quickly passed her the envelope. "This is for you, Rosa."

She glanced at the pesos in surprise, and shoved the envelope back at me. "You must keep, Lee-lee. You will need this."

"No, it's for your work. It's your pay. Mommy wants you to get away as soon as you can. You have to take it." She hesitated, but I pushed it back in her hands. "Mommy will kill me if you don't take it, Rosa. Don't be a ninny!"

She pursed her lips, smiling or crying I couldn't tell which, and pocketed the envelope. Crowds were pressing in on Rosa, and there I was glued to the bars like an eager orangutan at the zoo. I knew this was goodbye, and I babbled on, not wanting to let her go. I had a terrifying feeling that when she walked away, my whole old life would go with her.

"Can Warlito drive you to Baguio?" Our family often vacationed in Baguio, a lush, mountain village about 150 miles north of Manila. "The President still has some gas," I told her. *The President* was our 1936 Studebaker.

She shook her head. "Happy Japanese officer driving *The President*. You were right." She winked, showing the first sign of humor I had seen from her. "Other model was better idea. Fit his personality more."

She remembered! Rosalina had just started to work for us in 1936, when Daddy bought *The President*. I liked Studebaker's other model better. It had a futuristic V-shaped grille that surged into the road before it. I'd pleaded with Daddy to buy it, using all the wiles of an adored eight-year-old daughter, but he just snorted, said "Snow will blanket Manila before this family owns *The Dictator* model."

The Italian boss-man Benito Mussolini had just marched into Ethiopia and made it his own personal colony. Dictator Adolf Hitler had gobbled up the Rhineland and ogled Austria like it was a Viennese pastry. Japan's almighty Hirohito told his army to invade China. And an American car company trots out a car called *The Dictator*? Whose side were they on anyway?

"So, are you going to Baguio on carabao?" I was trying to make my voice light to match her humor, but my throat tightened painfully. Rosalina just smiled.

"We have way," she reassured me. "Don't worry, Lee. God be with you, and …. here." It seemed like an afterthought, but she took a wooden rosary from her pocket and folded the carved beads with their wooden cross into my hand. "This better than Panda. Mary is better than Max."

She held my eyes for a long moment, and my fingers closed over her gift. I had seen Rosalina pray on these beads to Mary, the Mother of Jesus, every day at noon. Now here they were, warm and solid in my hand. The sharp corner of the cross dug into my palm, but I held it tight. All I could do was stare at Rosa and shake my head—don't go.

"Bueno, es hora, niña!" A Spanish man barked at Rosa that he wanted to take her place at the gate, and was trying to push her aside.

Rosalina stood a second longer with love, fear, and uncertainty all shining in her liquid brown eyes. "Mahal Kita," she whispered the Tagalog for 'I love you.' "Goodbye, little Lee." She turned away.

Tears spilled down my cheeks as she melted into the crowd, and my throat ached as I called after her. "That sign was a great idea, Rosa. Thank you! Mah-hahl kee TAH to you too!"

She looked back, waved and smiled, but I could see she was crying. I clutched the beads and fought the sinking feeling that I would never see her again.

* * *

I headed for the package line, where it seemed like a thousand people jockeyed for position. Kay stood in a line marked "H-K," and as I came alongside her, the woman behind Kay tapped me on the shoulder, and pointed to the right.

"Princess." She spat the "p" sound and let the word linger in the air with contempt. "The Ps are over there. No cutting. Join the other princesses or go to the back of this line." She took a drag on her stub of a cigarette.

Kay wheeled around quickly. "She's not cutting. We're together—I'm her aunt," she lied with astonishing grace and Kay pronounced the word "ahhnt" like the southern belle she was. Well, how convenient that both Kay (Hodges) and Lee (Iserson) could retrieve our packages from the same H-K line. The cigarette lady just snorted, but said no more.

The ninety-degree heat and ninety-eight percent humidity closed in like a blanket. People were wearing the craziest hats to protect against the sun—floppy straw bonnets and giant paper mushrooms they had fashioned for themselves.

We inched further forward, and I saw five seated internees who sported red armbands, staffing rickety wooden tables covered with oil cloths. They had lists, and seemed to be checking off names as they funneled newly delivered supplies to lucky recipients. Japanese guards flanked them and scrutinized packages uncertainly, inspecting for radios, weapons, or anything else they didn't want us to have.

One thing about our captors had become clear: the Japanese were not wasting high-powered military officers and war-ready troops on a bunch of civilians, mostly women and children. They'd put a young, slightly dazed, and maybe even kind, former police-chief in charge. Lt. Hitoshi Tomayasu, our Commandant, was in his mid-thirties. He toted snapshots of his wife and children around, and I saw him show them to Mr. Carroll last week.

I'm sure the Japanese handpicked Earl Carroll to be head of the "The Internee Committee" because he looked so mealy-mouthed and timid. They probably thought they could bully him into anything, but this mild-mannered insurance executive was proving himself a Man of Steel.

"Since the Imperial Japanese Army refuses to feed us, why not let the Filipinos help with their contributions over the fence?" Mr. Carroll had argued through an interpreter.

Commandant Tomayasu had seen the wisdom in that, but disapproved of the bedlam at the Gate. Mr. Carroll had then offered to organize a package station, where all incoming items could be collected and inspected. Now instead of tossing things over the spear tipped iron bars, Filipinos turned them in at the package line, neatly marked with names of internees. (They still thronged the gate to wish us well, and pass messages if they could get away with it.)

The lines at the package station stretched from the front gate almost to the front lawn, and I braced myself for the long wait, but to the left of me, I could see friends standing in line with their parents.

"Pablo Diablo!" I called out to Paul Davis, standing maybe ten feet away with his mother and his little sister, Annie. He was in the D-G line. I waved like a crazy person.

Paul was my age and our families knew each other from church. He turned, flashing me his mischievous, wide grin, then raised his index finger and pinky, waggling them behind his head like devil horns. I closed my thumb and index finger in a circle and held it over my head, flashing an angel's halo sign back to him.

I don't know when we started calling Paul, "Pablo Diablo," which was Spanish for "Paul the Devil", but he loved it. It played into one of his strengths

—telling stories with his maimed hand. Paul was missing the second and third fingers on his left hand, but he never talked about it, and didn't seem to mind at all. He used that hand for telling the funniest stories, dancing his pointer and his pinky around to imitate little men walking toward the O.K. Corral, or flashing devil's horns. Paul could make anybody laugh. He nudged his mom, and Mrs. Davis and Annie now turned and waved at us.

Kay and I were almost at the head of the line now.

"Caroline Jones," the young woman ahead of us gave her name to the internee with the red armband at the table. The American glanced at his roster, found her name, then turned around to retrieve a large brown package tied with string, which he then passed to the delighted Miss Jones.

"You open now." A skinny Japanese guard with long whiskers stood next to the table and seemed to be in charge. He was the same guard who had glared at us five days before, and yelled 'No more in here!'

Miss Jones complied with his order, and out of the neatly tied box she pulled yards and yards of precious mosquito netting, two cartons of Lucky Strike cigarettes, numerous tins of canned meat and fish, an ill-disguised bottle of Scotch, and one cake-sized item, neatly protected with rounded cardboard supports.

The guard lost no time confiscating the booze, which was strictly forbidden in camp. He rifled through the mesh nets and tins, took none of them, but helped himself to one carton of Lucky Strikes, and then eyed the protected confection.

"Take off cover," he ordered.

Miss Jones removed the cardboard supports to reveal a heavenly sight: a frothy, white cloud of sweetness—a gold-tinged mound of meringue heaped high above a pie tin, and beading only slightly in the sweltering heat. A hush now settled over our little section of the line.

A pool of water filled my mouth, as I imagined the cool, lemon yellow custard beneath its snowy swirls—and then, I sampled in my mind, oh joy, the flaky, tender pastry crust, all of it bathed with marshmallowy meringue.

Now everyone in the L-P line turned to watch too—that lemon meringue pie, a reminder of the lost loveliness of our former life. What any one of us would have given for one luscious bite of that chilled treat.

"Put on ground." The wiry Japanese guard eyed the pie with grave suspicion.

Didn't the Japanese eat dessert? The internee with the red armband carefully placed the billow of sweetness on the bug-strewn dirt, and stepped aside. Muggy grit seemed to hang everywhere in the air, and threaten the snowy peaks.

"This clever trick. What you smuggle here?" The guard's eyes narrowed as he looked directly at the astonished Miss Jones. The sparse mustache on either side of his mouth twitched slightly like rabbit whiskers.

"It's just a pie," she responded in a clear, bell-like voice, and made a small motion like a fork being lifted to her lips.

"Message in here!" he shot back, and pointed his bayonet tip directly at the meringue masterpiece.

Then, in a lightning fast swish, he skewered the fluffy cloud with his bayonet, slashed back and forth rapidly, and sent sugary white gobs flying, leaving only a spoiled froth and a mud-yellow custard in the ravaged pie tin on the ground. Nobody spoke. The guard squatted on one knee, surveyed the pie tin, and stuck his finger gingerly in the cream, bringing it to his tongue and tasting with studied concentration. I saw his lips pucker, and startled brow knit, then he swallowed and nodded in grim satisfaction, the whiskered mustache quivering.

"You take now," he told Miss Jones.

Kay turned around and hugged me. To everyone else it must have looked like she was trying to comfort me for this shared internee loss, but I could tell Kay was laughing so hard she could not control herself. She whispered something in my ear and tried hard not to guffaw aloud. It took me a second to understand her. "Bugs Bunny with a Bayonet," she choked out.

My gaze darted to the skinny guard, whose long, straggly whiskers twitched even now. For at least thirty seconds, while Miss Jones collected her un-bayoneted wares, I buried my head in Kay's shoulder and we silently shook with laughter till both of us cried. "What's up, doc?" I whispered into her ear, and we shuddered and snorted all over again. Then Caroline Jones stepped away from the table and I freed myself from Kay's embrace. It was our turn, but Kay had not yet composed herself—though I saw her draw a hand across her mouth.

"Iserson Family," I rasped in a strangled voice as I stepped up to the table and wiped my cheeks. Bugs Bunny Guard narrowed his eyes at me, then walked away.

Chapter 4
SIDE BY SIDE

Sunday, February 15, 1942

The roast chicken simply melted in my mouth—succulent, salty, and rich. Its crispy skin crackled as I chewed. Mommy, Hope Miller, our roommate from New Hampshire, Betty and I all sat on woven grass mats on the front lawn, picnic style—eating intently and reveling in our good fortune, as jealous internees passed by. We'd invited Kay and Harry to join us, but they had a "Sunday dinner invitation" with cousins on the East Patio.

Betty tugged off the second wing of the rapidly disappearing bird and admired it, before chomping. She loved the wings.

"Betty, did you get any of the breast or thigh?" my mother asked. "You need more meat on those bones of yours."

"Mm-hmm," she nodded, lips compressed, while the fat dripped from a corner of her mouth. She wiped her chin, and swallowed before saying, "I hope Grandma's eating as well as we are tonight." We all nodded and kept eating.

In the five weeks since our internment, Grandma Naylor and the Package Line had been our salvation. Grandma sent in melons, mangoes, crackers, and tins of fish or corned beef. Some Sundays, like this one, brought a special treat when her driver, Alfonso, delivered a savory roast chicken to the gate—a chicken that miraculously survived the guards in the package shed.

We could no longer see the big-hearted Filipinos who kept coming to our rescue with food and supplies. The Japanese, embarrassed by how many came day after day, blotted out the sight of them by covering the entire front gate with *sawali*, a woven grass matting. Now when we looked to the iron spears on España Street, imagining the world outside, we saw only thatched grasses. Still, the Japanese let the packages in, and we Isersons lived for our roast-chicken Sundays.

The amazing part was how Grandma paid for these chickens: She sold Daddy's shirts. When Rosalina said Grandma had taken all our "precious treasures" from the apartment, I couldn't imagine a single one. But I was wrong: my father had dozens of handsome dress shirts.

Many of those were elegant "barong tagalogs," intricately embroidered Filipino dress shirts spun from a lightweight pineapple fiber. The fabric was so sheer that men wore it over a white undershirt. With its open collar and elegant drape, the Barong was classic evening wear for the tropics. Daddy also owned several pin-tucked shirts for his white dinner jackets and tuxedos, since he and Mommy attended dinner dances regularly. My father had run an embroidery business in the P.I. before the war, so garment quality was everything to him. Every time Grandma Naylor sold one of my father's flawless shirts to an appreciative Manila businessman, our family ate very well indeed. And every time we ate, we thought of him.

"Well, I hope *Daddy's* eating as well as we are," I added, as I polished off the chicken thigh and drumstick. Then the reality washed over me in a wave of sadness. We were selling Daddy's clothes, feeding ourselves from his finest shirts. My father had always been the breadwinner and now he still was, but were we really saying goodbye to him and all he treasured?

Betty turned pensive. "So, will he come here soon, Mommy?"

Zamboanga, where Daddy had been stationed, had fallen to the Japanese.

Leonore's Suite 43

Today brought more bad news about the British stronghold of Singapore. A mammoth air balloon floated over the camp, announcing in big red letters "SINGAPORE HAS SURRENDERED."

"Your father's probably in a military camp in Zamboanga." My mother tried to keep her voice even. "But we can hope they'll move him up here when they realize he's a civilian, who's just working for the army—not a serviceman."

Mommy tried to keep hope alive, but we hadn't heard from or about Daddy since January. And I didn't think the Japanese were looking for excuses to reunite broken families.

"He'd be very proud of you girls—the way you're making the best of a hard situation." Mommy was trying to change the subject, and keep Betty from worry. "He'd be proud that you're out of bed every morning at five-thirty, making yourselves useful."

"I'm very glad you're out of bed an hour before the rest of us, making yourselves useful. too" Hope's voice was jovial, low and raspy. "I do not budge until *'Good Morning, Good Morning, We've danced the whole night through...'*" She parodied the annoyingly bouncy wake-up tune blared over the camp public address system every day at 6:30 AM. Hope finished her chicken and lit a cigarette.

Hope Miller, a school teacher from New Hampshire in her late-thirties, had a lean, angular face, flinty blue eyes, and a trim frame. Her husband had worked as a mining engineer here in the PI, but he'd enlisted in the Army back in November. He was on Bataan now, with MacArthur's remaining forces. I knew Hope was trying hard not to think about Singapore, so she kept up a steady stream of conversation. "Five-thirty AM. That takes grit, girls." She exhaled a smoke salute to us.

We "gritty" Iserson girls rose and shone at five-thirty every morning to clean the first floor women's bathroom. That was a whole hour before everyone else, and it was a stinky job, but Mommy *volunteered* us for it, because when bathrooms were being cleaned, they were closed to all. Thanks to the plumbing efforts of men in camp, the Big House (our nickname for the Main Building) had more toilets and showers than a month ago. But forget privacy. Flimsy curtains separated the new toilet stalls, while two to four naked women shared any given shower head. You could easily wait twenty minutes in line for the toilet. In the early morning, the line stretched out the bathroom door and down the hall—fifteen or twenty women, not so patiently waiting their turn.

"Excuse me, are all the ladies in there reading the *Sunday Manila Herald*?" I'd heard Hope call from the hallway line in her gravelly voice this morning.

The women in line ahead of Hope had cackled their agreement.

But Betty, Mommy and I had not been in that line. We'd dragged ourselves out of bed in the dark, and locked the washroom doors, as we did every morning. Then we'd scrubbed the floors, scoured the toilets and washed the hand basins as fast as we could. That left us ten whole minutes to luxuriate in complete alone-time in the normally over-crowded bathroom. Sitting on the toilet without anyone hurrying me or parting the curtained door to see if the toilet was in use, was starting to be my idea of Shangri-La.

Then my gaze went back to the devoured roast chicken, and I snatched one last morsel of white meat under the rib. Maybe roast chicken Sundays were my idea of Shangri-La.

Sunday, March 2, 1942

"Is your homework done yet, Lee?"

Mommy and Betty tidied their cots in preparation for evening roll call in Room 4, but I was sitting on the edge of the large wooden bed I now shared with Kay. Harry had built it for the two of them, and it had drawers at its base and a real mattress, but since he had to sleep in the gymnasium, I was Kay's bed buddy. We both knew that mattress was a real luxury. Much better than a cot. And it was a good place to finish up vocabulary exercises.

"Finally." I nodded, folding the paper, which I then tucked it into a spiral notebook. "So much for Greek and Latin root words. Did you know "greg" is Latin for group and that's where we get 'gregarious' and 'egregious'?"

"I can understand gregarious," my mother replied briskly. She didn't even look up from cot-straightening. "But what does 'egregious' have to do with a group?" Mommy had eliminated every wrinkle and now adjusted the mosquito netting that protected her cot and Betty's.

Room 4 was tidier than it had been two months ago – partly because there weren't so many of us. Mothers of little children and all children under twelve had been moved out and over to a building behind ours, the Annex, where they'd get better food and milk. That exodus took Room 4 from fifty-six to forty women. We'd measured and sectioned it: each woman got 36 x 80 inches of space and no more. Most slept on cots donated by the Red Cross, we stored our belongings under them. We had to keep eighteen inches of aisle space clear around them. All the cots and beds were shielded now, with mosquito netting suspended from the ceilings in artfully placed wire frames. The nets dropped down at night, but were tied back by day.

"Egregious is *standing out from the group in a bad way,*" I parroted what I had just read. "Like us going to school in prison. It's egregious. How many prisoners of war do you think have to go to school?"

"I like school," said Betty, but I ignored her and pondered.

It seemed to me that if there was one thing Prisoner of War status should have earned us, it was the right to sack school. But nope. With more than seven hundred restless kids in camp, it didn't take long for the prisoner grown-ups (who served on the newly constituted "Education Committee") to decide we kids needed to go right back to our studies. Our Japanese captors loved that idea. They approved of anything that imposed order on the chaos of our crowded, disorderly lives. And, I guess it made sense. We were in a university filled with books and classrooms. Almost all our former teachers and principals were interned with us, along with mining engineers, missionaries, businessmen, and even some Shakespearean actors, happy to help teach English drama.

So, less than two weeks after our internment, Mr. Roscoe Lautzenhizer, the principal of my old school, H.C. Bordner, and Mrs. Lois Croft, the principal of our rival, the American School, announced the formation of the brand new Santo Tomas Internment Camp School or "STIC School," for short. By the third week of captivity, K-12 classes were up and running, and I was back in eighth grade. I would graduate in April.

Most of our classes met outside behind the Education Building, since the actual classrooms in the Main Building and the Ed building were chockful of cots, beds, clothing, and mosquito netting. Our parents and teachers had moved student benches and desks outside, and clustered them under large acacia trees that provided some shade. Those spreading branches didn't stop boys on the third floor of the Ed building (a men's and boys' dorm) from throwing spitballs and any other projectile they could on the studious below. Everyone knew our al fresco arrangement wouldn't last long. The rainy season was coming, and if we were still prisoners when the torrential downpours started, we'd have to find space inside. But, we'd be free by then, we all knew.

"Well, I'm headed out to the lawn now, where I will pursue gregarious activities with my egregious friends," I told my mother.

"Hold on, Lee. We haven't done roll call."

Oh, right. Mommy had been elected Room Monitor for Room 4. She had a clipboard, and her job was to call roll every evening at 7 PM, turn in the form, and make sure our room was ship-shape for any surprise inspection. Japanese guards came around unannounced to look down their noses at us and pass judgment. But they also gave out certificates for tidiness, and last week Room Four had been declared a "First Class Room." Oh joy.

"I'll vouch for Lee, Agnes. She's present." Hope lit a cigarette and flashed me a conspiratorial smile. (I had never seen Hope without a cigarette, but maybe her fifth grade students had.) "Let her go con*greg*ate with her ag*greg*ate of eighth *greg*gers before they se*greg*ate her."

My mother couldn't suppress a smile, but shook her head, and reached for her clipboard. "She's not going anywhere till we're finished here." Women's voices stilled as my mother began to call the roster. "Anderson, Marcia...."

Five minutes later I was out the door.

* * *

Evening was my favorite time in Camp. The Radio-Music Committee had rigged a public address system on the front lawn, then worked with the Recreation Committee to assemble a collection of records donated by the YMCA. They broadcast classical or big band music on the plaza from seven to nine in the evening (the Japanese said: no jazz allowed), while weary internees sat on lawn chairs or grass mats, just talking or playing mahjong and bridge. I could hear the strains of Artie Shaw's "Deep Purple" (*in the mist of a memory, you wander back to me...*) as I wandered outside looking for my new classmates. OK, where were they?

"Hey, Glamour Girl!"

A familiar voice called across the plaza. I looked left and squinted to see Paul Davis, waving at me. Paul stood near a mat, where a group of our new eighth grade friends had gathered picnic-style, as was the evening custom in camp. I picked my way around the numerous small groups seated on the lawn, eager to join my buddies, and breathe in what was left of the cool, twilight air in their company.

STIC School had some perks, I decided as I negotiated the human maze. Paul was now in my class, and having him as a classmate guaranteed fun— even in camp. Our families had been friends before the war, but he and his younger sister Annie attended the lily-white American School, while Betty and I went to Bordner, an international school for any applicant who met the entrance requirements and paid tuition. That meant at Bordner we had Spanish and Filipino classmates.

American School kids considered themselves a cut above us for that reason. "Now wouldn't you think the *American* school would admit kids based on merit and not where they were born?" I remembered my father saying. "Isn't that what 'all men are created equal' is supposed to be about?"

Daddy was the American-born son of Russian Jews, and discrimination like that bugged him.

I reached the edge of the woven mat where Paul now sat with Nellie Thomas, a friend of his from the American School, and two other Bordner friends of mine: Bunny Brambles and Bill Phillips.

Ellen Thomas—we called her "Nellie"—was rapidly becoming a friend of mine, too. Nellie was perfect: she was brainy, athletic, pretty, and just as nice as could be. Slender as a reed with sleek blonde hair, she was a year younger than Paul and me, but she was in our class because she was so darn smart. Nellie earned As on everything she ever did in her entire life and kept skipping grades and moving up. All the rest of us were turning fourteen, but Nellie was just twelve. We couldn't hate her, though, because she was always kind and fun.

Next to her sat Bunny Brambles, an angel-faced English girl with a blonde bob and easy laugh. Bunny's real name was Grace, but she had a little nose that twitched when she laughed, so her family had nicknamed her Bunny. To Bunny's right, but staring smitten at Nellie, was Bill Phillips, who could out-run, out-jump, and out-bat any boy in camp. Bill was an antsy, enterprising kid. School wasn't his cup of tea, but get him on the basketball court or baseball diamond, and our team's scores soared.

"So, you all settled over there in Glamorville? In tight with the Horsey Set?" Paul asked, making his maimed hand into a show horse that jumped hurdles.

"You're just jealous, Pablo Diablo. You Jungle Town boys can't compete."

Paul was talking about my family's new "shanty" in a campus cluster dubbed "Glamorville." As the camp population swelled and tempers flared, internees craved any kind of privacy, especially for family life. So STIC's newly-elected Executive Committee got permission for internees to build little shanties on the campus grounds. Those huts, made of bamboo, sawali, and grass nipa thatch, had to be left open on two sides, so our captors could keep tabs on us. The Japanese wouldn't let families sleep in the shanties, but if you had the money to build one, your family could gather in privacy and share meals or just talk.

My mother, with her pull-it-out-of-the-hat resourcefulness, lost no time in making sure that we had a shanty. I don't know where Mommy got the money to buy materials—probably from the phone company or maybe Grandma Naylor. Meanwhile, the Davis family had built their shanty in a different part of campus known as "Jungle Town." It was widely agreed, though, that the smartest shanties were in Glamorville. So Paul liked to needle me about being the 'horsey set.'

"So, you got an ice box and radio all up and running?"

"Nope. A charcoal stove, a table, some chairs ...and the dream of a private bathroom." I sighed and settled beside my friends on the woven grass mat.

"A radio, Davis?" Bill Phillips snorted and shook his head. "You'd be in jail so fast. Or worse."

"Isn't it loony that we can be in prison and still get tossed into jail?" Bunny Brambles said.

"Well, that's the charm of how they've arranged the whole thing, Bunny, old bag, old goat," said Paul in his Cary Grant accent. Then, mimicking the Japanese: *"Shu-ah, you locked up. But you could get even MO-AH locked up!"*

"I think that's the charm of how *we've* arranged the whole thing," Nellie reminded him, and he shrugged his agreement.

At Mr. Carroll's suggestion and with Japanese approval, we internees had agreed to police ourselves. It turned out the Japanese idea of hell was having to answer to thousands of opinionated, liberty-loving American and British civilians. They pretty much said, "Just organize yourselves, and don't escape. And by the way, we only want to talk to internee leaders, like Mr. Earl Carroll, not every blankety-blank one of you."

So, we—well, our parents—elected representatives to an Executive Committee of internees that pretty much ran the camp. We passed a constitution—a code of regulations, really—that was just a little shorter than the American constitution. We had our own police (the "Patrols

Department" who wore the red armbands), our own courts, and even our own jail in the camp. Jail was right inside the front hall of the Main Building. We also had our own slogan: *Let's show them how democracy works.* That's a pretty funny slogan for a bunch of prisoners.

Regulation Number One in our little democracy was: "No Washing Feet in the Drinking Water Fountain." You could be fined for that violation of the camp sanitary policy. And you could be tossed into jail for drunkenness or fighting or—brace yourself—fathering a child. Yup. The Japanese wanted no hanky-panky, not even between husband and wife. Our translation was: "When in shanties, keep on panties." Men were advised that they would get six weeks in jail for introducing a baby into the world. Two women had already given birth in the camp hospital, but of course those babies got their lease on life in old Manila.

"Well, at least, the Japs here haven't been the brutes they were in China," Bill said.

"Tell that to Tommy Fletcher or Henry Weeks," Bunny shot back.

Those two boys, and another Brit named Blakey Laycock, were the Santo Tomas internees who had attempted to escape two weeks before, and they had been executed. Bill didn't seem to notice Bunny's emotion.

"Complete morons," he said. "They go over the wall at night, and do they run to Manila harbor, hop a ship and cast off? No. They hit the nearest bar and get recaptured by the Japs while they're out drinking. What brainwaves."

"That's not true!" Bunny glared at Bill. "And even if it were, two of them were just boys, Bill Phillips—nineteen, twenty. They didn't deserve to die that way."

I remembered that Bunny had older brothers that age, and her family was British.

"Did you know them, Bunny?"

"They came to our house for parties before the war—friends of Ralph's and Jimmy's. They were sailors—two of them Australian and one English. Fun-loving chaps, with spunk."

"The spunk did 'em in," Paul noted a little too matter-of-factly.

"The Japs did them in!" Bunny hissed. "Tortured them, made them dig their own graves, shot them, even buried them alive!"

I couldn't breathe. The details made me sick. Now a silence hung in the air around our little mat and I glanced about nervously, but the strains of Glenn Miller lilted, and the other groups of internees nearby were engrossed in their own conversations. Not a guard in sight.

The unwritten camp rule of thumb was: no discussion of Japanese activities in public spaces. But this horrible execution of our own internees on February fifteenth, just two weeks earlier, had made a big impression on all of us.

Camp security had been loose in the beginning. Those three boys just jumped the wall one night, and we thought they'd be halfway to Australia, but the Japanese military police caught up with them four days later. They were hauled off to Manila's San Marcelino jail and beaten. Then they were sentenced to death by the Japanese military police in Manila. The "Kempeitai" (the Jap Gestapo's official name) outranked our Commandant Tomayasu. Tomayasu said he opposed the execution, but who knew.

Paul shook his head. "Imagine how Carroll and the others must have felt, forced to watch the whole thing as a lesson for other internees who might be thinking of escape."

"My father had to watch," Nellie said, her voice low. Nellie's father was a room monitor, and had been Head of Public Transportation before the war. "Dad said that when those three boys saw them coming, their faces just lit up. They were sure that they were being taken back to camp. But instead, the Japs drove them to the Chinese cemetery outside Manila and the rest was just as Bunny said." Nellie finished in a quiet, definitive voice, trying to end the conversation. But Bill and Paul didn't take the hint.

"I don't think they dug their own graves," Bill said. "I heard they took em to graves that had already been dug." He etched a hole next to the mat with one of his pebbles, put an *x* in the center, and tossed small stones at the *x*.

"Oh, for Heaven's sake!" Bunny sputtered, and her eyes glistened with tears, but Bill continued.

"Did you hear that Carroll gave 'em each cigarettes? Told them they'd be remembered as heroes, 'martyrs for freedom' in camp?"

"They will be." Paul nodded. "They got blindfolds too, but the Aussie didn't take his and said he'd 'die like a man not a rat.'" Paul paused and then lapsed into his wise-guy mode. "Which is a funny thing to say, when you think about it, because who blindfolds a rat before shooting it?"

Nellie, Bunny, and I stared in disbelief at our male friends, who seemed to need to recount every gory detail. Why were boys like this?

"Well, they were shot and buried, and that's all we need to say, because now none of us will try to escape." I said, putting an end to their retelling.

Tears streamed down Bunny's cheeks. All of us had been shaken by the gruesome event. Both the Commandant and his Lieutenant told the Executive Committee that if there was another escape, the room monitor would be shot too. My mother was our room monitor.

We internees didn't consider escape after that, and a new edge hardened between us and our captors. The Japanese had tried to seem so "reasonable" and "magnanimous" in the beginning, but now we knew that it really was *us* against *them*, and a kernel of fear and hatred had begun to harden inside me.

***

Saturday, March 14, 1942

"Look at those girls, swinging out the third-floor windows!" I motioned to Bunny.

She and I sat in folding chairs behind the Main Building on the West Patio and stared up, clapping so hard my hands hurt. My pulse raced in delight, and Bunny gripped my arm. "Breath-taking" did not begin to describe the graceful, high-stakes acrobatics of these dancers in their flame-red silks.

Waving their way-too-long gold, blue and red sleeves from high above, the Shanghai troupe swung and fluttered, but did not fall from their perches.

This was our third Saturday night variety show arranged by the Recreation Committee and hosted by Dave Harvey. It was by far the best. Dave Harvey had been an entertainer in Manila before the war, and the Recreation Committee decided he should be an entertainer during the war. The Executive Committee talked the Japs into letting us set up a makeshift stage out back, and once a month Mr. Harvey, a tall, elegant man in a white dinner jacket hosted variety shows featuring internee talent. The Rec Committee set up hundreds of folding chairs in front of the stage on the afternoon of the performance. Those without chairs just stood or sat on petates, our woven mats.

Tonight was an extravaganza. We had the good luck to be interned with an honest-to-God Chinese dance troupe. They'd been touring the Orient and gotten stuck in Manila after Pearl Harbor. The Chinese were sworn enemies of the Japanese, so they were interned with us, and they managed to get all their costumes sent in through the Package Line. The little troupe had been practicing for weeks. Tonight they performed not just on the stage in front of us, but above and around us, swinging gracefully and fearlessly from windows on the second and third floors of our boxy E-shaped building.

Commandant Tomayasu came for the show, as was his custom, and applauded louder than anyone else. I think our billiard ball Commandant was at this particular show, because it was the first since the execution. It seemed like he was trying to mend fences.

For the next two hours we almost forgot we were interned, as the dancers performed. Then finally, Dave Harvey and Phyllis Dyer took to the stage to wrap it up. It was a starlit evening and the duet, accompanied by piano, now launched into a final number—the hit song: "Side by Side."

> *Oh, we ain't got a barrel of money; maybe we're ragged and funny,*
> *But we're travelin' along, singin' a song*
> *Side by side*

As they sang, dozens of internees leapt to their feet, hooting their approval. Phyllis Dyer, the leading lady of this duo, was our own Judy Garland. Her rich contralto voice could put you right over the rainbow.

> *Oh, we don't know what's comin' tomorrow*
> *Maybe it's trouble and sorrow*
> *But we'll travel the road, sharin' our load,*
> *Side by Side*
>
> *Through all kinds of weather, what if the sky should fall?*
> *Just as long as we're together, it really doesn't matter at all.*

After all we had been through together, boy did those words sound right and uplifting. Miss Dyer and Dave Harvey crooned on to the final verse:

> *When they've all had their quarrels and parted*
> *We'll be the same as we started*
> *Just a-traveling along......*

They slowed down for the dramatic crescendo, and the whole audience was now on its feet, howling their appreciation. The crowd sang right along with them:

> *Singing our soooong,*
> *Side ......by ..... side!*

"Encore! Encore!" The crowds thundered. The singers beamed but hesitated until Comandant Tomayasu leapt to his feet, and nodded with enthusiasm. Miss Dyer whispered something to Dave Harvey, signaled for a ching-a-ling on the piano, and continued with the same tune:

> *So please allow us to sum up*
> *If ever a problem should come up*
> *We will fight like before*
> *But during the war, we're*
> *Side by side!*

They slowed for the socko-finish, drawing out each word meaningfully. We kids, and it seemed like every other internee in that electric moment, locked arms over each other's shoulders, and swayed, singing right along with them, echoing with new gusto and relish:

> *We will fight like before*
> *But during the war, we're*
> *Side by side!*

Now the night sky shook with applause and cheers. We all knew the real lyrics were "we will fight like before, but *after the war*, we're side by side." But tonight our crooners were telling us to put aside our own differences during the war, and stand "side by side" for each other and against the real enemy. Maybe at that moment Tomayasu realized his mistake. He didn't know the real words to the song of course, but nobody had locked arms with him. He had accidentally encouraged the kind of solidarity among us prisoners that would not be to the Japanese advantage.

Chapter 5
LEONORE'S SUITE

Sunday, June 28, 1942

I lay sweating beneath the mosquito netting on the big wooden bed I shared with Kay. It had to be almost midnight because out the window I saw the guards change. Kay, my mother, Betty, Hope, and most of the other women in Room Four had already drifted off to sleep, but I was too hot. April, May, and early June are "summer" in the P.I., and this summer didn't want to end. It had to be eighty-five degrees in here, and a symphony of snores filled the air: snorts, gasps, sighs, shallow breathing, and wheezing. My mind raced. My high school career started tomorrow, but it was coming on the heels of the worst summer vacation of my life. What a god-awful three months.

I closed my eyes and pretended I was in Baguio—cool, pine-scented Baguio. Rosalina should be there now. Had she gotten away safely?

Before the war our family always escaped Manila's oppressive summer heat by driving five hours north to Baguio's evergreen forests. There, high in the mountains, we basked in the mists of Bridal Veil Falls, and feasted our eyes on the red, orange, and yellow hibiscus in the vine-covered hills. During the day, we kids rode horses up lush mountain trails, or played tennis or practiced our skeet shooting. At night, we'd light a fire that snapped with pine resin. We studied the star-studded sky, and breathed in the crisp mountain air. Why wasn't I in Baguio?

I glanced through the iron grille to the night sky, and watched the Southern Cross slip to the horizon. Daddy had loved Baguio. Mommy would take Betty and me up there for the whole summer, and my father would join us on weekends, and then for a month in May. We'd stay at the Baguio Hotel, but in a private bungalow. We could walk to the hotel restaurant for meals. Somehow, Daddy always made sure we had an upright piano in our bungalow, and he'd play each night after we kids went to bed. So many nights like this—but lots cooler—I would drift off to sleep, listening to the melancholy strains of Rachmaninoff. With Betty softly snoring beside me. Well, some things hadn't changed.

Four cots away, Hope coughed in her sleep and rolled over. Smoker's cough. Hope and I shared a birthday—April third. That day was usually a doubly joyous event for me because it meant not just a party, but the end of school and the start of summer vacation.

In that sense, this year had been no different from others. Three months ago, on April 3, 1942, I turned fourteen and, along with sixteen of my new Santo Tomas classmates, graduated from eighth grade. We kids had sliced into a gigantic Honey Bee graduation cake that Mrs. Thomas had somehow gotten from a Manila bakery. The buttery, sugary, chocolatey masterpiece had made it in through the Package Line, and we kids greedily devoured it. But none of our families headed off to Baguio the next day. Instead, we'd all sweated behind the sawali-matted fence in the relentless tropical heat.

Hope coughed a second time, and I thought about the horrible news she'd gotten, as the war went from bad to worse. When our American troops evacuated Manila in December, more than seventy thousand of them had dug in on the jungle peninsula of Bataan across Manila Bay. Hope's husband had been one of those men. They planned to defend us—and eventually liberate us—from there. Bataan was strong, everyone said, and fortified by the heavily armed island of Corregidor to its south. Still, our boys had no reinforcements and no food coming in to them.

Then on April 3, the very day I'd turned fourteen, the Japanese launched a ferocious assault on Bataan. We'd heard the bombing and seen the plumes of black smoke cloud the skyline for five days. In camp, breathless rumors flew that the Americans had returned to liberate the PI. I had my wooden rosary from Rosalina going every night, praying for this great birthday present of freedom.

Instead, six days later, Bataan had surrendered. MacArthur had already high-tailed it to Australia, vowing "I shall return!"

Now horrible stories circulated. Did the Japanese make tens of thousands of shattered men march sixty miles north with practically nothing to eat or drink? Was it true they let them die by the roadside? Camp was always full of rumors so we didn't know for sure, but nowadays when internees said "Bataan," a sickening silence followed. What had happened to the men of Bataan?

Hope found out too soon: a Red Cross mail delivery informed her that her husband, George Miller, had died on the march north. My heart ached for her.

If I could only get some more air, maybe I wouldn't feel like I was suffocating. I sat upright for a minute on the edge of the bed with my feet on the cool concrete floor, looking through the mosquito netting at Hope, who slept fitfully. My school teacher friend was in her late thirties, like my mother. I breathed deeply and glanced through the iron grille of the window. Not a guard in sight, but the sky seemed to be clouding over. To my left, Mommy stirred in her sleep, and said something that I couldn't make out. Was she dreaming of Daddy?

Probably. We hadn't seen my father since November, when he'd gone off to train at Corregidor, the most heavily armored piece of real estate in Asia. One of Daddy's letters to me before the war said "You, Betty, and Mommy must not worry for a moment. Corregidor is rightly called 'the Rock.' It is impregnable." Before he signed off "with a flock of kisses," he'd written "and if my darling daughter does not know the meaning of that word, look it up in your Webster's." I did. It has nothing to do with pregnancy. It means: *Incapable of being taken by assault.*

I brushed a tear from my cheek. Corregidor was supposed to protect us from a Jap attack by sea from the west. But the Japanese had invaded from the north, not the west. Manila fell in their land attack, and the Rock came under siege from the harbor for months. Daddy was in Zamboanga by that time, but we internees counted on "the Rock." Even if Bataan had fallen, Corregidor had to stand, and those boys had to fight and get us out. Then last month, on May sixth, the unthinkable happened: The Rock fell. It crumbled. Poof. Our last hope gone.

That news, trumpeted by the Japanese and emblazoned on the front pages of the *Manila Herald*, hit us with the force of a quake and a typhoon. In fact, the disastrous news of Bataan and Corregidor were actually accompanied by an earthquake and a typhoon. We barely had time to focus on the catastrophe at Bataan before a hideous earthquake shook the islands. No one in camp died: we thanked God for our earthquake-proof building. But shanties fell and the new pipes in our plumbing burst. Then in early June, heavy rains and ferocious winds pummeled the camp. The storm washed shanties away a second time, and destroyed the little gardens we had started planting. The punishing weather even delayed the start of school in June—till tomorrow.

I lay back down on my bed, a little cooler and wearier. We all knew now that we were going to be "STIC-stuck" not just for weeks or months. Our parents were saying it could be another year. Another year of bugs in our beds, and weevils in our cereal, and spiders and ants crawling everywhere. Another year of shared bathrooms and no privacy. Another year of lines for chow, lines for packages, and lines for mail from home. Our family hadn't gotten a single letter through the Red Cross mail line. We still hadn't heard from Daddy. When I looked out the window from my bed, a cloud completely covered the Southern Cross. Not a single star winking at me.

Monday, July 6, 1942

One week after school started, I heard Paul's Cary Grant imitation behind me. "Lee, old bag, old goat!" I turned to see him taking two steps at a time, bounding up the Main Building's wide stone staircase. We were on our way to class. "Look at this!" Paul reached into his shorts pocket and revealed three white balloons. "Leftovers from Annie's party," he announced with a conspiratorial wink. Paul's little sister Annie had just turned twelve, and Betty' d been invited to that party on the Saturday after school started.

"Nobody wants white balloons. I don't know why they include those in the packet, anyway." I shrugged off his delight.

"Nobody except me and the Brooksies." He raced past me to catch up with the Brooks twins—Curtis and Barney at the top of the stairs. The Brooksies, as we called them, were American School kids who were in our class—smart and sometimes mischievous. They couldn't hold a candle to Paul in wise-guy devilry, though. I saw them whoop in immediate understanding when Paul showed them his find. They sped up to the next floor.

"What's Pablo Diablo up to?" Bunny asked as she came to my side, algebra notebook in hand. I shrugged, but suspected the boys' antics would make the morning lively.

Last week, when school began, our classes moved indoors. The Spanish priests who owned the university had given permission to use the empty chemistry labs on the rooftop of the Main Building as classrooms. They wanted to make sure we didn't asphyxiate ourselves with gas pouring from the spigots, so they cut that flow and opened an entire floor of labs from what had been their Pharmacy School for our new STIC School. These long, open rooms ran the length of the building. They were enclosed under flat roofs, but were up on the fourth floor, so we got our exercise.

Bunny and I emerged from the stairwell to the open-air section of the roof and took a deep breath of the mild morning air before heading into our make-shift classroom. Our teachers had divided the open chemistry labs into individual classrooms by inserting long chalk board dividers. That wasn't the ideal arrangement. When we were in Mr. Livingston's algebra class, we could hear Mrs. Maynard teaching tenth grade Latin on one side, while Father Monte taught eighth grade Spanish on the other.

Now, as we filed into the room, Paul and the Brooksies settled into their stools at the back, while Nellie, Bunny, and I slid into our seats in the front row. Pablo signaled me with his devil's horn fingers to watch him. That was going to be tricky because he was behind me.

Then Mr. Livingston—whom Paul had dubbed "Cuthbert" because he reminded him of the short, sturdy British boxing champ, Johnny Cuthbert—walked into the room, and nodded to us perfunctorily. Our Cuthbert was short and well built, a funny and feisty man, a mining engineer, whom we all respected. He occasionally lightened our day by throwing erasers or chalk at any boy in his class who gave a dumb answer. Now silence descended as he turned his back to us and started writing equations on the board.

I glanced behind me and saw Paul quietly filling his white balloons with water from the chem lab faucet in front of him. The gas spigots were off, but apparently, the water was not. The Brooksies could barely contain their glee.

I nudged Bunny to take a look, and she alerted Nellie. Then while Cuthbert's back was still turned, Paul lobbed not one, not two, but three water bombs over the chalk board divider behind him. We girls tried to stifle giggles, while we waited to hear the shrieks from the other side.

A hugely gratifying outburst of shouts and squeals followed, as the three water bombs drenched the eighth grade behind us. Bunny, Nellie, and I pivoted to the chalkboard, toward Cuthbert, our faces a mask of innocence and surprise. A STIC School tradition was born.

Friday, July 24, 1942

Betty and I returned from the newly built package shed, excited and stupefied. Everything was so much more organized at the gate these days. Our captors had agreed to let internee men build a shed out of bamboo and sawali to house donations from the outside. Mr. Carroll worked with the Japanese to set up a system of receiving packages for an hour or so in the morning, and distributing them every afternoon at three. There were lines, always lines, but our family got packages from Grandma Naylor, some German friends in Manila, and some Russian friends on the outside a few times a week. It was always exciting to go to the gate and see what awaited us.

Today's harvest was a bonanza. A note on the top of our exciting haul said:

Sweets for the Sweet!
Here are two for you!
(Sort of...)
Love,
Grandma N.

"What are we going to do with it?" Betty asked, as we lugged the enormous ten-pound tub of Ghirardelli's cocoa into our ramshackle Glamorville shanty, where Mommy fiddled with the charcoal stove.

We thought food gifts from Grandma Naylor were a thing of the past. She had sold the last of Daddy's shirts three weeks ago, and those luscious chicken dinners were fading into memory. But Grandma still scavenged Manila daily for what she could find, and ten pounds of unsweetened cocoa —- wow! Betty and I pulled up folding chairs, huddled around the large, lidded tin, and waited for our mother's pronouncement. Of course, she did make the best chocolate frosting in all of Manila, but how many cakes could we possibly eat? And this was an awful lot of cocoa to drink in the steamy tropics.

Our mother just stood and stared from our charcoal stove to the can. "Maybe we could give Mr. Whitman some competition," she said in a voice both amused and calculating.

Mr. Whitman, one of our shanty neighbors, was making fancy dipped chocolates and marketing his wares as "Whitman's Chocolates." He wasn't related to the real *Whitman's*, of course, but internees did what they could to be creative with names. He charged twenty centavos per chocolate.

Mommy drew her own folding chair over and sat down. "What if we made fudge? There's a bottomless bag of sugar outside that Red Cross canteen. They're not charging for sugar," Mommy continued. "And I bet Flossie would help too. She and Janet both have a sweet tooth." Flossie was a Room 4 friend, and she and her daughter Janet had been known to trade avocados for candy bars.

The food supply was not as dire in camp these days, because after six months of leaving us to our own (and Red Cross) resources, the Japanese had finally admitted they had a responsibility to feed us. So they allotted a miniscule amount of money per prisoner per day—40 centavos—and sent Executive Committee members, red armbands and all—into Manila under guard to buy food for camp. They'd also allowed some Filipino vendors to set up market stalls in camp, where we could buy coconuts, limes, cassava flour, cinnamon, onions and garlic, and some meat. Enterprising internees had even set up two little restaurants, for those who were bored with the Central Kitchen, and willing to pay for something different. If you had money, you could buy plenty in camp, but the key thing was to have cash—so internees were always on the lookout for money-making schemes.

"*Iserson Chocolates* sounds good to me," Betty said.

"Not compared to *Whitman's*," I countered.

"First let's make the fudge, and see if we can compete. Then we'll concentrate on advertising." My mother pried open the lid of the can and extracted a large, folded envelope, sitting atop the chocolate. "And, Lee, looks like this is for you, pet," My mother handed me a manila envelope, marked "Leonore."

Leonore is my formal name, and believe me, it is a burden of a name. I share it with one of my great-great Russian grandmothers, but I like people to call me "Lee" because they always scotch "Leonore." They turn it into *Lenore* or *Leonora* or *Leone* or something else wrong. Except for Daddy. When he says "Leonore" in his deep baritone voice, my name sounds like music.

My mother and Betty watched as I unfastened the clasp on the back, and slid four pages of hand written sheet music from the envelope. Daddy's sure, flowing script on top announced *"Leonore's Suite,"* and my heart swelled. My father had written this piece of music for me over a year ago—for my thirteenth birthday.

If I had been a devout Jew, like Daddy's mother, I would've had my Bat-Mitzvah on my thirteenth birthday—the time Jewish girls are officially considered women. Instead, my father had written this music for me and penned a little note on top, "Happy Birthday, dearest Lee, my darling grown-up daughter." He had played it to the oohs and ahhs of our delighted friends in April 1941, as his way of welcoming me to adulthood.

My father loved Rachmaninoff. He had heard him play in New York City in 1928, a few months before I was born, and I could hear echoes of the haunting Russian composer in the work he had written for me. First came dark, rich bass chords—sometimes passionate and then serene. Then the haunting silver melody. Daddy would play it in our apartment whenever I begged him to—I didn't play the piano. But I hadn't heard this beautiful suite since November 1941 when he left for Zamboanga. Tears streamed down my face as I wondered who would play it for me now.

Mommy and Betty saw what I was holding and immediately understood.

Mommy came over and knelt beside me, placing a protective arm around my shoulder and whispered, "Oh, how wonderful for Grandma to send that in, honey. You know, in a special way, that will keep Daddy here with us." She paused and announced, "Hope can play it for you." Hope taught fifth grade, and she frequently accompanied her little charges on the piano.

"You think she can play anything this tricky, Mommy? I mean *She'll Be Comin' Round the Mountain* is one thing. But *Leonore's Suite* is …well, you know."

"Daddy said 'passionate and romantic and a little melancholy too,'" said Betty, who was jealous that she didn't have her own suite yet, but then again, she hadn't turned thirteen.

"Like our very own Leonore?" My mother gave my shoulder a squeeze.

"We are going to have Hope play that for you, Lee." She nodded with conviction.

I tucked the sheet music back in its envelope and excused myself, so I could put it in a safe place: the deep wooden drawers of the bed I shared with Kay. Other women in camp had managed to hide their diamond necklaces and brooches by sewing them into the hems of gowns. Well, this was my crown jewel, and it would lie buried under all my clothes in my bed drawer.

That night Mommy asked our New Hampshire friend if she could play it for me, and Hope promised she would the next day, which was Saturday.

I could hardly wait for the morning to end. With all our Saturday chores done, Hope and I sneaked off to a little university practice room with a piano. There I waited for her to transport me to my pre-war world: the world of music and beauty and a father who loved me "more than words can ever say," he told me, when he handed me his composition.

Mommy thought I might rather be "alone" with Daddy, so she corralled Betty into making fudge with her and Flossie. Hope sat now at the piano bench studying the piece as she smoked, brows knit and a near scowl on her face. Then she extinguished her cigarette, straightened her back, and began to play.

Notes descended sharply, like stones chipped from a block of New Hampshire granite. They seemed to land in shattering, hard-edged showers, pelting a path from keyboard to eardrum. With a sinking heart, I realized that I might never again hear that piece as Daddy had written it. Dear Hope soldiered on, playing the piano with the same no-nonsense, workman-like dedication that made her such a reliable teacher and friend. But she played without nuance or sweetness. And she paused, puzzling over the numerous sharps and flats in the piece. Still, there were some moments when the grace of the music leapt through, and I knew for sure that the love of my father was still with me, right here in this piece of music from what seemed like a lifetime ago.

When she finished playing, Hope looked up at me apologetically, a frown on her face.

"I think this exceeds my Granite State certification," she said, reaching for another cigarette. Then she saw the tears in my eyes and rose to hug me instead.

"Thank you, Hope," I blurted out, trying not to show my profound disappointment, as I leaned into her bony, nicotine-scented shoulder. "For a while Daddy was with me." I tried to hold my tears in check and mask my discouragement.

Then Betty burst into the practice room. "Lee, come quick! There's a truck at the main gate full of new kids!"

I grabbed the manila envelope and raced to the main courtyard with my sister. New kids? Wow. Something to take my mind off the haunting piece that now belonged to another lifetime.

Chapter 6
LULU

July 25, 1942 (continued)

The second truck jostled through the iron gates just as Betty, Hope, and I got there. I had *Leonore's Suite* tucked safe beneath my arm. I'd get it back to my bed drawer soon enough, but I didn't want to miss this excitement. Thirty or forty dazed women and children swayed desperately atop the truck, gripping the side rails for dear life as the open-air convoy lurched to a stop.

"Where are they coming from?" I asked Betty.

"Cebu. They've been in two different camps down there. They look terrible, don't they?"

Cebu was a tropical island, hundreds of miles south of us. These new internees had come by ship and the journey, or maybe their two prior camps, must have been horrid.

I scanned the new prisoners in the convoy. Gosh, that was us seven months ago. Small children crying. Confused mothers gripping the hands of their little ones and clinging to whatever blankets or purses they had. Their clothes were filthy. A few older men in the group hefted bags and tried to keep their families together.

Then I saw her standing near the rail edge: a sturdy, determined girl about my age with a square face, penetrating blue eyes, and unruly sand-colored curls that were just as disheveled as my brown locks. She stood next to her frazzled mother, who struggled to comfort the sobbing one-year old in her arms. The girl my age clutched the hand of another little girl, who might've been eight or nine. She leaned over to whisper something that made her smile. Then she straightened herself and continued to look about with a probing stare.

I saw that gaze fly up to the clock and the cross tower. She scanned our boxy grey building, with its evenly spaced windows, and its missing columns. Then she took in the front plaza, where all of us milled about. Because it was Saturday, lawn chairs were scattered beneath acacia trees and Filipino vendors hawked their wares. She seemed puzzled.

There was something about her lively, alert, and searching face that drew me to her. She looked like she might burst into a radiant smile, even though she was completely serious. She didn't know it yet, but I had picked her out for my new best friend. Well, for my best friend period: because I'd never had a best friend. Betty didn't really count. I smiled broadly and waved at her. At first, she didn't see me, but then she looked right at me, clearly confused. I waved again. In two seconds, she beamed the radiant smile I'd known was there all along and flagged an energetic hand back at me.

By the time the guards opened the back gate of that truck, we each knew that we were heading for each other.

"Mary Louella Cleland, slow down!" I heard her mother calling, as her eldest daughter dropped the younger girl's hand, leapt off that truck, and darted toward me.

"You're Mary Louella?" I heard myself exclaiming to the bright-eyed girl right in front of me.

"How did you know?!" she squealed in delight. I pointed to her struggling mother. "Oh! Mommy only calls me that when she's mad. I'm Lulu. Everyone calls me Lulu."

"Lulu"—even her name seemed to promise fun times and looney adventures. Lulu was shorter than I was, but she looked about my same age.

"I'm Lee—well, actually *LEE-uh-nor* Agnes Iserson." I drew out each syllable with exasperation so she could see what a nuisance my name was too. "Lulu, we are going to have the best time together," I told her, a bubble of complete delight rising within me, and I hugged her.

"In prison?" she rasped. "We're going to have the best time *in prison*?"

Lulu had a very distinctive voice—she seemed to be scraping the upper limits of her range whenever she got excited, which, I'd learn, was often. Now she stared at me with a dazzling "this is too-good-to-be-true" gaze.

"Well, it is prison, and it's horrible," I conceded, "but we kids—" I was about to explain about school and fun times, when Lulu, whose gaze had wandered, cut me off.

"What is this—a country club?"

She gestured to the groups of adults settled on the lawn playing bridge and mahjong, then noticed some boys, who had a baseball game underway. "What's going on here?" She stared at industrious members of the Recreation Committee, assembling folding chairs on the lawn in front of a raised platform. Dave Harvey would be back on stage tonight, probably singing his hit tune *Cheer Up: Everything's Going to Be Lousy*.

"That's our "Little Theater Under the Stars." I pointed to the stage in front of the Main Building. "It's Saturday, so there's going to be a show tonight—a game show, I think. But Dave Harvey, our emcee, he's a good song and dance man too."

"You've got a theater?" Lulu's eyes widened and her jaw dropped.

"Well, we've got a stage. And the way it's set up now is a big improvement. We used to have shows on the west patio behind the Main Building, but it got too crowded back there because internees built shanties everywhere. It's like a slum back there now."

I remembered the fabulous Chinese dance troupe, hanging from the second and third floor windows of our E-shaped building. That was a thing of the past. As the Japanese corralled more and more prisoners into camp, internees had struggled to create living space, so our captors had allowed more shanties—little three-walled lean-tos—to be built in the palm fringed patios.

"The Recreation Committee asked the Commandant if we could have the entertainment somewhere else, and voila—they let us set up that stage in front of the Main Building permanently. Except for the folding chairs. We have to put those away between shows."

"Did I die and go to Heaven?" Lulu sounded as if she had laryngitis. "All those days in the dark, stinky hold of that ship. No toilets and no air and rats and all those Jap soldiers. And we were in ankle-deep water…" Her voice got soft and trailed off. "Maybe I did die …and I went to Heaven. Are you my guardian angel?" she asked incredulous.

"Mary Louella—get over here!" Lulu's mother brought her back to her earthly existence, and she raced in the direction of her mom and the little girls. I was right behind her. "Hold Margie's hand, so she doesn't run off," Mrs. Cleland ordered and clutched the baby.

Lulu thrust a sure hand out to her independent sister, and introduced me to her mother, her nine-year-old sister Margie (whom she called 'Mouse'), and her baby sister, Maureen.

"Mrs. Cleland, don't worry. We'll all help —" I started to say, when the voice of authority rang out from behind us.

"Listen up, folks." Mr. Carroll with his red armband now addressed the new arrivals. "Welcome to Santo Tomas. You've been through hell. We're going to do everything we can to make it better for you here, so help us out a little by following directions."

He informed the forty newcomers that mothers with small children would go to the Annex behind the Main Building. With its special kitchen, they'd get more milk and healthier food for the little ones. "Girls over ten and their mothers, and single women, go to the Main Building please—which we affectionately refer to as 'the Big House.' Men in the gymnasium and the Education Building."

Lulu stared up at her mother, who had little Maureen in her arms. Already Mrs. Cleland was approaching Earl Carroll, and I saw him nod and say, "Yeah, that's fine."

"Lulu, help me settle in at the Annex, and then we'll see whether you stay there or go to the Main Building."

With *Leonore's Suite* still tucked under my arm and the disappointing memory of Hope's rendition fading, I helped the Clelands collect their small straw bags, and head to the Annex. I spotted Betty and Annie Davis in the plaza with new kids their age, and suddenly all of life seemed brighter again.

* * *

While I helped Lulu and her family settle into their room, I told my new best friend everything, absolutely everything, about our life in Manila before the war, and our new life in camp, and how Grandma Naylor had sent us a tin of cocoa, and that we planned to make into fudge to earn some extra money. She stopped me on the word "Naylor."

"Is that right? The Naylors? Do you know Billy and Buddy Naylor?"

Billy and Buddy were Grandma Naylor's *real* grandchildren. They had lived with their grandparents in Manila before the war, but those lucky boys had gone back to the States a month before the Japanese attacked.

"Well, sure. They lived down the street from us. But do you know them? How do you know the Naylors?" I asked.

"Cebu—they used to live in Cebu near us before they moved to Manila. Isn't that something?"

Lulu and I were finding all sorts of parallels and coincidences in our lives. We both had fathers in the war. We knew many of the same people in the PI, even though she had lived in the tropical paradise of Cebu and we lived in Manila. Her American grandfather had been in Cebu since the late 1890s, just before my grandfather started his business in Luzon, and hers owned a shipping business there. Her grandfather played poker with MacArthur, when the MacArthurs were stationed on that island. Lulu's parents didn't like MacArthur either. Their family had spent a summer in Baguio too.

We chatted happily while we shoved cots into place, stowed the Clelands' small stash underneath them, and then fixed the beds. "Fixing the beds" meant tying up the mosquito nets, which were suspended from the ceiling by a network of strings. By day, the nets were tacked up and hung like spider webs—thirty or forty see-through flying carpets in mid-air—but they could be lowered each night and tucked under the mattresses in protection. This packed Annex room, like Room 4, now resembled the overcrowded scene of some Halloween prank—slightly organized squalor. I bet Lulu had grown up in a big, beautiful Cebu villa.

"Well, it's not much, but it looks about as good as it can," I said.

"You've even got mosquito netting." Lulu bit her lower lip in wonder and stared up at our handiwork.

My thoughts flew back to those first nights without mosquito nets, and I knew Lulu must have waged her own war against the creepy-crawlies. In fact, I could see two mosquito bites on her face. Lulu would stay with her mother and sisters tonight, but I was going to work on getting her into the Main Building if I could.

"It's a country club," she whispered shaking her head in wonder. Lulu turned to me, suddenly serious, her voice rising. "You just can't imagine the dark, stinky hold of that ship, the rats …the hideous smell. There were no toilets and it took six days to get here," she began to tell me. "I really thought we'd died and gone to hell."

Mrs. Cleland put an index finger to her lips and pointed her chin toward the two cots where Lulu's little sisters now almost dozed. She signaled for us to step outside the door, and Lulu said in a dramatic stage whisper to her mother, "We're going outside!"

Her mother flashed her an exasperated look and shooed us out of the room.

I grabbed my one precious possession from the window shelf, where I had stowed it. Secure in my grasp was the manila envelope bearing *Leonore's Suite*. We darted down the stairs and into the sunshine talking non-stop.

* * *

"I'll show you my room in the Big House," I said as we strode toward the Main Building. But Lulu stopped outside the Annex, and stared at the back courtyard, which to me looked like an overpopulated colony of mismatched ants at work. Swarms of people were everywhere.

"Is this the Ritz?" She gazed around in complete disbelief.

It took me a minute to realize that she was actually in awe. The newly expanded Central Kitchen behind the Main Building, was a hive of activity with internee crews peeling sweet potatoes, trimming green beans, and preparing tonight's dinner. Braised beef was on the menu—a big step up from our early picnic-style meals of Spam. Rows of recently constructed wooden tables lined the area adjacent to the kitchen. We could seat up to a thousand internees here. This open area was still exposed to the elements, but the men were working on getting it covered.

"Well, you should've seen it when we got here. This took a lot of work, you know. And we only get two meals a day. C'mon. I'll show you my room." I was anxious to get my music safely stowed in the wooden drawer of my bed.

In high spirits, we walked past the Father's Garden, and back out to the main plaza. Large palms ringed the perimeter and stately acacias dotted the patio and provided shade. People sat on mats, reading the camp's weekly newspaper, *Internews*, playing cards, and chatting. A group of four women washed their hair in a new outdoor tub the men had rigged up. Some Japanese newspapermen were even taking photographs—probably to show the world how great life was at Sanctuary Santo Tomas. But the internees turned their backs to him, and refused to be photographed smiling. We strode across the lawn toward the front entrance.

"What are you carrying?" Lulu asked.

I reached in to the envelope to show her my treasured music, but I felt my stomach plummet. The envelope was too light. Even before I reached in, I knew the truth. I'd left in a hurry. I hadn't put *Leonore's Suite* back in the folder before I left the practice room. Oh no. Maybe Hope took it. No, Hope had left with Betty and me. I stopped dead in my tracks. My heart sped up and my breath came in short gasps, while my mind raced.

"Oh, Lulu, it's what I'm *not* carrying." I blurted out suddenly near tears. "The music my father wrote me when I turned thirteen. *Leonore's Suite*. It's gone." She stared blankly at me. "C'mon—it has to be back in the practice room. We need to find it before a cleaning crew throws it out."

So Lulu and I ran. We darted up the stairs of the Main Building and flew through the long corridors, turning left, then right, then left again, and she continued to pepper me with questions as we ran.

"Is that right? He wrote you music? Your father wrote you your own music? That's unbelievable. And you have it here? Do you play the piano?" A breathless string of questions and exclamations poured from her. Lulu could talk even while she was running and bumping into people, but I couldn't answer or even concentrate on what she was saying. I was frantic, and hated myself for my carelessness.

As we rounded a final corridor and approached the little practice room, I came to a full stop and shushed her. Lyrical notes cascaded from the practice room and swelled in intensity as they poured into the hall. Daddy! Daddy was playing it!

For one moment, I couldn't move, as I listened to the virtuoso fireworks of those silvery notes streaming toward us—piano mastery that Hope had only dreamt of reproducing. I was mesmerized by the magic of my father's perfectly rendered piece. Even Lulu was awed to silence as the chords, first passionate and then romantic, slowed, turned dark and washed poignantly over the room I had left just an hour before. My father was in Santo Tomas at last!

I dashed to the door of the practice room, calling "Daddy!" and rounded the door jamb breathless, to see the arched back of a tall, slender man in khaki uniform hunched purposefully over the keyboard. The music halted abruptly, as he spun around, annoyed that we had broken his concentration. A Japanese guard!

His stern gaze took both of us in as he rose to his feet. He had to be six feet two inches tall, enormous for a Jap. Probably in his twenties. I stared at him, terrified, recalling his face from somewhere else. Where? The broad brow. The wide eyes. He was the guard who'd smiled at me—or had he *leered* at me?—six months ago when we were filling out those forms at Villamor Hall.

Dumbfounded, Lulu and I stood rooted to the tile floor of that little room. Then my new best friend, veteran of two other camps and a week in hell, had the presence of mind to step forward and bow politely to him, bow from the hips in perfect Japanese manner—as if she had been doing it all her life. I immediately followed her lead. The guard bowed back formally, but not as deeply as we had bowed, then pointed his chin dismissively to the door, as if he expected us to leave. But I couldn't. I stood planted in that spot and stared daggers at him.

"Let's go, Lee," Lulu whispered and tugged at me. But I was going nowhere.

"That's mine," I said to the guard as evenly and politely as I could manage, and pointed to the sheet music he had been transforming to pure magic. I couldn't believe I wasn't talking to Daddy. "That music is mine." I tapped my fingers on my chest to make him understand.

His wide forehead creased and he hesitated, but glanced back at the piano with dawning comprehension. Then he gathered the music on the stand, scowled at me and grasped the four pages possessively. Would he keep it or destroy it? Steal my last gift from Daddy? As he flipped through the pages, I noticed his very large hands and long, slender fingers, returning to the first page.

"What means '*Leonore*'?" he asked abruptly, pointing to the word penned in my father's hand just a year before. The guard made it sound like ree-OH-nore. My stomach churned to see him finger my precious gift, Daddy's own handwriting, with his grubby Jap hands.

"It's my name. *Leonore* is my name. My father wrote that for me." I held my ground, wondering if I was going to end up at torture-central, Fort Santiago for my sass, or made to stand for hours, tied to a post, in the unbearable heat and blinding light of the sun. We'd heard about all these things. But at that moment, I didn't care.

"*Suite* is a kind of music," I added, trying to sound authoritative.

"I know 'suite,'" he responded curtly. "Your *name* Lee-OH-nor?"

"Yes," I glared back at him and corrected him. "LEE-uh-nor."

"Ah," he nodded crisply and paused, as if weighing an important decision. "My name Haruo. Hah-ROO-oh," he repeated slowly, bowing with great seriousness. Then he handed me the music, turned on his shiny black boot, and walked out the door.

Lulu and I nearly fainted.

Chapter 7
OPERATION ARIGATO

Saturday, October 24, 1942

Lulu and I had been joined at the hip for three months now. Her mother, whom I called "Mim" (she was not my mother; she was my "Mim") and her little sisters remained in the Annex, but we'd gotten Lulu into the Big House, just a floor above us in Room 33. Lulu and I went to school together, sold fudge together, played bridge together, sang in the chapel choir together, and took whatever camp duties we could as an inseparable duo.

Today Lulu and I were on weevil duty, sitting across from each other at the end of a long picnic table behind the central kitchen. Bags of rice lay on the ground beside us, sieves and bamboo baskets sat in front of us, while we, like lab technicians, had tweezers in hand. Our job was to sift the rice and pluck the weevils, slithery long-nosed beetles, and other creepy-crawlies from the grain that would be tomorrow's dinner. A violent typhoon had pummeled Manila at the end of September, and our rice, which hadn't been stored in water-tight containers, was now home to weevils and worms galore.

"Should we be eating this even after we tweeze and boil it?" I squinted with disgust at the collection of vermin in my sieve.

So far, five internees had been hospitalized in Manila for dysentery, a stinky, horrid disease of non-stop, bloody diarrhea caused by contaminated food and water. Two internees had died of it.

Then out of nowhere Lulu said, "So, do you think they're still alive?" When she saw my puzzlement, she added, "Our fathers. Do you think they're still alive?"

My heart lifted. Lulu and I had this conversation about once a month. Both our fathers were with the Armed Forces, and neither of us knew where the most important men in our lives were right now, but talking about them seemed to bring them closer.

"They're alive." I nodded with more confidence than I felt. "But the Japs took Zamboanga back in February, a month after we got here. My dad's probably in a military prison camp down there."

"Oh, that would be hideous." Lulu sympathized. "Hideous" was a Lulu signature word. Anything that was horrible, ludicrous, or just plain bad was 'hideous.'

I plucked an enormous, glossy-shelled beetle from the grain, and tucked him under an overturned glass, taking care not to kill him because some of the little kids were collecting this kind as pets. They tethered the "salagubangs" or "sallies" to their shirt buttons with string and actually got the critters to sit on their shoulders. One little girl told me she'd had her "Sally" for six months.

"What was your dad doing in Zamboanga? That's really far south. *'Oh, the monkeys have no tails in Zamboanga...'*" she intoned, swinging her head rhythmically and chanting the popular ditty about the southernmost tip of the southernmost island.

"Building an airstrip, Brainwave. The Army Corps of Engineers thought we needed one down there."

"Well whatever *for*? Winter holiday?" Lulu's raspy, alto voice was completely engaged and full-throttle. "Did I tell you we went to Zamboanga once on vacation?" She didn't wait for my answer. "*Heaven*. Pink sand beaches, turquoise sea. You don't want to eat the fish because they're so gorgeous. Red, orange, purple. Does your father like fish? He better."

"He likes all food." I laughed, remembering our Sunday cookouts and my portly father's waistline. "I bet in his camp they've just got lugao, though." Lugao was the rice gruel we sometimes had for breakfast. "But at least, he's in a Jap camp. For him a Nazi camp would be worse. He's Jewish."

"What? Are you brain-dead?" Lulu lowered her voice to an urgent whisper, "Forget Nice-Guy Haruo. These Japs have been the worst! Reprobates. Complete reprobates."

Reprobates was another Lulu word, this one for any villainy. I didn't blame her for her vehemence, though. Dozens of captured army nurses from Bataan had arrived in our camp last month, and in hushed tones confirmed horrible rumors of cruelty, humiliation, and bayoneting of our boys, who had surrendered.

"What's Jewish?" she asked as an afterthought.

I dropped my tweezers and stared at her, dumbfounded. "Lulu, have you been living under a rock? '*What's Jewish*'?"

"Like Irish? Or Spanish?" she asked with complete sincerity.

Sometimes my best friend, the dearest light of my life in camp, completely astounded me. "Mary Louella Cleland, don't you Protestants learn anything in Sunday school? Wasn't Jesus Christ *Jewish*?"

She paused and thought for a moment, mentally inventorying her Bible stories. It was one of the rare moments I saw Lulu without a ready response. "Well, maybe before he became Christian," she said defensively. "So, are they still around? The Jewish?"

This was too much. "Yes! And Hitler's rounding them up in Europe, and killing them, or carting them off to be slaves or something. Nobody knows."

Except in Manila we knew something very bad was happening because dozens of Jewish families arrived in Manila in 1938—well-educated German Jews, fleeing Hitler. They built a synagogue in Manila, and some of them became my classmates at Bordner. Of course, those friends weren't captured and brought into camp with us because they were German—and Germans were on the same side as the Japanese. Go figure.

Lulu concentrated on her weevils, and became subdued. "Well, then I guess it's good the Japs have him—your dad, I mean. How'd your mother find a Jewish to marry?"

"A *Jew*, Lulu, not 'a Jewish.' There are lots of Jews in New York. OK, my Irish Catholic mother got restless on her family farm in Utica, so she decided to go off on her own and get a job in New York City. Her brother lived there. So she lived with her brother, took classes, and became a stenographer."

"That's like a secretary?"

"Uh-huh, a little less than a full-fledged secretary. Stenographers take shorthand and type letters for executives."

Lulu nodded, but kept her eyes on the pile of grain before her and the tedious task of de-bugging. I think she was a little embarrassed about not remembering who the Jews were. I continued tweezing out the vile, black-shelled vermin, and went on.

"So, Mommy answered an ad for a job in a garment factory in the city. And who did she see on the third floor when the elevator doors opened to the offices—none other than Harold Roland Iserson, my father. Jaunty. Handsome."

"Wait a minute. I thought you told me he looked like Don Ameche," Lulu objected. "That's shifty, not handsome."

Candor was Lulu's trademark. She didn't care whose bubble she burst.

"I think he's handsome! I love Don Ameche." It was my turn to be defensive about the buoyant young actor with the sparkling brown eyes.

She arched both eyebrows in doubt. "Well, was it love at first sight?" she said.

"Not for Mommy. She just went to her interview and hoped for the best. But the next week, Agnes Hanagan had a job on the lower East Side of Manhattan, working at Iserson Embroideries. My grandfather, Abraham Samuel, owned the business And A.S.—that's what we call him—decided Daddy should run the plant he was opening in the Philippines."

"The plant here was a smart idea." Lulu nodded. "Nobody embroiders like the Filipinas—fast, perfect, and *cheap*—that's what my mother says."

"Yup. And that was back in '26. They were even cheaper then. Well ... so guess who Daddy asks to go to Manila with him as his Secretary?"

I tossed two weevils out of my stash, and dumped the clean rice into the bamboo basket.

Lulu shrieked in delight, "Just like that? Your mother?"

"Uh-huh," I gave a smug nod. "Daddy said she was a real looker. Adventurous too. But Mommy still didn't know that Daddy was positively *mooning* over her. She just leapt at the chance to see Singapore, Hong Kong, Manila. Agnes Hanagan was on that boat before you could say 'Farewell, Flapper.'"

Lulu hooted and sang, "*Toot, toot, tootsie, goodbye.*" She parroted the song that was so popular in the thirties. "That's so romantic, Lee-lee. Puddles of purple passion."

Lulu would listen to my stories for hours—and I to hers. The truth is, besides school and camp duty, that's all there was to do sometimes. No radio. No place to go. Just tell stories.

"So, Daddy ran the new business in Manila," I continued. "And he proposed to Mommy. And they got married, and went on a round-the-world honeymoon trip—on the S.S. Mauritania. And they rode camels in front of the pyramids. And they sailed through the Suez Canal, and eventually got back to the PI. And then I came along thirteen months later." I took a deep breath and gave a satisfied nod.

"Tah-duh." Lulu mimicked a drum roll. "And the rest is HISTORY," she finished with a weevil-whomping flourish.

Hope came by with a wheelbarrow full of vermin-infested rice and replenished our nearly empty vats.

"I have never seen two girls jabber more in my entire life," she said in her rocky voice that always sounded like she had just put out a cigarette. But she was smiling. "This'll keep you going till quitting time."

"Ugh. Hideous." Lulu grimaced at the new grain, which was dotted with something besides weevils. "What's in here? Rat droppings? Maggots?"

"Uh-huh. Both." said Hope with a straight face. "We're going for variety, girls."

She pivoted the empty barrow toward the kitchen and almost left us to our task, but then stopped and turned back to us. "On second thought, you two girls come with me, and leave that for the next team. I've got a special project for you."

* * *

"I've got twenty-seven. How many do you have?" I asked Lulu, after ten minutes of intense swatting in the Annex kitchen.

"Thirty-two. Death to flies. Murder the maggots," she said, wielding her wire mesh weapon like Excalibur. Lulu almost landed her "Got-Ya" fly swatter on the head of Mrs. Elsie Harrington, the wife of the British consul, who ruled the Annex kitchen. But the lean and elegant woman was unflappable.

"Splendid, girls. Fifty more and you each get a coconut rice cake. Remember, every fly you kill is 500 to 2000 maggots unborn."

"One fly can lay that many eggs?" I was stupefied. We didn't stand a chance.

"Not all at once, but in the course of their one month life, yes." Mrs. Harrington replied.

I gripped the wooden handle of my fly-swatter and returned to duty. An hour later, both Lulu and I sat on the steps of the Annex, munching sugar-crusted coconut rice cakes. Their yellow-brown center was the color of maggots.

"You never answered me before. Do you think it's safe to eat this, Lulu? Rice treats made from grain probably infested with maggots?"

"After the rice gets boiled in the cauldrons, I think it's OK. I'm eating it." Lulu bit into the brown sugary top, and looked up at me. "I know we're getting two meals a day, but I'm hungry all the time, aren't you?"

Ten months into captivity, Lulu's stocky little frame was starting to look more fine-boned, and in the evenings we sometimes found ourselves taking in the waistbands on our skirts. Still, we didn't want to complain. The food wasn't abundant or terrific, but we got by. And we Isersons had our fudge too, now that Mommy was in the candy business. Maybe I was around the fudge more than Lulu, because I wasn't feeling hunger as much as she was.

"Well, I try not to think about it," I said, nibbling another piece and hoping not to find yellow-brown larvae embedded in the cake. "OK, your turn," I changed the subject. "Tell me about *your* father."

"Captain Morrison E. Cleland, Jr. He's tall. He's handsome. Everybody calls him Morrie. He ran the family shipping business in Cebu along with my grandfather. But he signed up as a naval officer just after Pearl Harbor. The last time I saw him," Lulu chewed with relish and smiled, "he was all decked out in his uniform." She swallowed the last bite of her rice cake, and turned pensive. "And he had gone back to wearing all his Catholic protection too."

"What's that?" I was Catholic, but I had never heard that expression.

As a convert, I felt like I was always learning something new about my faith. Since Daddy was Jewish and Mommy was Catholic, our parents let Betty and me choose which religion we wanted to be. When Betty was seven (Catholics call that the *age of reason*) and I was nine (with two more years of reason than I needed), we both chose Catholic. Probably because our mother took us to church every Sunday, and Daddy never went to synagogue. Besides, we liked all the gospel stories of Jesus, and most people in the Philippines were Catholic. In fact, before we were Catholic, our Filipino classmates sometimes narrowed their eyes at Betty and me and called us "black-hearted children of the devil!" That didn't scare us much, but we chose Catholic anyway.

Lulu was not Catholic, but her father had been. "Oh, maybe it's not protection. I don't know, but he had one of those St. Christopher medals and a St. George one, and a rosary in his pocket. And Mommy said that under his shirt he was wearing a brown and white flappy thing with Mary on it. I guess to keep him safe."

"That's a 'scapular'—the flappy thing. You put it over your shoulders like a necklace. And if you're wearing it when you die, you go straight to Heaven the Saturday after you leave the earth, and you skip out on most of the fires of purgatory," I informed her in sober tones.

Lulu looked at me as if I were nuts, but she didn't ask me what Purgatory was or why it happened on Saturday. I could tell she didn't know, though. I think she just didn't want to get into another debate about religion, which I clearly understood a lot better than she did.

"Well, I guess it's good my father has that," she said, and I could tell she was missing her dad and worried about him. Just like I was worried about my father. Every day I wondered if he'd be among the captives delivered to the gate.

At that moment two Japanese guards walked by, heading toward the Commandant's office. The tall one flashed us a nearly imperceptible nod of recognition, and almost, but not quite, smiled. *Don't stop. Don't ask us any questions.* We looked down swiftly, but followed them with our eyes after they passed. There was no mistaking it: the tall one was Haruo, who had played my music so beautifully.

I held my breath, and even Lulu was silent, waiting for the two men to be swallowed up by the crowds milling on the back patio. Then we both exhaled, and my mind fled back to that heart-stopping day in late July.

As much as I wanted to hate Haruo, I couldn't help being grateful that he had brought my daddy's spirit back to life for me. And I was more grateful still that he gave the music back to me, when he could have snickered and walked away with it. Or worse still, like Bugs Bunny Guard, he could have speared it with his bayonet before my very eyes and watched me shrink in screaming horror at his feet.

I had thought about it a lot. Haruo proved to me that not all Japanese were bad. When he returned my music, I was so shocked I said nothing. I should've said *arigato*. I'd learned that was Japanese for "thank you."

Lulu seemed to read my mind. "He's a nice guy, that Haruo." She nicked her chin in the direction of the vanished guard. "*NGH*. Let's call him NGH for Nice Guy Haruo."

"OK," I nodded. Lulu and I liked code names. "I've seen NGH around a few times since that day back in July."

"Well, I've heard him around." Lulu's whisper was conspiratorial.

"What do you mean?"

"After roll call last night, when you were helping Betty with her composition, Mommy put me in charge of Mouse. I took her to the practice room, thinking she could work out some tunes on the piano. At least I was going to, but when we came around the corner, music floated out of that room. Like an angel playing. Even Margie hushed up."

"Lulu, forget Margie! Was it Haruo? I can't believe you didn't tell me this. Are you sure it was NGH?" I wondered if he played every night.

"Yes!" she hissed. "Margie was quiet, so I tiptoed forward and peeked in, and it was NGH all right."

We both fell silent, as I absorbed the news. Gradually a tear trickled down my face.

It had been so long since I had heard anything from my faraway father. Max the Panda, my long-ago gift from Daddy, was a thing of the past. Yet I had my *Suite*, like a folded letter or muted radio broadcast from my own father, and I would probably never hear it again. The whole thing just tore me apart. Imagine, a Japanese guard being the only one who could play my Suite for me. The truth is I could have asked other people in camp, but after hearing Hope and then Haruo play it, I just didn't want to share it with anyone else. Haruo played it perfectly. You can't go back on perfection. Well, Daddy would play it for me again after the war.

"Did he see you?" I sniffed, pretending I wasn't at all affected. I wish I could stop missing Daddy so much.

"No." She shook her head. "At least I don't think he did. I got us out of there fast, but I think he really is just a nice guy, who happens to be stuck on the wrong side."

I snorted. "I think we're the ones stuck on the wrong side, Lulu."

We were both quiet for a while, then Lulu glanced up from her work and took in my tear-stained face. "You really want to hear it again, don't you? *Leonore's Suite*?" she asked, already knowing the answer. "Well, let's plan it!"

Wednesday, October 28, 1942

All Lulu's energies—and mine—became focused on Haruo. How could we get Haruo to play my piece again, get it back from him, and not get him or us in trouble? We walked the front plaza after dinner, while Bing Crosby sang, "I've Got a Pocketful of Dreams."

"OK, we need to find out if NGH practices regularly in that room. Then when we know his schedule, we appear there with the music." Lulu looked at me as if she had already solved our problem, but for my benefit continued. "We bow in stately Japanese fashion, present him with the piece, and then we sit down for the concert, and bask in musical magic. Of course, he'll give the music back at the end because he did before," she said with a satisfied nodded. "*And* …maybe we can even make a standing date for him to play. Every Saturday, let's say."

"That's crazy, Lulu. Even if he's willing to do it once, someone could walk in on us. Another guard might see him fraternizing with the enemy, haul him outside and slap him silly in front of all of us." By this time, we had seen those Japanese military slappings when they disciplined their own troops—young soldiers slapped till they bled or their jaw broke. "What if they broke Haruo's hands?" I worried aloud.

"Or you and I could be tied to some post and made to stand in the sun and stare straight at it for hours and be permanently blinded by its light," Lulu said. "They did that at my other camp."

"To girls?"

"No, to a man—a room monitor—but still."

"Or even worse, what if they punished my mother for being the room monitor who couldn't monitor her own daughter! We have to be really careful, Lulu. First, we find out when and where he practices. And we plan from there."

That task was right up our alley because Lulu and I excelled at sleuthing. In the evenings, we sometimes followed classmates around from behind—stealthily of course—since we were particularly interested in who was in love with whom. Were Nellie and Bill smooching? I didn't think so. Bill was sweet on Nellie—everyone knew that. But Nellie was popular with all the kids, and we just couldn't tell if she returned his affection. Besides, she was only thirteen and maybe not interested in that stuff yet.

Lulu and I (fourteen) were definitely interested in that stuff but no dashing suitors pounded down our doors. Even though he could do a great imitation of Cary Grant, Paul Davis was like a brother. The Brooksies were wiry wise-guys. Sure, there were other boys in our class, but they were all so immature. We continued our stroll on the front plaza and paused at a spot not far from the earthen basketball court, where the Brooks twins and Martin Rivers, a boy in Betty's class, hovered near the trunk of a small tree.

The boys stood watching an endless parade of large red ants scurry from the ground up the tree trunk to their nest in the branches.

"Get a black one. Throw it on," Barney urged Martin. The younger boy scrambled on the ground for a black ant, which he then tossed at the tree trunk.

"Look at 'em rip its legs and antennae off! Man, they know he's not one of theirs. See 'em taking those parts up to their nests to eat?" said Curtis.

"Just watch this," said Martin. He grabbed some red ants from the ground and tossed them on the trunk too. "See—they're tearing their own guys apart. They're fooled by the smell of my hand and they think the red ones I threw are intruders too."

Lulu and I paused on the path and stared disbelieving. How could they be so fascinated by bug cannibalism? This is why we wasted no time trying to charm ninth grade boys.

The "Haruo sleuthing adventure," though, fit Team Lee and Lulu like a glove. For weeks "NGH at 11 o'clock" or "NGH at Carnegie" were snippets of our conversation. We referred to the practice room as "Carnegie"—short for Carnegie Hall in New York City, where my father had once heard Rachmaninoff play. We even code-named *Leonore's Suite* "Moonlight Sonata," after Beethoven's triumph.

It was a silly code name because it had more syllables than *Leonore's Suite*, but both Lulu and I liked dramatic code names. We had grown up on *Nancy Drew* mystery stories that taught the value of carefully concealed messages. In fact, whenever Lulu muttered "Bluebells are singing horses," I became instantly alert; it meant: "something is not as it should be." That was the famous teaser line in Nancy Drew's best-ever mystery, *The Password to Larkspur Lane*. A carrier pigeon floated that cryptic message to Nancy while she tended her prize-winning delphiniums, and the code helped her rescue old people from being kidnapped, duped out of their fortunes, and imprisoned by a greedy doctor. Nancy Drew didn't have a partner, or she could have solved her mysteries twice as fast as she did. I had Lulu.

It didn't take long for Sleuth Lulu and me to discover that Nice Guy Haruo—NGH—did have a regular practice schedule. Sometimes he practiced on Saturday afternoons, but usually it was Tuesday and Friday nights at 7:30 pm. While internees lounged on the front lawn after roll call engrossed in their bridge, poker, and mahjong, NGH went off to Carnegie.

Weeks passed with school, fudge-making, weevil duty, bridge, and dish-washing opportunities to conspire. Lulu and I were both up to our elbows in suds one day at the central kitchen dish tub, when Lulu murmured, "OK, what about this. At roll call tomorrow night—that's Friday—you have Moonlight Sonata tucked under your shirt. Right after we're sprung, instead of heading out to the lawn, we run to Carnegie. We beat NGH to the practice room and leave the music on the piano stand. Then we hide in the room next door and we wait. When he starts to play, we hear everything. Or," she scrubbed more vigorously now, as new ideas occurred to her, "we go into the corridor if we want to hear better. He plays with the door ajar. We'll hear it all!"

"How do we get the music back at the end?" I had been through this scenario a hundred times in my head. "Do we go in? Isn't that too dangerous?"

"Not if we don't really go in...."

"I've got it!" Suds lashed me in the eye as I gestured in enthusiasm.

"Shhh..." Lulu hissed.

I lowered my voice. "We listen to him play it from the hall, so we can take off if we need to. Then, just as he ripples the last chord, we move to stand in the open door. We clap quietly. We bow and say, 'Arigato.' Then he gives us the music and we run like bats out of hell back to Room 4."

Lulu dazzled me with her that-was-the-best-idea-ever smile, and Operation Arigato was born.

"Tomorrow night," she said with the enthusiasm of a special operations officer. "Let's do it tomorrow night."

Chapter 8
SUPER GIRL

November 6, 1942

Cuthbert's Friday algebra class dragged on interminably. It was the last class of the day, and Xs and Ys littered the blackboard. I had lost track of their values, but to my left, Lulu was tuned in like a radio antenna. We kids sat on stools in long rows with a common lab-table desk in front of us. I glanced over at her paper, which she helpfully angled toward me. She hadn't missed a beat. Lulu and I were both good students, but she loved algebra and appeared undistracted.

And why not? She wasn't the one who was going to have "Moonlight Sonata" under her blouse at roll call tonight. I was starting to think of *Leonore's Suite* as a secret weapon instead of a musical memory. Operation Arigato approached.

While Cuthbert droned on about linear equations with two variables, my mind raced ahead. I had a lot more than two variables to think about: lunch and then afternoon work shift. Everyone had two hours of camp detail, and I was going to help Lulu on fly-swatting duty at the Annex kitchen again. Then homework. Then dinner. Then roll call and ... the moment of destiny with NGH. Only eight more hours to go.

When the bell rang, Lulu and I hastily agreed to meet after lunch. I headed back to our Glamorville shanty. It was strange that neither Mommy nor Betty were there, dropping daubs of fudge on trays. "Superior Fudge"—that was the name we chose for our candy business—usually needed all our talents at this hour. But coffee cans filled with melted chocolate now cooled and congealed on the dirt floor of our shanty with no one to stir them.

Flossie, Mommy's faithful, fudge-making helper, should have been there. So many afternoons, I knew I'd arrived at my own little shanty in Glamorville, when I saw the distinctive rhythmic swaying of Flossie's round posterior, rocking in time to whatever song she was humming as she stirred the fudge. All the chocolate would need to be re-melted if someone didn't stir it soon. I picked up the stick, and worked on it for five minutes, until I heard Flossie's clear voice ring out over my shoulder.

"Lee, your mother needs you in your room. I'll take over. You get up there. It's Betty."

Betty. My heart skipped a beat. She'd been a little woozy this morning. "Is she OK, Flossie?"

"Not right now, no. Go on to your room." Flossie was curt. "Agnes needs your help. Harry is on his way too."

Harry too? Not good. Betty had always been the fragile one in our family. Her tiny frame didn't seem to weather the assault of germs that were everywhere in the PI. I raced into the Main Building and tore down the corridor to Room 4.

The rooms were nearly deserted, since everyone was outside in line for chow. But a putrid smell wafted into the hall even before I rounded the door jamb. The foul odor overwhelmed Room 4. Mommy and Betty were near the corner by the window—Betty on her cot, moaning and flushed, seizing her stomach. I couldn't see everything, but a bloody brown mess lay clumped and spattered on the floor around Betty's cot. Diarrhea. Poor Betty. She hadn't even made it to the bathroom.

"Lee, I need to get Betty to the hospital. Help me clean her up and let's get her out of here." My mother's usually no-nonsense voice shook.

Harry Hodges charged into the room at that minute, took in the sight, and lost no time yanking a sheet off Kay's and my bed. He wrapped it around Betty, hoisted her in his arms, and moved rapidly toward the door.

"Agnes, she's got dysentery. This girl's on borrowed time. Let's go." Mommy's hazel eyes flashed a look of horrified recognition, and she sped after Harry. Then—ever the responsible room monitor—my mother turned back to me.

"Lee, just…" She pointed to the mess in the corner, mute with terror, but still inclined to command.

Betty shrieked in pain.

"I'll get it, Mommy. Go! Go!" I saw my mother overtake Harry in about one second and the two of them headed out the door.

I stood numb, watching them disappear down the grey corridor. Dysentery. Was it bacillary dysentery? The bad kind? Would Betty die? Would she ever be back in this room, clutching Cuddles and telling me about her day?

They'd have to get her out of camp and to a real hospital fast. There were special pills to take, but the sick person had to get them almost as soon as they got sick. Reaching into my skirt pocket, I folded my hand around the sharp edge of the wooden crucifix on the rosary from Rosalina. I squeezed it hard and murmured one prayer: *Lord, please don't take Betty. Please don't take Betty. Don't take Betty.*

I don't know how long I stood staring down the corridor out the door. The next few hours were going to be desperate ones. We had a camp hospital set up in the Sister's convent of Santa Catalina across the street, but they couldn't treat dysentery there. My mother would have to get a pass, speed Betty into Manila, and make sure she got to the Philippine General Hospital for the right medication. And Betty was so frail, even in the best of times. Desperate to think of something besides my little sister, I looked back into the room, and focused on the charge I knew my mother had given me.

Ugh. Double ugh. Somewhere in the back of my mind, I heard my father's voice commanding: *Do what your mother tells you.* With grim determination, I hauled the bucket, rags, and mop we used every morning out of the janitor's closet to do battle. Betty, my mother, and I had been scrubbing bathrooms and toilets every morning for almost a year, so I thought I'd seen and smelled it all. With tools in hand, I held my breath and walked to the offending cot to meet the enemy.

Fresh and foul, the milky vomit and red-brown slime puddled around the cot and stained its white canvas, too. The stench rose like a heat wave. I turned toward the door, covered my mouth with my hand, and retched an endless dry heave. How did little Betty produce all that? She was too small. She had to be dying. Don't think of that.

I dropped the tools and ran back to the cool janitor's closet, closed its door behind me, and breathed deeply. I drank in the heavenly scent of musty detergent and bleach, and weighed the options before me. If I stayed here in the closet long enough, someone else would probably come along and take care of the mess. What would my heroine Susan Walker, first mate of the Swallow, do? What would Nancy Drew do? *Do what your mother tells you.* I heard the insistent voice in my head. I inhaled. OK. I, Leonore Agnes Iserson, fourteen-and-a-half-year-old daughter of Harold and Agnes Iserson, destined to eternal fame in *Leonore's Suite*, I could do this.

Then I did something Mommy said never to do. I stole. There was one pair of precious rubber gloves in an unopened carton on the shelf in that janitor and supply closet. They had been expensive before the war when the Seamless Rubber Company first introduced them for household use, and they were very dear now. These were, I knew, to be used only for medical emergencies. In fact, this pair should've been over at the hospital.

Well, this was a medical emergency if I ever saw one. If I cleaned up that poop with rags and my bare hands, maybe I'd get dysentery. You could get dysentery not just from contaminated water and food, but from human excrement. My hands trembled as I opened the tightly sealed carton and yanked them on, feeling the talcum powder inside ease them into place.

Then I took a deep breath and marched back into the cot-strewn room, stopping first at my bed, where I dug through the deep wooden drawer for a bandana. I wound the scarf tightly around my nose and mouth to keep the smell out. *Don't breathe deeply.* I stared at Betty's mess two cots away, and at the rags, bucket, and mop strewn alongside it. If I could just blur the sight of that vomit and poop by squinting—not staring—at the revolting globs, I'd be OK, I thought.

With the bandana protecting me from the putrid odor, the rubber gloves covering my hands, and my squinty eyes blurring the details, I walked to the cot, righted the bucket, picked up the rags and got to work. Don't think. Don't breathe. I started to hum a low alto tune. *Just squint and slop and dump it in the bucket. Just squint and slop and dump....*

I don't know when I realized that I was humming the tune of "Swing Low Sweet Chariot," one of my mother's favorites. Well, I needed a chariot to carry me home right now. I cleaned a good-sized area, and walked on unsteady feet from the cot to the front sink, bucket in hand. After I sloshed the fetid contents down the drain, I rinsed my tools, and forced myself to walk back to the blighted bed corner. I was on the third round of Mop and *Swing Low,* when Kay and Hope hurried into the room.

"Smell of roses, Mother Mary!" Kay exclaimed in horror. "What foul odor is this?" she half-choked. Then she saw me at the sink, unsteady, stinky mop and bucket in hand.

"Oh, Lee, dahlin. We heard about Betty! And you," she said taking in the room, "you're all by yourself, cleaning up this atrocious mess?" Kay turned *mess* into a two-syllable word.

I gave a grim nod. "It's not so bad now," I murmured from under my bandana, but she could tell I was near tears, and near vomiting.

"You give me that!" she commanded, and snatched the rancid bucket from me, donning her own apron.

"I'll get us some bleach." Hope headed for the supply cabinet.

I had never been so glad to see two women in my entire life. Kay and Hope—they could solve any problem. World peace would be at hand if those two were free.

"I don't know if I could've finished it," I told Kay, and realized my hand was trembling. I shook my head in near-defeat, leaving the stinky mop in the corner. Kay hugged me fiercely.

"You don't have to finish, darlin'—just like the song, we're *side by side*. And you've practically done it all anyway. C'mon—hand me that mop now."

I handed her the matted brown mess and then washed off the gloves in the sink. I peeled them carefully from my hands, and turned them over to my bed buddy. "You'll need these, too," I told her and saw her eyes widen, when she realized I had stolen the Holy Grail Gloves.

"Well, good for you, dahlin'—and even better that you're givin' them to me." She nodded, smiling. "Get out of here, Lee. Get some fresh air, and don't think about any of this. Your mama and Betty are probably on their way into Manila—to the hospital. Betty will be just fine." I knew she was bluffing.

I hugged Kay one more time, untied my bandana, then went to our bed and stuck the scarf back in the deep wooden drawer. My hand brushed the manila envelope that held *Leonore's Suite*. Not tonight. No *Operation Arigato* tonight.

* * *

I spent the next hour trying to learn as much as I could about where Mommy and Harry had taken Betty. First I raced over to the Annex to find Lulu. Since Lulu was an outstanding sleuther, she and I could track down all the details together. When I told her my story, her blue eyes went wide with alarm.

"Not Betty! Oh that's hideous, Lee! Horrid and hideous. But Margie had dysentery once, and she got better. Puke and vomit, though! It was atrocious, worse than hideous. I just couldn't clean that up. How did you *do* that?"

Lulu was being Lulu and I had to admit that, after the wretched hour of cleaning poop and throw-up, I reveled in her amazement.

"Oh, I'm *so* glad I wasn't there to help you! You are a Super Girl, Lee Iserson," she rambled on. "If they invent Super Girl, she will have brown curls and a peter pan collar blouse, and a blue skirt, and bakias." Lulu was breathlessly describing what I was wearing. Bakias are carved wooden clogs. "And she will fly over stone walls and iron bars with a cape made of.... the American flag!"

By now I laughed and shook my head at her silliness. Lulu followed the first rule of friendship: she always built her buddies up. And as her best friend, I was on the receiving end of great devotion and praise. Lulu could be devastatingly candid too. I loved hearing her say she said was so glad she wasn't there to help me! That was so Lulu.

"Well, I didn't finish. Eventually Hope and Kay came, so they're taking care of it now." I wanted us to focus on finding Boops. "We've got to find out where they've taken Betty."

It didn't take long for Team Lee and Lulu to spring into action on the *Where's Betty Caper*. Our sleuthing paid off by late afternoon.

It turned out Betty's arrival at Santa Catalina had been well timed. The doctors were just loading an ambulance for transport to the Philippine General Hospital. Mommy and Betty got a much-prized medical pass, and would be out of camp for days.

Lulu and I stood in the front plaza with Flossie filling us in on all the details. All around us unconcerned internees spread their straw mats and blankets for the Friday bridge and mahjong. Flossie handed me a note from my mother.

"Lee, pet, be strong and pray. We will be back soon. Love, Mommy."

I handed it to Lulu. She read it and nodded.

"Operation Arigato postponed," she whispered.

"Yup," I answered near tears. Maybe forever, I thought. That adventure suddenly seemed frivolous. Here we were, planning a risky school girl prank just to bring back the memory of my father. But what if Betty never came back?

My sister. My only sister. We played dolls together, laughed together, made our First Communions together, sang together, and even learned to swim together. Betty could sketch anything, and she loved to put on plays with Annie. But little Betty had been on her knees scrubbing poop out of the toilets with Mommy and me for the last year. "Don't they have maids in this place?" I could hear her asking incredulously that first day when we arrived. I had laughed. Then she tucked on an apron, wrinkled her nose, and did whatever Mommy had told us to do. We didn't know if Daddy would ever come back. What if Betty didn't come back? Would it be just Mommy and me? Two stars missing from our Southern Cross?

Sunday, November 8, 1942

Two days had passed with no word from the outside on Betty, and it was tearing me apart. Lulu got permission to sleep on my mother's cot in Room 4 to keep me company. The room smelled fine now. Hope and Kay had worked wonders, even scrubbing Betty's cot clean, and Kay still heaped praise on me for being the first wave of attack against the deadly dysentery foe.

"No news is good news," Kay said. She sat on our shared bed, and finished writing a note to my mother. "I'm telling your mother all about your moppin' and your moxie." A truck would take letters into Manila tomorrow, and maybe we'd find out something later that day. I hadn't gotten an answer to the letter I'd written my mother yesterday.

Lulu and I sat on Betty's empty cot in the early evening and tried to figure out what to do. We'd finished our homework, and I felt like I had a pack of wild horses tied up inside me. I needed something to keep my mind off Betty.

"You need any help with the costumes or sets, Kay?" Hope and Kay had spent this week sewing costumes and painting sets for the children's Thanksgiving performance in a couple weeks in the Father's Garden. The two of them had been drilling Hope's fifth graders like little Marines.

"We're going to need both of you next week for rehearsals, that's for sure, but not now." Kay headed out the door.

"Want to climb to the roof and see if we can get up into the forbidden cross tower and look out over all Manila? That'll take your mind off your troubles," Lulu said.

I thought about it, but shook my head. "We can't. If we get in trouble before Mommy and Betty are even back, my mother will kill me. Forget Japanese punishments, they won't hold a candle to Agnes Iserson."

We'd reached the large foyer, where I saw Lulu's quick blue eyes scan the broad stone staircase with its hefty mahogany banisters. "I've got it!" she exclaimed. "The Climb and Drink Contest."

"What we'll do is climb up and down those stairs a hundred times, and every time we come down, we'll take a sip of water from the fountain," she proposed.

"How many flights are we climbing?" I asked dubiously, "and what makes it a contest?"

"OK, we climb to the first landing—what's that—about 12 stairs? And then we come back down and take a sip. The contest is that you and I will be the only two people to ever have done it! We will set the camp record and be the Climb and Drink champions!"

"And," I suggested, warming to the idea, "we could match our steps and swing our arms in perfect time, so that we look like a synchronized swimming team, but on the stairs."

"And we could chant!" Lulu said.

And so we did. Women walking up or down the broad staircase skirted us and shook their heads, but Lulu and I didn't care. Two fourteen-year-old girls marching in unison, chanting over and over:

Reaching the bottom step, we took a sip from the water fountain—first

Up the stairs,	*Up the stairs,*
down the stairs,	*down the stairs,*
march in time,	*march in time*
take a sip.	*never slip.*

Lulu, then me. First me, then Lulu. We alternated. On our fifty-seventh time up the stairs, we started to run out of steam, and stopped chanting. We concentrated on climbing, breathing, and timing our rhythmic moves. Two women, who climbed the stairs to their rooms hooted their appreciation, and Nellie—going up—said she thought we should lead the STIC Thanksgiving Day parade as "Grand Mistresses." Maybe a half hour later—and 43 trips later—we finished—exhausted, giggly, and water-logged.

"Lee-lee, I see stairs in your eyes," Lulu laughed as we sank on the floor near the fountain.

"You are a complete looney tune, Lulu. I can't believe I let you talk me into that. We aren't even athletic."

"We are the worst players on any team unlucky enough to have us," Lulu agreed, "but Super Girl, you and I are the Camp Climb and Drink champions!"

I hadn't thought about Betty for a solid hour.

Chapter 9
SOUTHERN CROSS

Saturday, November 21, 1942

Ten-year-old Freddy's voice rang out clear and true from the platform in the Fathers' Garden. In this private haven of eucalyptus, acacia, and palm trees, the university's Spanish Dominican priests often prayed and meditated. But they were generous and offered the garden for the Thanksgiving religious service and a small performance by the children two days from now.

Hope rehearsed her fifth grade class like a drill sergeant; Freddy recited:

And I died in my boots like a pioneer
With the whole wide sky above me—

Hope cut him off. "Good job, Freddy. But let's back up. I want to hear that Indian corn verse again. Make it louder and prouder," she said.

Hope seemed not to notice that her pupil, little Freddy Hopkins, had memorized the entire "Ballad of William Sycamore," a twenty-verse poem by Stephen Vincent Benet. I was stunned at his mastery of every word, but my roommate focused only on delivery and execution. Freddy closed his eyes, furrowed his brow, then launched:

When I grew tall as the Indian corn—"

"Whoa. Whoa. How tall is that? Stand up straight now—come on. Live the part. Start again. I want to hear it in the back of the Garden." She walked to the rear of the little alcove.

Freddy cast an exasperated look my way. I was there to help Hope with the thirteen other fifth graders, who now snickered and elbowed each othe. I sat down in their midst, hoping my fourteen-year-old presence would awe them. Hope, our five-foot tall drill sergeant, reached the back of the alcove and nodded, her slender frame ramrod straight. Freddy too straightened, took a deep breath, and started again—this time with volume and conviction.

When I grew as tall as the Indian corn,
My father had little to lend me,
But he gave me his great, old powder-horn
And his woodsman's skill to befriend me.
With a leather shirt to cover my back ...

Freddy regaled us in verse, recounting this pioneer's life from his Kentucky log cabin boyhood to the time he cleared the land for his own farm out west. With his "Salem clipper" wife, he raised two "right, tight" boys on the Great Plains.

Hope nodded in rhythm to the lines, her eyes glistening. Freddy's classmates quieted and listened too. Here we were prisoners of war, surrounded by twelve-foot walls and iron bars. And there was little Freddy spinning the tale of a free, adventurous American pioneer who loved the wild forest, the vast plains, and open skies. In the poem, hardy William Sycamore lost his two sons—one at the Alamo and one at Little Big Horn—"and still could say: So be it. But I could not live when they fenced the land, for it broke my heart to see it."

Would every single internee burst into tears at that point? High concrete walls ringed us on three sides, and sawali matting covered the iron bars of the front gate, while Cole Porter's "Don't Fence Me In," topped the hit parade of our evening P.A. list.

Yet our new Commandant, Akida Kodaki, *had* given us permission to celebrate Thanksgiving, that most distinctively American of holidays, openly. We hoped it would be our first and last Thanksgiving in captivity. Maybe Kodaki did too. Some of the internees thought him stern, but he told

Mr. Carroll that he liked Americans, and was thinking about getting a job in the United States after the war. Was he just trying to buy our good will for a peaceful camp? Maybe.

Mr. Grinnell, the Head of our Executive Committee, reminded us in the camp newspaper that "our camp enjoys an unusual degree of autonomy ... and if each internee will do his part in demonstrating our ability to govern ourselves, there will be no cause for criticism by authorities." *Let's show 'em how democracy works,* in other words.

For Thanksgiving, the grade school children planned skits and would recite poems for their parents. Kodaki drew the line at patriotic songs: no *Star Spangled Banner* or *America the Beautiful*. Well, if we couldn't have those, Freddy's *Ballad of William Sycamore* was going to do just fine.

Hope applauded with fervor when Freddy finished, as did his classmates, and Freddy himself smiled proudly, dipping into an exaggerated bow. We led her students back to the front plaza, and Hope asked about Betty.

A few days ago we'd gotten news of dizzying deliverance: Boops would live. She and Mommy had gotten to the hospital on time and Betty's little body absorbed the medication speedily. My mother and Betty were supposed to be back in camp tomorrow afternoon, and would be here in time for the Thanksgiving show on Thursday. I had missed them both desperately, and we needed to start churning out fudge again. Our main source of income was drying up.

"Now don't go expecting Betty to be fit as a fiddle," Hope cautioned. "She's gone through a lot and your mother too. We're going to have to help them get back into the rhythm of things around here."

I wondered whether Hope knew something that made her so cautious.

Saturday, November 21, 1942

That night, as I lay in bed and Kay dozed off, I stared through the iron window grilles at the four pulsing stars of the Southern Cross. As usual, when I saw the brightest blue-white light pointing south, I thought of my father—just as I had on that very first night in camp almost a year ago. Was he looking at it and thinking of me?

We still had had no word from Daddy. Many women knew their husbands were prisoners at Cabanatuan or Camp Donnelly up north. Hope knew her husband was dead. We didn't know anything about Daddy. My mind kept re-running the lines that Freddy had been reciting:

> *My father had little to lend me,*
> *But he gave me his great, old powder-horn*
> *And his woodsman's skill to befriend me.*

My New York City daddy was no woodsman—that's for sure. But he did teach me how to shoot. I remembered his arms around mine, showing me how to hold an air rifle and shoot those cone-topped Lucky Strike soda cans off the fence of our villa. I learned to sight those cans perfectly and ignore the gun's loud report. I became Daddy's "Little Sure Shot," his own Annie Oakley.

"My father had little to lend me…." That was truer than I wished. Our family's embroidery business had come to a screeching halt in 1938 when Daddy's own brother in New York stole lots of money from the company and ran off to who-knows-where. "Embezzlement" was the biggest vocabulary word I'd learned in 1938, and it was easy to remember because Uncle Eddie did the embezzling. "E" is for "Eddie Embezzles."

My grandfather had told Daddy to close up shop, and make his own decisions about the future. Iserson Embroideries just disappeared from Manila and the face of the earth. I had so hoped that meant we would go back to the States, where there was no humidity and there were no creepy-crawly bugs and spiders. But Mommy and Daddy loved Manila, and everybody talked about "the Depression" in the US. There were no jobs there.

Some nights after the embezzlement catastrophe, I lay powerless in bed, worrying about my parents and our happy home. I'd heard Mommy railing at Daddy one night about not stashing more of our own savings in the Bank of Manila, instead of vulnerable accounts in New York care of "Crooked

Eddie." My heart just broke for Daddy. It wasn't his fault his brother was a thief and a cheat. *Stop yelling at him, Mommy*, I had cried inwardly. It hurt me even more when he'd shot back at her about her "over-spending" and how Betty and I would turn into "pampered princesses" with "their Chinese amahs and special summer camps and fancy-dancy dresses."

Well, that had cut like a knife because it was so unfair to Betty and me. Yes, we did have a Chinese governess, but she was very strict. And yes, we had been allowed to go to Yosemite Camp, which was in Baguio and expensive, and where we learned to ride horses, but so did all my friends.

Betty and I did *not* get to go to the American School, where the real pampered princesses went. Our family did not have a membership at the Polo Club either, where the Horsey Set lounged at the pool every afternoon and on weekends. And never once in my life, had I gotten to pick out my own "fancy-dancy dresses." All the other American and British girls in the PI went to seamstresses on the Escolta, picked out their patterns and fabric, and ordered new clothes for every season. Even in Utica, New York, my girl cousins went to well-lit department stores and chose their own dresses from shiny chrome racks.

But not Betty and me. We were prisoners of Iserson Embroideries. All of our dresses had been samples—hand-made for the company in our sizes. The samples hung in the factory window for a while, or sailed off to Saks Fifth Avenue and Bonwit Teller in New York so they could see the fine quality of the workmanship and order lots.

Then the samples came back. And they were ours to wear. Intricately embroidered pink roses and green tendrils on smocked dress fronts, shiny pink satin sashes cinched at the waist, and puffy skirts that floated. Everyone who saw our dresses marveled at how beautiful they were. Betty never seemed to mind that we didn't get to choose our own clothes. But back then, when I was ten, it rankled. I resented the embroidered dresses everyone else would have killed for.

Things had quieted down strangely that night so long ago when Daddy and Mommy were arguing. The next morning at breakfast Mommy smiled like the Cheshire cat as she read her newspaper. Daddy had come through the door in white pants and jacket, and walked over to where she sat, squatted down, put his arms around her waist, and brushed her ear with a whispered something.

"There are children in the room," she hummed back in a low voice.

"Our greatest triumph," Daddy had replied. "You girls, be good for your mother," he'd smiled broadly at us as he reached for a Panama hat and headed out the door.

That day Daddy did something amazing. He trotted himself over to Manila's brand new, American-owned radio station—KZRH. It was a new division of the National Broadcasting Company. In fact, the call letter "K" meant the station was located west of the Mississippi River. Far, far west in our case. We were so proud that our father, Harold Roland Iserson, got himself a job writing and producing radio shows. 1939 would be the inaugural season for KZRH in Manila.

"Gimme that mop…" Kay mumbled in her sleep and rolled over. Was she re-living that horrible Poop Day? My bed-buddy usually slept like the dead.

I patted Kay's shoulder and she quieted, but my heart sped up when I spotted a ten-inch spider crawling up the mosquito netting on Kay's side. A huntsman spider. Its eight legs climbed crab-like up the net. Its revolting belly was all hairy and spurred. But it could not get at us through the netting. I knew that. It couldn't bite us. I just needed to close my eyes and think about something else. Something happy. Radio… radio….

Radio had proven a good fit for our creative Daddy. He'd always had a flair for the musical and the dramatic, and he was determined to increase the radio audience by making listeners part of the shows. It was thrilling when my father launched an audience participation show called "Jingle Swing." That was 1940. Listeners wrote "jingles," sung advertisements for our sponsors' products. Local vocalists sang them during the Saturday morning Jingle Swing hour. Then the radio audience voted by mail for the best jingle, and the winner (chosen by the listeners, not the sponsors) was announced the next week, and won a prize.

Jingle Swing was awash in catchy (and not-so-catchy) tunes, but Betty and I sang the opener. Daddy said we had "bell-like" voices and we never had any problem carrying a tune. Standing close to the large microphone, we intoned the familiar Christmas carol with a new twist:

> *Jingle swing, jingle swing, swings for you tonight,*
> *We hope you folks will send your votes and entries in just right.*
> *We want our sponsors here to know that you are listening there,*
> *So get those votes and entries in, and we'll stay on the air!*

We sang the last line with a synchronized jab in the air and a well-timed nod, imagining we girls were on stage, not radio. When we took off our headphones, Daddy winked at us from the control booth and held a finger to his lips. We'd tip-toe out as quietly as we could.

Daddy also arranged for Mommy to have a Saturday morning slot at the radio station. She introduced herself as "Senga Nagana," (pronounced SENG-gah Nah-GAHN-ah) and she was the silken-throated announcer for the Nash program, a show that featured popular singers and local instrumentalists. "Senga Nagana" sounded wonderfully exotic, but it was actually just Mommy's maiden name, *Agnes Hanagan* spelled backwards. Ingenious, we all thought. And it suited her. If you wrapped a sari around her willowy figure, and put a veil on her head, she could pass for a green-eyed Indian princess.

Sending her lilting voice over the airwaves was just one of our mother's jobs. That's when she got her position working full time as secretary to the Vice President of the P.I. Long Distance Telephone Company. Mommy knew her way around an office. Daddy balked at first when our mother proposed going back to work, but she flat-out insisted that it would do her good. And nobody had to point out that it would bring in extra cash for the family.

Betty and I had watched our parents grow closer together as our family moved from our palatial San Francisco del Monte villa to a small apartment on busy Taft Avenue across the street from where our factory had flourished and folded, and close to KZRH. No more swimming in our own private pool. No more shooting Lucky Strike cans off the fence in our big yard. We'd said goodbye to our Chinese amah and one of the cooks, but cheered when we learned that Rosalina could stay with us. Felix, our houseboy, and Warlito, our driver, stayed too.

Our little apartment housed a spinet piano for Daddy to play, and there was still enough money to spend on our cherished summers in Baguio. Mommy still had a closet full of evening dresses for the almost nightly dinner dances the ex-pats enjoyed at the Manila Hotel or the Marco Polo. The ex-pat community didn't care about your rising or declining fortunes—they bucked each other up in good times and bad. Whether you were the high and mighty President of Luneta Motors or the newly unemployed former manager of Iserson Embroideries, Americans in Manila were a small and close-knit club. For better or for worse.

Now, as Thanksgiving 1942 approached, worse was right on top of us. For the first time in a long time, I thought about how hard this had to be for Mommy. She and Daddy had said "for better or for worse" a long time ago. My once pretty mother was getting grayer and thinner in a Japanese prison camp without her husband to help her with their two daughters. At night, when I looked at the Southern Cross, I thought about how much I missed Daddy, but I knew she must miss him even more. That brilliant star at the foot of the Southern Cross pulsed brightly now. *Remember, I'm shining for you*, I could hear him say. I found Rosalina's rosary under my pillow and squeezed the wooden cross right back.

Thursday, November 26, 1942

"*Good Mornin', Good Mornin',*" the cheery strains blaring over the camp PA woke me on Thanksgiving Day, and when Rose Blane sang the part about the "sunbeams smiling through," I knew she was right. Mommy and Betty were back. We were a family again.

Yesterday, when they'd returned, Betty's angular face looked thinner and paler, but was lit by the same impish grin as ever. Also, my little sister had spent the day sketching our crowded room, which was a good sign. Betty was a real artist, but she only drew when she was in a good mood. I'd lost no time telling Betty that she'd darn well better make it to the bathroom next time, and she nodded and said she'd try. Betty was so earnest. You couldn't even tell a joke without her taking it seriously.

For her part, Mommy had gripped me in a big teary-eyed embrace when she'd returned, and told me how "immensely proud" she was of me for carrying on "like such a grown-up girl" in her absence. "I can hardly believe how you've grown," she kept saying, as if I had shot up a foot in her absence—which I hadn't. But word of my "super girl" exploits had reached her on the outside. And maybe Hope had told her that Lulu and I had been helping out with rehearsals for the Thanksgiving Day performance.

My mother seemed strangely withdrawn, though. She spent far more time weeding our little vegetable garden yesterday than I thought was necessary. Talinum, the only leafy green vegetable we cultivated, grew practically without any help. Still, it was probably hard to get back to camp life after being on the outside. I was just so happy to see her and not be in charge anymore.

Today, Thanksgiving Day, dawned bright, clear and delightfully cool—sixty degrees. This morning we attended a religious service in the Fathers' Garden before the performance. Then Lulu and I helped behind the scenes, keeping the ten- and eleven-year-olds orderly before their finale. *William Sycamore* had been a smash hit. Freddy Hopkins, in a cowboy hat and spurred boots, brought the house down. Now the fifth grade took the stage en masse to spell out the meaning of "Thanksgiving" in an elaborate rhyming acrostic they had written. Lulu and I stood offstage and listened, as the eleven-year-olds recited the last three letters.

"*I* is for Internees all sizes and ages, writing a new leaf in history's pages."

"*N* is for 'NO Pushing In Line,' waiting just peacefully every time."

"**G** is for Gate and behind it we stay, to celebrate this Thanksgiving Day." Thunderous internee applause followed. Proud children took their bows, and I could see Betty and Annie next to each other smiling, pointing, and clapping. Several rows back, Mommy sat next to Harry and Kay. Kay gripped Mommy's hand, and tears streamed down my mother's face. She was not alone.

"Look," I nudged Lulu. "My mother is all choked up. So is Mrs. Hopkins. I didn't think it was that great."

"Idiot," Lulu hissed. "They're thinking about all those other Thanksgivings, when they really did have lots to be thankful for—their husbands, us, their nice homes, their servants, a real turkey...."

"And freedom," I added, "Thanksgivings when they had freedom. *'G' is for gate and behind it we stay...*" I parroted the children.

Still, after the performance, when most of the internees were heading off to an impromptu football game, my gaze trailed my mother. She had grabbed Hope Miller's arm to congratulate her, and they hugged each other as if nothing could part them. Then, I saw them deep in conversation, walk over to a palm-fringed, hibiscus-studded corner of the garden, and sit on the flat stone bench.

"Lulu, my mother's acting strange. Let's sleuth over there."

Lulu nodded with bright eyes and the hint of a smile. Sleuthing was our tonic to boredom and a quiet adult conversation could be an interesting new code to crack. We slipped unseen behind the tall hedge of red hibiscus. It separated us from their stone perches, and we settled on the damp ground attempting to eavesdrop on their conversation. I was having a hard time making it out, when a generator from the Dominican seminary stopped humming, and all of a sudden we heard.

"It was pointless! Totally pointless," my mother spat out, "and here I am, left alone in this horrid prison camp to raise our two girls." I couldn't see through the dense hedge, but it was clear that she was sobbing and shaking.

"First of all," Hope responded, in her rock-steady manner, "you are not alone."

She moved closer, and her voice softened. "You may wish you were—what with all of us crammed in here and waiting in chow and bathroom lines forever—but you are definitely not alone. We are all in this together. Second, your girls are your greatest consolation. This damn war is raising them to their very best selves faster than any cushy ex-pat life in Manila ever could."

My mother sobbed, but Hope pressed on. "You should've seen Lee, mopping that crap out of our room, and not for one moment whining about needing any help. Did you know she had the moxie to swipe those expensive latex gloves? What a girl!" My mother wiped her eyes and nodded, trying to compose herself.

"And Betty," Hope continued. "Look at her coming back from dysentery as if it were chicken pox. She drew a sketch of me teaching yesterday, and signed it: 'Thankful to be back with you, Hope.' That little girl is a treasure." Hope paused, then spoke seriously. "Third, you should be so grateful that Harold died of disease and was not taken prisoner by the Japs."

At that moment, my heart stopped. My breath stopped. My whole world ended. Shattered in a million pieces. *Daddy died?* I grabbed Lulu's hand, and tried not to shriek aloud. Scalding tears blurred the hedge next to me, and one hand flew to my mouth in horror, as I struggled to stifle a sob. Lulu's eyes were wide in shock and her jaw was frozen open.

Hope was still speaking, hissing furiously now, but I couldn't concentrate. Then I heard "Bataan ... the most horrible and humiliating deaths, Agnes. The Japs marched those men with no food or water for more than a week. They fed them along the way with no bowls or utensils, spooned boiling hot lugao into their open hands, and when those boys couldn't hold it, *too bad Yankee devil.* They told them to eat it off the ground. If they stumbled to the side of the road on that death march, they were bayoneted. Our strapping American boys, bayoneted!" she raged. "That's how my George died. My husband, bayoneted. If there is a God in Heaven, I pray that He strikes dead every damned Jap on that Death March!"

My mother was wordless now, maybe as stunned at Hope's bitterness and fury as I was. Mommy sniffed. I think she reached to hug Hope, whom I had never heard so angry.

Now, my mother spoke with the low calm returning to her voice. "I *am* grateful they didn't take him prisoner." She paused. "Hope, you're a teacher. How am I going to tell the girls? Should I tell them before Christmas? Ruin their holiday? Betty's still so frail. And Lee is so happy to have us back. She's had to be brave and tough for too long. Once they know this, everything changes," my mother said in an anguished whisper. "Absolutely everything changes."

"Agnes, honey," Hope soothed, as she lit a cigarette and returned to her unshakable, reassuring self. "Everything already has changed. They need to know." She took a brief drag. "The girls have *you*. They have all of us. There is still a lot to be thankful for. And they're stronger than you think."

I almost stood up at that moment, burst through the tall hedge, and raced to hug my mother, but I didn't. I couldn't. I felt like I had been sucker-punched. I just sat there and cried silently. And somewhere in the back of my mind, I knew that if I cried by myself and thought about it on my own for a little while, I could be stronger for my mother when she told us.

We listened to Hope and Mommy murmur a little longer, and, through blurry eyes, I watched them walk away. Lulu had never stopped holding my hand or gripping my arm. A tear rolled over her still pudgy cheeks, and her blue eyes shone as reservoirs of love and sorrow.

"Oh, Lee-Lee," she sobbed and threw her arms around me. "You've got me, too" was all she could say. "You've got me, too."

* * *

Agonizing questions filled my mind: What did Daddy die of? How did our mother find out? Was she sure he was dead? Maybe I just hadn't heard it right.

Mommy chose that very night to tell us. After the internee football game, which ended 0-0, after the Red Cross feast with canned turkey, and after the roll call, she asked Betty and me to come back to the shanty with her for a while before lights out. There we sat, quite alone for a change, on small stools next to the charcoal stove in the bamboo shed that was our getaway home.

"Girls, as you know," Mommy began, "Daddy loved you and me and our country very much."

My stomach went into free fall. "Daddy loved." She did it. She put Daddy in the past tense. She was telling us he was gone. I clenched my teeth so tight it hurt. Betty looked at Mommy as if she were an alien from the Planet Mongo, and our mother pressed on. "He went to Zamboanga to serve our country. Remember how General MacArthur asked all patriotic men to do that—even before Pearl Harbor?"

Of course, we remembered. MacArthur had issued a call for the service of all able-bodied American men in September of 1941, when it became clear the Japs were up to no good. Daddy had trained on Corregidor for a month, and then left Manila for Zamboanga in the southernmost island of Mindanao, almost exactly a year ago, in November. That was the last time we had seen him.

Mommy spoke of Daddy's love of our country, how as a Jew, he could live his life in freedom in the United States, even though his Russian ancestors had been persecuted. She spoke of the good things he had been doing for the Army Corp of Engineers, helping to build that airstrip. "But ten months ago, back in February when we were still new in camp, Daddy got pneumonia working on that crowded military base."

Harold died of disease. I could hear Hope, and felt the lacerating shards of this morning's life-shattering crash.

"And he died just three days before Mindanao fell to the Japanese." My mother's low velvet voice held a note of finality. "Your father was not captured by the Japanese." Her tone was solemn, her green eyes steady. Her long, slender hands enfolded Betty's smaller one. "He did not suffer in their cruel military camps or endure their bayonet blows. He died thinking of us. And he died in God's grace," she said as if those were her final words on the subject.

But Betty was having none of it. She shook her head slowly, then emphatically, and tears rolled down her cheeks. Her entire frame shook with sobs and then anger.

"No, he did *not* die! He did not die! He told me he would come back!" her voice rose in desperation. "He told me we would go to the Metropolitan Theater and the Rendezvous Café every Friday night for the rest of my life after he came back!"

Betty was hysterical. My mother took her in her arms and murmured over and over again, "I'm sorry. I'm sorry," while tears streaked down her own face. Betty insisted that our mother was wrong, wrong, wrong. Tears scalded my face too, but I tried to be just a little brave for my shaken mother and despondent sister. Mommy had the presence of mind to reach one hand out to me too and I grabbed it like a lifeline.

"I will take you both to the Metropolitan and to the Rendezvous, when this is all over," Mommy soothed. "We will all go back to the Rendezvous Café, and we will positively stuff ourselves with papaya ice cream."

Oh, Mommy. It had been just a year, but that life seemed so long ago. Every Friday night before the war had been movie night for our little family. Warlito would drive us downtown to the Metropolitan, Manila's dazzling, air-cooled art-deco theater. When Ginger Rogers and Fred Astaire tap-danced across the ballroom floor, we traded our Pacific home for glittering American salons. Before going home, Daddy always treated us to papaya ice cream at the nearby Rendezvous Café.

"How do you *know*?" Betty was pressing our mother. "How do you know he's dead?"

"Because when you were in the hospital and sleeping, Boop," my mother replied, her voice even, "the hospital chaplain came by to give us Communion. He was a Jesuit priest, who had been working in Mindanao." Mother sniffed and straightened her back, determined to gut through this. Betty stared at Mommy fearful, but less hysterical now. "This priest, Father Rosario, saw the name *Iserson* on your clipboard, and asked if we were related to a Harold Iserson he had met in Zamboanga."

"He knew Daddy?" Betty's voice was a mixture of begrudging disbelief and delight.

"Yes, he did," our mother nodded. "Father Rosario baptized him the day before he died. And he was there with him when he died."

"Daddy got *baptized*?" I blurted out to my mother. This was nearly more shocking to me than his death.

My father's whole family was Jewish, and he never talked about converting, even when Betty and I became Catholic in 1937. Daddy proudly hosted a big party for us that day, but never for one minute did I imagine that Daddy would become Catholic.

"Father Rosario sat with your father for days before his death," Mommy explained. "He told him about our Catholic faith in ways that I guess were much more persuasive than mine," she reflected. "Though I never really tried to convert your father. But Fr. Rosario just sat with him and talked, and it had to be a very frightening time for him."

I never knew Daddy to be scared, so that was hard for me to imagine. But he was probably frightened for us, as much as himself. By that time, the Japanese had taken Manila. He knew we were prisoners and he couldn't help us. And the Imperial Japanese Army was rapidly moving south.

"When he was very near the end," Mommy continued, "Father Rosario asked Daddy if he wanted to be baptized. And your father said, 'I would like to die in the same faith and church as my wife and daughters. Yes.'"

This startled me and I saw Betty's eyes bulge. Mommy's voice got all raspy, but we hung on her every word.

"This good priest baptized your father," Mommy said, "and made the Sign of the Cross over him. Daddy joked with his new priest friend about squeaking through that Pearly Gate just before St. Peter closed the door," Mommy smiled. "Father Rosario said your father died the next day. The Japanese took the island three days later," she finished.

One shocking revelation had followed the next. We sat in complete stillness. Well, at least Daddy was going to be with us in Paradise, I thought incongruously. Betty and I had talked about this many times after our baptism. We worried he'd be in another place—wherever God decided to put good Jews who didn't have any part in crucifying Jesus.

Betty took deep breaths. She had stopped railing against the remote possibility of our father's death, and now just sniffed and stifled sobs. Mommy seemed exhausted, but resigned—almost serene. I closed my eyes, and for a brief moment let sorrow wash over me like a purple wave of the South China Sea. How many times had Daddy and I watched the sunsets over those seas? We'd nab a wooden bench on Dewey Boulevard, and stare out to Manila Bay. The sky would glow pink, orange, and then violet, turning the water a deep purple—the color of royal cloaks and endless sorrow.

"Well," my mother said, wiping her eyes and removing a folded piece of paper from her skirt pocket, "We have so much to be grateful for. You are well, Boop. Your father is well in the most important way too. I think we should say this prayer for him."

She showed it to Betty and me, but of course we knew it already, even before we started to recite it—the traditional Catholic prayer for the dead. "Eternal rest grant unto him, O Lord," Mommy began, "and let perpetual light shine upon him." Betty and I did our best to join in. "May the soul of your faithful departed servant, Harold Roland Iserson, through the mercy of God, rest in peace. Amen."

Moments later, we three Iserson women walked out of our little Glamorville shanty toward the Big House. The air was gentle and the lilac skies clear on this still Thanksgiving night. Jutting skyward in the distance was the dark silhouette of the boxy tower topped by its iron cross. We held hands and walked in silence, while in the distance internees laughed and shouted their picks for winners in an impromptu boxing match getting underway. As the skies deepened from periwinkle to navy, the massive stone tower disappeared.

Then I saw it—rising low on the horizon: the Southern Cross, the blue-white star at the foot of the cross pulsing more brilliantly than ever, right at me. My throat tightened, and my chest throbbed, but I held back my tears. I stared at our special constellation, Daddy's and mine, and addressed a silent prayer heavenward.

Maybe it was just a coincidence, but at that exact moment, the camp PA system switched from the bouncy jive of Glenn Miller's "In the Mood," to the rich contralto of Gertrude Lawrence crooning, "Someone to Watch Over Me."

> *He may not be the kind some girls think of as handsome*
> *But to my heart, he carries the key.*
> *Won't you tell him please to put on some speed,*
> *Follow my lead, Oh, how I need,*
> *Someone to watch over me.*

I glanced up, and that moment, the Southern Cross positively danced with light.

Chapter 10
HALO-HALO

December 1942

Mommy, Betty, and I wept for three days straight, and everyone in our room understood and comforted us. Nobody lashed out if we edged into their aisle space a little. Hope even offered to play *Leonore's Suite* for me again, but I told her it would be too painful to hear just now.

That was not entirely true. If Haruo had wandered in and asked me if he could play it, I would've said "yes" immediately. But after all, he knew nothing about my troubles, and Operation Arigato was out of the question now. The last time I had seen NGH, he was standing ramrod straight next to the Commandant, nodding approval of the new directives banning halter tops and short-shorts among the women in camp.

"Japanese soldier not respect American woman who not dress modestly," we had been told. And Haruo nodded gravely. There had been no instances of rape in the camp—which was amazing because we all knew what had happened to women in China when the Imperial Japanese Army invaded.

Kay thought the difference was that we didn't have a real Army commandant in the camp. Former Japanese businessmen or diplomats had been deputized to keep this pesky, demanding mass of Allied civilians in line. Some of them even remembered fighting on our side, as Allies in the Great War less than thirty years earlier. But in Manila itself, the I.J.A. ruled the city, and horrible rumors circulated about Japanese soldiers forcing themselves on Filipino girls, and selling women into prostitution. To our great relief, Mommy learned while on the outside, that Rosalina had successfully escaped Manila before that horror began.

So we grumbled a little about no short-shorts, but went along with the new rule. Santo Tomas became a Bermuda Shorts Camp. The added length didn't matter at this time of year, near Christmas, when Manila got a reprieve from its almost-always stifling heat.

Every night in those weeks before Christmas I heard the catch in my mother's voice when we prayed for those we loved and for the soul of our father, but by day Mommy seemed to me an unwavering tower of strength. She yanked weeds from our talinum garden till I could hardly spot the talinum. A grimly determined Agnes Iserson just poured herself (and us too) into work. Mostly, that meant FUDGE: the making, packaging, and selling of fudge.

Saturday, December 12, 1942

"You think they're going to be able to tell the difference?" Betty sat at the folding table in our shanty, crowding rounded daubs of cooled fudge onto large trays. It was a sit-down job, as she was still recovering from her dysentery. Lulu and I stood ready to cart them away.

"Substituting coconut milk for evaporated milk didn't change the taste that much," my mother replied, as she stirred a batch on the charcoal stove. "Nobody's complained so far."

My mother was right. I hadn't heard any complaints, but our fudge wasn't as rich and creamy as it used to be. "The problem will come after Christmas," she said, looking at her pot and not us, "when we run out of the Ghirardelli's and have to switch to a cheaper local variety of cocoa. Then we'll see how we compete."

We were one of fifteen licensed candy-makers in camp. The Executive Committee decided anyone who sold anything in camp had to purchase a license granted by the Committee itself, and the vendor (that was us) paid for it. The Committee used the money to buy extra supplies for the camp on the outside and to help prisoners, who had been caught in Manila without funds. Our little family earned an important extra income from our candy business. We only got two meals a day in camp, so fudge sales covered whatever we needed for lunch. Now we had to make up the many pesos lost while Betty and Mommy had been on the outside.

Lulu and I handled sales, and today we looked forward to making a killing at the STIC Hobby Fair, where internees would display and sell many items they had made.

"I know I can count on you two," my mother said as she surveyed Betty's work, and then passed two trays loaded with fudge to Lulu and me. "You and Lulu could sell ants at a picnic."

"Well, not the red kind," Lulu said. "They're hideous, but the black ones—they're big and crunchy, and if you fry and chocolate-coat them, they're not all that bad … well we could sell them." She barreled on, as if planning our next enterprise.

My mother laughed. "I rest my case." It was the first time I had seen a genuine smile on her face since her return to camp two weeks ago.

Lulu and I headed out to the front plaza, where almost a thousand internees milled about, inspecting the ingenious crafts: hand-carved bamboo steins for the beer nobody had (no alcohol allowed in camp), hand-crafted wooden pipes for the tobacco we didn't have (cigarettes and brown gold in very short supply), sketches of camp life, and water color renderings of Manila before the war. Betty had painted a magical watercolor image of the Manila Metropolitan Theater that I thought should sell for at least forty centavos. Our many camp seamstresses made aprons, doll clothes, soft dolls, and ornate string puppets. I even saw an intricately woven string bra for sale. Did I need that? I was losing some weight but still getting a little bigger in the bust.

"Superior Fudge for a Superior Christmas!" Lulu and I hawked energetically. "Ten centavos a daub!"

We were underselling Mr. Whitman. He cut his fudge in chunky squares and sold them for twenty centavos a piece. We dropped ours in rounded balls, and charged 10 centavos. Our fudge flew off the trays and we were pocketing lots of change that morning. Two hours later, after many trips back to the shanty for more fudge, Lulu and I sat down to rest with just a few pieces left on our trays.

Aubrey Man, the grizzled Brit from the Caddie, sauntered over to us. I had spoken with him a few times since that first day in the limo, and he no longer frightened me. He was just another unlucky British businessman trapped in Manila by the war. His kind wife and earnest little boy made up for his arrogance (one of the boys was in Hope's fifth grade), and Aubrey Man himself had taken on an unexpectedly helpful role: Camp Sanitation Engineer. That's right—this prominent British executive now drove two of the camp's garbage trucks. He advertised his knowledge of Shakespeare by naming one of his rigs "Rose" and the second "Any Other Name."

His play on the line from *Romeo and Juliet* confused his son, the fifth grader, until Lulu and I explained to him that the play was all about a starry-eyed teenage girl, named Juliet Capulet, whose parents hated the family of a starry-eyed teenage boy, named Romeo Montague. So Juliet wished that Romeo could just change his name and be "any other name," so her parents would like him, and because "a rose by any other name would smell as sweet." The fifth grader asked: "Why did Juliet want Romeo to smell like a rose?" We gave up trying to explain.

Now Sanitation Shakespeare approached us. "If sack and sugar be a fault, God help the wicked!" he proclaimed. We stared blankly at him. "A line from *Henry the Fourth*."

Lulu recovered first: "Superior Fudge for superior quoting!" she urged.

"Ladies, fair, I am a man of modest means, but freely will I loose my purse for your fine fudge, if you can but answer these riddles."

"What is he saying?" Lulu turned to me wearily, as if he had spoken in a foreign language.

"For my part it is Greek to me," I answered Lulu with a cocky smile, quoting a line from Shakespeare's *Julius Caesar*. We had just studied that play in class. She rolled her eyes.

"It's Tagalog to me," she scoffed, and looked away from the Brit.

We had been on our feet, shilling fudge for two hours in the late morning heat, and Lulu was ready to call it a day. Having lost my own father, I guess I felt more kindly toward Aubrey, the hard-working, garbage-truck-driving dad, and toward all the men in camp who were working jobs they never thought they'd endure, just pushing on with the business of life. Besides, Aubrey Man had challenged us, and Super Girl did not shrink from a challenge.

"I shall quote a line from Shakespeare and you identify its provenance, and I will pay you fifteen centavos for your fudge," he said.

Peso signs flashed before my eyes since we sold our fudge for just ten centavos a piece, and he was offering fifteen.

"Its what?" Lulu scowled, feigning ignorance to annoy him.

"Its provenance, Lulu. He wants us to tell him which play he is quoting." Lulu knew full-well what provenance meant.

She and I were good at English literature, and besides, we were interned with that troupe of Shakespearean actors, who had been caught in Manila when the Japs invaded. They performed pretty regularly, so we knew a lot of the plays.

"Twenty centavos," Lulu said. "If we guess correctly, we get twenty centavos each."

"The lady doth protest too much, methinks." Aubrey shook his head with a smile.

"*Hamlet*," I pounced, and Aubrey smiled, showing yellowed teeth but genuine amusement, and he forked over fifteen centavos.

"And not to Miss Louella, but *to thine own self be true*," he said.

"Another *Hamlet*. All the best lines are in *Hamlet*," I said, turning to Lulu. "Remember: *To be or not to be*?" Lulu shrugged, but she looked Aubrey Man straight in the eye.

"*Brevity is the soul of wit,* so purchase quickly and be gone!" she commanded with her own line, partly from Hamlet.

"Ah, thou wouldst have me show mercy?" he bantered back. "*The quality of mercy is not strained. It droppeth as the gentle rain from heaven.*"

"Merchant! *Merchant of Venice!*" Lulu leapt. And so it went.

We guessed five of his six lines. When he said "the game is up," we thought he was finished and didn't continue. But it turned out that was a line from Shakespeare too—a play called *Cymbeline*. Well, who ever heard of that one? We were very proud to have sold our last five pieces of fudge for seventy-five centavos instead of fifty, and we headed back to Glamorville for lunch.

* * *

In the late afternoon, Lulu and I strolled through the Hobby Fair on the front plaza, taking in the sights. Market stalls lined the entry to the Main Building with Filipino and Japanese vendors selling vegetables, peanuts, carabao meat, and candy. Our friend, Bill Phillips, had a little shoe-shine business going between the Big House and the Education Building. You would've thought all STIC men reported to penthouse offices every Monday because the line was five deep. Bill was charging ten centavos a shine.

The Red Cross comfort kits had arrived too—one for every two prisoners (we think the Japanese took the other one). The camp's smokers were selling canned tomatoes, marmalade, and condensed milk from their kits for a pack of cigarettes from the kits of others.

"NGH at ten o'clock," Lulu muttered. We watched him head to the forbidden Southwest Territory, where the Japanese military had their offices.

"I think we need to give this up, Lulu. I can't take a chance on Operation Arigato now that Daddy's dead. My mother and Betty are barely holding it together. If we got caught, all hell would break loose."

"Halo-Halo!" Lulu sputtered. She was using our favorite Tagalog slang, telling me I was "all mixed up." Filipinos had a tutti-frutti dessert called "Halo-Halo."

"We don't *have* to get caught. And what about YOU, Super Girl? Maybe you just can't take being so lonely for your dad and so strong for everybody else any more. Did you ever think about that? Halo-Halo."

Lulu's exasperated rant penetrated like a well-aimed lancet. I missed Daddy so much—more now than before because I knew I'd never see him again. We didn't even know where he was buried. And every time I caught a glimpse of that music in the bottom of the drawer, it just pierced my heart. *Leonore's Suite* whispered to me like a distant message from another world. Was Lulu right? Was I just trying to be strong for everybody else?

"Somebody has to," I shot back. "Somebody has to be strong for everybody else! You don't listen to Betty bawling at night or see Mommy weeding at that stupid talinum garden like a demon possessed," my eyes were filling with tears now, and I was angry. "It's terrible." I spat. "It's hideous!" I threw her own word back at her.

My mother was starting to scare me. After hours of fudge-making and camp duty and settling room squabbles, she went back outside to pull at weeds that weren't even there. Like maybe she could yank Daddy right out of her heart. Like maybe she could make everything clean and spotless and right again for all of us.

"*Somebody* has to be strong, Lulu," I repeated, madder now. "Maybe it's the only way I can help." Hot tears streamed down my cheeks even as I railed at my best friend.

Lulu listened, but she didn't hug me or budge one inch. She urged more softly in her low raspy voice, "Maybe NGH would like to help. Maybe he would like to give YOU a present for a change."

What wishful thinking. I sniffed and brushed the back of my arm over my face, blotting tears. "NGH doesn't know a single thing about me," I said, remembering those last tense moments we had talked. "Except my name, and that once I bullied him into giving me my music back." Still, I was touched by Lulu's words.

"By this time, he must have heard that we're good at fly-swatting." Lulu was trying to make things lighter between us.

I sniffed again. "And he's probably heard that we were named the camp Climb and Drink champions," I said sarcastically.

"He knows one other thing," Lulu continued in a more solemn voice than I had ever heard from her. "I could tell by the way he plays the piano. He knows that music heals and lifts us up."

A deep ache welled inside me. *Music heals and lifts us up. Music binds us to those we love*, I thought. Now what? I really was Halo-Halo.

Chapter 11

O HOLY NIGHT

Tuesday, December 22, 1942

If music could heal, the Christmas preparations at Santo Tomas should have emptied STIC hospital beds. The Japanese had given permission for a Christmas Eve community sing. This would be our first—and we all fervently hoped only—Christmas in captivity, and while some had suggested that Christmas be "cancelled" this year, more buoyant spirits prevailed.

I was trying hard to stop thinking about Daddy's death. So, along with Lulu, Bunny, and Nellie, I joined a Women's Chorus that would perform on Christmas Eve. We practiced such pop hits as "Santa Claus is Coming to Town," and "Rudolph the Red-Nosed Reindeer." The Men's Chorus worked on "O Tannenbaum" and "Come All Ye Faithful." For the Christmas Eve performance, both choruses would back up the soloist in "O Holy Night."

Lulu, Bunny, Nellie and I sat under an acacia tree on the front lawn, and pored over some hastily copied sheet music.

"This is tricky—we're going in three different directions here." Bunny pointed to the divergent tenor, alto, and soprano notes. We had been trying to untangle the complex harmony for our favorite verse of *O Holy Night*—the part about "His gospel is peace. Chains shall he break and in his name all oppression shall cease." We wanted to sing that part about *no more oppression* with full voice.

A loathsome, red speckled gecko slithered across my mat. I took off my wooden sandal, pounded an end to his existence, and swept him away. In the battle against creepy-crawlies, it was us against them, and my Christmas cheer did not extend to lizards. I turned back to the music.

"Well, I can take the tenor part," Nellie offered. Despite her age, her voice was low enough to sing it.

"Lulu and I have alto covered. You do soprano, Bunny." I said.

Just then the P.A. system sizzled to life and Guy Lombardo's band struck up, "Sleigh bells ring, are you listening? In the lane, snow is glistening … walking in a winter wonderland." We all paused to listen. Wouldn't that be beautiful?

I looked down to see a wobbly line of red ants heading straight for my petate. Why me? Where were the spiders when you needed them? Weren't they supposed to eat these guys? I threw gravel on the invading army and they skittered off in another direction.

"I have never seen a winter wonderland," said Bunny. "Even when we made it back to England once for Yuletide cheer, we didn't have snow."

I looked up at her, surprised. "I have. I remember one winter wonderland Christmas—1937. I was nine and Betty was seven. We went back to the States to visit my grandparents on their horse farm in Utica, and it was just like the song says: snow glistening and sleigh bells ringing. It was magical."

"Lucky you," Bunny answered, and I smiled at the memory.

My mother had wanted her parents to meet us for the very first time, so we girls sailed from Manila to San Francisco, and then took a train east to Utica. Daddy had to stay in the PI and run the embroidery plant—which was a good thing because my Grandfather John Hanagan didn't approve of his rogue daughter Agnes marrying a Jew. In fact, during that whole vacation Grandpa never even called Daddy "Harold." He'd constantly referred to him as "Earl." As if he couldn't be bothered to remember a two-syllable name. Still, we'd loved that white Christmas—tasting the downy flakes of snow on our tongues, chopping down our own tree in the quiet woods, stringing popcorn with my cousin Francis, and of course, "dashing through the snow" with Moxie the Mare pulling our sleigh. Not a single creep-crawly in sight.

"In the meadow we can build a snowman…And pretend that he is Parson Brown," the male trio sang.

"C'mon we can't concentrate here." Lulu stood up abruptly. "Let's go to your shanty, Lee, where we can work on the harmony."

We ambled over to Glamorville, where Mommy stood at the charcoal stove, making fudge. The four of us settled into folding chairs around the card table, and Bunny unfolded the music. When we sang the second verse and reached the climatic "His power and glory ever more proclaim" notes collided in a shockingly screechy cascade. Lulu was decidedly off-key.

"We're wretched!" she wailed. "Let's do it again."

We bumbled through it one more time, but, without piano accompaniment, it was hard.

"I know—let's hit the practice rooms tonight," Lulu said. "We'll torpedo the entire piece if we don't get this right." I nodded my approval: it was good to see Lulu so insistent on musical excellence, for once. She didn't usually go the extra mile for these occasional performances.

"Aggie, could you and Betty help us, too?" Lulu called to my mother, who was stirring chocolate. No one called my mother "Aggie" except Lulu, and for some bizarre reason my mother tolerated it. "Senga Nagana can coach us," Lulu warmed happily to her own idea, "and Boops can keep the beat."

"You really don't need me, Lulu." My mother shook her head and focused on fudge.

"Oh yes, we do, do, do, do, do!" Lulu insisted, making sure the last "do" was a sotto voce lilt. "We are hopeless without a coach. Can't you hear us? 'Ever more proclaim ….." she howled in a strangled feline voice.

My mother looked at my best friend with her 'oh brother' face. "Well, maybe you do." She smiled and gave her consent. Dipping into her radio voice, she said, "Senga Nagana will be there."

"You're being a perfectionist, Lulee," Bunny said, "but I'll be there. I'm head over heels for this piece when we're on key."

That was a relief. Lulu or my mother or I could have tapped out the melody line on the piano, but Bunny played better than we did, and she could work through the challenging harmonies in the chorus. Nellie declined because she and Bill were "going walking" that evening—which is as close as it came to having a date at Santo Tomas.

Lulu babbled on about the importance of this rehearsal because it was "the very last possible night" to practice. The performance was on Christmas Eve and none of us wanted to miss the movie tomorrow night.

That's right. Nobody could believe it, but the Recreation Committee had gotten permission to screen motion pictures in camp. "While winning the war, we can afford to be magnanimous," Commandant Kodaki had decreed, when he gave the green light for films to enter through the package line. Well, when you think about it—any activity that kept almost four thousand internees motionless for two hours had to be a good thing from the Japanese standpoint.

Our "Little Theater Under the Stars" sure wouldn't rival the Metropolitan, but the prospect of watching Don Ameche and Rosalind Russell spar on screen had everyone buzzing. *The Feminine Touch*, a movie that came out last year, was to debut tomorrow night, December 23. Betty and I were especially excited about it because Don Ameche reminded us so much of our Daddy—if Daddy had been slender and fit. But on this first Christmas after his death, and this first Christmas without him, we'd take any vestige of him that we could.

***

That evening after roll call Mommy, Betty, Bunny, Lulu, and I gathered around the piano in one of the two practice rooms. My mother was quick to correct our many errors. She was a good sight-reader, and her years of singing harmony alongside Daddy had paid off. Boops, meanwhile, was our metronome, and her soprano voice was a good assist for Bunny. We worked through all three verses of *O Holy Night*, and by 7:30, had the complex harmony down pat. As we packed up to head back to the Big House, a lush, minor chord sounded from the room next door.

"Shh!" Lulu hushed us all.

A weighty silence followed, then a single bass note tolled. Silence again, and then a rich minor chord answered by a deep bell tone. Then the rippled chords and the haunting melody built, measure after measure, bar after bar, until the piece exploded passionately. Then it softened, silver melody notes streaming like shooting stars in a midnight sky. A tear streamed down my cheek and I couldn't move. It was *Leonore's Suite*. I knew who was playing it.

Mother and Betty stood in shocked silence unable to believe what they were hearing. But Bunny had already tiptoed into the hall. Lulu took my hand, and as the melancholy chords swelled, we advanced silently behind Bunny. Peering through the partially opened door, our friend grew stiff, and backed away quietly, standing motionless. Lulu approached, opened the door even wider, and signaled to me. I came to her side, and from the door, we watched Haruo at the piano.

He leaned forward into the music, his arms in fluid motion, his hands lighting on notes like birds in flight. The music itself took flight, and I closed my eyes, letting the chords float me heavenward—high as a fearless gull into a stormy sky, gliding through thunder clouds, and soaring higher until my fingers seemed to touch the stars of the Southern Cross. In my mind's eye Daddy sat on that bench playing the haunting piece for me. "Soar on," his music seemed to say. "Spread your wings to match the gale, Leonore." *I will, Daddy. I will.* And then the lush chords of the tempest-tossed piece calmed like gentle waves on the shore, and the silver song melted into stillness.

I opened my teary eyes to see Haruo's broad brow and impassive face staring at me. He was still seated on the bench, held, as was I, by the spell of the last notes. For the first time ever, I was not afraid of a Japanese guard. My heart swelled with such gratitude, I thought I would burst. I had rehearsed this scene in my mind so many times that instinct took over. I took one step forward, straightened my back, as we had been taught, crossed both hands in front of my legs and bowed deeply, saying "Arigato."

This seemed to surprise him, but Haruo too stood, smiled slightly, and bowed formally with his hands at his side, saying something I took to mean, "You're welcome." Then he gathered the four pages of my father's music, advanced to the door, and handed them to me.

"Leonore, beautiful," he said. I couldn't tell if he meant me or the music, but I was betting on the music. "Your father compose well."

"He died," I blurted out in a moment of stupidity. As if a Japanese guard would care. "He died in February in Zamboanga." A shard of pain pierced my heart even as I said it.

"Leonore Agnes!" I heard my mother's shocked voice behind me. I don't know when she and Betty had edged into the hall, but I turned to see her horrified stare and blanched face. Then I looked at Haruo.

A cloud seemed to shadow his features, but Haruo just nodded soberly, as if he understood. "My brother die at Midway."

Midway. It had been the only U.S. victory in the Pacific all year. Word of the triumph had filtered into camp in mid-June, and what a tonic for our spirits. We Americans had gotten clobbered at Corregidor and Bataan, but we got them at Midway. For the first time, though, I understood that this vast, horrid war was killing all of us. Good guys and bad guys. And good bad guys too.

"I'm sorry, Haruo." I hoped he didn't mind that I used his name.

But after a moment he said "Arigato. We not meet or talk again," he spoke decisively now. "Too dangerous for all. You must follow rules and stay obedient." He bowed deeply and formally to us all. "Goodbye, Leonore. Goodbye friends of Leonore."

I saw the back of his neatly pressed khaki uniform turn toward us, as he strode briskly away. From that angle, he looked just like every other guard in camp. *Goodbye, Haruo.*

* * *

When Haruo walked away, my mother didn't know who to yell at first. "Leonore Agnes and Mary Louella, do you have any idea how dangerous that was?" she gasped.

"Lulu, how did you do it?" I gushed almost simultaneously. My heart still thudded at the thrill and joy and glory of what we'd just witnessed. Daddy had been with me!

Lulu, jubilant in her triumph, chose to ignore my mother. "I slipped into Room 4 this morning, and snatched *Leonore's Suite* from your bed drawer. And did you like my caterwauling in the shanty this afternoon?" Her eyes shone with mischief. "I sang off-key on purpose, but I didn't have to work very hard at it. I just *had* to get all of us over here on Haruo's practice night."

"Haruo? You girls are on a first name basis with a Japanese guard?" My mother practically breathed fire at us.

Then we blurted out the entire story: that we had met him once before, that he found and played *Leonore's Suite* the day Lulu arrived in camp, that he'd given it back to us, that we nodded to him in camp sometimes, and that Lulu had just masterminded this unforgettable performance.

"Not all Japs are reprobates, Aggie." An earnest Lulu attempted to mollify my mother. "Lee and I could tell. Back in July, he could've just ripped up the music or kept it for himself to play some other time. But he didn't. Instead, NGH just bowed, and gave it back"

"NGH?" Mommy's horrified and relentlessly disapproving stare had not wavered.

"Nice Guy Haruo," I offered. "That's our code name for him. NGH—we've seen him around camp—being a nice guy to the internees."

"He gave Patty some hard candy last week," Bunny said, reminding us that her younger sister was fighting tonsillitis. "Just on the QT," she continued. "You know those Jap vendors at the camp market in the mornings? He bought the candy from them, and Patty was coughing two feet away. He slipped her a piece. I saw it."

"And you're sure it was the same guard?" Betty asked Bunny.

"Right-o. He's a bit tall for a Jap, don't you think?"

"Now, I could've just dragged Lee over here by herself, Aggie," Lulu barreled on breathless, "but you've been missing Mr. I. so much that I thought you and Betty would want to hear the music too. You needed to hear it just as much as Lee did."

Then my mother just fell apart—that's all there was to it. Her face crumpled. She fell forward and smothered Lulu in her arms and sobbed, and told her what a dear and wonderful friend her eldest daughter had, and how grateful she was to hear those familiar chords played so beautifully one last time. And that we should never *ever* do anything like that again. She told us how important it was that we not acknowledge Haruo in friendly fashion around camp in order to avoid getting him into trouble with other Japanese soldiers or officers.

"He has taken great risks to be kind to us," she reminded us all, as she wiped away tears. "We cannot give so much as a hint that we know him or like him."

That night, we walked hand in hand down the dark corridors of the Main Building back to Room 4. I held *Leonore's Suite* under my arm, and the bird of hope in my heart.

***

And so the Christmas of 1942 unfolded. Nobody forgot that we were prisoners, but *The Feminine Touch* the next night made internees laugh, and our Christmas concert lifted weary hearts.

Even in captivity, Christmas turned out to be a strangely joyful and chaotic day. A giant Christmas tree, complete with ornaments, rose behind the Big House in the east patio. The Internee Committee had arranged it, and to their credit, the Japanese had allowed the symbol of hope in through the front gate. Santa made a surprise appearance, too, delivering presents to the children, who squealed in delight over freshly painted wagons, scooters, and doll houses, which their parents had cobbled together from scraps foraged in camp.

Mr. Carroll said one-thousand-eight-hundred-and-one Filipinos lined up at the gate on Christmas morning to deliver packages for many of us on the inside. We couldn't see the crowd of well-wishers, of course, because sawali covered the front gate, and a second wall of the reed matting hid the human line in front of the package shed too. But the Executive Committee took the tally of visitors and packages and reported tolls.

That day Mommy and I got small gifts from German and Spanish friends on the outside. Some Russian friends of Betty's sent drawing supplies for her. Grandma Naylor made sure we got extra evaporated milk and a stash of toilet paper (now in short supply).

Grandma also delivered what for all of us was the best gift of all: an envelope marked "To Iserson Ladies. Care of Grandma Naylor." Inside we found a hand-drawn sketch of a small family in a nipa shed, their baby lying in a manger. The wide-eyed infant was flanked by a dozing carabao (its horns pointing to a star) and a bushy-tailed Asian bearcat. In the palm tree behind their shed, a cockatiel rested, and hovering at the baby's feet was a silly looking, bug-eyed tarsier, who seemed to make the child laugh. All these native Philippine animals honored the infant, while familiar handwriting announced: "The Prince of Peace is born. May He Reign. Fond greetings from Rosalina, Warlito, and Felix."

A lead weight lifted from my heart: they were still safe.

Chapter 12
SPREAD YOUR WINGS

Sunday, March 21, 1943

"Truly, truly I say to you, when you were younger, you girded yourself and walked where you wished, but when you grow old, you will stretch out your hands, and another will put a belt around you and lead you where you would not want to go." Father Kelley read the gospel for the day.

Sunday morning mass in the emerald haven of the Father's Garden almost always lifted my spirits. Today about a hundred internees gathered on a sweltering morning to hear the "good news," which is what "gospel" really meant—as Father Kelley constantly reminded us. We always needed it—good news, that is. But today's gospel—being read in every Catholic church around the world—came too close to the truth for us: "someone will put a belt around you and lead you where you would not want to go."

I tried hard to concentrate on Fr. Kelley's next words from the makeshift altar, but my heart was in Room 4. The first three months of this year had been a trip to Hades and back for my roomies. Hardly a week went by without one of them learning of her husband's death or her son's capture. Sixteen of the forty women in our room were now widows. Six others knew their husbands and sons fought to survive in Cabanatuan, the hard-labor military camp just seventy miles north of us. There, captured Americans hauled gravel, slaved barefoot on farms, loaded dirt from garbage dumps to trucks, or paved rock roads for the Japs. Smuggled notes from those men described the hardships, and their wives were frantic with worry. Many of our roommates, who did not know where their husbands were, dreaded the monthly Red Cross mail deliveries. Who had died?

Lulu stood next to me at this outdoor mass, worrying a wrinkle in her skirt, as Fr. Kelley read. She still didn't know where her father, Captain Cleland, was, but despite my father's death, she remained an optimist. Her father was shielded from harm by his "Catholic protection," she continued to tell me. Lulu's bottomless well of optimism and signature confidence in right endings still lifted everyone in her presence.

We'd passed the one-year anniversary of our internment in January with Japanese planes flying overhead in formation. How we longed to gaze heavenward and see stars on the wings of those planes instead of red suns. Black New Year's, just a year before, seemed a whole lifetime ago. I remembered peering through the shutters of our Taft Avenue apartment on New Year's Day, just before the Japs picked us up, and watching that crazy looter's parade. Was the lady on the barber's chair with the stack of Panama hats on her head better off than those of us imprisoned here at STIC, I wondered. And how many of those beefy American soldiers who fought for us from Bataan were dead now?

"*And after this, he said to him, Follow me….. The gospel of the Lord*," Fr. Kelley finally proclaimed, and we settled into the canvas folding chairs behind us for his sermon.

"Well, brothers and sisters, we have followed Him into this land where we did not wish to go," he began his sermon. Father Kelley got that part right. "What reward awaits us? More disease? More hunger? More suffering? More squalor?"

Wrong answer, Father. Wrong answer. But I could see how he'd reached that conclusion. There were so many gaunt new faces in our midst—hollowed, deeply lined faces. Between New Year's and the end of March, hundreds of new internees had crowded into Santo Tomas. They came from prisons in the southern islands of Leyte and Negros, many fighting beriberi, malaria, or tuberculosis. Beriberi was a horrible disease that would eventually kill you. It came from lack of thiamine in your diet—not enough wheat, bran, yeast—that sort of thing. None of us had seen wheat bread in months, but a newly arrived matron, who sat three seats down from me, took deprivation to a whole new level: wizened face, reed slender body and tree-trunk legs.

My mother sat to my right, stared at her lap, and frowned, as Fr. Kelley continued to tick off the possible ways we could continue to suffer. As room monitor, Mommy had been the one to get out the tape measure and calculate reduced aisle space for each of us to fit in the extra cots for the new internees.

Our roommates groused, but softened when they heard the new arrivals' stories. Most of the newcomers had endured a horrific ten-day passage in the dark hold of a cargo ship, and many had lost their husbands. Many army nurses came with that group, and they had seen the ravages of hand-to-hand fighting in the south. Those girls now labored tirelessly in our hospital, pulling eight-hour shifts, while the rest of us moaned about our two-hour camp duty.

On that Sunday morning in March, we knew that someone was leading us "where we would not want to go." But we were still waiting for the reign of the Prince of Peace that Rosa's Christmas card promised. Somehow Father Kelley managed to wrap up by reminding us of Jesus's words, "I came that you may have life and have it more abundantly." I squeezed the wooden cross on the rosary in my pocket, and prayed, "Any time now, Prince of Peace. And, any time would be fine for that abundant life part too."

Friday, March 26, 1943

"Being a room monitor has its perks," my mother answered my astonished stare. We strolled in the front plaza a week later, holding hands and talking in what we hoped looked like a casual manner.

Mommy had arranged for Paul Davis and me to get out of camp on an overnight pass for "family medical" reasons. Grandma Naylor suffered from "consumption" and was near death, my mother had told the Internee Committee. I don't know how much of this they actually believed, but they agreed that I could go into Manila with buyers from the camp to visit my aging grandmother, and bid her farewell. Paul Davis was given permission to accompany me as a family friend and personal escort. We were to go to Grandma's home in the city, nurse and care for her, shower her with affection, spend the night, and return the next day, having said our goodbyes. That was the official story.

"And you'll need to sew the pesos into the hem of your skirt," my mother continued gravely. "I know you can do this, pet. It might be our last chance to take advantage of their largesse."

My mother was referring to the generosity of her friends at the Philippine Long Distance Telephone Company, where she'd worked before the war. They'd sent word of their willingness to assist our family, and their heart-stopping note—with its promise of funds—had arrived through the package line, carefully concealed in the slit of a melon.

"I don't know how much longer the fudge business will keep us afloat," Mommy confided. The Japanese had started rationing sugar, and when it ran out, we would be out of business. No more of Daddy's shirts to sell, no more fudge, and no more money.

"We can't risk smuggling that much money through the package line," my mother continued. "And my going to see Edith Naylor would raise eyebrows since I was out with Betty not that long ago. The fact that you want to see your grandmother before she dies is more touching and believable."

My heart raced at the thrill of it. I could not believe my mother trusted me enough to undertake this grown-up mission. But she'd been looking at me in a new way since Daddy's death, and every fiber in my being wanted not to disappoint her.

"Does Grandma know she's about to die?" I lowered my voice, and pretended to adjust my sandal. *It's just a casual conversation. That's all it is.*

"Not exactly. But you can tell her," my mother said. "She has the money from the Telephone Company for us."

"Couldn't Lulu go with me, instead of Paul? We've been sleuthing together in camp for a long time and..."

"No." My mother cut me off. "I want a man with you, Lee—even a young man. The Japanese military are in charge of Manila, and a pretty young girl should not be alone. Harry couldn't get permission, but Paul's mother has complete faith in his abilities."

So did I, for that matter. Tall, wiry, and wily, Paul could talk his way out of any scrape, and I swear he had eyes in the back of his head. When he filled water bombs from the chem lab spigots, his precisely timed efforts always escaped the notice of Cuthbert or Father Monte. Besides, Paul knew Manila well. Like Betty and me, he and Annie had grown up in the city and never lived anywhere else. He knew its back alleys, its main drags, and its crowded quays. And his Tagalog was better than mine.

My stomach did somersaults at the thought of the risky errand entrusted to me. I was to smuggle five hundred pesos—about $250—into camp. *Spread your wings to match the gale,* Daddy's music said. All right, Daddy. I was turning fifteen in six days.

Friday, March 26, 1943

"Hear you're stepping out tomorrow!" Bill Phillips waved me over to the petate, where he, Nellie, Paul, and Lulu were playing bridge. The bouncy strains of the *Boogie Woogie Bugle Boy from Company B* filled the evening air and the patio hummed.

"Were you bragging, Pablo Diablo?" I sat down next to Lulu to keep an eye on her hand.

"Just letting them go chartreuse with envy." Paul's gave me a smug wink. He was playing dummy, so his cards were on the mat. He used the fingers of his maimed hand to mimic two internees scaling the wall and leaping to freedom. "GBA!" he announced triumphantly—that was our code for "God Bless America." Everyone smirked.

Getting out of camp was an event, but not unheard of. "Mum and I have been out three times on medical passes." Nellie focused on her cards, but continued. "I think you'll be eager to get back in, though." She played a low club.

"Why?" I asked.

"Dewey Boulevard is still Dewey—sunsets, palm trees, Manila Hotel—but the Fried Egg is everywhere." She was referring to the Japanese flag. "The Filipinos just stare at their feet when they pass you, and the soldiers are the only ones laughing. They even parade on the Luneta now."

Could that be true? Before the war, Filipinos always shouted bawdy greetings to us and to each other in the busy streets. "Pasok ka!" they would hail us, signaling "Come in, Come in," to their market stalls. You never saw a warmer or friendlier people. And American troops were the only ones marching on the vast expanse of the Luneta, a beautiful parade ground built by the U.S. Army.

"Take that red armband off the minute you hit the street, so they don't stop you," Bill cautioned.

The red armbands identified us as enemy nationals, and they were actually supposed to protect us from the military police, the Kempeitai. Supposedly, those bands told the Japanese Gestapo that we were already locked up somewhere else, and were out and about with permission.

"The Jap military picked up two of our red-armband guys last week," Bill continued. "Carted them off to their favorite torture center, Fort Santiago, and nobody's seen 'em since."

I went cold inside, and shot Paul a "Holy Cow!" look. He gave me a "no big deal" shrug. Well, Paul was fearless.

Bill lowered his voice, and said in completely matter-of-fact tone, "Truth is, our jailors got clobbered at Guadalcanal, and they're mad as hell."

Guadalcanal, the largest of the Solomon Islands in the western Pacific, practically sat on the shoulders of Australia. We knew from the *Manila Tribune* that the Japanese had seized it in May—almost a year ago—and started building an airstrip to pound our Aussie allies. But—we'd heard from newly arrived prisoners—US forces didn't let them finish it. In August, American Marines fought their way on to the beaches of Guadal, and a major battle had raged there for months.

"How do you know that? That they got clobbered?" Lulu murmured, playing her ace, as if nothing unusual had been said.

"Dad's shortwave," Bill responded in low tones, trumping Lulu's ace and taking the trick from the mat.

We all knew that Bill's Dad was a Navy reserve officer, who'd been interned as a civilian after the invasion, but none of us knew Mr. Philips had a radio till Bill mentioned it. That was dangerous, and I'd be scared to death if I were Bill. The Japs conducted surprise searches for radios in camp, and if found, his father and maybe his whole family could go straight to Fort Santiago.

"The battle took seven months," Bill spoke matter-of-factly, as if he were describing Hoyle's rules for bridge, "but we pummeled 'em in February. Dad says the Japs in Manila are taking it out on any Americans they see wandering around."

"Thank you for that heartening thought, Phillips," said Paul. "Fortunately, I have a Germanic countenance. I could be Heinrich Davis."

"You do look German." Nellie looked up at him. "Something about those Prussian blue eyes and that wide forehead. Besides, they won't stop teenage kids."

As Nellie raked in cards and tallied the score from the hand, she reminded us how many of our German, Spanish, and Swiss friends from school were free on the outside. Neutrals and Axis civilians carried on with their lives as normally as they could.

"Remember Juergen Goldfarb, Paul? He was with us at the American School?" Nellie shuffled and started to deal.

"Yeah, sure. He's free. I left Juergen my entire Lionel train collection before we got nabbed. Promised me he'd take care of it during the war." Paul sorted his hand.

"Isn't it something?" Nellie shook her head. "His family's German—so they're free. Axis Allies and all that. But the Goldfarbs are Jewish. If they were in Germany, they'd all be carted off to some horrible place by now."

"The Japs can't figure out the whole Jewish thing," Paul said.

"I haven't been able to figure it out either," I said, recalling my father's goodness and decency. "Judging someone by their religion or race—but it's been going on forever, right?"

We had wrapped up the year in English with Shakespeare's *Merchant of Venice*. "Remember how they hated Shylock 'cuz he was a Jew, and he launched into that *If you prick us, do we not bleed? … If you poison us, do we not die?* speech?" I said to no one in particular.

My friends counted their points silently and got ready to bid. "Well, that's why *all men are created equal* is a really big deal," I continued, remembering how proud my Jewish father had been of our country. "And that's why the United States is special. Religion and race don't make you any less when all men are created equal." I sounded pompous and school-girlish even to myself.

"Halo-Halo," Lulu wagged her head, but did not remove her gaze from her hand. "Why do you think Ginny McKinney and her sister are sleeping in that second-floor alcove in the Big House?"

Ginny, who was a few years ahead of me at Bordner, looked Filipino to me—golden brown skin, wide almond-shaped eyes, brown-black hair, and an easy smile. Pure Oriental glamour. But her American father was black, and had served in the U.S. Army eons ago. Mr. McKinney settled in Manila after World War I, and married a Filipino woman late in life. Now Ginny, her sister, two brothers, and dad were all interned at STIC, but not Ginny's Filipino mother because the Japs had no desire to intern the entire island of Luzon.

"What do you mean, Lulee? That's a great private space they've got. I've been kind of jealous," I admitted.

"She means they've got that 'great private space' because the all-white Horsey set didn't want their cots anywhere near the brown *hoi polloi*." Bill crudely finished Lulu's thought.

I was stunned into silence. "Hoi polloi" meant riff-raff.

"I talked to Ginny about it once," Lulu eyed her cards and tallied points mechanically. "She and her sister got assigned to room 16, but Bill's right. The room monitor couldn't bear the thought of brown ladies sleeping with white ladies. She assigned them their own little bedroom area in that alcove."

I sat looking over Lulu's shoulder and tried to digest this jarring information. At Bordner everyone loved Ginny. Her brothers could be hellions, but Ginny was a great student, a voracious reader, and athletic too. I couldn't believe the room monitor, would isolate two terrific girls on purpose. Of course, Ginny and her sister would be fools to complain about their space because they could luxuriate in PRIVACY, something the rest of craved every minute of every day. The McKinney girls could change clothes without seventy-six eyes watching them. They could sleep without hearing thirty-eight other women snore. I was glad that in this one case, bad intentions led to good results. As I stared at Lulu's cards, I resolved not to envy their space ever again.

Lulu had a strong hand. She should open with two clubs. She did.

"Anyway, if you take off your red armbands, the Japanese won't guess your nationality," Nellie continued. "Paul here is right about looking German, and Lee, you could pass for Spanish any time."

"*I'm jealous ....*" Lulu crooned, parroting Julie Gibson's tune from *The Feminine Touch*. "I wish we were together on this Lee-Lee. I can't believe Pablo is the Chosen One. You're safer with me!"

"*LU-lee-LU-lee-LU-lee,*" Paul chimed in with his best Cary Grant accent, "*What do you think I will do—kill her?*" Pablo tweaked the famous line in our favorite Hitchcock thriller, Suspicion.

"Cary Grant here is going to protect me," I said, trying to summon a lot more confidence than I felt.

Chapter 13
PURPLE SMUDGE ON THE PEARL

Saturday, March 27, 1943

Manila Mission Day dawned hot, sticky, and hopeful. I raced through my early morning chores, dressed in a black skirt, kissed my teary-eyed mother goodbye, and headed for the Southwest territory to board our charcoal-powered bus. Gas cost a fortune in the PI these days, but the round contraption mounted to the side of the bus burned coal to produce a gas that would jerk us forward. Paul waved to me, and I sped to his side.

"Lee Iserson, Paul Davis," Earl Carroll held a clipboard and called the names of internees boarding the dilapidated bus.

"Right here, sir," Paul responded before I could answer. Pablo took my elbow and steered me to the front of the little troop.

Mr. Carroll handed us red armbands emblazoned with the Japanese characters for Enemy National. "These are yours, courtesy of our magnanimous hosts," he said, and peered over his glasses to make sure we put them on.

We donned the armbands, keeping straight faces, but I felt insulted. Our label—Enemy Nationals—rankled because everyone knew that the Philippines were American territory. The only "Enemy National" here stood uniformed, ramrod straight, and scowled at the open door of the bus while balancing a bayoneted rifle.

"Miss Iserson, promise me you'll protect young Davis here, all right?" A smile played at the corners of Mr. Carroll's lips.

"He's safe with me, sir."

Paul rolled his eyes heavenward, as we boarded the bus with fellow scarlet-letter prisoners. Sitting next to each other on a wooden bench seat, Paul and I and strained to see ahead as the bus lurched forward. The iron gates swung open, and for the first time in fifteen months, we broke free of Santo Tomas.

I drank in the jasmine scent of Manila. No smoke now. No soot from explosions in the harbor, but the city seemed a mauve shadow of its former self. The once-busy boulevard of Calle España yawned open and empty. Our bus sped over the Pasig River bridge, which had been a choke point of traffic before the war. We passed just one Japanese tank going in the other direction, and then turned onto an eerily quiet Taft Avenue.

To our left rose Intramuros, the walled Spanish city built in the 1500s. Most Filipinos thought the old town picturesque, but I never liked it. Its black stone ramparts and chunky walkways screamed "medieval Europe," and now, with Japanese flags flapping from the sooty watchtowers of Fort Santiago, the effect was even more bizarre.

You're twelve, Lee. You're ready to understand the darker side of human nature. I tried to fight back the memory, but the last time I had been in Intramuros was with my father. He'd taken me to see the dungeons of Fort Santiago, where Spaniards had tortured rebel Filipinos centuries ago. I'd practically vomited when he told me how they were used. Imagine being held prisoner in a stone pit chained to a wall, while the pit filled with water. Only your head above the water, while snakes and rats swam around you—your toes and hands gnawed away day by day.

American forces had turned Fort Santiago into a museum and preserved its hideous torture chambers so that Filipinos could visit it "and remember what bastards the Spanish were," my father had told me.

Well, we should've knocked that fort right down because the conquering Japanese decided to use those cells and chambers just as they were intended.

There the military police, the Kempeitai, brutalized American and Filipino prisoners for information, which they might or might not have. I couldn't bear to look at it.

I let my eyes wander just past Intramuros to the broad expanse of the Luneta park and parade ground—no vendors, no picnickers, or bands. No resplendent American military parade.

"Listen!" Paul commanded. He leaned out the open window next to me.

"What?"

"Nothing. That's the point. It's like the city's been smothered. Suffocated."

He was right. A few Filipinos drove horse-drawn caramatas or pulled two-wheeled wagons on empty thoroughfares. An occasional carabao ground to a halt and snorted in disgust, but a hush blanketed the city. No toothless peddlers shouted greetings from their stalls. Not a single car moved in this petroleum-starved ghost town.

"Son of a gun!" Paul jerked his torso off the wooden seat, and waved his hand frantically over his backside. "Ani! Termites!" He stood up and steadied himself with a hand on the back of the seat. I didn't feel anything, but I had on black stockings, a slip, and a very voluminous black skirt I'd borrowed from Kay to provide lots of folds for the pesos I'd sew inside.

The bus finally halted in front of the University of the Philippines, and when the door opened, a Japanese guard descended the steps with a clipboard in hand. Mr. Carroll stood and signaled for us to follow him. When I stepped out of the bus, the scent of nearby sea washed over me.

"OK, you two," Mr. Carroll said, "You've got exactly twenty-four hours to go through the woods and visit Granny. Watch out for wolves. Hold on to your picnic baskets. And be here tomorrow at noon sharp for our return to Oz," he said mixing metaphors. "Oh, and have fun." His bright blue eyes glinted behind his rimless glasses.

Paul and I both nodded as the bus, the guard, Mr. Carroll, and the camp buyers headed off toward the Escolta or maybe the market at Quiapo. I reached into my reed bag and pulled out a large black lace mantilla, a typical

Spanish veil that covered my head, shoulders, and arms. When I tossed the musty veil over my head and shoulders, and slipped off my red armband, even Paul was impressed.

"Carmencita Iserson?" he joked, his eyes widening. "Man, you really do look Spanish. The painted fan from Seville is the only thing you're missing."

"I got the idea from Nellie," I admitted. My black-brown hair, mud colored eyes, and fair skin did make me look Spanish. And we all knew that German and Spanish kids were free.

For his part, Paul quickly tousled his short brown hair, and produced—to my complete horror—a swastika pin, which he fastened to his shirt. He then made short work of his armband, stuffing it in my bag.

"OK, dream-dish Spanish girl and hot-to-trot Gerry boy about to take a stroll down Dewey Boulevard," he said, grabbing my hand as if we were sweethearts, and giving me his cocky wink.

My heart somersaulted with the thrill of it all. War and camp be darned! Who cared if the Japs were in charge? We were going to have a good time.

* * *

Alfonso, Grandma Naylor's aging chauffeur, was supposed to meet us at the Manila Hotel on Dewey in half an hour. What would he be driving these days, when tanks and charcoal-powered buses owned the streets? Paul and I hurried toward our rendezvous, walking briskly down Taft before turning the corner towards Dewey.

"Oh, Paul, the Jai alai Club!" I tugged at his hand, and jerked him to a halt in front of Taft Avenue's most futuristic building. Its cylindrical glass front pulsed into the street and soared heavenward, topped by a flying saucer disk roof. The magnificent building seemed poised to jet off to the Planet Mongo with Flash Gordon.

"If only we had the time for the Sky Room…" I sighed.

Before the war, the glass-enclosed rooftop restaurant was the place to see and be seen in Manila, but what I loved best was its modern air cooling. You practically had to wear a sweater. My full black skirt and the heavy lace veil already hung limp in the heat and humidity.

"If we only had money for the Sky Room," Paul countered. "Dad took the whole family there to celebrate my thirteenth birthday, and Mom said she could've hired a house girl for two months for the price of that dinner. But we had T-bones. Yum."

"Think they're still playing Jai alai inside?" I loved the fast-paced Basque game, and so did every Filipino I ever met.

At that moment four Japanese military police officers emerged from the glass doors, one officer shouting to the others in short staccato bursts. They swerved left and seemed not to notice us, but almost simultaneously, Paul had his arm around my waist and turned us sharply right towards Dewey.

"Not exactly," Paul's eyes bulged, and his voice was low. "Looks like they've got the Kempeitai in there now. Did you see the number of white armbands behind the door when they came out?"

The Japanese Kempeitai wore olive uniforms, and on their left arms sported broad white armbands emblazoned with a red character. That's how you knew they weren't regular army. No, I had not seen the armbands, but eyes-in-the-back-of-his-head-Paul didn't miss a beat. "We gotta get to Dewey," he whispered and tugged me forward.

For a moment, when we reached the tree-lined boulevard and feasted our eyes on the waters of Manila Bay, I remembered being free and carefree just two years before. Slender palms still swayed in the breeze and lined the shore, while wrought-iron benches faced the sea for the sunset spectacular. Massive acacia trees still graced the median. Travel companies could write reams about the city's Jai Alai Club or the posh Manila Hotel, but Manila's real treasure was her bay and her sunsets.

How many times had our family sat here watching an orange sun sink into a purple sea? How many times from this very spot had we stared across the bay at Corregidor, imagining its mighty guns and rock-hewn tunnels? *The Rock.* The Rock that Crumbled.

"There he is!" Paul nudged me. I saw nothing but the elegant Manila Hotel with its white adobe walls, red tile roof, and arched windows. "Over there. Alfonso!" he called, and sped us toward a wooden cart.

I hardly recognized Grandma Naylor's leather-skinned driver without his silver-grey chauffeur's uniform. Alfonso sat barefoot on the bench seat, holding the reins of a gaunt horse. He wore a long-sleeved white shirt with Mandarin collar buttoned at his neck. It topped loose cotton pants that were rolled to his knees—the outfit of a Filipino peasant. Alfonso also seemed to have traded Grandma's sleek 1940 Packard for this rickety, two-wheeled "caretela" that seated six.

Alfonso's face split into a wide grin when he saw us, and he sang out "Mabuhay" or "welcome," as Paul helped me up into the back of the caretela. "We go to Malate and you enjoy ride," he called from the seat.

***

Grandma had moved from the city of Manila to the northern suburb of Malate in early 1941, several months before the Japanese invasion. That was lucky because the Japs had not yet commandeered homes distant from the city, and her Malate garden with its avocado, mango, and papaya trees could still supply some of her (and our) needs. I could hardly wait to see her and her fabulous pastry chef house girl, Valentina, again.

Edith Naylor, a white-haired pixie of a woman in a blue-checkered apron, waited on the screened verandah of her home, and nearly burst out the door and down the stairs when we arrived. I couldn't stop myself either. Clunky wooden bakias or no, I leapt from the caretela as Alfonso yanked the cart to a halt.

"Grandma, we're here!"

"Oh, you're here, and you're all grown up—and you're so beautiful, Lee!" she gripped both my arms and smiled up at me, her blue eyes glowing. "But you're really too thin!" She wrapped me in a fierce embrace, then held my face in her bony hands and kissed me smack on the lips. She had to stand on her tiptoes to do it.

Then she turned to Pablo. "Oh and Pauly!" Paul got away with a ferocious hug, and a promise. "Do I ever have a surprise for you two! In you go," she waved us forward. A widow in her late sixties, Grandma looked her age now, her paper-thin skin creased like an accordion fan, but her love of life undiminished.

"Oh, they told me today was the day," she jabbered away, "but not to plan on it, just in case, but— how was I not going to be ready for you?" The Internee Committee had gotten word to Grandma of our impending visit. She, in turn, had arranged for Alfonso to meet us.

Grandma led us through the porch into her terrazzo-tiled living room. A wicker palm-frond fan circled overhead, wafting a breeze. Grandma's house girl, Valentina, gave us a shy smile and offered us both frosty Coca-Colas from a silver tray. But Paul squinted at figures in the corner shadows, and immediately bolted toward a shaded area of the large room.

"Juergen! I can't believe it!" Paul shouted, taking two long strides to the sofa in the corner.

Juergen Goldfarb, caretaker of Paul's Lionel train set, was a blue-eyed blond, a poster child for the Aryan race—even if he was Jewish. Paul's classmate from the American school grinned broadly as he shot to his feet and raced to bear-hug Paul.

Next to him, smiling brightly was chubby Ramón Ayala, a former neighbor and Spanish classmate of mine from Bordner. He had lost some weight, I noticed, but was still no beanpole. Grandma knew both their families from the Polo Club, of course. She also knew they were classmates of ours. I wondered for a second why Grandma didn't invite any girls.

"Como estás, Leonora?" Ramón smiled at me, his chestnut brown eyes liquid warmth, as he tried to get me to practice the modest amount of Spanish I knew. Since Paul was pounding Juergen's back, I figured I'd better at least shake Ramón's hand. When I grasped it, he surprised me by leaning over to kiss my cheek. I had forgotten that about Spanish men—they always kissed you on the cheek in greeting—usually when you least expected it.

"Muy bien, Ramón, pero sorprendido." I thought that meant "I'm well, but surprised."

"You mean 'sorprendida' since you're a girl," Ramón said.

That was the problem with Spanish—so many endings that changed from *o* to *a* depending on gender. I liked Spanish, but I sure hadn't mastered it.

"Bueno. Sorprendida." I corrected myself. "Or is it 'Buena'?

"No, it's 'bueno,'" he laughed, his pudgy cheeks full and rosy, and his eyes bright.

Ramón had unusual eyes. They were mostly brown, but were rimmed at the edges in blue and framed by impossibly long dark eyelashes and a straight hedge row of black brows. I shook my head in exasperation at his language.

None of us could stop smiling or talking. Valentina served the Cokes and then brought a tray of cheese and crackers, followed by ham sandwiches on real white bread. I had skipped breakfast because I didn't have time for the line, so Paul and I greedily helped ourselves to two sandwiches each. How did Grandma get these luxuries? We hadn't seen Coke in a year, and white bread had disappeared from camp, along with wheat flour ten months ago. These days STIC bread was made from rice flour, and it tasted like chalk.

For an hour, here in Grandma's familiar living room, we were catapulted happily back in time. Remember the Daisy air rifle competition at the Polo Club? Remember Sonia Henie's skating in *Happy Ending*? There on Grandma's wicker coffee table were old copies of *Good Housekeeping*, *Collier's*, the *Saturday Evening Post*, and our other favorite pre-war magazines.

Grandma came in and sat down with us for a while, then sensing our desire for unbridled teen talk, excused herself for a siesta, assuring Paul and me that she'd catch up with us that evening. Meanwhile, Paul and I pumped Juergen and Ramón for details on life in occupied Manila.

Some things hadn't changed, they said. The Swiss Club still organized dances. The Yacht Club held regattas too. The Capitol and Lyric theaters on the Escolta were still air-cooled havens showing movies. Ramón and Juergen had just seen Flash Gordon's latest, *The Purple Death from Outer Space*, and we almost turned purple with envy.

"So the earthlings are all dying of a plague that leaves strange purple smudges on their foreheads," Juergen said, "and of course the weirdo epidemic is traced back to the Planet Mongo and Flash's archfiend, Ming the Merciless. Earth can be saved only if Flash can get the antidote—Polarite—ASAP from the frozen wastelands of Frigia—and guess what? He does. No more purple smudges. No more purple death."

"Man, I can't believe I didn't see that," Paul moaned.

"You don't need to—you got your own saga going, Pablo. You can write *The Yellow Peril from Santo Tomas*," Juergen smirked.

"They're not really yellow, you know," I corrected in a stern voice. I don't know why I felt the need to defend our captors. Maybe because of Haruo. Maybe because of one Japanese guard and his simple act of kindness in my topsy-turvy world.

Paul dismissed me. "Lee, Old Goat, Old Sack," he started off in his best Cary Grant, then dropped it. "Let's face it: they are a peril. I've never seen the Luneta that empty or that dead. No concerts, no ice cream vendors, no families picnicking—nothing." Paul turned to Juergen. "Is it like that all the time?"

Juergen and Ramón snorted almost in unison.

"Not during the 'gratitude rallies,'" Ramón scoffed. "That's when we all line up in pretty rows on the Luneta, wave Japanese flags, and cry out our thanks to our Asian Brothers for liberating the PI."

"Last month," Juergen told us, "the Japs made a big show of announcing Philippine independence—independence *maybe, probably, when and if* Filipinos recognized 'the magnanimity of the Imperial Japanese Forces' and acknowledged the blessings brought to them by participation in the Greater East Asian Co-Prosperity Sphere."

"Now that you mention it," I said, "I think I read that in the *Manila Tribune* we got in camp."

"Can you believe the Filipinos did not leap up to thank them?" Ramón continued, his brown eyes alight with mischief, and his voice a melodic lilt. I suddenly remembered that Ramón played some instrument. "So the Japanese"—he said it like "hah-po-NACE"—decided to organize a Gratitude Rally—supposedly organized by the Filipinos in thankfulness."

"They strong-arm as many Filipinos as they can," Juergen continued "to parade down Taft Avenue in caretelas, waving Rising Sun flags, 'Heil Hirohito,' and all that. We kids—even the neutrals and Axis kids—had to leave school, line up on the Luneta with our little flags, yelling 'Banzai!' And 'Nippon-go!'"

"Did you do that?" Paul looked appalled and wide eyed. Paul, who was wearing his swastika pin....

"Of course, we did. We want to live, don't we?" Juergen continued.

It was shocking to think of Juergen and Ramón out there on the Luneta waving their Japanese flags and cheering our captors.

"But when we shout 'Nippon-go!' we turned to each other and whispered, "American come!" Ramón added with a warm smile.

"They're training us for next month, the one year anniversary of Corregidor's fall," Juergen snorted. "Tojo—the Jap Prime minister—is coming to town to receive," and here Juergen switched into his best Japanese accent "the sin-see-ah and over-werming jubiration and tanks of Firipeen peepoh."

We all laughed, but for the first time ever, I was glad that in May I was going to be stuck in Santo Tomas, and not free in Manila. Tojo was once step closer to the Imperial Japanese Empire than I ever wanted to be.

According to our friends, these gratitude rallies had been the least of the burdens placed on civilians by the occupying Japanese army. Soldiers on the streets felt free to stop and take what they wanted from the civilian population—watches, lace veils for wives. They demanded identification for no reason, and might flare up unpredictably. Ramón said that by now the kids had learned to show no emotion if stopped—and never, ever to laugh near a Japanese soldier. The soldiers assumed they were being laughed *at*, and quickly advanced to slap smiles right off the faces of the merry children.

I wondered why Grandma hadn't invited any of my Spanish girlfriends from Bordner, but as the afternoon stretched on and the light grew golden, I understood why. Ramón lowered his voice when he told us that women were suffering terribly in Manila. Officially, Spanish women, as neutrals, were safe, he said, but they always carried papers with them, and tried to keep off the streets when at all possible. Filipinas routinely suffered leers and humiliating detentions—if they were lucky. If they were not lucky, they could be cornered and abducted by soldiers "out for a good time," as Juergen put it.

The boys told us about Japanese soldiers visiting a Filipino school—a class of eighth graders. The teaching of Japanese in school was mandatory now, and one teacher taught her class of girls to sing a Japanese folk song. The visiting soldiers applauded the performance loudly and proclaimed themselves so impressed that they would come to pick up two of the girls the next day and take them for a special award for their performance. They came back the next day, collected them, and those eager little girls had not been seen since.

My stomach knotted, and I excused myself to go talk to Valentina in the kitchen—mostly to assure myself that this innocent Filipina, who reminded me so much of Rosalina, was safe. Valentina let me help her dry some dishes, and chatted merrily about a new blouse she was making for her sister and about polishing the floor before leaving. Her easy chatter soothed me and I basked once more in the friendliness of the Philippine people.

"Are you safe, Vale?" I asked, as I dried the last dish. "Juergen and Ramón told us terrible things—about those girls in the school."

Valentina's face clouded and she grew unnecessarily energetic with her scrubbing.

"Just thirteen—those little girls just thirteen. Young as you, Lee when taken. Americans never do such crap." I saw a tear running down her cheek.

My head spun with sickening speed as Valentina hissed out more of the story. The four-story apartment building on the corner of Dakota and Herran Streets had been converted to a brothel, for Japanese officers. "Japanese call it 'Comfort House.' For who? Comfort for who?" Valentina spat out the words.

Dozens of soldiers pushed in and sauntered out each day, buttoning and zipping smugly as they descended the steps. Most of the captive women there were Korean and Chinese, carted off from the conquered territories—women who couldn't speak Japanese or English or Tagalog. Women who stood no chance of escaping. I couldn't even imagine the horror of that life for innocent young girls. How foolish I had been waltzing down Dewey Boulevard as if all were right with the world.

"We don't know about Fatima or Angela—where they went, if they still alive," Valentina said of the missing girls. "Who knows if Jap soldiers still hold them prisoner and use them like Three Hole Girl," she hissed bitterly. The Filipino slang for prostitute turned my stomach. She told me more that I didn't want to hear. "We stay out of city," she concluded.

Valentina, Alfonso, and Narciso all had routines that kept them out of the way of Japanese patrols, she stressed. For how long? I wondered. And didn't I still have to get back to the bus by walking those streets?

When I re-entered the living room, the boys were murmuring grimly, and Paul abruptly turned the conversation to sports. He told them how in camp our "Green Bay Packers" had defeated our "Chicago Bears." Juergen, who followed American football with passion, told us last year's Western Division championship had actually gone to the Bears, who trounced the Packers back in November. But we already knew that, because American sports scores were one thing the Japanese didn't bother to censor. For a fleeting moment, I missed my mother, my sister, and Room 4.

***

That night at dinner, hours after Ramón and Juergen had left, Grandma kept the conversation light. She proudly reminded me that she had salvaged all our photos from the apartment, and they would surely survive the war. She was pleased with the good price Daddy's shirts had brought, and told me she was going to continue to send as many fruits, vegetables, and as much native cocoa, as she could find, though all were scarcer now. There would be no more Ghirardelli's, but MacArthur's forces would surely liberate us soon.

I'm not sure what else Grandma talked about because Paul and I were so greedily wolfing down the abundant dinner that we hardly heard a word. Our stomachs remembered every moment, though. We ate a mouthwatering stew of roast pork and white beans to which Grandma had added little purple eggplant and some "pechay," a green cabbage both milder and softer than our coarse, camp-grown talinum. Valentina served the stew with "kamote" or sweet potatoes, and flaky biscuits Grandma herself had made. Then at the end of the meal—green coconut ice cream topped with chocolate shavings greeted us. Our tummies felt like they had died and gone to Heaven.

Valentina removed the dishes, and smiled warmly at Grandma. "We not eat like this every day, you know. Mrs. Naylor find special treats for you today."

I had suspected as much. Everyone in the PI looked thinner, but there were still ways to get basics and a few luxuries: most of them involved connections and money. As if reading my mind, Grandma urged us back to the living room for coffee. From a drawer in a wicker side table, she extracted a fat envelope and handed it to me.

"Time for the sewing circle," she smiled.

I opened the envelope to find a stack of twenty peso notes. My heart raced as I counted: twenty-five of them—each worth approximately ten dollars. The perfectly symmetrical Mayon volcano on the front and "VICTORY" imprint on the back, marked the bills as authentic gold-backed peso notes drawn on the Bank of the Philippines. These were not the worthless "Mickey Mouse" notes that the Japanese were printing willy-nilly. These funds would go very far in camp. Grandma cast me her most conspiratorial grin, then handed me a pair of scissors, black thread and a needle. I started to snip and sew.

Chapter 14
RETURN TO OZ

Sunday, March 28, 1943

Cold hands...

"Amah! Your hands are freezing! Go warm them up!"

Our Chinese governess scowled at me, but left the room to run her hands under hot water before helping me dress. Hadn't I told her a million times about warming her hands up? Groggy with sleep, I squinted at the gauzy cloud of mosquito netting that swayed in the tropical breeze, then closed my eyes again. The hum of morning household activity rose around me.

On the terrace Rosalina laughed as she scraped the inside of a split coconut. She swapped stories in Tagalog with our house boy, Felix. But moments later the whoosh told me Rosalina was at work, skating across the terrazzo tile floor, one bare foot securely mounted on the rounded coconut husk, and the other free to push off and accelerate, as she swept from side to side. The oils and soft fibers in the coconut meat polished the floor tiles to a pool of satin cream. Rosalina would have that outdoor terrace gleaming before we finished breakfast.

Breakfast... I'd have mango for breakfast. The mangoes hung heavy on the bushes in our yard, turning red as they ripened. Amah needed to stop poking at me, even if she had warmed her hands up.

I protested. "Stop, Amah!"

"I'm not your Amah, princess. C'mon, now, time to rise and shine. It's nine o'clock."

I squinted to see Grandma Naylor, smiling down on me. It took me a full five seconds to realize that I had been dreaming. I was not a spoiled ten-year-old with a governess, but a determined fifteen-year-old on a mission. *Halo-Halo*, as Lulu would say. Still, so much about this moment echoed my old life. I lay in a soft four-poster bed draped in mosquito netting. The familiar whooshing from the other side of the house was Valentina polishing the tile on coconut skates. Monkeys chattered in the banyan trees outside, and as I blinked into wakefulness, I could see plump mangoes turning red in the courtyard. And there was Grandma, pale blue eyes aglow, smiling at me.

"Is Paul up?" I bolted into wakefulness.

"He's been in and out of the pool already," Grandma smiled. "Grab a shower, honey. It's time to have breakfast and get you back to camp with the goods."

The pool! Darn. I wasn't going to be able to use the pool. Well, that was OK. I hadn't slept that long or that well in a year—no Mommy calling me to bathroom duty at 5:30 AM, no bouncy *"Good Mornin, Good Mornin"* blaring over the PA. And there would be nobody, not a single human being, in line for Grandma's mosaic-tiled bath and shower. The thought of having the whole bathroom to myself propelled me out of bed.

After a heavenly shower and a breakfast of soft-boiled eggs, mangoes and real coffee, I stood outside with Paul and Grandma Naylor to say our good byes.

The three of us had talked for hours after dinner. The lights had flickered and died, but Grandma had candles at the ready, and she explained that the nightly blackouts were routine to save electricity. Meanwhile, my camp sewing lessons paid off. I'd carefully stitched the twenty peso notes in the hem of my skirt, and spaced them at even intervals in the row above it. The bank notes gave my black skirt a fuller, fluffier appearance, but not one that attracted attention.

I glanced over at Paul. Jaw clenched, his hands played nervously with something in his pocket. We'd both donned our red "Enemy Nationals" armbands, as we prepared to re-join Mr. Carroll. Alfonso would be here any minute to return us to the city. Teary-eyed and not wanting to let go of the moment, Grandma and I stared at each other.

"I told you that you were dying, didn't I?" I sniffed. "If the Japanese ask you, you had consumption. But you can miraculously recover, now that we've said goodbye."

"What's *consumption* anyway?" Paul asked, his wise-guy mode almost returning.

"It's a kind of tuberculosis, honey. A wasting away of the body." Grandma grinned now. "At my age, everyone has consumption."

"Well, thank you for ours, Mrs. Naylor," Paul nodded heartily. "All our consumption I mean. Those were the best 24 hours in food history for me. T-bones in the Sky Room do not compare."

The screen door slammed behind Valentina, as she hurried to present Paul and me with waxed paper packages. "They're just some calamansis, and pilipit, but you'll like," she half-explained and half-apologized. Small Philippine limes, calamansis, were much in demand in camp and I'd give some to Mommy to sell, but I knew the mouthwatering figure-eight pastries —pilipit—would be gone before we got off the bus. Valentina darted back into the house, before we could smother her with kisses. Then, Alfonso pulled up in the horse-drawn cart, and with hugs, tears, and admonitions to stay safe, we left Grandma Naylor alone on her front step.

***

Clipboard in hand, Mr. Carroll checked off our names as we boarded the bus. "We've got one stop at Quiapo market before returning to Oz," he told us. "And Davis, keep that armband on. You're with me at Quiapo. Miss Iserson, you stay on the bus. We're not taking any chances with our girls in the market."

I nodded to Mr. Carroll, relieved. I remembered Ramón telling me Spanish women stayed out of the crowded markets patrolled by Japanese soldiers. And Valentina's story of the kidnapped thirteen-year-old girls turned "Comfort Women" still haunted me.

Paul and I took our seats near the window. When our bus roared to life and headed down Taft Avenue, my heart hammered and my mind raced. Nellie was right—I desperately wanted to be out of blighted Manila and back in camp. But first I had to get five-hundred pesos through the front gate. I fumbled for the wooden rosary I usually had in my skirt pocket, but had I'd left it back in Room 4. Why hadn't I stuck it in the pocket of this skirt?

I glanced over at Paul, whose bright blue eyes radiated tension—or maybe adventure. My thoughts fled back to the previous evening. "What were Juergen and Ramón telling you last night, when I came back to the living room?"

Pablo gave me a puzzled frown.

"After I talked to Valentina. You three were whispering like conspirators in that corner, but I heard something about Rizal Stadium, before we started talking football at STIC—"

Paul cut me off. "You don't want to know"

"We're in a grown-up world now," I said. "I need to know. Maybe we can do something about it."

"We're in a screwed-up world, and we can't do a damn thing about it," Paul responded sharply, and then seemed embarrassed. The boys usually saved their profanity to impress each other, and hardly ever swore in front of us girls. He was shaken about something.

"What is it, Pablo? I want to know." Silence greeted me.

"I'll spill to Phillips," he finally said. "If you can get the gory details out of him, go ahead. But you're not gonna hear them from me. I was awake half the night thinking about it. I took that swim this morning to wash the filth out of my head."

I tried to let it go. But what could be bothering Paul so much? Did he know about something worse than the Comfort Women?

Our bus crossed the Pasig River bridge, and lurched to a halt in front of the Quiapo market. One of the oldest sections of the city, Quiapo still teemed with activity. Here, Manila's vendors hawked fish, rice, vegetables, duck eggs, and whatever meat still existed. Swarms of flies blanketed the produce and fought over refuse. Religious articles crowded the shelves of stands selling rosaries, scapulars and tiny carved statues of an almost-black Jesus carrying his cross. The market's covered stalls snaked maze-like on the shore side, while flat-bottomed boats, loaded with woven baskets and hats, rimmed the river edge. Boatmen shouted their best deals to passers-by.

The air stank of dead fish and the rotting remains of overripe vegetables, but my heart still leapt as I drank in this familiar scene. Here was *life*. Manila's irrepressible people—bantering, haggling, buying, selling—willfully determined to survive, even as the bayonet-toting Japanese soldiers strode through the narrow aisles.

As we waited, Mr. Carroll strode to the front of the bus and spoke to the Japanese guard and Filipino driver. My gaze strayed to the triple-domed Quiapo Church flanking one side of the market. Even now worshippers entered for noon-day mass, as if life were normal. I had been in that cavernous stone basilica before and could still see the altar's centerpiece—a life-sized wooden statue of Jesus hefting his cross. The three-hundred-year-old sculpture from Mexico had been charred in a ship fire before it ever arrived in Manila in the 1600s, but it survived. Robed in maroon velvet, a crown of thorns woven tightly around his brown, wooly hair, and three flames of gold foil shooting from his bloodied head, the "Black Nazarene" had become an icon for the dark-skinned Filipinos. They identified with the blackened Jesus, suffering with and for them.

It was Lent now. And Friday. There would be Stations of the Cross later in the day. Maybe practicing that old devotion, when Catholics stopped to remember every step of Jesus' agony and passion, made Filipinos feel like their own suffering was not so bad. Or at least in suffering, they had a friend in Jesus, as the old Protestant hymn went.

When you came right down to it, my mind was wandering now as I stared out the window, Protestants had a much tidier and more cheerful religion than we Catholics. Our churches—like Quiapo—were all gloomy, dark, and dirty with horrible, bleeding, Spanish statues, and nobody knew how to sing. Nobody even tried to sing, really.

Before the war—and before I became Catholic—Mommy let me go to the Presbyterian church sometimes with my friend Mildred Cooper. Her church was clean and bright, filled with British and American white people, and there was not a single depressing statue in sight. Jesus was not always suffering at me in the Presbyterian church. And everybody sang full-voiced—wonderful reassuring hymns like "His Eye is On the Sparrow" or "What a Friend We Have in Jesus." I could see why Protestants liked being Protestants.

"I'm outa here, Lee." Paul rose abruptly from our seat, and for a moment I was afraid for him. Why did he have to go out there again, and with the tell-tale red armband no less? But Mr. Carroll was in charge, not me, and it made no sense to protest. I waved at my buddy, and he smiled nervously at me. Paul, Mr. Carroll, and two other men from camp descended to the crowded market.

* * *

The red armbands proved good markers for our little troop, and I watched as the four men made their way from stall to stall. Mr. Carroll, clipboard in hand, kept lists and bargained for purchases, while merchants bantered, then dumped their produce into the woven-mat bags of the others. I lost sight of our men for a moment; then there they were again—Carroll shaking his head at over-priced papayas, saying yes to rice and bruised avocadoes, and making one fishmonger a very happy man indeed.

When our men purchased an entire basket of his silvery fish, the gap-toothed Filipino flashed a blood-red smile, his teeth and gums scarlet with the residue of betel nuts he was chewing. In the Philippines, fire-red betel nuts were the poor man's tobacco, caffeine, and alcohol all in one: people said they packed a rush of energy and a feeling of euphoria in every chew.

They also left the user with a terrifying Halloween mouth; it was widely agreed that no sight was scarier than a smiling chewer of betel nuts.

Twenty minutes into the excursion, I saw Paul—his red armband still in place—steal away from the fishmonger and our men. *What was he up to?* Mr. Carroll didn't stop him, or maybe he didn't see him break away. Paul darted through the twisting market aisles before I lost sight of him, and my stomach tightened. Pablo—daring and wily—was often too sure of himself. Every instinct I had told me he was up to no good.

He re-emerged in front of a neatly dressed Japanese cigarette vendor, who stood no more than twenty feet from our bus. Paul bowed deeply to the man, whose glasses made him look scholarly. The seller seemed to recognize Paul. This could be real trouble. Paul was wearing the red-armband and haggling with a Japanese merchant? One who would surely be well-protected by rifle-toting soldiers on market patrol.

When the merchant gave a vague smile, and returned a perfunctory bow, Paul reached into his pocket and pulled out—what? I couldn't see it. But the man's clouded face suddenly cleared and lit up. He smiled broadly, took the tiny object from Paul, and rolled it in his hand with reverence, his entire countenance one of disbelief. Paul said a few words hurriedly. Then the merchant's head bobbed rapidly up and down several times in appreciation. What had Paul given him?

The man turned his back to Pablo and squatted down, looking for something behind the curtained section of his stall. As he did, I saw Paul sweep what had to be thirty packs of precious Akebono cigarettes into his coconut reed bag. *Paul was stealing cigarettes from a Jap!* Well, they were a cash crop in camp—that's for sure. You could support a family on those thirty packs for more than a few months. But the risk… The Japanese merchant straightened, turned toward Paul, still smiling, and didn't notice the theft.

My friend remained ramrod straight, and smiled as the pleased merchant flashed the cover of some plastic-wrapped magazines—maybe comic books. Paul nodded nervously, prompting the merchant to wrap them quickly in brown paper, and whisk the packet into Paul's extended hand. He turned away from me, and when he turned around again, the magazines had vanished, but Paul was tucking his tee shirt into his pants. His skinniness helped him now; I couldn't tell that he had stashed the contraband under his shirt. Pablo Diablo bowed to the merchant one last time, and then headed toward our bus.

Mr. Carroll and the others strode back to the STIC-mobile too. I stared at the delighted Japanese merchant, who at that exact moment noticed the empty space on his counter—so recently occupied by Akebono cigarettes. He started to shout after Paul—then stopped himself, seemed to think better of it, and re-arranged his counter display. What was that all about? Why didn't he sic the guards on Paul?

Paul boarded the bus and slipped into the seat next to me, grinning like the Cheshire Cat. He was full to bursting with pride, his cheeks flushed and breathing rapid. "OK, Pablo Diablo—spill," I whispered as the bus roared to life. "What'd you give that Jap? And how do you think you're going to get those cigarettes into camp?" Paul's face registered surprise, but not annoyance as I hissed on. "I watched the whole thing from up here. He almost had the guards on you."

"Really?" Paul looked doubly pleased now. "Nah, he wouldn't have done that. That was Mr. Funabiki. He's a nice guy. He's also a collector, and I traded him something worth a lot more than those forbidden *Time* magazines or those cigarettes. He'd wanted it for a long time."

"How do you know?"

In low tones, Paul explained that his family had done business with Mr. Funabiki before the war. The well-educated merchant from Tokyo was a collector of *netsuke*, tiny Japanese sculptures carved from ivory, walnut, or even rhinoceros horn. Some shapes were rarer and more valuable than others.

"I traded him an ivory baku—which is very rare," Paul confided in a conspiratorial whisper. "*Bakus* are monsters that devour your nightmares."

Where would Paul get that? I loved Paul, but the "true north" on his moral compass often pointed in a direction different from mine.

"You didn't take it from Grandma's, did you?" I was almost afraid to know the truth. It was a relief to see his brow furrow in indignation.

"No, it was my mother's. Juergen's mom stored all our stuff for safekeeping before the Japs took the house. She had Juergen give it to me in case we needed some bargaining chips in camp. Mr. Carroll and I thought it would be better to use the bargaining chip outside of camp."

So that was it… Mr. Carroll knew. And let Paul do it.

"Was it very handsome—this *baku*?"

"He had the head and trunk of an elephant, claws of a tiger, and horns of a bull, so he's not gonna win any beauty contests, but he's more than three-hundred-years-old. And ivory. And the carving was unbelievable. So maybe that baku can take away Mr. Funabiki's worst nightmares—if any of 'em have to do with money. Meanwhile, I'm bringing home the bacon for Mom."

Paul's mother, like mine, was alone in camp and trying to support her teen son and Paul's younger sister, Annie. Mrs. Davis taught fourth grade in the camp school and didn't have a fudge-making business, so these cigarettes were going to be a windfall. I watched Paul rapidly re-arrange the items in his bag, so that the numerous packs of Akebonos sank to the bottom, covered by vegetables on top.

The bus coughed to life and began its trip toward the Quezon Bridge. I handed Paul one of the pastries Valentina had made for us, and he smiled as he took a big bite.

"How do you think you're going to get that bag past the guards?" I asked, as I bit into my own pilipit. If the Japs discovered his contraband, we'd all get extra scrutiny and maybe camp jail time. Were my pesos going to get through?

"Same way as you're going to bring in the moolah, Lee, Old Bag, Old Goat," he reverted back to his cocky Cary Grant self. "Right under their noses. Oh—almost forgot. This is for you."

From his pocket, Paul pulled a tiny plastic object, and pressed a sloppily painted statue of Jesus, the Black Nazarene, into the palm of my hand. Three inches tall, clothed in red, hefting his cross, while blood dripped from his thorn-crowned forehead, this suffering patron of the Filipinos stared right up into my eyes. His eyes were liquid pools of brown gold. I thought about the wooden cross on Rosalina's rosary that I'd forgotten to bring with me, and my fingers closed around the little statue. I didn't want to think about whether Paul had stolen this too.

"And by the way, one of the Filipinas in the market took one look at my red armband and *gave* him to me," he said as if reading my thoughts. "I didn't steal it." He drew the fingers of his maimed hand into a pencil-shaped cone and dashed a decisive stroke. "I draw the line at pilfering the Passion."

I thanked him, pocketing the little treasure. "We're going to need him now."

The speared tips of the iron gates loomed ahead of us, and swung wide. Looking straight ahead to the Big House, I saw the familiar clock tower and right on top, the spare metal cross profiled in the blue sky. Now, if only we could get past the guards.

When the bus jerked to a stop, Mr. Carroll was the first to stand—clipboard still in hand of course, armband in place, as he descended the steps. He positioned himself to check prisoners back into camp with a Japanese sentry by his side. *Oh no.* It was Bugs Bunny Guard—whiskered slayer of lemon meringue pies, bayonet-wielding foe of fluff. Bugs was only a Private First Class in the army—"Ittohei," as the Japanese said—but he conducted himself like a Major General.

Seated near the back of the bus, Paul and I watched eagle-eyed as five STIC patients, newly released from the Philippine hospital, made their way gingerly down the steps. Mr. Carroll nodded to each in turn, checked off their names, collected their armbands, and sometimes extended a hand to steady each one. Bugs Bunny eyed them with suspicion, barking orders to turn over satchels and pouches. He rummaged through each bag, but seemed to find nothing. The infirm hobbled to the waiting arms of loved ones. I could see my mother waiting in that crowd. And Mrs. Davis too.

When the fifth emaciated man descended the steps, Bugs Bunny Guard decided "No More Mr. Nice Rabbit." He snatched the reed bag from the hand of the man, who probably stood five-foot-six when healthy, but was now bent like a wilted blade of grass. Judging from the contents of his bag, the man had been passing time in the hospital sketching. Bugs scrutinized each page of the pad he had tugged from the bag. *Was it code*? he seemed to be wondering. Then in an abrupt show of might and spite, he ripped several of the illustrated pages to shreds and tossed the whole thing into a metal pail, and then set it aflame for good measure. I saw the frail man shake his head with a sad smile, but step into the embrace of his anxious wife.

Despite the ninety-degree morning heat, every hair on the back of my neck stood on end, as both Paul and I climbed out for our inspection. The camp buyers were behind us. With any luck Bugs Bunny Guard would be focused on the grown men with the real haul, and not look too carefully at Paul or me. I wore the now-padded full black skirt and carried a bag filled with limes and four remaining pastries from Valentina. Paul had his contraband-stuffed tee shirt tucked into baggy pants, and sported a large coconut reed bag filled with vegetables and of course, the cigarettes.

As I stepped onto the familiar plaza, Mr. Carroll nodded at me as if this were all routine. I remembered his whispered instructions to me at the University. *You are sad that your grandmother is near death. But you are very thankful to have seen her one last time because of the magnanimity of our Japanese hosts.* I handed Mr. Carroll my armband and dipped into a respectful bow to Bugs. Predictably, he snatched my bag, and glowered as he emptied the prizes of calamansis and pastries onto the table next to him.

"You buy these for camp?" he demanded in a curt staccato, his eyes meeting mine.

"No. They were gifts from my grandmother," I answered truthfully, casting my eyes down in what I knew was modest Japanese fashion. At least, he was not staring at my quite full black skirt.

"I think they gift for me," he sneered.

My heart sank, but the limes and pastries were nothing compared to the smuggled pesos in my skirt. I glanced briefly at Mr. Carroll and saw him nod almost imperceptibly at me.

"I am happy to present you with them," I said, hardly recognizing my composed voice and dipped into a bow again. "Thank you for allowing me to see my grandmother."

Bugs Bunny Guard stilled and lifted his chin in surprise. He peered through heavily lidded eyes, regarding me with his best imitation of a seductive smile. His eyes roamed freely up and down my body, where they lingered rudely on my full skirt and my bare legs. I had not put on the black stockings this morning. *Stupid.* Now my blood ran cold.

Mr. Carroll looked up for a moment and tried to appear unconcerned. "That's generous of Miss Iserson, but unnecessary, isn't it Ittohei-san? They're from her grandmother."

I stared at the ground and wished I had at least worn bobby socks with my bakias, so that my legs weren't so exposed.

"We take," announced the brisk voice of another guard who seemed to have appeared from nowhere.

Broad-shouldered and no-nonsense, he swept my prizes off the table and into a box of confiscated items. Even though he was bent over, I could tell he was quite tall. The white star and yellow stripe on his shoulder insignia labeled him a "Gocho" or corporal, outranking Private Bugs. In fact, Bugs had snapped to attention when the new guard took over. I stared disbelieving for a moment. It was Haruo.

"You go in now," Haruo's wide-spaced almond eyes seemed not even to notice me as he flagged me forward.

I wasted no time, darting into the arms of my mother, thankful I had gotten in with every one of my pesos, and not believing my good fortune. Her embrace was warm and bony, and she whispered, "Good work, Sunshine." We both turned to watch Paul now standing for inspection, and while I looped one hand around her waist, I reached for the Black Nazarene in my other pocket, squeezing it in wordless prayer.

Haruo fixed Paul with what appeared to be a gruff stare, and pantomimed for him to open his vegetable-crowned sack. Rummaging through its contents and digging deep to the bottom, Haruo's almond eyes widened, turned cold, and then dismissive. Still, he did not remove a single one of the vegetables or cigarettes.

"These all for camp?" He interrogated Paul and seemed to stare hard at Paul's newly expanded chest. The Time Magazines bulged ever-so-slightly under his tee shirt.

This time Mr. Carroll answered. "These vegetables are all for camp, Gocho. Mr. Davis helped us at Quiapo."

"He help himself too." Haruo nodded brusquely, but he waved Paul forward.

Chapter 15
STARLIGHT ARENA

March 28, 1943

Lulu, Betty, and Annie rushed forward to welcome us, folding us almost instantly back into the familiar world of kids at Santo Tomas. Paul and I, who had been so eager to get out, could hardly wait to burst back in.

"Was it hideous? Was it completely hideous?!" Lulu demanded with sarcasm as she hugged me and grabbed both my hands. Smiling broadly, she sought affirmation of the great fun and good times we'd had on the outside, her entire being eager for the details of our marvelous adventure. But when she saw I could only nod and was tearing up, she looked at me startled.

"I was kidding, Super Girl! Oh, I was just kidding! It couldn't have been hideous. Tell me every single thing you ate at Grandma Naylor's!"

"The Sky Room does not hold a candle to Mrs. Naylor," Paul called confidently, as he and his mother walked toward the Big House in conspiratorial closeness.

Then Lulu, Betty and Annie had pressed me for all the rich, meaty, buttery, sugary details. Did Grandma really have Coca-Cola and shortbread cookies? Do they still have wheat flour in Manila and did Grandma have sandwich bread? Did I bring any back? They were horrified to learn that the Polo Club now served as headquarters for the hated Kempeitai. I didn't tell them about the Comfort Girl-Women.

My proud mother couldn't take her arm from around my waist, and soon urged me to go back to our room to "change into something lighter." She walked beside me, and Lulu tagged along, while Annie and Betty set off to join a group of their newly graduated eighth grade friends, who were planning a performance of *Mid-Summer Night's Dream*. In our corner of the never-empty Room 4, I stepped out of the heavy skirt, and Mommy declared in an off-hand manner that she would take the waist in for me and bring in that side-seam, since I had been losing so much weight. She was off to the shanty to work on the fudge, she declared, but she'd have time to do it while there.

I nodded as if this was exactly what needed to happen, and watched her fold the skirt efficiently then head for the door. Agnes Hanagan Iserson—chocolatier and financier par excellence.

"She was cool as a cucumber the whole time you were gone," Lulu rasped with admiration. I had confided every detail of the plan to Lulu, of course, and sworn her to absolute secrecy. Even my mother wasn't allowed to know that my best friend knew.

"And look at her—trotting that Fort Knox skirt off for *mending*. Your mother's a mover and shaker—you know that?"

"Let's not talk about it, Lulu." I reached into the drawer of Kay's and my bed and found my Bermuda shorts. As I tugged them on, I recalled the stern urgency of my mother's warning to tell NO ONE of our plan. All too many internees were stealing from each other these days, and one of my mother's biggest challenges would be finding a hiding place for our new stash. I didn't want to know where she put it.

As I tugged on a pair of now-loose shorts, I too marveled at my mother's capacity for enterprise and, let's just say it, deception. Of course, my mother was first and foremost a mother, and all her clever initiatives (IJA acronyms, agreeing to be room monitor, figuring out how to get us a shanty, starting the fudge business, secret communications with the telephone company, and now this money-smuggling) were ways of protecting her brood. But she pulled off these little ruses with smoothness that dazzled me. Where did my church-going, law-abiding mother learn all that?

"But I guess if you're the seventh of ten children, like she is," I speculated, "You learn to hustle just to keep up with your older brothers and sisters. Or maybe if you ditch farm life to become a flapper and working-gal, it goes with the territory."

"She's got moxie, that's for sure," Lulu agreed.

I didn't know where it came from, but I was aware that my mother was different. Not like Mim—Lulu's mom. Mim, had always lived a high-society life surrounded by servants and amahs, and promptly had a nervous breakdown three weeks into captivity in the Jap jail in Cebu. She pretty much left Lulu taking care of Margie and the baby, while she fell apart. Fortunately, Lulu had enough resilience for the two of them. Mim recovered and made the best of it here at STIC, but she was typical of society ladies of leisure who'd had their whole world turned upside down by the war. Whereas my Utica farm-girl mother had a toughness and steely determination that awed me. If I had to be a teenage prisoner of war, which I obviously did, I was very glad to be Agnes Hanagan Iserson's daughter.

Friday, April 2, 1943

Back in our crowded room two nights later, my spirits were lighter, but voices rose in anger as we got ready for bed. All eyes turned to two women in the middle of the room squabbling.

"Put that damn case under the cot, Lady Macbeth! That is the second time I've tripped on it trying to get to the can! " Hope glared at the chronically overspread Mrs. Randolph Meade, British society matron par excellence and pre-war friend of Douglas MacArthur. Hope likened Mrs. Meade to Shakespeare's evil heroine, Lady Macbeth, because Mrs. Meade constantly connived to get more of everything for herself. More food. More space. More creature comfort.

"Eighteen inches," Mrs. Meade sniffed with the haughtiness of a British Headmistress. "You've got eighteen. Make do."

She was referring to the mandatory eighteen inches of aisle space we had to keep clear between our forty cots in this hopelessly overcrowded room. Hope was having none of it.

"If that's eighteen, so am I," Hope growled and without further ado kicked the straw case with its elegant leather snap under the cot, and headed to the snaking bathroom line as Mrs. Randolph caught her by the collar and jerked her back screaming "You arrogant bitch!"

Hope had a small frame, but was every inch the tough Granite State fighter, and whirled around to strike her adversary with the small tin bucket that held her toothbrush, towel and comb. Before the edge of the bucket struck Lady M's face, my room monitor mother darted to the fray, and pulled them apart. She scolded them both, brandishing the only weapon that was truly respected in this sweaty, heat-soaked room: the tape measure. Hope was right: a mere eighteen inches separated the two cots, so there was no room for the protruding maleta.

"It stays under the cot, Mrs. Meade," my mother instructed firmly, at which point the haughty woman harrumphed and stormed out of the room.

When she cleared the door, Hope growled: "Out, out, damned snot!" The entire room erupted into peals of laughter, as we returned to the business of preparing for lights out.

Mommy picked her way back to our corner oasis, but she was looking at me now and scowling, as if Mrs. Meade's insolence had reminded her of something else. Ugh. I knew what was coming.

"And Leonore Agnes Iserson, I had a conversation with Roscoe Lautzenhiser today," she wasted no time in upbraiding me when she reached our spot. "Or I should say that YOUR PRINCIPAL had a conversation with me. If I ever again hear of you involved in anything as idiotic as that April Fool's prank you pulled with Lulu yesterday, you will not be playing bridge for a month!"

I met my mother's angry gaze, biting my lower lip and nodded. I didn't blame her for being mad.

The day after I got back from my "spread your wings to match the gale" escapade of smuggling money into camp, my best friend pulled the most outrageous stunt. Lulu (OK, I helped her) arranged for our entire STIC High School—all eighty-six of us—to boycott classes on the fourth floor, and assemble outside on the front patio as an April Fool's joke on our teachers. They were not amused by our strike, and we got a sharp tongue-lashing from the principal, Mr. Lautzenhiser, who reminded us that our captors needed only a small excuse to cut our rice ration even further.

"Disorder and insubordination are just such excuses," he snapped. Fortunately, the Japs couldn't figure out what the outside assembly was about and just looked the other way, when they saw our principal dealing with it.

At the end, stern and balding Mr. Lautzenhiser pulled "the instigators" aside. (Lulu and I confessed when he threatened to punish the whole school.) He professed himself to be "particularly disappointed in you, Miss Iserson. After securing special permission to be out of camp overnight, you return to instigate mischief that could have had sorry repercussions for this camp. It's dangerous and ungrateful."

Of course, I teared up, profoundly ashamed of myself, as he turned and walked away. Lulu waited till Mr. L had rounded the corner of the Big House before slipping her hand into mine and mimicking his voice:

"I am particularly proud of you, Miss Iserson. After securing special permission to be out of camp overnight, you returned to spread joy to your classmates with hilarious repercussions for this camp. It's edifying and inspirational," she concluded seriously. I burst out laughing, and hugged her as hard as I could.

Still, I had been waiting for that other shoe to fall with my mother, hoping against hope that she wouldn't hear about it. Or maybe that she would think our little prank was harmless and funny like we did. Dream on.

Now my mother just shook her head in exasperation at me, and turned to reprimand my artist sister Betty for "dawdling with your doodles" instead of getting ready for bed. I reached for my nightgown and headed to a corner of the room where, hidden by other women, I could change without being seen from the outside. The ground floor windows of our room were grilled, but had no curtains, and anyone strolling on the outside could look straight in to see whatever was going on.

When I returned to our corner, twelve-year old Betty was in her nightgown and propping her very ragged bear Cuddles on her cot. I don't know why, but suddenly tears welled up unbidden and a great sadness washed over me in a wave. I still missed Max, my giant panda, my twelfth birthday present from Daddy. Now Max was gone. Daddy, the one who loved me best, was dead. We were prisoners. And my mother, who had risked so much for Betty and me, was disappointed in me.

Mommy sat on the edge of Betty's cot, ready for our little family's evening prayers, and as I approached tears welling, she motioned me over with a begrudging smile. I sank down on the cot next to her, newly secure in the arm she reached around my shoulders. Then suddenly she groped for something in her pocket, and produced a small object that she pressed into my hand.

"I found him in your skirt pocket," she said in her silken alto. I stared at the face of the Black Nazarene and felt my heart lift. He was still bleeding sloppy red paint from his crown of thorns and his shoulders still sagged under the weight of the cross, but the brown-black eyes stared up at me with tenderness.

"Do you believe in good luck charms?" I asked her, not taking my eyes from the little figurine.

"Yes, pet, and more," she answered with quiet conviction. "I believe we are not alone—even here."

"You are definitely not alone here, Agnes," Kay drawled as she sat down across from us on the heavy bed she and I shared.

The rising voices of our nearly three dozen roommates almost drown her out. "For God's sake, who could entertain such a looney idea, dahlin? And, Lee, this is for you, my Bed-Buddy."

Kay presented me with a slender, rectangular package, neatly wrapped in *Internews* paper tied with a string bow. Confused, I untied the string, stripping away the newspaper gift-wrap. A slender red leather book four by six inches wide stared up at me. The word "Autographs" was tooled in gold on the cover. Genuinely perplexed, I opened to the first of its blank pages: "A very Happy Birthday to dear Lee from Kay and Harry Hodges. Manila, April 3rd 1943."

I had almost forgotten. Tomorrow was my fifteenth birthday.

Saturday, June 19, 1943

Lulu could be very persuasive but she was having a hard time convincing Bunny Brambles to join us for tonight's boxing-smoker. Amateur prize-fights were called "boxing-smokers" because thunderheads of smoke swirled overhead during indoor matches. But the outdoor location of our "Starlight Arena" and the price of cigarettes in camp ensured that tonight would be more boxing than smoker. In one of the matches, our friend Curtis Brooks (aka "Squeaky") would square off against fellow classmate Jimmy Rockwell for the Junior Fly Weight championship.

"C'mon, Bunny. Curtis needs us there!" Lulu's fist pumped the air.

"Could either of you tell me why it's jolly fun to watch our gnat-sized boys pound away at each other in front of our captors?"

Bunny sat on the edge of her cot, face darkened by the rain-spattered window. The storm had let up, but typhoon force rain and winds had trapped us inside for nearly a month, which meant more frayed tempers, more overcrowding, and more disease. Today Bunny's mother and sister had been hospitalized for dengue fever.

"Actually, they're fly-weight," Lulu corrected. "Gnat Weight, Atom-Weight and Electron-Weight are all next week. Tonight's Flea Weight, Moth Weight, and Fly Weight."

"Don't forget Paper Weight," I smirked, hoping to get a smile out of Bunny. Boys as young as eight boxed in camp, and there really was Paper Weight division.

"And besides," said Lulu, "Aren't you Limeys the ones who invented 'Boxing Day'? You don't see any Americans spending the day after Christmas boxing. Come with us, Grace Brambles. This sport is in your blood."

"We don't box on Boxing Day!" Bunny was incredulous. "Boxing Day is a way of thanking servants for their hard work." On December 26, she told us, English domestics were given "the Christmas Box" filled with gifts for their service, and of course, the day off. "Other than that, Boxing Day is just an excuse for another holiday. We visit with friends, eat Christmas leftovers, or take in a rugby match—that sort of thing."

"You mean not a single Brit puts on the gloves and boxes on December 26th?" I asked.

"Not unless, he's donning gloves to watch that outdoor rugby match." Bunny shook her head, but a smug smile played on her lips. "Actually you're right about one thing. We Brits did invent boxing."

"I knew it!" said Lulu. She and I exchanged quick satisfied nods, knowing we had turned a corner in rescuing Bunny from her sulk.

"All right, let's go watch the He-Men." Bunny rose from the bed. "Side-by-side, and all that."

***

Our English golden girl had been pelted by far too much bad news lately. Bunny's father and brothers had been gone for two months now, ordered south with 797 other STIC men to build a second prison camp for our overflowing population.

In mid-May when they left, we had more than thirty-six-hundred prisoners in a camp that should never have held more than twenty-five-hundred Every shower, toilet, and university classroom overflowed with internees. One toilet for every hundred prisoners. Three or four women standing under every shower head at any hour of the day. Interminable lines and fraying tempers. Even the Japanese had come to the conclusion that another camp had to be built.

Fifty miles south of us lay the tropical haven of "Los Baños," where fresh springs and a former agricultural college existed. The Japs were determined to convert that college into a camp too, and announced over the loudspeaker one May evening that all of us would be moved south when the Los Baños barracks were completed.

The announcement was met with complete shock. All of us? We would be far from the heartbeat of busy Manila, cut off from the flow of information through the package line, far from Filipino and German friends who still sent food to us, distant from hospitals and medical facilities, and miles away from everything pre-war that we knew and held dear. It's true that we would be safe from the destruction of battle when the Allies returned to seize Manila, but would those troops ever find us in the jungle?

The Executive Committee, headed now by diplomatically inclined Mr. Grinnell, protested, insisting that studies had to be done to see if water supply sufficed to host the 7000 prisoners the Japs wanted to intern. Still, everyone knew that another camp was necessary, and many thought it had to be better than our overcrowded slum dwelling. So while the Japanese and our top guys argued about whether to close STIC, plans were made to build Los Baños.

Most of the able-bodied men in our camp were drafted to build the new facility—some volunteered and others were forced to volunteer. Off went Kay's husband, dear Harry Hodges. Off went Bunny's father and her brothers, Ralph and Jimmy. We had heard nothing from any of them in the last six weeks. Bunny and her mother knew only that the men in their lives were seventy miles south—digging ditches, laying pipes, and building barracks, while fighting wind, rain, mosquitoes, and disease.

You would have thought the removal of those eight hundred men would lessen the crowding at Santo Tomas. And the chow line did get shorter for a couple days. But three days after all the men left, hundreds of new internees poured into camp—Americans, Brits, Australians, Dutch, Mexicans, old people, young people, little children, weak and diseased people. The Japanese were herding all prisoners from the southern islands north, bringing our Santo Tomas numbers over thirty-six-hundred again.

Many of these feeble prisoners suffered from tropical diseases: tuberculosis, beriberi, dysentery, dengue fever, even pneumonia. Our Santa Catalina hospital was full to overflowing, and infections spread quickly. Bunny's mother and sister had just been admitted with the dreaded dengue. That was two strikes for Bunny.

The last month had been excruciating for all of us. We were supposed to be back in school now that it was June, but our sophomore year barely staggered off the starting line. Typhoon-strength winds and torrential rains had pounded the camp for the last month. Our family's little Glamorville shack had survived, but the storms washed away several dozen shanties, many of the little vegetable gardens, and the big general camp garden—taking with it precious crops of yams and mongo beans.

During the worst of the storms, the power snapped off and we were trapped in the Main Building for days on end. You couldn't walk down a hall without tripping over chairs and card-tables for the non-stop mahjong, bridge, and poker games. And the din in the Big House was mind-sundering. While winds howled outside and rains pelted, it seemed that everyone indoors shouted. Voices were constantly raised across the two courtyards and the four floors. You couldn't hear yourself think.

So, Lulu, Bunny and I all desperately needed this clear night outdoors with the soft breeze blowing.

* * *

"They're over there," I shouted to Bunny and Lulu, as we elbowed our way through the crowd. Nellie, Bill, and Paul had already claimed a spot ringside and we joined them.

Hundreds of internees milled around the makeshift stage just in time to see Ginny McKinney's seventeen-year-old brother Tommy step into the ring for the only light heavy-weight competition that evening. Ebony black, his chest a rippled sculpture, Tommy McKinney often dominated the ring, but tonight he'd square off against red-haired, green-eyed Danny MacDonald, who was easily a head taller. Danny's pasty skin and nasty smirk made him nobody's darling.

"Battle of the Micks—McKinney versus MacDonald!" shouted Aubrey Man, who stood not far from us: as a Brit, he felt it his duty to belittle all Irishmen. Of course, Tommy McKinney—with his black Spanish-American War vet father and Filipino mother—was not Irish in the conventional sense, and Aubrey's slur only served to enrage the MacDonalds, who were proudly Irish-American and did not regard black-Filipino-Americans as part of their clan.

"Danny Boy is the only Mick in that ring, and he is Fighting Irish!" Mr. MacDonald shouted back at Aubrey. "Tommy Boy better run for cover."

"Tommy is Black Irish! Ain't got no need to run for cover," Bumblebee, the good-natured Negro cook interned with us shouted his support, then caught sight of Tommy's elderly dad and made eye contact, flashing him a V for victory. Mr. McKinney, also black, but graying at the temples, nodded his appreciation. I saw Ginny applaud her brother enthusiastically and say something that made her friend Lizzie Lautzenhiser laugh.

Cigarettes were scarce and alcohol forbidden in camp, but a surprising amount of smoke wafted heavenward and the smell of gin scented the sweat-soaked air. Two Japanese guards watched amused and apparently unperturbed, ready for the three rounds. The Japanese allowed boxing-smokers for the same reason they permitted variety shows: they kept us occupied, and out of trouble.

At the sound of the bell, Tommy and Danny danced around each other, stabbing the air and feinting back to the shouts and jeers of their friends. Choruses of "Deck him, Danny! Deck him, Danny!" alternated with "Two-Step Tommy, make your move!" Hard, square blows to the abdomen, to the face, and to the neck on both sides marked the match as an even fight. Then in the third round, from nowhere, Ginny's brother Tommy unleashed a sweeping left hook, and Danny McDonald hit the canvas with a thud. Silence and a collective intake of breath seemed to stop time. Somebody hissed.

We never had knock-outs in our fights at STIC, and nobody liked having them now. As the ref counted slowly, we were all relieved to see Danny stagger to his feet, and the crowd cheered. But Tommy came right in for the final pummeling. I'd been rooting for Tommy in that match because Ginny was my friend, but her brother proved an aggressive hitter, and that bothered me—the way he moved right in for the kill after Danny had fallen. It was the way I imagined the Japs racing in to bayonet our boys fallen in battle. Danny managed to remain standing through the rest of the match, but Tommy won on points.

The crowd was wild with both jeers and cheers as the ref held Tommy McKinney's gloved black arm aloft. Danny MacDonald glared at his shorter but stronger opponent before limping out of the ring.

In our group Bill Phillips applauded the loudest. "There's nothing like the fights!" he shouted with satisfaction, turning to Paul, Nellie, Lulu, Bunny and me. "You square off against your rival, land those rock-hard blows above the belt." He mimed the fight. "Take the best he can throw at you. Endure. Triumph."

"And why is that so ducky?" Bunny looked over at the Japanese guards, and frowned. "We're doing their work for them. The Japs are watching us beat each other up."

"No, they're not. They're watching us prove we're men," Paul summoned a bass voice and broadened his not-so-large shoulders. "You stand your ground. And you get to pound the hell out of your opponent!"

"And he pounds back...." I ventured.

"With all his might, but it's a fair fight," Bill said. "It's the manly art of self-defense. The Japs admire it too. Look over there."

He was pointing to two animated Japanese guards, rifles butts temporarily on the ground, nodding their approval and clapping.

"Men. Bad as brutes," Bunny did not hide her disgust.

"I actually felt sorry for Danny in that fight," I admitted. "Tommy didn't cut him one bit of slack when he got back on his feet after that knock-out punch."

Paul and Bill snorted. Danny MacDonald deserved anything Tommy McKinney could throw at him, they insisted. Hadn't I seen what a swaggering bully Danny-Boy was in school? Hadn't I seen him baiting McKinney for a year and a half about being a half-breed? Tommy and Danny were two classes ahead of us, and no, I hadn't noticed, but now I understood better what had happened in the ring. Looked to me like justice triumphed.

"Well, what about Squeaky? Will he just endure or will he triumph?" Lulu changed the subject.

"Triumph for sure," Bill replied—"watch that right jab of his. Jimmy Rockwell doesn't stand a chance."

"Rocky's a goner by the second round," Paul pronounced confidently.

Oh, for Heaven's sakes. But it was great to see our gang in such high spirits. For a couple hours outside in the cool June breeze, we kids, parents, even the Japanese guards, all forgot we were prisoners. None of this: "Just surrender and be meek. And by the way—bow low when you walk by your captor." Just two feisty boys in a ring—brave boys, proudly duking it out. Dads, Moms and siblings cheered their little boy's courage. I saw Haruo smile slightly when the little eight year-olds showed their stuff. I wondered if he had any little boys.

When our buddy Curtis Brooks took on Jimmy Rockwell, Bill's words proved prophetic. Squeaky danced to victory in three rounds, landing his right jab with stunning precision but no real injury. The best part was that Rocky was a real gentleman in defeat. The *Internews* quoted him as saying: "Squeaky may have a high voice, but he gets high marks for the jab."

Bunny announced that from now on, she was sticking to bridge.

Chapter 16
LESSONS FROM OVID

Sunday, July 9, 1943

"I didn't know my heart could beat like this," Lulu sighed as we left Santa Catalina chapel on Sunday. "He's dreamy, isn't he, Lee? It's such a shame he's a priest. Never able to fall in love and marry…"

Newly arrived Father Robert Sheridan stood six foot three inches tall, had penetrating blue eyes, enormous shoulders, and a full head of strawberry blonde hair. Lulu's new heartthrob was probably in his mid-thirties, and radiated manly energy, standing erect, purposeful, and strong. If Maryknoll, the missionary order of priests to which he belonged, ever needed a face for a recruitment poster, it was his: compassionate, smiling, and at times, mischievous.

Girls I knew who had no interest in religion whatsoever had started going to mass on Sunday. Lulu and I had been singing in the church choir for the last year, so our rekindled devotion to the Lord was not quite so transparent. But oh, how we treasured our front row seats in the chapel choir loft when this newly arrived missionary celebrated mass.

"It's perfect that he's a priest," I countered. "If he were your average American Joe, he'd be target practice for Rommel in Tunisia, and would definitely not be here with us. It's absolutely perfect that he's a priest."

We knew from Paul's contraband *Time Magazine* that the Allies had tried to invade North Africa in February. Time reported heavy American losses against Rommel's panzer divisions. Rumor had it that the Americans and Brits were rallying now, but who knew? It was a very good thing Father Sheridan was FATHER Sheridan.

"I did see you practically swooning over him during the Gloria," I teased Lulu. "I thought you weren't going to be able to hit that high C."

"Of course, I could hit that high C," my alto friend said in a silly falsetto. "His love has given me wings! I think I might be able to hit the E over high C at his masses."

Last week, the Japanese had stunned all of us when two trucks bearing dozens of American, British, and Dutch priests had rolled through the camp gates. Maryknoll and Jesuit missionaries in their full-length black cassocks and white collars had spilled from the convoys, dusty from their journey but hale, fit, and apparently unfazed by their new mission. We sophomores had been changing classes on the open-air rooftop, and looked down to the spectacle in the front plaza below. Had the Vatican sent a delegation? We knew the priests couldn't be prisoners, since the Japanese were not interning priests or nuns in the PI.

Securing their side-belt rosaries and large pendant crosses, the self-possessed men of all ages and shapes leapt to the ground and took the lay of our chaotic land. I wondered what they thought as they looked at the long lines of prisoners in front of the Filipino market stalls in camp. What did they make of the women debugging rice? The men picking bedbugs from mattresses? The chain line of skinny boys bearing low open cauldrons of mush to the mess hall? What did they think of the front plaza itself, almost denuded now of its once lovely acacia trees?

One of the priests—a redhead—fixed his gaze on the spare metal cross topping the Big House tower above us, and then looked up at us kids. He waved, and we waved back enthusiastically. Paul thought maybe the Filipino archbishop had arranged for a pastoral visit. Heaven knows, a lot of people around here needed to go to confession.

But all our idle speculation about the black-robed visitors proved false: The priests were indeed new prisoners among us, and here at STIC for the foreseeable future. The Japanese were convinced that too many of the Allied priests and nuns had been helping the Filipino guerillas and should be locked up with their fellow countrymen. Their large group was immediately herded to the Gym, the roughest of the men's living areas, now partly vacated by the men who had gone to Los Baños.

Those priests pitched right in to help Father Kelley. This was the second Sunday that Father Sheridan had stood in for Father Kelley at the nine o'clock mass.

"By 'His Love has given you wings' I assume you mean the love of God?" I nudged her.

"Of course. Him too," Lulu acknowledged with smile. "Do you think he plays bridge? Father Sheridan, not God."

"He's probably too busy for bridge. Priests have to pray and teach and mentor a lot, but it would be swell if he played bridge, wouldn't it?"

Since summer vacation in April, Lulu and I had morphed into complete and fanatical bridge sharks. Any free moment we had together (after school and homework and jobs) found us as partners at the bridge table. It made sense. A mere year and a half ago, we had been silly eighth grade girls who sleuthed around camp, inventing Nancy Drew-like codes for any curious sight we saw ("bluebells are singing horses").

Now, we were mature sophomores in high school and deadly serious about the greatest code game of all: bridge. Its elaborate bidding conventions dazzled us. Instead of thinking about how much we longed for a thick, juicy steak (beef not carabao, thank you very much) or a giant bowl of green coconut ice cream, we pored over the camp's only copy of *The New Contract Bridge* by Harold S. Vanderbilt. It was the Bible.

Indeed, as the kitchen failed us, bridge fed us and consumed us. When I had a hand with 22 points in front of me, I couldn't think about being hungry or bored or imprisoned. I was only thinking about my opening bid, what

Lulu was telling me with her response, what our opponents were saying, and then how to make the contract. For all her zaniness, Lulu was a great bridge player. She was a whiz at math, and that helps a lot in bridge, because at any given moment you need to know how many cards of each suit have been played and how many trump are out.

We were a good team, too—analytical but risk-takers. We read every bridge article we could find in camp magazines and learned to communicate our strengths and weaknesses almost flawlessly. When Lulu said 'Four No Trump,' I knew she was asking for my aces, and we were going for a slam—maybe a grand slam, taking all thirteen tricks. I was happy to be her "dummy" in those risky situations, and just prayed that the bridge gods were smiling on us as she went in for the kill.

Bridge gods…. Inspiration struck.

"Lulu, I've got it. Maybe we can ask Father Sheridan if he could mentor our new Catholic Teens Bridge Group. We could include Paul, Annie, and Betty. They're all Catholic."

"We don't even know if he plays and I'm not Catholic!" Lulu wailed in dismay. "Couldn't we just call it our Christian Bridge Group?"

"Why don't you become Catholic?" I urged her. It saddened me that my best friend didn't share this important part of my life. "Your father's Catholic. I've taught you everything I know about scapulars and purgatory. You love singing in our choir. I bet you we Catholics have a patron saint of bridge too. St. Bridget? I don't know. But we can find out."

"And then what?"

"And then we'll meet privately with Father Sheridan at least once a week when our club convenes. He'll open every bridge game with a prayer to our patron saint and we'll probably win even more than we do now. And Father Sheridan could help you individually with your conversion classes too."

"Who said I wanted to be converted?" Lulu's protest was feeble, as if she were seriously considering the dream world of private classes with Father Sheridan.

"OK, on Monday we ask Mrs. Maynard who the patron saint of bridge is.

Then we'll impress Father Sheridan with our knowledge when we invite him to mentor our holy card group."

Monday, July 10, 1943

Leila Maynard was our Latin teacher for the second year in a row. Square-shouldered, fine-boned, and calmly demanding, Mrs. Maynard was Protestant, but she knew more arcane Catholic trivia than any person had a right to because she worked every afternoon in the priests' private library, cataloging rare books.

Proficient in Latin, Spanish, and French, she had stumbled into this plum of a job in 1942, when the Dominican priests unearthed several crates of old books in a musty corner of their wood-paneled library—some of them *from the 1500s*. They asked the Education Committee if any internee had the language skills to help them catalogue their treasure trove, and Leila Maynard volunteered.

Lulu, Nellie and I—the only students in her Latin II class—were jealous beyond words of this job because while the rest of us battled lines, crowds, and roommates every moment of every day, Mrs. Maynard luxuriated for four hours daily in the solitude of that off-limits library. She didn't speak of this quiet haven often, but we knew she thrived on the work.

After class on Monday, Lulu and I put the patron saint question to Leila Maynard, and she hesitated not one milli-second.

"Saint Benezet of France. In the 1100s, he had a vision that he was supposed to build a bridge over a turbulent section of the Rhone River, and he managed to do it. Bridge-builders have been praying to him ever since."

"Oh, not the patron saint of bridge-builders. Bridge, the card game," I said. "Who's the patron saint of bridge players?"

A small smile flitted across her face, and her brows lifted. "Well, I'm not sure there is one. I think it's a little like asking who's the patron saint of poker. Even Catholics don't believe the Lord plays favorites in games of chance."

Even Catholics, I thought. What was that supposed to mean? That we were a superstitious lot? Protestants were probably jealous because they didn't have hard-working patron saints like we did.

"Bridge is not a game of chance!" Lulu's voice broke, as it always did when she got excited. "It's a game of skill and strategy. And telegraphing messages with complex codes. And here I was, almost converting." She turned to me in disgust. "I can't believe there's no patron saint of bridge."

Cuthbert, our math teacher also for the second year in a row, happened by the door at that minute, and overheard Lulu's outburst. An avid bridge player himself, he poked his head in.

"Saint Balthasar," he said. "It's Balthasar. Gets me results every time."

"Who's St. Balthasar?" we demanded in unison of our frequent opponent at the bridge table.

"He of the Three Kings," Cuthbert responded. "Casper, Melchior, and Balthasar—the black king, King of Egypt actually, and the patron saint of playing cards."

"I don't recall the Magi bringing the baby Jesus gold, frankincense and playing cards," said Mrs. Maynard.

"They didn't. But the first decks of cards had the King as their high card, so it made sense to have one of the Three Kings as a patron. Balthasar turned out to be the guy."

I knew it! I just knew we had to have a Patron Saint of Bridge.

"OK, Lulu, after classes, we're off to see Father Sheridan." I nodded and she flashed me her five-thousand-volt smile.

Friday, July 23, 1943

"Two squares?" the haughty British matron sputtered. "We're down to two? Or have you hoarded them for yourself, Miss Issue Tissue? Oh, privileged princess daughter of the Room Queen?" Mrs. Randolph Meade glared down at me, and was living up to her Lady Macbeth alias. I tried to ignore her insults. The toilet paper ration had been cut this morning.

"The Red Cross shipment was short, Mrs. Meade, and the men decided to make do with leaves and newspaper. We women need to cut back so we can make the toilet paper last."

Handing out two squares of toilet paper to each woman in line for the stalls was my afternoon job three days a week. Because we had to leave space in the halls for the long lines, I sat on a folding chair just inside the smelly bathroom with the prized commodity. It hadn't taken long for women of the camp to dub the toilet paper girl, "Miss Issue Tissue." In the early days of internment, Miss Issue Tissue dispensed five squares each, and then we were down to four and then three. Those scarcely sufficed because of the diarrhea we all had from the poorly washed, poorly cooked, and sometimes contaminated food we ate—especially at the beginning. Now we were down to two squares.

The stinky Issue Tissue job annoyed me, but I knew it wasn't as bad as some jobs. Ginny McKinney had nabbed the worst: Once a week, she was in charge of washing the menstrual rags. That meant emptying the fetid used rags from dozens of foul-smelling bags taken from the Big House and the Annex. She boiled them in a large shallow pot with whatever detergent we had, and stirred them to make sure they were properly sterilized for re-use. The putrid smell made everyone keep a wide berth, but Ginny had to stay right with it and keep stirring. Then she squeezed, dried and hung the rags to dry. Other women shared this task, but Ginny was the only one of our group of friends assigned the wretched job.

In any event, Ginny's burden wouldn't last much longer because most women had stopped getting their periods. Our doctors said that the poor nutrition and stress had dried them up. I myself had had only three periods in camp before they just plain stopped. Lulu had two. She and I thought not getting our periods was the best part of camp.

Today's decision to restrict toilet paper to two squares per customer had met with collective groans from most women, but not surprise. Even in our school work we were conserving paper—and sometimes that was very hard indeed—as Nellie Thomas knew all too well.

Last week Nellie wrote a beautiful two-page essay on "The Ibis," a poem by

Ovid. Publius Ovidius Naso (Ovid's real name) had penned this long, nasty ballad while in exile from his beloved Rome. Embittered old Ovid spends 630 lines raining curses down on some enemy who's been persecuting him in exile. He shows off his knowledge of Roman gods by wishing his foe every mythological mishap that ever happened to any of the gods. "While swimming, may the waters of Styx choke your mouth. Or as shipwrecked you ride the stormy sea, may you die on land, like Palinurus. As Diana's guardian did to Euripides … may a pack of vigilant dogs tear you to shreds… As Althaea's son burned in the distant flames, so may your pyre be lit…"

We translated enough of the poem to know that Ovid loathed this guy and wished him every sort of ill. Our assignment was to translate part of the poem and reflect on its meaning to us.

Nellie's paper was called "Lessons from Ovid." She translated thirty lines and then drew a parallel between Ovid's exile from Rome, and our own exile from the United States and from freedom. She said our greatest challenge in exile was not to give in to the bitter hatred that consumed Ovid. She wrote that every day we faced temptations to hate fellow internees who made life difficult for us, or to despise our captors, the Japanese. But hatred divides, and even poisons the hater himself, she wrote, "and we are called to something higher." Nellie concluded with a quote from Cicero: "We were born to unite with our fellow man, and to join in community with the human race."

When she read the paper aloud to our little foursome, Mrs. Maynard—whose husband was in the brutal military camp of Cabanatuan—had tears in her eyes. Lulu and I sat in shocked awe. Nellie was a full year younger than we were, but fourteen year-old Ellen Spencer Thomas was both brilliant and compassionate. Lulu and I exchanged looks that told me my best friend was as grateful as I that the class was over, because neither of us wanted to read our papers now. I had been proud of mine but my first sentence was: "Publius Ovidius Naso is a whiner, who should buck up." That was not exactly comparable to Nellie's call for human fellowship and world peace.

Anyway, about the shortage. Mrs. Maynard collected the compositions and returned them a day later with Ellen's A+ and effusive comments penciled in—and Lulu's and my Bs with less effusive comments. Then she instructed us to start erasing. The camp, she explained, was short of lined notebook paper, and from now on we needed to reuse every sheet as many times as possible. I felt not one pang of regret, but Lulu and I immediately looked to Nellie in horror and sympathy, and read momentary frustration in her face. Still, when she returned our glance, she just shrugged her shoulders, offered a quick smile of resignation, and picked up her white block eraser.

As I offered two squares to the next weary woman in line, I tried to mimic Nellie's cheerful goodwill.

Monday, August 2, 1943

My first glimpse of Father Robert Sheridan that afternoon took my breath away. The newly interned missionary priest stood shirtless, wielding an axe, his muscles rippling, his massive shoulders bathed in sweat, a gold cross swinging from his neck with each well-timed stroke. Clothed only in khaki shorts tied with a rope, his cassock tossed on the ground next to him, the young priest was chopping down one of the few remaining acacia trees in the front patio. Cheering him on was a rag-tag circle of aging men, content to let him do the work.

Lulu and I halted—mesmerized. Father Sheridan swung the axe yet again, and landed another powerful blow

"He's absolutely gorgeous," Lulu sighed. "I don't care if he is chopping down my favorite shade tree."

The camp was running out of wood for cooking fires, but the kitchen still had to feed four thousand people twice a day. This massive acacia, a thorn tree of at least three decades, would provide green lumber, but we needed any wood we could find to heat the "cawas," shallow cooking pots for our stringy stews. How we hated to see those giant patio trees come down, but meals trumped comfort on our list of priorities. The Japanese had even given permission for some of our men go outside the camp, and start felling the stately trees along Dewey Boulevard.

Meanwhile, the newly interned priests had pitched right in to help the enfeebled men in camp.

"Padre, can I steal some of your picadura?" one of the aging internees shouted to him. The wire-framed man held up several leaves of native smoking tobacco that had fallen from the young priest's cassock.

"Oh sure. A native chief in Iloilo stuffed those in my pocket to help me bribe my way out of trouble up here. But I guess we're already in trouble, so they're all yours."

To think that our Father Sheridan had been stuck on the southern island of Iloilo—his good looks totally wasted on a mission to elderly native Ilonggos. Thank God, he was in the right place now.

The men chuckled appreciatively, and one drew a wrapper from his shorts pocket and started rolling. The last American cigarettes (Lucky Strikes) had disappeared from our Red Cross packages more than a month ago. Paul's "Akebonos" were still selling on the camp black market for a pretty penny, but "picadura" the tobacco leaf of the PI provided a good alternative for the nicotine needy.

For some reason, it pleased me that Father Sheridan didn't keep the leaves for himself, and I felt sure he didn't smoke. My romantic image of him as a pure, fair-haired, blue-eyed knight on a white charger remained intact.

"You should ask him to be mentor for our bridge group when he finishes, OK? You know all the right Catholic things to say." Lulu spoke breathlessly.

"Maybe it's not the right time. He's surrounded by men, and he's going to want a shower when he finishes." I murmured, glancing at the sharp-sided tub shower where women often washed their hair outside.

"We could watch him shower too," sighed Lulu.

Like most teenage girls in camp, our hearts quickened at the thought of handsome young men, but until Father Sheridan's arrival, they were just dream men. All the boys our age at Santo Tomas had string-bean bodies and personalities inspired by the cartoon character, Goofy. What did they know about how to treat a lady? And most of the grown men who populated camp after the Los Baños recruitment were candidates for the Old Folks Home. We kept hearing about their exploits during the Spanish-American War. The Spanish-American War? That was last century, for Pete's sake.

"I have pass! I have OK! No spying, just vegetable!" The last word sounded like "VEJ-tah-buh."

Desperate shouts in the distance interrupted my reverie, and I saw Father Sheridan straighten in mid-swing as we all turned to watch a panic-stricken Filipino struggling against two Japanese guards. Their wild-eyed prisoner was a scrawny camp vendor in an open-neck, white-collared shirt, sleeves rolled to his elbows. Two khaki-clad soldiers flanked him, each gripping an arm, and dragging the flailing prisoner between them. They headed in our direction. My stomach knotted in horror and despite the ninety-degree heat, a chill rippled through me when I recognized Haruo gripping the left arm of the terrified man. Haruo?

"No spying! Just vegetable! No spying! Just vegetable!" the man kept shouting.

Fewer than ten Filipino vendors were allowed in camp, and their activities were strictly monitored by the Japanese, but the loyal Filipinos sometimes managed to slip contraband messages into camp from prisoners at Cabanatuan. More than half the women in Room 4 had husbands and sons in that hell-hole, and lived for some word of their fate. Sometimes camp doctors smuggled much needed medicines out of STIC and north to Cabanatuan through the Filipino vendors who had access to both places.

As the trio passed us, NGH did not look at me or at any of us, but fixed his resolute gaze on his objective, the Japanese offices in the southwest corner of the camp. The "Southwest Territory" became our shorthand for all the official Jap offices on camp. The voice of the terrified prisoner grew fainter as the guards hauled him away.

"No spying! Just vegetable!" echoed like a failed incantation in the air, and tears welled in my eyes.

I couldn't watch this. The Filipinos had befriended us every day of our internment, still bringing food and smokes to the Gate, always offering a friendly word. They risked their own lives to help us and the Americans in the military camps of Bilibid and Cabanatuan, who needed medicine twenty times more than we did.

What would they do to that man? Would they torture and kill him? I had almost turned away, when I saw the fed-up guard across from Haruo jerk the howling prisoner to his feet and slap him three times so hard that the Filipino fell silent, and sank to the ground unconscious. Then the two guards picked him up and dragged him away, disappearing into the distant Southwest Territory.

Everyone watching the spectacle stood immobile, seconds passing in complete silence. Then, Father Sheridan, whose jaw was clenched and whose chest now heaved, picked up the axe. His blue eyes aflame, his face a mirror of rage, the young priest seemed poised for retribution. As a Japanese guard neared us, Father Sheridan hoisted the axe, and instead swung savagely at the wounded acacia. In one mighty blow, it fell.

Chapter 17
THE LOCUST RULE

August 2, 1943

Lulu and I didn't ask Father Sheridan to mentor our bridge group that afternoon. The horror of watching that Filipino dragged to his probable death penetrated even our fifteen-year-old psyches.

Late into the night, we could hear the man screaming from the Southwest Territory, as we lay in bed and tried not to listen. I turned on my side, and curled up as small as I could, pressing an index finger into each ear. Rubbing my head against the pillow, I prayed, "Make them stop, Lord. Please make them stop." The rubbing produced a noise that obscured the man's cries, so I kept it up.

We had not seen killing or horrible torture in camp. At the very beginning, when those three escaped sailors were caught, beaten, shot, and buried alive, only the male room monitors witnessed the executions. The rest of us just heard about them. In the last year and a half, some of our own men had been carted off to Fort Santiago for interrogation. There, horrible things happened to them, but we learned of their fate mostly from rumors, for they seldom returned.

Lately though, internees with passes to get out of camp, returned with grim stories of lacerated Filipinos bound to stakes on the roadside, or shot and left in the street. And now we had seen with our own eyes the scuffle with the vendor, and most of us heard his wails through the endless night.

Who was he? My heart broke for him. He might be Rosalina's cousin or Valentina's boyfriend. He could be the husband of the Quiapo lady who gave Paul the Black Nazarene.

Kay tossed on her side of our shared bed, and Betty pulled her pillow over both her ears. Changing strategies, I flipped on to my stomach, gripped Rosalina's rosary in one hand and the Black Nazarene in the other, locking both forearms over my ears, and kept silently repeating "Make them stop, Lord."

When the man's screams finally died away, part of me still strained toward the window, wondering what the weighty silence meant. Had they just paused or was he dead? Could that beating happen to one of us? Was Haruo part of that? What if I had been caught with the money in my skirt? What if Haruo had denounced Paul's *Akebonos*?

I don't remember falling asleep, but I must have, because the mocking strains of "Good Morning, Good Morning" came bouncing over the camp loudspeaker. I shot into wakefulness, realizing that I was late to my bathroom cleaning task.

"It's OK, pet. Kay and I took care of it." My mother stood by my bed. "We wanted you and Betty to sleep as late as you could after…" She didn't finish the sentence. "Time to get a move on, though."

I dressed quickly and headed for the now-long line for the toilets. Women waited their turn, slumped against the wall, eerily silent, as if we had a pact not to talk about the night before. A half-hour later, when Betty and I queued up for chow, Aubrey Man ladled one spoonful of bug-studded corn mush into our bowls without tossing me a single "name that play" line from Shakespeare.

Betty peeled off to join Annie at a table, and I started to look around the patio for Lulu and Nellie. I wanted to be with my gang this morning, and find out what they knew. Nels and Lulu were nowhere in sight, but I saw Bill, Paul and Squeaky jabbering like conspirators at a table in the corner of the patio. Their tin bowls were empty, so I knew they'd be leaving soon, but I headed over to join them, thinking Lulu and Nellie couldn't be far behind. I heard Bill. "Pried his eyes out?! What kinda bastards do crap like that?'

"The same kind that smash your balls with a club and skin you alive in front of hundreds of your friends," Paul spat out.

"Jesus…" Squeaky shook his head.

"What did they use to pry his eyes out?" Bill leaned into Paul, and pressed his question with almost surgical interest.

They hadn't seen me yet. I could've walked away, but I didn't. I needed to know what happened last night. I put my bowl on their table, and sat down next to Paul, and across from Bill and Curtis.

"Whose eyes?" I asked. They looked up startled. "That Filipino vendor? Did they pry his eyes out last night?" I could barely get the question out without choking up.

Paul and Bill exchanged uneasy glances. Squeaky puzzled over the wood grain in the table. Then Bill, always less squeamish about blood-and-gore-in-front-the-womenfolk, looked at me and shook his head.

"No. We don't know what happened to him. Paul was telling us about some Filipinos tortured at Rizal. Juergen and Ramón saw it."

Then I remembered the weighty silence that had descended on Grandma Naylor's living room that March night when I'd re-joined the boys after talking to Valentina—the mysterious, interrupted conversation they hadn't resumed after I sat down, the secret Paul said he'd tell Bill. My heart pounded.

"They saw that? At Rizal?" Rizal Stadium was used for soccer matches before the war.

Paul didn't wait for Bill to explain. "They had to be there," he said. "The Japs rounded up as many local civilians as they could find, mostly Filipinos but even the neutrals and Germans—to show how they treated 'traitors' and 'spies.' Juergen thinks they were trying to scare the Filipinos and impress the Germans." Then he added, "I didn't think you should know, Lee. Girls shouldn't have to know."

"Why not?" I spat. "You think we're so weak and you're so strong, and you can handle all this so much better than we can? Well, you don't know half of what I know about what the Japs are doing to girls." I hadn't told him about the "Comfort Women." It ate me up to think about it.

Suddenly, Lulu plunked her bowl down next to me, and Nellie was on her heels. They both had dark circles under their eyes, but settled on the splintered benches, and seemed to sense the angry words that hung in the air.

"What's up, Bill?" Nellie knew she'd get the straight scoop from her sometimes boyfriend.

Bill gave the gist of our conversation—that the Japs were trying to make examples out of Filipinos who betrayed them. That our friends Juergen and Ramón and their families, had been forced to watch a man having his eyes pried out, a Filipino being bludgeoned to death about the testicles, and a third—this one the worst—a man being skinned alive with—

"That's enough, Phillips!" Paul cut him off. "We don't know what happened to that Filipino vendor last night. But we hope it's not any of those things."

Nellie bit her lower lip and nodded to Paul appreciatively. Curtis discovered more fascinating wood veining in the table, and I found I really did not want to know how that Filipino had been flayed alive. Lulu managed to down a bite of her straw-colored corn mush, but I could no more eat than dance the Charleston at that moment.

Paul's maimed left hand lay still on the table next to me—his two missing fingers a reminder of how cruel life could be even without torture or war. He must have sensed me staring at his hand, as he quickly jerked it to life, snapping out of the dark place he had been and back into wise-guy mode.

"Hey—did you hear the one about the man with the withered hand asking Jesus for a cure?" he said, all sunshine and shenanigans again.

Of course, we knew this Bible story of healing, but it was so close to Paul's own predicament, that Nellie winced a little even as she tried to smile. We watched as Paul reached his left arm forward, crooked at the elbow, show-casing a crabbed left hand with contorted pinkie, two missing center fingers, one arched index finger and a grotesquely hooked thumb, forming the letter C.

"Oh, Jesus, if you *will* it, you can heal me," Paul mimicked the high pleading voice of the invalid to the Savior. "Please, Lord, make my one hand like unto my other hand." Paul the Beggar cast his eyes from left hand to right, and shook his deformed paw dramatically at the imaginary Jesus.

"I *do* will it," our comedian changed his tone and features, imitating the compassionate Jesus. He nodded his head in a gesture of "so be it."

"Aaaargh!" Paul reverted to the invalid, who shrieked as he saw his perfect right hand jerk into mid-air, now crooked at the elbow, missing two middle fingers, with pinkie, pointer and thumb hooked hideously—an exact replica of his misshapen hand. "No! Not that one!"

All five of us exploded into laughter and positively guffawed for five minutes. We laughed until our sides ached, until our stomachs hurt, until tears streamed down our faces. "No, not that one!" one of us would shriek as the laughter died down, and the howl started all over again. Lulu banged her head down on the table, convulsed in fits of laughter, making an unabandoned spectacle of herself. Internees turned to watch us in puzzlement, but we just couldn't stop laughing. How long had it been since we'd laughed like this?

Cuthbert passed our giddy, fit-ridden table, and shouted that class started in five minutes. All we could do was nod wordlessly, our eyes glistening, our mouths clenched shut. He passed out of sight.

"No, not that one!" Mindless hilarity reigned all over again. When we stood up to head for class, I hadn't eaten one bite of that buggy corn mush.

Wednesday, August 11, 1943

In the days that followed, I tried not to think about that screaming Filipino vendor or the teenage "comfort women" or the horror at Rizal. But every time I passed a guard, I imagined myself spitting at him, and I positively glared at Haruo, who'd helped drag that Filipino vendor away.

Whenever I thought of Nellie's "Lessons from Ovid" paper, urging me to resist hatred and "unite with our fellow man," I wanted to throw up. Sure, Nellie could write that because both her parents were alive and with her in camp. Nobody in her family was dead or tortured. Well, I wasn't ever going to unite with these evil-doers.

Thankfully, my raging spirit stilled when I was in class. Geometry. Label the x intercept. Got it. Find the slope closest to zero. OK. Deduce the surface area of the pyramid. Yup. Write the equation for line-of-best-fit, using the board scatter plot. Trickier, but more interesting because you had to noodle on it.

Evenings on the front patio brought distraction too. The relentless camp rumor mill churned out nightly torrents of new "what-ifs." The *Teia Maru* was back in port in Manila. It had been used as a repatriation ship earlier in the war, and would take hundreds of us back to the US in exchange for Jap prisoners. I didn't believe that rumor for a second.

More than anything else, though, in the evenings we had our music. The tinny public address system was now housed in a surprisingly sophisticated booth on a corner of the front lawn. At 7:15 PM its blinking red light signaled solace—the start of a two-hour broadcast.

Clarence Beliel, who'd work with my Daddy at KZRH, masterminded it, choosing our crooners and big bands from the more than three thousand platters donated by internees through the Package Line. Mr. Beliel was hiding in plain sight. Before the war, he'd been a famous Manila newscaster known as "Don Bell," and when he'd reported on atrocities in China, he'd blasted the Japs over the airwaves. The Japanese knew this, and wanted him dead or alive, but when they took Manila, Don Bell just went back to using his real name, "Clarence Beliel." He was a shoe salesman, he told the Japs, at Heacock's Department Store. But Don Bell continued his broadcast career in camp, sometimes sending us not-so-coded messages.

Tonight, when Dorothy Lamour sang "This Is the Beginning of the

End," the heartbreaking song became a source of hope. This had to be the beginning of the end. Even the Japanese-controlled *Manila Tribune* had published stories about new fighting on the nearby Solomon Islands—islands the Japs had held securely since the beginning of the war. We'd be out soon, we whispered to each other. But would we?

Now, in the bed I shared with Kay, hideous images reared their heads and ravaged my imagination. Valentina had told me something about those abducted teen girls that I hadn't told anyone—not my mother, not Lulu, certainly not Betty. I'd just stuffed it. Stuffed the horror of her words deep down and refused to think about them. But hearing the screams of that Filipino man nights ago and learning about those horrors at Rizal, brought the buried image to life at night. Could it happen to one of us or to me? My gaze instinctively fled to the grilled window, but the sky was covered in clouds: Daddy's star was nowhere to be seen.

And when I closed my eyes, Valentina's words echoed. "They didn't just abuse those girls in their private parts down below," she spat out. "One girl was forced to kneel every day with her mouth pried open, so Jap soldiers could do all sorts of ugly, cruel things to her. Day after day." The girl had escaped, Valentina said, but she'd gone crazy—literally insane. Tears pooled now, and my insides twisted and retched, fueling a rage that surged and roiled inside me. As on other nights, the horrible image of the kneeling girl and the jeering soldiers came to me, and I couldn't it bury it. And something else had come with it: a rock-solid *hatred* of our captors had hardened like a weight inside me.

Two days ago, I'd even confessed my "mortal sin of great hatred of these Japs" to Father Sheridan. I really did think my hatred was a mortal sin—that's the worst kind for Catholics. You get two choices: venial sin, which is like a misdemeanor and no big deal, or mortal, which is a spiritual felony and means your soul is in "mortal danger." Well, this was granite-hard mortal hatred.

Father Sheridan had told me there was a difference "between *hatred* which is sinful, and *righteous anger* which is not." Maybe I was simply angry at injustice, my hero priest prompted softly, and there was nothing wrong with that, he assured me. And even if I actually hated, well, he, as a priest, now absolved me from my sin in the name of the Father and of the Son and of the Holy Ghost, and because I was sorry for my sin and would say my penance, I was totally forgiven.

Well, that was the problem. I said my penance, but I was not sorry for my sin. I was not one little bit sorry. I still hated them, and it was more than "righteous anger." So, I knew I wasn't forgiven. I took one last look out the window. No stars.

Thursday, August 19, 1943

I planned to hash out all my hatred and anger with Lulu tonight while we studied in the hall outside Room 4. We had a geometry test tomorrow on congruent and similar forms. Candle light flickered over mismatched triangles on the pages of the textbook we shared with six other girls in class. Bunny, Nellie, and two other classmates had used the book earlier that afternoon, but Lulu and I had agreed to take it last because we were night owls. She and I often studied in the hall like this after lights-out, sometimes till midnight, and if we were quiet, nobody minded.

We sat huddled close together, our backs pressed against the cool concrete wall of the corridor, the book propped on our knees between us, solving sample problems and whispering observations. A parallelogram on a stray review sheet puzzled us, but my mind was taking a break. Who cared whether these angles were "congruent"?

"Any more news on your dad?" I whispered.

Yesterday the Red Cross mail delivery had brought gut-wrenching news that Captain Cleland's ship had been torpedoed, and he'd been taken prisoner off the coast of China. What were the Japs doing to Lulu's dad if they could do those horrible things to young girls? I expected a rush of "hideous reprobate" fury to gush forth from Lulu, but she didn't seem to want to talk about it. In fact, she seemed determined to drill down harder on geometry.

"No," Lulu shook her head, hunched toward the book, and kept her eyes on the flickering page in front of us. All I could see was the wispy hedge of her blonde eyelashes. "But he'll be OK," she said without looking up.

Why wasn't Lulu as angry at these Japs as I was? All she did was purse her lips and keep her eyes on the text.

"Do you hate them, Lulee? Do you just hate them for taking him and what they're doing to him?" I launched into the conversation I really wanted to have, hoping she would say "YES," and together we could rage and froth and fuse our hatred of these monsters, but she just shook her head.

Straightening her back, she leaned against the wall, then turned her blue gaze on me, her eyes heavy with sadness.

"No. We're taking their guys too you know. I used to think all Jap soldiers were reprobates, but there's Haruo. I bet some Nice Guy Haruo is being rounded up in the Solomons right now. And maybe my father is lucky, and he's got an NGH guarding him in China too. The Japs aren't all bad guys, you know."

"No, not all," I agreed, but my heart sank, and Lulu's allegiance to Haruo annoyed me. "You know Haruo helped drag that Filipino vendor away, don't you?"

"Lee, he's a Jap soldier. He can't always help our side. Sometimes he has to be a Jap soldier, and we don't know what that Filipino did."

There it was. My chronically big-hearted best friend clung to infuriating kindness and hope. How could she be so resigned when her own father might be at the wrong end of a bayonet? Ever since I saw that screaming Filipino being dragged away and heard about those comfort girls—I had been hungry for revenge. Downright revenge! None of this sappy returning good for evil stuff, that Father Sheridan was always talking about. None of Cicero's "born to unite with our fellow man" claptrap.

"Besides, the bad guys will get theirs," Lulu rasped with quiet conviction that both mystified and irked me. Don't go all Pollyanna on me, Lulu, I was thinking. I hated that she was being loving and kind, when I could only be furious. "It's the Locust Rule," she said.

Lulu and I had been best friends for almost two years now, and this was the first I ever heard of the Locust Rule.

Even in the flickering candle-light she saw my puzzlement, and continued in a whisper, a new energy in her voice. "Did you ever see locusts swarm?"

I knew farmers on the southern islands lived in fear of the clattering hordes of winged grasshoppers that could devastate a crop. Locusts hatched just once every seventeen years, and we'd never seen a big infestation in Manila, so I shook my head, and Lulu hurried on. "I've seen it once—at our second camp in Cebu."

She closed the book propped on our knees between us, allowing the review sheet to flutter on my lap, and turned toward me.

"The Japs had all of us caged behind the barbed wire in our camp, and two of the soldiers had been complete reprobates to one of the men that day. They thought he had a radio hidden—and maybe he did. They beat him with a rubber hose, tied him to a stake, made him stare up at the sun, and told him he would go blind before the end of the day if he didn't confess." Lulu squinted her eyes toward the ceiling.

"They yanked his head back and forced him into that position for hours until he told where the radio was, but he didn't tell them. In the end, he collapsed on the ground, and got hauled back to his barracks. Then the two soldiers who'd beaten him reported to the Commandant." She pushed a wayward curl off her face and focused on the candle. "When they came out of his office, they headed for a Jap army plane parked just beyond the gate and barbed wire. Maybe they were going back to Manila. Maybe Tokyo. Who knew?"

I hung on her every word. I couldn't believe she hadn't told me this story before. But then again, Lulu seemed to parse out these gems of her past in tiny bundles, just a few at a time, as if she had forgotten that she had them to share.

"So the little plane lifts into the air and we're all staring at the propellers and the red fried eggs painted under the wings, but we could hear a strange buzzing noise coming from the plane." Her brow furrowed at the memory.

"And then all of a sudden, we see this dirty cloud that's growing and swirling and spreading in bands. The shape keeps changing. And we realize the buzzing isn't coming from the plane. It's coming from the cloud. It's millions of locusts—hordes of 'em—churning and buzzing, heading straight for that plane."

"Are you making this up?" I demanded.

She shook her head. "No, swear to God. We saw it. This cloud stretched for miles—miles," she rushed on. "And maybe the locusts thought that plane was a crop—I don't know. Because pretty soon the hum of the plane and the buzz of the locusts were all one thing—one huge rumble and gigantic fuzzy smudge."

Lulu described how the frenzied locusts seemed to swallow up their strange prey, their tumbling bodies feeding on propellers, crusting the silver shell of the plane, obliterating the red suns painted under the wings, surging into the open glass of the cockpit—until finally, only the sound of the gnawing, buzzing horde remained.

"You couldn't hear the plane anymore," her voice grew agitated. "The plane just disappeared in the cloud, as if they'd eaten the whole thing. And then all of a sudden, we saw it again," she stared just past my shoulder, "the chewed-up plane—tumbling right out of the sky in a death spiral. And it crashes smack in front of the barbed wire of the camp—right in front of us."

Awed silence fell between the two of us in the darkness of the hall. Our candle flickered, its flame momentarily reflected in Lulu's now radiant blue eyes. I held her gaze in disbelief, and she went on.

"And for one minute, we all forgot we were prisoners, and we cheered. Loud and wild cheers. But then we caught ourselves and stopped—right away before the guards could get mad and shoot us—or haul somebody else up to the stake. I clapped my hand right over my mouth when I realized it.

But the Jap soldiers were all so busy, racing to the plane and dragging out their dead soldier pilots that they didn't pay any attention to us. None at all," she concluded in quiet triumph.

Not wanting to break the spell of her story, I sat motionless for a moment before whispering, "So, what's the Locust Rule?"

A sad smile crossed her lips. "In the end, the bad guys get theirs. God takes care of it. I don't have to hate them. Not one bit."

My eyes smarted and hot tears welled unbidden. Lulu's radiant blue stare became a blur, and I started to sob miserably as she hugged me. Here was Lulu—the one with the captured father in a horrible death camp—undaunted, and here was I, doing the hating.

Hating because my own father was gone. Hating because of screams I heard, and horrible stories that ravaged my imagination. Hating because I was afraid, and wanted to go home, but there was no home anymore. I don't have to hate them, Lulu said—as if hate were a heavy burden we placed on ourselves, and she had a choice.

Did I have a choice? Through my tears, I suddenly realized she was right. I didn't have to hate them. I could choose to believe that there were good guys on both sides, and that evil really would be punished. That losses could be made whole. For a moment, stillness settled on me, and a great weight lifted slowly from my shoulders. The tight knot inside me loosened its grip, and I could feel the taut cords within me slacken and slip. When I lifted my face to brush away tears, I saw Lulu's triumphant smile.

Then I caught sight of the symmetrical shapes on the review sheet we had pondered minutes before, and the geometry question leapt out at me: *Are the opposite sides and angles of this parallelogram congruent or incongruent?* The line on top of the slanted shape paralleled the line on the bottom, and the line on the left mirrored the angled one on the right. Opposite sides and opposite angles. Balances on some invisible scale.

That's just what Lulu and I had been talking about. Balances on a cosmic scale. They were congruent, I realized. Completely congruent.

Chapter 18
GOING TO GOA

Saturday, September 4, 1943

Saturday brought extra camp duties. Bunny, Lulu and I worked at a picnic table outside the central kitchen on vegetable detail—a coveted task because it allowed us to handle FOOD! Lulu separated stringy, spinach-like talinum from the prickly weeds that had been yanked up with the root, while Bunny removed the leaves from the stalks. My job was to peel shrunken sweet potatoes from the camp's garden. I kept cutting myself with the dull paring knife I'd been given, and thought we should just leave the wormy skins on: everyone was hungry enough to eat them anyway.

None of us were really concentrating on vegetables, though. Instead, the entire camp buzzed with news that the repatriation rumors were true. More than a hundred STIC internees would be among the three-hundred-fifty Americans sailing home at the end of the month via the neutral Indian port of Goa (pronounced like "I wanna **GO A**way from here!")

"Do you want to be on that ship?" Bunny asked Lulu. Our English friend barely looked up as she plucked bug-bitten leaves from a scraggly stalk.

"Well, sure, but I wouldn't want to go now. Ouch!" Nettles from the weeds dug into Lulu's palm, and the thorny task distracted her. "What I wouldn't give for gloves."

"What I wouldn't give for air-cooling," Bunny replied as a bead of sweat trickled down her forehead. "OK, why not now?" She whisked a drop from her brow with the back of her hand.

"The Japs are losing." Lulu returned to the topic in a much-lowered voice, nearly whispering. "The war's gotta be almost over, and my father's in a Jap camp here somewhere. How will he know where to find us when the GIs come storming back?"

None of us doubted for one second that our Intrepid Jumbo-sized Americans would come storming back. Paul's *Time* magazine confirmed that our boys had re-taken Guadalcanal in February. Then in March, the hidden camp radio reported that Allied airpower had obliterated a Rising Sun convoy that was carrying thousands of troops to nearby New Guinea. Those islands had been in Japanese hands since the beginning of the war, but were now under assault. August brought news that New Georgia in the Solomons was ours.

"Once our boys have nabbed the Solomons and New Guinea, the PI can't be far behind," Bunny nodded in agreement. "That's what FDR meant, when he said *you will soon be redeemed from the Japanese yoke.*"

Two weeks ago, the Jap-censored *Manila Tribune* took the unusual step of quoting President Roosevelt's promise to the Filipinos. The editors mocked his radio broadcast as "another vain promise" of "the imperialist president" on the forty-fifth anniversary of American occupation of the PI.

But FDR's words—*you will soon be redeemed from the Japanese yoke*—sent our spirits soaring. They also sent camp scholars scurrying to their dictionaries for the exact definition of "soon." Did Roosevelt mean "promptly without delay" or did he mean "in the near and immediate future"?

My heart was lighter and my hopes brighter than they'd been in months. Since our Locust Rule talk three weeks before, the rock-hard burden of hatred I felt had been lifted. I managed to take STIC one steamy day at a time. My mother, Betty, Lulu, and fudge buoyed me, as did Hope, Kay and all our gang. Sure, I was hungry, but I could pass Haruo in camp these days and bow without loathing him. I thought that he bowed extra low back to me and that his eyes softened a little when he saw me. We'd be out by Christmas.

Still, it was tantalizing to think about going home NOW. In the prisoner exchange, freed Americans from the Philippines were supposed to be traded for an equal number of Japanese prisoners. One hundred thirty STIC internees were to be sent home—our weakest, sickest, and oldest prisoners, those most in need of medical attention.

Not surprisingly, hundreds of internees suddenly developed life-threatening illnesses and clamored for the right to be on that ship. But not all. My mother, Mim, Hope, and Kay all had doubts about seeking repatriation.

"That ship, full of sitting-duck-Americans, may not even make it to Goa—or from Goa to San Francisco," my mother cautioned Betty and me in our shanty last night.

The Japanese ship *Teia Maru*, chockful of American captives, would sail west from Manila to the Indian Ocean. Then in the Portuguese colony of Goa, the Japs would supposedly exchange their cargo of Allied civilians for an equal number of Japanese nationals, and the freed US nationals would sail home on an American ship.

"It could just be a ploy to get hundreds of us out to sea, and then torpedo us." I voiced my mother's fear to Bunny and Lulu.

They both nodded.

"Well, my Mum says, we're not leaving STIC when Pop and the boys are building the Hilton for us down at Los Baños," Bunny quipped. Her father and brothers sent regular reports of construction on the new camp.

"Maybe you'll get your air-cooling down there," I kidded her. "I think they call it tropical breezes."

We peeled and sorted with greater energy. We were in this together and making the right decision. Not that we had any choice since our names would never be on the list, but the Clelands, the Brambles, and the Isersons were here for the duration. And besides, we'd be free by Christmas.

Friday, September 17, 1943

Paper-stuffed clipboard in hand, our fair-haired dream-priest in a clean white tee shirt, and Bermuda shorts, roamed from one chatting group to another. A pendant cross hung from his neck. What was he doing? Bridge and poker players on the front lawn stopped their play mid-hand to answer his questions. Mahjong addicts looked up from their boards in expectation, keen to have their say. Even those deep in conversation on the grass mats watched Father Sheridan's every move, occasionally gossiping about those responding, but eager for their turn at the clipboard.

Over the P.A. Tommy Dorsey's orchestra played the heartbreaking strains of "I'll Never Smile Again," but Father Sheridan was smiling again. His hair shone red-flecked or amber, like the setting sun that glinted on the cross he wore. By turns jovial, then serious, Father Sheridan asked his questions, checked answers on his many-paged list, and jotted notes in a side margin. What was he up to?

Lulu and I were partnered against Nellie and Paul in the never-ending bridge game. We sat cross-legged on our mats, the petates serving as protection from the dusty ground and a clean surface for our tricks. But we all kept an eye on the priest with the clipboard, who'd just finished checking responses at a mahjong table. Paul could not resist.

"Padre! Come over here and ask the Catholic Teen Bridge Group! We want to vote!"

"You told him?" Lulu hissed at me. "You told Paul about our plan for the Catholic Teen Bridge Group?" Nellie (who was Protestant) looked up in puzzlement.

"Well, he would've been part of it anyway. Why not?" I couldn't understand Lulu's annoyance.

Father Sheridan headed toward us with a spring in his step.

"The bridge-playing teens can go for a grand slam, but they cannot vote. Only those over twenty-one may cast ballots," he answered in good humor. Happy for a break, he settled his manly frame on our mat just to my left. Looking at the dummy across from me, he peeked in my hand, and whispered, "Don't miss that finesse." I arched two eyebrows at him: I wouldn't have.

"No outside help, Padre!" Paul objected, then pointed his chin at the clipboard that was face-down in Father Sheridan's lap. "What are you up to? Everyone's ogling you like you're MacArthur come to liberate them."

"Don't insult him, Pablo. They like him much better than MacArthur." Lulu shot Father Sheridan one of her high-voltage smiles.

Picking up his clipboard, he read: "*Question Number One: If it is consonant with the policy of your government to arrange for the release and transportation of yourself and your immediate family to the continental United States ... would you wish to go?*" All eyes widened. "*Question No. 2: If your answer to Question Number 1 is YES, would you still wish to go if it means a separation of your family by reason of only women and children, aged and sick, being permitted to go?*"

He looked up at us. "It's about the prisoner exchange. I'm taking a survey of Americans in camp for the Executive Committee. Grinnell and Carroll just *might* have some say on the repatriation list. Chairman Grinnell wants to know where everyone stands. No sense sending folks home if they want to stay right here in Shangri-La."

Carroll Grinnell, the new Chair of the Executive Committee, was not to be confused with Earl Carroll, our first chair, who'd been appointed by the Japs. A few months into captivity, Mr. Carroll had asked the Commandant to let internees elect their own Chair, and the Japanese brass said: "Sure, you internees can vote as long as Earl Carroll stays on the Executive Committee, and we can say NO to someone we don't like, and put Mr. Carroll right back on top." Well, Mr. Grinnell won handily, and the Japanese seemed to like him too. He'd had been VP of General Electric in the Far East before the war, and even spoke some Japanese. And he poured himself into the Chair job—always sending out feelers to determine how internees felt about camp problems. Then, since he had to make decisions that many internees disagreed with, Mr. Democracy was always accused of being Mr. Dictator, trying to run "Mine Camp."

"Whooeee…" Paul whistled through his teeth and drummed the two good fingers of his left hand on the mat. "Well, who WOULDN'T want to go back? Put the Davises in the 'yes' under any circumstances column, Padre. What are you finding—five hundred to one for repatriation?"

"You'd be surprised," Father Sheridan replied. "As of now, Shangri-La is winning. A little less than half say they want to go to Goa." The priest's calmly delivered bombshell took a minute to explode.

"What?" Paul demanded. "Cowards? Are we all cowards? Is everybody afraid of being torpedoed at sea? What about 'screw your courage to the sticking place' huh?"

We had just finished *Macbeth* in English, and the boys loved that line because it involved both *screwing* and *courage*—even though Lady Macbeth had been urging her husband to commit murder. But was Paul right? Were we cowards?

"Maybe *this* is the sticking place. Maybe we're not cowards so much as companions." Father Sheridan said with glacial calm.

Nellie laid her cards face-down on the mat, and spoke for the first time. "My father said that after all that the Filipinos have done for us every single day we've been here, we shouldn't even think of abandoning them. That's what it would be. We'd sail home while they're left alone with the Japs"—she lowered her voice—"who hate them. It's like saying 'Sure, we had a good time running your country, but that's all over now. Good luck with these new guys.'"

Paul's jaw dropped. "And what good are we doing the Filipinos staying here and living off their charity? How do we Package-Line-Parasites help the Filipinos?" he demanded.

"We're bearing witness," Father Sheridan replied evenly. "Or that's what a lot of folks here think. We're standing with our friends against a common foe."

"Priests aren't supposed to have foes," Paul muttered darkly.

I could tell Pablo didn't like this explanation one bit, and I had to think about it too. I had been in the "Prefer-Not-To-Be-Torpedoed" group. But *bearing witness*—what did that really mean? Was this about loyalty? To Rosalina, Warlito, Valentina and Alfonso and all the others who came every day to that gate? Even now.

"So, we hang around and die in solidarity because we don't have the pluck to get on that ship? Sounds like cowardice to me." Paul grumbled.

Father Sheridan smiled a little. "I think we've got the pluck. But some people are making a different choice." The young priest glanced at the tower of Main Building, where the black silhouette of the cross stood against a mauve sky. "Sometimes bearing witness or taking a hit for someone else— can seem that way—like cowardice," he said almost to himself.

I thought he was going to say more, but he didn't. Instead, he jumped to his feet, his usual upbeat self, with clipboard nestled firmly in his right hand.

"You kids have a good game, and Mary Louella," he said in a conspiratorial tone, "when are you going to come see me about those catechism classes? Otherwise, how can you keep playing with this Catholic Teen Bridge Group?"

Lulu's face flushed crimson, but the radiant smile she beamed could've illuminated a path to the Main Gate.

***

Father Sheridan's poll results proved prophetic. Of the two-thousand seven-hundred-thirty-six adult Americans interned at Santo Tomas and Los Baños, only one-thousand-three-hundred-thirty-four said they wanted to be on that repatriation ship. More than half chose to stay. To me that said: more than half our camp had true grit. And now that I'd heard Father Sheridan's explanation—about loyalty to our Filipino friends—I was proud to be in that group.

The chance to go home roiled waters in camp, though, because the half that wanted to go, REALLY wanted to go. Internees connived to be on that list, and like busy rats scheming to jump ship, they gnawed at whatever rope was nearest to them. Pay off the Commandant? Sure. Did he want stock in Meralco? Sleep with the guards? Fine. Shanties weren't just for family fun. Eat traces of rat poisoning to develop a desperate health crisis? Yes and ugh! Rat poisoning? That burns your intestines like acid.

In Room 4, Mrs. Randolph Meade continued to make life insufferable. The still hefty matron moaned theatrically through the night, feigning "gnawing pains in my entrails, at the very heart of me," and twice had herself hospitalized. How could a friend of General Douglas MacArthur's be allowed to languish in such straits? Astonishingly, when the Repatriation List was posted, Mrs. Meade's name was on it. She edged out numerous feeble men, women and children, who actually were in dire straits and needed immediate medical attention. How did they make up the list? Everyone wanted to know. Was Mr. Grinnell responsible for this?

"I don't know whether to weep or throw a party," I heard Hope telling my mother when she saw Mrs. Meade's name on the list.

"A party," my weary Room Monitor mother responded. "Let's definitely throw a party."

In fact, the entire camp decided to throw a party, a farewell extravaganza for those leaving as a way of saying *Good bye and we'll miss you!* Or in the case of Mrs. Meade and others, *Goodbye and good riddance!* Dave Harvey promised that Friday night the "Little Theater Under the Stars" would host the minstrel show to end all minstrel shows for departing internees.

Friday, September 25, 1943

Furious preparations had been underway all morning. By the time we kids got out of class, nearly a thousand lawn chairs stood in neat rows before our makeshift stage. The raised wooden platform with its white curtain backdrop stood in readiness, and several wiry men knelt beneath the stage floor, rigging KLIM cans to its edge.

"Ah, the Good Ladies Iserson!" Aubrey Man called to us, as we tried to rush past the scene. "Ta to your Red Cross."

Betty and I were heading to our Glamorville shanty to help whip up several extra batches of fudge for tonight's performance. My entrepreneur mother anticipated brisk sales before the event, since Commandant Kodaki was scheduled to speak first and the socko show to follow. That combo was sure to bring nearly all four thousand internees on to the front lawn.

"Ta?" I stopped and stared at him. Betty tugged my hand, but Aubrey's British slang proved an irresistible riddle to me, and he made a game of coming up with new expressions to puzzle me.

"Many thanks," he translated with a smug wink and waggled the long cylindrical can in his hand.

A can of KLIM (which is MILK spelled backwards) accompanied every Red Cross care package, and the American-made powdered milk disappeared all too quickly in camp. KLIM had been popular in the tropics for years before the war because regular milk spoiled quickly in the heat. Since we hadn't seen a Red Cross package in nearly a year, the small amount of KLIM remaining fed calcium-deprived children at Holy Ghost Convent or simply assuaged hunger if it was in private hands. Mommy kept a nearly full can stored high on the shelf in our shanty, and sometimes, when she wasn't looking, Betty and I dipped clean teaspoons right into it. We just let the sweet milk crystals dissolve in our mouths, savoring the buttery richness that reminded us of fresh cream and all good things before the war.

Ingenious internees on the Entertainment Committee had found another use for the empty KLIM cans: Aubrey Man was wiring them as footlights for the big show.

"Well, ta, for the lights, cameras, and action! Keep calm and carry on!" I called back.

Betty and I sped past what looked like a suitcase demolition derby on the front lawn. Departing internees were allowed one maleta each, and had to have all their possessions packed for inspection on the lawn by yesterday. Explicit instructions had been given. No personal papers except passports. No books. Only family photos, no camp photos. No newspapers could leave camp. Above all, no comprehensive report on conditions in Santo Tomas—recently written and submitted by the Executive Committee—was to leave camp.

Maybe our little band of pilgrims actually *would* make it to the US, I thought, because the Japanese seemed obsessed with confiscating any information about camp harships. Guards on the lawn unwrapped every item in each suitcase. They unwound hoarded rolls of toilet paper looking for secret messages. (How infuriating that some internees hoarded *toilet paper*, while the rest of us were making due with two squares!) They bayoneted their way through precious packets of Kotex provided by the Red Cross. They even confiscated Mrs. Meade's knitting instructions. *K3* and *P1* (knitting shorthand for "knit three stitches and pearl one stitch") looked like a code to Bugs Bunny Guard.

The Japanese were nothing if not orderly, though, and tidiness reigned supreme by show time. In the rosy light of dusk with a pale moon above, four-thousand of us milled about on the front lawn, waiting to hear a rare speech from Commandant Kodaki. The former Japanese businessman-turned-officer mounted a wooden soap crate, and a wary silence descended. Dressed in official olive drab with the pressed collar of his white shirt worn open over lapels of his jacket, Kodaki seemed to drink in the evening air. He drew a pensive breath before speaking.

"We try to be good to you," he began in halting English. "You have moving picture," he said pointing to the makeshift screen on his left. "You have music." He nudged his chin in the direction of the PA station. "You have shanty for family. You have good place to study and exercise and pray."

Did he mean "play?" I wondered. But then I thought of the Santa Catalina chapel.

"We wish all prisoners well. Those who return, we hope you speak kind and true of us in America."

He's scared, I thought for the first time. They're gonna lose the war, and he's afraid of what will happen to him because of how they've treated us.

My heart leapt a little higher. Lulu was standing right next to me, and she squeezed my hand. We both understood the same thing. The war had to be almost over because the Japs were covering their tracks.

What would Kodaki say about the repatriation list I wondered? That was important because many internees felt cheated out of a spot on the ship, and blamed our own Executive Committee chaired by Mr. Grinnell. Kodaki had the power to make Grinnell and the Committee look squeaky clean by attributing the whole list to Tokyo and Washington. But he didn't.

Maybe it was his poor English, but the Commandant concluded by saying that the Executive Committee was "not complete responsible" for the names on the list. That made all who suspected Grinnell of determining the winners really furious. "Not complete responsible" meant "partly responsible," right? But maybe Kodaki meant: "Not responsible in any way" and just said it wrong. Who knew? No one said a thing, but the rapid exchange of incriminating glances, and the barely audible whisper of "Mine Camp" floated in the air.

Who were we becoming? Just a year and a half ago, we had all locked arms and sung "Side-by-Side" with gusto, vowing to stand united against the foe. Now we were turning on each other. Lots of internees were more furious at our own leaders than at the Japs.

After Kodaki bowed, we did the same, and some internees even clapped: a curious wave of applause rippled over the plaza for our Japanese captor. Before anyone could puzzle over how odd that was, a jazzy trumpeted version of *"My Bonnie Lies Over the Ocean"* blared from the stage, and we raced to claim lawn chairs in front of stage and screen.

I grabbed a spot on a mat next to my gang, with Hope, Kay, my mother, and Betty in lawn chairs to my left. I spotted all-business Haruo at a post near the projector. In the deepening twilight, a movie projector loosed a tube of insect-crazed white light, while black numerals raced down a makeshift screen. Martial music swelled as the screen flashed a gray-white globe radiating search lights from its heart in the Pacific. THE LOST TRIBE OF THE PHILIPPINES. The movie title flashed on the screen, and we all applauded madly, as we read in smaller font: "A Dave Harvey Traveltalk Accompanied by the STIC Traveltalk Record Collection. Animation by Donald Dang and Commentary by Dave Harvey and Clarence Beliel."

How did they do this? The home-made film started off just like *Voice of the Globe* travel reels we saw at the Manila Metropolitan before feature films. "Traveltalks" tantalized you with the dream of sailing to exotic places like Siam, the Arctic Circle, or Egypt. The *Voice of the Globe* narrator delivered flowery commentary like: "Gazing over this vast, panoramic plain, we espy the majestic ruins of ...."

Just then, the booming baritone of Clarence Beliel (aka Don Bell) pronounced, "In a remote corner of our earth, stands the lost, verdant colony of Big House, where recently, in the year A.D. 2000, an English-speaking tribe of natives has been discovered."

We hooted. Two decrepit stick figures hobbled across the screen barely supported by their coconut reed canes. "The revered ancestors of this charming people," Beliel informed us, "hail from a place they refer to as "Stick" in the lovely Philippine island of Luzon." Now internees leapt from their chairs, yelling in enthusiasm and whistling.

The cartoon characters bantered about *Stick People's* peculiar habits of always bathing six to a shower head and standing patiently in line for chow, though plumbing and food were plentiful in 2000 and "the fabled war" had long since passed. The old coots were being interviewed on screen by the cartoon granddaughter of an internee who had "Gone to Goa" in September of 1943, and returned safely to America. The curious woman had traveled to "Big House" as an archaeologist to learn of her family's origin. Internees exploded in mirth at the spoof.

I laughed too. The whole thing was ingenious. Part of me wondered: how would it be sixty years from now? I'd be seventy-five. Would the folks who were going to Goa make it home and recover their normal lives, while those of us left behind—what? Ate each other alive with petty squabbles? Or went crazy? Or died in some battle to liberate us? I didn't want to think about that just now, and Dave Harvey made it easy to forget.

An all-out minstrel show followed—vaudeville acts of every sort, sarcastic comedy teams poking fun about accidents at sea, tap-dancers tracing paths across the Pacific, and even a song titled "Going to Goa." The slam-bang finish came when the phonograph blared the instrumental for *My Bonnie Lies Over the Ocean*, while Dave Harvey in his white smoking jacket and Patricia Dyer in her pale green evening gown sang heartily for all departing internees:

> *Next week I am sailing for Goa,*
> *Cuz Goa means freedom to me;*
> *But if Portugal gets in the woah,*
> *I'll come back from Goa to thee!*
> *Come back, come back,*
> *Come back from Goa to thee,*
> *Come back, come back, come back from Goa to thee.*

Funny verses followed, but even as we laughed and shouted and sang the refrain, we knew our fellow countrymen were never coming back from Goa to us. They might get out and they might get home, but would we? Would this war really end by Christmas? The confidence I felt by day slipped away by night. The final strains welled, and our emcees managed big smiles, as they belted out:

> *So, here is our last Aloha*
> *To the folks who are goin' to Goa*
> *See you all once mo-ah,*
> *When the war is o'ah!!*

Harvey and Dyer signaled the audience to join in, and the entire camp rose and sang, arms waving rhythmically to the stage, many in tears:

> *See you,*
> *see you, see you all once mo-ah*
> *when the, when the, when the woah is o-ah!*

Overhead the waning moon shone in a cloudless black sky. I squinted to the front gate completely covered in sawali: none of our Filipino friends in sight. Could they hear us singing? Did they think we were happy? Even as the music swelled to its crescendo and crowds cheered, I felt very alone. Another group was leaving us. Six months ago, we'd lost eight-hundred men and twelve nurses to Los Baños for who knows how long. Now the Lucky 127 might be going home, and we remained STIC-stuck.

I shot a glance at Betty and Mommy smiling uncertainly, their hands locked together as if holding on for dear life. Hope had just put out a cigarette, and crushed it into the ground, while she frowned at the stage. Kay made some sarcastic remark in her ear that made her laugh. Haruo, in the back on a raised block, re-shouldered his bayonetted rifle, and fixed his gaze ahead. I looked right to Lulu, Nellie, Bill, Bunny and Paul, all applauding with more hope than conviction. Not one of them had an all-out-happy grin plastered in place.

What was in the air tonight? I couldn't name it. But I was thinking that those "Goans" darn-well better go home and tell every single person in America how much we needed to be sprung from this god-awful camp—and by Christmas!

A light breeze ruffled my curls, and a seagull screeched overhead. I glimpsed the bird's tubby silhouette against the moon and followed his flight to the four pulsing stars of the Southern Cross. It had been many months since I'd stared intently at my father's favorite constellation, closer to us now, it seemed, further east in the sky than I'd ever seen it. For a second, the dark, passionate chords and silver melody of *Leonore's Suite* washed over me. How long had it been since I'd heard it? Ten months? An insistent voice repeated, "Spread your wings to match the gale, Leonore. Spread your wings to match the gale."

I closed my eyes and felt one tear roll down my cheek. OK, Daddy.

Part Two

OUR DAILY BREAD

October 3, 1943
Room 4, Main Building
Santo Tomas Internment Camp

Dear Francis,

My health is good. We are well-fed. Tell it to Sweeney.

Your loving cousin,
Lee I.

Chapter 19
BREAD OF LIFE

Thursday, September 28, 1943

Bamboo rods, sawali matting, and heaps of nipa roof material lay behind the camp kitchen and across from the dining sheds. The piles were shrinking, though, as our men framed a large covered pavilion.

"Do you think they're building that playhouse to make the little kids feel better about being stuck here?" Betty asked, as we sat down at a table with our tin bowls. Lugao, a watery rice mush, had just replaced cracked wheat as our new breakfast porridge.

"Do you feel better now?" I asked her.

"Hardy-har-har," Betty shook her head at me. Her brown eyes were still alight with mischief, but her face was gaunt, and her wrists looked like the wooden slats on our old Venetian blinds. "I'm turning fourteen for liberation you know."

I nodded. Betty's birthday was Christmas Eve. Surely, the GIs would be here by then, but this new construction—begun the very day our internees left for Goa—made me wonder.

Well, the kids needed the shade. So many of the camp's big acacias had been felled to fuel cooking fires that it was hard for kids to find shelter from the sun. So, when Mr. Grinnell pointed out to Commandant Kodaki that bamboo still abounded, and nipa—which was just dried grass—could be found anywhere, the Commandant had given permission for this new structure to be built. (Maybe the GIs wouldn't be so hard on him, when they arrived to save us....) Scrawny aging men and still muscular young priests pounded the final touches on a big playhouse.

"Are you and Annie planning to do a puppet show there for the kids?" Paul had mentioned something about that.

"Yup. *Columbus Sails the Ocean Blue.* In two weeks." Betty squinted at the bugs in her lugao, and edged them to one side of her bowl. "The fifth graders are helping us. They're making the Columbus and Queen Isabella puppets. We're not the only ones who want that space, though. There'll be a crafts table, a story corner, and the children's choir will get to practice there. And don't forget the dance."

I snorted. The Recreation Committee had announced a dance for us teens in the new playhouse in November, but that didn't thrill me.

"Who am I going to dance with? Pablo Diablo? Squeaky Brooks?" I shook my head and swallowed my grainy lugao, self-pity overwhelming me. "I feel just like Mary. *I ain't got nobody.*"

Betty looked at me as if I were a complete moron. "Mary had Joseph."

"Not *that* Mary, Brainwave. Judy Garland Mary." Two weeks ago at our "Little Theater Under the Stars," we'd watched *Strike Up the Band* with Judy Garland, who played teenage Mary Holden and sang, "I Ain't Got Nobody, and Nobody's Got Me." I practically wept. That was me—completely boyfriend-less. "And even if I had a boyfriend," I stirred the sandy remains in my dish, growing despondent, "what would I wear? All my dresses are too loose and too short."

"Mommy could use some of our cloth coupons and have the Sewing Committee whip something up, but that's kind of expensive." Betty nibbled one edge of her lugao-filled spoon, and frowned. "Or maybe Kay can loan you something."

"It doesn't matter. Who cares about dancing anyway? You want me to finish that for you?"

Saturday, October 30, 1943

"What about this one from eighth grade? Can I bear to part with it?" I dangled a sheet of paper in front of Lulu with the straightest face I could manage.

She and I sat in the first floor hallway of the Main Building at a folding table where we usually played bridge. Women jostled for spots in the bathroom line directly in front of us, but we ignored them. No. 2 pencils in hand, pink erasers at the ready, we each had a stack of old assignments in front of us. Our job, Mr. Lautzenhiser told the sophomore class on Friday, was to erase enough work to produce ten clean sheets of paper for next month. Lulu glanced at the short text I had scrawled on an unlined sheet.

"It's short and easy to erase. Is that a poem? Read it," she rasped. Lulu hadn't lost her ability to observe, ask questions, and give commands all at once.

"It's about a friend I had before you." I smiled, cleared my throat, and read with mock mock conviction.

A Friend
by Lee Iserson. Grade 8

A tree that's a friend and a friend indeed,
Is a tree that you've known from a wee, small seed.
For then your labor is many times blest
When 'neath its branches you lie to rest.
But whenever I
start to plant a tree
The seed, if it's edible,
Ends up in me.

Lulu's cornflower blue eyes widened and her smile grew before she burst out laughing, throwing her chin to the ceiling, tilting her chair back against the wall, and accidentally knocking her papers to the floor as she shrieked.

Women in the bathroom line turned to stare at us, as she continued to guffaw.

"OK, I had tapioca for brains." I forced a smile, but didn't think my poem was that funny.

"I am so glad not to be a tree seed friend!" Lulu gasped and then started laughing all over again.

Sometimes Lulu could be really annoying. She wiped her eyes and kept giggling as she picked up her papers. "I think you can let that go, Lee-lung." She used her new nickname for me. "But you know what it means, don't you?"

I had already started erasing my pathetic text. "That my favorite poet, Ogden Nash, has no competition from me?"

"Nope. It means you've been hungry for a long time," Lulu swiped the back of her hand across her cheek. She righted her chair and pulled it close to the table. "You were thinking about eating tree seeds almost two years ago."

Those words stopped me cold, and I stared at her. *The seed, if it's edible, ends up in me.* I'd written those words at the end of eighth grade. We'd been in camp for only two months then.

"Well, probably just hungry for variety. I wasn't really hungry back then."

"No?" Lulu arched two eyebrows.

"I don't think so. You weren't here then, but Grandma Naylor was sending all sorts of goodies through the Package Line, and the kitchen started serving a couple of meals a day in February—just a little after we got here." I was thinking aloud.

"Do you hear yourself?" Lulu shook her head, as she returned to her task. "A couple of meals a day? I used to think three squares with snacks was the bare minimum." Lulu's stocky little frame held none of the baby fat she had arrived with. "I'm pretty sure I've been hungry that long—at least two years. I bet you have too."

Betty raced by us on her way to Room 4, and reminded us to hurry up. We had to be at choir practice in half an hour to rehearse some tricky new music we were singing for the feast of Christ the King. Every choir member was going to put heart and soul into that music because the Spanish nuns who owned Santa Catalina convent were hosting a party for the choir after mass—and party meant food. I wondered what kinds of food they had that we didn't have in camp.

My mind raced as my eraser flew. When had I started to be really hungry? Camp chow had been boring from the start, but we weren't starving in the beginning. Anyone with connections on the outside could get treats through the Gate. Sure, Bugs Bunny Guard might bayonet a lemon meringue pie or two, but the Japs didn't want to pay to feed us, so they let tons of food come in through the Package Line—like our Sunday roast chickens paid for with Daddy's shirts. And early on, the Commandant let the Red Cross set up a kitchen in STIC to feed the camp. Of course, the Red Cross got the honor of paying for the meals too.

Within a month, we had a system of queuing up for chow morning and evening: four lines, each internee holding a ration ticket, each ticket featuring a neat grid of squares for every meal, every day of the week. (Maybe that's why we were running out of paper—all those paper cards produced every week.) That card was punched by someone sitting at the dining shed entrance, so you couldn't cheat by going through the line twice.

Breakfast had always been cracked wheat porridge and some version of tea or coffee. Dinner might be carabao stew or a stringy pork dish or boiled duck eggs, along with sweet potatoes, a roll, a banana, and some tea. Sometimes we got a sweet satisfying bread pudding for dessert too. STIC dining wasn't exactly the Sky Room, but it was filling enough, and of course, we Isersons had started making our Superior Fudge.

I flicked away the pink eraser shavings, and paused. Four lines of text to go. Now all that had changed—except for the lines and meal tickets. Our food rations had been cut twice in last month. Sugar was so expensive that my mother said we'd be making our last fudge for the Christmas fair. Wheat flour had disappeared more than a year ago, and with it all fluffy white bread and mouthwatering cakes. I don't know who killed or stole all the hens and cows in the PI, but we hadn't seen real beef, chicken, eggs, milk, butter, and cheeses since January. Tiny little mongo beans were our new main course. Our camp garden kept coughing up as much garlic as anybody wanted, and scads of stringy spinach-like talinum. And if you had money, you could still buy rice, sugar, lard and duck eggs at the canteen, but it was getting hard to buy cooking oil, and everyone complained about soaring prices.

I carefully erased the last line of my eighth-grade masterpiece ("*The seed if it's edible ends up in me*") and a memory jolted me.

"I remember now." I turned to Lulu. "I remember when I *knew* I was really hungry. It wasn't two years ago. It was about six weeks ago."

"Six weeks ago?" Lulu looked up, but exasperation crept into her voice.

"Mrs. Meade was moaning about her empty entrails one night, and all of a sudden, I found myself fantasizing about a recipe. I'd seen this photo of a "Grand Slam Bridge Dessert" in a cookbook on the library table earlier that afternoon."

"Did it guarantee we'd make our next slam?" Lulu smirked, then went back to erasing. A grand slam was when you took all thirteen tricks. Lulu and I had done it at least four times.

"It was to celebrate our slams. The picture was heaven on earth—a giant, nut-topped meringue torte." My mouth watered even as I recalled it. "That night, with Mrs. Meade groaning, I was in bed next to Kay—who was already asleep—and the torte suddenly danced before my eyes. Four layers of sweet, sugary fluff filled with a thick, custardy vanilla pudding that you make from egg yolks and sour cream and confectioners' sugar."

"You're killing me, Lee-Lung." Lulu had stopped erasing and stared at me.

"That's what the recipe called for. I studied it then and there at the table. But to make it perfection," I hurried on, "I decided I would add two cups of semi-sweet chocolate chips to the filling, and then scatter chocolate chips over the top of the meringue, and bake them right in." My mouth held twice as much water as Manila Bay. I swallowed and continued. "That way they'd melt, spreading dark, chocolatey goodness through and through. And that's how I'm going to make it when we get back to Utica," I concluded, triumphant.

"So that's it? That's when you knew you were really hungry?" Lulu's voice held a note of disbelief. "That one tiny food fantasy that I've had three million of in the last two years?"

"No. Not then," I interrupted. "The next morning. When I woke up and realized I was still hungry and still thinking about the Grand Slam Bridge Dessert. In fact, I'd dreamt about it. I saw myself serving it to my mother and Betty."

"Not me?" Lulu's jaw dropped.

"Sorry—Lulee. I don't know why, but just Mommy and Betty. That was new. Dreaming about food was new."

Suddenly, an idea streaked like a comet before me. "Lulu, maybe I'll start writing a recipe book with all of my ideas. Jot 'em all down quick before liberation and sell it afterwards as *The POW Cookbook: Lee's List of Favorite Foods.*

Lulu's face lit up at the idea of spending endless hours contemplating rich and decadent food. "You should call it *The Captive's Kitchen!*"

"Perfect!" I nodded my agreement. "Perfect. *The Captive's Kitchen.*"

Now I just had to come up with the paper.

Sunday, October 31, 1943

The next day I knelt in the first row of the choir loft with Lulu next to me. The calm, white-washed interior of the Santa Catalina chapel always lifted my spirits. It was such a relief from the never-ending squalor of camp, where too many bodies competed for too little space. And it was such a switch from our old churches in Manila. Most Catholic churches in the city were dark, foreboding places. The stone floors were always filthy. And some Filipina, draped in a lacy black mantilla, rosary in hand, was always crawling up the aisle on her knees, making a disgustingly servile spectacle of herself.

Santa Catalina was different. The Dominican nuns had broken with tradition and built a pretty white wood convent across the street from the giant stone edifice of Santo Tomas. Everything about their chapel radiated light. Tall windows. White walls and ceilings. Luminous quartz floors that were mopped down twice daily. And the sisters wore white too—a snowy tunic and cape, squared white wimple and veil. Some of the older nuns were Spanish, but most were Filipinas, their brown faces and eyes a happy contrast to their habits.

In fact, that's what I noticed about the sisters every time we came here—that they still seemed happy. Even now, after their orderly little convent had been turned into a camp hospital. That's right. It hadn't taken long for us internees or the Japanese to realize that STIC needed more space for the sick, so back in August of last year, the Executive Committee persuaded the sisters to lend their convent out as a hospital, which they did—sending a big group of their nuns to live on the outskirts of Manila. Eight or nine nursing sisters still lived at Santa Catalina, but nowadays their conference rooms were quarantine centers for internees with dengue fever or dysentery or beriberi, and we had even taken over their chapel for our nine o'clock Sunday mass.

The nuns had their own mass at seven-thirty, but a few came to ours at nine o'clock too because they loved our music so much. We had some magnificent voices in our choir, and first-rate direction from a former opera director interned with us, but the music itself drew them in. Our twenty-five-person choir sang original work composed by a Dutch priest, who came into camp with Father Sheridan. Father Visser's music soared and lilted so gracefully that Lulu and I often caught ourselves singing snatches of his Credo and Gloria as we played bridge. At least until Paul and Nellie shushed us so they could concentrate on their hands.

On this Sunday morning, our choir had just finished the "Agnus Dei," and the notes of the prayer for peace hung in the air, a haunting invitation to the Communion rail. That was good because I was hungry.

I shook my head and closed my eyes. This was so pathetic. I couldn't believe that I was actually physically "hungry" for that one tiny wafer of bread they were going to give us for Communion. Maybe I was growing in my faith, I rationalized hopefully, but I knew the truth. Lulu, kneeling next to me, was transfixed too. In fact, every eye in the chapel was riveted to that large round, white host Father Kelly held up as he whispered sacred words.

I tried to yank my thoughts back to lofty spiritual things. The whole gospel today was about Jesus as our King, but his kingdom was not of this world. That didn't comfort me very much because all I longed for right now were things of this world, like BREAD and Grand Slam Bridge Desserts. But the scripture did remind me that Jesus knew what it was like to be a prisoner. He stood flogged and beaten in front of Pilate when he said those things about his kingdom. I was grateful nobody had flogged me so far.

Along with most of the choir, I rose from my kneeling position to go to Communion, when Lulu touched my wrist, and whispered conspiratorially, "Bring some back for me."

I tried to keep a straight face. "Think party," I whispered to her.

Lulu remained kneeling with her head down pretending to pray, but she was smiling. As a non-Catholic, Lulu couldn't go to Communion. Anybody could go to a Catholic mass, and Lulu came almost every Sunday because she loved singing in the choir with me. But communion was only for those who believed the host was truly the body of Jesus, not just a symbol. It was the bread of Eternal Life. I had a lot of reasons to believe that with all my heart today. When I received that host on my tongue, went back to kneel in my pew, and let it dissolve slowly in my mouth, I almost sighed aloud. I felt physically revived.

Fifteen minutes later, after Communion, after the last notes of the final hymn echoed through the chapel, the sisters opened the doors to their convent refectory. With impish grins on their faces, young Sr. Ignacia and kindly old Sr. Nora motioned us forward, ushering eager choir members into their private sanctuary. Squeals of delight and laughter rose all around us as other choir members entered the cheerfully decorated room.

"I am in Heaven," Lulu breathed as we both took in the heart-stopping sight.

"We're in this dream together," I said.

Our eyes were glued to a long, linen-topped table, where three platters overflowed with large wreaths of golden Ritz crackers. This would have been a miracle in and of itself because we hadn't seen crackers in more than a year. But the crackers ringed huge wedges of edam and cheddar cheese—newly cut, we could tell because of their untouched red wax casings. I was mentally stripping the red paraffin away, when I realized that cheese and crackers were just the beginning.

Flanking the cracker trays were tumblers of orange and mango juice, each topped by a sprig of fresh mint and garnished with a cherry. Next to the drinks, fruit platters held spears of papaya, mango, pear-like guava, golden jackfruit, and star-fruit. But the ends of the table completed the bounty. Each held a footed china cake stand: the one on the right heaped with freshly baked hot-cross buns, and the one on the left piled high with "ensiamadas," the traditional snail-shaped cheese brioches that Filipinos loved.

Where to begin? My heart raced and my mouth watered furiously. Lulu had already bolted for the table and I saw Betty moving swiftly in that direction too.

"Leonera, bienvenido!" a smooth Spanish baritone rang out to my left.

I was so enraptured by the food that I scarcely noticed the tall, dark, and handsome owner of that voice nearing. The vaguely familiar young man was not in our choir, nor was he from camp, but he approached me with plate in hand, holding it out to me as if he knew my favorites. Buttery cheddar cheese chunks, Ritz crackers, red cherries and golden mango spears were all artfully arranged. I pretended to know him and eagerly accepted the plate. I did not wait one second to pop the first chunk of cheese into my mouth, all the while puzzling over his brown-blue eyes trying to figure out who he was.

"Have you been to any Gratitude Rallies yet?" he asked, and waved his hand as if waving a flag. "Nippon-go! American come!"

Ramón Ayala. Chubby Ramón from Bordner and Grandma Naylor's! But Ramón wasn't one bit chubby anymore. Broad-shouldered and trim, he seemed easily a head taller than the last time I saw him—seven months earlier in Grandma's living room. Now he smiled confidently at me. His large chestnut eyes were still ringed with that distinctive powder blue edge, framed by impossibly long black lashes, and a lush sweep of straight black brows. High cheek bones, squared jaw, perfectly straight nose, a warm smile and the whitest teeth I had seen in a very long time. He should have been in Hollywood, playing across from Judy Garland.

"Ramón, I can't believe you're here!" I recovered. "You look wonderful. I am just so … sorprendida," I blurted out, remembering to put my adjective ending in the feminine. "Why are you here?"

"Helping the monjitas, the sisters. With all the shortages, it is hard to find crackers or flour or sugar - even butter, but Sr. Ignacia wanted to do this last one thing for all of you. My father still has supplies—so when they asked, of course we helped find these treats."

Ramón's lively demeanor lifted my heart and freed some long-buried bubble of hope and memory. We had been neighbors once, he and I. When I was ten, Ramón's extremely musical family owned the home next door to ours in San Francisco del Monte. At twilight, when the light was golden and the air was soft, my family often sipped cool drinks in our garden patio, waiting for strains of music to float across the hibiscus hedge from his house next door. Ramón, his parents and sisters played a concert every evening, and if we couldn't be on Dewey Boulevard watching the sun set on Manila Bay, our back yard was almost as delightful. Those memories flooded back to me and the sheer beauty of the music in the sunset welled within me and lifted my spirits

"I miss your concerts at twilight. What instrument did you play? The violin?"

"The piano." He pointed his chin to the upright in the corner. "I still do. Maria Luisa, my little sister, plays the violin. But we're not playing outside any more. The Japanese" he still pronounced it *hah-po-NACE*, "took your old house, and if they knew we had such fine instruments, we would not have them much longer."

The Japanese had occupied our old villa with its swimming pool and its tennis courts and its three-foot-deep mosaic tile tub in the main bathroom? That was infuriating.

Ramón just kept up a steady stream of conversation. "Either that, or we would have to invite them to our concerts. Which actually some of them would like." He smiled mischievously.

For a moment, the image of Haruo hunched intensely over the piano flashed before me, but Ramón's vital presence glued me to this time and place. The rest of our conversation was light, magical, animated. I ate the whole time. After wolfing down the entire plate of treats Ramón had prepared for me, we went to the table, where I devoured two hot-cross buns and one ensiamada, feeling truly satisfied for the first time in months. My heart raced. My spirit soared, and a flood tide of joy rose within me.

"Are you going to introduce me to your friend?" Lulu appeared from nowhere.

But I didn't answer right away. *I'll dance with Ramón,* I was thinking. *I'm going to dance with Ramón.* How could I get him into camp? There had to be a way....

Chapter 20
SHALL WE DANCE?

Friday, November 5, 1943

I'd been floating weightless for five days, and it wasn't just because I was starving. Before leaving Santa Catalina, I'd told Ramón about the November nineteenth dance in our newly built pavilion. His eyes lit up. He said he'd never imagined breaking into a prison camp—especially for the social life—but he could try. On Fridays, his family delivered duck eggs, limes, and whatever medicines they could scrounge to the sisters. If he made the delivery run, Ramón thought he could slip into camp for the dance that night.

Was that even possible? I got goose bumps just thinking about it, but Santa Catalina had been incorporated into the camp with two high-board partitions forming a corridor across the street to the main campus. In a tower between the two facilities, a Japanese guard stood watch to ensure that only authorized internees came and went. Ramón said one of the guards was friendly to him, and he thought he could sneak in.

"If you have such courage as to smuggle money for your family into camp," he said, "I could smuggle myself in and out for an evening dance."

Had Grandma Naylor told him about the money I'd snuck in? Well, I didn't mind that he knew. His eyes had swept my form with such admiration that afternoon, my heart did joyful somersaults.

"That was seven months ago." I'd shrugged. "And I was shaking like a leaf. You should've seen me when I stood at the gate, and Bugs Bunny Guard was staring at my skirt."

"You are a lioness, Leonera. I'm sure you stood fierce and proud—just like your name."

My cheeks burned. "Actually, did you know my name is *Leonore* and not 'Leonera'? *Leonore* comes from the Greek 'Eleanor'—which means 'light' not lion." I sounded like an English teacher in search of a classroom, but Ramón's hot chocolate gaze made me self-conscious. And my father had explained the exact meaning of my burdensome name to me many times.

"You are both light and lioness," Ramón insisted. "In Spanish, 'leonera' means lion's den. You have lion in you. And besides, look at your wild, curly hair—a lion's mane."

He pushed one of my unruly curls off my forehead. When he left, I could still feel where he touched my brow. I floated back to camp that afternoon with a happy heart and satisfied stomach, thinking about exactly one thing: the dance on Friday, November nineteenth.

Saturday, November 6, 1943

"This is as close to being a Vanderbilt as I'll ever get," I told Lulu, as we tied on our pinnies with their faded V monograms and frayed oak leaf crests.

Our girls' basketball team, the Vanderbilts, was named after the wealthy American family that claimed the oak as their family symbol. Mrs. Baskerville, head of the internee Sewing Committee, whipped up these pinnies for our team a year and a half ago when cloth was still plentiful in Manila and imaginations lively. Nowadays, we needed ration coupons to buy fabric, and it was a big deal to make a new blouse, skirt, or playsuit. Nobody wasted much time embroidering oak leaves into the letter V.

"Speak for yourself, Lee-lung. When I'm at UCLA, I might snag one," she mused, as she tied her shoe. "Mary Louella Vanderbilt has a lovely ring to it, don't you think?"

"Lulu, Vanderbilts don't go to UCLA. You have to come east—Vassar or

Smith, then you'll be close enough to snag Mr. V at Harvard or Yale, and I'll be right around the corner at Cornell."

Lulu's family, the Clelands, were from California, but since my family was from Utica, I'd stay closer to home for college. One thing was for sure: we were both leaving the PI after the war was over, *if the war was ever over...* My stomach growled.

"Are there any Vanderbilts at Cornell? I could go there and we could room together."

"I don't think so. But you could still go there and we could still room together."

Lulu and I had no idea if we could ever get into the prestigious colleges, but talking about it gave us something *besides food* to dream about. In fact, lots of our STIC girls' basketball teams were named after high-end women's colleges: Our "Vassar" team squared off regularly against "Wellesley," and our "Bryn Mawr" took on "Smith."

We didn't stick to elite women's colleges for names either. Our gang's Vanderbilt team—named for the plutocrat family, not the college founded by the plutocrat family—challenged teams like the Rockefellers and Astors—about whom, we knew next to nothing except that they had gorgeous mansions on Fifth Avenue, lavish "cottages" in Newport, and moolah to spare. That sounded like our pre-war, ex-pat life, so we liked that idea and pretended we were one of them. It made up for having to play a sport we had no interest in.

Early into internment, the grown-up powers that be decreed that we teens must participate daily in one sport after classes. This was part of their never-ending quest to keep us so busy we could cause no trouble whatsoever. Lulu and I chose basketball because Nellie was good at it, and she really wanted us to join her team. Which says a lot about Nellie's big heart, because the only part of basketball Lulu and I excelled at was putting on the pinafores. Other than that, we were terrible. My attempt at a layup usually ended in a lay-out—of me splat on the court.

Nellie, on the other hand, had been throwing softballs with her dad, dribbling basketballs with her brother, and practicing her two-hand set shot since she was five. She was as skillful on the court as she was in Latin class, and was so unfailingly kind and humble, that of course, we all elected her Captain. With her blonde hair bobby-pinned neatly off her face, navy shorts cinching a tiny waist, and open-collared blouse topped by the V pinny, she was the epitome of Wholesome American Girl.

"OK, girls—listen up. Here's the schedule," Nellie squinted at the clipboard in her hand, the basketball roster's clip glinting silver in the nearly blinding sunlight. "The boys lead off this afternoon. It's Sioux versus Cherokee at 2 PM, then Iroquois against the Crow at 2:45, then Vanderbilts are up at 3:30, and we're taking on the Cabots. Tomorrow it's the Lodges. You can go wherever you want till 3:25, or stick around and watch the boys."

Hoots and whistles rose instantly from our six-girl team.

"Is that even a choice?" June Darien called out. "We're starting with the Sioux, and I'm crazy for Crazy Horse!"

"Woo-woo-wooh," we all swooned in unison. "Crazy Horse" was the nickname for June's sometimes "Sioux" boyfriend, seventeen-year-old Jack Aaron.

"They're playing shirts and skins, and I'm betting the Sioux are barebacked," Lulu shouted.

Awash in almost-sixteen-year-old silliness, we six girls seated ourselves next to the university's only basketball court. This hard-pack dirt court on the southeast corner of the front lawn was installed just before our internment, and was getting a workout by both genders.

Sure enough, the seventeen-year-old Sioux boys were skins that day. Lulu and I sat next to each other, bumping shoulders in companionable delight, enchanted with the spectacle of rippling muscles and broad shoulders on the older boys. Some of the guys were painfully skinny, but not all. The seventeen-year-olds who boxed still boasted solid, if thinning, forms.

Sitting cross-legged and courtside, Lulu and I tried to forget it was four hours till dinner by humming upbeat rhythms, rocking against each other, and putting the boys' game to Fred Astaire's music. I sang a line from his song, and Lulu kept the beat with an improvised basketball command.

"*Shall we dance? Or keep on moping?*" I led off.

"Dribble!"

"*Shall we dance and walk on air?*"

"Pass!"

"*Shall we give in to despair or shall we dance with never a care?*"

Jump, jump, jump! Take the shot now!

"*Life is short. We're growing older.*"

Dribble!

Don't you be an 'also-ran.'

Pass. Pass!

You better dance little lady, dance little man.

Sink the jump shot!

Dance whenever you can! We both crooned that final line heartily as we could, jostling and bobbing happily, and everyone ignored us, riveted to the boys.

The guys really did play a fast-paced, tap-dance of a game - the way they hustled down the court, tossing rhythmically, heaving the long passes till they closed in on the net. Then one gaunt frame would float up to sink the basket. *That's the only good thing about starving,* I thought. *Nothing to weigh you down on the layup.*

We cheered loudly when our own Bill Philips sank his shot. Our boy Bill was not particularly tall, but he was great at this game which involved timing, rhythm, and teamwork more than height. How fifteen-year-old Bill got to play with the seventeen-year-old Sioux today, I don't know, but Bill managed to pull off lots of unusual feats—most of which had to do with impressing Nellie.

"Wouldn't you love to see Ramón, out there?" Lulu poked me with her elbow and pumped me for as many details about my new love-light as I could remember.

"So, how'd you meet him again?"

"I already told you." I focused on the game.

"Tell me again. I like that story." Out of the corner of my eye, I saw her impish grin.

"When we lived just outside Manila, he was our San Francisco del Monte neighbor. He and his family played a concert in their garden next door to ours every night at twilight. AND, he was my classmate at Bordner."

"Your chubby classmate…" Lulu chided.

"Right. Nice guy, but I never thought he was my type."

"Nobody has a type in eighth grade. You have to be at least fifteen years old to have a type. So, what's your type, Lee-lung?"

Lulu knocked into my shoulder playfully, but our eyes remained on the basketball action. Ten sets of shoes raced to the rhythm of a fast dribble. The guys darted to the other end of the court. Lulu's question still hung in the humid autumn air, so I closed my eyes and inhaled deeply.

"Tall… dark… handsome…. Musical. Romantic. Writes me poetry. Brings me flowers…."

"What kind?"

"Red roses," I answered without hesitation. "Like the ones they grow in Baguio. Not the floppy orange-red hibiscus you find around here."

"Picky, picky…"

"And gardenias too … don't you love snowy white gardenias? Their perfume? So elegant."

"Does Lee's Type need to play basketball?"

"Hah! Never. But he needs to be able to dance. Better than I do, I hope."

"Well, let's rack our brains now: Ramón Ayala compared to 'Lee's Type.' Is he tall, dark, and handsome? Check, check, check. Musical? A classically trained pianist, right? Check." Halting abruptly, Lulu turned full face toward me and inspiration lit her features. "Lee, he can play *Leonore's Suite* for you! Hasn't it been almost a whole year since you've heard it?"

The Sioux and Cherokee rushed past us again, scattering small stones from the earthen court as they flew by, but I could only stare at Lulu. Why hadn't I thought of that? As we moved closer to Thanksgiving, the one-year anniversary of my father's death, approached. Lulu and I had uncovered that horrible news on Thanksgiving Day just one year ago, but it seemed like forever now.

I thought of Daddy living for me now in the gently pulsing star of the Southern Cross or sometimes when "Deep Purple" came over the loudspeaker. "In the mist of a memory, you wander back to me." I just loved that song about lovers reunited, "here in my deep purple dreams." But in real life, my father's love for me only burned brightly when released from the pages of *Leonore's Suite*, now buried in my bedframe drawer.

Could Ramón bring Daddy and my music to life, as Haruo had nearly a year ago? My heart vaulted at the thought. Wasn't there an upright piano in the refectory of the Sister's convent? I'm sure I saw one there during the Christ the King party. He could get in there easily and I bet Sr. Ignacia would let me in there too. Maybe that's where Ramón could play it for me.

"Remember Operation Arigato?" Lulu asked.

"It was your finest hour," I said, already planning the next performance.

"You ain't seen nothin' yet, Lee-Lung. At the dance, we'll get that music to Ramón, and he can play it for you. Now, about the other *Lee's-type* requirements."

Did Ramón write poetry? Who knew? Lulu was convinced Ramón had to be a good dancer, though. Didn't those Spaniards invent the flamenco? Yup. He was a good dancer, alright. Did I know how to dance? Basic swing, of course. Lulu and I decided we'd better put on our dancing shoes and start practicing. Right after the Vanderbilts trounced the Cabots.

November 9, 1943

My mother persuaded twenty-eight-year-old Maurice Naftaly, a Russian-born American Jew interned with us, to offer dancing lessons at the Children's Pavilion after school. Maurice's family had emigrated to the United States when he was five, and like my own Russian-Jewish father, he'd grown up in

New York City before making his way to the PI. His family even knew the popular songwriters, Israel Beilin and Isidore Gershowitz, who by that time had changed their names to Irving Berlin and Ira Gershwin. Can you say: "Alexander's Ragtime Band" or "Embraceable You"?

Our quick-witted dancing teacher told us that growing up in the Yiddish theater district in the twenties was like being a spoiled pup in a wild, close-knit pack. Jewish geniuses Jerome Kern, Oscar Hammerstein, Richard Rodgers (whose father had changed his name from Abrahams) and Lorenz Hart were composing, and the rest of the world was dancing. Waltz, swing, jitterbug, and foxtrot—Maurice knew them all.

The number of girls who signed up for Mr. Naftaly's little class exceeded the number of boys. But eager to dazzle Nellie, Bill Phillips had joined Bunny, Lulu, and me. Paul Davis decided to come along too, insisting that he was already "Astaire Out East," but he wouldn't mind polishing his skills. Curtis Brooks came (but not Barney) and we all thought that was because Squeaky was sweet on Bunny, and hoped to dance with her. Paul's little sister Annie tagged along, so that meant Betty did too. When Maurice fired up the phonograph with his 78 RPM of "In the Mood," we forgot about being hungry prisoners, and let Glenn Miller's fox trot whisk us off to the ballrooms of our imaginations.

Gee, I loved Glenn Miller. Even though he was thirty-eight-years-old when the war broke out and didn't have to enlist, the famous bandleader had joined the U.S. army. The army put him in charge of re-fashioning military bands and entertaining our boys in Europe. Those lucky GIs in London listened to him live on a regular basis.

"Slow-slow-quick-quick." Maurice was instructing us in the fox trot, as we uncertain teen couples did our best on the pavilion's dirt floor. I was paired with my buddy Paul. "Gentlemen, right hand higher on the back of your partner. Near her shoulder blade not her hip."

"I'm no good at being noble," Paul called out, parroting a line from *Casablanca*, and every boy in the room snickered. Still, Paul obliged, and locked me into a high stance embrace with our hands held high.

Lulu was paired with Bill Phillips, who didn't know anything about dancing but was an athlete, and had natural grace on the dance floor. Bunny and Curtis Brooks were partners, as were Annie and Betty, but Maurice was going to cut in every so often and take the lead for each of them.

"Ladies, watch the toe release. Get ready to turn on the slow-slow. Gentlemen, raise your left arm on the quick-quick, signaling the ladies' turn for the slow-slow. And she turns and… "

Paul and I did a flawless twirl, and so did Lulu and Bill, but Bunny and Squeaky collided to our right, and Betty and Annie spun smack into each other on our left, landing on the unforgiving hard pack amid hoots and giggles. Glenn Miller didn't notice. He kept right on playing but we could hardly stop laughing.

Three hours later, though, we considered ourselves experts. I imagined myself in Ramón's arms, floating off to another world. November nineteenth couldn't come fast enough for me.

Chapter 21
THE TEMPEST

Sunday, November 14, 1943

Mommy and Flossie were making fudge like maniacs, and that meant Betty and I were roped into every spare minute. Four stomachs growled, protesting the injustice of cooking a bubbly sweet treat we could not eat.

"Agnes, how long can we keep up this pace?" Flossie stirred the molten chocolate on the charcoal stove, wiping her brow with the back of her forearm. We'd used empty coffee cans for pots, and one of them sat on the ground cooling, while Flossie stirred the second, and Mommy mixed up a third batch. On this cloud-darkened afternoon, a damp breeze blew through our three-sided shanty.

"Just till Christmas, then it's over," my mother replied, glancing at the leaden sky above.

"We'll be sprung by then?" Betty's hope sprang from an inexhaustible well. She spooned daubs of chocolate on to trays, and didn't even look up as she asked her question. I loaded the hardened fudge into tightly sealed tins that Grandma Naylor had scrounged for us, and glanced in Mommy's direction.

"No, pet," my mother said. "We'll just be out of sugar and chocolate by then. Out for good. But with any luck the Red Cross kits will be our gift from Santa."

Betty stopped what she was doing and looked at me thunderstruck. Her eyes said: *What? No liberation for my birthday? Did you know this?* I looked away, and concentrated on filling my tin.

I did know. But I'd been too head-over-heels for Ramón to despair, especially with the dance just five days away. Besides, the camp rumor-mill was always pushing back the date of our liberation. Two weeks ago, our hidden camp radio confirmed that the Allied push across the Pacific had stalled.

Bill Phillips, whose dad had access to the radio, told us the Japs had sent fresh troops to the Solomons and were fighting to the death on every island. So in camp, exhilarating rumors that we'd be out by Christmas had been exchanged for sugar plums visions of Red Cross "Comfort Kits." They'd bring tins of Spam, corned beef, and bars of chocolate for sure. Maybe tubs of oleomargarine and more KLIM, the milk substitute too.

STIC's new English-speaking commandant, Konichi Kato, stood in for Santa Claus this year. Commandant Kato assured the Executive Committee that Red Cross packages were on a ship in Manila harbor and would be distributed for Christmas. A former Japanese consul in London, Kato had replaced Kodaki at the end of October and seemed like a decent guy. He'd been interned at Kensington House in London at the start of the war. "I bear no ill will toward British or Americans," he'd told the camp, and confided to Mr. Grinnell (who told the Room Monitors) that his time at Kensington House "was very, very nice. I had two eggs for breakfast every morning."

Well, lah-dee-dah, Commandant Kato. We starving internees would like hen fruit for breakfast every morning too. More than one of us had that thought as we ate our lugao, a thin rice gruel.

"Girls, let's wrap up here," Mommy directed abruptly. "I don't like the way this wind is rising. Flossie, pull the pots and douse the fire." The wind had become a small gale and skies darkened ominously.

"Agnes, if we pull these cans now, the fudge will harden and we'll need to reheat, re-melt and re-mold," Flossie objected.

"If we don't pull them, we're going to lose everything." My mother could be very stern when she was in one of her increasingly frequent no-nonsense moods. Flossie complied. "Lee and Betty, take everything—finished and unfinished fudge—into the Big House and get it under Lulu's bed upstairs on the second floor. If this is a typhoon, the first floor might take water," my mother continued.

I froze in disbelief. November was a funny month in the Philippines. Clear blue skies often greeted us, but just as frequently, banks of leaden clouds hovered, bringing high humidity and rain. Then from nowhere a major typhoon could descend.

I helped Betty get her gooey chocolate into an unoccupied tin. There were still six days before the dance. I consoled myself with that thought. Everything would be cleaned up and back to normal by Friday.

* * *

It had been a rain-spattered late afternoon, turned black as night well before dusk, and the wind howled violently as we prepared for bed.

Hope whipped off her blouse and tugged a frayed, white nightgown over her head. She was standing right in front of our un-curtained ground floor window, but apparently didn't care who saw her - or maybe she thought that on this stormy night not even the Japanese guards wasted time peeping.

"Number Four? That's ridiculous." Hope's hard-edged dismissal cut through the buzz of voices and reassured me. I could see the outline of her bony arms under her nightie, unclasping her bra, and whipping it out like a pocket hanky from under the gown. The camp rumor mill was working overtime on this storm, and many hand-wringers predicted the worst. "We are not going to get a Number 4 typhoon."

Hope was used to calming fifth graders with that authoritative tone, but nobody else seemed quite so sure that we'd dodge disaster. A Number 4 typhoon was a calamity, as bad as you could get—with winds blowing over 120 miles per hour. I had never been in one that bad.

"It does not matter, Hope, darlin'" Kay drawled. She was stowing her clothes in our shared drawers. "We are not doin' our Christmas shoppin' tomorrow anyway. In fact, I believe I have nowhere in particular to go."

Kay still possessed her sense of humor and her drawl. If I had to share a bed with anyone, I was glad it was Kay. Kay had promised me her brightly colored skirt for the dance—one with red and white roses.. We had cinched it in the waist to fit me perfectly. She sank onto the large wooden bed beside me now, and our overstuffed kapok mattress rustled as we both settled in for the night.

"Aren't you leading the Swat-a-Fly campaign in the Annex kitchen?" I reminded her—only half in jest. Kay worked like a beaver, and she actually was supposed to be in charge of fly-swatting at the Annex tomorrow. Lulu and I had been conscripted to help too.

"I'll either be swattin' or swimmin'." A resigned smile flitted across her face, as she closed her eyes. "The possibilities are endless."

I sure hoped those flies would feel our wrath tomorrow because I didn't want to think about what a typhoon could do to my well-laid dance plans.

The bed Kay and I shared was right next to the window, and I usually liked that because I could look out and see the Southern Cross above me, and talk to my father. But tonight the glass was rain-streaked and a fierce, gusty wind pelted the panes.

A plague upon this howling! I heard the line echo in my head. Some sailor shouted that during the storm in The Tempest, which we were studying in English II. He had it right. I felt for the wooden rosary Rosalina had given me nearly two years *ago*, and pressed the sharp-edged cross into the palm of my hand. "Lord, please protect us and let this noisy storm just peter out," I prayed and fell asleep surprisingly quickly.

In the middle of the night, I awoke in a clammy nightgown to pandemonium. The wind charged the glass like an approaching train, and the rain drove its way right into Room 4 through the frames of the windows, as if someone had left the glass wide open. Our mosquito netting, my night clothes, and our shared reed mattress were now soaking wet. Kay stirred beside me, sleeping, still oblivious to the chaos. I nudged her, but even as I did other women near the windows were stirring, shrieking their dismay, and my Room Monitor Mother awoke.

Mommy shouted directions over the bedlam. "Somebody turn on a light!"

From near the door came the reply. "The power's off, Agnes. No lights."

"All right everybody up! Ladies! Wake up! Move all the beds away from the windows and to the center of the room."

This was not easy because every woman in that room stored her whole life under her bed. Boxes, baskets, and straw maletas filled with treasured possessions had to be shoved along with cots toward the beehive cluster of bedding in the center of the room. By now Kay was awake and though soggy like me, leapt to the side of our sturdy framed bed and motioned me to come alongside her to help shove. Kay didn't shout because I couldn't have heard her over the gale. A rising chorus of moans rose from the center of the room as women roused themselves to wakefulness and staggered to action.

Even in the chaos and confusion, though, every woman there seemed to awake with purpose, putting shoulder to the task, and moving with determination rather than complaint.

STIC is always best in time of emergency, I thought and marveled at how easily we moved together like a single organism.

Hope had finished moving her cot, and hurried over to help Kay and me. "No Lady Macbeth to complain!" Hope shouted in my ear. That was it! No Mrs. Randolph Meade to insist that she could not possibly move her precious self! I smiled for the first time that night.

Thursday, November 18, 1943

Three days later it was still hard to believe: we *did* get a number four typhoon. On Monday and Tuesday, the rain fell in relentless sheets and winds tore through the camp, uprooting trees, downing power lines, leveling shanties, washing out vegetable gardens, and sending a foot of standing water into the entire compound, including the first floor of the Big House. Before the storm, some families had been sleeping outside in the shanties, but by midnight all of them—hundreds of them—had crowded into the Main Building seeking shelter. They filled its corridors with new bodies clutching hastily retrieved bedding. There wasn't a dry, quiet, or uncrowded space in all of Santo Tomas. The smell of unwashed bodies mingled with odor of raw sewage unleashed from broken pipes.

The storm had savaged power lines and even toppled the steel towers that supported the power lines. With gas and electricity off, Manila's water filtering plant failed, so no tap water could be used for drinking. Now all drinking water had to be boiled, and water pressure was so low that there was not enough water to flush toilets. We had to bring buckets of water into the bathroom to flush with us each time we went to the bathroom. Meanwhile, drowned pigs, slithering snakes, scrawny rats, and even a five-foot python came floating into camp. A *baby* python, everybody said, but Jumpin' Jiminy Crickets—a mammal-swallowing python came into camp! The men got rid of it and I don't even want to know how.

On Tuesday, it was still raining, and I was heading for the bathroom, bucket of filthy water in hand. I paused for a moment next to Hope, who was watching the men build cooking fires on a high stone base in a protected corner of the west patio. Water swirled around them, but they worked on, and Hope's face was full of wonder.

"Hard working, aren't they?" I said looking at the tireless men who had built the makeshift base, and grateful for the chance to put down my buckets for a minute.

"Unbelievable. Do you see them swimming like that?"

Nobody was swimming, but I followed Hope's gaze to the muddy surface water and then I saw it. Hundreds of them. Agitated swarms of displaced ants paddling frantically in the water, seeking a dry surface just like the rest of us.

"Their nests are at ground level," my school teacher friend pointed out. "So in monsoon season they have to rebuild with the rest of us." Hope seemed mesmerized, but I abhorred all creepy, crawly things.

"Well, I'm not shedding one tear of pity for those ants, Hope Miller. If I had any kerosene, I'd go over there right now and put them out of their misery!"

Just then one of Hope's fifth graders raced up to her and announced breathlessly, "Mrs. Miller, the playhouse is all caved in! A giant acacia fell right through the roof!"

"I know, Jimmy," Hope nodded, brow furrowed as she glanced over at the Annex. "We'll rebuild it."

My heart broke at the irony of it all. One of the few trees in the patio that the men had not yet chopped down for firewood had crashed through the thatched roof of the new Children's Pavilion, where, of course, the dance was supposed to be on Friday. If Mrs. Hildegaard Jones, my English II teacher were here, she would call that a "metaphor." A tree crashing right through the one pavilion of hope in my life. There would be no dance any time soon.

I knew better than to mention my disappointment to my mother. Since the rain continued, all our cots were still pushed together in the center of the room. Tempers flared at the slightest provocation.

Despite my mother's best efforts to create neat eight-inch aisles between the beds, trip hazards abounded and the "all for one and one for all" spirit of that first night had been replaced by "Grapes of Wrath." Mommy had to break up more than one cat fight, but when Mrs. Turner accused Dodie Peterson of stealing her cigarettes and intentionally slashing her mosquito netting, there was almost a whole room brawl. It took Agnes Iserson standing on a soap box, and brandishing her tape measure and waving a newly found pack of smokes, to quiet Mrs. Turner, induce an apology and restore order.

On Wednesday, the skies remained gray, but the rains ended, and at about eleven AM, the PA system announced the return of electricity, blaring "Happy Days Are Here Again," over the loudspeaker, while internees cheered wearily. Days of mopping, dredging, and rebuilding lay head. Many shanties were simply lost, but ours was salvageable. Mommy got the little charcoal stove back in place and what remained of our fudge business staggered back to life.

Thursday, November 18, 1943

My mother could not understand why on Thursday afternoon when the worst was long over, I was sitting glum and immobile on the edge of my still-damp bed in Room 4. Mommy, Betty, and I had returned to the Big House to retrieve some cooking utensils.

"Lee, I know we've been through a tough time, but the worst is over now, and you need to snap out of this funk. I need your help," my mother pronounced.

"She's moping about Ramón Ayala," Betty said, and I glared at my little sister. I vowed that was the very last time I would ever share a secret with Boops. Even at almost-fourteen, she could not be trusted.

"He was going to come in for the dance tomorrow," said Betty, "and now there is no dance. Annie and I think he asked Haruo to sneak him in."

"What?" my mother's eyes widened and she turned the full force of her incredulous stare right at me. "You asked Haruo to sneak Ramón Ayala into this camp?"

"No!" I was as horrified as she was. "I did not! I just told Ramón about the dance, and he said he had a Japanese guard friend, who could probably get him in."

"And you encouraged that? You led Ramón to believe that it was all right to break into this camp for a dance?"

I was dumb-struck. Well, I didn't *dis*courage him—that was true. But he had suggested it.

"Do you know how many people are trying to get into this camp right now?" My mother raged in disbelief.

I shook my head. Was she serious? What kind of idiots were trying to break into a prison camp?

"Hundreds!" she spat. "More than five hundred men here have Filipino wives and children desperate to get INTO this camp because Manila is a nightmare. Food riots. Kempeitai raids. They're pleading, they're desperate, and every day our Executive Committee has to tell them NO. We don't have enough room. We don't have enough supplies!"

Now, Betty had come alongside me and stared at our raving mother. "Mommy, it wasn't like that. Ramón wasn't going to stay," she tried to interject on my behalf. I was grateful my little sister stepped in because Mommy was always gentler with Betty. "Ramón was just coming in for the dance, and then he would have snuck right out again. He's sweet on Lee," Betty said, "And besides, we need him because there aren't enough boys who dance."

Sometimes Boop's innocence pushed even my mother over the edge. She clapped two hands over her eyes, and sank on to the cot across from us, struggling to get hold of her emotions. The next time she spoke, it was in a dangerously low voice.

"Girls, what you almost did was life-threatening for everyone involved. If Ramón had been caught, he could've been jailed and tortured at Fort Santiago!"

"Why?" I demanded. She was being ridiculous and I could not grasp her fury or outrage.

"The Japanese would consider him a spy for the Filipino resistance, passing or seeking information from contacts in camp. They would not have wasted one thought on puppy love!" My mother rushed on, "If Haruo had been caught helping him enter, the best friend we have among the guards would've been slapped down publicly, thrashed to an inch of his life, and then sent to the Solomons on the front lines. And Lee, if anyone knew that *you* had encouraged this, I would've been held responsible, and as your mother and Room Monitor, our entire room might have suffered repercussions—cuts in food rations or hours of standing at attention at roll call in the sun!"

"Nobody would've found out, Mommy—it was just a dance," I muttered. But she raged on.

"Just a dance? Is that what you think? The one thing I can do right now is resign as Room Monitor, and spend more time being your mother, so that reckless, addle-brained schemes like this do not come up in the future!"

She looked around at the crowded cots and disheveled swaths of mosquito netting and clothes strewn everywhere. "You girls need to understand that we are prisoners of war. We have been spared much of the worst so far, but if we do *anything* the Japanese think suspicious, we could be jailed at Fort Santiago. We could be tortured or raped. We could be killed." She paused and glared at us. "We are not guests at a summer camp!" Her green eyes blazed fury. My mother had turned forty in August, and at that moment, she looked every year of her advancing age.

"Leonore, when you go to church on Sunday," she concluded with one last round of unspent rage, "you should spend a great deal of time on your knees, *thanking God* for that typhoon!"

***

Mommy's explosion contained so many bombshells that it took me a while to defuse them all in my mind. Filipinos were trying to get into camp? That was news to me. But the next day I learned that a group of our American men who had Filipino wives and children on the outside had petitioned the Commandant to admit their wives and children. They had been trying to get them admitted even before the typhoon, but the storm had made everything more desperate. It had wiped out homes and crops, flooded basements and bodegas full of grain and sugarcane, and even medical supplies. Internees who had their shanties near the edge of the compound complained their things were being stolen by Filipinos hopping the wall at night to see what we had. I remembered how eager I had been to return to camp after just one night on the outside in May. Now all the Filipinos knew the secret: camp was safer than the outside.

My mother's resignation as Room Monitor met with surprise and some resistance. Despite what I considered her sternness, Mommy was admired in our room for her impartiality. Twenty-three women wrote a letter of protest, asking her to re-consider, but when Agnes Iserson made up her mind about something, it was made up. Mommy did not tell our roommates what prompted her resignation, just that the typhoon had reminded her how precious our family was, and that she needed to be more available for Betty and me. (She didn't say "for my addle-brained daughters.")

Two days later, the thirty-eight adult women in our room (Betty and I couldn't vote) elected Mrs. Linda Lee Todd of Mobile, Alabama to the next three-month term as Room Monitor.

Big-boned and soft-spoken Mrs. Todd was grandmotherly benevolence and sugar-coated despot rolled into one. She began her term by thanking "our dear Agnes" for all her "hahd work" and assuring "you sweet girls" that "Room Four is your home, and I shall strive to keep it that way." Then she smiled, lit up a cigarette, and a blue cloud of benevolence instantly ringed her large cherubic face.

Chapter 22
UNDANCED DANCE

Sunday November 21, 1943

I knelt in one of the pews of Santa Catalina chapel. Father Sheridan had said it was OK if I stayed to pray for a few minutes after mass, while he cleaned up the sacristy. I was definitely not on my knees thanking God for the typhoon. I knelt before the cross, telling Him that I didn't like his timing, and was really disappointed about how He wasn't working things out with Ramón ... or my mother. Then I was going to follow Father Sheridan's advice from religion class and "humbly beseech the Lord" to change all that.

Sr. Ignacia touched me on the shoulder. "This is for you, Lee."

The young nun did not look me in the eye, but tugged from her white sleeve an envelope emblazoned "Leonera" in looping script. My heart hammered so loudly that I thought she must hear it, but Sr. Ignacia just genuflected at the altar and turned back to the refectory.

I clutched the envelope and stared at the cross. This happened to me with God sometimes. I would be complaining to Him about something—complaining and "beseeching" constituted most of my usual communication with the Almighty—and then some normal everyday thing happened that turned out to be kind of an answer. Lulu and I had talked about this, and decided you had to be alert for answers, because God used codes—kind of like Nancy Drew. He wasn't sending the obvious messages that I longed for.

What I wouldn't give for one loud thunderclap followed by a snowy white dove floating down with a message in its beak that began: "Dear Lee, Meet Ramón at the gate" and ended "Thinking of you, God." Well, this might be it!

All these chaotic thoughts went through my mind as I eased myself back on to the pew, and gingerly fingered the envelope that had to be from Ramón. No one else called me "Leonera." Hot tears welled in my eyes.

I didn't want to open it. What could he tell me? "Sorry I couldn't come to the dance. I hope you realize it was cancelled." How pathetic.

On the other hand, I ached to open it. Was he as heartbroken as I was? I considered waiting to read it, but at least here in the chapel, I'd have privacy. When I slipped an index finger underneath the flap, the envelope opened easily. Good. Ripping an envelope from Ramón would be a crime. I unfolded three crisp pages, full of text. The carefully inked letters were small as if he'd tried to fit more on these pages than he had room for.

November 20, 1943

Dear Leonera,

Forgive my Spanish nickname for you one more time. Remember you are part lioness and that will sustain you. I am sad not to have seen you on Friday. Our home in the hills endured the storm, but we had no electricity or gas, and I could imagine the ruin at Santo Tomas. I knew there was no dance. I played piano in our family library for a while —then I looked to books to distract me. I wanted to read adventure, but I pulled poetry instead. Ruben Darío. Do you know him? He is a poet I like and admire.

I actually *had* heard of Ruben Darío. In Spanish II, Father Monte taught us a unit on "Poets of the Americas," and Ruben Darío was from Nicaragua. Darío wrote a simple poem about the "Three Kings" that I liked a lot - maybe because I could understand it and translate it easily, and that didn't happen often in Spanish. Still, I couldn't believe Ramón was writing me about poetry. I loved poetry.

> *I read his poem about autumn, and it made me sadder because in the first verse Darío describes a lonely dreamer, who watches clouds go by, just like me. But the second verse lifted my spirit and reminded me of you. He wrote (if I don't translate poorly):*
>
>> *'In the pale afternoon*
>> *A friendly fairy maiden comes to me*
>> *... with the spell and music of the moon,*
>> *And from her I learned what wonder the birds sing,*
>> *And what the breezes bring over the sea,*
>> *All that lies hidden in the mist or gleams,*
>> *A fleeting presence, in a young girl's dreams.'*

Now my eyes brimmed with tears, and I reached into my skirt pocket for the embroidered hanky that Hope had given me. Never in my life had anyone compared me—curly headed, muddy-eyed Lee Iserson, to a fairy maiden who could weave the spell and music of the moon. Or teach the song that birds sing or .... Now I couldn't even see the page through my tears. Something about breezes from the ocean.

I closed my eyes and let tears roll down my cheeks, then quickly dried them because I didn't want them splotching Ramón's fountain pen ink. With a sniffle, I turned to the second page.

> *So you see, Leonera, here I am the dreamer and you are the autumnal fairy, and you bring me beauty and hope. Those I will need because my family has decided to return to Spain.*

Did I get punched in the stomach? My breath came hard and fast, but I forced my eyes back to the text.

> *Spain is neutral in the war, so there is no fighting there. The civil war in my country drove my family out years ago, but that is over. My parents say it is better now for our family to return to Madrid and build a new life in our homeland. Better than to stay in war-torn Manila.*

I knew the Ayalas had three children, two younger than Ramón, and they needed to protect themselves as best they could, but still—leave their beautiful home in Manila?

I turned the page. Ramón said how hard it was for their family to continue living where there was so little food, order, and safety. His family had money and connections, and they could travel to Spain because the Japanese didn't care what the Spanish did. Of course, Ramon wrote, they planned to leave all that they could to the nuns. I turned to his third page:

> *Leonera, the two brightest days for me in the last two years have been seeing you at Mrs. Naylor's and talking to you at the party of Christ the King. To me, you have been a shining light, "the spell and music of the moon," a language of hope. Stay strong, Leonera. Be a lioness. Roar as you can. I am looking forward to receiving a first edition (bound in leather, I hope) of the Captive's Kitchen when the war ends. It will end. "Nippongo. American come!"*
>
> *Yours,*
Ramón

Yours, he signed. *Yours.* But he wasn't mine. Scalding tears blinded me and while I blinked them back, an outraged voice inside me screamed at the injustice of it all, and all the opportunities I had missed.

Seven years ago. I was in fourth grade when Ramón's family moved into that house next door to ours, and we heard strains of heavenly music floating over the hibiscus hedge. The next day at Bordner, our teacher introduced us to our new classmate: chubby-cheeked Ramón Ayala.

And right through eighth grade, I hadn't given him a second thought, but he'd been there all along! Now, he would never play *Leonore's Suite* for me in the refectory of Santa Catalina. He would never even be here again. I sat there, staring at the empty altar and the cross.

"Ready to head back, Lee?" I hadn't heard Father Sheridan come out of the sacristy, but he stood beside me now, hand on my shoulder. I looked up at him grief-stricken, and my once redheaded, now graying priest-hero knelt down in the aisle next to me, and stared at the open letter. "Not the answer you were hoping for?" he prompted gently.

I shook my head. "No…" was all I could muster.

Saturday, December 4, 1943

Two weeks after the typhoon, camp was staggering back to life. But on Thursday, Lulu's youngest sister, two-year-old Maureen had awakened feverish, struggling to breathe, her neck swollen. That "bull neck" was a dead give-away for diphtheria, the horrible respiratory disease caused by overcrowding—so many people sleeping, breathing and coughing in the same rooms. Little kids sometimes died of diphtheria because we couldn't treat it in camp. Mim rushed to the Release Committee, got a medical pass, and the two were whisked off in the bus to San Lazaro Isolation Hospital in Manila.

Lulu had been on pins and needles for two days waiting to hear from them, but now she was jubilant. "Mouse is OK! Daddy's OK! They're hunky-dory!" she enthused.

A wonderful note from her mother had come through the package line: Maureen was going to live. But that wasn't the end of my best friend's postal jackpot from the rare Red Cross Mail delivery. Lulee got a three-month-late birthday card from her State-side grandmother with news of her dad. Captain Morison Cleland was alive in a Japanese military camp, which she now learned was in Formosa. Lulu's grandmother promised her the largest hot fudge Sundae she could eat upon her return, and my best friend was practically dancing across the patio singing.

"They're OK, they're OK, they're hunky dory. Well, we don't know if they are really hunky-dory, but at least we know both of 'em are still alive and Daddy's probably got an NGH for a guard." Lulu continued to cling to the bright side of absolutely everything.

"He probably does. There's got to be more than one Nice Guy Haruo in their army." I tried to echo her enthusiasm and hide my disappointment at No-Mail-Whatsoever for the Iserson family.

We Isersons never got mail from the States. It seemed like all the other internees got letters and cards with every Red Cross sack that arrived (even if only five had arrived in two years), but not my family. Of course, maybe I shouldn't have expected it. I knew that my parents' Jewish-Catholic marriage rankled both sides of the family, but I loved my cousin Francis, who was just a year older than me. Francis had taken me under his wing in Utica in the winter of 1937, and shown me how to sled and skate. Why didn't Francis ever write to me?

I wrote him the short, censored forms that we could send from camp sometimes. *To Francis Maher. My health is good and we are well fed. Tell it to Sweeney. Your cousin, Lee I.* "Tell it to Sweeney" was a code the English invented that meant "Only a dumb Irishman would believe that." The Japs never caught on, but Francis would. No letter came from him, though.

I knew Ramón couldn't write me from Spain. Americans had the Red Cross to send mail to prisoners, but the Spanish Red Cross (if they had one) was not delivering to Santo Tomas.

"Well, good thing, you've already had the most romantic letter a girl could ever get in her whole life." Lulu seemed to sense my every thought and mood. "You wrote Ramón back before he left, didn't you?"

She knew I had, and I nodded. "Through Sister Ignacia." I hadn't told Lulu what I'd written to Ramón, and that bothered Lulu.

"Lee Iserson, am I not your very best friend? You let me read his letter to you. So, what did you write to him?"

Lulu had stopped in the front plaza, where hundreds of internees milled around in pre-Christmas bustle, some heading for the Package Shed, some for the Red Cross mail, and others to the long line for the canteen, which was rumored to have rice and duck eggs for sale. Hordes of children stood on the makeshift stage of the "Little Theater Under the Stars" practicing Cinderella for a holiday performance.

Lulu grabbed my wrist and tugged me to the ground, where we both fell cross-legged. "I've waited long enough, Lee-lung!" she demanded. "Did you sprinkle fairy dust in his letter and promise to wait for him forever?"

"Don't be ridiculous, Lulu. I'm probably never going to see him again."

"So you broke it off. That's sad. But you probably did it by quoting Shakespeare—something tragic from Romeo and Juliet." She parodied: "Good night, good night, sweet prince, parting is such sweet sorrow." This was a trick of Lulu's. She thought if she could make you laugh or mad, she could get you to talk. Usually. it worked.

"I didn't break it off, Lulee! Life broke it off! The war broke it off. Anyway, what I told him wasn't nearly as poetic as what he told me. Just that I would miss him very much and that I still dreamt of our undanced dance."

Lulu nodded solemnly, waiting for more, her blue eyes wide and her brows arched in anticipation.

"I did send him something though." I pushed my shaggy curls forward. "A lock of my lion's mane tied with a red ribbon."

"Perfect! Oh, that's perfect!" Lulu sighed.

" and The Black Nazarene," I concluded solemnly.

She stared at me. "That cheap plastic statue of Jesus carrying his cross with the red paint all over his face—the one that Paul gave you?"

"Yes." I felt anger rising.

She looked at me stunned. "Well, that's not romantic! I never told you this, Leelung," she rushed on, "but I always thought that thing was hideous."

"You see why I don't tell you these things, Lulu?" Resentment crested like a wave inside me. "That little statue of Jesus protected me during a very scary time. Remember when I had to come back in through the gate with all that money in my skirt and Bugs Bunny Guard was staring at me? Giving me the once over?"

She nodded.

"I had the Black Nazarene right in my pocket, and the moment I wrapped my hand around it, Haruo—Nice Guy Haruo," I raised my voice for emphasis, "appeared from nowhere. My salvation." I glared at her, daring her to speak, but she didn't. "Ramón and his family just might need some help on their journey home. That trip is dangerous, you know, with both navies prowling for enemies. And besides," I paused still annoyed, "Spanish people love bloody statues and paintings. Where do you think the Filipinos get it from?"

Lulu nodded and seemed chastened. "Well, that was really good of you, Lee." She looked to the ground, but the air hung heavy between us.

At that moment Clarence Beliel's resonant voice came over the camp P.A. system, announcing with the most cheer he could muster that sugar, lard, soap and rice were no longer for sale in the camp canteen. "For the time being, these luxury items are Gone with the Wind," he quipped, "a casualty of the typhoon." We watched exasperated internees leave the long canteen line, some muttering, others swearing. Lulu's brow was furrowed, and she still held her head down, thinking.

"I'm sorry about what I said," she looked up at me, her blue eyes all sincerity. I nodded my acceptance of her apology. Then she pursed her lips and seemed to be trying to keep from smiling. "But that was a really hideous statue." She burst out laughing.

Chapter 23
COMFORT KIDS

December 11, 1943

"I'm trying so hard not to sneak one of these." Lulu inhaled the scent of her fudge-laden tray.

"If you pretend it's human excrement, you can diminish your craving for it," Hope said, as she sped off the corridor towards Room 4.

"Ugh! Hideous! That's hideous, Hope!" Lulu shouted.

Lulu and I were hawking tempting morsels of fudge on the first floor of the Main Building, yelling, "Superior Fudge—fifteen cents a daub! Superior Fudge—fifteen cents a daub!" Betty was doing the same thing upstairs.

The Iserson price was higher than last year, but we were still underselling Mr. Whitman (who continued making squares, not daubs) and business was brisk. The typhoon had worsened scarcity of all sorts. For the first time ever, no meat of any kind was being served in the chow line—not even the tough, chewy carabao we'd all come to know and loathe. Vegetable stew topped the dinner menu three times this week, along with "peanut loaf" doused in imaginary-meat gravy that wasn't too bad.

Maybe the food would improve after the roads were repaired and the Comfort Kits arrived, but sugar was going to stay scarce, and this was the end of our fudge-making business that made "extras" possible in lives – extras like soap, eggs, evaporated milk. What then? my mind and stomach asked. Would we be reduced to watery Line Chow?

Thanks to my mother's business savvy, we Isersons had stockpiled enough sugar, coconut milk, and native cocoa for one last fudge-making extravaganza—all to be sold, she insisted, before the distribution of the Comfort Kits.

We knew the Red Cross Comfort Kits—laden with corned beef, spam, cigarettes, and chocolate bars - were in camp. Mrs. Maynard told us they were in the library for safekeeping, and Commandant Kato had promised them for Christmas distribution. But the Japanese hadn't tipped their hand about when and how they would distribute them. Maybe they didn't even intend to distribute them. Maybe they would keep them for themselves.

In the meantime, internees were ravenous, and the price for our fudge stayed high. Iserson Superior Fudge Company made a record total of two hundred forty-seven pieces in December 1943, and our sales were netting a tidy sum for our final stint as chocolatiers. We could only hope that the money we earned now would tide us over till liberation—which had to be in the next few months, everyone agreed.

Betty bounced down the wide stone stairs from her second floor rounds, empty tray in hand. "I'll head over to the shanty and load up. Then why don't we go out back and sell at the Annex," she said. "The little kids will point us out to their moms and dads."

"Margie and her friends will be all over us," Lulu agreed.

Lulu's little sisters and her mother still lived in the Annex, but Maureen and Mim were not back from the hospital yet. Lulu stopped by frequently to see Margie, and she also tried to earn at least one meal a week at the Annex (sometimes by being official Kitchen Fly Swatter) because the food was better over there. Whenever milk or eggs became available, the Executive Committee made sure the little kids got them.

Lulu and I sold the last pieces off our trays, refilled in Glamorville, and then followed Betty out to the Annex. Aubrey Man and three other rail-like men were at work there, rebuilding the Children's Pavilion. When Sanitation Shakespeare saw us heading in his direction with trays laden, he called out,

"If sack and sugar be a fault, God help the wicked!"

"Henry the Fourth!" I shouted back to him. And when he flashed his gap-toothed, yellow smile and nodded, I walked over to claim his cash. Aubrey reached into his pocket, handed me twenty centavos, and helped himself to a piece of fudge.

"'Sweets to the sweet'?" he challenged, never taking his gaze from at me, as he devoured the daub in a single bite. His gaunt, grizzled face was now alight with pleasure.

"I wouldn't say you're that sweet," I stalled for time, as Lulu came up alongside me. "Which one is *sweets to the sweet*, Lulee?"

"Hamlet," came the immediate reply.

Of course. All the best lines are in Hamlet. Our own STIC troupe had performed the play just two weeks ago. Aubrey fished another 20 centavos out of his pants, pocketed a large piece, and said, "Thy fudge is too dear for my possessing. But this treasure" he touched his shorts pocket, "shall I bestow on my own sweet little ones."

I was willing to bet that "fudge too dear for my possessing" was probably a line from Shakespeare too, but by now, we were besieged by our own sea of little ones. Children from three- to eight-years-old clamored at our knees, so we held the trays high, and worked our way over to their mothers sitting near the entry to the Annex door.

As Betty predicted, we sold every piece, but tears rolled down the cheeks of one little girl, whose mother had shaken her head at the child's plea. Money was tight in camp. That mom might not have any extra to spare for candy, and could be saving her centavos for milk and eggs instead. I had one small piece of fudge wrapped in my skirt pocket that I was saving to eat with Lulu at the end, but the girl's face broke my heart. The mother whispered something else in the child's ear and she brightened a little. Still, when I finished selling, I went over, squatted down to be on eye level with her, and fished the wrapped piece out of my pocket.

"This is for you. It's mine, but I want you to have it."

She couldn't have been more than four. Her green eyes danced, and the smile that lit up her tiny face melted my heart.

"What do you say, Dottie?" Her mother prompted.

The child was looking at me awe-struck, as if I were an angel dropped down from Heaven.

"Are you a Comfort Kid?" she asked breathlessly.

Her mother burst out laughing. "I told Dottie the Comfort Kits would be here soon," she said, "and that they'd have chocolate bars and lots of other treats. Are you a Comfort Kid?" her mother repeated with a smile, and I laughed. The mother turned back to Dottie. "Can you say thank you, honey?"

"Thank you," she whispered breathlessly, and still held my gaze.

"I'm happy to be your Comfort Kid, Dottie." She had begun to tug ineffectually on the wax paper. "I'll help you open that."

Wednesday, December 15

"Bastards!" Paul muttered under his breath, as Barney and Squeaky reported what they'd just witnessed on the east side of the Main Building.

In our rooftop classroom, we'd been waiting for Cuthbert to walk in and start geometry class, but every one of us wanted to be downstairs, where an explosive drama had unfolded. Curtis Brooks (aka Squeaky) told us that Japanese guards were plunging chisels and knives into our Red Cross packages, slashing and puncturing precious tins of corned beef and God knows what else.

"Our food! Our food! They can't do that!" I shouted, not caring how I sounded. I had spent so many nights dreaming of crackers smothered in butter, cheese, and jam. I didn't know about crackers, but butter, cheese and jam were all supposed to be in the Comfort Kits.

"Well, you tell them that," Barney muttered darkly.

This was supposed to be such a happy morning. Commandant Kato (whom Lulu and I had dubbed 'DG' for Decent Guy) had announced that the distribution of Red Cross Comfort Kits would begin this morning, following their inspection. DG then promptly left the camp, though God only knows why.

Nearly a hundred of our starving, eager internees volunteered to lug the forty-seven pound Red Cross cartons from the library upstairs to the ground floor outside the Big House. They laid them for inspection in long, neat lines in a newly roped-off area. Naturally, hundreds more internees—maybe a thousand—flocked to the ropes to ogle the wooden crates, watch the inspection, and stand first in line for the distribution.

When the Military Inspectors arrived—Kempeitai from the city of Manila, not our own guards—Kato and his second-in-command were still nowhere to be found, but the Kempeitai didn't care. Squeaky said they'd just whipped out their knives and chisels, and pried open the wooden crates to reveal four Heaven-sent food kits in each container. These they'd dumped unceremoniously on the filthy ground, pried off the kit tops, proceeded to rip apart cigarette packs, and then plunge their chisels and knives into canned meat tins, oleomargarine tubs, and raisin packages. They had speared our rich meaty corned beef and then smeared into the muddy ground! I suddenly felt faint and looked over at Nellie, Lulu, Bunny, and Paul—all as white and livid as I was.

"When the raisins spilled on the ground, swarms of ants devoured 'em," Barney said, "but the Japs just kept up their rampage. They ripped labels from every packet and can, and tried to read the backs of each. They're destroying it all."

"Everything? All of it?" Lulu could not believe it. "Reprobates! Why? What are they looking for?"

"Secret messages, of course." Barney snorted as he said it.

My mind flew back to September, just before repatriation, when the Japs had been ransacking internee luggage, tearing apart Kotex packages and confiscating knitting instructions - all in search of secret messages. I wondered what kind of life they thought we had here. Who among us was

Mata Hari, receiving and sending signals to the Philippine guerillas or military prisoners in Cabanatuan or Bilibid? Then I thought about the radio and Bill Phillip's dad. Maybe somebody was. But destroying our Red Cross packages. This was too much.

"I don't know if they've destroyed everything," Curtis said. "We saw them tearing up two kits, but Grinnell was at the front of the rope line, wearing his red armband, and shouting at the top of his lungs. At the end, they seemed to be listening to him."

At that moment, Cuthbert burst through the door, clipboard in hand, face red with either fury or disgust. He turned his back to us, and slashed on the chalkboard "Degrees of Freedom in a Random Vector." Then he rested his hands on the chalkboard tray, seemed to breathe deeply, his shoulders rising and falling once before he and turned to face us. The class had fallen completely silent, awaiting news of what he'd seen.

"Vectors," he began in a solemn voice, "have both magnitude and direction. When Euclid first speculated…" Almost immediately a chorus of protest greeted him.

"Mr. Livingston, what happened?"

"Are the packages OK?"

"Are the Japs trying to starve us?"

"What are they looking for?"

Cuthbert stood grim-faced, lips pursed, and seemed to be making a decision. Then he reached into his pocket and extracted a pack of Old Gold cigarettes. Nobody had Old Golds any more. Cuthbert was holding up a pack of American-made cigarettes crafted from fine Virginia tobacco. In camp, our smokers were all desperately trying to fashion "fags," from various Philippine grasses.

He held the pack up before us, rotating its pale yellow label with red print, front to back, as if it were a tool for experimental demonstration or a prop in a magic trick. Then he carefully peeled the rectangular wrapper off the pack, and showed us the backside, on which something was written in small print.

A title and then something underneath. We all strained forward. What was that?

Cuthbert flipped the wrapper around and read aloud: "FREEDOM. Our heritage has always been freedom. We cannot afford to relinquish it. Our armed forces will safeguard that heritage, if we do our share to preserve it."

Total silence in the room. I was staring at the face of the Old Gold label. Under a pile of gold coins, it said "The Treasure of them All."

"That's what the Kempeitai found," Cuthbert said. "That's what set them off. For that they tore into I don't know how many packages, figuring if there were messages like this in the cigarettes, they'd find more "secret code" in the chocolate bars and corned beef and spam. But they've stopped now."

"Why?" Barney asked the question on all of our lips.

"Carroll Grinnell used his Japanese and got them to hold off until the Commandant returns. I think the Japs saw they had a full-scale rebellion on their hands. The inspectors had bayonets, chisels and knives, but there were only four of them and almost three thousand of us." He drew a deep breath. "Now back to Euclid."

"Euclid, Shmooklid," Paul's inner-smart aleck roared to life. "I say we go down those stairs and claim our comfort kits! We are men, not mice! 'Freedom! Our heritage has always been freedom! We cannot afford to relinquish it!" Fifteen-year-old Paul Davis, reborn as Paul Revere, tried to rally our class with words on the Old Gold wrapper.

Cuthbert's eyebrows shot to the ceiling, and he shook his head in disapproval. Tugging the wrapper out of his pocket again, he read the last part one more time. "'Freedom....Our armed forces' " he emphasized "will safeguard that heritage, if we do our share to preserve it." Everyone stared up at him.

"We," he paused dramatically, "are not the armed forces. Our share is our work in this classroom right here and right now—preparing you for a free and decent life after liberation." Silence hung heavy in the room. "In this classroom, we are free. Free to learn. Free to think. We are doing our best to preserve our heritage—some modest degree of freedom," he concluded.

I glanced to the left of my front row seat to see Nellie, Bunny, and even Lulu imperceptibly nodding. We all knew Cuthbert was right. I knew from opposing him at the bridge table that he was a strategist. He bided his time. But I wondered what Paul—my wise-guy, hot-blooded buddy—thought. Five seconds passed as Cuthbert glared at us.

"Well, just call me 'Randy.'" Pablo quipped from the back, his tone suddenly light-hearted, and as I turned around, I saw him thrust his chin at the chalk board. "I'm just Random Vector in search of as many degrees of freedom as I can get."

Cuthbert smirked and threw an eraser at him. The whole class erupted in laughter.

December 31, 1943

"Oh, tidings of comfort and joy, comfort and joy," Betty half-sang and half-laughed, as she dug into her stash. "Oh tidings of comfort and joy!" My sister gleefully extracted a package of processed cheese. She ripped it open, offering the treasure around—a New Year's Eve treat.

In our Glamorville shanty the empty coffee-can fudge pots rested on shelves up high and the charcoal stove lay cool in a corner, enjoying its holiday break. Mommy was smiling for the first time in what seemed like forever, but she had called this "Family Council," as she dubbed it, to discuss our newfound wealth and to plan strategy.

Each and every internee had received a forty-seven pound comfort kit from the Red Cross—every single one of us! That was partly because Commandant Kato did turn out to be a decent guy. He picked a bad time to be out of camp, but smoothed things over with the Kempeitai inspectors when he got back, and actually, apologized to Mr. Grinnell for the destruction of what turned out to be just a few Comfort Kits. All the kits were inspected, but no longer with chisels and knives. The Saturday before Christmas, when thousands of kits were finally distributed, seemed like Christmas itself.

Each kit held four cans of KLIM (powdered milk), fourteen cans of butter spread, four tins of Spam, eight of corned beef, four cans of salmon, eight chocolate bars, four packages of sugar, more envelopes of bullion than we could count, four cans of chopped ham and eggs, one can of party loaf, six tins of corned pork loaf, eight cans of powdered coffee, four jars of jam, various packs of unlabeled cigarettes. The list went on and on—forty-seven pounds of Red Cross bounty for each and every one of us!

The Executive Committee made a gloom-and-doom announcement over the PA system that no major foodstuffs—no rice, no flour, no corn, no meat of any sort—had been delivered by the Red Cross, and reminded us that these kits were just "GI supplementary rations" and should be preserved for an emergency. Well, if starving in a prison camp wasn't an emergency, what was? I wondered. Besides, all the items were tiny and many (like the prunes and raisins) were not in tins that were ant-proof. We might as well eat them now.

We'd had a deliriously happy Christmas. More than two-thousand Filipinos lined up at the gate to deliver packages. I felt sheepish about accepting gifts from Rosalina's family because with our newly delivered Red Cross packages, we probably had more food than they did right now. Grandma Naylor got us one last roast chicken from God-Knows-Where, but mostly we were thrilled to learn that Grandma had survived the typhoon. Santa, clad in red cotton and a white beard, even came through the front gate of the camp at 11 AM Christmas morning, bearing a stash of toys that internee parents had been busy making for months.

It was a cafeteria Christmas. Santa lined up all the toys on a table and children from the Annex got to pass by and choose two. Betty and I were too old, but we loved watching the little kids. I kept my eye on Dottie, who chose some tiny wooden dolls carved of bamboo debris from the recently rebuilt Children's Pavilion.

Christmas week itself brought many treats. Dave Harvey led a minstrel show that poked fun at absolutely everything. His theme song, "Cheer Up,

Every Thing's Going to Be Lousy" was a hit. A men and women's chorus sang Handel's *Messiah* with such grace and power that silence followed for a solid thirty seconds after the final note, then internees burst into applause. Another night we saw the movie "Honky Tonk," starring Clark Gable and Lana Turner. And whenever we knew we were without guards, everyone toasted: "Out the Door in '44."

Now here it was, New Year's Eve. Our family was all going to watch the kids perform *Cinderella* at the Little Theater Under the Stars. Then we teens had a bridge tournament scheduled to bring in the New Year (the Japs had lifted curfew for that night), but Mommy had insisted that our "Family Council" needed to meet this afternoon to make our own resolutions.

"Girls, the advantage of growing up on a farm is that you learn the rhythm and demands of the seasons," my mother led off.

Agnes Hanagan Iserson, daughter of Irish immigrants, seldom talked about her girlhood on a farm in Utica, so my ears perked up. Her face was lined, her brow furrowed, her lustrous brown hair graying, but her jade green eyes were still determined and bright. "There are seasons of plenty—just after the harvest. But there are also seasons of want, waiting for the harvest to come in."

"Good thing our harvest came in!" Betty piped up.

"Yes, but here's a rule about the harvest," Mommy's low velvet voice soothed and warned, "You have to use it wisely and save for the season of want."

Neither Betty nor I liked where this was going. I saw Boop's face fall, even as she stuffed the remaining piece of cheese into her mouth. I snuck a chocolate bar from my box.

"We had the season of want, Mommy," I said brightly, unwrapping the slender bar and munching. The job of being my mother's sunshine was starting to be a full-time task. Her smile was half-hearted and dismissive.

"Remember your Bible stories? Remember Pharaoh's dream that Joseph interpreted for him?" It was odd to hear my sophisticated flapper mother quoting Bible stories. We Catholics said prayers and the rosary more than we read Bible stories, but I had a vague memory of that tale when Father Paschal talked about it in my confirmation class.

"The one about the fat cows and the skinny cows?" I asked.

She nodded. "What do you remember?"

"Joseph, one of the good guys in the Old Testament knew how to interpret dreams. Then Pharaoh had a dream about seven fat cows coming out of the Nile River, followed by seven skinny cows who ate the fat cows, and the Egyptian head-honcho couldn't figure out what it meant. But Joseph could, and that's how he got to power in Egypt."

"What did the dream mean?" my mother asked.

Betty and I remained mute. Who knew?

"The seven fat cows represented seven years of plenty, bountiful harvests in Egypt," my mother said in a level, no-nonsense tone, "but the seven scrawny cows meant seven years of famine would follow. Pharoah needed to build silos and store the surplus of the first seven years to save for the famine."

"Mommy, we already had the famine," Betty insisted. "We're gonna be out the door in '44."

"Yes, probably, pet, but when—in May? August? Six or eight months from now? There was no grain with the Red Cross shipment. No fresh meat. We have a bountiful harvest this month for sure." My mother's callused fingers caressed the tops of the KLIM cans, but she held Betty's gaze. "We made good money from the fudge sales too, and I've saved it; there's still food for sale in the canteen, and these Comfort Kits are a great harvest. But we need to build our silos and plan for the time of skinny cows."

"If they're skinny cows, at least we're gonna have meat," I countered, but my joke fell flat. I took a quick bite of my chocolate bar. Mommy looked up at the empty coffee cans on the shelves.

"Those are ant-proof." She pointed to them. "We're going to transfer the raisins, prunes, and unprotected food into those coffee can silos, seal them, and then we'll commit ourselves to a schedule, making these three Comfort Kits last for one year."

"A year!" I erupted. "Mommy that's ridiculous, these packs are GI extra rations for a month—just a month! We're not even gonna be in here another year!"

"There were ninety-six food items in each pack," my mother continued, ignoring my protest. "We each have ninety, after this one week of feasting—that's two-hundred-seventy items. There are also eight bars of soap and twenty-four vitamin C tablets in each kit. And there are some cigarettes that we will sell. But we are going to make these kits last for one year."

She then whipped out a schedule specifying our pace of consumption—or non-consumption, and Betty and I looked on appalled.

"We need to be a team, girls. 1944 is going to be hard. We've been blessed in many ways these past few weeks, but there's a rumor that Kato is leaving, and that the Japanese military police are taking over the camp soon."

Betty and I froze in place. It was a warm afternoon, but I felt every hair on my head and arms lift. The Kempeitai? The same Japanese military that was in charge of Fort Santiago? The ones who had abducted those Filipino and Korean girls? The ones who had been ripping apart our Comfort Kits?

"It's just a rumor, right Mommy?" Betty whispered. Rumors were a dime a dozen in camp. This might be the product of some crazed internee's nightmare imagination.

"So far it's just a rumor, but Commandant Kato has been out of camp a lot lately. And we've seen more and more jack boots coming through the gate. No one knows why."

I heard some drunken internees careening too close to our shed. Drunk at 6 PM on New Year's Eve? I couldn't blame them. I dug in the pocket of my skirt for the Black Nazarene, then remembered I had given him to Ramón, who was now two continents away. The wooden rosary Rosalina gave me was stashed under my pillow in Room 4. An iron vise seemed to be gripping my chest.

"Old clothes. New Clothes. Stitch! Stitch. So it goes." Reedy voices floated sing-song lyrics from the Little Theater Under the Stars, where the girls were rehearsing *Cinderella*. For us, Old guard, New guard. So it goes? How terrifying.

I pushed stray curls out of my eyes, and remembered the lock I had sent to Ramón. *Stay strong, Leonera. Be a lioness.* Ramón's blue-rimmed brown eyes floated in front of me. Then daddy's deep chestnut brown ones. *Mind your mother.* The iron vise started to ease its grip, and a new stream of resolve surged within me.

"I guess we better start planning for the year of skinny cows," I tried to sound matter-of-fact, as I rewrapped my chocolate bar. "What's your schedule, Mommy?"

Chapter 24

PRISON CAMP NUMBER ONE

Tuesday, January 11, 1944

"That's not sixteen inches, it's twelve. Move that cot over!" Hope snapped at the newcomer to Room 4. The ladies of room four were merrily trying on new clothes sent by the Red Cross, but Hope could hardly turn around in the area next to her cot.

Tape measure in hand, Mrs. Linda Lee Todd, our room monitor since Mommy's resignation in November, headed toward the disputed area. "My dear ladies, it's just a misunderstanding. Let me help." Our Southern belle monitor of advancing years measured the space and adjusted cots, receiving a satisfied nod from Hope, and an eye roll from the newcomer. Hope shrugged into her new playsuit, but her mood still seemed to mirror the last ten days.

So far January had been a terrible month. Three hundred sickly new prisoners from the southern island of Davao had been herded into camp, and we squeezed to make room for them. Mrs. Todd decreed that aisle space between the cots had to shrink from eighteen to sixteen inches. Walking sideways between cots was my solution for reaching the door without crashing into someone's bedframe.

Even Commandant Kato saw the need for more space and decreed that STIC families—who had been separated by gender with men in the gymnasium and women and children in the Annex or Main Building—could now live together in their outdoor shanties, making room for the feeble newcomers inside.

Still, with so many of us packed in the buildings, disease spread like fungus. Diphtheria, measles, and whooping cough ricocheted through the camp. Lulu's little sister, Maureen, had recovered from her bout with diphtheria, but our hospital, with its one hundred fifteen beds, was chockfull, and the gravely ill from Davao had been rushed to Manila hospitals.

Then the Executive Committee announced that our corn, rice, and bean rations had been cut again, and chow line chatter turned to grumbles. *The Iserson Family Distribution Schedule* for those Comfort Kit treats seemed wiser every day. Betty and I divided a special treat from the stash three days a week. Sometimes a handful of raisins, sometimes a square of dark chocolate. Very seldom a can of spam. We made a four ounce can last three days. Our mother, Agnes the Invincible, often didn't take anything for herself, but made sure Betty and I did, and that our sealed coffee tins were invisible to anyone entering the shanty. Hanging over all this gloom was the rumor of the military take-over of the camp.

Today brought the only bright spot in the new year, and once again, it came courtesy of the American Red Cross. The Japanese had authorized distribution of new clothing to internees this morning, though rumor had it that the duds had been in camp since Christmas. Aside from Hope's outburst, Room Four positively hummed with delight.

"My dear children," Mrs. Todd tried to get our attention above the din in the room. She never addressed us simply as "Ladies." We were either "my dear children" or "you sweet girls." Mrs. Todd had the easy grace of a hostess accustomed to directing large, social gatherings at her family plantation.

"You sweet girls do indeed look lovely!" she tried again.

Mock wolf-whistles and lively chatter filled the room, as dozens of women modeled their idntical floral print playsuits. For some reason the

Red Cross had chosen a green, blue, and maroon print for this one-piece design. To them, an open-neck top with squared shoulders, cinched waist, and modestly long shorts seemed just the thing for internee life. When the clothes were distributed earlier today, Lulu had immediately pronounced them "hideous," but we both snatched one anyway. The delight in brand new clothing from home was universal.

"Didn't Betty Grable wear one of these in *Million Dollar Legs*?" Kay asked no one in particular. She stood next to me and modeled her own suit provocatively, doing a pretend Gable pinup. Kay had really good legs.

Across the aisle Betty twirled in hers, which hung loosely on her. Mommy tried to keep her in one place to pin it. Gleeful shrieks came from all over the room, as we ladies examined carbon copies of ourselves in all shapes and sizes. Finally, Mrs. Todd reached under her cot and produced a silver bell that pierced the air with a sharp ring. We "sweet girls" quieted.

"My dear girls, so lovely all of you!" Mrs. Todd began. "I almost dropped my drawers when they announced we were all receiving new garments!" The last word came out gah-ments. "And now we are just like an Army of the Andrews Sisters!"

Laughs and hoots rippled across the room. Everyone appreciated Mrs. T's relentless attempt to make us feel like special guests at her party, instead of captives of the Japanese.

"And speaking of Army," Mrs. T. continued or *ahhmy* as we heard it. "My dear girls, I do have sobering news."

Silence descended. We all knew about Commandant Kato had met with the Executive Committee, and they with the Room Monitors this afternoon.

"It seems that for the last four days," Mrs. Todd soldiered on, "we have all been prisoners of the Imperial Japanese Army. As we will be for the duration of the war."

The collective intake of breath stifled any conversation. My stomach plunged and my heart stopped. It got worse.

"Unfortunately, I must say 'prisoners,' my dear girls. Our Asian brothers,"

Mrs. Todd continued with genteel sarcasm, "have decided we are no longer to be 'Internees in Protective Custody.'"

Mutters rose from around the room.

"I never felt very protected," Betty whispered to me.

"We are now officially 'Prisoners of War.' The Imperial Army has changed the name of our beloved home from '*Santo Tomas Internment Camp*' to 'Prison Camp Number One.'"

More silence, till Hope's hard-edged voice broke the spell. "So, we're no longer STIC? We're PC-1? We won a contest or what?"

Hope had a knack for lightening the mood even while she pronounced doom and gloom. None of us had any idea what that name change meant, but it could not be good.

Mrs. Todd continued, "I myself am always inclined to look for the silver lining in stormy times such as these, and there is one. The regular Japanese Army has taken control of this camp, my dear girls, and not the Kempeitai."

Not the Kempeitai. Not the Jap Gestapo. Not the evil Secret Police who so cruelly tortured our men at Fort Santiago. The clamp gripping my heart eased slightly.

"Is Kato staying on as Commandant?" I heard my mother's all-business voice ring out, and her question hung in the air. Kato had been decent to us. We all knew that.

Mrs. Todd lit a cigarette. "No. He is passing on his wisdom to his army replacement, and he will be leaving us the first week in February. But consider this," Mrs T. took a long drag on the cigarette she had just lit. "The Japanese are probably not going to waste mean, nasty, bloodthirsty warriors on starvin' little old us." She squinted at us in hopeful calculation, exhaling a curved plume of smoke that hung in the air like a question mark. "They need their wildest warriors, their most rip-roarin', fiercest, most head-buttin' bulls right up there on the front lines of those islands, where they're fightin' our brave boys. So it is possible," she said hopefully, "we shall have the Guardianship of Ferdinand The Bull."

Betty and I had read that children's picture book so many times as children, and then to Lulu's little sister Maureen in camp. We marveled that *Ferdinand the Bull,* the massive beast who hated to fight and loved to sit under the cork tree smelling flowers, calmed Maureen's nerves when nothing else would.

"You may recall that 'Ferdinand the Fierce,' was carted away for the Bull Fight Day, but when he got to the middle of the ring…" Mrs. T. paused for another drag.

In a silvery voice Betty finished her sentence, "he sat down just quietly and smelled the flowers, so they had to come and take him home. And for all I know," she was quoting directly from the memorized text now, "he's sitting there still under his favorite cork tree, smelling the flowers, just quietly. And he is very happy."

Mommy looked over at Betty and winked at her. Some women in the room applauded.

Hope announced in her gravel-edged voice, "Well, I don't give a rat's ass how happy that bull is, but let's just hope they cart in a God-Damn-Ferdinand."

Sunday, February 6, 1944

The back of my throat burned and I struggled to swallow. I was lying in bed, but felt like I was trying to fight my way out of a burning building.

"Lee. Wake up, honey. Lee." My mother was stroking my forehead. Opening my eyes, I glanced right and saw that Kay had already evacuated our shared bed. It was Sunday and our wake-up was later than usual, but still, how had I slept through "Good Mornin' Good Mornin"?

Mommy smoothed some damp curls off my brow. "How do you feel, Pet?"

"Not good," I rasped and didn't recognize my own voice. "My throat's on fire. Everything else too."

My mother lifted a damp washcloth, mopped my forehead and cheeks, then moved into her Executive Secretary Super-Mother Mode.

"You're going to have to get up and get dressed now, honey. I'm taking you to Santa Catalina."

"Are we going to Church?"

"Not you, pumpkin. You're going to the hospital. This is either diphtheria or quinsy or God forbid, measles. We might need to get you into Manila."

Even in a feverish fog, I knew diphtheria or measles would be bad, life-threatening even. Quinsy was just an infection caused by tonsillitis. I had been struggling with sore throats and tonsillitis for the last month. So had Lulu. Our crowded dorm rooms had become breeding grounds for all three sicknesses. I never asked my mother how she came to be sitting by my bed that morning, waiting for me to wake up and announce my throat was aflame. But the next hour passed in a series of blurry, fever-stoked images of me being carried out of the Main Building.

When I emerged into consciousness again, Sister Ignacia was bundling me into the clean white sheets of a hospital cot. The large room held about a hundred women and every bed was full.

Dr. Fletcher came by to look down my throat. "OK, I want you to roar like a lion, Lee," he ordered, and held out his tongue-depressor.

My roar sounded like the last gasps of a strangled goat. I thought of Ramón's letter. *Be a lioness, Leonera. Roar as you can.* Well, that's the best I can, Ramón. Pathetic. This lioness has been laid very low.

"Quinsy," Dr. Fletcher concluded scribbling on my chart, as my mother walked up from behind him. "Peri-tonsillar abscess. Look."

As I "roared" again, he showed my mother "a large pus" mass in the back of my throat, making it hard for me to swallow, and causing a raging fever. "I need to lance that, and get her on sulpha drugs."

"Doesn't she need to go into Manila? We don't have sulpha drugs in camp, do we?" Mommy remembered leaving camp with Betty a year and a half ago because we couldn't treat her dysentery. We just didn't have the medicine—a drug called sulphathiazole.

"We do now. The Red Cross sent the drug in powdered form but we've been making it into tablets," Dr. Fletcher said. "Let's get you into the operating room, Lee."

We didn't have any anesthetics in camp, so when the doctor lanced my throat I screamed my strangled goat best, then fainted. When I woke up, I was in bed again, and Sr. Ignacia was standing at my side with a young man about my age, who was holding a bottle full of tablets.

"Just off the press, Sister," he nodded efficiently, and spoke with a clipped British accent. "That tablet machine from the Pharmacy School is coming in handy."

"Thanks, Len," Sister took the bottle from his hand, extracted a tablet, and offered it to me with a glass of water. I could barely swallow it, but managed and promptly fell asleep.

***

The next day, I slept past noon, but awoke feeling lighter and cooler. And Lulu sat by my side. She squeezed my hand.

"Welcome back to the Prison Camp of the Living!" she beamed at me. "You have to get well, Super Girl. I can't face all this fun without you." Defiant optimism was Lulu's trademark, but there was a fear in her eyes that I had not seen before.

"What's up?" I forced my voice, but it came out as just a whisper.

"Pretty much our life," she squeezed my hand again. "The Jap military announced that the Package Line is closed for good. Fini. Done. Over."

The package line? Our two-year lifeline to the outside world and to our friends in Manila? I felt as if I had been punched in the stomach. If the package line was closed for good, there would be no more packages from Grandma Naylor. Or anyone. No more helpful Filipinos lining up outside with everything from mosquito netting and roast chickens to meringue pies.

"And by the way, no more Filipino vendors allowed in camp either," Lulu continued. "Only Japanese vendors, from now on. And if that's not enough," Lulu rushed on, "the Jap army is providing all the food supplies for the camp from now on."

"No more camp buyers going out?" I couldn't believe it. Our camp buyers had typically been the ones scouring Manila to get the best deals on food from friendly Filipinos. Those Filipinos wouldn't be nearly as generous to the Japs.

"No more Red Armbands," she confirmed. "The new Commandant says: Santo Tomas is a prison camp, and prisoners stay in prison."

I suddenly came to life as if Lulu had given me a shot of adrenalin and a handful of vitamins. "I can't believe all these things are happening while I'm in the hospital! Lulu, I get sick for twenty-four hours and my whole life changes! Who's Commandant? Do we know yet?" My voice sounded as scratchy as our PA system, and my throat still burned.

"A lunatic. A reprobate. Yasu-yoshie something. I dunno. His whole plan is to cut us off from the rest of the world. Nobody gets out of camp anymore."

"What about polio? Dysentery? Stuff we can't treat?"

"We treat everything now. No more Manila hospitals. Santa Catalina Hospital has to do the job. It's us against them." She gripped my hand. "Hang in there, Super Girl."

I did. Three days later, thanks to those sulpha tablets, I was back in Room 4. Dressed in our identical playsuits, Lulu and I sat on the side of my big wooden bed, doing homework. We froze when we heard a hysterical rant in Japanese coming from the front courtyard. A clipped voice ran up and down the scale, followed by a loud slap. It was our new Commandant berating his own troops. Gravel footsteps stormed away. We barely exhaled.

Chapter 25
CURVE BALL

February 10, 1944

Lt. Colonel Yasunksa Yoshie did not have a toothbrush moustache. Aside from that, our wild-eyed, madly gesticulating Commandant could have been a stand-in for Charlie Chaplin in *The Great Dictator*. Did the Japanese see that film and take it seriously? Did they admire the maniac Hitler-character with flailing arms and crazed eyes? In that movie, Chaplin had made me laugh so hard I couldn't hear the soundtrack, but I wasn't laughing now.

Now, we had our own Great Dictator—"Yo-Yo," Lulu and I had dubbed him for his wild mood swings—who'd called a special assembly of "all prisoners" (not internees) on the front plaza this warm morning. Just shy of five-feet tall, Yo-Yo mounted a soap box and commanded four-thousand of us to attention.

"Ohio, Ohio!" he shouted energetic greetings to us.

I struggled to control my every facial expression. We still didn't know what to expect from the erratic military regime—in power for just a week—so we all stood ramrod straight waiting, trying not to make a false move. Now Yoshie thrust out his arms like a kabuki actor, brandishing weapons. He was armed with ... gardening tools.

"Prisoners! You grow own food!" Yo-Yo barked, as if we should all be thrilled. He waved a shovel and hoe. "Japanese generous! We give you land near offices. You plant vegetables." The last word sounded like vej-tubahs.

"Who desire to eat good food? Who work?" he demanded.

Yo-Yo seemed to be calling for volunteers, but we just stood there. Six months ago the Japanese had given us plots of land to garden, and we'd all pitched in. Then at harvest time, the those plots were declared out of bounds for prisoners, and gosh, maybe Japanese soldiers should reap the squash and mongo beans we'd sown. Just for safe-keeping until they could be used in the camp kitchen. We hadn't seen that food since.

Mr. Grinnell, Head of the Executive Committee, stepped forward and bowed deeply from the hips. "Commandant, our best gardeners are at work, plumbing the toilets you ordered built two days ago," Mr. Grinnell explained calmly. "I will assemble a team of volunteer gardeners for tomorrow."

Every internee glared at the head of the Executive Committee and silently cursed Grinnell. Collaborator. Traitor. Wasn't there something in the Geneva Convention prohibiting forced labor? Yoshie narrowed his eyes in suspicion, but nodded at Grinnell, who again bowed deeply and stepped back into line with the rest of us. (In the last five days, Yoshie had insisted on additional bowing lessons.) Our new military Commandant soldiered on in his broken English.

"More food necessary, because prisoners are more. Every day more."

Everyday more hungry? I wondered. We had a stinky new fish on the chow line these days, but the Japanese had cut food rations three times since November. Then I looked around and realized Yo-Yo meant more people—more prisoners just kept on coming.

Last month, the hundreds of internees from Davao squeezed in—filthy, starving, diseased, stick people. When those refugees looked around and told us how well-fed and well-groomed we all looked, we didn't know whether to laugh or to cry.

Then just today, the Army closed the Holy Ghost Children's Home in Manila, and ordered all those orphaned kids into camp with us. We kept squeezing tighter to create spaces for newcomers in the Big House, the

Ed Building, the Annex, and the Gymnasium. Now you tripped over cots whenever you walked into a room.

"So!" wild-eyed Yoshie continued, hoe and shovel still in hand, "with large number prisoners, sport is good. Baseball is good. Tomorrow you play ball with me. I play ball with you!"

He gave a decisive nod, and we bowed deeply, torso parallel with the ground—as we'd been taught in the last week. Usually, we just made a half-hearted attempt at the Nip Dip (we teens called it) because we all resented it so much, but this hip-deep bow worked well now because no one could hide huge smirks that were creeping over all our faces. You play ball with me, I play ball with you? From our stooped position we watched our new Commandant turn on his black leather boot and march off to the Southwest Territory, hoe and shovel in hand. Maybe we had gotten lucky. Maybe we really had landed Ferdinand the Bull.

Clarence Beliel, our disc jockey, didn't miss a beat. When the PA system sizzled to life for the evening hours, scratchy-voiced Edward Meeker started singing, "Take me out to the Ball Game." Appreciative hoots rose from the front lawn. Thank God the new military regime hadn't taken away Glenn Miller Time on the front lawn. And thank God they didn't understand sung English either.

***

In the cooler evening air, Lulu and I met our gang on the front lawn, straw mats and decks of cards in hand for a guys-gals bridge game. I'd brought a frequently used score pad for two tables (or two straw mats in this case). Bridge was one way to stop thinking about being hungry and being scared.

The Japanese military takeover had terrified all of us. Army trucks and supplies rolled in and out of Santo Tomas all the time now, becoming as much of a Japanese bunker as prison camp. We knew from the hidden radio, and even reports published in the Manila report that our boys were getting closer, and Japan was losing the war. Now the IJA was stockpiling weapons in camp, where large acacia trees once stood. In our first two years, a handful of guards had stood watch over all of us, but now dozens of soldiers roamed the camp, building pillbox defenses as if they expected attack. And if that happened, would we be hostages?

The Imperial Japanese Army wasn't changing everything about STIC overnight, though. Rumor had it, the military was amazed that Japanese civilians managed to run this camp of nearly 4000 prisoners for two years with just 8 guards. How did Kodaki and Kato do that, they wanted to know. ("Let's show them how democracy works." I could hear my buddy Paul quipping.) Yoshie had spent much of January pumping Kato for information, preparing for the IJA takeover in February. Kato told him all about our Committees and self-policing and internal jails and so on.

Internees clung to some of the familiar routines of the last two years, and for us kids that meant school and bridge. Tonight Lulu and I were taking on Paul and Bill first, while Nellie and Bunny were challenging Curtis and Barney Brooks. Then we'd switch after one rubber, and at evening's end, declare a victor in the war of the sexes.

"The ladies are here to clean house!" Lulu announced confidently.

"Just like real life?" Paul smirked. "My space in the Ed Building is looking shabby, Lulu. Could you start there?" Most of the boys were housed in the Education Building. Some in the Gymnasium.

"Dream on, Pablo Diablo," Lulu unrolled her mat, and I settled on mine, eraser in hand. We were re-using score pads, so I got busy rubbing away evidence of our last game. Nellie and Bunny found us, settled themselves across from the Brooksies.

"Lulu said you all would clean house, Nels, and I just wanted her to start in my room," Paul called over his shoulder. He wasn't ready to let go of the dig and sat with his back to Nellie, facing Bill.

"Hardy-Har-Har. No maid service for you, Pablo," Nellie dismissed him, and started erasing. "You boys do live on Easy Street, though. Why don't I ever see any of you washing laundry with us at that tub?" Nellie finished erasing, and watched Barney shuffle the cards.

"What I can't understand is how the Executive Committee came up with that ludicrous work rule." Bunny changed the subject in her beautiful British accent. Only a Brit could make "kahnt" and "ludicrous" sound so lovely.

Smiles spread across all four boys' faces, at the memory of this regulation. In camp, everyone was required to do two hours of communal chores a day (like peeling vegetables or washing dishes) starting at age sixteen for girls and age seventeen for boys. Of course, a lot of us had been helping since we got here, because our parents decreed that we would. But the one-year age difference rule for boys (promulgated by the Executive Committee) was just plain nutty and unfair, we girls thought.

Barney was dealing, and so was Paul.

"The guys do heavier work," Bill offered his conjecture, "so we need mature, seventeen-year-old muscles." Bill was only sixteen, but he was a go-getter. He worked the chow line, and was already helping to lug incredibly large, heavy pots of hot mush from the kitchen to the line. "You think Squeaky over there could do what I do? Not a chance."

Curtis was fifteen like me. He probably could've done Bill's job though. After all, he boxed.

"It's not that we need more brawn," Curtis objected with mock seriousness and a wry smile. "It's just we boys are wilder and less mature, so we need more time to play sports."

Snorts from all four girls followed. "Well, you got the 'less mature' part right," said Lulu. Then we fell silent, sorting our hands, and listening to Bing Crosby and the Andrews Sisters croon "Lay that pistol down, babe" from their hit tune, "Pistol Packin' Mama."

"And what do you think Yo-Yo meant at the end—all that sports stuff?" Lulu asked, studying her cards. "You play ball with me, I play ball with you."

"Yoshie's a baseball nut," Bill said. "Claims he saw some Japanese pitcher strike out Babe Ruth and Lou Gehrig, when our All-Stars toured Japan in thirty-four."

"Our American all-stars toured Japan?" I was only six in 1934, and I never heard anything about this. I had a good hand. Six spades and 16 points. I was a pistol-packin Mama.

"Yup," Curtis said from the mat next to us. "Our guys trounced the Jap teams in all eighteen games, but this Edgy Sawa-something did strike out Babe Ruth and Lou Gehrig."

"Are boys just born knowing baseball stats?" Lulu asked her brow knit, puzzling over her hand. She and I had no brothers, and it was amazing to us that boys just rattled off this obscure trivia about games that happened decades ago.

Across from us, Curtis reached into his back pocket, extracting a bright yellow card with a red band at the bottom, and he turned it towards us. Some player had just swung his bat and seemed to be taking off from home plate. White block letters on the red trim proclaimed "Big League Chewing Gum." Squeaky reversed the card to show us the back, with its full paragraph of information about the player and his career.

"Baseball cards - secret to our success," he replied smugly.

"Let me smell that!" Lulu snatched the card from Squeaky's hand and inhaled the faint sugary sweetness of bubblegum. "Oh, Heaven... Do you have any bubble gum? I'm starving."

Squeaky shook his head.

"Yoshie has some respect for Americans because we invented baseball," Nellie said. She probably heard that from her dad. Nellie's dad sat on every important Committee and spent long hours in meetings with the high-mucky mucks, who actually talked to the Commandant.

"One spade," I started the bidding at our mat. "So what was that about 'you play ball with me and I play with you'?" I repeated Lulu's question to Nellie, as my opponent Paul considered his bid. "Is he just saying we need to cooperate?"

A smile snuck across Nellie's heart-shaped face, making her look prettier and more mischievous than ever. Bill was not studying his hand. He was staring at Nellie like a love-struck puppy, but her eyes didn't leave her cards.

"Nope. Yoshie learned that saying from Kato the Worldly." She looked up amused. "Yoshie asked Kato how the civilian Japs kept order so well, and Kato said he lived by the helpful American saying: 'you play ball with me and I'll play ball with you.' Dad thinks Yoshie took him literally. Anyhow, tomorrow afternoon we're all playing baseball."

"One No-..." Paul stopped in mid-sentence, turned around on his mat and stared across at Nellie.

"*We* are?"

She looked up, smiling broadly. "Well, not really *us*. The men are. Yoshie wants Mr. Grinnell to assemble "Prison Camp Number One's Finest Players," to square off against an IJA team. Yoshie's gonna pitch."

"You're kidding me!" Bill was both flabbergasted and excited. "Us against the Imperial Japanese Army? Oh, I am going to be on that team if I have to kill to do it."

"Don't do that, Bill. Then you'll be in jail and you won't be able to play." Nellie grinned.

February 22, 1944

Hope, Kay, Mommy, Betty and I hurried out of Room 4 together, and headed to the southeast corner of the Camp. In the last two weeks the Japanese military had insisted on twice-daily roll calls, torso-deep bowing, and "none of our guff," as my mother put it. But we didn't want to miss the entire last game of the Japanese-American All Star series—now in its second week. This last game had to be in the seventh inning by now. Although the Japs may not have realized it, today was Washington's Birthday, and they were going to get trounced.

Without a doubt, these baseball games between the IJA (conscripted by Yoshie) and Prison Camp Number 1's Finest were the best entertainment our camp had offered in a long time. The comical sight of five-foot tall Japanese soldiers running the bases and trailing their sabers in the dust was topped only by the frenzied antics of Wildman Yoshie on the Mound. He reveled in power, craved an audience, and acted flamboyantly as both captain and Sole Pitcher for the IJA.

As we approached the well-used diamond, Hope, Kay, and Mommy peeled off toward Flossie and their friends. Betty and I sidled up to the first baseline, where Annie and Paul were standing. Wide leather belt around his middle, sword at his side, Yoshie was on the mound and wound up for the pitch, delivering a startlingly good curve ball.

"Strike 2," Mr. Beliel announced over the loud speaker. Our buddy Bill Phillips was at bat.

"Bill's just biding his time," I told Betty confidently. "Our strategy is to win, but keep the score down so as not to embarrass the Japanese. We don't want to make Yoshie fuming mad. But we're gonna beat 'em."

"How can you say that? We've lost some games," ever-earnest Betty quizzed me.

"We haven't lost any games. We've thrown games," Paul told her in a low voice close to her ear. "These guys are terrible."

We heard a fierce crack and strained over the heads of those in front of us in time to see a baseball sailing over the barbed wire fence, well on its way to España Street. Gee whiz, Bill. What about face-saving?

Two of our guys on base ran in for the score, and our own Bill rounded the bases with effortless grace. I knew Bill wouldn't be able to hold back for long if he got the right pitch. Yo-Yo raged at his men, who of course, couldn't do anything about the long-gone ball, and were powerless to rage against the pitcher.

In the eighth inning, Fr. Sheridan pitched for us and spent a lot of time throwing easy-to-hit softballs to allow the Japanese to catch up. Too much as far as I was concerned. In the bottom of ninth, with the score at 7 to 6 (prisoners in the lead) and one man on base, Haruo came to bat for the IJA.

Haruo had been out of camp for the last two weeks, probably on duty at Los Baños. The Japanese sometimes moved the guards around between the camps, but the upshot was that we'd never seen him play. At six-foot tall with willowy grace, he looked like the only guard who might actually belong in that game. For one thing, he removed his prestigious saber. Sabers (given only to corporals and officers) were badges of honor to Japanese soldiers, and their pride kept them from setting them aside - even on the baseball diamond. But Haruo was Mr. Practical and Mr. Humble.

Danny MacDonald was pitching for our side now. Pasty Danny was a bully and a braggart, and none of my gang liked him, but he was a no-holds-barred pitcher—one who wouldn't toss any face-saving soft balls.

Danny narrowed his eyes, squinted toward the catcher, and streaked his first pitch, a curve ball, across home plate for Strike One. Yo-Yo screamed bloody-murder at Haruo for the strike, but his face remained impassive, as he stood tall, rolled his shoulders, and repositioned the bat. The crowd quieted. We all liked Haruo, who kept doing countless small favors for us, and Yoshie's wild-man rants directed at our favorite guard made more than a few internees knit their brows. Still, we knew enough not to show our feelings. If we showed any support for Haruo, he himself might be punished by the mercurial Commandant.

Danny MacDonald fired a second merciless curve ball over the plate.

"Strike 2," Mr. Beliel announced, and Yoshie erupted, spewing venom at NGH, but only for a moment because his eyes too shot back to Danny, who had the ball in his glove again. We internees were silent. If Haruo could just get a hit, that'd be good, I thought.

I was expecting another curve ball, but Haruo must've seen the angle of Danny's arm, because after the streaking fastball left the pitcher's hand, NGH swung with absolute authority. The solid crack from the bat brought high-pitched cheers from the Jap bench, and a few delighted gasps from some of us on the sidelines too. Until we saw what it meant.

That ball did not sail over the barbed wire to España Street, but it made our men scramble and weave for the catch, while the man on base raced home, and Haruo tore around the bases to score as well. The Japanese had taken the lead at the bottom of the ninth. An ecstatic Yo-Yo jumped up and down in delight, bear-hugging his new favorite guard. The gut-wrenching final score of 8 to 7 was a sucker punch to every American internee gathered around that diamond. We lost Prison Camp Number One's All Star Series.

***

That night, in the Father's Garden with the loss still heavy on our hearts, there was a reading of excerpts from George Washington's famous letters and speeches. The Ed Committee had told the Commandant it was a literary presentation, and Yoshie'd given the OK, thinking this was how Kato ran things (which was true). There wasn't a single Japanese soldier in the garden. They were probably celebrating with as much sake as they could find, toasting themselves and recalling the good old days when Eiji Sawamura struck out Babe Ruth.

I sat down next to Lulu, with Curtis Brooks was on my right. Curtis was a history buff and probably knew more Revolutionary war history than George Washington himself. Mr. Carroll stood up front, reading from Washington's address to his troops before the Battle of Long Island.

> *The time is now at hand which must determine whether Americans are to be freemen or slaves… The enemy will endeavor to intimidate by show and appearance; but, remember, they have been repulsed on various occasions by a few brave Americans. Every good soldier will be silent and attentive—wait for orders and reserve his fire until he is sure of doing execution.*

Total silence descended. Sure of doing execution. That meant sure of striking at the right time. Sure of doing damage. My heart pounded furiously, swelling with the dawning conviction that maybe I was part of my country's great drama for liberty. I could do my part. Every good soldier will be silent and attentive …reserve his fire. Wait for the right time. Reserve fire. Then act.

"We lost that battle." Curtis leaned across and stage-whispered to Lulu and me, his brow knotted. "We lost the Battle of Long Island."

Just like today, I thought.

"Well, we won the damn war!" Lulu hissed back at him.

That was the first time I ever heard Lulu swear.

Chapter 26
ADVANTAGEOUS TO OUR GROWTH

Wednesday, March 29, 1944

"Our boys are only five hundred miles off the coast," Betty breathlessly repeated the ten thousandth rumor about American forces nearing the PI. "Maybe we'll be out for your birthday, Lee. That'd be a Sweet Sixteen gift you'd never forget."

My sister and I were standing in the endless, snaking chow line, and the stink of dili fish fouled the air. "Gangway! Hot Fish Stew!" Bill Phillips shouted, as he passed us in a three-man line, hauling two boiling cauldrons of putrid fish-lings between them. These minnow-like survivors of an increasingly squalid Manila Bay still had their heads on, and we were supposed to eat those too. Since the Japanese buyers took over two months ago, dili fish constituted our main source of protein, and I was beginning to think, starvation might be a better option.

"Yup, but April third is just around the corner, and you know how the STIC rumor mill works, Boops. *Rumortism.* It's the camp disease. Everybody's got rumortism."

Betty scowled at me. "I heard it from Annie, who heard it from Paul, who overheard Mr. Brooks, who is friends with Mr. Phillips, who listens to—and here she stopped speaking aloud and mouthed "the radio."

There was at least one radio in camp, maybe two, but none of us kids knew who had it or where they were hidden. The Japanese suspected we had a radio in camp, and since they were desperately trying to cut off all internee communication with the outside world, its probable existence drove them nuts. Occasionally, they'd mount surprise mid-day raids on shanties, turning everything upside down. They hadn't found it though.

In the meantime, actual news and our ever-flowering grapevine ensured liberation rumors aplenty. Hope said we got the war news several months before it happened. She'd be tickled about liberation for our shared April third birthday too.

I wanted to believe Betty, but I refused to allow myself to get excited about the latest unfounded rumor. Yoshie and Grinnell both told us that we'd have black-outs and air-raid drills when Manila was "in danger from the Imperialists" as Yoshie put it - and there hadn't been a single drill or blackout yet. Every time planes screamed overhead, we looked heavenward in hope— only to see red suns under their wings. Usually they were Jap Wild Eagles. How we longed for a single American star.

It was getting harder and harder to wait—even though I considered myself an honorary member of Washington's Long Island brigade, and remembered his admonition: "every good soldier will be silent and attentive—wait for orders and reserve his fire… till sure of execution." We got lots of practice these days.

On March first, the Commandant decided we needed twice daily roll call, so at 8 AM and 6:30 PM every single day, we all lined up outside our rooms as Japanese guards came by to collect checked rosters from Room Monitors and confirm counts.

Reserve fire till sure of execution, Washington insisted. What fire did I have? Was I going to drop a piece of sheet music on a Jap guard? Pummel him senseless with my two remaining pieces of fudge or a jar of Ponds Cold Cream in the Comfort Kit? My only fire, I decided, was my own lioness spirit and life. What good was that going to do? I didn't know, but I felt like I was waiting for an answer. In the meantime, while I was busy being vigilant, friends, school, and bridge filled my days. And there was work to do on *The Captive's Kitchen*. Future chef Leonore Agnes Iserson had transcribed 48 recipes so far—the latest, "Salmon and Egg Casserole" with a buttery white sauce and grated American cheese.

Friday, March 31, 1944

Mrs. Hildegaard Jones heard the moans as she scribbled the debate theme on the board, and turned around to feign a scowl at us. She must have wracked her brain for weeks to come up with this doozy. "Resolved: That the Internment Camp Experience is Advantageous to Our Growth." What? Our sophomore year of English was concluding with a unit on debate and persuasive speaking. Classes would stretch into the stifling days of early April because of November typhoon delays, but it was almost unbearable to think I might have to wax effusive about hunger and captivity.

Sitting next to each other in the front row, Lulu and I gripped hands. We were debate partners, of course, and now we had to draw straws for sides—affirmative or negative, supporters or opponents of the revolting resolution. Paul stood before us with a smirk on his face and an artfully arranged row of matchsticks in his hand. When Lulu reached, I closed my eyes and prayed. Please God, let us be Negative. Disadvantageous! Wretched for our growth!

My partner tugged and boldly flourished—a broken match stick. Ugh! Affirmative! Our job was to argue that the internment camp experience helped us, while a few moments later, it became apparent that Nellie, Bunny, Paul, Squeaky and it seemed like everyone else got to argue the negative. Ugh! Triple ugh!

Lulu's exasperation was equaled only by my own, as the two of us clattered down the wide stone stairs after class. "Are you kidding me? This is what we have to throw our hearts and souls into for the last week of school and a final English grade? 'Advantageous to our Growth'?" she sputtered. "Has anybody noticed that we are all about fifteen pounds skinnier than when we came in here?"

"But two inches taller," Paul quipped as he passed us on the stairs. "And everyone knows—it's up that counts."

"Hideous, Pablo! Hideous!"

I couldn't tell if Lulu meant Paul's remark or our debate prospects, but it didn't matter. It was better just to get started on this loathsome task. We hit the wall of oppressive late morning heat, and sought the shade of the one remaining acacia tree, while sounds of construction and destruction filled the air.

To our right, thirty of our sweat-soaked, beanpole men were pounding away on a high bamboo fence meant to separate the Gymnasium, where our men lived, from the University Seminary. The new barrier had been ordered by Yoshie to block the men's view of Filipino family members, who were attending church at the seminary on Sundays. That barrier infuriated a lot of men in the gymnasium because some of them had non-interned Filipino wives and children, whom they hadn't been allowed to talk to in months. But from their perch at the Gymnasium windows, they had been able to *see* their families coming to mass at the seminary every Sunday—so they knew their loved ones were safe.

In its infinite wisdom, the IJA had concluded that being able to see outsiders made communication too easy, so Yoshie ordered the tall fence built, and insisted our men volunteer to build it. Forced labor (not essential to camp functioning) was against all the rules of the Geneva Convention for prisoners, but the Japs had never signed the Geneva Convention, and Mr. Grinnell did not put up a fuss. Not because he was a "collaborator," my mother insisted, but because he was smart. If our men built the fence, they could design it with lattice-work openings wide enough for desperate husbands to scrutinize church-going wives and children. That's exactly what they were doing, and amazingly Yoshie OK'd it.

To our left, another group of men were tearing down shanties built, according to the new Commandant, too close to the camp wall, making communication with the outside world too easy and encouraging theft by Filipinos, who were sneaking into the camp. The Japs had caught two Filipinos in camp a few nights ago, and we didn't know what happened to them. But a twenty-foot cordon of space—a protective dirt moat—was being created where thatched roof shanties, lawn chairs, and charcoal cooking stoves once stood. Everyone was outraged that at a time when our rooms were sardine-like mazes, and people were pretty much sleeping in the halls, shanties were being torn down, and rebuilt in the rabbit warren of already crowded patios.

Lulu and I unrolled our petates in an unclaimed patch of acacia shade, and sank to the ground, the tropical heat anchoring us in place. We were used to ignoring the crowds of people always around us, so I whipped out a pencil and a half-blank piece of paper, and started to think about our affirmative argument. My blouse clung to my sweat-soaked back. How had this experience been advantageous to our growth? What had been good about it? I glanced at the clock on the cross tower, and did my best to ignore the hollow gnawing in my belly. Just forty minutes till the lunch that wouldn't begin to satisfy my cravings.

"Well, what do you want to start with?" Lulu was eyeing our skeletal men and their thankless tasks. "The great chow or the superior recreational activities?"

She was being sarcastic, but my thoughts fled back to our first show on the West Patio more than two years ago—that Chinese dance troupe and the "Side by Side" chorus. And we'd had lots of good variety shows and a great performance of *Hamlet* and *Twelfth Night*. "Well, the entertainment's been pretty good, Lulu, you have to admit. Where else would we get the kind of shows we've been having for the last two years—totally gratis?"

I started to scribble away, when a black metallic spider—at least three inches across—climbed on my mat. Dropping my pencil instantly, I whipped off one of my wooden clogs, and beat the loathsome creature to death—taking an extraordinary amount of satisfaction in his demise. After shoving him back on the dirt with the bakia, I brushed my damp curls off my forehead with the back of my hand, and returned to my list, reciting as I wrote: "Broadened our horizons with Dave Harvey's Follies. Quiz Shows. Shakespeare. Free movies. Baseball exhibition games." I listed them mechanically.

Lulu's head sank to her chest, and then snapped back up. "Lee Iserson! I can't believe you're actually going to sit here and list the things that are good about us being held captive by these reprobates!"

"Lulu, we have to do the assignment. We're gonna get a grade. I personally still have my eye on Cornell. And aren't you planning to look for Mr. Vanderbilt at UCLA? Grades count, you know."

"From a prison camp? Are you out of your mind? Nobody is going to care what our grades were—if and when we get out." Lulu's exasperated gaze drifted to an Imperial Japanese Army convoy truck rumbling through the gate with at least twenty bayonet-bearing soldiers in back. It wasn't the first time I registered a new look of fear on my friend's normally upbeat face. "They're everywhere now," she whispered. "You still think we're gonna get out pretty soon?"

I put down my pencil and reached for her hand. "Out the door in Forty-Four," I parroted our New Year's toast with more confidence than I felt. "Betty says our boys are only 500 miles off the coast."

Lulu and I had an unspoken rule of friendship: build up the buddy who is down in the dumps. Building up was getting harder, though. The hunger, the soldiers, the heat, the bugs, and the ever-present mass of dirty, skinny humanity everywhere. Still, I clung to our ridiculous debate assignment like a life preserver. Thinking was the only way to keep my mind off the gnawing monster in my belly. What other positive things could we say?

"At least, it hasn't been Nanking. The army's been here for two months. Nobody's raped us or anything," I said.

"They've starved us, Super Girl! They *are* starving us!" Lulu spat out. She glared at me, her fiery blue eyes wide and wild with indignation.

A week ago, our egg and even banana rations for camp had been cut again, and yesterday Yoshie's office announced rice flour was a thing of the past too. That meant our ersatz bread—with its reliably chalky aftertaste—had been snatched from our mouths as well. The chow line, serving no more meat, just awful, stinky dili fish, was starting to be an exercise in mutinous muttering.

"Did I tell you I found a squash in the trash the other day?" Lulu was breathing quickly. "A big juicy, yellow *calabasa*, just sitting in a rubbish heap outside the Jap kitchen, so I filched it - to eat it right there on the spot! And..." Her face was flushed crimson, and she stopped.

"And?"

She swallowed hard. "And there was a rat inside it. A big dead rat."

I stopped breathing. "What'd you do?"

"I took that stupid rat out by its tail, tossed it in the rubbish, and ate the squash any way," she spat out.

"You didn't!!" My hand flew to my mouth. "Lulu, you didn't! You'll get plague! They're testing for bubonic plague over in the hospital lab right now!"

"Well I don't have it yet," she replied defiantly. "Actually, we cooked the squash first. I took it to Mom. She borrowed a little charcoal stove and cooked it for the four of us. Probably killed all the plague germs." She closed her eyes and smiled. "It was really wonderful."

"Lulu...." I was stunned and frightened for her, but didn't want to keep scaring my best friend with my theories on her imminent death.

Before I could utter another word, Bunny Brambles' voice rang out, and we saw her racing towards us, eyes alight, and straw mat in hand. She unrolled it and sat down next to us. "We're leaving in ten days," she announced breathlessly. Bunny confirmed a rumor that on April seventh, a whole new group of internees were being transferred to Los Baños, where her father and brothers had been helping to build the new camp for the last ten months. Bunny would finish the school year with us and then head south with her mother and sister to the new "jungle resort," as she called it.

"I'll miss you mates here, but no more cheek-by-jowl in Room 22," Bunny sounded optimistic.

"Out the door in Forty-Four," I played along, parroting the lame slogan for the second time that day, trying to sound pleased for her. I should be. She'd be with her family.

The Jap military had decided that they had too many prisoners in the PI to close Santo Tomas and move us all up north. So, only those with families there—and lots of the priests and nuns—were being moved. Our best British buddy, her mom and sister, would soon be reunited with her dad and brothers, and maybe Los Baños was a better camp—less crowded, more food. We'd all heard families could live together in that camp—unlike Santo Tomas. But I found myself tearing up anyway, smiling a watery, insincere smile, and I couldn't speak anymore. All the losses. Rosalina. Daddy. Ramón. Now Bunny. Would Kay be leaving too? Harry Hodges had been sent south with Bunny's father and brothers to build that camp.

In the lunch chow line, Kay hugged me and told me I'd be bunking by myself as of April eighth.

Sunday, April 2, 1944

Max wouldn't have liked it here. It had to be close to midnight, but random, childish thoughts raced through my overheated brain as I lay sleepless in the sweltering heat of Room 4. Once again, I recalled blissful pre-war nights in our San Francisco del Monte home, sleeping with my overstuffed panda Max. *He doesn't like the heat,* Daddy told me, when he gave me the be-ribboned bear on my twelfth birthday. But the wicker ceiling fans in the bedrooms of our villa wafted gentle breezes through the mosquito nets at night, so I thought Max was pretty comfortable there. I wondered for the thousandth time what Rosalina had done with Max.

I couldn't believe that I'd be turning sixteen tomorrow, and was still thinking about my panda bear. I flipped over on my back and wriggled both legs free of the sheet, trying not to wake Kay or kick off the mosquito net.

I had a real tear-jerker fantasy that when the war was over and we were back in Utica, I'd go to the mailbox, and find a big package addressed to "Leonore Agnes Iserson" in that familiar looping script. And when I tore open the brown paper and ripped off the packing tape, out would pop Max with a note from Daddy, saying "news of my death was greatly exaggerated. I'm coming home." Then Daddy would walk in the door! Just as large as life, and with a belly as big as Max's! And we'd all be together again—Daddy, Mommy, Betty, me ... and Max.

It could happen that way, I tried to convince myself as my bare foot brushed the mosquito netting, but, if it didn't, I could write a short story with that ending and send it to *The Ladies Home Journal*. After all, in *Twelfth Night*, Viola's brother comes back from the dead—supposedly after being drowned at sea. So, why couldn't my father come back just like that? The wishful thought always made me smile and tear up, so I glanced out the grilled window looking for the reassuring wink of my father's star on the Southern Cross.

Instead my blood ran cold. I saw bayonets in motion, and moonlight glinting off rapidly moving rows of gunmetal. Then the thump of dozens of pairs of black leather boots grew thunderous, as row upon row of soldiers marched toward our building. A siren pierced the air. Lights blazed on everywhere around us, and the camp loudspeaker blared to life.

"Prisoners stand to attention immediately! Stand immediately! Prisoners, all stand in hall! Wait search teams!"

Kay awoke with a start and stared at me befuddled, squinting at the blinding light suddenly switched on. "What the..." she began. I bolted out of bed, batting the mosquito net aside, and wishing I had slept in something besides a skimpy T-shirt. My mother was right behind me.

"Prisoners stand attention now! Now! Out of bed! All stand in hall!" barked an insistent Japanese voice on the loud speaker. It was not Yoshie. I fought a rising wave of terror.

"Lee, put this on." My awake-on-a-dime mother handed me her

knee-length cotton robe, and I snugged it on. Where did she get this sixth sense? Mommy's own night gown was calf-length, and Betty's too, but our mother had Betty tugging a blouse over her see-through nightie. My own words from this afternoon echoed in head. *Nobody's raped us or anything.*

We stumbled out into the hall as a now alert Mrs. Todd, proclaimed: "Girls, let's humor them. Move swiftly now."

"That woman could host a plantation party in hell," Hope muttered with a certain amount of admiration. "What time is it—2 AM?"

I was too terrified to answer. The bedraggled knot of Room 4 ladies surged into the stone hallway, many still fighting the fog of sleep, but I was wide awake. My mother also seemed alert, making sure that willowy little Betty was lodged almost imperceptibly between the two of us as we lined up along the wall. We had roll call in the halls sometimes, so we knew the drill and took our usual places, but not before we saw maybe fifty bayonet-bearing Jap soldiers marching down the hall towards us. I didn't see Haruo. In fact, as I squinted, I thought I had never seen any of these soldiers before. My heart stopped when I realized that each wore a white armband emblazoned with red characters. Kempeitai! The Jap Gestapo from Fort Santiago was surging towards us like a wave.

Room 4 was almost at the end of the hall. We watched them advance, peeling off in groups to search room by room. Search for what? Probably the radio. The Japs were convinced that some internees were in radio contact with Filipino guerillas—maybe even with American military prisoners at Cabanatuan and Camp O'Donnell. Could that be true?

One Kempeitai team brushed past us and tore into the room across the hall, while still another stormed into Room 4—knocking from our door Mrs. Todd's beautifully penned sign: "Room Four Is Your Home." Through the open doorway across the hall, I saw bedding and mosquito netting flying, while a sailing wooden crate spewed a cold cream jar and brushes. Framed in the doorway briefly, a frenzied soldier overturned cots. He moved out of sight, but I could still hear the cots clatter to the ground.

What was happening in our room with our bedding and treasures? I had a horrible thought: what would they do to my sheet music? *Leonore's Suite* was hidden in the bottom drawer of the wooden bed I shared with Kay. Inside our room some soldiers seemed to be scouring the janitor's closet, dashing cleansers, jars, and cleaning supplies from the shelves. Glass jars shattered and tin pails clanked. The din rose on both sides of us as the Jap Gestapo ransacked our pathetic home.

If they were searching for the radio, I was pretty sure it wasn't in the Main Building, and I doubted that any of us women knew where it was. The men in our camp would never endanger the women by hiding it here. It had to be in the Gymnasium or the Ed Building.

Almost before I finished that thought, I heard shots fired outside near the Education Building, where our men and teenage boys lived. Shouted orders came from the central hall of the Main Building. In seconds, the furious Kempeitai raiders stormed out of our room and back down the hall as brusquely as they had stormed in.

I raced back into the rubble of Room 4 and stuck my head out the grilled window, looking left and trying to see what was happening there in front of the Education Building. In the light of the half-moon, I saw furious white-banded soldiers slap down three shoeless men in skivvies, then drag them across the patio, and toss them into the rear of the army convoy truck. Dozens of heavily armed soldiers jumped in behind them and three trucks roared out the gate. Were they taking them to the horrible torture chambers of Fort Santiago?

"Lee, get away from that window!" my mother shouted from across the room.

I turned quickly, expecting to see Agnes Iserson's fierce mother-bear stare, but my mother was lost somewhere in a sea of distraught women, and all I saw instead was the havoc of Room 4. Splayed before me was mayhem—a surreal explosion set to the soft cries and moans of my roommates. All the baskets and maletas under our cots had been emptied, every dear possession we owned was scattered and strewn yards from its home. Even the wooden drawers beneath Kay's bed and mine, were now wrenched at a horrible angle - slashed with a bayonet and they held nothing. For a minute my heart stopped: Where was it?

I scanned the littered room frantically, my eyes skimming over slashed mosquito netting, past the full black skirt I'd used for smuggling, and over my rumpled blouse in the aisle. Then I spotted it—the desecrated sheet music near Betty's cot—four disheveled pages. I darted over and gently lifted them from the floor. The first page was torn, but it could be taped. I smoothed its tattered edges, and held it, as hot tears scalded my eyes. The bold lines of Daddy's familiar looping script leapt out at me. "Happy Birthday, dearest Lee, my darling grown-up daughter." Today was my sixteenth birthday.

Chapter 27
UNUSUAL SKILLS

Monday, April 3, 1944

Even with all forty of us girls working, it took more than an hour to clean up the mess the Japs had made in five minutes. But Mommy reminded Betty and me that we were lucky we could go back to bed at all, and not be carted off to Fort Santiago like those three hapless men. What if the Japs had chosen to cart off three women instead? I hadn't forgotten Valentina's horrible stories of "comfort women," and the thought terrified me.

I was in a dazed fog all morning, despite my mother's big birthday hug and the beautifully embroidered hankie she gave me at breakfast, and despite Betty's artfully drawn "Sweet Sixteen" card that included a sketch of our Glamorville Shanty with an overhead banner reading "No Me Olvides." That means "forget me not" in Spanish. Boops was really an artist, and I was going to treasure this reminder of our family "home" here at STIC. Both of their gifts had been stowed in our shanty last night, and escaped the Great Raid.

Over breakfast of rice mush and coconut milk that morning, the tables were abuzz with rumors about what last night meant, and what the Japanese had actually found: no radio. But the Kempeitai carted off three men who had diagrams of electronics under their cots. Were those guys just taking one of the adult education classes on engineering that the Education Committee offered? Or were they actually working on a radio? No one knew.

***

"It's a masterpiece, Agnes! How did you manage it?"

Flossie was already at our shanty by the time I got there, and she was ogling the BIG SURPRISE - my birthday cake. Just the sight of this single-layer, one-inch tall cake glazed in chocolate lifted my spirits as high as the cross tower.

"The good old fashioned American way. Money still talks," my mother replied, her velvet voice tinged with sarcasm. "And the Jap vendors will sell you whatever they've got for a price. But Lee's sixteenth birthday—well, that's worth a splurge."

My mother was hosting a special birthday luncheon for me in our shanty. The little card table had been set with tin plates, and a cup in the middle held three red hibiscus blossoms - probably plucked from the Fathers Garden. Betty, Lulu, Flossie, Janet and Hope (who shared my birthday) had all been invited to the feast, and my mother had even broken out the Spam from our Comfort Kits. But best of all, Mommy had scrounged some powdery cassava flour, a duck egg, and enough raw sugar from Jap vendors to make me this birthday confection. Before the war, if Rosalina had made this pancake-sized cake for dinner, Mommy would've told her to throw it out and start over. But now it looked like the work of a master pastry chef.

"Besides, someone I know has a sweet tooth," my mother added.

"That would be yours truly, Aggie," Lulu chimed in, but she knew that my mother meant me.

I just loved chocolaty, buttery, creamy, sugary desserts that we never had any more. I was making up for that by devouring them in my imagination - copying every mouthwatering dessert recipe I could find into my collection. Of the fifty-nine recipes I had copied from books and magazines in camp so far, thirty-seven were desserts. (My most recent was Eggnog Ice Cream.) I was running out of paper for *The Captive's Kitchen*, since I had used the last ten pages of a notebook left over from Latin I in 1942. But I wasn't going to think about that now.

"Lulu, we shouldn't even share this cake with you," I chided my best friend. "You didn't invite us to feast on that big fat squash you found."

"The bubonic plague squash?" Betty chimed in. I had told my sister all about Lulu's exploits. "I wouldn't have touched that with a ten-foot pole, Lulu. I'm not holding a grudge about that."

"Besides, there was barely enough for me and my starving family," Lulu was trying to sound sarcastic and light-hearted, but she and her family—we all—truly were starving.

Usually, I could smell Hope's cigarette before I saw her, but when she ducked her head through our shanty's bamboo door, she was not sporting an Old Gold. Instead, she was toting a small woven basket topped by a floppy bow made of red thread. She handed it to me with a smug smile.

"This is for you, Birthday Buddy."

I gave her a big hug of thanks. "And here's for you, Hope!"

Hope and I had traded small gifts on our birthdays for the last three years, and I had two full-sized pieces of white chalk tied in a blue ribbon ready for her. Teachers were so low on chalk these days. Then I peeked inside my mystery basket. Atop a colorful collection of….well, stuff —was a note inked in Hope's back-slanting script. The fountain-penned verse was on real, honest-to-goodness stationery with beautiful yellow and pink hibiscus blossoms in the corner. I started to tear up already. Nobody had real stationery any more—now I had a personal letter on beautiful stationery. After "Happy Birthday, Lee," Hope had written:

> *When you are old and grey like me,*
> *Yet charming as of yore,*
> *Let's send us word on our birthdays*
> *To wish us many more*
> *And I so old and feeble then*
> *Will cry, "Oh boy, oh boy!"*
> *And say to all, "I knew her when*
> *She filled Room 4 with joy!"*

Then came the detailed instructions for my gift:

> *Hang on a nail in your shanty*
> *This beautiful basket of junk.*
> *If you need a pin for your panty*
> *Or for want of a thumb tack are sunk;*
> *Paper clip, pencil or notebook,*
> *Of crayon or chalk a slight dab;*
> *A button or thread, you don't have*
> *To look* ——
> *Just reach in the basket and grab.*

I laughed out loud. Hope was never going to rival Ramón's favorite poet, Ruben Darío, but treasures here abounded—two safety pins, several thumb tacks, three paper clips, one-half a pencil (but the eraser half), a red crayon, one needle and some white thread, along with … here my heart almost stopped. Lying flat on the bottom was booty beyond my imaginings. I tugged out a completely blank, spiral-bound notebook with gently rounded corners. Its cover was a muted olive green, but to me it was pure gold: *The Captive's Kitchen* was about to have a new home.

Tuesday, April 4, 1944

"It's tomorrow, Lulu. C'mon, we have to finish this assignment."

The Great Debate was almost upon us, and I really wanted to get this prep done so we could declare an end to our sophomore year of English. The clock on the cross tower tolled four, and a gentle breeze stirred, but it had to be ninety degrees out here in the shade on the main lawn. My sweat-soaked blouse felt like a quilt, when Lulu and I unfurled our mats and sank to the ground. Off in a corner of the lawn, Nellie's softball team was at bat. Just beyond them, a group of Japanese soldiers on ladders unfurled more barbed wire to top the already high stone walls. *Protection! Keeping thieves out.* Commandant Yoshie had cheerfully informed us, but of course, it worked just as well to keep us in.

We still had no word on the fate of the three men who had been hustled out of camp two nights ago. Mr. Grinnell told Nellie's dad that they had been taken to Fort Santiago—which is what we all figured. That meant unspeakably horrible torture. Grinnell also learned that Yoshie, who was regular Jap army, had been as surprised by the raid as we were. The ruthless Kempeitai liked it that way: keep the prisoners and the army on edge and guessing. I guess they thought they could discover more secrets that way.

Yoshie had been flummoxed by the raid—mightily embarrassed that we all hadn't bowed like bobble-head dolls to the Kempeitai as they stormed down the halls. The P.A. system informed us that tonight at 5 PM, there would be "mandatory bowing lessons" on the front lawn. *Must show respect all times with good bowing to Japanese superior. Bow from hips not shoulders, not waist.* This subservient Japanese custom really rankled. Here we were starving to death, going to school every day, working in steaming kitchens or broiling vegetable patches, or the hospital, and what was Yoshie worried about? How we bowed.

"Did you finish your cake last night?" Lulu asked as she sank next to me on the ground.

"Of course. I wasn't going to let those ants have one morsel of my scrumptious birthday cake. It really was delicious, wasn't it?" Lulu nodded, while I turned to the task at hand, my new half-pencil at the ready.

"OK, so we've got Horizon-Broadening Recreational Activities—better shows than we'd ever have seen without the war. We really lucked out with that Shakespearean troupe interned with us."

"Yup. And Dave Harvey's no slouch."

"I've been thinking about your bubonic plague squash, Lulu. What if we have a category called Ingenious Survival Strategies and we tell your story there. You showed true grit, girl, with that rat." I was scribbling away. "How are you feeling by the way?"

"Hungry. A touch of the plague coming on, but otherwise OK. Ingenious Survival Strategies." She rolled the phrase around on her tongue. "I like it.

Well, what about the fudge-making you did for two years? And the fudge-selling we did. Don't forget that."

"Hawkers par excellence, that's us. Oh —- how 'bout a Fending Off Boredom category—amazing ways we've learned fended off boredom. Remember Climb and Drink?" I shook my head as I recalled our silly, synchronized routine on the stairs. "We were such idiots."

"Write that down! We were brilliant," Lulu's natural optimism was gaining traction. "And don't forget *The Captive's Kitchen*. How many recipes have you got copied now?"

"Fifty-nine. But I have to transcribe them into my new notebook. Does *The Captive's Kitchen* go under Fending Off Boredom or Ingenious Survival Strategies?

"I say Survival Strategies."

"Right." I was writing furiously now. "And Lulu, under Fending Off Boredom—BRIDGE." I stabbed the paper decisively.

"We might've learned to play bridge without camp. I knew how to play bridge before I got here."

"Well, we wouldn't have been world-class, like we are now. We beat Cuthbert last week, and we've memorized all of Vanderbilt's *Contract Bridge*."

A brown marbled gecko slithered on to my mat and inched toward my leg. I felt merciful, so I picked him up by his disgusting striped tail, and tossed him as far as I could. Just then, I saw a Japanese army truck rolling through the gates. Were they bringing the men back? I strained to see, but I couldn't tell.

Lulu seemed lost in thought, then announced, "OK, I've got a category—Unusual Skills Acquired: things we would never have learned otherwise—like de-bugging rice and weevil removal."

"Very important," I agreed. "And de-lousing mattresses for bed bugs." This pencil would be used up in no time.

"Fly-swatting champs too," Lulu went on. "And I just thought of something. Don't hit me. Should we put in Japanese Bowing Skills?"

I felt like I'd just been socked in the stomach, and my hand froze in place. Our new twice-daily roll calls made bowing more ridiculously loathsome than it had been at the start.

"You want to argue that bowing lessons are advantageous to our growth? No, no, no, no! For one thing, Pablo, Squeaky and all the guys in the back row will start throwing things at us. And if Cuthbert sits in, we'll get an eraser in our faces."

"He never throws at girls. And isn't there a rule against heckling?" Lulu demanded. "You gotta admit, it's an unusual skill we would never have mastered otherwise. And it got us out of a jam once. Remember the first time we met Haruo?"

How could I forget? That was the same day I met Lulu. When I realized I had left my sheet music in the practice room, the two of us had made a beeline over there, and heard *Leonore's Suite* being played so beautifully that I was sure Daddy was in camp. I remembered how Lulu and I just blasted into that room, interrupting the piece—only to find a Jap guard at the piano. If my new best friend hadn't had the presence of mind to bow, I might never have gotten my music back. Haruo might never have been our friend. Oh, but those hateful bowing lessons as advantageous to our growth? That was an explosive argument. We could be shunned as pariahs by all our friends forever… But still…

"OK, will you argue it as Second Affirmative? Because I, Lee I., as First Affirmative, do not wish to use that example."

Our high school debate rules staggered presentations. I'd open the argument in favor of the resolution as "First Affirmative." Then the opposing team, "First Negative" would present an overview of why we were all wrong. Then would come Lulu, as "Second Affirmative," who would expand on the case I had already made and rebut the negatives.

"Done. I'm gonna do it."

Lulu was so gutsy. "OK, any other unusual skills?

"What about learning how to weave a bra out of string?"

"We've never done that."

"No, but June Darras has. She's amazing. She's been making socks out of string too."

The ideas just kept on coming. "Dysentery poop clean up skills!" I shrieked, recalling Betty's accident of a more than a year ago and my escapades with the precious latex gloves.

"Yes! And bladder control. Learning to wait our turn in long bathroom lines."

For the next hour—and in honor of the year 1944—Lulu and I generated a list of forty-four ways "the internment camp experience has been advantageous to our growth." We included learning how to live with all sorts of crazy, whacko people—from Out-Out-Damn-Snot Mrs. Randolph Meade to Sanitation Shakespeare to Bugs Bunny Guard. And we started feeling sillier and giddier with each passing minute—the raid of just two nights ago relegated to some far corner of our brains. By five o'clock we had wrapped up our last sophomore year English assignment, and felt enormously pleased with ourselves. Even eager for the debate.

"You know, Lee, except for the starving part," Lulu's impish eyes crinkled with her high voltage smile, "we've had a really great time."

The P.A. system crackled to life with Clarence Beliel reminding all internees to assemble on the front lawn immediately for mandatory bowing lessons. Commandant Yoshie to instruct.

"I wouldn't go that far, Lulu."

Chapter 28
ABIKO

June 30, 1944

Dear Bunny,

How are you in the jungle resort? Miss you terribly. You wouldn't recognize this old place. We are so well fed. Tell it to Sweeney. We are bowing so regularly and well that we should get diplomas at the end.

Speaking of diplomas, you missed HS graduation. Ginny, Lizzie, and all the girls wore white dresses and received diplomas and flowers. Jack Aaron (remember Lulu had a crush on him?) graduated too. He posted this invitation to ceremony on camp bulletin board: "To my Uncle Sam—I sure hope you can make it for my graduation. More than two years since I've seen you, and having you here would make my 'commencement' the beginning I hope for."

All your best friends are juniors as of one month ago. Lulu, Nellie, and I have Mrs. Maynard for Latin for the third year in a row. We are studying Cicero who is a bore and a whiner, and no earthly good at all. Do you have school up there?

Regards to your dad, brothers, and mom. Give a special hug to Kay for me, and tell her the bed is hers whenever she wants it. Lulu comes down to sleep with me sometimes, but she is such a restless sleeper that our friendship won't survive being bed buddies. I hope to see you soon.

Your friend,
Lee I.

I really did hope to see Bunny soon. A few weeks ago we had learned through the Jap-censored *Manila Tribune* that Allied forces had actually landed in France. "Barely a single Yankee dog or British wog survived the mighty German defense," the *Trib* editorialized with their pidgin English. But our boys were in France. And yesterday the Nishi-Nishi tossed off a sentence about Hitler wisely ceding "the ancient, venerable city of Rome"—as an act of heroic restraint to save all art, architecture, and civilization there.

"Is that ready to go, Lee?" Fr. Sheridan ducked into our shanty with a stack of letters in his hand. He and two other men from camp had been drafted by the Japs to haul construction supplies to Los Baños with an army convoy truck. Fr. Sheridan told those of us with friends at LB that he'd take letters if we had them ready and kept them short.

"Sure," I folded the letter and dashed "Bunny Brambles" on the top flap. "I don't have an envelope, is that OK?"

"I can't accept a letter for delivery without an envelope," he said, smiling broadly and snatching the hastily penned note from my hand. "What? No stamps either?"

In tired Bermuda shorts and a loose-fitting, open-necked shirt, Father Sheridan still bore his trademark smile, but his shoulders, once so broad and muscular, seemed lost in the shirt he filled amply more than a year ago. My priest friend wasn't wearing his Roman collar today, but I knew he was partly on a religious mission too—taking several months of Communion supplies down to Fr. Reuter and the other Jesuits imprisoned down there. One factory in Manila was still churning out Communion wafers, and the Japs were actually allowing that. Our men would be back tomorrow, hopefully with some letters from our friends to us. Father Sheridan glanced at my hastily folded note.

"You didn't tell her about Abiko or anything awful, did you?"

"No! What if they found the letter?"

"Exactly, you smart girl. Exactly." He then tucked what had to be twenty letters inside his shirt, snugged his belt, and headed out the door, looking slightly less skinny than when he'd walked in.

July 2, 1944

Abiko—Lieutenant Nanakazu Abiko—was our newest nightmare, and Bunny was lucky to have missed him. "AH-bee-koh" - we even spat out his name like a foul curse. A month ago, this big-bodied, short-fused, bully had been transferred to Santo Tomas from the fighting in the Solomons and named Commander of the Prison Guards.

He relished telling internees what cowards and "third class" soldiers our boys were at Guadalcanal (though we knew that we won that battle). In STIC he'd found the new satisfaction ordering our emaciated civilian men around. In violation of every rule of the unsigned Geneva Convention, he'd ordered them to build two watchtowers on the outside walls of the camp— one at the northeast and another at the southeast corners. Abiko's unusually broad shoulders and muscular frame fueled wild internee speculation about his background—the camp rumor mill quickly pronounced him a 1936 Olympic swimmer for the Japs. But that was just rumortism. Who knew?

What we knew for sure was that he was a bully. Railing and sputtering at everyone, including the guards under his command, Abiko specialized in prisoner humiliation—usually in the form of *how low can you go bowing*. During our twice daily roll calls, he gave refresher courses. The good news was that he could not be in all places at once. Roll was called in individual halls, buildings, and shanties, so on any given night the Abiko Brigade might be somewhere else. But tonight, on the first floor of the Main Building, it was our turn.

Big Boy Abiko, heavy gilt sword at his side, swaggered through the first floor of the Big House at 6:30 PM, accompanied by his interpreter. Hundreds of women were lined up outside our rooms, standing at respectful attention, and bowing as the two Japanese soldiers came by. After plucking a checked roster from the hand of Mrs. Todd, he paused and stared at her. She was almost as tall as he was, and leveled her green-eyed, don't-mess-with-me Confederate matron glare at him to considerable effect.

Big Boy moved down the hall to Room Three, squinting at the assembled ladies, who bowed to him. Mrs. Davis, Paul's mom and the monitor for Room Three, proffered the roster, but Abiko seemed not to see it.

"Bow from hips, from hips! Not waist! Spine total straight!" he ordered. "Do again!" He walked down the line.

The ladies bowed lower, while he snickered and grunted. We had been through this before, and usually that second Nip Dip was the end of our troubles for the day. But tonight Abiko walked back to Mrs. Davis, stood less than a foot from the petite woman and slapped her hard across the face.

"You not bow low enough, Yankee dog woman. Dog bow better than you. Do again, third class persons!"

The stone hall, lined with motionless, women froze. I caught the horrified look on Annie's face, but the entire room acted as one and bowed lower. Abiko snorted. He snatched the roster from Mrs. Davis and moved on. I had never been so scared of anyone in my life.

Later that night, Lulu and I lay in my big double bed. I was glad that she was my bed buddy tonight and didn't even mind if she kept me awake all night with her wild girl tossing and turning. It was good to have a friend so close—she literally had my back. We struggled to fall asleep, and whispered about the new turn of events with Abiko.

"You know, we would never have won that debate now," I tried to sound non-chalant, but my voice trembled a little and for once, I didn't feel hungry because my stomach was in a knot.

"Not a snow ball's chance in hell," she agreed. "Good thing that grade is on paper and unchangeable."

"Boosted us right into English III," I said.

I turned my head and saw Lulu smiling, remembering our unexpected triumph three months ago at the end of our sophomore year. And that made me smile too. As Second Affirmative, Lulu had argued brilliantly that proper bowing (an Unusual Skill Acquired) was actually a handy Japanese cultural skill, and a way for both sides to show respect to each other. Who bowed first or lower wasn't that important, she insisted. It was just a way of showing respect—the way we Americans sometimes tipped our hats to one another or shook hands. And now we knew how to do it right.

Jimmy Flood and Eric Sollee, who had argued the Negative, were so flummoxed that they didn't even rebut the argument, but had moved right on to name-calling, concluding that "the Affirmative team consists of two Pollyannas who just fell off a Christmas tree!" That got a howl of laughter from some of the boys in the back, but in her decision, Judge Hildegaard Jones had soberly informed the young men "that personal insult and *ad hominem* derision is the lowest form of public discourse," and earned them no points in high school debate. Mrs. Jones then stood up and bowed deeply to us, congratulating us on our grade and our debate victory. And the class (mostly the girls) applauded. The memory warmed my heart every time I thought about it.

Well, Lulu could make that bowing argument with a straight face three months ago—in the days before Abiko came—but not now. Not ever now.

"We taught them a lot in that debate. Did you see how many of our classmates are copying your *Captive's Kitchen* idea, by the way?"

"Everybody. Not just our classmates. Anyway, I can't take credit for that. It's just natural that starving people like to think about food."

Most internees now had some form of recipe collection and menu planning going as the new hobby. It seemed to help just to talk about food, and the camp was very lucky that the Manila YMCA had donated its whole library of books, with many cookbooks among them. What I hated was the way some internees were actually cutting out the photos of food for private viewing, and not leaving them in the magazine with the recipes.

"Your recipe book is the best though," Lulu built me up.

"I'm furthest ahead I think. One hundred ninety-eight recipes so far."

"Well, what are we having for breakfast tomorrow?"

I closed my eyes and thought for a moment. "How 'bout ham pancakes? I found this recipe that had slices of thick, juicy ham soaked right into the pancake batter, and there's a trick to keeping them fluffy, but you can do it, so we'll serve fluffy, buttery, thick ham pancakes with apple sauce on the side."

"Mmmmmm. Wake me for chow if I oversleep."

July 9, 1944

It was Sunday morning, but we weren't going to Santa Catalina for mass. Instead Father Sheridan had invited Mommy, Betty and me to a special mass at the university's museum at 5 PM. Two days ago seventy new priests had been brought into camp from Manila and the Southern islands — Australian Redemptorists and American Holy Cross priests. They had been under house arrest until now, but the Japanese had decided the priests were probably helping the Filipino guerillas (just like the Maryknollers they had rounded up a year ago) and had to be imprisoned. So in they came, seventy men who should've been in black cassocks, but now wore Bermuda shorts. Many would head off to Los Baños the next day.

Yoshie thought religion kept us out of trouble, so he agreed to let all the new priests say mass daily as was their religious duty. But it turned out the only space large enough for seventy priests to say mass was the university's Museum of Natural History—which had been off limits to prisoners. But no longer. The Spanish Dominican priests, who owned the university, agreed to allow daily mass there, so later today, we'd have a first: mass in the museum.

In the meantime, mandatory sports filled my day of rest. I had talked Nellie into coaching my new lost-cause basketball team, called the Whites. Father Sheridan said our name was meaningful because "white is the color of martyrs' robes, whose trials and sufferings have not yet ended." But we girls weren't that creative. We named ourselves "the Whites" because the only pinafores left bore no embroidery and were completely white. We were "lost-cause" because my teammates had been silly enough to elect me as "Captain." That showed how little they valued winning. My first move was to plead with Nellie (not even on the team) to be our coach.

So on this muggy July morning, when Lulu and all the other Whites were assembled and practicing on the southeast court, I trotted Nels over from the Big House to whip us into shape. As we approached the front gate, we spotted a group of internees gathering in the Southwest Territory near the gate. They were watching something through the wire fence that now cordoned off the military compound.

"Is Yoshie making an announcement?" Nellie strained to see ahead and tugged at my hand. "Let's go find out." We started for the Southwest Territory, but I wish we had just gone straight to the basketball court.

As we neared, I heard Abiko's voice shouting something, and someone screamed back in what I thought was Tagalog. Nellie and I hurried to the rapidly forming crowd. Peering over the heads of those gathered, I could make out Abiko and two Japanese guards taunting a struggling Filipino. No Haruo there to help him. I glimpsed Aubrey Man on the other side of the crowd.

We all knew that Abiko reserved his greatest contempt and brutality not for us internees but for the Filipinos, who sympathized with us and tried to help us. Like most of our Japanese captors, Abiko loathed the Filipinos as traitors to the East Asian cause. He considered them stupidly devoted to us "colonialist oppressors," and a "fourth class people." Commandant Yoshie had banned all Filipino vendors from camp back in February, but sometimes—camp being camp and pretty chaotic—a Filipino courier slipped inside, sneaking notes or money to prisoners who were desperate for news of their families on the outside.

Abiko and his henchmen now had the bloodied Filipino tied to a chair, but the man had clearly put up a fight, before being roped down. One side of his face was purple and his eye grotesquely swollen—probably from the butt of the guard's rifle.

"Oh, Nels…" I whispered to Nellie, but I couldn't drag my eyes from the scene, and my friend seemed not to hear me.

We inched a little further forward. I saw one guard yank the man's head back and shove a funnel down his mouth, while another grabbed a water hose. The frantic, young man thrashed his face from side to side while the first Jap clamped the funnel in place and put his writhing man's face in a headlock. Another guard shoved the water hose into the funnel and yelled something to the third. When the water came on full force, the man's screams went to gasping, guttural gurgles.

I was sickened by the horror, but for some reason, I couldn't stop watching. Abiko, bayonet rifle in hand alternately laughed uproariously and then ranted. Nellie and I were both frozen to the spot, about ten yards from where it was happening—our view of the gasping man partly obscured by the internees in front of us. Abruptly, Abiko ordered the guards to stop the hose, and then taunted the coughing, drowning, gurgling man. Abiko railed on in Japanese, which another guard translated to Tagalog. They demanded an answer to some unintelligible question, while their bloated victim tried to suck air.

Two women in front of me blocked my view, so I couldn't see him entirely. But when the Filipino prisoner did nothing but gasp, wretch, and shake his head, Abiko ordered the funnel back in and the water released full force. A collective mutter rose from the internee crowd all around me. Then, the two women in front of me fell on their knees with their faces in their hands, weeping for the battered man, and when they did, I saw him clearly.

His stomach swelled to an unbelievable size, and I almost vomited. They had to stop! They had to stop! My hands flew to my mouth, and I screamed, but I don't think any sound escaped me. I just kept watching. Then Abiko did something more horrible. He leveled his bayonet at the man's middle and stabbed, stabbed, stabbed. Water and blood gushed out of his victim's ballooned belly like a hellish fountain, but he jabbed on. Finally, after what seemed like an eternity of water and blood spewing, the man's bloated belly collapsed. The gored, crumpled, shell of the man, hung forward in the ropes of his chair, his lifeless form bowed and broken.

And Abiko laughed. That bastard laughed. The other guards didn't. I grabbed Nellie's hand and she gripped mine back. Only when Abiko turned toward the gaping crowd, and waved his dripping bayonet at us did we turn slowly and in shocked silence start to walk away. Abiko yelled at us as if we were not supposed to be watching, but he had done it in the open for a reason. Somewhere in the back of my mind, I knew he was glad we internees had seen what we saw—that we'd seen what an evil, murderer he could be.

From the ranks of the thinning crowd, Father Sheridan in his loose black shirt and Roman collar came up from behind us, a lifeboat presence in this churning sea of horror. He slipped quietly between Nellie and me, placing one hand on each of our shoulders as we walked. I looked up at him in shock, tears streaming down my cheeks, and my throat so tight I could hardly ask the question. "Why would they do that? How could they be so horrible and cruel?"

"I don't know, Lee." He shook his head and glanced at the cross tower and clock on the Big House. It was noon. "Human nature at its very worst."

We walked on slowly, and I was trying hard not to think about what I'd just seen, but I couldn't shake the grotesque images from my mind. Especially, the bloated stomach fountain. And the end. That man slumping forward in his chair, hanging on his ropes, water and blood everywhere.

"I wish we hadn't seen it," Nellie whispered up at Father Sheridan, tears streaking her pretty face. "I couldn't look away. Does that make me evil too?"

The same question had been gnawing at me the whole time. Why did I watch? Was I secretly a horrible torturer too?

Father Sheridan paused mid-stride, and both Nellie and I waited for him to answer. He too seemed to be replaying the monstrous scenes in his mind, his brow knit, and his green eyes glassy, but he spoke firmly. "I didn't turn away either." For a minute, I thought he was finished speaking and felt a stab of disappointment, before he added, "Maybe that man needed some friends at the foot of his cross."

"But we didn't help. We didn't stop them," I choked out. I was so ashamed of us.

"We witnessed," Father Sheridan corrected me. "Sometimes that's all a friend can do. He was not alone."

Then he squeezed both of our shoulders, as if we three had been there on a mission and for a reason. Without waiting for Nellie or me to respond, he started walking us toward the basketball courts, and said quietly, "Eternal rest grant unto him, O Lord, and let perpetual light shine upon him."

The words of the traditional Catholic prayer for the dead were barely out of his mouth, when I saw Lulu, on the distant basketball court, peel off from the team and come racing towards us. I froze.

"We can't tell her." I looked from Nellie to Fr. Sheridan frantic. That lightning flash realization seemed like the most urgent message I would ever have to deliver. "We can't tell Lulu what we just saw. Her dad's in a military camp, and she keeps telling herself he's got some Nice Guy Haruo for a guard."

Nellie's sorrowful eyes cleared and she straightened instantly, and gave a quick nod. "We won't say anything," she agreed.

Father Sheridan played along. "You two are just a little late to practice," he said, "because you asked me to come over and bless your team before its opening season. "What did you say your name was again?"

"The Whites," I answered quickly.

He stared at me. "Yes, the Whites."

Chapter 29
MASS AT THE MUSEUM

Sunday, July 9, 1944 (continued)

"Cranberry Turkey Mold? Are you out of your mind? Even I wouldn't eat a cranberry turkey mold."

Lulu and I were killing time before mass, and had settled into folding chairs around an empty table outside her second floor room. My best friend stared at Recipe Number 217, which I was penciling furiously into *The Captive's Kitchen*. Open on the table beside me was *The Junket Book*, a 1932 cookbook that featured "cool-creamy-desserts." As a way of blocking out the morning's horrors and keeping Lulu from learning about them, I focused on food—a pastime that now rivaled bridge for our attention. I'd transcribed into my notebook all the Jello-mold and mousse recipes I liked: Apricot Mousse, Key Lime pie, pudding, and now—"Cranberry Turkey Mold."

"When you live in the free and fertile United States of America, a country that hasn't been invaded or fire-bombed or shelled to smithereens," Lulu railed, "a country that still has flocks of big fat white turkeys and juicy red cranberries galore, what kind of idiot puts them together in the same recipe? Hideous. I can't believe you're copying that one."

"If we're home for Thanksgiving, I'm going to try it. It sounds pretty good to me. Actually, Lulu," I glanced over at my once-chubby friend's now hollow face, "I can't believe you're developing standards. Aren't you the one who stopped me from pummeling that locust the other day, because you were thinking about eating it?"

"If you fry them and put some chocolate on them, those are crunchy and good," she insisted. "The problem is finding something to fry them in. The peanut oil line was two hours long yesterday."

I continued copying the elaborate list of ingredients as if my life depended on it, the exercise a powerful distraction and the only thing that stood between me and my grotesque morning memories. I wrote very neatly in small, penciled script, and squeezed two rows of text onto each blank line. I had already filled more than half the notebook Hope had given me, and I didn't want to run out of pages. Then I heard the echo of Lulu's words 'something to fry them in,' and smiled at a flash of memory.

"Did I tell you about Hope's trick yesterday when she was trying to make the talinum taste less horrible?" Scrawny talinum greens looked more like weeds than food, but they were the only vegetables that still grew in camp.

"What'd she do?" Lulu was instantly alert.

"Pond's Cold Cream. Hope still has half a jar left from the Red Cross Comfort Kits, so she scooped a blob on to the frying pan and sautéed the talinum right then and there on the charcoal stove in our shanty. I can still hear 'em sizzling away."

Lulu was hanging on my every word. "How were they?"

I looked up. "Greasy, but good. Kind of like spinach, but the cold cream made them taste," I fumbled for the right word, "heartier maybe. This mold's going to be really hearty too." My mouth was watering as I turned back to the recipe. "It's got two cups of minced turkey in a clear broth base jelled at the bottom. Some chopped onion and celery in that layer too—all chilled of course."

"Then what? I reserve the right to loathe it, but tell me every detail," she demanded. Somehow just talking about food, describing luscious ingredients, and key steps in preparation made us less hungry.

"Then you make the second layer," I read my notes "boiling water, sugar, cranberries, apple, cloves, chestnut meats, cinnamon stick, and orange rind. Mix those together with gelatin and you pour that all over the congealed turkey."

"And it goes back in the fridge?" Lulu was riveted. "So you mean the cranberries aren't crushed and mixed in with the turkey? They're two separate layers—one brown and one red?"

"Right. Then you chill it overnight and serve it for lunch the next day on lettuce—with mayonnaise, pimento, and green pepper." I concluded with satisfaction. "Happy Thanksgiving!"

"Hideous," she shook her head. "I still say it's hideous." She took a deep breath and stared at me intently. "What's the matter with you today, Lee-Lung? At basketball practice, you played like you were out there on the Planet Mongo. Come to think of it, Nellie was on another planet too. I looked like Babe Didrikson on that court compared to you two."

Just the thought of Lulu as champ Babe Didrikson on the basketball court made me laugh out loud. Babe Didrikson was the US Olympic star who'd led her women's basketball team—the Golden Cyclones—to national victory in 1938. Then in classic Lulu stream-of-consciousness style, my best friend switched topics again.

"You think we'll be out by Thanksgiving—now that the boys are in France and MacArthur's leapfrogging across the Pacific?"

My heart lifted for the first time that day, recalling the blissful news of our boys landing in France, and recent word of MacArthur. "Maybe, and by the way, Lulu," I stopped writing and looked up at her in mock seriousness. "It's *frog-jumping*, not leapfrogging. Didn't you see that *Manila Trib* headline: 'General MacArthur's Frog-Jumping From Island to Island Is Proving Very Costly and Far From Successful.'" The Japanese-run *Manila Tribune* was still being distributed in camp.

"Oh, right—'frog-jumping.' Well, that headline's a sure sign he's probably just a couple hundred miles off the coast of Mindanao," Lulu speculated. "We're definitely free by Thanksgiving. Probably less than sixty days to go."

"Maybe, but we haven't had any air raid drills yet. Even Yoshie says we'll have air raid drills *'if Yankee imperialists threaten futile attack,'* Grinnell says so too."

Lulu scowled, and changed tacks again. "Are we going to that special mass at the museum?"

I finished the last sentence in the recipe, closed my spiral-bound notebook gently, and met her restless blue gaze. "OK, you heathen. You can come too, even though you haven't converted yet. If you converted, Lulu, you could go to communion, you know."

***

The museum was on the mezzanine between the first and second floors of the Main Building, and I told Lulu to wait for me on the landing, while I walked down to Room 4 and tucked *The Captive's Kitchen* safely into the drawer of my bed. A year ago Lulu would've come with me, but we were hungry enough now to avoid making extra trips up and down the stairs. Besides, my quick mission gave me welcome time alone to pull myself together and stop pretending I hadn't seen what I saw.

Earlier in the afternoon, I had stolen a few minutes alone with my mother and told her everything about Abiko's cruelty and that poor Filipino's death. She hugged and rocked me for a long moment, and whispered how unfair it was that I should be "trapped in a place of such barbarism." Then she took my face in her hands and told me how deeply sorry she was that she and Daddy hadn't gotten us out of Manila before the war.

I'd told her that was ridiculous. How would they have known what was coming? It helped me, though, to know that my mother knew about the monstrous cruelty of Abiko, and thought it was as appalling as I did. She hadn't just shrugged her shoulders and say "that's a Jap for you" - like Aubrey Man. She'd ordered me not to tell Betty. Of course, I wouldn't tell Betty. Betty still liked to believe the best about everyone, and would probably go mad with something like this.

Even before the sign *Room Four Is Your Home* came into focus, I heard

Hope's acid voice ring out in the first floor hallway. "So help me, if either of you ever go near my cot again," she raged, "you will learn how Granite State women handle mountain lions!"

I rounded the door jamb to see two frightened women, recent transferees into Room Four, backing away from my school teacher friend. Hope gripped a straw maleta that usually lived under her cot. Cat fights happened all the time these days, partly because our rooms were so crowded and roomies so short-tempered, but partly because internees were stealing shamelessly from each other. Across the room, another group of women, two in matching playsuits, glanced up from the mahjong game on their cots, and warily eyed the quarrel. Unfortunately, Mrs. Linda Lee Todd was nowhere in sight.

"What's up, Hope?" I tried to lighten the situation and headed across the room to the corner near my bed and her cot.

"You could remind these tramps about STIC's Eighth Commandment," she replied without ever shifting her gaze from the two women apparently caught in the act.

"*Thou shalt not steal.*" I announced.

"And the tenth commandment?"

"The tenth is like it," I quipped. "*Thou shalt not covet thy neighbor's shanty nor his room space … nor anything that is thy neighbor's.*"

In the first month of captivity, the Executive Committee instructed the Religion Committee, led by Rev. Walter Foley, to produce *The Camp's Ten Commandments*. We had people of all faiths in camp, so our set was modeled on the Bible's big ten, but tailored to our circumstances. They applied to everyone.

"We were only looking," replied the gaunt woman with unkempt hair, who kept backing away from Hope. Her bedraggled accomplice nodded. These ladies had to be totally new to camp. I still didn't know their names.

"Well, don't! Don't look!" Hope snapped and defused the situation by plopping down on her cot, suitcase snug on her lap. She snapped the locks open, while the two newcomers darted towards the door.

"Did they take anything? Is it all there?" I asked as she rummaged through her precious possessions.

To me it always looked like Hope had a lifetime supply of cigarettes in there, since she traded "food for fags" as she said. You could get 12 packs of cigarettes for a one pound can of powdered milk, and Hope said milk should be for kids anyway. Hope was five foot four, and at this point, couldn't have weighed more than 95 pounds. She nodded perfunctorily and snatched a pack of Akebonos from the case along with a slender book. I squinted at the cover—Maxwell Anderson's play, *Valley Forge*.

"Thieves. Cheats. We're losing all honor, Lee." She shook her head, lit a cigarette, and returned the three-quarters full cigarette pack to her suitcase, stowing it once again under her cot. Then she took a drag, stood up, and taking in my worried face. "I heard about the Filipino and the water torture," she said, exhaling. "You're strong, Lee. And you're a smart girl. Now you know what they're capable of. The question is: what about us? What are we capable of? We have to be able to count on each other."

Hope shot an annoyed glance toward the silhouettes of the two women who fled through the door. Then she brandished *Valley Forge* at me. "That's what this is about. You coming to our reading tonight?"

My mother had mentioned the performance earlier in the day. I nodded. "Sure."

"Father's Garden, after roll call," she reminded me.

As Hope headed for the door, I slipped *The Captive's Kitchen* into its home, and struggled to close my wooden drawer tightly. The frame was still hopelessly jammed from the Kempeitai raid three months ago.

***

As I trudged back up the stairs, I realized I was relieved to be going to mass. Nothing else in our lives was quiet, safe, or beautiful any more. But mass still was. We often just sat or knelt in silence and drank in the quiet. I forget which famous saint said "God is in the Silence," but that's why God was so hard to find at STIC. The camp rumbled with the din of four thousand short-tempered prisoners and angry guards. Mass wasn't all silence, of course. Sometimes we listened to centuries-old chant of the priests or sang Fr. Visser's beautiful glorias and credos. We heard readings that were often hopeful. We watched candles flicker on makeshift altars, and saw an unflappable priest in Bermuda shorts lift a spotless white host or makeshift chalice.

I paused halfway to the landing to catch my breath, a little weak, and squinted at the outline of an empty gray space in the stairwell, where some dramatic painting had once hung. It had been removed for safe-keeping during the first month of our internment, and I couldn't quite remember it now, but I missed seeing color in that drab space. This place was "Bleak House" now—grey stone walls on the inside, beige stone walls on the outside—festooned with barbed wire, of course. Endless dirt and dust and squalor. It was all so unlike our tropical island home before the war, which burst with color—lush green lawns, pink and crimson bougainvillea in every garden, orange hibiscus and purple orchids on every hillside.

"Huuhlloooooh" Lulu hollered down to me from the mezzanine landing, and I snapped out of my reverie and climbed the remaining half flight of stairs, as she sped down to meet me. "Mass at the museum instead of Santa Catalina. This'll be a first. I've never been in there," Lulu siad

"Me neither. We're not allowed, remember?" I tugged on the door. It was still locked.

"Just Mrs. Maynard." Lulu reminded me that Mrs. Maynard's work in the library was just off the museum. "So they've got too many priests to fit in any other space?"

"Yup. Big new group of Australian and American priests. Seventy of 'em."

Priests had a religious obligation to say or serve mass daily. But it was against the rules for all the priests to just say one mass around a single altar, so we were going to have the unusual spectacle of thirty-five individual masses taking place here at the museum.

I heard the click of the lock being turned, but nothing prepared me for the sight when the iron-hinged door swung open, and we stepped into the forbidden space. Dark, cool, and three floors high, the cavernous museum could not have looked less like a church. Twin rows of balconies overhung the second and third floors, and my upward gaze immediately was met by the hoary snout of a bearded wild pig.

I almost screamed before recalling that this was a Natural History museum. The colossal Palawan pig's head was just one of a weird chorus of onlookers - the walls between the balconies featured the heads and carcasses of every animal species in the PI. A Bengal tiger, a snarling lion, and a furious leather-faced gorilla glared down at us. The armored snout of a Philippine rhinoceros practically charged off the wall. Only the elongated snout and slender antlers of the local deer looked vaguely benign. Oh, and a life-sized stuffed carabao standing in the corner. Lulu gripped my hand painfully.

I forced my gaze straight ahead to the long museum hall, where tiny crucifixes topped dozens of dusty glass display cases. A few dozen internees sat in folding chairs in front of the numerous make-shift altars. I spotted Paul, Annie and Mrs. Davis at one end, and then my mother near the middle, who waved us to two seats she and Betty had held for us. Paul shot me a "can you believe this?" glance, as we moved toward them and slid into our seats. I could not.

Settling in the rigid in the wooden chair, I stared at the improvised altars smack in front of us. No starched, white altar cloths covered the cases. I squinted through the grimy glass, and realized with a jolt that the priests had placed their crosses and missals smack on top of the ghastly reptile collection. Serpents, iguanas, pythons, and all manner of dead, slithery thing reared their heads up at the mass paraphernalia. Ugh! Disgusting.

Leave it to the PI to have enough different creepy-crawly things to fill three dozen cases. Is this where they put that baby python that floated into camp during the typhoon? Today had been a day of horrors, and now even mass was ghoulish.

A tinkling bell rang precisely at five, and our little congregation rose to the sight of thirty-five priests processing in all manner of wrinkled Bermuda shorts and knotted rope belts, hands clasped in prayer. They processed calmly to their individual altars with an equal number of similarly clad server priests right behind them. The green satin vestments they would've worn before the war had been left behind in some ransacked seminary. Minus their vestments, this was like watching rehearsal for a mass, the unsynchronized performance of seventy players, in which each recited the familiar Latin words and made the same gestures of blessing at just slightly different times.

"In nomine Patris, et Filii, et Spiritus Sanctus... Amen," the male chorus intoned, and they genuflected almost simultaneously in front of the altars. My heart raced and I was riveted to the scene, knowing that every single one of those priests had just come eye to eye with a serpent staring back at him. They didn't flinch. I wondered what Fr. Sheridan thought.

Where was he? It was hard to tell because the cases lining the hall ran three across and twelve deep, and the priests had their backs to us, so they all looked alike. Then, I spotted him at the altar furthest to the right in the third row—distinctive red-gray hair, but balding at one spot in the back. I hadn't noticed that before. I nudged Lulu, and pointed stealthily.

Her eyes widened. "He's going bald!" she whispered as appalled as I was. My mother cast a withering glance in our direction, and we quieted—instantly reverential.

As we sat and listened to the Latin readings, I closed my eyes, hoping to clear my mind of the day's horrors. But images of Abiko jabbing his bayonet through that poor bloated, fountain-of-a-man flashed before me. Then the bowed and broken Filipino hanging forward in the thick ropes of his chair. I looked up to distract myself, only to be glared at by the open-mouthed Bengal tiger, his four spiky incisors poised to rip into my flesh. The scowling gorilla next to him was standing in line for the leftovers.

I blinked away, looked into my lap, and instead focused on the embroidered pocket of the faded skirt I was wearing. It was the same skirt I'd worn the day I met Ramón. *Be a lioness, Leonera. Roar as you can.* Ramón's encouragement came back to me, and I felt a new resolve. These stupid monsters were all dead and glued to the wall. I glared back up at them. I couldn't help thinking, though, that's what Abiko and his henchmen had been today—snarling beasts, Bengal tigers, gorilla brutes.

By the time we all stood for the Gospel and listened to the Latin, I knew exactly which reading I wanted to hear. I hoped it was the one about Jesus getting furious with the money changers in the temple, knotting a thick rope, and whipping the greedy blood-suckers out. Rage. "Righteous Anger," as Father Sheridan would say. That's what I wanted, and besides, that's the only gospel where Jesus really lets the bad guys have it. He lands on them like a ton of bricks and scatters them to kingdom come.

I had a fleeting thought that if we got the "turn the other cheek" gospel today, I might consider becoming Jewish. At that exact moment, I glanced up to see the enraged lion snarling down at me. OK, maybe I would not become Jewish. But I sure hoped we weren't going to get any "meek and mild" advice.

A towering, blond priest turned towards our little congregation to read the scripture in English (the only part of the mass they translated for us.) "A reading from the Gospel according to St. Mark," he boomed with the basso profundo voice of God himself —if God were an Aussie. It echoed wondrously in the cavernous room. "In those days, when a great crowd had gathered and they had nothing to eat, Jesus called his disciples to him…"

My heart lifted and a bubble of hope rose. It was the miracle of the loaves and fishes. Jesus has five thousand hungry people in front of him and he's worried they'll faint dead away on the long walk home if they don't eat before they go. He blesses a few loaves and fishes and suddenly, multiplies enough food for everyone to eat. When the priest concluded that there were even seven big baskets of food left over, Lulu poked me in the ribs and rolled her eyes longingly.

The promise of that reading lifted my heart, but it was the Consecration in that dark, forbidding room that would stay with me my whole life. The Consecration was the time in the mass when ordinary bread became the body of Christ. The priest would hold high the round, white host and it was transformed not in shape but in reality to the true presence of Jesus himself.

That day we knelt on the stone floor and at the moment the bell chimed, I looked up to see thirty-five, full-moon hosts raised simultaneously over the cases of serpents and to the chorus of snarling beasts. My heart grew very still. God wasn't just in the silence, I suddenly knew. He was in the horror and above the horror. No basso profundo voice boomed, but I heard Him. *I am with you in the darkness and the beasts don't win. The serpent is crushed.*

A warm flood of memories washed over me: Rosalina pressing the sharp-edged cross of her wooden rosary into my palm, a gift to make up for Max. Haruo, our prison guard and enemy, bringing *Leonore's Suite* to life. Me, standing terrified before Bugs Bunny Guard at the gate, squeezing that plastic Black Nazarene only to have Haruo appear. Lulu refusing to hate her dad's captors and insisting on the Locust Rule. And in the darkness each night, stars shining brightly in Daddy's own constellation—the Southern Cross. *I am with you in the darkness.*

When mass ended, Mommy, Betty, Lulu, and I left the museum silent, each of us lost in our own thoughts. The contingent of newly interned priests were scheduled to say mass at the museum daily for the next few months, and we internees could attend whenever we wanted, but I knew this Sunday would stayed etched in my mind and heart forever.

"The chow line will be a mile long by now," Lulu broke the spell. "If we don't hurry, we're only going to get the dregs of those little dili fish our cooks have multiplied for us."

"I've been hoping for the bread, myself," said Betty. We hadn't had bread in months.

I needed a recipe for bread, I suddenly thought. The four of us shuffled down the steps and neared the empty space on the gray stone wall.

"Do you remember what painting used to be here, Mum?" I asked her as we moved past the spot. I was trying out "Mum" because "Mommy" was starting to sound childish to me.

She paused, glanced at the outline of a missing shape, and furrowed her brow. My mother had always had a good eye for art, and she painted a little herself. "Dramatic blue sky and Jesus crucified with a bunch of Filipinos at the foot of the cross, and a light shining from his heart to them."

That was it. I remembered it now. The kneeling Filipinos, whose faces were pure sorrow.

"They witnessed," I muttered. "Sometimes that's all a friend can do."

My mother looked at me strangely. "The Filipinos weren't even there, Lee."

"It's symbolic," my artist sister chimed in. Fourteen-year-old Betty was taking every art history book she could find out of the camp library. "It's like all of us being there. The light from Jesus's heart means he already suffered for them and their sorrow won't last long."

"Like our chow," said Lulu, annoyed that we had all paused on the landing. "It's not gonna last long if we don't get downstairs soon."

Chapter 30
WINGS

Thursday, September 14, 1944

The Japanese banned their own *Manila Tribune* in camp by the end of July because even the most contrived headlines ("Americans Lose 90% Soldiers in France") could no longer hide the decisive turn of the war. We knew through the still undiscovered camp radio that our boys were marching through France, and had liberated Paris in late August. By early September rumor had it that Hitler had surrendered too, but that was just the camp disease, *rumortism*. We didn't know that for sure. All the joyful events seemed to be in faraway Europe, but good news in Europe had to be good news for us. How long could Japan fight on without Germany?

Besides, we had seen soldiers hoisting anti-aircraft guns up into the watchtowers our men had built at Abiko's order. That meant the Japanese anticipated our planes any day now, right?

All these thoughts vied for my attention, while I fought to concentrate on English III, our last class of the day. A sweltering blanket of heat enfolded our rooftop classrooms. Miss Margaret Whiteley had just chalked a short poem on the board: "The Caged Skylark" by Gerard Manley Hopkins. I loved poetry, and this title was promising, since there wasn't a single day I didn't feel like a caged songbird. But the fourteen lines proved impenetrable, beginning with:

> *As a dare-gale skylark scanted in a dull cage*
> *Man's mounting spirit in his bone-house, mean-house, dwells —*

For Pete's sake… Whoever heard of "dare-gale" or "scanted"? Dead Brits specialized in words we American teenagers had never heard in our lives. Was *dare-gale* a medieval English word, like chain-mail? Didn't "scant" mean "scarce"? How could you be "*scanted* in a dull cage?" And why was the house "mean" to that man's mounting spirit? I couldn't begin to decipher it.

"We need Bunny," Lulu whispered to me. "She'd crack this code. It's like Boxing Day."

I nodded, wondering if at Los Baños, Bunny still had school. Miss Whiteley turned, having scratched the last line on the board—something about *rainbow footing* and *bones risen*. From end-to-end the poem was an impregnable fortress.

"As we continue our study of late nineteenth century English poetry," she began in a British lilt, "we turn to a Victorian who refused to be caged by the conventions of his time, one whose experimentation in imagery and rhythm delight us still."

"They do?" Paul couldn't resist the easy jab from the back of the room, and we girls giggled. Miss Whiteley chose to interpret the sarcastic question as sage agreement.

"Mr. Davis, the very first image - *dare-gale skylark*—surprises, but charms the reader. Could you explain it, please?"

I turned around to watch this, as did Nellie and Lulu. Paul specialized in flippant humor, but he was also sharp and competitive—particularly in anything that had to do with words—his forte. He squinted at the board for a moment, then bluffed.

"That caged skylark was gutsy. He dared to fly into a storm or gale. He was a *dare-gale skylark* not a ground-bound skylark."

I was about to burst out laughing, but Miss Whiteley seemed satisfied and nodded, giving Paul the encouragement he needed to ramble on in wise-guy, know-it-all fashion. "Skylarks do that - fly into the storm just for fun. They can't sing unless they're flying."

"Is that true?" Squeaky pressed him. Paul was always coming up with instant statistics, and we were often suspicious.

"That is true," Miss Whiteley wrested control of the class back from Paul. "They sing only in flight, so they live to be aloft," profound meaning implied in each syllable. Margaret Whiteley's ordinary speech was like poetry. "Well done, Mr. Davis," she added.

Well done, indeed. Pablo Diablo showed flashes of brilliance, I concluded. Lulu nodded her appreciation in Paul's direction.

Over the next forty-five minutes our teacher explained that "scanted in a dull cage" meant "short-changed" into living in a cage, and that "mean house" translated to a "modest home" rather than "nasty." Hopkins, she concluded, was comparing the soaring spirit of every human being to the caged skylark, because we are "caged in the modest home of our bodies, imprisoned by flesh and earthly cares."

As she lilted on, I was debating whether to plunk Gerard Manley Hopkins into my Whiner Category—right up there with Ovid and Cicero. I bet Hopkins wasn't trapped in a real prison and starving to death when he wrote this. I personally would love to be caged in my earthly body in some "mean home" in Utica. Still, as we worked through the verses, I started to soften toward old GMH. A line late in the poem about the freed skylark seeking rest "in his own nest, wild nest, no prison" won me over.

"Your next assignment," Miss Whiteley informed us, "is to analyze the imagery of flight employed by another late nineteenth century poet, Walt Whitman."

Already my spirit lifted. Whitman was a dead American poet, who did not use mystifying words.

"Perhaps you will identify with his ballad, "To the Man-of-War Bird," she concluded.

Just then an ear-piercing siren screamed over the public address system and we all leapt to our feet - conspiratorial smiles on the faces of every kid in that room. The mind-sundering wail was an air raid siren. Just a drill, of course—it came so conveniently at the end of the school day— but the fact that we were practicing for air raids on Manila—rehearsing the day when American planes retook our city—thrilled us.

Our troops had to be on the way. So sure were we, that last night's music program on the front lawn included "Columbia: The Gem of the Ocean," and "Yankee Doodle." The Japs didn't even know it was patriotic music until we all applauded wildly. Then they figured it out, and announced there'd be no music tonight. Bastards. (I was starting to sound like Paul.)

The only question was how soon would our boys be here?

For the last month search lights had probed Manila skies at night, watching for Allied planes. In camp, Japanese soldiers mounted a growing number of anti-aircraft guns. Meanwhile, we kids, all three hundred of us, had been trained to clear our rooftop classrooms in under a minute. Classes near the stairs exited first, which left Hope's seventh grade, and Hope herself, to bring up the rear, but the exodus was swift and joyous. Every kid going down those stairs had a spring in his or her step.

***

"Pablo, you were an absolute brainwave today," Lulu called to our wise-guy buddy when we spilled out on to the west patio after the drill. We were headed to the Central Kitchen lunch line, where a thin talinum-based soup, awaited us. Would there be any meat in it? We were down to about 900 calories a day now.

"Right. That's why I'm getting steak for lunch," Paul snorted back, and said no more.

Paul, our comedian buddy who'd loved to banter, was changing. His jokes were harsher and more sarcastic now. His humor darker. I knew his mother was in the hospital—fighting dengue fever. What if Paul lost his Mom before the GIs got here? At sixteen, Paul couldn't help but feel he was in charge of the family now, though he could do nothing to protect his mother or little sister.

Annie came alongside her brother and uncharacteristically slung her arm around his waist.

"I hear there's iguana for lunch!" Lulu teased, as we moved nearer to the brother-sister pair. Annie beamed a knowing smile at Lulu.

Three days ago Annie Davis, Betty's buddy, had been chattering through breakfast and dawdling with her cornmeal mush. Camp bully Danny Boy, seated next to her on one of the picnic benches, couldn't stand it. He leaned over and spat—yup, he spat—into Annie's tin bowl, so that he could wrest the untouched mush from her and eat it.

Paul saw the whole thing, sprang up, grabbed Danny by the shoulder with his bad hand, and tried to deck him. But Paul was too scrawny, Danny was too big, and a scuffle followed, with both boys wrestling and throwing punches on the ground, till our own Red Armbands pulled them apart.

Danny got carted off to the Discipline Committee. When a muddied and bloodied Paul turned back to Annie, she proudly showed him her empty bowl. She had eaten all her mush (Danny's spit included) while they were fighting.

That didn't square things for Paul, though. Yesterday, a prize two-foot long iguana that had resided happily in one of the museum's glass cases had gone missing. The stuffed specimen had slithered into Danny MacDonald's bed in the gymnasium during the night. When Danny Boy awoke this morning and tore screaming through layers of mosquito netting to escape his reptile bedmate, Paul had his sweet revenge. Word spread quickly through camp at breakfast.

"All's fair in love and war, eh what?" Paul called to us as we came alongside him. For one second, he flashed his cocky, true-self smile.

"Never more deserved," I congratulated him. "And don't you worry, Paul. We'll see those stars and stripes any day now." I tried to buck him up, but it was the wrong thing to say. His face darkened and his scowl retuned.

"Don't be a complete fool, Lee. We'll be lucky to be out by Christmas, and how many of us will be dead by then?"

He stalked off to the line, while Annie looked back - regret and apology on her face. We had no idea if we'd be out by Christmas.

September 18, 1944

"So you're not last off the roof in the air raids anymore?" my mother quizzed Hope, as they sat on the cots in Room 4.

I had come back to the room to get the notes for my latest English assignment ("write a poem about flight") and walked in on their conversation. Hope took a drag on her cigarette, and shook her head.

"Sometimes, the hardest times bring out the best in kids. Freddy came up to me after the last drill and reminded me that not only was he the tallest, but also the oldest boy in his class, and that he should take the risk."

Freddy Hopkins, of "Ballad of William Sycamore" fame two years earlier was in seventh grade now and was now easily a head taller than Hope was.

"He volunteered to be the last off?" From my mother's pleased smile, her admiration was clear.

Hope nodded. "Wanted to protect me. This camp has turned boys into men, Agnes."

"Did you let him, Hope?" I asked. "Take your place? Be the last off?" I was surprised. Hope was usually so protective of her kids.

"Of course, I did. When a boy is trying to be a man," she took a drag on her cigarette and exhaled, "in the best of ways—and at the worst of times—no busy-body mother hen should stand in his way. Besides he'll be just a millisecond behind me." Hope would have been such a good mother. I wondered why she and her husband had never had any kids. "His father was very proud of him, by the way. For having the courage to think of it and to offer."

"What did his mother say?" my own mother asked. Grace Hopkins was the proverbial Mother Hen.

Hope just pursed her lips and smiled, allowing a thin stream of blue smoke to furl into the air from the corner of her lips. "Let's just say, Dad prevailed."

As I removed my English notes from my drawer, I thought about Hope's warning to me months before: *what about us? What are we capable of?*

So much had changed in the last year —since last September when a hundred of our fellow internees had been repatriated. We'd sung and danced about them "going to Goa," but I remember feeling so alone that early morning when they left.

Looking back, that was the beginning of the hard times. Food that had been boring then was a tantalizing memory now. Now, there were no shows or movies. Some internees, like eighteen-year-old Danny Boy, cheated and stole food even from little kids. They connived to get ahead at every turn. Others, like Paul, sank into depression. Some of us stayed afloat by copying recipes or writing poems about flight and going to mass. And here was Freddy Hopkins, offering to be last off the roof to protect his teacher and be a man. It made me want to cry.

September 20, 1944

"American imperialists threaten closer," our new Commandant informed us at a rare, all-camp assembly and we collectively strove to repress our glee. "So we practice black out and air raid. Japanese protect you."

Commandant Juichiro Hayashi had replaced Wildman Yoshie of baseball fame. Hayashi seemed to share Yoshie's conflicted desire to be both feared and loved by internees. "We protect you," he repeated and we all tried to look suitably grateful. "But you work. Now you go back to grow vegetables. Continue good harvest in camp garden."

At a signal, we bowed deeply, while Hayashi dipped slightly to us, stepped off the wooden crate, then turned on his heel to go. We were not dismissed, though. Pot-bellied Abiko stepped on to the soapbox, and we steeled ourselves for what we knew would be unpleasant. The commander of the guard addressed us through an interpreter.

The camp vegetable harvest had been good, he decreed. Betty and I exchanged glances. So where was the evidence on the chow line, we wondered. My mother and Flossie, their chocolatier days long behind them, spent every spare minute working in the camp garden, and they said the mongo bean harvest had indeed been good. So where were the mongo beans? Where was the cornmeal for that matter? The Red Cross had sent in tons of that, and nowadays we were lucky to get a cup of it at breakfast. Meanwhile, our Japanese guards looked extremely well fed.

The camp garden, Abiko boasted through the translator, had been so successful that no extra food from the outside was needed. His interpreter went on:

"Ignorant Filipinos bring cart with fruits, vegetables and eggs. We ignore. We refuse. We let rot in sun at gate because Filipinos insult Japanese."

Muscles tensed. Anger welled like a warm wave inside me. We were starving, and they were turning away food! Free food from the Filipinos! I tasted bile bitter in my mouth. I could practically feel the four thousand of us rising in mutiny.

"Filipinos not know Japanese take good care of prisoners," Abiko continued. "Have all food you need, third class people."

Then he stepped off the soap box, signaled for the deepest bow we could muster, and the seething mass did not surge forward to kill him. Everyone wanted to, but we did not. Instead, we bowed as low as we could go, while he left with a sneer and cursory dip to us.

"Bastard," my mother muttered. She'd never used that language in front of me before.

I stood there for a minute longer, rage engulfing me, and remembered a time two weeks ago, when we had all thrilled to see Jap soldiers digging air raid shelters—deep trenches right in front of the Commandant's office.

"Let them sweat and dig—their captors will be our liberators," Aubrey Man had muttered in a low voice to me as he passed by the scene. And then in a quiz voice added: "Revenge should have no bounds."

"Hamlet," I answered. Our captive Shakespearean troupe had performed Hamlet just last week for maybe the fifth time. "All the best lines are in Hamlet."

Thursday, September 21, 1944

Mr. Roy Bennett, our bespectacled, scarecrow history teacher stood at the front of the rooftop classroom. He had two tough jobs: teaching modern European history without maps, and keeping his first period students awake at 9:05 in the morning. Early in our internment the Japs gave the Education Committee permission to teach World History up to 1900, but they nixed the use of maps. "No geography," they decreed. That was especially irksome last month when we studied the "Age of Exploration"—the time when Columbus discovered America for Spain, and the Portuguese were "going to Goa"—gobbling up as many ports in India and Africa as they possibly could.

According to Curtis Brooks, our in-house history expert, the Japanese put the kibosh on maps to keep us from realizing how puny and insignificant Japan was compared to the great Allied powers they were up against. Or maybe our captors just didn't want us to understand the course of the war. Whatever the reason, no maps appeared in our classroom or—theoretically—in our textbooks.

But textbooks were harder to sanitize than classrooms, and at night some of us ogled forbidden maps in books the way GIs hunted for bare-all photos of Betty Grable. Where were our boys now? Hadn't they taken Saipan back in June? How many miles was that from the PI?

This morning we didn't need maps. Our class was staggering through a month-long study of "The Scientific Revolution," and today's lecture on Isaac Newton unmasking the laws of motion promised to make Mr. Bennett's second task of keeping us awake, even tougher. As he droned on about Newton playing by the seashore discovering "smooth pebbles in the great ocean of truth," I nodded off.

Then an ear-splitting whoop of a siren shattered the early morning air, and jolted me awake. But just one whoop. Roy Bennett's thick glasses made him look surprised all the time, but now he looked really startled. Usually our air raid drills came at the end of the day, not at 9:30 in the morning. We'd had them every day for weeks, and our teachers and parents emphasized the importance of speedy, orderly evacuations. We kids could now clear that roof in twenty-five seconds flat at the end of the day.

Now, though, I could hear the drone of planes though, and a distant booming. Were those anti-aircraft guns? For a split second, we turned to each other in puzzlement. But Mr. Bennett had regrouped, and hustled everyone out the door.

"Air raid drill, let's go," he announced with annoyance.

"This'll wake us up—" Lulu elbowed me cheerfully. "You were drifting off you know."

"I know," I said, leaping to my feet.

Our class was out on the roof in seconds, moving purposefully toward the stairwell as we had done dozens of times in the last two months. I glanced up to what I thought would be an empty sea of blue, but a heart-stopping sight greeted me. Coming towards us, in perfect V-formation were dozens of silver planes - some at low altitude. How many? Lots. Dozens and dozens. Every rooftop evacuee slowed, stopped, and looked up. My heart pounded and my mind raced.

Were those Jap Wild Eagles? Wild Eagles often screeched overhead in mock dog fights, but usually in groups of five or six not fifty or sixty. These planes looked too big. All three hundred kids and at least fifteen teachers poured out to the roof now, but no one moved toward the stairs. Instead we stood transfixed, and stared skyward, watching the streaking, silver formation thunder towards us.

I was close to the edge of the roof, and glanced down to see internees on the front-lawn like us: frozen in place, gaping at the incoming planes. Commandant Hayashi had been walking with Mr. Carroll, and they both paused: Hayashi pointed up at the incoming flyers with what seemed like pride and approval. Now, the banshee siren began to wail, and my eyes darted back to the skies.

Mr. Bennett's excited baritone voice suddenly boomed louder than the wailing siren. "They're ours! They're American planes!" he shouted. "They're ours!"

I didn't dare believe it, but a wild ripple of joy cascaded across the rooftop. The planes were nearly over us now, and I saw what he had seen under the wings—white stars on a blue field, red and white stripes to the side! Stars and stripes! Not a single fried egg among them! A sea of red, white, and—oh God, love our Navy-blue—under the wings!

"They're ours, they're ours, they're ours, they're ours!" Lulu hollered, leaping up and down next to me. She grabbed my hand and lifted it and we shouted, jumped, and cried for joy all at once, along with three hundred other crazy people on the roof

"Hurray! We love you!" I yelled, as we blew ecstatic kisses to the sky.

Every kid and every teacher, every single one of us who had been trained to evacuate that roof in twenty-five seconds flat, stood our ground, jubilant. We stared heavenward exultant, as if we had all the time in the world. We stared past the nearby stone cross tower that jutted skyward in ecstasy toward the answer to our prayers. Frantic with joy, we waved at the incoming planes, arms lifted like sun-worshippers, all our faces split in grins, like we were celebrities in a *Life Magazine* photo shoot being taken from above.

"Our boys are back for us! They're here!" Did one of them just drop down and rock his wings at us? Yes! They were breaking formation. There he was, dipping his wings again in a salute to us! They knew it was us! They knew us!

"I bet he's adorable!" Lulu shrieked. "Lover, come back to me!" she sang to him.

The joyful rooftop mayhem lasted a solid fifteen minutes, while the siren wailed to deaf ears. I glanced down once to see dozens of Japanese soldiers bolting into the air raid trenches they had dug for themselves outside the Commandant's office. Didn't they know the little boys had been using those for toilets? Haruo looked up to the roof, and waved his arms toward us, signaling us to get off the roof. Well, I didn't care one whit what Haruo thought we should do! Somewhere in the background, Fr. McSorely bellowed, "Get downstairs, kids! Move! Move."

I stayed. We all stayed. And we cheered those big-bodied, silver saviors, as they thundered over us and headed for nearby Manila harbor—home to Jap tankers and oil reserves. Then in the direction of the harbor, a new group of smaller, bent-wing planes burst out of a cloudbank to the northwest. Were they ours too? Yes! Navy blue and gull-like, shimmering their way through puffs of anti-aircraft fire, they swooped like birds of prey. How many - another sixty planes? Stars and stripes streaked across Manila skies as if it were the fourth of July. Oh boy, there would be fireworks in Manila harbor tonight!

We couldn't see the harbor from our rooftop perch, but we saw the planes break formation, crisscross, and dive-bomb decisively, brilliantly. Forget *Swan Lake*: this was the most beautiful ballet ever performed: each steel-muscled plane peeling off at its precise moment, sloping seaward over its target. White streamers unfurled from blazing guns, black dots floated in the air as planes loosed their bombs. High columns of white smoke shot up in fluffy plumes from the harbor.

Only when those first American bombs triggered an explosion of oil and a stupendous scattering of shrapnel, did any of us consider that this was an actual air raid. With fires blazing in the distance and the sky turning ashen before us, shells from the guard tower-based anti-aircraft guns and jagged debris suddenly pelted the air. Our air! Shrapnel whizzed by us and peppered the shanties below.

Hope's gravel voice cut through the jubilation. "Off the roof, kids, off the roof! This is a real air-raid. Get downstairs! Get off the roof!"

Only then did we move. I glanced at the sky once more before ducking into the stone stairwell, and my heart turned gleeful somersaults to see more planes incoming. Thank you, God! Thank you!

A minute later, in the main hall of the Big House, we were all so wild with joy, that no one could stop talking or laughing. Bombs thudded in the distance, and the siren kept wailing. I felt like my teeth would fall out from the concussions of shells so near, but we were all radiant with joy.

Then the lights flashed once, and though bombs continued to pound, the air raid siren screamed no more. Our boys had cut the electricity. Well, not a single STIC internee gave a damn! Did I say that? My new experiment with profanity sounded just right—not a single one of us gave a damn!

Chapter 31
HOPE RETURNED

September 28, 1944

Prisoner euphoria followed that first raid. Had our boys invaded the Philippines? Was liberation just days away? A month at most, we thought. Some internees, who still had tins of Spam or corned beef squirreled away from Comfort Kits, polished them off that very night. Agnes Hanagan Iserson, said "no"—that to celebrate the raid we Iserson girls could split one six-ounce tin of Spam among the three of us, but we were going to make that December 1943 kit last for one solid year in case we needed it, and it was only September. And that was that. (But my three mouthfuls of Spam tasted so good.)

Clarence Beliel (aka Don Bell) made the evening music sing for us that joyful September night. When Lulu and I strolled out to the front lawn, we heard Bing Crosby crooning "Every time it rains, it rains pennies from heaven." Later Billie Halliday's sultry voice floated over the P.A. system. "I cover the waterfront. I'm watching the sea. When will the one I love be coming back to me?" The Japanese didn't understand any of those references, and just let the music play.

For the first few days, the raids continued, and then they stopped. After four straight days with no American planes, Mr. Beliel piped the smoldering voice of Mildred Bailey over the loudspeaker belting out "Lover, Come

Back to Me." And is if our pilots heard her, Our lovers did! Those American planes—thirty, forty, fifty—were back the next day bombing, strafing. Giving us hope.

Sometimes we watched dog-fights in the sky, as Jap Wild Eagles took on our boys. Once, I saw a plane of ours burst into flame and spiral toward the sea, and tears sprang to my eyes. No parachute ejected. That could be my cousin, Francis from Utica, for all I knew. He was a year and a half older than I was, and probably in the service now.

We could watch the air raids only from secret perches now, because after that first day of hoopla, our captors made watching an air raid a crime. They issued an ultimatum: anyone caught staring up into the skies watching a raid, would be tied to a post in the bright sun and made to stand there all day and look up at sun in those skies. No water. No shade. For one day. Two men had already suffered that fate, and their wives said they might never recover their sight.

Meanwhile, our hearts sank when the Japanese moved hundreds of additional Jap soldiers into camp with us. Curtis and his brother Barney, and lots of men living on the first floor of the Ed Building were ejected—banished to the crowded second and third floors of that building, or to the shanties, Gymnasium, or into the Big House, so that the Ed Building's first floor could house Japanese troops. Ugh. Jap troops living in the same building as our men and boys!

Camp was crawling with Japanese military now. They set up tents in front of the Main Building, where they collected truckloads of ammunition and army supplies. And still more army trucks rumbled through the gates. STIC, Prison Camp Number 1, was becoming Imperial Japanese Army Central. Every morning, newly arrived soldiers trained on the front lawn. They marched and drilled, their goose-stepping followed by bayonet practice, sharpened spears thrust forward into an imaginary soldier. Or prisoner? Would that be our fate? Would we all wind up on the end of a bayonet?

Sometimes, though, the whole spectacle of training was downright comical and looked like a Charlie Chaplin movie. One morning, when I was making my bed, I glanced out the grilled window to see dozens of newly arrived Japanese soldiers marching, and oblivious to a handful of little kids behind them. The four- to eight-year-olds, earnest faces screwed in concentration, strutted an exaggerated version of the menacing march routine.

I could not tear my eyes away from the sight. There was little Dottie (my Comfort Kid admirer) and Aubrey Man's son, goose-stepping and thrusting imaginary spears in the air, a bayonet kiddie chorus line. Fortunately, Abiko was nowhere in sight. But Haruo was. He was not part of the drill of these rookie troops, but strode by at that exact moment and tried unsuccessfully to suppress a smile when he saw the kids. I liked him even more than ever then. *You are a nice guy, Haruo.*

***

Saturday, September 30, 1944

"What are you two doing?" I couldn't believe my eyes. The beastly morning found most internees prone in the shade on this sultry Saturday, but Hope Miller in a red bandana, and my mother in ragged Bermuda shorts and a man's shirt - were down on their hands and knees in the full sun, pulling up withered grass and weeds from hard-baked earth outside our shanty. They had marked off a new strip of land about four feet wide and ten feet long. My mother looked up at me, grim distaste on her weathered face.

"Ask the Farmer's Daughter," she replied in an acid tone—which was ironic because my mother was a farmer's daughter too. But Hope had grown up on a hard-scrabble farm in New Hampshire, and seemed accustomed to coaxing life from flinty soil.

"I scrounged this basket of talinum cuttings," she pointed to a woven bowl laden with scraggly greens. "We've also got two garlic buds and some mint." Hope sat back on her heels, shielded her eyes from the sun, and looked up at me. "Then I sweet-talked your mother into helping me. We're planting a garden to take us through the duration,"

"*Duration!* Hope, didn't you see those planes last week? We're gonna be out in days or weeks! You don't have time to grow those!" My heart sank. Did Hope know something I didn't?

"Talinum grows almost overnight," she shot back, returning to her work, "and have you seen today's menu?"

I had seen it. The camp menu was posted outside the Central Kitchen every day. Today it read:

Breakfast:	1 ladle mush; 1 cup tea
Lunch:	None
Dinner:	1 ladle boiled rice; 1 ladle gravy

"I'm planting anything that adds bulk and flavor," Hope continued without looking up, "some extra greens for rice or a soup. And I told your mother that I would do it myself." She smiled up at me in wide-eyed innocence.

"However, I will want to eat it with you, my Little Red Hen friend," my mother responded to Hope in her red bandana, "so I had better help plant it and water it."

"Besides, Agnes, what else do we have to do on a Saturday morning?" Hope asked, as she tugged brown roots from the baked earth.

"Watch for more planes or lay on our cots and conserve our strength," my mother replied, but I noticed she had cleared more weeds and brown grass from her patch than Hope had.

Then my mother glanced up at me.

"Well, don't just stand there, Leonore. Either pull up some weeds or go get us a bucket of water."

I opted for one round of water brigade, then remembered I had to babysit Mouse and Maureen with Lulu. Lulu's mother, Mim, was in Santa Catalina hospital, trying to get vitamins for her beriberi. But for the next two days, Hope took care of the watering, and sure enough perky green talinum stalks poked up from our new Glamorville shanty patch within 48 hours, and small purplish flowers burst from the main stalks. New leaves sprouted almost overnight and we ate them just as quickly—usually chopped on top of our watery rice or in a soup made with hot water and salt. The mint was also growing by leaps and bounds and made good tea (the tea was mint in hot water). Hope said we needed to wait a little longer for the garlic.

One of the rookie Jap soldiers strode through the shanty area and stepped smack on top of the budding plants by accident, and Hope lit into him like he was one of her seventh graders. He spoke no English whatsoever, but could tell by her rapid-fire speech and pointing that she was furious. And he looked mightily embarrassed. He bowed very low repeatedly and backed away apologetically.

October 4, 1944

We lost a few days of school with the ongoing air raids, but our poems about flight were due tomorrow, even though a black-out was in force tonight. Lulu, Nellie, and I bent over a table on the second floor in the hallway, furiously composing our poems by candlelight—at least Nellie and I were. Lulu was slumped in her chair.

"I can't believe we're doing this," she protested to no one in particular. "We could be liberated tomorrow. We are definitely home for Thanksgiving." Lulu's half-sheet of paper was blank, and she pushed it around with her eraser the way my little sister Betty used to play with peas she had no intention of eating.

Lulu seemed intent on resisting our most recent assignment, stared at the ceiling, hesitated a moment and said, "My poem is: *I cannot write a single word, for I will be free as a bird ... pretty soon. And no one needs a poem on flight, when I eat turkey Thanksgiving night ... or at noon.* You think that's long enough?"

I glanced up from my Baby Hermes typewriter, smiled, and shook my head at her, trying not to break my own concentration. I had borrowed an old typewriter from Mrs. Maynard, and was pounding away on my epic ballad. Gosh, I loved poetry.

"Lee-Lung, you might even get to make that disgusting Cranberry Turkey Mold in Utica, so everyone can throw up," Lulu needled, just to see if I was listening.

"Uh-huh."

"Our boys have to be in the PI by now. Leyte - don't you think?" Lulee said. "To fly these bombing runs, make their drop, and get back to base?"

Leyte was an island about 600 miles southeast of Manila. Everyone agreed MacArthur had to take Leyte before he could liberate Manila's island of Luzon. That's where he'd have to enter the Philippines.

"Maybe," I said and pounded on. "But maybe those silver babies are launching from an aircraft carrier.'"

"Those big bombers cannot launch from an aircraft carrier," Lulu said. "I bet they're B-29s." Lulu, like everyone else in camp, was learning as much as she could about plane models and payloads. (Even before the war, *WINGS Cigarettes* had included aircraft recognition cards in every packet, so many of us kids had stacks of these from our smoker parents.)

"Maybe they're B-25s … Darn!" This Hermes typewriter had a "w" key that stuck, and every time I typed a word with the stubborn letter, I had to re-finger and hit the "w" key with my index finger really hard. Then the key struck like a wet spitball. All the "w"s were coming out like solid blocks of print.

"Lay-tee, lay-tee, give me your answer do. I'm half-crazy all for the love of you," Lulu sang her parody of the "Daisy, Daisy" or "Bicycle Built for Two" song we all knew. Then she reached out and put her hand on Nellie's rapidly moving pencil, forcing her to pause.

"Nels, do you know? Are the boys in Leyte yet?"

"Not yet," Nellie shook her head decisively. "Dad says not yet."

Lulu slapped her pencil on the table in disgust. Well, that was that. We knew Nellie's Dad had access to the radio. My stomach knotted at her news. I wanted to be out, out, out - especially by Thanksgiving. Our men were so sick and emaciated—many were battling to stay alive. A rickety wooden death cart left the hospital daily, often carrying bodies to their graves—ninety-one internees dead this year. The Brooksies' father was in the hospital now.

"Our boys are getting close though," Nellie added quickly. "Really close."

"Well, they were close enough to fly overhead and rock their wings at us," I tried to regain my lost emotional momentum, then turned back to my work with fierce determination. "And they are close enough to inspire my opus magnum!"

I rolled the onion skin paper off the cylindrical carriage, and fed the paper in sideways, typing the last two lines of my poem at a right angle up the side to get it all on one page. Then I whipped the finished piece off the carriage and sat back in my chair to re-read it. It looked great typewritten—even if the "w" blurred.

This limping typewriter came in very handy because you could fit more text on a page than with cursive, and we were constantly short of paper. I had stretched the limits of my 6x9 sheet from Hope's Birthday Basket by typing almost all my poem in neat single-spaced, horizontal lines, and finishing with the last two lines at a right angle to get it all on one page. It was more than forty lines long.

Lulu squinted at my epic in disgust. "Lee-lung, that Hopkins poem we read was only fourteen lines long, and 'Man of War Bird' was just twenty-something."

"I know."

"Man of War Bird" was the best. We studied it the day after the air raid, and even though Walt Whitman was writing about a giant black sea bird, he could've been describing our planes. "Thou born to match the gale, (thou art all wings)/ To cope with heaven and earth and sea and hurricane/ Thou ship of air that never furl'st thy sails ... " Walt Whitman really knew how to write.

Lulu cocked her head and squinted in the candlelight to read my title sideways. "Hope Returned. That's a good title. Where's the part about flight?"

"I get to that at the end."

Nellie looked up from her work, blonde bangs brushing her long lashes.

"Read it," she urged.

"It's kind of long, and it's really a ballad of Santo Tomas. I'll just start at the part where we get taken into custody. The Japs are just rounding us up in this part."

"It's not about flight?" Nellie quizzed.

"Wait for the end! OK, here we go." I cleared my throat. "This is about ten lines into it.

> *Alien nationals, all report,*
> > *Pay up for your dreams of imperial sport.*
> *Internment? Call it custody:*
> > *The place—Santo Tomas University.*
> *Duration—that's how long we'll stay,*
> > *Thru sleepless nite and hopeless day.*
> *The spirit—American thru and thru,*
> > *'Gone now, but we'll be back for you'*

"Yes, they will! They will, they will!" Lulu couldn't resist leaping in. "They are back for us!" I glanced up at her, and she stilled. I continued:

> *The blow—the fall of Singapore,*
> > *Soon after, "impregnable" Corregidor.*
> *Men of Bataan, in vain are you brave,*
> > *The Death March leads to your wayside grave.*

"Oh, good that you put that in," Lulu interrupted. "Hope needs to know we haven't forgotten lost husbands. Did you get Bilibid in? Or Cabanatuan?"

"Of course. Just listen." I was a little annoyed that she had disrupted my recitation again, but of course Lulu had to be thinking about her captive dad. Oh, this part was going to be hard.

> *For those who're still living—Cabanatuan.*
> > *Work and starvation and death go on.*
> *At Santo Tomas, we think we're lucky,*
> > *To endure their lot would take more plucky*

"Plucky can't be a noun," my supposed best friend broke in. "It's an adjective. You can be brave—plucky—or you can show pluck, but you can't take more plucky."

"Lulu, this is my poem and I'm using poet's license to change things," I snapped. "Remember how the skylark was 'scanted in a dull cage,' and Hopkins made 'scant' a verb?" She stared back at me skeptically—even a little cynically - none of the usual Lulu-Love in her eyes, and that made me mad. "Well, plucky is a noun for me, and it means 'courage.' I'm gonna repeat this part, so just listen all the way to the end without interrupting, OK?"

Lulu arched her brows, pursed her lips and gave me an "oh-brother" look, but I continued.

> At Santo Tomas, we think we're lucky,
>   To endure their lot would take more plucky
> Than we, with gradual starvation
>   Added to minor, tho' much privation:
> Rollcall, rumors, camp detail,
>   A cup of cornmeal in a 5 lb. pail,
> Lines for chow and lines for shower,
>   Lines for everything, every hour;
> Bedbugs, mosquitoes, ants and flies,
>   Beriberi, deceit and lies,

I glanced up briefly, surprised to see tears streaming down my best friend's face. She was rocking slowly in time to the rhythm of the poem, her face contorted in anger or sorrow. I read on.

> Nerves on edge and everyone waiting,
>   Pessimists, faithless, anticipating
> Death before the promised return
>   'Til the spark of hope can no longer burn,
> And then September of '44

> And hope flares up to burn once more —
> The silver eagle of death now flew,
> No sun on its wing, but red, white, and blue.

I concluded with in a triumphant whisper. Nellie gripped Lulu's hand and smiled like she was trying not to cry. Lulu's pond-like blue eyes were now alight and resolved.

"No sun on its wing, but red, white, and blue," Lulu repeated softly, and nodded, staring sadly at her blank page.

"I don't know about you, but my hope has returned," Nellie decreed, and gave me a thumbs-up.

"Not mine, I still have to write this hideous poem," Lulu said, and turned to her task.

The next day, when Miss Whiteley asked for volunteers, I read my poem aloud and uninterrupted to wide-eyed appreciation from my classmates. Our British teacher nodded her approval and said I had expressed my ideas clearly, concisely, and with a strong rhyme scheme. She collected all our poems, but a week later returned my ballad at the end of class with a disappointing B+ because "although very well executed, this poem is not really about flight, which was the assignment."

It was flight of the spirit! I raged to myself. Didn't she recognize a dare-gale exercise in free thinking when she saw one? Brits were so tragically rigid.

"This is infuriating," I grumbled to Lulu as we marched down the stairs, unable to contain my indignation at Miss Whiteley. "She is so …"

"Leonore," Lulu interrupted with pedantic gravity and a barely concealed smile, "She is 'scanted in a dull cage.'"

"Right!"

***

For the next two weeks, rumors about Leyte abounded, and we had air raids both morning and afternoon. Then on Saturday, October 21, a month to the day after that first joyous air raid, Clarence Beliel made all the usual morning scheduling announcements for the day over the PA. Everyone lapsed into silent attentiveness when he concluded his reveille reminders by urging internees working in the vegetable garden to report in timely fashion.

"You'd better hurry. Don't be late," he urged. "But you know it's better LAY-TEE than never."

Everyone froze in place, but conspiratorial smiles broke out across the lawn that golden morning. Not a single Jap guard understood, and not a single internee missed his meaning. Our boys were in the Philippines. Our boys had taken Leyte.

Hope Returned —
Lee Agnes Iserson

The day—the first of '42
    The sky- an inky black, not blue;
The hush—the Open City; gone
    The forces, just before the dawn;
The smoke—bodegas burning down,
    Leave nothing useful on the ground;
The policy—by name, "Scorched Earth",
    A blackened path to want and dearth;
The terror—vengeful Sakdalists
    The villains enter, hear no hists;
The "Conquering Heroes," small and wan,
    Slit eyes, the light of freedom gone.
Alien nationals, all report,
    Pay up for your dreams of imperial sport.
Internment? Call it custody:
    The place—Santo Tomas University.
Duration—that's how long we'll stay,
    Thru sleepless nite and hopeless day.
The spirit—American thru and thru,
    Gone now, but we'll be back for you.
The blow—the fall of Singapore,
    Soon after, "impregnable" Corregidor.
Men of Bataan, in vain are you brave,
    The Death March leads to your wayside grave.
For those who're still living—Cabanatuan.
    Work and starvation and death go on.
At Santo Tomas, we think we're lucky,
    To endure their lot would take more plucky
Than we, with gradual starvation
    Added to minor, tho' much privation:
Rollcall, rumors, camp detail,
    A cup of cornmeal in a 5 lb. pail,
Lines for chow and lines for shower,

      Lines for everything, every hour;
Bedbugs, mosquitoes, ants and flies,
      Beriberi, deceit and lies,
Nerves on edge and everyone waiting,
      Pessimists, faithless, anticipating
Death before the promised "return"
      'Til the spark of hope can no longer burn,
And then September of '44
      And hope flares up to burn once more—
The silver eagle of death now flew,
      No sun on its wing, but red, white, and blue.

Chapter 32
SPOT SEARCH

Saturday, November 18, 1944

"Leyte, Leyte, give me your answer do. I'm half-crazy all for the love of you." It was only mid-afternoon, but Lulu lay in bed next to me, staring at the mosquito netting suspended above us, and making up whimsical song lyrics, while I read *Gone with the Wind*. "I'm waiting for liberation," she sang, "to go back to my nation. And when I'm there without a care, I'll eat steak and cake for two."

I couldn't help laughing. *Gone With the Wind* slipped from my hand and clattered onto the floor. It was a chunky book. Was it worth the energy to pick it up? Was Scarlet O'Hara that interesting? In the part I was reading, she was almost as hungry as I was. "Steak and cake, huh?"

"Yup. Aren't you going to pick up that book?" Lulu spoke to the intricate web of nets suspended by strings above us.

"I'm thinking about it. Do you think if I pick it up I'll be hungrier than I am now?"

"Maybe. Probably."

We had gotten into the habit of resting after lunch—when there was lunch. Today's lunch on the line had been one ladle of lugao—a watery, rice mush that had more than its fair share of small black critters in it. If Lulu and I had been in charge of de-weeviling, that rice would never have gotten through. Then again, maybe there were more vermin than grains of rice these days.

At lunch, I heard one little boy complain about the worms, and his mother told him to eat them because they were good protein. *Mommy, do I have to eat all the worms?* I could still hear his plaintive little voice.

Despite this disgusting protein supplement, I was starting to think that eating made me hungrier than not eating. One ladle of lugao just left me wanting more (maybe not more lugao), so reading after lunch was usually a welcome distraction. But did I have the strength to retrieve that heavy book?

"My mom's getting better you know," Lulu's spirits had been high all morning because the vitamin supplements were working on Mim's beriberi.

"That's such good news, Lulu." My mother had squirreled away two bottles of vitamins from our comfort kits, and given one to Mim.

"Oh, listen to this! I was taking care of the girls yesterday," Lulu said. The girls were Lulu's two younger sisters, eleven-year-old Margie and four-year-old Maureen. Maureen had spent almost her whole life in camp.

"Mom had to rest for a while, so I was in charge of them over in the Annex. We were playing restaurant," Lulu said, "I was the waitress, so I said, 'Well ladies, I'll take your order now. What would you like?' I'm scribbling in the air on my little pretend pad. Margie says 'I would like a sandwich.' And I ask 'What kind?' Maureen pipes up and says—all earnestness— 'I would like a sandwich with some bread on it.'"

Lulu shook slowly with laughter, and then I started laughing, and we both started laughing so hard we cried. I rolled over on my side and I put my arms around my best friend, and she hugged me back, laughing and crying hysterically. We had almost no laughter left and no tears left, when the banshee wail of the air-raid siren split the late afternoon air, and brought us both to our feet. Thank God! The boys were back for another foray! Liberation had to be any day now.

November 24, 1944

Thanksgiving came and Thanksgiving went. No Cranberry Turkey Mold in Utica. No annual internee football game either.

Days before Thanksgiving our weekly rice and cornmeal rations were slashed again, so weary internees sat around talking about football, but nobody had the energy to play on the muddy field any more. We teens hadn't played had sports in a month.

Mrs. Croft and Mr. Lautzenhiser hinted there'd be no more classes after Christmas break. We lost weight every time we climbed those four flights of stairs. I was five foot four now, a good two inches taller than when I came into camp, but tipped the scales at just 94 pounds. Mommy and I were the same height, and she was down to 90 from the 130 she weighed BI—that's *Before Internment*.

And our family was doing much better than many. A year ago Betty and I thought our mother was an overprotective kill-joy, for not letting us devour every item in those Red Cross kits. Now the two of us thanked God she had forced us to squirrel away provisions. And Hope's garden outside our shanty was proving a godsend too.

The Japanese, meanwhile, were stocking up on food supplies right before our very eyes. Just this month they brought four hundred fifty-pound bags of corn into camp, three sacks of sugar, and more than 2000 cartons of cigarettes (OK, that's not food), socking them away in their military supplies warehouse or "bodega" on the front lawn. Abiko made no secret of the fact that Japanese troops were well supplied.

That rankled, especially on Thanksgiving Day, when the Central Kitchen menu announced:

Breakfast:	Cornmeal Mush, no sugar, no milk
Lunch:	Lugao
Dinner:	Rice and Vegetable Stew of Camote Tops

Well, at least we got lunch. And Betty and I knew we could count on Mommy, Flossie, and Hope to make things special for Thanksgiving.

For our third Thanksgiving dinner, we got our rice and vegetables from the line, then headed to our Glamorville shanty, where we gathered around our charcoal stove with the red clay pot that had cooked and bubbled many special stews for us over the three years. The little clay pot had a hole in it now, but we had been plugging it with a wadded scrap of fabric from an old shirt for the last few months. It worked fine.

In honor of Thanksgiving, Mommy and Hope broke open a small tin of corned beef and another of apple butter from our nearly depleted Comfort Kits. But something smelled marvelous. Flossie and my mother had also prepared a Thanksgiving stew with talinum, garlic, salt and pepper, chopped canna bulbs, and some hibiscus leaves, fresh from our own garden. It was so hearty and flavorful, that we almost felt full.

It wasn't until Betty and I were washing the tin plates and the clay pot after dinner, that we realized the pot was draining itself. Its tight fabric plug was no longer in place. We looked frantically on the ground for it, but it was nowhere to be found.

"Do you think it was in the stew? Do you think we ate it?" Betty stared at me in wide-eyed horror. Silence descended.

Then Mommy and Hope burst out laughing and just couldn't stop. Flossie and Janet followed and Betty and I started laughing too.

"Well, now we know why that stew was so filling and tasty," my mother choked out as she continued to shake with laughter, reaching into her skirt pocket to dry her eyes.

***

Lulu, Mim, Maureen and Margie had their own celebration, and Lulu and I were going to meet for bridge later, so after dinner, I went outside to sit for a while and look at the stars. The bombing had been constant for the last two months. There seemed no end of targets for our boys to pulverize, but I was starting to wonder if they had forgotten about us.

I remembered another Thanksgiving night two years ago—the sorrowful night when Betty and I learned of Daddy's death. And come to think of it, just last year on Thanksgiving, we were still trying to bounce back from that merciless typhoon and the "dance-that-wasn't," and I was head over heels for Ramón Ayala, who never played *"Leonore's Suite,"* for me and never danced with me. He'd left for Spain a week later. Was I always going to associate Thanksgiving with loss?

Still, even on that purple twilight two years ago, the strains of "Someone to Watch Over Me," had rippled across the front lawn, and one star of the Southern Cross had pulsed vibrantly just for me. Then a year later, Ramón had written me such a beautiful letter, comparing me to an "autumnal fairy." Imagine me bringing light to his cloudy days. That was really sweet of him. Where was Ramón now? Did my Black Nazarene protect him? I looked up to see the pulsing star of the Southern Cross. Ramón was probably just fine.

"You looking for planes?" my mother asked as she settled down next to me, and we watched a cloud float in front of the moon. "It's a beautiful night for bombing."

I smiled. My mother wasn't kidding. She was referring to the clouds. The bombers needed some cloud cover to come in undetected. Or at least the clouds helped them. Tomorrow would be cloudy for sure.

"They'll skip tonight, don't you think?"

"Uh-huh," she nodded. "It's Thanksgiving." She looped her arm over my shoulder and pulled me close. "It won't be long now, pet, and we have things to be thankful for." My mother wasn't a snuggly person, so her embrace meant a lot to me. "I'm thankful for you and Betty, and for still being here. Well, not being here, but still being alive."

"Me too." I whispered back. "Maybe tomorrow."

December 11, 1944

I don't know when I realized Betty was spending an awful lot of time on the third floor of the Main Building, but after eleven straight days of rain in December, even Lulu realized we hadn't seen much of her.

When we kids weren't in class, our gang had been entertaining itself in the halls of the first and second floor of the Big House with a non-stop bridge tournament. Lulee and I had just beaten Lizzie Lautzenhiser (our principal's daughter!) and her buddy, the glamorous Ginny McKinney, who had the private alcove because she was brown. They were seniors, and infinitely more mature than we were, so Lulu and I would have felt quite smug about the whole thing, if Ginny hadn't been so distracted because her dad was very sick. She wasn't playing her best game, but Lizzie was too nice to say anything about the hand they just lost.

Betty whizzed out the door of Room Four, scraps of paper in hand, and swept by our table to head back up the stairs.

"What are you doing up there?" I called after her.

"See for yourself. It's a Christmas present for Dottie over in the Annex, and you just won't believe it."

"Little Dottie of the "Comfort Kids" Dottie? The one I gave the fudge to last year?"

Betty nodded. "She and her mom are in the Annex, but her dad is up on the third floor. He's going to surprise her with the most amazing doll house ever. Made it out of four empty Comfort Kit crates. It's big. It's got everything - front steps and a porch, a little handrail. Annie and I are making some tiny rugs, and paper dolls. Martin's working on some miniature chairs. He's a great wood worker."

Annie had always been Betty's best friend, but Martin's name had come from her lips increasingly lately. Fourteen-year-old Martin Rivers had moved into the third floor of the Big House with his dad a month ago - displaced by those Jap soldiers in the Ed Building. I was pretty sure my little sister had a crush on him, and that was sweet because Martin was Jewish and our dad was Jewish so, so maybe she felt a connection to him too.

"Come see it when you're done here!"

At that moment, an announcement blared over the loud speaker. "Residents of the first floor Main Building report to rooms now for roll call and search!"

Betty froze in place, then turned, and scowled at me in disgust, and started back to our room. I got to my feet, exasperated too. We were just starting the second rubber. And even standing up took effort. Well, at least Betty and I were on the right floor.

This spot search was a new Japanese military technique—they plundered one floor of a building or one section of shanties at a time in surprise searches. The Japanese were still looking for the radio or anything that could be made into a radio or anything that looked like radio code. Two weeks ago, we had been ordered to turn over all typewriters. God only knows how Mrs. Maynard's limping Hermes could be turned into a radio, but I was glad that I had whipped off "Hope Returned" before she had to fork it over. "Hope Returned" was going to be my Christmas present to my mother.

"See you after hide and seek," Lulu muttered to me, as she moved away and toward the stairs. Lulu's room was on the second floor, along with Lizzie and Ginny. They had to be out of the way for our spot-search.

"To be continued," I nodded and slipped the score sheet into my skirt pocket. Tables and chairs were quickly stowed, clearing the hallway for the Japanese search team, and we Room 4 ladies moved to our roll call positions outside our rooms. Mrs. Linda Lee Todd snuffed out a home-made hibiscus leaf cigarette that couldn't have been very good anyway. It smelled like camp fire.

"Let's show them how it's done, ladies," Mrs. Todd smiled at all of us. "Surely, our last runway parade before the boys arrive."

Mommy, Hope, Flossie, Janet, Betty, and I all headed to our spots on the wall. It was our third search, and we knew the drill. We also knew the Japs weren't paying as much attention to us, as to whatever they could find in the room. Still, when three uniformed, bayoneted soldiers strode down the hall in front of us, we bowed as low as we could go.

I didn't get a good look at the three-some, but I knew Bugs Bunny Guard was one of the team, and that Haruo was not. I hadn't seen Bugs Bunny in a while, and rumor had it he'd been transferred to Los Baños, which made me feel bad for all the Los Baños internees because that be-whiskered screwball was oily and treacherous. Here he was. Back again. We heard the usual tossing of crates, overturning of cots, rummaging of drawers, and clanging of tin pails as the trio ransacked Room 4 in search of something—anything they hadn't found before.

Then as quickly as they had entered, they exited and pressed on to Room Three, where Annie and Mrs. Davis and Mrs. Brooks and thirty other women stood at attention. Bugs Bunny Guard had some papers stuffed under the pit of his arm. What had they taken? I had a sinking feeling in the pit of my stomach. An eternity passed while they repeated their Viking pillage routine next door. They came out empty-handed. The three-some began to storm back to the main door, when Bugs, who seemed to be the senior guard, halted in front of our Room 4 line, and whipped out from under his arm the tattered papers taken from our room.

"Who have this code?" Bugs demanded as he splayed the four dog-eared, yellowed pages in his stubby hand.

My heart stopped, as I saw the five-lined staffs, the musical notation and unmistakable handwriting. "Happy Birthday, dearest Lee, my darling grown-up daughter."

"That's mine," I heard my mother's unwavering alto voice before I had time to react. She stepped forward and bowed so low, that even Bugs seemed taken aback. Except that when she rose to face him (she was exactly his height), he slapped her hard across the face.

The women of Room Four now flattened themselves against the wall, and my mind screamed at the injustice of the blow, but Agnes Iserson didn't flinch. She just stared back at him. I could only see the back of her brown-gray curls, but I knew her eyes were boring into him like emerald drill tips because I had been on the other side of that unyielding stare many times. Then I couldn't stand it.

"No, that's mine," I heard myself say, and stepped forward. I bowed very low (*From the hips not the waist*, I could hear Abiko chiding) and rose slowly, bracing myself for the blow that didn't come. Bugs Bunny Guard turned from my mother to me, and just ogled me: his whiskered mustache twitched; his brown eyes mocked. "That's music," I said in the simplest, clearest English I could muster, thinking that maybe he would actually understand the word "music," and give it back to me.

Instead he fanned the four pages, leered at me, and drew his finger suggestively across the top of each page.

"This radio code," he decreed. "You come with me."

And before I could say another word, the two guards on either side of him grabbed my arms and marched me down the main hall and out the entrance of the Big House toward the Commandant's office, while my mother and Betty screamed in the background. I heard Lulu shriek from the second floor "Reprobates! Hideous reprobates!" But their voices echoed from a fading, distant realm. The only thing I was conscious of were two vice-grip hands that clamped my bare upper arms so hard, I was sure they would snap off above the elbow.

My heart thudded against my ribs, and a cold terror seized me on the long march to the Southwest Territory, where I had seen the horrible water torture months before. I glanced back over my shoulder once to the Main Building with its cross tower, hoping to see dozens of angry prisoners storming after us in protest, but no one raged. Internees just stared, open-mouthed. I was alone with these brutes.

Wild incoherent images and memories raced through my mind. Jap guards hauling that protesting Filipino vendor away from his vegetable stand a year ago, and all of us hearing him wail through the night. Then that roped prisoner in the chair, the hose forced down his mouth, his balloon belly pierced by the bayonet. The painted Korean ladies who sat around in their slips all day near the officer quarters, and kowtowed to Jap officers. The last image filled me with more horror than the first two. They wouldn't make me a Comfort Girl like Valentina's friend, would they?

As the two soldiers gripped my arms, we jerked abruptly to a halt to let one of the death carts roll by. A humiliating sight.

The wooden cart pulled by two bone-thin men bore four short wooden coffins - the end panels of each knocked off. Swollen ankles and feet of the dead dangled out the end. These coffins, designed for Filipinos, were too short for Americans, but the corpses they carried were internee starvation deaths. Bugs Bunny Guard pointed and snickered. He murmured something contemptuous to the two guards who gripped my arms. *That was not going to be me*, I resolved. *That was not going to be me.*

I could make a break for it at the gate, I thought wildly. The vice grip of the two thugs hauling me tightened, and they shoved me forward, but not toward the gate. Bugs Bunny Guard rounded a far corner away from the gate to drag me in a back door to Commandant Hayashi's headquarters. There I had the first welcome sight of the day.

Bugs seemed startled to see Corporal Haruo Tanaka seated at the desk outside the Commandant's office, doing paper work. He looked like a secretary or maybe a watchdog for Hayashi. I could hear animated voices, both Japanese and English inside the closed doors of the Commandant's office. Haruo immediately rose to his feet and gave no sign of knowing me. He barked something in Japanese at Bugs and his goons.

The two guards released me, sheepish looks on their faces, and stepped back. Bugs Bunny snapped at Haruo, rattled off a string of rapid fire Japanese, and thrust out to him the offensive papers. Haruo's eyes widened as he looked at the sheet music, which he did not accept. He stared at Bugs as if he were lower than a toad, and I heard him say something like:

"Koray-WAH-nan-DESkah?" which I took to mean, "What the hell is this?"

Then another rapid fire string of Japanese, as Bugs Bunny clearly elaborated his theory of evil radio code. Then Haruo snatched the papers from him, and rattled something back, which I hoped meant: "You complete idiot. The only radio code here is in bass and treble clefs. Now get out!"

Because Bugs did. He and his two goons turned on their ugly jackboots, and headed out the door as Haruo stacked the four sheets neatly in front of him, and stood facing me, his face impassive but his eyes sympathetic. We could hear English and Japanese in the office behind him, but we were alone.

"Thank you," I said. And then I remembered my manners and my limited Japanese. "Arigato," I said and bowed.

Haruo dipped back slightly, but his gaze lingered on the musical notation scrawled in my father's hand. Then he held the four pages out to me. "Hard to give back," he said.

"Do you want to copy it?" I asked, and held myself very erect. "You can copy it, and give it back to me later."

His almond shaped eyes widened, and for the first time in three years, I saw a warm, genuine, Nice Guy Haruo smile. The only one I ever saw. No teeth, no laughter, just a slight smile with his liquid brown eyes looking right through me. Then he dipped low to me. "Arigato, Leonore." I almost smiled, but more of me felt like crying because I was so relieved that I was safe, and I hadn't lost my father's last gift to me. Haruo tucked the pages into a manila envelope on his desk.

"You're welcome, Haruo." I dipped back, just as Mr. Grinnell and Mr. Carroll emerged from Commandant Hayashi's office.

"Is Miss Iserson filing a report?" Earl Carroll was trying to make light of the unusual situation, but he stared at me with concern.

"There was just a mix-up during a spot-search," I said. "They thought I had radio code but it turned out to be…"

"Let me guess - knitting instructions," Mr. Grinnell interrupted. "K2, P2; repeat across, end K2. Sounds very sinister. We've had that before."

I just nodded. I don't know why. I didn't mean to lie, but I didn't want anyone to know that I had given Haruo my music to copy. I rustled the folded bridge score sheet in my skirt pocket, as if it were the offending document.

Mr. Carroll put his arm around me. "Take you back to your room, Lee?"

I nodded, and the three of us headed out the door.

Chapter 33
CHRISTMAS CONCERT

December 24, 1944

"How will he get it back to you?" Lulu was practically pulverizing her white cotton slip in the aluminum wash tub. "Honestly, Lee, we've got a conundrum here."

More than a week had passed since the spot search, and Haruo had not yet returned *Leonore's Suite* to me. I tried not to think about it. "He knows where I live, Lulu." Water spattered in my eye, as I wrung out my favorite white blouse with its Peter Pan collar.

Lulu and I had gotten up before the *Good Mornin'* reveille to get our family's laundry done at the communal wash stand before the hordes arrived. Mommy and Betty usually took care of this while I did the bathrooms, but the men had started to clean the bathrooms now to spare the women the toll of calories from harder physical labor. So it was my turn to pitch in at the galvanized iron trough where we washed our clothes. Lulu and I stood next to each other with metal buckets before us, a rack for "clean clothes" above, both up to our elbows in cold, grey, not-very-sudsy water because the entire camp was running out of soap.

"OK, so let's imagine this." Lulu wrang out her slip and plopped it on the damp Bermuda shorts that were "clean." "Haruo marches to the door of Room Four, and says 'Mrs. Todd, I have a delivery for Miss Iserson. Will you please convey this unto her hands?' Then he hands her a mysterious envelope, bows, and marches off?"

"Something like that," I said, growing more uneasy as she spoke.

"Are you out of your mind? A Jap soldier leaving a written message for an American prisoner—a teenage girl prisoner? Halo-Halo! They will clap him and YOU in Fort Santiago so fast it'll make your head spin. Conspiring with the enemy! Passing secret messages!"

"Lulu, aren't you supposed to be my friend?" I didn't like to admit it, but Lulu could be right, and my stomach knotted painfully.

Just yesterday shock waves rippled through camp when four members of our Executive Committee—the head honchos—had all been dragged to Commandant Hayashi's office, screamed at, and summarily arrested by the Kempeitai. Mr. Grinnell, Mr. Dugglesby, Mr. Larsen, and one other man seemed to be accused of something dastardly in Jap eyes. Aiding and abetting prisoners in Cabanatuan! How the heck could they be doing that?

Still, their quarters were searched, and they were being held in the camp jail, but everyone was worried they'd be sent to Torture Central - Fort Santiago. And for what? Mr. Carroll was the only one to survive the Jap purge. None of us knew why he had been spared.

Lulu and I filled our small woven baskets with the last of our wrung underwear, and I arched my aching back. We washed small loads of laundry at a time because there wasn't a lot of space to hang wet clothing, but even so, being hunched over the tub for three-quarters of an hour on an empty stomach took its toll. I'd hang our family laundry in the shanty. Lulu would take her family's back to the Annex, where Mim and the girls had a communal space.

"Keep me company," I said. "Then I'll walk you over to the Annex."

"Sure." Lulu and I breathed in the rosy early morning air, and walked in silence toward the Glamorville shanties. Camp was never completely quiet, especially with so many Japanese trucks and troops making STIC their headquarters these days, but for this brief moment, nothing seemed to move except us. Rose Blane hadn't chimed in yet, and the dawn was blissfully cool.

We didn't talk because lots of families were still sleeping in their shanties, but just as we rounded the bamboo stake, marking Hope's talinum garden, a bright, blast of Abe Lyman's orchestra and Rose Blane's "Good Mornin, Good Mornin" came chirping over the camp loudspeakers, and practically jolted me into dropping my basket. Only willful refusal to rewash those clothes accounted for my athletic recovery. Small children started to cry, hungry for their breakfast, and the overcrowded camp stirred to life all around us.

We entered the shanty with its card table and folding chairs. I deposited my basket on the canvas seat of a folding chair and reached up to the shelves for the line we used to string laundry. Lulu sat with her basket in her lap. She reached for something on the table, while I strung the line.

"Lee," she whispered a minute later. She didn't have to whisper. It was past reveille now.

"What?" I answered at full voice as I started to drape damp clothing. I was trying to hang my Peter Pan collar blouse so I that wouldn't have to iron it very much. There. That was fine.

"Lee, he knows where you live." Lulu said just a bit louder.

I spun around to see my best friend, holding a buff colored, 8x11 envelope that had been lying on the card table. I had walked right past it, but now Lulu held it out to me.

I snatched the treasure, peeked inside, and a wave of relief washed over me. The pages of *Leonore's Suite*, neatly stacked and none worse for the wear. I'd been sure Haruo would get it back to me. I pressed the envelope to my chest. Then I laid my treasure back on the table, ready to return to clothes-hanging, but was surprised to see crabbed, childish script on the front. The indecisive fountain pen ink proclaimed:

44-12-25 19:30

That stopped me in my tracks, and I slowly turned the envelope toward Lulu, who frowned.

"What do you think it means?" I quizzed.

"That he used an old envelope someone else had scribbled on?"

"Or that we now have the combination to some important safe—maybe in the Commandant's office, and it has a lifetime supply of Spam inside," I fantasized.

"Or ….." Now Lulu's periwinkle blue eyes were alight with mischief, "that bluebells are singing horses."

I stared at her a moment and burst out laughing. Lulu and I hadn't used that Nancy Drew code for years. Not since the early days of our sleuthing around camp together and Operation Arigato. In the best Nancy Drew mystery ever, Nancy used that expression all the time to mean: "Things are not as they seem."

"You think it's a code?"

"I think it's a message," Lulu speculated. "44 sounds suspiciously like the year we happen to be in, and 12 is amazingly akin to the current month, and 25 is tomorrow—Christmas! It's an appointment!" she declared with glee, sounding very much like Nancy Drew herself.

"And 19:30 is the time!" I filled in and suddenly saw everything in a new light. Lulu had to be right about this. Seven-thirty PM on Christmas night. My heart beat wildly and seemed to catch in my throat. "Where?"

"The Practice Room, of course. Haruo's got his own music!"

For the first time in many months, maybe in a whole year, a bright flash of pure joy surged through me. A Christmas concert! A glorious rendering of *Leonore's Suite*. A visit from my father. Nothing could be more beautiful. Or more daring. Why would Haruo do this? Could he have any idea of how much this meant to me? Maybe it was his way of saying thank-you for the chance to copy music I knew he admired. But wouldn't it be dangerous if he got caught? Or what if we got caught fraternizing with a Jap guard? Would they take us to Fort Santiago? I didn't know the answers to any of those questions, but my heart raced furiously at the prospect. I was going to keep that appointment.

Monday, December 25, 1944

Most internees agreed that it was our best Christmas in captivity ever, because hope filled the air. American planes had been pounding the city for months now, but today they dropped thousands of leaflets instead of bombs. Some of the fliers had fluttered right into camp and been snatched up by internees before the Japs could destroy them. They proclaimed:

> *The Commander-in-Chief, the officers and men of the American Forces of Liberation in the Pacific, wish their gallant Allies, the People of the Philippines, all the Blessings of Christmas and the realization of their fervent hopes for the New Year.*

The realization of our fervent hopes for liberation! Our boys were going to spring us any minute.

When Father Sheridan celebrated 9 AM mass at the museum, it was packed. Today he settled a worn cloth on the wide, flat back of a stuffed carabao, and made that his altar. He said being surrounded by all these animals was like being with Jesus in the stable. Then he spoke of the birth of Jesus as our light in the darkness—even in the darkness of our captivity.

My mind wandered. Our darkness had to be pretty short-lived at this point. After communion, I began to bargain with God. I always formulated my prayer like a letter. *Dear Lord Jesus, remember how your parents snuck you out of Bethlehem when Herod was trying to kill you and how they spirited you away to Egypt? I'd like to be spirited away to Utica instead of Egypt, but please save us now. Get us out of here soon, before the brutes kill us.*

I was trying to figure out my closing, when my thoughts fled back to that breath-taking moment when I was dragged from the Big House by those two Jap soldiers, who gripped my arms with their vice-like claws. I saw clear as day Bugs Bunny Guard tromp ahead of them with my father's precious music shoved under his smelly armpit. I saw how they shoved me into the Commandant's office, and I was so afraid they would make me a Comfort Girl. All that dread and fear—only to see Haruo sitting there and to hear Mr.

Grinnell and Mr. Carroll's reassuring voices floating from Hayashi's office. Mr. Grinnell – he was another person to pray for. He had been carted off to Fort Santiago.

I knelt now and had my face buried my face in my hands, trying to clear my mind. But that familiar echo from the long-ago mass at the museum floated back to me, *I am with you in the darkness. The beasts do not win.* Maybe I didn't need a closing line after all, because I think He heard me. But it was just a habit. "Thank you, Lord, for your consideration of this request. Love, Lee."

***

Everyone was abuzz with news of the leaflets when we exited mass on that mild Christmas morning. On our way to the chow line we passed the Annex where Dottie played outside with her brand new dollhouse. The little girl brimmed with delight, as she arranged paper dolls and furniture. Dottie's parents sat on the steps, her mother leaning on her husband's arm, admiring their daughter and her favorite present.

The Comfort Kit dollhouse was a marvel to behold - with its staircase to a front porch, elegant living room, dining room, and kitchen all on the first floor, then a bathroom and three bedrooms on the second. Goggle-eyed five-year old Dottie, who didn't even remember living in a home of her own, could hardly believe this is what American homes looked like. Betty, Annie and their friends had cut out intricate paper dolls for the little girl—a mother, father, three children, the neighbor's children, and some extra playmates too. Dottie lined the whole series of dolls in an ascending row from outside up the front porch through the first floor stairs, and up to the second floor hallway.

"What's happening in your doll house, Dottie?" Betty asked as we moved past her and toward the chow line. Janet and I came closer to ooh- and ahh.

She pointed to the second floor bathroom door. "It's first thing in the morning. They're waiting to use the bathroom."

Betty, Janet and I bit our cheeks to keep from laughing. Betty squatted down next to Dottie, and said, "When you get back to the United States, Dottie, you won't ever have to wait in line for a bathroom again. There are enough bathrooms that people don't have to wait in line—especially in your own house."

Little Dottie just looked at Betty like she was telling a funny joke and shook her head, and returned to her game.

***

The three of us headed to the chow line, where the Christmas menu read: "One ladle rice mush with sweetened chocolate and coco milk." Well, that was something! Sweetened chocolate and coconut milk—where'd they get that? Betty, Janet, and I collected the breakfast ration for all five of us, and headed back to our shanty, where Mommy and Flossie had prepared a special Christmas breakfast.

Today marked exactly one year to the day from which my mother decreed we must conserve our Red Cross kits for one year. We were going to have a spectacular finale. We Isersons still had one can of tiny Vienna sausages, a little tin of Log Cabin maple syrup, and —God-only-knows how my mother had scrounged it—a duck egg and one cup of rice flour. She and Flossie were making pancakes! All of us were studiously avoiding the question of how we would make do without any Red Cross reserves. There hadn't even been a rumor of Comfort Kits this year. Well, there had been a rumor: the rumor was that the Japs stole them all.

After a marvelously filling breakfast, we exchanged Christmas gifts. Betty had drawn an absolutely perfect rendering of our little shanty for our mother with the banner "Glamorville Days" inked above. Underneath she had penciled, "1942-1944."

"Are we 'out the door in 44?'" Mommy smiled and chided Betty, thinking back to our toast last January.

"It's in pencil, Mommy. I can change it if we go another few weeks."

'To *Out Alive in Forty-Five!*'" Hope toasted, as she waltzed into the shanty unsteadily, holding what looked for all the world like a mostly consumed glass of champagne with some mint in it.

"Where'd you get the bubbly, Hope?" my mother was impressed.

"The Hopkinses invited me to their shanty for a little Christmas cheer. Some teachers get apples, and others get Champagne Juleps." Hope wore a smug grin, raised the glass to her lips and sipped appreciatively. "My contribution was the mint. It's doing very well. Did you see, Agnes?"

"There's almost as much mint as talinum out there," my mother confirmed. Their little garden was flourishing and had been a life-saver. None of us could've imagined how we would have gotten through December without it.

"I would've preferred bourbon to champagne," Hope continued, "but beggars can't be choosers. God only knows how long they've had that bottle squirreled away."

My mother showed Hope Betty's drawing, and Hope fussed over it. Then I handed the gift of my poem to Mommy, wrapped in the envelope Haruo had used—it was festooned with a red crayon bow I had drawn on top. (I had managed to completely erase the pencil-marked "B+" from my typewritten poem, "Hope Returned," and even steamed the onion skin paper a little bit - and with extreme care- to make sure the impression of B+ was gone.) When she slipped it out and read the poem, it was clear that in my mother's eyes, my opus magnum surpassed B+. Tears rolled down her cheek, then she hugged me close for a long moment, and she told me she would frame it on our return. And that her hope had returned!

For her part, my mother produced two Christmas miracles for Betty and me. Her gift to each of us was one can of Spam. "To be eaten whenever you wish. Love, Santa." was penned on the little card taped on top. How did she do this? I knew our Comfort Kit reserves and tallies as well as she did, and we were out of Spam. We were out of everything.

My mother's ability to pull a rabbit out of a hat in these darkest days never failed to amaze me. Did she still have money left over from fudge-making or my smuggling more than a year ago? And who was willing to sell Spam? The camp black-market still operated, but prices were astronomical now. People were selling wedding rings and gold jewelry for a couple pounds of rice. A can of spam was going for the equivalent of fifty dollars. Maybe last year Mommy sold our cigarettes for more than she said she did. That might explain it.

Hope reached in the pocket of her shirtwaist and produced three little packages—one for Janet, one for Betty, and another for me. They were wrapped in discarded pages of *Manila Tribune*.

"It's about time you girls had some new *joolery*," Hope slurred and nodded, pleased with herself. "Made 'em myself," she added, as I pulled mine out of the packet.

Suspended from a heavy piece of string was a whittled—maybe three-inch long - piece of wood hanging like a pendant. A bomb-stick! Lots of people in camp were using them. When the bombs began to fall, the concussion was so loud, you felt like your teeth would fall out. If you clamped down on a piece of wood—it seemed to help. The bomb stick had to be a good chunk of wood—three times the thickness of a pencil maybe. Internees swore by them and said the vibration went in your ears and out your mouth. We couldn't bite the bullet, but we could bite the bomb stick!

We all donned our most useful jewelry ever, and thanked Hope profusely.

I bided my time carefully, and played Santa last. After Flossie and Janet set off for a Christmas morning stroll, Mommy, Betty, Hope, and I were left alone. Lulu waltzed in at exactly that moment and right on cue.

"There's one more present here, Mommy, and it's for all five of us," I said.

I turned the manila envelope over, pushed it across the table toward my mother and waited for her to focus on the shaky hand-writing.

"That's a lovely manila envelope, Lee," Hope was a little tipsy, but she continued with good cheer. "Do you know why they named that envelope after our fair city?" Hope was ever the teacher and totally oblivious to my intent, answering her own question. "Because it is made from the fibers of the abaca plant, which grows only in the Philippines and mostly near Manila. Manila hemp, it's called."

I never knew that. "So you have given your mother a very meaningful native present. But it will be hard to divide among all of us." She toasted me and drained her glass.

My mother, who had not imbibed any champagne, just stared intently at the cryptic message. "What is it, Lee? What does it mean?"

Betty's eyes were boring into me as well.

"There will be a concert for us tonight in the practice rooms at 7:30 PM. Our favorite pianist will perform."

Stunned silence followed. There were no rules against going to the practice room, but 7:00 was usually lights out nowadays. Betty looked as if she might burst out of her chair.

"Isn't curfew…" my mother started.

"Curfew's been extended to 8 PM tonight—for Christmas," Betty answered the unfinished question.

My mother's jade green eyes turned impish for the first time in many months, and a smile spread across her lined face, as she stared down at the envelope. "Should we wear our formals?" she asked conspiratorially.

***

In the end, we decided not to wear our formals. They might draw too much attention to us as we headed off to the practice rooms, at 7:25. I wore my flouncy black skirt, with my white Peter Pan collar blouse, and in my hair, a red cloth flower barrette that Betty had pieced together for me as a Christmas present. In attendance were Hope, my mother, Betty, Lulu, and me.

I missed Bunny being there. She had been with us two years before - the first time Haruo had performed *Leonore's Suite*, and she had always liked Haruo. But Bunny was in Los Baños, which in some ways was supposed to be better than Santo Tomas. They weren't as crowded down there, and families could actually sleep together, but they had no real hospital.

My fourth grade teacher, Mrs. Gewald, had gone to Los Baños with Bunny's family, and with her own daughter Betty Lou. One day nine-year-old Betty Lou got appendicitis and died just because they had no clinic or doctor to remove her appendix. What a tragedy. The clenched black knot of hunger or fear that I carried around constantly these days tightened for a minute. I forced myself to breathe deeply. I wasn't going to think about that now, as we headed toward the room. I hoped Bunny didn't get appendicitis.

Lulu moved into take-charge mode when we entered the practice room. There was only one wooden folding chair in the room, and my best friend foraged extras from rooms on either side. At 7:28, we ladies sat arrayed in our almost-finest on the hard wooden chairs awaiting the entry of the pianist, hardly daring to believe that this was going to happen. I sat in the middle with Mommy and Betty on one side of me, and Lulu and Hope on the other. The piano and bench stood sideways to us, and the chairs were slightly to the right. We were going to be able to see Haruo's finger work, and maybe his face.

At precisely 7:30 PM, Corporal Haruo Tanaka entered the room, and an electric thrill coursed through me as we rose to our feet. Crisply attired in khaki, with a starred red and yellow striped band on his collar and a star on his cap, Haruo's face remained impassive, but he bowed deeply to us, and we bowed back. How strange this was. We were waiting for the enemy to give us a concert. Then NGH seated himself at the piano bench, removed his cap, adjusted the position of the bench, and we slipped into our folding chairs.

Only then did I realize that Haruo was carrying no sheet music. Didn't he copy it? Wasn't that what he was supposed to be doing with it for the whole week he had it?

Seated at the bench, Haruo seemed to forget about us completely. He closed his eyes, drew a deep breath, and a look akin to peace or prayer crossed his face before a lush minor chord filled the room. Every fiber in my being stood alert in the silence between the echoing minor chord and the single bass note, which he struck with such conviction and gong-like clarity that my heart welled in remembrance. As the intervals between minor chord and the bass note shortened, and his finger work quickened, a warm, light flooded my entire being. The familiar strains of *Leonore's Suite* filled the room.

Rippling chords cascaded into a haunting melody that surged and flowed effortlessly under Haruo's sure hands. His fingers caressed the keys and moved lightly along the ivory reaches, the melancholy melody mounting explosively. I remembered watching Daddy play this part, his left hand undulating rhythmically, while his right worked apparently unrelated magic of its own. Here was Haruo doing the same thing, until the piece unexpectedly erupted, and lyrical silver notes sprang from the upper reaches of the keyboard. The music itself took flight. I closed my eyes, and the clenched black knot of fear that I had carried deep inside me for three years quietly loosened and slipped.

It seemed like my whole being floated free of this dirty, overcrowded camp. My father was playing that music just for me, and I was a strong gull on the wing, braving the torrents of a stormy sky, gliding through thunderheads, going higher, beyond the clouds. A cascade of silver notes lifted me, and I touched the stars of the Southern Cross in a velvet sky. "Soar on," my father's music reminded me, as it had two years before. "Spread your wings to match the gale." I was sailing high above the camp.

In my mind's eye, I floated among the stars one minute, then looked down from the black velvet to our squalid world below, as the passionate, chords swelled. I saw myself scrubbing latrines and de-weeviling rice. I floated over an image of me cleaning up Betty's poop, and then climbing the stairs with Lulu. I was selling fudge and becoming Dottie's Comfort Kid one minute, then smuggling money in from Grandma Naylor's the next. I saw myself with Lulu as we peeled vegetables. Then I was writing in my recipe book, pounding out the verses of "Hope Returned" on that Baby Hermes, and facing down Bugs Bunny Guard. I wheeled in flight near the cross tower, and silently witnessed that poor Filipino's death by water torture. I felt a tear on my cheek. That death still made me so sad. "Soar on," my father's music said. *I tried, Daddy. I really did try.*

But the music didn't let me stay sad. The music, my *Leonore's Suite*, leapt to a playful section, where notes bounced brightly off the keyboard, and I stopped flying abruptly. I opened my eyes wide in surprise to see Haruo's finger-blurring technique. His hands dazzled, as they raced in sprightly grace up the ivories and down. This was magical. The melody leapt with fierce lightness off the keyboard, an indomitable joy lifting each note. Haruo's lively toccata had all of us glued to the speed of the notes and his fingers. It had been too long since I'd heard *Leonore's Suite*. I almost didn't remember this impish part, but Haruo's mastery of it was superb. This part of the piece made you want to laugh and shout. I glanced from Hope to Mommy to Betty and Lulu, and saw each of them leaning forward in their chairs, as mesmerized as I was, each of them almost smiling.

Then the free-spirited notes floated into meadows of calm, and the lush minor chords rippled, and the bass note tolled melancholy once more. Haruo's face was a mask of concentration and commitment, as he played. The rippling chords of the piece softened, and the silver melody melted into waves of stillness. Silence. I blinked to see his broad brow furrowed, his quiet eyes resting pensively on the keys. Then suddenly, a softness, peace, and calm suffused his features into a near smile.

We leapt to our feet, clapping, but all of us so awed that we dared not approach him. I glanced at the clock and realized Haruo had been playing for fifteen minutes. My father's piece did not take fifteen minutes to play. Then it hit me. Haruo had added a part. It was a gift! He added that playful part at the end just for me, and it fit so seamlessly I thought it was part of Daddy's original *Suite* to me!

Haruo rose from the bench and bowed deeply to us. We bowed back and we applauded furiously, looking like alternating windshield wipers, I was sure. But it didn't matter, and it didn't seem to be enough. I took a step toward him, and bowed as low as I could go.

"Arigato," I said as I rose. I brushed unruly curls away from sweaty temples. "I loved your new part. Thank you. Do you have a copy?" I asked stupidly because for Pete's sake, he had just played the whole thing from memory.

"I have here," he pointed to his the banded epaulet over his heart. "You have copy. New part free and playful, like Leonore." Except he said *Rike Ree-oh-nore,* which made me smile. *"Merikurisimasu,"* he said, dipping toward me.

"Merry Christmas, Haruo." Again, I dipped as low as I could go. Before I rose he was out the door.

Seconds later, I heard two men engaged in a sharp exchange in the hallway. Haruo was arguing with a fellow guard. I prayed it wasn't Abiko. Two seconds later, Bugs Bunny Guard strode imperiously through the door, and turned the light out. "Curfew! Rights Out!" he announced. "Go to Big House." I looked at the clock. It was 7:55.

Chapter 34

ROLL OUT THE BARREL

Thursday, February 1, 1945

"November—twelve. December—fifteen. January thirty-one." I ticked off the list wearily, as I settled on the edge of my solid wooden bed across from my mother in Room 4. Mommy lay on her cot with her swollen ankles propped on its wooden frame. I had just returned from visiting Lulu at Santa Catalina hospital.

"If only those were dates," she murmured.

"I know…" I'd listed the number of internees who had died of starvation in the last three months. Twelve in November, fifteen in December, and thirty-one in January. That was the latest count from the hospital. Would my mother make it?

Mommy was all bones, but her legs looked like sturdy tree-trunks, the same width from knee to toe, despite the fact that she was down to a skeletal eighty-nine pounds. Those swollen legs were a sure sign of beriberi, the horrible vitamin-deficiency disease that sapped your lungs and circulatory system. We hadn't had wheat flour or bread since April of '42.

She closed her eyes, brow furrowed. "Thirty-one in January." She was trying to take it in. "We were supposed to be out by January."

I nodded. When those first American planes overflew camp back in September, our spirits had been so high. They were here! They would save us! Then on Christmas Eve, when our boys dropped those leaflets wishing us "the Blessings of Christmas and the realization of your fervent hopes for the New Year"—oh, we were so sure.

On New Year's Eve, freedom had been in the air. We kids could practically taste it. Lulu, Betty, and I palled around all night with Nellie, Bill, Lizzy, and Ginny and we just sang our heads off. The Japs were so busy burning documents and building bunkers out of old rubber tires that they paid no attention to us whatsoever. We roamed the Main Building and sang everything from "Mairzy Doats and Dozy Dotes" to "Chattanooga Choo-choo" and "There'll be a Hot Time in the Old Town Tonight."

But that was more than a month ago. My bomb-stick now looked like it belonged to a family of beavers. And we were still trapped here—moving into our thirty-seventh month, for Pete's sake! School, our great distraction for the last three years, closed after Christmas because we were losing too much weight climbing up and down four flights of stairs. There was really nowhere else to hold school: the camp teemed with human beings in every room, patio, and plaza. Besides, everyone just knew our liberation would come any day.

Meanwhile deaths from starvation mounted. Ginny McKinney's dad died just before Christmas. A week ago, Mr. Brooks, Curtis and Barney's dad, lost his battle with beriberi. My mother's tree trunk legs signaled that she had begun to battle the disease too. Mommy wasn't critical yet, but the onset of the sickness depleted the little energy she had left.

"Did you hear about Glenn Miller?" my mother asked, her face a mask of sorrow.

"Yup." My throat tightened.

Glenn Miller, the famous swing band leader whose recordings entertained us nightly on the front lawn, joined the army at the start of the war. Our secret camp radio delivered news that Miller's plane had been shot down over the English Channel in December. He was flying from London to Paris to perform for the troops. Glenn Miller—dead! I don't think the Nazis knew enough about American culture to actually target him, but—killing Glenn Miller... Nothing could've been more devastating to our morale.

I changed the topic, but hardly to something cheerful. "Dr. Stevenson is in the camp jail. They threw him in because he refused to lie on the death certificates. The Japs told him malnutrition and starvation could not be listed as 'cause of death.' He was supposed to change them to - I don't know what—maybe 'appendicitis.'"

"Ted Stevenson has never told a lie in his life," my mother's eyes were closed, but she was almost smiling. "And I bet he's down fifty pounds himself."

I nodded. "He refused to cover up for the Japs, so now instead of helping sick internees, he's in jail. Dr. Fletcher and Dr. Allen are still working though."

"But those people did die of starvation, didn't they?" Betty had come into the room and settled next to me on my bed.

"Of course. Or beriberi, caused by starvation," my mother said. "But if he lists 'malnutrition' or 'starvation' on a death certificate, the Japs are worried they'll be charged with war crimes when this is all over. "

"Well, they should be charged with war crimes!" Betty let loose in an uncharacteristic torrent of fury. "Did you hear about that huge fish and dressed hog they brought in yesterday, for themselves? Stored it in OUR internee ice box! Annie said they slaughtered a big carabao, and are eating that too. And here we are starving!"

Betty was repeating the latest camp rumors. Bill Phillips, who worked in the Central Kitchen, confirmed the fish and hog story. And truth be told, the stew served on the line yesterday had some marrow in it - probably from carabao bones.

"How's Lulu?" my mother rasped from her cot, not even opening her eyes. Mommy didn't like to see Betty upset, and her distraction worked.

"She's repenting, and the nurses say she'll recover. I still can't believe she did this."

Two days ago my best friend got herself hospitalized for a tonsillectomy because she was convinced the food in the hospital was better and more abundant than on the chow line. That's what everyone said. And Lulu was absolutely desperate for more food. Sitting around at night with me, making up menus, didn't seem to take away her hunger any more.

I tried to talk her out of her looniest scheme ever, but hunger possessed her, ravaged her, and ruled her every waking thought. Lulu had faked numerous sore throats in the last two months to create the impression of susceptibility to bronchitis, and convince camp doctors they should take her tonsils out. Actually, they took her tonsils out once. But not successfully—they grew back. Finally, this week Dr. Fletcher gave in and obliged her.

"But they don't even have anesthesia at Santa Catalina any more, do they?" Betty saw the stupidity instantly.

"Nope. They've got some Novocain, but Lulu said it was so old and watered down, it didn't work. Going 'under the knife' she was on her own. She said she felt like someone was slicing her insides out, carving her throat up—which they were."

"Oh my God, how excruciating!" My mother propped herself on her elbows, and looked at me. "Your Lulu is the bravest *idiot* I ever met. Well, are they at least giving her ice cream?"

"Ice chips. A little cold coconut milk. They don't have any ice cream; that was just a rumor." The injustice of it all broke my heart. "I took the *Captive's Kitchen* over and read her my 'Pineapple Raisin' recipe though, and that seemed to cheer her up."

"Pineapple Raisin what?" Betty asked.

"Pineapple Raisin Ice Cream. Recipe number 361. You make it with scalded milk, tapioca, sugar, crushed pineapple, lots of raisins, whipped cream, vanilla and some shaved orange rind." I took a deep breath, satisfied.

Betty's eyes grew wide as saucers, and my mother stared at me as if I had just started to tell a good story, so I continued. "You scald the milk in a double boiler first, then mix in the tapioca and sugar, cook it, stirring it all the time until it thickens. Then you run the mixture through a sieve to get any clumps of tapioca out." I paused and they were still hanging on my every word. "Let it cool off before you fold in the whip cream. You have to beat that really stiff. Then you add the crushed pineapple and raisins. You freeze it over night before you eat it."

In my mind's eye, I could still see the scrumptious photo from *Good Housekeeping*. It was a Betty Grable pinup for a hungry teenage girl. A long delicious silence descended over all three of us as we closed our eyes and imagined our first icy cold, creamy, fruity, spoonful. It was almost as good as the real thing.

"You have three hundred sixty-one recipes?" my mother asked moments later, breaking the spell. "Are you going for one for every day of the year?"

I hadn't thought of that. "That's a great idea. It'll be: *The Captive's Kitchen— Lee Iserson's Culinary Companion for a Year of Plenty.*"

"That's good. That'll sell," Betty nodded. "When's Lulu getting out?"

"Tomorrow. Friday. She's not exactly good as new, but she thinks there's going to be a dance on Saturday, and she keeps hoping Jack Aaron will notice her."

"A dance! Are you girls out of your mind? Do you hear those bombs falling and see those explosions over the wall?"

My mother couldn't contain herself. And she was right. There had been air raids and ear-splitting detonations all day long. On the front plaza we could see the hellish glow of numerous fires burning in the distance. "There is not going to be a dance," my mother dropped her head back on top of her pillow as if disgusted that she had given birth to such nitwits.

"I know, Mommy, but don't tell Lulu, OK?"

Saturday, February 3, 1945

Lulu and I lingered at a table in the dining shed, trying to decide on our plan for the evening. "I say we get dressed up anyway. It's Saturday night," I urged Lulu "Maybe we can rustle up a bridge game."

It was clear there'd be no dance, but I was so glad Lulu was out of the hospital and even had a spring to her step. It was around 5:30 PM, a balmy, humid evening, and we had just finished our line dinner such as it wasn't. "One ladle rice mush," the menu proclaimed.

Curtis, Bill, and Paul sat further down on the bench, with Squeaky extolling the virtues of the B-24 heavy bomber, while Bill expressed his preference for the P-38 Lightning dive-bombers, and Paul looked at them both as if they were deluded morons. His mom had recovered from her bout with dengue fever, but Paul's spirits hadn't changed much. Annie told me he was down to 105 pounds from his 145 before the war, and he looked like a walking cadaver.

Nearby bombing and detonations rocked the camp all day, along with ridiculous announcements over the loudspeaker earlier in the afternoon, reminding us to observe "correct angle for bowing," and "show more respect to Japanese guards." That was clearly Abiko's work. We just rolled our eyes, stood roll call, bowed very correctly, went to dinner, and now waited. Our boys just had to be here soon. Fires blazed all over the city and our planes had been strafing nearby Grace Park, where the Japanese had an airfield.

Today one of our own hot-shot fliers flew unbelievably low over the camp. We waved to him, he waved back to us, and actually dropped a pair of goggles on the lawn with a message attached. "Roll out the barrel—Santa Clause is coming to town Sunday or Monday." Everyone in camp was on edge, and nearly frantic with expectation.

"Did you hear Hayashi took the Jap flag off the wall in his office?" Lulu's raspy voice was scratchier than usual after her tonsillectomy. She was still too distracted by the wonderful rumors to think about bridge games. "He just folded that Fried Egg up and stuck it in his drawer!" she squeaked in delight. "We're gonna eat fried eggs, and they'll taste delicious!" she prattled on.

That rumor was lifting spirits all over camp, and I believed it because I'd heard it from Aubrey Man too, who'd been in Hayashi's office yesterday to mop the floor. The Japs were burning as many as papers as they could, and were pretty much ignoring us completely. I'd seen Haruo only once in the last month, but then again, I didn't spend that much time at the Commandant's office.

"They're runnin' scared. It has to be any day now, Lulee," I said with more confidence than I felt.

"You two are such looney-tunes," Paul had grown weary of his conversation with Squeaky and Bill, and now turned his contempt on us. "We won't be out of here for another month. Half of us will be dead by then!"

Paul's strategy of "expect the worst and you won't be disappointed" grated on us, and Lulu was having none of it. The sky had turned a magnificent orange-purple, a glorious Manila sunset that seemed to bode beautiful things. Sweeping both hands toward the rainbow Heavens, she challenged, "You can look at all of this and say that?"

Then Lulu launched into a giddy impromptu imitation of Snow White's quavering voice. "To-day, my prince will come, and away to his castle we'll go, to be happy forever I know." I clapped. Her solo took me back to glittering pre-war days at the Manila Metropolitan when the beautiful cartoon movie came out. I was nine: that was a lifetime ago. But was today the day?

Paul stood. "And I just feasted on steak and mashed potatoes." He shook his head at both of us and walked off toward the Ed Building.

"OK, let's get dressed up!" Lulu snapped back to the present, and my most recent suggestion.

"Shall we be Bobbsey Twins?" I suggested. Lulu and I (and half the other women in camp) shared identical floral print playsuits given us by the Red Cross last Christmas. She and I sometimes dressed exactly alike (including matching hair ribbons) just to be silly.

"Oh, hideous. Maroon, blue, green—who chose that print, anyway? No. We're going for chic and understated."

"You still trying to get Jack Aaron to notice you?"

"Or my prince. You never know what could happen on a Saturday night." Lulu smiled mischievously.

An hour later we were "chic-ly" understated. I wore a faded red and white print blouse that Mrs. Baskerville had just taken in for me, and a white crepe skirt I had inherited from Kay before she left for Jungle Ville—or Los Baños by any other name. ("I'll never be able to keep it clean there," she told me. As if it were easier here.) Lulu wore a once-forest green shirtwaist dress with big black buttons down the front and tucked front panels. She had been a stocky little girl with a mop of sandy curls when she first came into camp, but both of us had grown a couple inches and lost dozens of pounds. Lulu was still two inches shorter than I was, but she had a figure, and that belted shirtwaist looked terrific on her.

We stepped out on to the front plaza in search of a bridge game—or at least our gang - but not-so-distant detonations and a new sound stopped us in our tracks. A ground-shuddering rumble shook the ground. I felt the low-pitched roar in my bones more than heard it. Was an earthquake was in the offing? Thousands of internees milled expectantly on the front lawn—talking, then listening. What was that shudder? It was getting louder.

The roll of thunder surged from the west, behind the gym and the Father's Garden. Boys and men on the third floor of the Ed Building had a view. They were leaning out windows, pointing, and shouting. Japanese guards in the watch towers shouted too, but I couldn't see a single Jap on the plaza. Maybe they were all in the Commandant's office or on the first floor of the Ed Building.

Paul Davis raced towards us from the Ed Building, and Lulu spotted him. "Pablo! Over here!" she shouted.

"Where are Mom and Annie?" he asked, as he approached. Paul's mother and sister lived in Room Three, the corner room right next to ours, while Paul lived in the Ed Building. Paul seemed genuinely excited, and it was good to see his spirits lifting.

"Inside, I think. What do you see from up there?" Lulu asked.

"Tanks! Those are tanks beyond the wall! That's the rumble. Lots of street fighting too. We can see the tanks and firing. This might be it!"

"Jap tanks or American tanks?" I asked, hardly daring to believe our boys might finally be in the city to spring us.

"I don't know. We think they're ours. The soldiers have huge helmets, though. Not like our guys in '42, so maybe they're not ours. I can't tell."

At that moment, as if he had just vaporized from Hell, big-bodied, broad-shouldered Abiko appeared on the front lawn, and stood on a soap box, bullhorn in hand to address the delirious crowd. This was ridiculous. If we were going to have bowing lessons now, even Abiko would have a mutiny on his hands. He surprised us by ordering, "All internees inside the Main Building now!"

Abiko couldn't have enforced that order on his own. People were too wild with expectation and there were too many of us, but our own Red Armbands, the self-important Guard Patrol, seemed to agree with Abiko. "What if those are Jap tanks out there?" some of the GPs said. "What if the Japs are about to storm in and kill us? Take us out before our own boys can liberate us?"

"All internees return to the Main Building," the camp loudspeaker instructed, Clarence Beliel at his finest. "Seek shelter in the Main Building. All internees evacuate the shanties. Now hear this: The Japanese have decreed: any internee looking out the windows of any building will be shot!"

Part Three
THIS IS MORE LIKE IT

"We've been liberatin' jungles and swamps.
Now, women and children! This is more like it! Hoo-ee!"

American GI on the Ole Miss
February 3, 1945

Chapter 35

TOO DAMN BIG

February 3, 1945 (continued)

What? We couldn't even look out the windows?

Lulu, Paul, and I pressed inside with the throngs. It was about 7:30 PM, and we were all so keyed up we couldn't stop jabbering. Some internees peeled off and went to their rooms, but many of us milled around in the lobby and lined the halls expectantly. More than a few of us teenage girls were dressed up because it was Saturday night, and the hall had the atmosphere of an impromptu party. We were cheek by jowl, buzzing with nervous excitement.

Mommy, Betty, Annie, and Mrs. Davis found us in the big central hall, and my mother seemed to have magically recovered from her bout with beriberi. Her tree-trunk legs were still swollen, but Agnes Iserson was out of bed, with her ash-blond hair neatly waved, her eyes bright, and in high spirits; she knew something was in the air. Fr. Sheridan had been caught in the crowd outside and was now inside the Big House lobby with us. Lulu and I scanned the crowd for all our best buddies. Lulu's mom and sisters were still over in the Annex.

"Have you seen Nellie or Bill?" I asked Paul.

"Nellie *and* Bill?" he corrected me and arched both eyebrows. For one moment he became the old, mischievous, fun-loving sarcastic Paul.

Were those two off smooching somewhere? I wondered. Bill was just ga-ga over Nellie, but she kept him on the string. "He's really carrying a torch for her." I said.

"Got a light?" Paul said in his suavest Cary Grant voice and I burst out laughing. We'd seen *Only Angels Have Wings* at the Little Theater Under the Stars more than a year ago, but Paul knew every Cary Grant line in the movie.

"Where are Barney and Squeaky?" Lulu asked Paul.

"In the Ed Building. Up on the third floor. They've got the best view."

Internees near the grilled windows at the front of the Main Building were eager for a view, and didn't seem to care what the Japs had said. In the foyer, two men poked their heads out through the iron grille to watch what was going on in the front plaza. And for the first time ever, in all our internment, a Japanese guard in the watch towers shot at the internees. Shot at us just for trying to see what was going on for Pete's sake! Fortunately, Jap prison guards are not exactly sharp-shooters. They missed every one.

"This could be it, Lee-lung. This could be it!" Lulu couldn't stop smiling and gripping my arm. "Say a prayer!" Then she saw that we had a prayer expert in the crowd. "Father Sheridan!" Lulu called to our hero-priest, who stood five people away from us. "How 'bout a good battle prayer?"

Father Sheridan's red-blond hair had gone gray months ago, his long frame was gaunt and meatless, but his blue eyes were still impish. "St. Michael the Archangel," he intoned solemnly, as people near us quieted, "defend us in battle; be our protection against the wickedness and snares of the devil. May God rebuke him we humbly pray. And do thou, O Prince of the heavenly host, by the power of God, thrust into hell Satan and the other evil spirits who wander the world seeking the ruin of souls. Amen."

"Amen" several nearby internees shouted. It was more like a cheer. They had all noticed the special emphasis on thrusting the bad guys into hell.

"Abiko is one of the evil spirits wandering the world, don't you think?" Lulu could not stop smiling.

***

A nervous hour dragged on. The group of internees in the Central Hall thinned, as some went to their rooms to sit, and wait for whatever was coming. Mommy and Hope headed back to Room Four. Not us kids, though. We stuck together. When the roar and rumble of the tanks seemed to come from the back of the building, along Dapitan Street, we all raced to the rear exit, and parked ourselves near our little lending library—which was a folding table piled high with books from the pre-war YMCA.

We couldn't exit from the rear, because we didn't want to risk the Japs shooting at us, but the nearness to the rumble made us feel closer to freedom. While we huddled in the back foyer, I glanced at the mountain of books on the folding table, all with familiar titles. Nothing to do but wait.

"Pablo, have you read this one yet?" Lulu was brandishing a chunky little book called *Tom Mix, the Fighting Cowboy*.

"In which Tom Mix, brave and agile as a lynx, rides into Snake Prairie, Texas," Paul narrated as if on stage "and vanquishes the thieving Conway band with its bum card shark leader, Durham 'to make this country a decent and safe place for our ranchers, their wives and children.'? That *Tom Mix*?" There were at least thirty "Tom Mix" books, and before the war boys collected them like baseball cards, or like we girls collected *Nancy Drew*.

"Your role model?" I kidded him.

"Definitely my role model."

All of us were trying to hide how nervous and scared we were, and Paul's bravado helped. I was relieved to see him so cocky, so like his old self. We kids now strained to see through the grilled bars of the windows, but none of us dared poke our heads out. We squinted at the shanties lining Calle Dapitan, and the pathetic remains of a vegetable garden off to the right. But then I glimpsed a skinny stick-figure climbing the north wall. Was that Bill Phillips? Oh no. What was he doing? He'd be shot! I motioned to Paul, Lulu, and Betty. And we watched in horror. This was such a stupid time to try to escape.

"Phillips!" Paul gasped. "What the hell...."

Bill was on top of the wall now, motioning with his arms and yelling. No shots rang out before he practically leapt off that fifteen-foot wall, and disappeared back into the shanties. "Agile as a lynx," the silly *Tom Mix* phrase came back to me. Had he just saved himself from the Japs? Or were they American?

The thundering rumble no longer emanated from the rear, along Dapitan Street. Probably the tanks had rounded the block at Forbes, and were heading towards España, the front of the building. We rushed back to the central hall, where a crowd was gathering again.

It was well past curfew now. It was past lights out. In fact, the Japs had pulled the plug on the electricity at six-thirty, and the waning crescent moon cast so little light, I strained to see the outline of the closed massive doors that stood between us and freedom. We huddled at the foot of the stairs, caught between terror and exhilaration. I knew that in the Annex, weary mothers, like Mim, might be putting their kids to bed now regardless of the rumble. Most internees here in the Big House hunkered down nervously in their rooms, but nobody slept. We kids couldn't drag ourselves away from Central Hall, where more and more excited internees gathered to wait.

"Lee, is that you?"

I squinted into the crowd, trying to locate the source of the familiar gravel voice that was barely audible above the rumble. "Betty and I are near the water fountain, Hope!" I shouted as loud as I could. In no time my mother and Hope pushed through the crowd, and found us. We clustered together in that hall—maybe a hundred sweaty bodies jostled for space as the din grew louder. The place smelled like a locker room. But the earth-shaking rumble outside grew louder still and promised that something big was going to happen. I reached into my skirt pocket and grasped the hard, wooden crucifix on the rosary Rosalina had given me. I squeezed it so hard that it bit into my palm. Please, God, bring us the good guys.

Then we saw a flash from the outside. What was that? A flare? Tracer bullets? Machine gun fire shattered the night, and an iron-crunching, stone-scraping rumble roared perilously close. Our own Red Armbands patrolled the hall, telling us to stand back. Then they opened the doors of the Main Building just a crack, then wider, and all of us strained forward with them to see into the flare-streaked distance.

An enormous dark hulk of a tank, an armored monster with a terrifyingly long lead gun had crashed through the front gate, and was rumbling right towards us with another behind it! Huge uniformed men with submachine guns walked by its side. Its lights blared right at us, and I couldn't see a single star or stripe.

"Stand back! They might be Japs!" one of our men yelled, but no one could stop the starving, frenzied crowd from pushing forward.

Lulu and I pushed right along with them. If they were Japs, we might be walking to our death, but weren't we all dying anyway? Starving and dying?

Then suddenly, from the hatch of the lead tank, rose the tallest, burliest mountain of a man, I have ever seen. His torso sprang from the well of that tank like a fast-growing sequoia sprouting a machine gun. We all gaped open-mouthed at the impossibly broad-shouldered, beefy giant of a man in an enormous combat helmet. Time stopped. My heart stopped.

"He's too damned big to be a Jap!" someone in the crowd yelled. "They're ours! They're American!"

The crowd of internees exploded. We surged forward like a crashing wave, erupting on the plaza in delirium and cheers, shouting and laughing, as four more American tanks rolled through the gates, and dozens of US jeeps plowed right in behind them.

"Look at them!" Lulu pointed to the side walls, where dozens of GIs were climbing over the stone ramparts, cutting barbed wire as they went.

I cried, jumped up and down, and laughed all at the same time. I didn't let go of Lulu's hand for one second. We could now see Stars and Stripes on the sides of jeeps and tanks. The tanks were painted with names like *Battlin' Basic*, *Georgia Peach*, *Ole Miss*, and *San Antone*. Hundreds of American GIs poured in—huge boys in tanks, on jeeps, on trucks, by foot.

Internees went berserk. Shots rang out somewhere, everywhere, but at that moment, nobody in camp cared. Our boys were here now. Nothing could happen to us now. I stood transfixed with one arm gripping Lulu, and listened to fellow internees shouting, "They're here! They're here!" Internees rushed, poured, burst out on to the plaza.

Twelve-year-old Freddy Hopkins, Aubrey's son, and even little Dottie started to scramble up the sides of the tanks to welcome our boys and hug them. Worried GIs shouted, "Wait a minute, kids! Get down now. Don't climb up yet, OK? Moms and Dads, hold the kids!"

Our boys, the GIs, looked both delighted and wary. It seemed too easy. Where were the Japs? A shot rang out from the watchtower aimed at Battlin' Basic, the first tank, but the Mountain Man in the hatch spun around and took out that bayoneted Jap rifle-toter with a well-trained volley of fire. He toppled from his tower. As we cheered, the GIs stared at the thousands of us, looks of disbelief on their faces. I heard one of the boys on the Ole Miss, the third tank, call out in deep southern drawl, "We been liberatin' jungles and swamps. Now, women and children! This is more like it! Hoo-eeee!"

Pandemonium reigned, and in the shouted greetings we learned our saviors were from the First Cavalry Division of the United States Army, and the 44th Tank Battalion. More shots and fire rang out just beyond the gates, but inside the camp joyous bedlam continued, with internees mobbing the GIs who were on foot, hugging and kissing them. Lulu and I cheered with the delirious crowd, watching awe-struck. The boys were having a hard time bringing more tanks in because so many internees thronged the plaza to welcome them.

"Lee, they're colossal," Lulu shouted above the din. "They're giants! Look at our boys! I love them!" Then she flung a melodramatic, two-handed kiss in the direction of the Georgia Peach, shouting "We love you!" to no one in particular.

But one of the boys on top of the tank in an enormous helmet was looking right at her, and called back, "We love you too, sister! What are you and friend doing later tonight?"

Lulu didn't miss a beat. "We're gonna teach you how to jitterbug!"

He just hooted back. "Let's tango, baby!"

"What's your name?" Lulu shouted.

"Trimm!" he yelled back.

"Pleased to meet you, Trimm!" Lulu was practically glowing in the dark, radiant with joy.

Then a larger GI, a curly-haired Errol Flynn look-alike, popped up next to him, and lifted his helmet at us, as if we were the only two girls in the wild crowd. "Sergeant Hoy Moffett at your service, ladies!"

Shots rang out from the roof of the Ed Building, and suddenly, our Georgia Peaches turned all-business, as they ducked into the tank, turned the hatch toward the source, and fired with deadly accuracy. A Japanese soldier fell from the Ed Building roof, and hundreds of us watching in the plaza roared approval— everyone marveling at the glory and deadly accuracy of the First and the Forty-Fourth. How did they get these boys so big and so deadly? After months, maybe years of seeing only IJA soldiers and emaciated shrunken shells of men, we just could not get over it.

My eyes then moved to the Mountain Man with a machine gun in the hatch of Battlin' Basic. He seemed to be searching for more enemy to conquer. Two Japanese officers stepped forward into the beam of Mountain Man's tank light, each holding an 8x11 leaflet American planes had dropped into camp days earlier for Jap benefit. It said in large letters "I Surrender." I couldn't make out who the surrendering men were in the glaring light, but I could tell by their swords that they were officers, and while Mountain Man threatened from above, four other GIs took their first prisoners away.

Then out of nowhere, Abiko rushed forward, waving a surrender leaflet in his left hand, while his right hand reached for something in his shoulder bag. Would our boys hold their fire and accept the surrender of this brute who'd never shown mercy in his life? Who'd turned that poor Filipino into a human water fountain, for God's sake? Ten feet away from me, an army major with a pistol shot Abiko from the hip so fast it made my head spin. It was like watching a western. Our own *Tom Mix*! Then Mountain Man in the hatch shot him from above.

Abiko hit the ground twenty feet in front of me. Our long-hated taskmaster, the water torturer, and sadistic instructor in the fine art of bowing, took a bullet in his belly, and my heart leapt.

"They got Abiko!" I heard myself shouting. Cheers and roars of approval rose from the crowd. He writhed in pain on the ground, taking yet another bullet from one of our boys. In the glare of the tank light I saw an angry knot of black-red tentacles seep out from his belly and grip his torso before the crowd surged in on him.

"They got him!" I shouted to Lulu. "Look! They got Abiko!" Good! Good! Good! Even at that moment I was horrified at how deeply satisfied I felt. I knew death and revenge shouldn't make me happy, but Abiko had humiliated us time and again. I hated him, and I was glad to see him meet his end. Angry crowds now crowded around Abiko's fallen body, spitting and kicking, and I looked away.

"They got him before he got us!" Lulu yelled back.

She was still staring, and now pointed to two GIs, who had raced forward to remove an unexploded grenade from our tormentor's hand and another grenade from his shoulder bag. Abiko had been reaching for a grenade to kill us all.

Chapter 36
A FINE FELLOW

February 3, 1945 (continued)

Nobody thought about going to bed. Jubilant chaos reigned as thousands of internees poured out of the shanties, the Annex, and the Gymnasium and on to the plaza to welcome our liberators. We had to be ordered to stand aside so that two more monster tanks—*Block Buster* and *Crusader*—could come roaring in.

Lulu and I spotted my mother, Hope, and Betty near a jeep, where they were pouring out their thanks to the GIs. Mommy hugged and lifted Boops, whose wild mop of curls danced in the evening breeze. Tears ran down my mother's face, and they seemed to wash away the worry; she looked ten years younger to me. When I raced over, she threw her arms around me, and hugged the breath out of me.

"Home alive in '45," she whispered into my ear, repeating our New Year's toast. "We made it. Daddy'd be so proud of his girls."

"And our boys. They're here, Mommy—the IJA." I was laughing and crying. She looked at me as if I were nuts. "Our Intrepid Jumbo-sized Americans. They're here." A smile lit her face as we both recalled that horrible day more than three years ago, and her clever answer to keep us safe. Our Intrepid Jumbo boys didn't look very happy though.

The soldiers in their jeeps kept wary watch on the Education Building, where some kind of stand-off was taking place. The GIs on foot dug into their K-rations (K is for Kombat, because somebody in the army doesn't know how to spell) and were tossing candy bars to the children who mobbed them, and tried to kiss them. Lulu and I each nabbed a Hershey's Bar and practically swooned with delight as we ate it.

"Wanna smoke, sister?" a GI in the jeep asked Hope, and didn't wait for her to answer before tossing a pack of Lucky Strikes, which she deftly snagged.

"Lucky Strike, indeed!" she called to him in her granite voice.

Then in the west corner of the camp, a small group of internees started singing "God Bless America". Their voices swelled and the din quieted, as more internees took up the tune. *Land that I love*, Lulu and I chimed in with everyone around us. *Stand beside her, and guide her.* I heard my mother's husky alto voice raised for the first time in three years, as the strains of Kate Smith's signature song welled everywhere around us.

At that moment, pride in my country so deep it was almost painful, rushed through me. *Through the night with the light from above.* A silver crescent moon gleamed overhead and one brilliant star of the Southern Cross winked right at me. *From the mountains to the prairies, to the oceans white with foam.* On the banks of Manila Bay, the entire camp sang now, even the Brits and Aussies were singing. I sang as loudly as I could, and still heard Aubrey Man—of all people— belt out: God bless America, my home sweet home! *God bless America, my home sweet home!*

In the stillness after the last note, one of GIs in the San Antone said, "I ain't never heard that sung better." Tears streamed down his face, and another cheer erupted.

Now, shots rang out from beyond the gate, and machine gun fire seemed to be growing louder and coming from the direction of Malacañan Palace across the river. We guessed that our boys were taking out the last Japs in Manila, but we internees had won our prize. We were free! We were going home!

"Let's go meet Trimm, and your Sarge," Lulu urged. We pushed through the crowd and found the Georgia Peach. All of the tanks were now lined up in front of the Education Building, fanned six abreast and arrayed like a firing squad. "You boys ready to tango?" Lulu shouted up at Trimm.

He sent her a smile that could've melted the North Pole, but Sergeant Hoy looked worried. "You girls better go back in that Main Building. We gotta finish taking out these Japs." My Sarge pointed to the Ed Building. "They're doin' Custer's Last Stand in there. And if you're church goers, ask the Man Upstairs for reinforcements. We got twenty thousand Japs on the other side of that river, and nine hundred of us here. So, get safe, OK?"

What? It wasn't over?

"We don't have Manila yet?" I called up in shock, and realized I had just enlisted myself in the U.S. army.

"Nope. We got you, though," my Sarge answered, and winked at me. Then he got serious. "Our orders were 'Get Santo Tomas first.' MacArthur didn't want the Japs to kill every last one of you while we took the city."

Kill us? They'd been holding us prisoner for three years. Would they actually have killed us in revenge for our boys taking Manila? The horrifying thought hadn't even occurred to me.

At that moment, the Camp PA echoed the GI advice. "All internees, seek shelter in the safety of the Main Building." Before we turned back, Lulu and I blew our Georgia Peaches kisses.

We crossed the lawn and saw more GIs pouring in through the open España Street Gate, carrying scores of wounded now. Everyone stood aside as the medics carted dozens of our fallen heroes into camp. Lulu and I were back in the crowd, but we could see that most of the injured boys lay on stretchers covered with flimsy blankets, a bloodied bandaged foot protruded or a hastily crafted arm cast. The medics with their white armbands emblazoned with red crosses hurried them up the stairs.

What broke my heart were the walking-wounded. One moaning soldier was being carried piggy-back by a medic about half his size. A bloodied white stump flashed from his pant leg. He was missing a foot. That boy couldn't be any older than my cousin Francis. How would he ever live a normal life? Another tall boy staggered toward the Big House on his own two feet, supported on either side by medics. The bandages around his head formed a giant, puffy O, revealing a dazed face. Brown hair, bright blue eyes, but below the nose, a sea of blood that walked. He had been shot in the mouth— or maybe the jaw—and it looked like someone had sloshed red paint all over the bottom third of his face. My throat tightened and tears poured down my cheeks, but that sure didn't help him. The bandages soaked up all the blood he could pump out, and the broad disfiguring slash of crimson grew. So this is what war looked like.

"Take the wounded to the Main Building," I heard Earl Carroll shout, organizing amid the chaos as he had for the last three years. "We can't get to Santa Catalina yet. The Japs have the Ed Building."

The Ed Building stood between the Commandant's Office and Santa Catalina Hospital. For the past year, the Ed Building's first floor had been home to the Jap garrison, while our men and boys slept on the second and third floors. Amid all the chaos and jubilation, I remembered that Curtis and Barney were over there now. And lots of the little boys we knew too. Mrs. Linda Lee Todd's grandson lived there, as did Nellie's brother, Joe. They called themselves "the Boys' Club." The Japs might have two hundred men and boys as hostages in that building.

A group of our own bazooka-bearing GIs now stormed past the wounded and internees, rushing into the Main Building. We watched from outside as they charged up the wide stone staircase, heading for the roof, where they could sight the Ed Building.

"Do they know our men and boys are over there?" Lulu asked as we watched them race up the steps.

"Mr. Carroll would've told them, don't you think?"

***

The stand-off at the Ed Building continued through the night. The GIs did start to fire from the roof of the Main Building before they realized our own men and boys were in there with the Japs. When the Commander of *Battlin' Basic* ordered his men to train tank guns on the site, Mrs. Linda Lee Todd raced out of the crowd, shouting. "You certainly will not do that, young man! You stop that right now!" She laced into that tank commander like he was an ill-behaved house-guest, and railed at him in full plantation matron ire. "Our children are in there! Our sons and grandsons are in there!"

Scarlett O'Hara could not have done it any better. Mountain Man shouted to his fellow tank commanders to hold their fire.

Was Haruo in the Ed Building? I didn't know, but I hoped so because I knew he would never kill our men and boys. Hayashi, on the other hand, prided himself on being "samurai." He wouldn't hesitate to be a warrior to the end.

Major James Gearhart, the same officer who shot Abiko, was now in charge and started negotiations with the Japs. Ernest Stanley, a British internee who spoke Japanese and translated for our Executive Committee, offered to translate for the GIs. But the First Cavalry even had their own interpreter. Here's something I never thought I'd see: a Jap dressed like a U.S. soldier. And not just a private either—this Jap was dressed like a U.S. Sergeant.

I found out later that he *was* United States Army Sergeant Kenji Uyesugi—born in California, and just as American as I was. His family, though, was locked up in an internment camp back in the States. Still, our GIs treated "Sergeant Ken" like he was one of us, and I guess I started to see him that way too. Unarmed and bearing a white flag, lead negotiator Colonel Charles Brady and Sergeant Ken entered the Ed Building. They shuttled back and forth all night between Hayashi with his armed Japs on the inside and Major Gearhart with the First Cavalry on the outside.

So much excitement, joy, and sorrow fought for our hearts on that great and beautiful night. We were free. We were saved. But a dozen stretchers bearing our wounded soldiers lined the wide corridors of the Main Building.

A first floor dorm room now served as a clinic, but the overflow of wounded waited in the halls. The metallic stench of blood mingled with human sweat and vomit. Most of these beautiful GIs couldn't have been more than eighteen or nineteen years old, but bandaged stumps of limbs announced this soldier had lost a foot, and that one an arm or a hand. And for what? For us! They did it for us. My heart just overflowed with love for these boys I didn't even know.

Father Sheridan, in Bermuda shorts and a loose white shirt, but a makeshift priestly stole around his neck, came out of the clinic room where he had been giving last rites to the wounded. His face was peaceful. "They're gonna make it," he told Lulu and me. "There's not a boy in there who will die. I just gave 'em last rites for peace of mind."

"Father, I'm Catholic," one of the boys called from a stretcher. "What about me?"

"Where are you wounded?" Father Sheridan shot back at him in good spirits. We knew all the seriously wounded were in the clinic room. The boy lifted his blanket and it looked like his belly had been gnawed by a hyena.

"Get that boy into the operating room," Father Sheridan shouted to medics in the hallway, and they leapt to attention. Our priest friend was at the boy's side in a shot, his thumb on the boy's forehead. "Through this holy unction may the Lord pardon thee whatever sins or faults thou hast committed." I heard him pray as he strode behind the stretcher. And I remembered some priest had said those words to my father in the middle of a war zone too.

So much joy and so much sorrow all on one night.

For an hour or so, Lulu and I roamed the halls in the Main Building, and squatted next to each unattended stretcher to thank the injured GIs, and tell them how much their bravery meant to us. We were wiping tears from our eyes, but you should've seen the smiles from those broad, gentle, faces. They looked up at us like we were angels.

Lulu knelt next to a blond boy with a bandaged head, sparkling blue eyes and a dangling right arm. She took his left hand, and said something.

He smiled proudly and nodded. "A pleasure, miss. Saving you's a pleasure. Name's Desmond."

"I'm Mary Lou," she squeezed his hand and rose.

There were shouts in the main entry, so we hurried toward the hall where a raucous crowd was gathering.

"You decided to be 'Mary Lou' with the GIs?" I asked.

"It more sophisticated than 'Lulu,' don't you think? If they find out we're only sixteen, we won't be in their league."

I laughed out loud. I had seen the way the GIs were ogling every woman they saw here. "I don't think we need to worry about that, Lulu."

***

Catcalls, jeers, and shouts now rose from the front entry, so Lulu and I jostled and shoved our way there to see what was going on. Maybe we could get a spot on the stairs and watch. We wriggled our way to the sixth step, about half way up to the first landing. We could see the makeshift camp jail that had its home in a corner of the foyer now boasting an open door. All our internee prisoners had been sprung from it. Dr. Stevens—sentenced a week ago for refusing to falsify death certificates—had been liberated and was hard at work in the dorm-clinic, operating on GIs. Hundreds of internees flanked either side of the Main Entry inside and out, and we could hear boisterous heckling and boos.

I could make out the silhouette of large GIs hauling a captured Japanese soldier up the steps of the Big House. Then the Savior GIs burst into the light of the foyer with Bugs Bunny Guard.

"Booooooo!" jeered everyone around us. Lulu, standing next to me, shouted her rage and I joined her, "Boo! Booo! Boo!" I remembered how he'd snatched my music, leered at me, grabbed my arms when he hauled me off to the Commandant's office. An image of him bayonetting that Lemon Meringue Pie flashed through my mind. I remembered how he ogled me when I had that money sewn in my skirt! The booing and hissing came from all sides and I saw something in his lecherous, be-whiskered face that I had never seen before—fear.

Paul called out "What's up, doc?" and then spat at him from the sidelines. Another man tried to claw at him but the GIs held back the seething crowd. There was blood lust in that foyer.

"Good riddance, bastard," somebody shouted. "Lock him up. Get him behind bars." The GIs turned left into the foyer and shoved him through the open door of the internee jail, slamming it behind him. Our soldiers were on the offensive, dragging in more Japs to more sneers and insults.

Then came a sight I do not want to remember, but can never forget. Two brawny GIs dragged up the stairs and into the foyer, the mangled, bloodied body of Abiko and he was *alive*—writhing in pain, his face contorted in agony, but alive. I thought I might throw up. I wanted that bastard dead. I wanted him to be dead! Then once again I wondered what I was thinking. Who had I become?

A male voice shouted, "I ain't never gonna bow to you again, Shitface!"

Internees formed a tunnel opening on either side to let the GIs through, but they spat on Abiko and kicked him. Aubrey Man tried to burn him with a cigarette, and one man tried to cut off his ear. But the GIs blocked that.

I watched as if I had toothpicks supporting my eyelids. I couldn't turn away. This was wrong. We shouldn't be doing this—we were the good guys, weren't we? Lulu and I gaped in horror—or was it fascination?—when I heard a familiar gravel voice ring out.

"Stop that! We are not brutes! We do not sink to their level!"

I spotted Hope in the crowd off to the right. Hope, who had lost her husband in the Bataan Death March. Hope shouted that at the frenzied human gauntlet, but the crowd would not be stilled.

The GIs seemed to realize they might have a riot on their hands, and quickly hauled Abiko to an off-limits room down the hall where—we later found out—Dr. Stevens treated him but could not save him. Internees would've been furious if they had known the GIs insisted on treating our captor and tormentor, but those boys were such heroes and saviors that night, nobody considered stopping or confronting them.

Still, the bloodlust in the foyer raged on. Not all the Japs had been holed up in the Ed Building because another GI bounded up the stairs of the Main Building, hauling an uninjured Jap soldier he had caught. I couldn't make him out in the darkness beyond the main door, but into the lights of the mobbed hall burst my Errol Flynn look-alike, my own Sergeant Hoy Moffett manhandling and strong-arming a Jap who was almost as tall as he was. His hands were tied behind his back.

Suddenly, my heart was in my throat. Haruo! He had Haruo! I stood mute and frozen. Lulu saw it too. She stilled and gripped my arm. Internees flanking the GIs tunnel stared for a minute, looking at who was being brought in, and the enraged crowd quieted. How many people in this crowd had Haruo helped?

Bunny said he had given her little sister candy. Haruo let Paul smuggle in those cigarettes at the gate. How many people's contraband had he overlooked? I remembered Haruo on the baseball diamond, not just saving face for the Japanese with his hit, but helping us not incur their wrath. Most of all, I remembered him at the piano, concentrating, as if in prayer, playing my music. I was pretty sure I was the only one he had written music for. But here he was, Nice Guy Haruo, on that night of bloodlust, bound and standing before us. And the crowd stilled.

Then one person in the hushed mob began to clap. I don't know who. And then another. I scanned the crowd. By now my mother and Hope were clapping, and a few others joined in, but most just watched. Lulu and I started to clap too. An English lady on the stairs behind me called down, "Don't hurt him. He's a fine fellow!" Haruo looked straight up the stairs toward her, but he saw me instead, and his eyes softened.

I wish I had said it. I wish I had said "Don't hurt him. He's a fine fellow!" Why didn't I say that? Instead, I just stared at him bug-eyed, clapped both hands over my mouth as if in prayer, and bowed quickly to him. When I looked back up, the GIs had loosened their grip and were very courteously escorting him to the jail. They knew he had helped us.

And ever so faintly, Haruo smiled.

I was proud of my camp at that moment on that night. That the starving mob of STIC internees, newly sprung from their cage, hell-bent on pay-back and vengeance, did not forget kindnesses. We did not abandon our friends, even when they were our foes. Maybe we were the good guys after all.

Chapter 37
GET STRONG

Monday, February 5, 1945

I rose at dawn on this second day of freedom. There was no "Good Morning, Good Morning" reveille and no roll call. Freedom is a beautiful thing, though, and I awoke eager to see the sunrise. Mommy, Betty, and most of my roomies were still asleep, but I dressed quickly and went outside to see the sky turn pink with the promise of a new day.

What gifts would today bring? Yesterday a GI gave me an entire can of evaporated milk. I drank the whole thing at once, and then spent hours in the bathroom with the runs that followed. I had many companions there because our shrunken stomachs just couldn't take all the rich, concentrated food we were gobbling down as fast as we could, but we were wild with joy in that bathroom. That evaporated milk tasted so good.

When I bounced down the stairs to the plaza and breathed in the cool morning air, tanks, guns, and soldiers were reassuringly everywhere. U.S. army reinforcements of all sorts had rolled into camp on Sunday—soldiers, trucks, jeeps, medical supplies, and food. Yesterday they'd served the most delicious beef stew.

Santo Tomas looked like the center of operations for the U.S. Army in Manila—which it was, I guess. There had to be more than fifteen hundred

American GIs in camp now, commanded by General William Chase. I could see a crowd of Japanese soldiers gathering near the España Street gate. They were flanked by an equal number of our GIs.

"They're letting 'em go," Bill Phillips appeared at my side from nowhere, and nicked his chin toward the scene. His blue eyes radiated intensity and maybe disapproval. "The whole Jap garrison, including prisoners—they're letting 'em go."

"What? Why?" Even as I sputtered the questions, the answer dawned on me. It had to be a swap for our guys in the Ed Building. Tense negotiations had dragged on all day yesterday, with Major Gearhart and Sergeant Ken Uyesugi going back and forth, while Hayashi made more demands. Father Sheridan offered Sunday Mass in the Father's Garden for our hostage men and boys. That mass was such a joyful mix of gratitude for our liberation and worry for our men. "It's a trade for our boys in the Ed Building? Are they free?"

"Yup. Barney, Squeaky, and Joey, Nellie's brother—all of 'em. But most of 'em are still asleep."

"Do you ever sleep, Bill?" I marveled at Nellie's suitor, who was so restless and omni-present. "You're always at the scene of the action."

"Some. As little as possible."

"We saw you climb that north wall when the Japs were shooting at us before the GIs came in. Were you trying to get killed?"

"Nah—there were no Jap guards in the rear watchtowers. I could tell that from our shanty back there."

"So?"

"So, I heard the rumble and wanted to see it up close. I got to the top of the wall, and there was the 44th tank battalion. Lost like Red Riding Hood in the Forest. They were at a dead stop on Dapitan, and one of their guys yelled up to me—'Kid, where's the entrance to the camp? So I showed 'em."

"You mean the mighty First Cavalry could not figure out how to get into Camp?"

"Nope. They had maps, but the Japs had taken down the street signs."

"So, we should all thank *you*, Bill Phillips, for our freedom." I studied his pleased face and a smile snuck across it.

"That'd be nice."

"I thank you, Bill." I said solemnly, then looked back toward the gate. "C'mon let's go see the Exodus."

***

We hurried down the front lawn, skirting fox holes, tanks, and gun emplacements. The GIs just smiled when they saw us approach, and let Bill and me work our way up by the gate to watch. I saw proud, bespectacled Commandant Hayashi in his modified combat gear. The lanky American lieutenant standing next to him dwarfed him, but Hayashi stood with his chin high and eyes forward, ready to lead his seventy-man garrison out the iron gates.

Abiko would not be going with them. He'd died yesterday, and his mutilated body had been on display under the backstairs of the Main Building all day, where anyone who wanted to could kick or spit on him. The grisly spectacle sickened me. I was glad he was dead. (I'd have to confess that horrible sin to Fr. Sheridan sometime.) But why did they have to leave him in the back hall like that, encouraging the worst in everyone? They should've just buried him right away—very far away from any of our dead GIs or internees, of course. That's what ended up happening on Sunday night anyway.

I scanned the troops behind Hayashi. Where was Haruo? There.

Corporal Haruo Tanaka, sword at his side, proved easy to spot. He stood almost a head taller than the others, erect and alert, his broad brow unfurrowed, his almond eyes wary, but his face impassive, betraying nothing. I remembered him leaning into the piano and into my music itself on Christmas night, his face then a mirror of concentration and commitment. Why couldn't Haruo be one of *our* Japs? I pondered in frustration, thinking about Sergeant Ken.

Then the iron gate of Santo Tomas swung wide, and the column of Japanese soldiers, flanked by their American escort, marched silently into the war-weary city of Manila. There was a lull in the fighting now—a truce arranged by both sides for the Japanese garrison to exit. Most internees were still in their beds, so no one jeered and booed. The men marched in muffled silence, and the American troops on the outside of the column were so tall, that even if the Japs had looked around, they couldn't have made out anybody on the sidelines.

But the Japanese soldiers didn't look around. They just stared forward. Corporal Haruo Tanaka stared forward. He didn't see me. And it was the last time I ever saw him. He never heard me whisper "Arigato, Haruo," as he swept past that gate.

Bill Philips didn't hear me say it either. "Good riddance, bastards," he pronounced at exactly the same moment.

***

By noon, the laughter and shrieks of children and the deliriously happy voices of shanty-dwellers next to us filled the air. We were eating well for the second day in a row—rich army grub now—beef stew, baked beans, vegetables, and limitless chocolate from the GI D rations. (I had no idea what D stood for. Probably DELIGHTFUL because most of the D rations were chocolate.)

Line chow improved immediately after the liberation. On that magic night of February third and in the wee small hours of February fourth, internees had broken into the Jap storerooms and found bags of mongo beans, cornmeal, and stashes of canned beef. Enough to tide us over in style till this morning when the Army trucks rolled in with real food, and lots of it! The Army set up chow lines for us now, and we were in heaven. We could even go back for seconds.

On this second day of freedom, Betty and I toted our line lunch back to the shanty, where Mommy laid the table with our tin-ware finest. I noticed there was not a single talinum garnish in sight. Ever since October, Hope's little garden had been our main stay—chopped talinum, chopped mint, and chopped garlic topped every watery rice stew. No need for that now.

"No home-grown greens?" I kidded my mother.

"Funny you should mention that." Mommy placed tin cups on the table for the can of milk we each had from the line. "Just a couple hours ago, Hope dragged me outside to look at what she said was 'the most wonderful sight you ever saw, Agnes.'" My mother was smiling like the Cheshire cat. "Sitting on that stone curb around our vegetable patch was a big GI and a little boy right next to him, swapping stories like an older brother to a kid brother: both of them had their feet planted squarely in our garden—crushing all the stalks of talinum. "That is so beautiful," was all Hope could say.

I laughed and remembered how Hope had lit into the Jap soldier who accidentally stepped on her plants at Christmas time. How time and our fortunes had changed. I distributed the heaping plates of stew, as we sat down.

"And, a gift from the GIs," Betty announced proudly, plunking a round twist-key tin of CHOPPED HAM and EGGS in the center of the table.

We stared at the solid black lettering on its top, as if it were scripture, and said a quick grace. Then the three of us ate in silence for a few minutes, savoring the most delicious army lunch ever served—beef stew and baked beans—and pondering our new heroes, the GIs. When we weren't eating, we couldn't stop talking about them.

"My Sergeant Hoy 'is just a pore boy from a Texas farm,'" I mimicked his accent to Betty and my mother as best I could. "But have you seen him, Boops? What looks! Got my own Errol Flynn." I was jabbering on at about fifty miles an hour.

"And he paid you a bushel of compliments on the most exciting night of your life, right?" Betty said.

"I'll bet he did," my worldly-wise mother smiled and arched both eyebrows knowingly, as she dipped a spoon into her chockfull tin bowl.

I nodded, smiled, and kept right on eating. "Anyway, Lulu and I invited Hoy and Trimm over to the shanty for dinner tonight. OK?"

My mother nodded, but seemed distracted. She shouldn't have been. Inviting someone over for dinner just meant that we'd tidy up the shanty and set extra places, but we'd all get our food through the new Army chow line that had been set up. Betty and I relished the food and the freedom, but Mommy's eyes rested on the twist-key tin of ham and eggs that was our centerpiece.

"Now girls, I know these boys are generous," our mother began to lecture, "but I do not want to see you girls cadging food off the GIs anymore." Betty and I both gaped at her in astonishment. "They have brought us ample supply now, and they need their strength to fight. They are still battling for Manila."

"Mommy, they want to help us!" Betty protested.

Betty'd been thrilled with that tin a GI had given her. She and I had been walking from the Central Kitchen to the shanty with our lunch on a tray. Fortunately, I was carrying the grub because—as usual—Betty wasn't watching where she was going, and she tripped over a shovel that a soldier had left on the lawn while he inspected his fox hole. There were fox holes everywhere now, and Betty could just as easily have tripped into a fox hole.

That husky young soldier leapt out of his pit, so embarrassed. He kept apologizing, as he helped my skinny little sister to her feet. He stood holding her reed-thin upper arm for a minute too long, tears coming to his eyes. I swear to God, his fingers were thicker than her arm. Then he dug into his sack, and produced this tin of ham and eggs. "This is yours, miss. You eat it and get strong, OK?"

We thanked him profusely, of course, and headed for our Glamorville shanty to meet Mommy. But as we left, I heard him tell his buddy, "I am going to kill every damn Jap soldier on the face of this earth!"

"He was being kind, Betty," my mother's voice jerked me back to reality, "but he needs his nourishment. Those boys are fighting for you and me and all the other prisoners who aren't free yet. Los Baños is not free yet. I will not have you girls imposing on the generosity and sapping the strength of the GIs."

My mother returned to her stew, and Betty threw me a look of complete exasperation. I snuck a smile at her. Our cadging days were not over.

Chapter 38
SMOKE ON THE WATERS

Tuesday, February 6, 1945

The next afternoon we gathered on the front lawn around Curtis and Barney Brooks, our new heroes. The Brooksies had endured the two-day hostage ordeal in the Ed building. They were full of stories about how they raced from one side of the building to the other to stay safe when the GIs started firing. Then they hid underneath their beds, and finally slept—sometimes with Japs curled on mattresses above them. Barney awoke under his cot to see a hand cradling a grenade just a foot from his head—its owner dozing above him.

"I still can't believe they let the Japs go." Paul Davis shook his head.

"General Chase didn't let them take machine guns or grenades," Curtis, our military expert, informed us. "Just defensive weapons—pistols and swords."

"Yeah, well, which Filipino is gonna be happier because he got killed by a pistol or sword?" Paul scoffed.

"You planning to lodge a complaint with MacArthur when he gets here?" I asked.

A rumor was circulating that Dugout Doug, *I-Shall-Return* MacArthur, was actually going to visit camp. If he came, he'd be thronged by grateful internees, but was it true? *Rumortism* was still rife in camp.

"Two hundred of our internees for seventy Nips is a good deal if you ask me, Pablo—even with the guns." Lulu echoed the camp sentiment. "Besides, we've got the camp to ourselves now. The Big Bad Witch is dead."

"Gone, not dead," Paul corrected, but he couldn't squelch the delight we all felt at no longer having a single Japanese soldier among us.

"And all thanks to the First Cavalry and the Forty-Fourth Tank Battalion," I said. "The handsomest men and the best fighting force in history."

"You're not kidding about the fighting force. Did you meet Robert E. Lee yet?" Curtis asked.

We all stared at him. Maybe our friend's hostage ordeal had pushed him over the edge.

"Isn't he dead?" Paul asked the obvious. "The Civil War ended a long time ago."

"That one's dead, but his great-great grandson, Lieutenant Robert E. Lee is right over there on that tank." He pointed to *Crusader*. "He's in the 44th, but he can tell you all about the history of the First too; that was his great-granddad's unit."

"Civil War Robert E. Lee was in the First Cavalry?" I couldn't believe it. We were liberated by historic Titans.

"Yup. Before the Civil War, obviously. Jefferson Davis and George Custer too," Curtis added.

"Let's see—Lee, Davis and Custer. You notice that all three of those guys ended up on the wrong side of history?" Paul's sarcasm was unrelenting.

"Not while they were serving in the First," Curtis shot back.

Curtis could've told us anything about those men and their units and we would have believed him, but learning the history of the First made us adore the GIs all the more. These boys could do no wrong in our eyes. *So strong, so healthy, so polite,* you heard people marveling all over camp. *Such fine young men,* all the mothers agreed.

"But so *yellow*," Lulu pointed out the day after our liberation.

It was true. The GIs were taking malaria pills that stained their skin a strange shade of maize. We got used to it: they were sunshine to us, we said. And they sure got used to us. Hope said that we reminded them of their families at home.

Heart-warming scenes from yesterday flashed through my mind: indulgent GIs letting the little kids climb all over their tanks during the pause in the fighting. The little boys begged to play with their guns too, and most of the GIs were smart enough to say no to that, but they still showed them how they worked.

"You gotta get from holster to bang in less than a second," Major James Gearheart instructed an awe-struck group of little and not-so-little boys. Major Gearhart was the one who shot Abiko from the hip, and it turned out he actually *was* a cowboy and sharp shooter from Montana. Our own *Tom Mix*, who impressed all the boys with his fast-draw techniques.

Lulu, Nellie, and I had run around all day yesterday with our autograph books, introducing ourselves, and getting war-weary, but very happy GIs to sign them. They couldn't believe their good fortune to be surrounded by a "gaggle of gorgeous gals," as one of them put it.

And they seemed to think we had suffered more than they had. Hope, Lulu and I chatted with two GIs at a card table outside Room 22 late in the afternoon. One of them rambled on and on about his wartime adventures, while the other remained very quiet. His eyes followed the skeletal men who walked passed us on their way to the bathroom. He took in the dingy, gray walls, the overcrowded rooms with their jimmy-rigged mosquito netting, and the squalor that surrounded him. Finally, this Still-Waters-Run-Deep boy put his hand gingerly on Hope's forearm and said, "Tell me. Did you ever despair?"

We all quieted. If anyone had reason to despair, it was forty-one-year-old Hope Miller, who'd lost her husband in the Bataan Death March, and would return to Sunapee, New Hampshire, widowed, childless, and penniless, to start over. But Hope's eyes brightened in her gaunt face. She couldn't suppress a small smile, as she took a drag from her cigarette, and exhaled with satisfaction.

"No. You see," she turned toward Still-Waters as if it were very important that he understand each gravelly word. "We *knew* you'd come back. We just knew it." She held his eyes for a moment, and we all relished the childlike smile that suffused his face.

"Out alive in forty-five!" Lulu squealed in delight.

We had to keep reminding ourselves this wasn't a dream. It wasn't. When Hoy and Trimm came to dinner at our shanty last night, it was all so real and so joyful. Shy-Guy Trimm brought his guitar, and played all the latest cowboy songs—*Pistol Packin' Mama, San Antonio Rose*, and my new favorite, *Smoke on the Water*. Trimm lost all his bashfulness as he sang about how we'd "rejoice on that great day when the powers of dictators shall be taken all away," and "the Sun that is Risin' will go down on that day!" Lulu's Georgia boy could really strum that catchy tune, and the rhythm hooked us.

Pretty soon I was leading the singing. "There'll be smoke on the water, on the land and the sea, when our Army and Navy overtakes the enemy." My heart was full to bursting at the sheer satisfaction and justice of it all—singing about how "when the Screaming Eagle flies, that will be the end of Axis. They must answer with their lives." Maybe we were a little loud, because other internees flocked to our Glamorville shanty to sing along. At the end, Hoy admired my singing voice—which Lulu had always told me was very good. I got it from my mother.

All these joyous memories from just a single day flashed before me in a kaleidoscope of light, color, and triumph. Not all of my Santo Tomas memories would be grim. No siree. And to be standing here now on a glorious afternoon, FREE and alive with Lulu, Paul, and our buddies, the Brooksies, knowing we'd never have to fear another Jap bullet, I just couldn't stop smiling.

"Lee! Up here!" I heard Betty shout from the Main Building. She was standing with maybe a dozen other women on the massive stone portico that jutted out over the front entrance, waving at me.

You could get out on that large landing only by crawling out the window of a second floor dorm room, but it had been totally off-limits for the last three years. Some of the ladies were tacking a red, white and blue striped bunting across the thick face of the portico.

"Get up here," Betty called and mimed for me to come up. Something was about to happen.

I took off like a shot, Lulu right behind me. We raced up the forty-one steps to the second floor and burst through the door of a nearly empty Room 22. Everyone had crawled out the window onto the portico, so Lulu and I wedged ourselves out to join them. Mrs. Baskerville, the leader of our team of seamstresses, and Mrs. Linda Lee Todd, our Room Monitor, were now unfurling what had to be a ten-foot long American flag. Did they make this? They secured the flag's edge and let it drop below the portico, stars and stripes flapping gaily in the breeze.

From the PA speaker in the plaza, I heard the scratch of a record, and then Jimmy Cagney with fifty of his best friends belted out "You're a Grand Old Flag, you're a high-flying flag, and forever in peace may you wave." Internees milled around on the front lawn whooping and waving, some singing right along with the tinny recording as they looked up at us. "Every heart beats true to the red, white and blue, where there's nary a boast nor brag." Well, that wasn't true. We had been boasting and bragging for three solid days since our boys got here, but the crowd bellowed on, jubilant in the knowledge that not a single Japanese soldier remained in camp. "Keep your eye on the grand old flag!"

Some GIs on the tanks hurrahed, and hundreds of internees on the front lawn cheered. I looked out to a sea of skinny stick people smiling up at us, and maybe a thousand toothpick arms, waving like reeds. We waved right back, and a bubble of pure joy and pride welled inside me. We were almost home-free.

In the distance lay beautiful Manila. Looking past the gate of Santo Tomas and over the river, I could make out the Metropolitan Theater—completely unharmed.

"Lulu, see the pretty pink building over there—the one with the spires? That's the Metropolitan, where Betty and I saw every great movie ever made before the war—from *Snow White* to the *Wizard of Oz* to Sonia Henie in *Happy Landing*."

"We're going to have a happy landing," Lulu said with delight, and gripped both of our hands. "Maybe the Filipinos will too. Manila looks beautiful."

She was right. The city seemed largely unscathed. The GIs had told us that the Germans marched out of Paris in August without razing the city. Would the Japanese leave Manila that way? Not go on a big rampage and just evacuate? I sure hoped so.

"The Rendezvous Café is right around the corner from the Metropolitan" Betty said, "ready to serve us the most luscious green coconut ice cream— just as soon as these Japs pull out."

"They're not gone yet," I said, pointing to the flag of the Rising Sun still afloat over the magnificent Post Office with its scroll-top columns and huge semi-circular wings. "That Post Office is where I'm going to mail a letter to our cousin Francis just as soon as this is over."

"No, let's go to lunch at the Manila Hotel first," Betty said and pointed, our fantasies running wild at this point. "Then you can mail your letter."

The white adobe walls and red tile roof of the Manila Hotel rose along the bay. Mommy and Daddy would never go to another dance there, I realized, but maybe Betty and I would. For a fleeting moment, I wondered if Ramón would come back after the war and take me to a dance at the Manila Hotel. That was silly. We weren't even going to be here; we'd go home to Utica when this was all over. Still, I was filled with joy just knowing that these beautiful landmarks, the much taken-for-granted touchstones of my childhood, survived. The Filipinos would go back to them. Maybe Rosalina would go to a dance at the Manila Hotel someday.

Or would she? A black plume rose from the bay, where our American bombers pummeled Japanese ships and oil reserves. There was smoke on the waters, all right. To the east, near Grace Air Field, another inferno roared—souvenir of a shell exploded earlier that day. The bright spark of hope, kindled briefly by the sight of so many of my childhood haunts, dimmed for a moment as I gazed south across the Pasig River.

The ancient black-walled city of Intramuros hulked on its hill, one corner anchored by the citadel of Fort Santiago—Japanese Torture Central. Were Mr. Grinnell and Mr. Duggleby still prisoners there, still suffering? The leaders of our Executive Committee had been carted off in December and nobody knew what happened to them. The fort's sooty stone turrets with their spiked cupolas poked above massive walls. And flying from one charred medieval tower was a blood-red Rising Sun. "Keep your eye on the grand old flag," the scratchy platter reminded us. The clenched black knot of fear loosed on February third tightened once again. Manila was still in Jap hands. We weren't out of here yet.

Chapter 39
THE SECOND COMING

Wednesday, February 7, 1945

Betty poked her head through the window of the second floor room, and shouted across to Lulu and me, "He's coming! Don't you want to shake his hand?"

At eight-thirty AM, Lulu and I had again parked ourselves on the massive stone portico over the main entrance, along with dozens of other internees, for a birds-eye view of the most exciting event since the night of our rescue. Five-star General Douglas A. MacArthur, liberator of Santo Tomas and Supreme Commander of Allied Forces in the Pacific, was returning in glory. Betty wanted us to join her downstairs in the packed hallway, with a thousand other internees waiting to shake his hand or, as Lulu said, kiss the hem of his garment.

"We're staying here. We've got a great view!" I shouted back, and my sister vanished.

My heart pounded, as I stared into the morning sun waiting for the arrival of MacArthur's motorcade. This man was partly responsible for our imprisonment, but completely responsible for our liberation. Well, if he could save Manila and free the PI, maybe I'd forgive him for my three years in a Japanese prison. But what would Daddy think of me standing up here getting ready to cheer for MacArthur? *MacArthur is an ass.* I could still hear him saying that.

"Did I tell you MacArthur used to play poker at my grandfather's house in Cebu back in the thirties?" Lulu said, peering hard into the distance, watching with me. The Clelands ran the biggest inter-island shipping company in the PI and were rich before the war. They ran in MacArthur's circle. "He's a braggart—nobody's idea of a gracious guest."

"That's what Daddy thought too."

MacArthur had lived in the Philippines from 1935 to 1942, mostly in Manila, but sometimes in Cebu. The American community in the Philippines was small enough that many of us knew him. At first, he was U.S. Field Marshal, in charge of helping the Philippine government come up with defense plans against possible attack from the Japanese. *How did that work out?* I could almost hear my father scoffing from above. Then he became Commander of US Forces in the Far East, and lived in the penthouse suite of the Manila Hotel, taking up an entire floor overlooking Manila Bay. *A pompous ass*, I heard my father's voice again.

The truth is that MacArthur's oversized ego was as famous as his corncob pipe, and despite the fact that he was tall, fit, and good-looking, he was heartily disliked by many in the ex-pat community, even before the war. Everyone knew he was brilliant—he never let you forget that. MacArthur had a photographic memory, and delighted in reminding anyone he happened to be talking to about what appeared on say, page eleven of the *Manila Herald* six months ago.

Lulu's family agreed with ours in judging MacArthur harshly. "But my grandfather was no prize either," Lulu added. "Maybe they were kindred spirits. Terrible womanizer, real reprobate."

"Your grandfather or MacArthur?"

"My grandfather. Maybe MacArthur too—I don't know." Lulu's trademark candor never failed to make me laugh. "Both of them were full of themselves, especially before Pearl."

For Americans in the Philippines, MacArthur's reputation sank another notch after Pearl Harbor. His vaunted defense plans allowed the Japanese to take the island of Luzon almost without a fight, landing all of us in Santo Tomas. He then directed the Philippine campaign from the bowels of the earth, inside the fortified tunnels of Corregidor off the Manila coast. That earned him the mocking nickname of "Dugout Doug."

Then finally, before Corregidor fell, MacArthur high-tailed it out of the PI with his wife Jean, their five-year-old son Arthur, Arthur's Chinese amah, and (according to rumor) all their nice Oriental furniture—while the American civilians he was supposed to protect ended up in Japanese prisons. All the while he announced, "I shall return!" And he had. I had to give him that. Thank God he had.

Shielding my eyes from the glare of the early morning sun, I spotted MacArthur's olive green staff car roll up the front walkway toward the Main Building. A red flag with five gold stars flew from its long, pointed hood.

"There he is! Look—see the five stars," I nudged Lulu, but of course she'd spotted it too. I'd learned from Curtis that the brand new Army rank of five stars meant seniority over generals from other Allied nations serving with him. A five-star US general outranked any foreign general in his theater. Eisenhower was five stars. So was George Marshall.

"He got that fifth star in December. Curtis told me." Lulu said. She and I were both applauding now.

He got the fifth star before he liberated us? Why? I wondered. Well, I wasn't going to begrudge him his fifth star—maybe he was planning our liberation at the very moment it was pinned on his chest. I clapped harder.

The moment MacArthur's car slid to a halt in front of the Big House, wildly enthusiastic internees ringed the vehicle (at a respectful distance) and prepared to welcome their old friend and now liberator.

"He's gonna eat this up," Lulu shouted to me above the din. "He's at his best when he's working a crowd."

"He'll see a lot of neighbors, that's for sure."

For a brief moment, when MacArthur's staff car door opened and the Great Man stepped out, the sea of internees quieted and parted. General Douglas MacArthur drew himself up to his full height of six feet, smiled confidently, and spread his arms wide, like Jesus, in what could have been greeting or blessing. A thunderous ovation rose on all sides.

Lulu and I clapped and roared our approval right along with everyone else, but MacArthur's reception came as close to "Adoration of the Blessed Liberator" as I ever wanted to see. At first, internees just gawked and applauded, thundering their delight. Then "Mighty Mac" was being pushed by a sea of humanity into the Main Building.

"OK, let's go downstairs now," Lulu tugged at me. "Let's see if we can shake his hand."

We slipped through the window into the second floor dorm room, sped through the hall, and worked our way down the crowded flight of stairs but we couldn't get past the first landing. That was OK. We could still see. Every internee pressed toward the same point and the same man. And there he was, working the adoring crowd, shaking every hand proffered, beaming a cocky crooked smile, but for once, minus his trademark corncob pipe.

General Douglas A. MacArthur greeted Manila friends and neighbors he hadn't seen in three years, and he was doing it in triumph. "Manila has fallen!" he assured us all. Nobody could get enough of him. Our family and the Clelands cheered right along with everyone else. He got us in, but he also got us out. So this morning, watching the military Titan press the flesh, I found myself shouting my approval too. In the back of my mind I was answering my father. "Well, he got us out of here, Daddy. At least he got us out of here." But a voice in my head answered. *No, he hasn't. Not yet.*

***

Hours after MacArthur left, the glow of his presence seemed to linger for many in Room 4. As we sat around, dozens of women told stories of how they'd shaken his hand, how great he looked, how the war hadn't aged him a bit. Most smoked contentedly, satisfying the craving that had stalked them for more than three years. My mother didn't smoke, but she was lighting Hope's Lucky Strike and they were exchanging state-side addresses.

Camp buzzed with the news of a Red Cross mail delivery tomorrow: We'd get letters from home for the first time in three years. I wondered if my cousin Francis had written me. He might even be in the army now. My mother had two letters ready to post: one to her family back in Utica and another to Mrs. Onus Moffett, Sergeant Hoy Moffett's mother in Roby, Texas. Mommy had written to her about what a fine young man her son was, and how he had brought us such nourishing food, and came back from the fighting lines every night to visit with her and her daughters. She hoped to congratulate Mrs. Moffett on all this in person one day when we returned to the United States.

Everyone was in high spirits. We'd had bread in the lunch chow line today for the first time in two years—luscious white bread with a firm dark crust—and we could take as much as we wanted. The army was so good to us. If they were baking bread, and MacArthur was confident enough to show up at Santo Tomas, assuring us "Manila had fallen," the city had to be ours soon. We prayed that it was only a matter of hours or days before the last Japs pulled out— this time leaving Manila an Open City, an uncontested prize, for American troops.

Betty and Annie dashed in from Room 3, in search of a costume. They were part of a show for the GIs maybe as soon as Saturday night. Did mother have that old evening gown? They scoured the boxes under my mother's cot. What could they use for the ballroom scene? Annie had a sudden flash of inspiration and ran back into Room 3 to look for something, while Betty continued the search among my mother's treasures.

Meanwhile, Lulu and I sat on the edge of my big wooden bed, trying to figure out how to repair the damage Lulu caused last night when she broke Trimm's heart. At least, that's what I was trying to figure out because trampling on the tender soul of one of our liberators horrified me. When Lulu rejected him, Trimm had drunk himself into a stupor and sulked around all last night, saying, "Ah've nevah had anythin' lak' this happen to me befo…" He was from Georgia or "Jo-jah" as he pronounced it.

"Well, I can't believe Hoy was looney enough to bring the two of them into camp together!" Lulu was exasperated. "And I like them both, Lee—really I do. Trimm is sweet, but gosh, Andy is *dreamy*!!" She turned the last word into three syllables "duh-*ree*-me."

I don't blame Lulu for swooning over Sergeant Andrew Anderson, a wavy haired, blue-eyed, lady-killer who just might be twenty-two. This love triangle started shortly after the joy of liberation on Saturday. Staff Sergeant Hoy Moffett was my new beau of four days, and he and his shy-guy buddy Trimm had been our first dates. When that Georgia farm boy strummed his guitar, and the four of us sat outside my shanty singing cowboy songs together, we had the best time. Trimm felt lucky to be in the company of a girl as cute and fun as Lulu. We girls were thrilled to be serenaded by those enormous American GIs, who had ended our horror.

But GIs have assignments, so the next night when Trimm had duty outside camp, and my platoon Sergeant Hoy wanted to double-date, he came into camp with a different friend—Sarge Andrew Anderson. Of course, I got Lulu again. And boy, did Andy sweep Lulu off her feet! Next night, in came Hoy with Andy, and out went Lee and Lulu —Lulu completely over the moon for Andy. And then last night, my Brainwave Hoy waltzes into camp with both Andy and Trimm at his side! Well, Lulu made her choice for Andy, and poor Trimm left camp with a broken heart, and a load on.

"I can't just pretend, can I, Lee?" Lulu pressed.

Before I could put on my *Advice to the Lovelorn* thinking cap, a gigantic explosion rocked the ground beneath us, and the light in our room flickered. We froze. A quake? Then seconds later, a faint high-pitched whistle pierced the air and screamed ever closer.

"The hall, girls! Get into the hall!" After three years of captivity, my mother still had the presence of mind to protect her brood.

Lulu and I leapt from my bed, but Betty seemed frozen in place, clutching an aqua chiffon dress to her chest. I grabbed my little sister's hand and she tripped over the dress before releasing it, as we darted toward the door. Mommy and Hope raced behind us, as did every woman in that room, dozens of us pouring into the hallway. A second earth-shaking, ear-splitting concussion rocked the ground, and we dove for cover in the chaotic hall. Where were the shells coming from? Where would they hit next?

Cowering terror-stricken in a corner of the hall, I squinted back into Room 4. Through the iron bars on the window, I could make out frantic GIs in the patio, yelling orders at dazed internees. Soldiers dove into foxholes, mounted automatic weapons, leapt into their tanks, and whirled guns into position amid clouds of dust, shrapnel, and debris. When a third ear-piercing whistle and blast erupted, I had a clear view of my old room, and saw my ponderous wooden bed shoot straight into the air like a feather-weight cot.

That third shell didn't hit our room though. It smashed a gaping hole through the concrete wall of the Main Building and detonated Room 3 — our neighbors, forty women and girls, the room Betty had just left. Glass shattered and shards flew. Straight iron bars twisted like ribbons in the window. Those thick, concrete walls, built to withstand Manila's frequent earthquakes, cracked and rocked, and I prayed they wouldn't tumble. We ran again and raced for the main hall and the stairwell, while another shell pounded Room 3. Women were still pouring out of Room 3 screaming, crying, and taking cover. Betty stared back at the exodus wide-eyed, watching.

The barrage continued. The Japanese seemed to have found their target, and we were it. I spotted, what looked like a safer place to hide behind the stairwell near the men's bathroom. I shouted and signaled to Mommy, who could not have heard my words over the relentless whizzing and concussive thuds of shells, but she saw me. She nodded and we ran for it, while shrapnel whizzed through the air as if self-propelled. A steel-edged piece of flying debris nicked my leg, but I ran on. We ducked under the massive double stairwell, and I gripped my bleeding ankle. Lulu wrapped it with her sock, and together we watched yet another shell, take out more of the building's southwest side.

The acrid smell of smoke saturated the air, and for a brief moment something like silence descended. Helmeted GI medics with stretchers came running down the hall.

"Keep your cover! Stay down!" they shouted.

We all wanted to follow them. These heroic men burst into Room 3, with our own nurses right behind them. Another explosion rocked the far side of the building. The water tower had been hit. The medics in Room three hurried with their task, freeing trapped internees from the rubble and scrambling out with the wounded before the next shell. Down the hall they bore mutilated bodies on blood-soaked stretchers. They had to get them to Santa Catalina, the hospital. Around me rose the plaintive wails of women who watched their neighbors and friends fight for life. An afternoon of terror on the heels of this morning of freedom and joy.

From behind the stairwell, I squinted at a stretcher bearing the body of a girl whose face and head were completely covered in blood. Or was her head was gone? With horror, I realized there was only blood where her head should be. I *knew* that blue flowered dress. Whose dress was that? Betty peeked out too, braced herself against me, and emitted an anguished half-cry, half shriek. "Annie!"

Annie Davis. Fourteen-year-old Annie, Paul's loyal little sister and Betty's bosom buddy. Annie—who never lost her smile after three years of hunger and captivity, who was so proud of her brother Paul when he defended her against Danny Boy. Annie, who was planning the ballroom scene with Betty—Annie was gone. *Where was Paul?* I thought in a state of panic. Betty and I just hugged each other and wept. My little sister sobbed inconsolably.

I cried too, but my tears were part grief and part relief. What if Betty had stayed longer in Room 3? What if she hadn't come back to look for that gown when she did? What if she'd gone back to Room 3 with Annie? I'd be burying my little sister instead. *Oh, Lord, thank you for saving Betty.* I closed my eyes and prayed again. *Thank you for taking Betty out of Room 3.* When I opened my eyes Betty was still crying, but I stared now at the faded mural of the Sacred Heart of Jesus painted just to the left of the stairwell. Jesus was staring right back at me, and his brown eyes were so sorrowful; his heart was ringed with thorns—as if he were suffering right along with us. Maybe he was. I tore my gaze away to more stretchers bearing neighbors and friends.

Another blast rocketed us back under the stairwell. For the first time since liberation, it dawned on me that we might not get out alive. It's strange—the things I remembered at that moment. My tenth birthday party with all the candles on the cake. Mommy had made me a fabulous checkerboard cake. Daddy was teaching us kids to shoot soda cans off the fence in the backyard of our home. When I fired the Daisy air rifle, and the last soda can fell, Daddy, Betty, Paul, and Annie, all applauded. That's right —the Davises had been at that party. We knew the whole Davis family from church.

Another earth-shattering shell burst the west wall of the Big House, bending the steel reinforcements. That direct hit cracked the frescoed image of the Sacred Heart of Jesus left of the stairwell. The heart of Jesus literally broke in front of me.

"Lee, I see my mother," Lulu shouted right in my ear. "I think she's over there!" she pointed. "See the playsuit?" Lulu started to make run for it, but I yanked her back under the stairwell.

"Lulu, don't! Wait till they stop shelling!"

Another shell pounded the building. Mim and her two other daughters could be anywhere. So many women were wearing the same green, blue, and maroon print playsuits delivered last Christmas. It was easy to mistake identities now. Was that really Mrs. Cleland? Lulu was frantic to reach her mother, but we stayed huddled together. The woman who looked like Mrs. Cleland stood and ran. It wasn't Mim. Another shell hit the building.

An hour later, we saw Nellie's mother, Mrs. Thomas crying uncontrollably as she walked down the hall near a stretcher, holding the hand of another bloodied woman. Who was it? At one point, I had seen Nellie race out to the back of the building. She and Bill had put the whole Main Building between themselves and the shelling. So I knew it couldn't be Nellie. Mrs.

Thomas sobbed, "Emily, stay with us. Stay with us, Emily." Mrs. Brooks! It was Curtis and Barney's mom! My heart broke in two thinking of how the Brooksies had lost their dad last month to starvation, and now might lose their mom to the shelling.

The bombardment continued through the night and our little group moved three times. From the broad-shouldered stairwell near the men's bathroom, we raced for the women's bathroom on the northeast side, and hunkered down with the toilets for our best friends. Just in time because the men's bathroom exploded less than half an hour after we fled the stairwell. The barrage was relentless. Eventually we decided the main stairwell was safest, and moved yet again.

"Where are the shells coming from?" I yelled to one of the medics, as he raced past us.

"The old walled city!" he yelled back.

Intramuros. Of course. Probably Fort Santiago. The shells were being lobbed from the medieval fortress on the south side of the Pasig River where just yesterday I'd seen the Rising Sun flapping angrily in the breeze.

"Why would they do this?" Lulu screamed into my ear, tears streaming down her cheeks. "They kept us alive for three years! Why kill us now?"

We were so close that the two of us held hands but we could hardly hear each other in the din of shells. I didn't answer aloud. *Because the army's here*, I thought. The Japs had finally figured out that most of the US army was headquartered right here in camp, and the soaring cross tower of Santo Tomas, the highest landmark in the city, made an easy target.

"They need to just leave! It's over!" Betty screamed hysterically. My mother put her arms around her.

But our captors were not simply leaving the city, as we had all naively hoped. Before we'd been taken captive, just three weeks after Pearl Harbor, MacArthur declared Manila an "Open City" to spare civilian bloodshed and terrible destruction. Our American troops marched out in orderly fashion, and the Japanese marched in unopposed. It had been too much to hope, I guess, that they would return the favor in 1945.

The Japanese were going out in a blaze. They trained mortars, shells, and artillery on Santo Tomas, and probably every other remnant of American power in Manila. My leg throbbed. My heart thudded. Our GIs fired right back through the late afternoon and long into the night, but the bombardment went on and on. When total darkness fell, we could see flashes of the night sky explode in fire as the Japs ignited the city's bridges and warehouses, and attempted to pulverize us.

Our American tanks with their huge guns answered every shell fired. I knew my Sergeant Hoy, his buddy Trimm, and Lulu's new heartthrob, Andy were right in the thick of it, pounding right back. Those strapping boys—so big and so deadly. Huddled near the stairwell, I couldn't see them. But I imagined them all in their tanks: *Battlin Basic, Georgia Peach, Ole Miss,* and *Crusader* ... manned by Lieutenant Robert E. Lee.

What had Paul said about that? *Lee, Davis, Custer—notice how all three of those guys ended up on the wrong side of history.* And Curtis snapped back: *Not while they were in the First.*

My leg throbbed. My heart thudded. I was so afraid. But I couldn't believe we'd come so far to have it all end in complete horror. I closed my eyes, and said the only prayer that occurred to me. "Lord, let the First be first. Save the First. Save the Forty-Fourth too. Save us all."

Chapter 40
CHOOSE LIFE

February 9, 1945

Two days had passed since the bombardment began, but it went on. In the Big House, we'd learned the safest place to be in the shelling was right on this main stairwell. It sat well back from the outer walls of the large, earth-quake resistant building. When concussive shells punched through the concrete exterior the building itself held, and the recessed central staircase remained unharmed. During this lull in the bombardment, dozens of internees and off-duty GIs hunkered down on the wide stone staircase of the Main Building, waiting.

We waited and ate, waited and talked, waited and wrote—but mostly waited, either for the all-clear from our boys or the next blast to rock our world.

"You can't possibly be writing a recipe." Chocolate bar in hand, Lulu sat down on the clammy stone stair next to me. She eyed the Red Cross stationery that I was populating with tiny letters and as many details as I could cram onto a single page.

The Hopkins family was right in front of me and Freddy had his lunch pail with him. He chowed down greedily, determined to finish every last bite before the next explosion. He was not alone. The smell of stew mingled with the stench of sweat, and the clink of spoons in tin pails alternated with detonations in distant Manila. We'd left an open path for internees going up and down the stairs, but our stepped seating reminded me of a Greek amphitheater—the audience waiting for the tragic performance to begin. I was not eating. I was writing.

"It's a letter to my cousin Francis in Utica," I told Lulu. "He hasn't written me yet, but he's probably in the Army by now, and I'm filling him in on what he's fighting for—us."

I glanced down at the tiny sheet of paper. How annoying that the Red Cross had taken up valuable space on this page by emblazoning *Form 539A* in the corner. I had only three sheets total: we weren't allowed to write on the back, and I had so much to tell him. "Oh, Francis, you will never know what we've been through." I re-read my opening.

I'd told him that in the beginning, Santo Tomas was really quite the place—with shows, movies, dances, and of course, School. But all that had changed. I told him about starvation, and how, in the end, women who still had diamond rings sold them for a couple kilos of rice, and how some of us planted our own gardens and tried to grow extra to feed ourselves. "Hunger in camp being what it was," I wrote, "by the time the produce was ripe someone else would have eaten it. Stealing in camp was terrible. People lost all self-respect & honor & everything." I still got mad thinking about Hope slaving over that talinum and mint in her garden only to have other internees steal it at night.

"Are you telling him about the shelling?" Lulu asked.

I shook my head. "That wouldn't get past the censors. General Chase said not to give any battle details—or they'd be scissored out—remember? Have you written home yet?"

"One to my grandmother in Seattle. I told her Mommy went from 170 pounds to a hundred, and that she had been knocked out by artillery 'in the recent unpleasantness,'—I didn't say 'battle'—but she wasn't really hurt. Told her that a piece of shrapnel grazed Maureen's tummy, but she was fine. That they're in the hospital now, but they're OK."

"Really trying to cheer Granny up, huh?"

Lulu beamed her five-thousand watt smile. "I also told her that the soldiers are VERY nice to us, that they give us all their rations. They keep cooking even while the shells are flying." She paused to flick her six-square chocolate bar before my eyes, "that we girls are having the time of our lives, and that we all have lots of boyfriends."

"That's more like it." A bubble of hope and triumph rose in me. We sure did have lots of boyfriends. Hoy, Trimm, and Andy led the hit parade, but they often had assignments on the outside, while many others transferred in, and we loved them all. "We're gonna get out of here, Lulee." I saw the answering impish twinkle in her blue eyes.

My spirits had lifted with the long pause in shelling. Maybe our boys had breached Intramuros today and stormed Fort Santiago. Maybe they'd taken those Jap trench mortars out. "It's gotta be almost over," I said, hoping that saying it would make it so. "I met this gorgeous new Lieutenant last night—Boyd Davis from New York. He said they almost had Fort Santiago. Oh, but Lulu, the Japs are destroying the whole city—really letting the Filipinos have it."

"Andy told me," she nodded. "The three Bs: burning, bombing, bayoneting. The Japs are hell-bent on revenge against the Filipinos for choosing us over them. Hideous reprobates." Lulu's signature denunciation had not changed in three years. Then as abruptly as she'd come, my best friend sprang to her feet. "I'm off to visit Mommy and Maureen in the hospital."

A distant explosion made the building shudder again and my stomach twisted in a knot of fear. Ahead of me, twelve-year-old Freddy Hopkins grabbed his little sister's hand, as if to protect her. "Be careful," I called after Lulu, as she darted down the steps. On her way, she nearly tripped over the carelessly tossed crutches of Aubrey Man, whose leg had been hit in the first shelling. Don't die, Lulu was all I could think. Don't die.

My pencil hovered over the Red Cross stationery and my unfinished letter to Francis, but my mind kept replaying the jarring contrasts of the last six days. After liberation on Saturday night, we'd been bursting with joy. I still felt that exhilaration well up inside me just thinking about February third. The euphoria of knowing we were no longer prisoners.

But then came the shelling. Nineteen internees had been killed so far: Little Annie Davis. Mrs. Brooks. And all through that horrible night of February 7, a persistent male voice called over the loudspeaker at one-hour intervals: "Will Dr. Foley please come to the clinic? Dr. Foley, please report to the clinic to assist your wife."

Where was Dr. Foley? For the last three years, that unfailingly kind Protestant minister had leapt up to help anyone who needed him. He was the one who'd written our Camp's Ten Commandments. I knew Mrs. Foley had been wounded in the Room 3 blast.

That woman was a pillar of strength, though. In the chaos between the second and third shells, I'd seen her stagger with determination from the rubble toward the room medics were using as a clinic, and she clutched her arm to her side. When I looked closer, my stomach lurched into a sickening downward spiral—Mrs. Foley's arm wasn't attached to her body. She'd been holding it where it ought to be, as she trudged toward the clinic. All through the night the announcement had droned over the loudspeaker: "Dr. Foley please report to the clinic. Will Dr. Foley please report to the clinic." He'd never came, though. Dr. Foley had been killed in the men's bathroom when it blew up.

When we learned of his death yesterday, a wave of sorrow washed over me. That devoted couple had endured so much in the last thirty-seven months to be severed from each other at the end. Not just an arm severed, but a marriage and a life. Should I tell Francis about that? How could he ever understand?

Just then a stronger concussion brought everyone on the stairway to silence and attention. Aubrey Man righted his crutches as if he were prepared to leap up at a moment's notice and hobble God-knows-where. But nothing followed. The blast was still outside of camp. I noticed that my left hand had instinctively fled into my skirt pocket and wrapped itself around the sharp-edged wooden crucifix on my rosary. "Mary is better than Max," Rosalina had insisted when she shoved that rosary through the iron bars of the gate into my hand thirty-seven months ago. She was right. Now I squeezed it hard. Squeezing the crucifix had become a habit in these last three years—my way of praying without saying a word. This time, though, I did talk to God . *We've been here—on our own cross—for three years, Lord. Haven't we had enough? Isn't it time for Easter yet?* I waited for a new shell to explode in response to my insolence, but it didn't.

That's probably because the saviors God already sent us were hard at work. Our boyfriends of six days—Hoy, Trimm, Andy, my new Sergeant Boyd and so many others—came back into camp from the fighting each night somber and grim. They didn't want to talk about the battle, but assured us they would get "every last Nip." Then Clarence Beliel—aka Don Bell—piped "In the Mood" or "Chattanooga Choo-Choo" over the P.A. system, and it was as if those battling boys, our weary warrior saviors, just flipped a switch. They went from Sad Sack Sams to Good-time Charlies.

That was beautiful to see—that pivot. How these boys—near my age—reached deep inside themselves and found the strength to do hard, horrible, but necessary things during the day. And then those same battle-scarred GIs, bruised and partly broken, came back to camp each night, listened to the strains of Glenn Miller, and put it behind them. They softened. They laughed. They shared their chocolate bars. They played guitars and sang. That's over for now—they seemed to say—we choose LIFE.

Then it hit me for the first time. Maybe that's what we'd all been doing for the last three years: finding ways to choose life. Lulu and me with our friendship, our schemes, our school work, and The Captive's Kitchen. My mother with her fudge, our shanty, and her careful stewardship of our Red Cross packages. Betty with her drawing and dancing, and her ready smile. Hope with her fifth graders and her vegetable garden. Haruo with his piano. Even Aubrey Man with his Shakespeare games. We'd all clung to the one freedom we had—to hope and to choose life. That's what little Annie Davis had been doing just before she died—planning a show with Betty. Now the tears streamed down my face.

Not everyone chose life, I knew, wiping the back of my hand across my cheek. Some people didn't even try. I closed my eyes and remembered Mrs. Randolph Meade, who'd wallowed in woe-is-me selfish complaint every minute of every day—a slave to her own ego. And what about Danny Boy, who'd become the permanent Camp Bully, the menace to life. Even our own Paul had lost his buoyant sense of humor near the end, and seemed to despair under the weighty burden. And I knew so many people in camp right now, who still spoke as if they were tragic victims—even now that we'd been liberated, for God's sake. We'd been given the gift of life. We had a blank slate and could start all over.

I put my pencil to paper again to try to explain to Francis. "Even now when we can have all we want," I wrote, "and the army tries to give us everything, some people still want to chisel and cheat to get a little extra. You can't imagine what an experience like this can do to people, even the best. But you know, Francis, I wouldn't give up this experience and what I've learned for 10 yrs of my life."

I stopped and stared down at what I had written—appalled. *I wouldn't give up this experience and what I've learned for 10 yrs of my life.* Was that true? Just two weeks ago this camp was my enemy—holding me back from everything I desperately longed for: food and freedom—in that order. Two weeks ago I would never have written that. But now, I re-read it and wondered why that sentence seemed exactly right. Then I knew. Camp taught me—without my ever realizing it—to dig deep, find the good, and choose life. STIC never took that freedom from me. The Japs never took that freedom from me.

Well, I was one hundred percent free now and I resolved that I was not going to waste one minute of one day ever again—especially on self-pity. What I'd written was absolutely true, I decided. And besides, I was at the bottom of Red Cross *Form 539A*, and out of room. "Love & God keep you, Francis—Lee."

Chapter 41
BIRDSEYE VIEW

Wednesday, February 28, 1945

It took our GIs nearly a week to rout the vengeful Japanese soldiers firing on Santo Tomas, and they made horrible discoveries along the way. The bodies of Mr. Grinnell, Mr. Duggleby, and two other members of our Executive Committee who'd been taken from camp in December had been found in Manila—slain, beheaded. Those men had done so much for us and gotten so close to freedom.

Though camp was secure, the horrible battle for Manila raged day and night. For two weeks we heard the rapid fire of cartridge-loaded automatic weapons, and the high-pitched whistle of shells, as the enemy made a ferocious suicide stand—intent on taking every last Filipino and American down with them. Artillery pounded, fires blazed, and explosions ravaged the city. Until yesterday. Yesterday our boys took out the last Jap garrison.

Manila was free. And the Army lost no time in announcing a big dance tonight to celebrate the city's liberation

"I think this slinky silk is perfect for you." I pulled an ice-blue evening gown out of my mother's straw suitcase, and handed it to Lulu. "I can shorten it for you before nine, and nip in the waist, but the color's a knock-out with your eyes."

Lulu and I were on the second floor of the Main Building in her room, and she held the gown against her five-foot-three-inch frame. She and it looked stunning, and her face registered longing.

"Are you sure Aggie won't mind? She's probably been saving it."

"No, she told me to take what we wanted. She's on the mend; she's going to be fine, but she won't be there tonight."

My mother was in the hospital, recovering from pneumonia. Because our room suffered so much damage in the shelling, we Isersons had been sleeping on the cold concrete floor of the hallways for a few nights. Mommy ignored the congestion in her chest until it became almost impossible for her to breathe. Then the GIs rushed her to their own field hospital, where they had penicillin.

What if I had lost both my father and mother to pneumonia? I pushed that thought aside. I was not going to think about one more tragic thing. Mommy had begun to recover and she was going to be just fine.

In the meantime, internees who'd lived in the now damaged first floor rooms had been re-assigned to other areas. We Isersons moved to "the model home," a small building once used by the university Home Economics Department to educate students in everything from meal preparation to household management. If there hadn't been dozens of us sharing the "model bedroom," it would have been a great place to live, but I wasn't complaining.

We'd also received thrilling news that a division of paratroopers and marines had surprised the Japs at Los Baños, and liberated the entire camp without a single Allied casualty. Every prisoner in that camp came out alive—Bunny Brambles and her whole family, Kay and Harry Hodges, Mrs. Gewald, my fourth grade teacher, Sr. Olivette, Fr. Reuter, and so many others. They were all safe and alive. My heart was singing, because we were all free, safe, and tonight we were going to a dance.

"How many just-sprung prisoners of war have such great evening gowns?" Lulu asked, impish eyes alight.

"About five hundred of us by my tally," I said.

It really was a stroke of luck that almost all internee women who'd lived in Manila BC (*Before Camp*) had their evening gowns sent into Santo Tomas well before the package line closed. We always thought that liberation was just around the corner and wanted to be ready. The truth was that before the war most American women in the Philippines probably owned more evening gowns than street clothes—because every single night brought a social event at the Manila Hotel or the Sky Room or the Polo Club. So, we'd asked for them to be sent in. We'd worn formals for the Christmas Concert in 1943, and for high school graduation in early 1944. And of course, if performing in shows led by Dave Harvey. The Japs didn't seem to care. (They actually kind of liked it.)

Nellie popped her head in Room 33, spotted us near Lulu's cot in our Coco Chanel mode, and made a bee-line for us. Her eyes radiated excitement. "Bill got the key to the cross tower. Shall we go up and take a look? Watch the sunset on Manila Bay?"

My heart leapt and my pulse raced.

"How did he get the key?" Lulu was incredulous.

The Main Building's boxy cross tower, the highest perch in the city, soared one hundred and seventy feet off the ground. It had been forbidden territory for all three years of our captivity since anyone scaling it could see the whole expanse of Manila, and observe Japanese troop movements. The Japs always worried that our guys were in contact with Filipino guerillas, so during the three years of our internment, the doors to the base tower had always been padlocked and guarded.

"How does Bill Phillips get anything?" Nellie shrugged her shoulders, and hurried us. "Let's go. Maybe we can still spot the Metropolitan or the Manila Hotel."

***

Nellie held out that beautiful hope, but we'd been listening to non-stop explosions for three weeks. Was a single building in tact? Only one way to find out.

We stashed our ballroom choices under Lulu's bed, headed for the stairwell, and bounded up three flights of stairs to the rooftop classrooms. A month ago, starving and weak, it would've taken us a solid ten minutes to make that climb. But after three weeks of hearty stews, evaporated milk, wheat bread, and chocolate bars, we took the steps two at a time.

Bill Phillips and Paul Davis waited for us on the roof at the tower entry, and Bill brandished the key triumphantly. We three girls applauded.

"They don't call him Fast-Fingers Phillips for nothing," Paul said. It was good to see a flash of Paul's old humor. He was trying to bounce back, but he and his mother had buried Annie just two weeks ago in the "K.I.A." funeral. Little Annie Davis had been Killed In Action.

The Main Building's squared cross tower rose in two chunky segments above our rooftop classrooms: the first, a solid, crate-like tower, six stories high, opening to a wide, railed landing, and then a narrower, light-house-like spire shot up another five stories to a squared platform just below the cross itself.

I stared at the smoking city of Manila from the rooftop and now had grave doubts about whether we really wanted this birds-eye view above. Was the whole city in ruins? But Bill had already opened the heavy iron door and disappeared inside the first stone tower, leading the way. Nellie and Lulu followed, while Paul waited for me, holding the door. I slipped into the darkened stone cube with Paul behind me, and there was still enough light to make out an iron staircase leading up six flights. Ever onward.

The cool limestone entombed a somber silence, broken only by our footsteps and our rhythmic breathing. Each of us mulled over the momentous events of the past month, and hoped against hope that we'd find something glorious and redeeming on top. If only a nostalgic look at the graceful palm trees on Dewey Boulevard and maybe the first flashes of sunset on Manila Bay.

Bill led the climb up six flights at a brisk pace, and when he opened the door to the first landing, late afternoon light flooded the boxy tower. We scampered out behind him and onto a spacious, limestone terrace that overlooked the city. But my first instinct was to look up: the Santo Tomas cross rose from yet another slender lighthouse-like tower in the center of the terrace. Perched on a cupola, the cross— the highest point in the city, the most conspicuous target—still stood by some miracle, solid and unharmed. If we went inside that slender tower, there were another five flights to the top—to a small landing just one story below the cross, and overlooking the campus and the city.

Bill was already racing for the door of the lighthouse tower, intent on climbing as high as we could go and getting the best view he could. We all followed. More steps, more silence, more breathing—until we emerged from a final door to a breathtakingly high perch on a small landing right beneath the cupola and the cross. I looked up and felt like I could practically touch the solid stone cross.

"Shit…" I heard Bill swear and not even try to mask his language. The boys hardly ever swore in front of us girls, and Bill especially never swore in front of Nellie, but when I looked out to the sooty, smoke-shrouded Manila, I understood.

The five of us pressed against the stone rail of the landing and stared across the Pasig River at a flaming chaos of destruction. Manila smoldered and burned, a lone church tower stood in Intramuros, but block after city block had been razed to the ground. Oh my God. Had Grandma Naylor survived?

"Bastards," Paul muttered. "Damn Japs have been on a rampage for two solid weeks."

Every night our teen boys relentlessly pumped the GIs for details about the battle for Manila, and now Bill scanned the horizon, trying to make sense of what he'd heard.

"Sometimes they targeted a single building—like the Spanish consulate— it used to be over there, remember?" Bill pointed to one of many charred, exploded heaps. "The Japs sealed everybody inside, locked it up, and burned it to the ground. Fifty people dead in that attack—and the Spanish were neutrals." Bill's voice dripped contempt. "They weren't even the enemy."

For the first time in months, I thought about Ramón and how glad I was that he and his family had left the PI. Why would they kill neutrals and civilians?

"And that Red Cross attack…" Paul was repeating what he'd learned from Lieutenant Robert E. Lee. "Japs stormed the Red Cross building, bayoneted and shot everyone in there—doctors, patients, refugees, Filipina mothers and kids trying to get food. Bastards burned and bombed any place they couldn't hide in, any place they weren't lying in wait to ambush our guys."

I saw a tear roll down Nellie's cheek, and fought to hold back my own. "There's nothing left to hide in now," Nellie's voice seemed distant and lost.

She was right. I peered out to what I knew had been the business district, now a mass of rubble. Heacock's Department store, where Betty and I bought every Christmas present we'd ever sent to our cousins in Utica, was gone.

"The Japs made their last stand in the best buildings," Paul nicked his chin toward the city center. "The National Assembly and the Post Office—turned 'em into kamikaze fortresses." Smoke partially shrouded the view, but my eyes flew to the collapsed temple-front roof of the National Assembly, which looked like a fallen Parthenon.

"How did they do this?" Nellie whispered. "And why blow up yourself and everything around you?"

"I'll tell you how," Bill answered almost too eagerly, ignoring the philosophical question. "They dragged *artillery*—the big guns, cannons and rocket launchers—into those buildings to ambush our guys, and bring the whole damn building down on top of all of them. Destroy and murder as many as possible."

"'Never-surrender,' 'death-before-dishonor' maniacs,'" Paul spat. "They waited to ambush our guys in the tunnels of Intramuros and in the corridors of City Hall."

We kids had been hoping against hope, but we knew the rest. Our GIs had been forbidden to use airpower against the enemy because—ironically—MacArthur wanted to avoid civilian casualties and not destroy Manila. But that meant American troops had to go building to building, house to house, often in hand to hand combat to dislodge the enemy.

In frustration, they rolled tanks into occupied buildings or shelled from mortars and howitzers into enemy-held structures. "Sometimes we just pounded like hell with artillery," my Sergeant Hoy had said. One by one all the great buildings had fallen—blown up by angry Japs or by American avengers.

Here lay Manila in the purple twilight, debris-bedecked and covered with ashes. Buildings gutted, knocked to the ground, classical columns broken, stone foundations exposed, laying bare the squared grids of what were once neighborhoods. Beams lay like matchsticks across the ground. The once-neat rows of palms on Dewey Boulevard sprawled chaotically along the bay and the harbor spewed flames. Black soot misted the darkening skies.

As I gazed on the city's complete devastation, I thought about all our friends on the outside who had helped us. Was Grandma Naylor still alive? Valentina? Alfonso? Juergen Goldfarb? And what about Rosalina, Felix, Warlito and Valentina? Did they survive? We, in camp, had endured the shelling, trembled with the explosions, and worried about our own safety for weeks now, but how could anyone in Manila have escaped this carnage?

It just shouldn't have been like this. A tear rolled down my cheek. The day after our liberation, when we jubilant internees had unfurled that giant American flag and I'd stood on the stone portico looking out to the city, the Pearl of the Orient, still had her luster. That was just a little over two weeks ago. Now, as I pressed against the stone rail, with Paul on one side of me and Lulu on the other, the ashen violet skies announced the funeral of a city.

I glanced down for a minute to look away from the horror and saw Paul's maimed right hand, gripping the stone rail firmly. That image seemed to say it all—a damaged boy looking out at a broken city, while the skies turned plum.

"*The Purple Death from Outer Space,*" Paul murmured.

His words rocketed me back to another time and place. Was that just two years ago or two lifetimes ago? Paul and I had sat in Grandma Naylor's living room with Juergen and Ramón—listening to them recount the latest Flash Gordon movie adventure. "Ming the Merciless" had unleashed a plague from the Planet Mongo, a "purple death" that left an eggplant-colored streak on foreheads of doomed earthlings. But Flash Gordon came to the rescue, of course, finding the antidote just in time.

"No antidote this time," I whispered back, and put a hand on Paul's forearm. His jaw was clenched and I saw the muscles in his throat working to maintain a stoic exterior. I knew he had to be thinking of Annie. His own personal purple death.

Bill pulled a newspaper clipping from his back pocket maybe to distract from the horror and give us some hope. "Listen to this. MacArthur met with big wigs and the new Filipino President—Osmeña—yesterday to congratulate themselves on the end of the battle and their new start." He scanned to the key paragraph and read aloud. "'My country kept the faith,' MacArthur announced to the assembly. 'Your capital city, cruelly punished though it be, has regained its rightful place—the citadel of democracy in the East.' Osmeña acknowledged gratefully that peace had indeed been restored."

We fell silent and looked out to the smoking ruins.

Nellie stared, her eyes misting. "Ubi solitudinem faciunt, pacem appellant." Our Latin-scholar was quoting Tacitus. Mrs. Maynard had drilled that line into all three of us.

The boys, who were not in our Latin class, stared at her perplexed. "Is that a secret code, Nels?" Bill prompted.

She translated in a detached voice. "They make a desolation, and call it peace." Bill and Paul stared at her as if waiting for another translation, and she continued. "The Romans were proud of bringing peace to the whole world or at least their empire. Pax Romana and all that. But they did it by one war of conquest after the next. Conquest, plunder, destruction, then peace." She paused as if waiting for them to get it, but their puzzled expression kept her going. "Tacitus was skewering the Romans when he said that: 'Ubi solitudinem faciunt, pacem appellant.' They make a desolation and call it peace. Just like MacArthur—'we kept the faith. Here's your peaceful ruined city.'"

The razor-sharp edge of Nellie's intellect never ceased to astound me. But wait a minute, didn't that make us, us Americans, the rapacious Romans? Everyone knew that the Japs were the bad guys here.

"You don't think we're responsible for this, do you, Nellie?" I objected. "I mean if the Japs had just left the city—like MacArthur did in '41 or like the Nazis did in Paris in August—if they hadn't fought like suicidal maniacs, Manila would still be whole and beautiful." I was aware that my voice sounded desperate and a little hysterical, but I couldn't help racing on. "We could still walk down Dewey Boulevard and go dancing at the Manila Hotel, and watch Deanna Durbin at the Metropolitan. And Rosalina and Felix and Valentina would be fine, and Grandma Naylor too—they would all be fine and…"

And suddenly, I couldn't go on. I started to cry, sob really, for all that had been and was not going to be. For the innocent, pampered children we'd once been, and were never going to be again. For the magical place we had once lived, that was forever lost. For the courageous Filipino friends who stood by us, and now had no home, no city, and maybe no life. Was it just two weeks ago that I was certain I would not give this experience up for ten years of my life?

Lulu reached me in a second, put her arms around me, and held me. We stood there for a few moments with her rocking me. The sporadic explosions in the harbor sounded like a requiem salute, and one final blast jolted me from her arms.

I pulled away from Lulu and looked up at the massive stone cross that had watched over us these thirty-seven months. What did I expect to see there? The first time I glanced up at that cross was when we'd entered camp in January of '42, and the clock below had been striking noon. Now a narrow shaft of magenta light brightened the sky and illumined the clouds above the cross. Manila sunset.

"It is finished," I whispered to no one in particular, but Lulu heard.

"You bet it is," she said.

And then, from our high perch, we heard the crisp scratch of a 78 RPM over the PA system. Six bright chords blared before Guy Lombardo's orchestra launched into the lush, lazy strains of a 1930s jazz hit.

I looked below and could still make out laughing women talking to handsome GIs and self-assured officers. Was that Betty down there joking with the beefy GI whose shovel tripped her? Hordes of happy kids swarmed all over tanks, while skinny men bantered, smoked and played cards. A heightened joy thrummed in the early evening air. The bad stuff was all over. The welling music meant a magical night was about to begin, and hearts and minds were already leaping ahead to the dance tonight.

"What's that tune—can you tell?" Lulu was straining to hear.

"Deep Purple," I said without thinking. "Deep Purple" had been my favorite song for years. About lovers separated, but reunited in the deep purple twilight. After Daddy died, I used to imagine him coming back to me when that song played over the PA in camp. Now I imagined all the lovers and families reunited with the war over, and all the new loves beginning tonight and every twilight hereafter. "Here in my deep purple dreams," as the song went.

Lulu's suddenly impatient voice snapped us out of our reverie. "Don't we have a dance to go to?"

"Puddles of purple passion, you are correct, Miss Mary Lou!" Paul shot back. You never saw five pairs of feet fly so quickly down those stairs.

Chapter 42

KEEPSAKES

Sunday, March 4, 1945

"OK, this needs to be done quickly and without any whining," my recuperated mother announced as if Betty and I were cranky toddlers. Sometimes Agnes Iserson positively specialized in Aggravation Techniques.

"Whining? Mother—when was the last time Betty and I did any whining?" I could not keep the irritation out of my voice. Still, I was having a hard time keeping up with her determined stride as we headed down the wide stone hallway of the Main Building.

My mother, like most internees, had a spring in her step these days. She was fully recovered from a bout with pneumonia. She, like all of us, had been feasting on delicious army grub for nearly a month now. But most important for everyone's morale: the battle for Manila was over. We'd slept two nights in a row without being jolted from sleep by explosions. Today Grandma Naylor sent word through the Red Cross that she—along with Valentina and Alfonso—were alive and well. And, as Dave Harvey bantered in a show last night, "Repatriation has replaced starvation as the very best topic of conversation."

The U.S. Army in the Philippines had a big job on its hands: finish the war in the Pacific and at the same time, get thousands of us liberated civilians back to the States. Two groups of internees had shipped out already, and tomorrow Clarence Beliel would read another list of the homeward-bound over the loud speaker. We had to be packed and ready to go with ninety minutes notice, but one important task remained for our little family: retrieving our treasures from Room Four. Room Four had been badly damaged and off-limits since the shelling two weeks ago, but clean-up crews had been hard at work, and we now had permission to go back and collect whatever personal items remained.

When my mother suddenly stopped short in the doorway of our old home, Betty and I practically collided into her. She stood motionless for a moment before edging inside, leaving the door frame to Betty and me. All three of us now gaped at the pile of rubble that was once the only predictable place in our lives. The top half of the carefully lettered sign—*Room Four is Your Home*—jutted defiantly from a pile of trash in the corner. The iron window bars, through which I'd stared at my father's star on the Southern Cross, now bowed and sagged, their cement frame crumbling. Battered cots with torn mosquito netting lay scattered in haphazard rows. A dozen piles of debris rose like termite mounds around us. The clean-up teams had worked hard to sweep up the shrapnel, the chunks of cement, and the shards of broken glass, but Room 4 still looked like what it had been—a battle zone.

My stomach knotted in dread. Were my treasures still here? Did *Leonore's Suite* survive? What about *The Captive's Kitchen*? Was my letter from Ramón still here? Betty had to be thinking about her treasured keepsakes too. We made our way to the corner we'd claimed three Januarys ago. Long gone was the student bench I'd tried to sleep on that first night, when I'd been attacked by bed bugs. But to my relief, the sturdy wooden frame of the bed Kay and I shared seemed to be intact.

"OK, girls, you each have a maleta." My mother used the Filipino shorthand for suitcase, and took a deep breath. "Pack what's really important to you, but we'll get new clothes in the States—and the Red Cross has some for us too—so just take what you need for our stop in Leyte and the ship home," my mother ordered.

I sank to my knees, and tugged on the wooden drawer of my bed, but it was jammed. How to pry it open? I stood and looked for anything that resembled a crowbar, thinking about the lucky internees who'd already shipped out. Like the Brooks twins, who'd left camp a week ago. They *flew* from Manila to the Philippine island of Leyte further south. They flew, courtesy of the U.S. military, in a C-47. We were going to have our first plane ride soon too, and then board a Navy transport ship from Leyte to San Francisco. Would we be on tomorrow's list of families to be repatriated?

My heart did crazy somersaults just thinking about our return—somersaults of excitement and joy, to be sure—but also of worry and loss. What if tomorrow was the last day I'd ever see Lulu? She and her family planned to settle in California when they got back to the States, but we were going to Utica—three thousand miles away. I desperately wanted the Clelands and the Isersons to be on the same ship home. But I knew it wasn't likely.

"He's here!" Betty shrieked with delight to find Cuddles dozing under her shattered cot, and my mother and I both applauded. My fifteen-year-old sister hugged that skinny, nose-less wonder of a bear.

Cuddles, like us, had once been chubby. He'd been stuffed with cheap mongo bean filling, but back in January, when we were desperate for food, it occurred to my mother that Cuddles would not mind losing a little weight for the family. Mommy had deftly slit his side seam, portioned out a meal for the three of us, and sewn him back up again. Betty had been distraught to see Cuddles looking like a bear cadaver, but Mommy assured her that he could be restored to his former glory right after liberation. That hadn't happened before the shelling and he'd been stranded here, but Cuddles would be looking more like his old self before dinner tonight, I was pretty sure.

Ah. Here was an iron rod from the damaged window's grille. I returned to my spot, knelt beside my bed and pried the stubborn drawer that still held my hopes and dreams. I got it open maybe three inches. Betty foraged under her cot and extracted the basket where she'd stored her clothes and other treasures.

"We'll need a formal, don't you think, Mommy?" Still kneeling, Betty held up a demure white gown with butterfly sleeves and exquisite embroidery on the bodice. It was a young girl's formal, and it used to be mine. Her question elicited a quick nod from my mother.

"There'll be dances with the GIs on Leyte and probably on the ship going home," my mother said matter-of-factly, and then with uncharacteristic lightness added, "We may be just-sprung prisoners of war, but we are going to be well-dressed, just-sprung prisoners of war." It was good to see my mother smile again. Especially at the prospect of our return.

The trip home promised both excitement and danger because war still raged in the Pacific, but we'd have a Navy escort, the GIs told us. A couple of destroyers were going to float right along with us. I was sure that we'd get home alive and safe with almost everything that was really important—if I could ever open this blankety-blank drawer.

"Boops, can you help me with this?"

Betty placed a set of drawings she'd retrieved in her suitcase, and then knelt down next to me. Together we tugged on the drawer and wedged it open a full eight inches.

"Oh, you have to take that." Betty pointed to my ruffled, black "Spanish lady" skirt on top, and returned to her work.

I agreed. The flouncy skirt that topped the treasures within was loose in the waist, but it reminded me of my adventure on the outside, when Paul and I visited Grandma Naylor in Manila and I sewed those illicit pesos into its folds. I'd smuggled that money into camp right before the eyes of Bugs Bunny Guard, I recalled proudly. I was also going to take that Peter Pan collar blouse next to the skirt—the blouse I'd worn for Haruo's Christmas concert, and the white crepe skirt I'd worn on February third, the most exciting night of my life. But I hadn't found what really brought me here yet. I dug deep beneath the folds of clothing and felt for it.

"Eureka!" I announced as I tugged the plump manila envelope out, my heart rocketing skyward when I saw *"Leonore"* emblazoned on the front in Grandma Naylor's handwriting. My mother and sister stopped what they were doing and looked over. *"Leonore's Suite,"* I added as I waved the prize back and forth.

A sad smile creased my mother's deeply lined face. She looked so much older than her forty-two years, but her voice was still velvet. "Grandma could never guess how much that music would mean to you… To us," she corrected herself.

My mother was right: that evidence of my father's love kept with me these three years had lifted me up, kept me going. When Grandma had sent the music into camp along with the Girardhelli's chocolate that started our fudge business, she'd given me food for both body and soul.

"Is it all there?" Betty asked.

I peeked inside, withdrew the pages, and nodded. *Leonore's Suite* my father's handwriting proclaimed on the top. Then underneath: *"Happy Birthday, dearest Lee, my darling grown-up daughter."* Grown up at thirteen? I didn't feel that way then, but now I felt like I deserved my father's words: I would turn seventeen next month. I had survived prison camp and starvation. I was going to be a free, top-of-the-heap senior in an American high school. I allowed myself a moment of pleased-as-punch pride, before tucking the pages back inside the envelope and placing the envelope face down on top of the skirt in my maleta.

Then I caught sight of the crabbed scrawl on the back of the envelope—*44-12-25 19:30*—and a warm wave of memory washed over me. Haruo's coded message and the glorious Christmas concert. Haruo hadn't copied my music—he'd memorized it and added his own. He'd pointed to his heart—"I have here," he said, when he gave it back to me. He knew it by heart—an expression that took on new meaning for me. Where was Haruo now, I wondered. Was his heart still beating? Yes. I decided to believe that somehow, somewhere Haruo had survived.

I kept packing, but it was easier now. Here was Ramón's letter, comparing me to an "autumnal fairy" and reminding me to roar like a lion. I silently roared with delight as I tucked it into the *Leonore's Suite* envelope. My thin red leather autograph book with the names of my classmates and the signatures of GIs who liberated us came next, and I found the poem that Hope wrote me for my sixteenth birthday stuck inside it. Then I dug deeper and found my second greatest treasure on earth—the olive green, spiral bound note book with three hundred seventy-four recipes: *The Captive's Kitchen*. Would I ever publish my magnum opus, I wondered as I snapped shut the fasteners on my maleta. Just then Lulu came tearing into the room.

"Lee! Oh, Aggie—thank Heavens you're here too." Lulu was still the only person in camp who called my mother 'Aggie' and got away with it. "Two really nice lieutenants are heading up to Muntinglupa now, where all the Los Baños internees are. They invited Lee and me to go with them. We'd be back later tonight. Is that OK?"

Muntinglupa was twenty miles south of Manila, but a safe haven high in the mountains, where, we'd been told, more than two thousand liberated prisoners from Los Baños had been taken after their daring rescue.

"We can see Bunny and Kay!" I leapt at the prospect. "That's all right, isn't it, Mum? I'm sure those lieutenants are nice guys."

"Who are they? What do you know about them?" my mother asked wearily and almost as a formality because the GIs could do no wrong in her book.

"One's name is Boyd and the other one is Dick," Lulu announced as if that cinched it.

"Boyd Davis—oh, he's a great guy, Mum. You've met him. He's from New York. His friend Dick has to be wonderful too."

"They're both from New York," Lulu confirmed. She knew my mother was from Utica, New York, and had a special fondness for New York City where she met Daddy.

My mother gave a resigned smile, and waved us off wearily. "OK, but get those New Yorkers to bring you back before dark." I quickly entrusted my maleta to Betty, then sprinted for the door. "And tell Kay how much we've missed her!" my mother called after us.

Leonore's Suite

***

The Army jeep careened wildly from side to side along cratered roads as we roared our way into the hills. We sped south of devastated Manila and into the scent of jasmine wafting from the densely forested hills. We'd left behind collapsed buildings, exploded shops, and the rubble of my former home at 690 Taft Avenue. I'd asked our lanky lieutenant driver, Dick Church, to take us by there, but we couldn't even tell where the building had been. We'd woven through the streets past weeping refugees and wounded carabao. Now in the hill country, ripening mangoes hung from trees, and lime green avocadoes offered themselves.

Lulu and I would have admired the fire-red hibiscus and the purple orchids poking through the vines, if we hadn't been so terrified. In the back seat of the jeep, we held on to each other for dear life, while shots rang out in the distance, and the reckless zig-zagging continued.

"We're swerving to avoid ka-booms," Boyd shouted back to us. "These roads are mined, but we've got a pretty good idea about where most of the mines are. You just have to stay alert."

"I'm as alert as I ever want to be!" Lulu shouted back to him, and flashed me a look reflecting our mutual thought: what kind of girl idiots decided to do this?

The battle for Manila was over, but the war was very much still on. These roads were mined! Or maybe the GIs were just trying to impress us with their driving skill and daring. Well, gunfire definitely rang somewhere in the distance. What had started out as a lark with handsome GIs was proving harrowing—at least to us.

"You girls want to stop and collect shrapnel?" Dick's cheerful voice rang out. Sunlight glinted off the silver wedding band on his left hand. "There's some nice pieces up ahead for souvenirs."

We'd just passed a road sign saying "WATCH OUT FOR ROAD MINES, BOOBY TRAPS, AND SNIPERS IN TREES," so I almost shouted "no thanks!" but Dick had already slowed the jeep a little, and pointed to some applauding Filipinos at the side of the road ahead of us. The women clapped and waved flowers at our oncoming jeep. Broad-smiling men were emerging from nipa shanties behind them, and cheered too. I forgot the sign, and had a thought that made my heart race: Could Rosalina be up there? Would I see her again?

"You should stop and accept the flowers," I shouted up to our guides over the roar of the engine.

Dick braked sharply and pulled up next to the jubilant Filipinos, who were shouting "Sa-LAH-maht! Sa-LAH-maht!"

"They're saying thank you in Tagalog," Lulu called to the front seat, but I think the GIs both knew that.

At the urging of the applauding Filipinos, we all got out of the jeep and our uniformed lieutenants were immediately showered with orchids and hibiscus that the young women placed in their breast pockets or on their heads— they had woven them into wreaths. Both men looked embarrassed but delighted. Lulu and I clapped too.

"Salamat! Thank you!" the Filipinos switched from Tagalog into English and bowed happily to the boys. No Rosalina among the women. But maybe one of them knew her.

I waited for the little "thank you ceremony" to be over, then turned to a young woman standing next to me. "Do you know Rosalina Ramboa?"

She smiled broadly and nodded vaguely but said nothing. She probably didn't understand me. "Rosa-LEEN-uh Rahm-BO-uh?" I asked again very slowly. "She's about your age." I pointed to her.

The young woman nodded again, vigorously this time, still beaming. "My cousin. She OK. She lucky."

Now I was the one beaming and clapping. I hugged and kissed this girl I didn't even know, and felt like a huge weight had been lifted from my shoulders.

"Where is she? Will you see Rosa soon?" I asked

"Two weeks," she nodded enthusiastically. "She was hiding north, but come back."

I reached into my short-shorts pocket and produced the brown wooden rosary Rosalina had given me through the bars of Santo Tomas three years before. I pressed it into her hand. "Would you give this to her from me, please? She'll need it now. Tell her she was right—it got me through. It's from Lee." I pointed to myself.

"Lee? Like Chinese name?" the young woman asked.

"Right." I nodded, too happy to be offended. "But I'm not Chinese."

"You fine American girl," the Filipina smiled so broadly that I hugged her again.

Minutes later, lighter by one rosary and lifted by the tide of good news, we were on the road again. Ten miles to go. Still swerving. Still careening, but I didn't have a care in the world.

***

"Oh my God, they're in a palace! Look at that!"

Lulu pointed ahead to what looked like a crenellated stone castle from medieval Europe, but American and Filipino flags flew from its towers. New Bilibid Prison in remote Muntinglupa looked like anything but the penitentiary it was designed to be. Filipinos had built this new prison just before the war, but it positively sang Middle Ages. Two imposing towers flanked a gate house with a draw-bridge arch. Except there was no drawbridge. And right now, innumerable American jeeps, armored trucks, and Red Cross vehicles poured through that wide open arch.

When the U.S. Army rescued the prisoners at Los Baños a week ago, they'd decided New Bilibid was the safest place for them to be. Dick now slowed our jeep, Boyd waved to a sentry, and we drove cautiously into the dusty, open courtyard, where thousands of jubilant ex-POWs milled about with chocolate bars in hand. The chocolate bars appeared to be dessert.

I could see the chow line, but lunch was winding down. Maybe a hundred people still stood in line for the hearty soup or stew that was being served from what look like large, aluminum garbage cans. Garbage cans? That didn't look very reassuring but the Army was scrupulous about cleanliness when it came to feeding civilians.

"OK, ladies. We're here—safe and sound." Boyd announced in triumph.

"How are we going to find Bunny?" Lulu asked, as we stared mesmerized at the crowds. More than two thousand prisoners had been rescued from Los Baños, and every single one of them was here with what seemed to be the same number of servicemen.

"First step is to see if she's checked in. Right over there."

Dick pointed us to a long, makeshift, folding table in one of the shaded inner arcades. Former internees stood in line while four uniformed servicemen sat with clipboards and lists, checking off the new arrivals. Posted above the servicemen were letters: A-F, G-M, N-R, S-Z. For a brief second, I thought of the package line a full three years ago, when we'd been standing underneath similar lettered signs, and I had spotted Pablo Diablo across the room. He'd waved his Devil Horn fingers at me, and we'd laughed—both full of bravado before our ordeal began. Kay and I had stood patiently waiting our turn, while Bugs Bunny Guard bayonetted that beautiful Lemon Meringue Pie intended for the lady ahead of us.

"She's B—for Brambles," I heard Lulu telling the guys and Boyd skipped the line, and went right over to the serviceman with the A-F list for a quick check. Meanwhile, as we stood watching, a smiling young mother with a scrawny little baby, waved happily to a U.S. Signal Corps camera. Dick said the Army Signal Corps was filming the new arrivals and even interviewing ex-prisoners. They had a little stage set up in the far corner of one arcade.

"Wait, Lulu, there she is!"

I pointed to a stick-figure of a young woman who stood on the U.S. Signal Corps stage. Our Bunny, her blonde hair swept in two scroll-like curls above her brow, wore high-waisted shorts and an open-necked white blouse. She was talking to a uniformed emcee with a clipboard, and between them stood a shiny, black tripod topped by a furry microphone. For brief seconds, I felt myself transported back to 1939, when my father worked in radio. I remembered that when KZRH recorded outdoors by Manila Bay, they would wrap the sides of the microphone in kitty-soft fur to filter out wind and other noises. There was a lot to drown out here.

"Bunny!" Lulu shouted, and waved furiously at our friend.

"Boyd, we found her," I shouted back to the boys, as we raced quickly to the broadcast area.

Lulu and I and wedged ourselves as close as we could to the stage, and sat. Here was our Bunny, being interviewed as if she were an important person in the war. We couldn't wait to hear what she had to say.

Chapter 43
VICTORY ROLLS

March 4, 1945 (continued)

Bunny hadn't seen us. Her attention was riveted on the young lieutenant with the clipboard, who'd asked her something about exercise—but maybe I hadn't heard him correctly. Bunny was nodding.

"The rescue caught the Nips exercising—as they did every morning—calisthenics between a quarter to and quarter past seven." Bunny's lovely British accent lilted into the microphone. "Hundreds of them in their skivvies."

"So when the rescue forces came, the Japs were all out there doing calisthenics?"

"Except the guards who had sentry duty—six or ten maybe—in the watch towers or in the Commandant's office. The others—hundreds of them—pranced about, striking poses, making horrid guttural noises, and shouting 'Banzai' to the Emperor."

"Pretty well-timed for our side, wouldn't you say, Miss Brambles?"

Lulu and I wriggled our way closer to the stage. The microphone didn't amplify Bunny's voice well. Instead, it was attached to recording equipment for newsreels. Maybe they'd show Bunny's interview before some feature film. Maybe she'd be a star!

"Were you in your barracks when it all began?" the interviewer queried.

"No, we were all outside. Roll call, you know. A bit haphazard. Everyone milling about. Our monitors—fellow prisoners—took roll call every morning at seven." Bunny waited, as if for another question, but the lieutenant just urged her on.

"Then suddenly, there was this roar of planes—nine of them nearly black against the pale sky, coming in very low. At first, I couldn't tell if they were Yank planes or not. But then dozens, maybe a hundred parachutes, bloomed like camellias from above. It was the most beautiful sight." She looked up as if she expected to see them again. "And so close to us! I felt I could practically reach up and touch them. Well, they just had to be American. The Japs had no reason to parachute into their own territory."

"Those boys jumped from four hundred feet—you practically could touch them. Were you frightened, Miss Brambles?"

"No. Thrilled! Five of our men had died of beriberi the day before. We were desperate."

Bunny told her interviewer that the rapid-fire rescue happened so quickly, she couldn't remember the exact sequence of events. But to her it seemed the minute those paratroopers appeared, machine gun fire erupted, and American and Filipino soldiers on the ground stormed the camp from all sides. The army paratroopers landed and joined the fight. Then huge amphibious vehicles crashed through the gates.

"Bullets flew everywhere. People dropped into ditches. My mother and I ran to hide in the barracks under our cots. We prayed the Yanks would finish the Japs off quickly."

"They certainly did, didn't they, Miss Brambles?" the emcee filled in. "You couldn't see it, but our boys took out the sentries in the towers, blew up the storehouse, and made short work of those athletes out there in the fields."

"Who were defenseless because they'd laid down their arms while they were exercising," Bunny added.

"Did you feel sorry for them?"

"Not one bit! Good God! They fed themselves, but not us. Ate on lovely porcelain dishes—fine painted china, and always had fresh fish from the lagoon. No seafood, no meat, no protein, for us. They turned away food that Filipinos tried to bring us," she continued in disgust.

Lulu and I sat mesmerized, and I instinctively gripped Lulu's hand, listening to Bunny. Their horror and hunger had been as great as ours: I remembered our rage when Abiko refused the papayas, mangoes, and camotes that the Filipinos tried to bring us. The Filipinos, our forever friends, our pre-war-servants-turned-saviors, had stood by us every step of the way. That infuriated the Japs.

"So after the take-down, you were free and safe," the GI interviewer prodded.

"Hardly," Bunny corrected decisively. "By then all the Yanks were in camp, urging us to hurry because another Jap force was just down the road. We had to run to the amphibious vehicles, the amtracs. They helped us. They had stretchers and medics. The amtracs took us down to the lake and across the lake to secure territory. And here we are. All of us. Two thousand of us. Alive."

I had goose bumps and wasn't breathing, as I thought of our big, gutsy American boys pulling off this split-second perfect rescue. I saw Bunny draw a deep breath, and we all waited spellbound. "There are no words to express our gratitude to the brave Yanks, who acted with such daring." She swallowed hard. "Shakespeare wrote—I think I've got this right— *O Lord, that lends me life, Lend me a heart replete with thankfulness.* Our hearts are replete with thankfulness. Thank you." She stepped away from the microphone and closed her eyes, a tear running down her cheek.

Lulu and I and everybody gathered around the stage applauded energetically. Listening to Bunny, I partly wished I had been born British. The Brits spoke so beautifully, and always knew the right thing to say. It was in their mother's milk: They nursed on Shakespeare, while we American kids devoured Nancy Drew and Tom Mix. But, then again, I thought as I continued to clap for my eloquent friend, it was our big, brash, American boys—sharpshooters from Montana, rangers from Texas, farm-boy paratroopers from Indiana— who had pulled off that daring rescue. Boney Shakespeare, the skinny Brit boy bard, could go ahead and write about it, but he could never have done it.

Well, my heart was "replete with thankfulness" too, but I didn't have much time to think about that because when the applause died down, Lulu leapt up and shouted to Bunny, who now let out a delighted screech and jumped off the stage.

"Lulu! Lee! Gorgeous beanpoles!" Bunny's nose twitched and her bright blue eyes glistened, as she reached out and hugged us.

"You're a pretty sensational string bean yourself, Bunny Brambles! I love your hair! You look so sophisticated!" Lulu cooed over the large scroll curls Bunny sported on her forehead.

"They're called 'victory rolls'—like the aeroplane maneuvers when the fliers go in for the kill. You like?"

We lost no time exchanging news about each other's families, telling stories of our time in camp, and remembering our time together at STIC. Bunny asked if we'd been to any good fights lately, recalling our time at the boxing-smoker in the Starlight Arena almost two years ago. "How are Squeaky and Rocky?"

"Repatriated on the first ship," Lulu said.

We had the sad task of telling Bunny how the Brooks twins had lost both their parents in the last three months, how terrible the shelling was, and how Paul had lost his sister Annie too. Bunny grew sorrowful and pensive, as we all felt the weight of death settle over our moment of jubilation. Then Bunny told us about Mrs. Gewald's daughter, Betty Lou, dying of appendicitis, about those who'd died of Dengue and beriberi just days before the rescue, but also about a baby born in camp the day before the liberation. Life in the midst of so much chaos.

"Mah Bed Buddy!" I heard the North Carolina drawl before I spun around, and then saw both Kay and Harry Hodges approaching. "Is my custom-made bed ready for me to pick up and take home?"

"You can't get it on a C-47, Kay!" I yelled as I ran toward her and they approached. We exchanged squeals and grateful hugs.

Kay was a rail, but her hair was swept off her face in a fashionable style, and to me she looked prettier and more vibrant than ever. Harry, though, was a walking skeleton with arms shrunken to the bone, beriberi's tell-tale tree-trunk legs, and cheeks that sagged under sharply defined cheek bones. Still, his eyes burned brightly and he seemed undefeated.

"Now Kay, who said we're leaving?" Harry joked. "International Harvester probably wants to keep some people here." I couldn't believe he was saying this. International Harvester was the company Harry worked for before the war. Would Kay and Harry stay to help with the post-war rebuilding? Kay jabbered away at a thousand miles per hour before we even had a chance to sit down.

That afternoon was golden. We ran into my spunky nurse friend Sister Olivette, who'd come to Los Baños with Bunny, and kept her bright smile even as she lost everything else—including her signature pie-plate headpiece, the white coif that made Holy Cross nuns look like they carried halos around with them. She wore just a simple white veil now. We saw emaciated Father Sheridan, who had been here saying mass, and visiting with all his Jesuit friends. There were nearly a thousand priests and nuns up here, living in four barracks that the Los Baños campers referred to as "Vatican City."

It turned out that the Jesuits had been side-splittingly funny entertainers at Los Baños. At Santo Tomas, we'd had Dave Harvey and Phyllis Dyer emceeing our monthly shows till July of 44, when the Japanese decided show time should be over. But at Los Baños, they'd had vaudeville Jesuits all the way through. Those lucky-ducky internees had nightly shows, and the Japs never cracked down on that.

"We sang coded lyrics, and our captors didn't really catch on," Sr. Olivette told me. "Father Jim, sing something for my friend Lee here." Sr. Olivette addressed a handsome, young man in an open-necked shirt and Bermuda shorts, standing close by. Aside from the cross he wore, he bore no outward sign of being a priest. "Father Reuter was one of the most outstanding vocalists in camp," Sr. Olivette said.

Rail-thin Father Jim Reuter might have been thirty, had a waist that wasn't more than 28 inches, but he had stevedore arms. Sr. Olivette said he'd been on "wood detail," chopping wood every day for cooking and boiling water. He looked at her and at us with uncertainty.

"Look—that stage is empty! Entertainment, please!" she urged him.

"Sing for us, Father!" Lulu seconded, and everyone around us clapped and hooted.

"Do *Shuffle Off to Tokyo*, Father! *Shuffle off to Tokyo!*" someone in the crowd yelled, and people began to assemble around him and the stage.

Ruby Keeler and Dick Powell made "Shuffle Off to Buffalo" a big hit in the 1930s, but I'd never heard "Shuffle Off to Tokyo." The young priest flashed Sr. Olivette a reluctant smile, then hopped up onto the stage, and everyone near us began to quiet down. Somebody pulled out a pitch pipe and gave him a musical note. From nowhere welled the warmest, jauntiest tenor voice I had ever heard

> *They will pack their porcelain dishes*
> *and a string of little fishes,*
> *and away they'll go!*

The entire crowd sang back as if on cue: "*Whoo, whoo, whoo… Off they're gonna shuffle, shuffle off to Tokyo.*" The growing audience hooted, swayed, and clapped in expectation as he solo-ed the next lines.

> *When the moon is at the quarter,*
> *They'll be out there on the water,*
> *where the typhoons blow.*

With visions of Japs overturned on the high seas, the crowd roared back, "*Whoo, whoo, whoo …Off they're gonna shuffle, shuffle off to Tokyo!*" The sung spoof went on to imagine the Japs at sea detonated by "*a cute little calling card—from the Brooklyn Navy Yard!"* And the last line was *"we'll get them down in Tokyo!"*

Shouts, cheers, exultation, delight. A thunder of applause and laughter. It was all there in that golden afternoon. We were young. We were free. We were alive and victorious. God was good. Bunny, the Hodges, Lulu, and I made plans to get together at a dance for the 37th Infantry near Grace Park next week—if we hadn't shipped out yet. So we put off tears of farewell, and parted with hugs of joy. Now all we had to do was survive the treacherous road back to camp.

***

"Look at this one—it's like a giant Indian arrowhead," said Dick.

Our two lieutenants had pulled over to the side of the road on our return trip to Santo Tomas, and were rummaging on a hill among the shrapnel for their own souvenirs. Lulu and I had climbed out of the jeep and plunked ourselves down on the hillside, staring out to Manila Bay and watching the glorious day's end. I decided that twenty-five year old Dick Church, with his long face, puppy-dog hopeful eyes, and wavy blond hair, looked for all the world like Danny Kaye. He moved with grace and was probably a great dancer. His wife had to be head-over-heels for him.

"That's a shell fragment," Boyd said, turning the banded six-inch piece of metal with the pointed tip in Dick's hand. "Funny how our newest weapons look just like our oldest weapons."

"Pack more of a punch, though." Before he pocketed the arrowhead shrapnel, Dick turned to us. "You girls want one?"

"No thanks," Lulu and I both called simultaneously.

"We've had enough war. Plenty of shrapnel back in camp," I added, hinting—I hoped— that now would be a good time to get going.

The skies were turning fuchsia, and I'd started to worry about getting back to camp before dark—especially on mined roads. We'd had a wonderful afternoon at Muntinglupa, but now our gentlemen escorts didn't seem particularly eager to get us home.

Dick settled down on the hill next to me, took a pack of Lucky Strikes from his pocket, and offered me one. I shook my head, thinking about how Hope would leap at the prospect, and how many people in camp had traded food for tobacco, right down to the last days of starvation.

"I haven't taken up smoking," I said, a little embarrassed that this worldly GI would think me a child. "In camp, they were hard to come by. You think I should?"

Dick smiled, took a deep drag on his cigarette, and exhaled. "Nah..." When he shook his head, a blond curl fell across his forehead, and his impish blue eyes swept my form with admiration. "You look like the kind of girl who just put out a cigarette anyway." He smiled at me with such genuine warmth that my heart leapt.

"I'm gonna take that as a compliment, Richard Church."

Dick laughed, stared out at the beautiful bay, and seemed to be the happiest guy in the world, just savoring the moment. Meanwhile the sun was sinking.

"We'd better get going don't you think?" I called to Lulu. She was giggling over some joke Boyd was telling her, but Boyd heard my reminder.

"You sure you girls don't want to sit here with us a little longer and watch the light of the silvery moon on the silvery shrapnel?"

Dick's hopeful face lit up at those words, and like something out of a movie, he crooned in a surprisingly good baritone: "Those silvery beams will bring love's dreams, we'll be cuddling sooooon.....by the silvery moon." Then he looped a long arm over my shoulders and pulled me close to him.

The gesture was charming, funny, and gave me a thrill, but when he didn't take his arm away, little alarm bells went off inside me. Dick was married. Both these boys were our liberators and they were definitely handsome fellas, but they were also grown men, and soldiers well into their twenties. *What do you know about them?* I could hear my mother saying. Were Lulu and I in over our heads? My years of singing *Jingle Swing* on Daddy's radio show paid off.

"Honeymooooon...." I drew out the next line in Dick's song in my best, purest alto voice and they both looked at me in surprise and delight as if they'd never heard a gal sing before. *"Keep a shinin' in Juuuuune...* Wait!" I broke off dramatically, and out of Dick's grasp. "It's only March, not June! Too soon, boys. Time to go. We told my mother we'd be back before dark." I jumped up.

They both remained frozen for a second, then hooted, and looked at each other, laughing like they'd been had.

"Her mother's VERY strict," Lulu confirmed, leaping to her feet.

Boyd shrugged his shoulders at Dick, and heaved himself off the ground. Lieutenant Dick Church smiled a sheepish grin, shook his head, crushed his cigarette into the ground, and drew himself up to his six foot three inch Danny Kaye frame.

"Race you to the jeep," Lulu tugged at me, and I tore after her, with the boys at our heels.

Our two perfect gentlemen escorts opened the rear door of the Jeep for us, and tipped their caps before they shut the door. Then they hopped in the front, fired up the engine, and we roared off to Santo Tomas. I noticed that on the return trip, we didn't zig-zag nearly as much.

Chapter 44
NOT BEFORE LUNCH

Saturday, March 10, 1945

My mother, Betty, and I sat in our Glamorville shanty, making lists and checking them twice. Our three straw suitcases stood packed and at attention on the far wall—*Leonore's Suite* and *The Captive's Kitchen* stowed safely in mine. We had to be ready to leave for Nielsen Air Field with ninety minutes notice if our name was called over the P.A. Last Monday, the day we got back from Muntinglupa, the Davis family had been called up, and they were now on their way home. We'd parted with tears from Paul, but I'd been so happy for him. When would our turn come? And Lulu's? And Nellie's?

"Don't get your hopes too high, girls," my mother cautioned, distracted, even as she glanced around the shanty doing one last inventory. "Mr. Carroll says some of us won't ship out till April or May. The fighting is still intense."

"Mommy, take this for a souvenir." Betty was holding out one of the tin coffee cans that our mother and Flossie had used to make fudge, but my mother dismissed it with a laugh.

"I think we could live without that."

My mind was still on what Mommy had said about the fighting. "Dick says the Japs are doing Custer's Last Stand on every island in the Philippine Sea," I repeated his exact words. Horrible reports arrived daily of hand-to-hand fighting on a little island called Iwo Jima, northeast of the Philippines.

"Five thousand of our boys are dead—trying to take that one tiny, fortified island."

"Are Hoy and Trimm up there? In Iwo Jima?" Betty asked.

"No, Boyd said they're down in Mindanao. They're probably OK."

All three of us sat in silence for a moment, remembering that Daddy had died on the southernmost island of Mindanao. Mindanao was supposed to be secure in American hands now, and we thought about Hoy and Trimm, those two boy liberators, who'd come to visit us here in the shanty every evening for the first two weeks after our liberation. I loved that night Trimm had strummed his guitar outside our shanty, and we all sang "Smoke on the Water." I'd seen enough smoke on the water by now. I was so sick and tired of war. I just wanted it to be over.

"Agnes, ready for lunch at the Jai alai Club?" Hope leaned into our shanty with her ever-present Lucky Strike in hand. "I made a reservation for us at the Sky Room, but we have to queue up at the Central Kitchen first."

A grateful smile lit my mother's lined face as she rose. An image of Manila's Jai Alai club, that impressive, air-cooled, cylindrical building soaring heavenward, rose in all our imaginations. It was still standing when Paul and I had made our great excursion into Manila, but had to be flat as a pancake now. "The elevator there's been spotty the last few days, hasn't it?" my mother dead-panned.

"Well, hardee-har, you two," Betty chimed in. "Good thing that army grub is just as good as the Sky Room ever was." Fourteen-year-old Betty was nothing if not loyal.

"You can be forgiven your impaired memory, my dear," Hope shot back.

My mother rose. "Lunch starts in fifteen minutes. Hope and I will hold your place in the chow line." My two favorite women waltzed out the door of our bamboo shanty, and over to the Central Kitchen behind the Main Building.

I was glad to have the chance to be alone with Betty for a little while. There was a sadness in her eyes and spirit these days, even as we packed to go home. A big part of that sorrow had to be Annie's death in the shelling a month ago—her best friend gone in a bloody moment of horror. But I also wondered if Boops was weirdly sad about leaving. She was only eleven when we came here, and maybe didn't remember much else.

Betty's eyes swept the shanty, our home-away-from-home, and seemed to be taking in all its details. The little card table, the family gathering place, where we'd eaten so many terrible meals, still formed its center. Boops and I sat on folding chairs, the third one now empty. The clay stove, with its missing (consumed) plug, still waited on the shelves along with some tin plates and empty coffee tins. And outside, although the mint and talinum garden had been trampled, the young banana tree Hope planted right after the first air raid unfolded its leaves to the sun. Our bamboo walls and thatched roof still gave the same shade they'd always provided, both inside and out.

"Will you miss this place?" Betty asked me, as we looked around.

"Not for one second," I said, and she burst out laughing, then unexpectedly started crying.

I was at her side in a second, and put my arm around her shoulder even as I knelt next to her chair, trying to understand the flood of tears. "Boops, we're going home!" was all I could think of to say, but the tears just kept on coming.

"Home to what?" she eventually blurted out. "Home to no Daddy? Home to no friends? Home to live with Mommy's family who hasn't even written us since we've been here? Home to cold and snowy Utica—when I've always loved Manila?"

Betty's sober assessment of our future stunned me. I'd been so eager to be free and *full* these last three years, that all my dreams focused on liberation, food, return, and now, one last year in a real American high school before going on to college and a brand new life. I'd never loved Manila or the Philippines the way Betty had. Manila, with all its creepy-crawly tarantulas and bed bugs and five hundred kinds of spiders. Manila, with its pious peasant ladies crawling on their knees along a dirty church aisle to praise bloody statues. Manila, with its oppressive humidity and never-ending heat.

"Home to freedom, Boops! Home to safety and food. Home to see Francis. Home to a new life. Home to a real American high school, where kids are …. free!" I said, perplexed and exasperated. "And people have fun, and nobody bows to any Japs." I tried to jolly her, as I knelt next to her, "and nobody worries about how many pieces of toilet paper they're using."

Betty snuffled, kept her eyes lowered, then spoke quietly. "Is that enough for you?" She finally met my eyes and looked straight at me, as if she were the older sister and I had a lot to learn. "Is that enough? Food… fun … toilet paper?" Her voice trailed off, but her disdainful gaze tore right through me.

Anger surged in me like a tidal wave: fierce, full, and thunderous. "Elizabeth Ann Iserson! Daddy would be so ashamed of you! You are an ungrateful nitwit of a sister. Haven't you learned anything these past three years?" I glared at her, but she just stared at me defiantly. "We've been through hell—a gale-force typhoon, for Pete's sake! We learned to fly right though that gale and we survived. All of us—the three of us—with our fudge, and your drawings and my recipes and sneaking out of camp for money, and you surviving dysentery, and us squirreling away our Red Cross supplies, and praying like crazy, and keeping our wits about us," I ranted, unable to stop myself. "And here you are longing for …more? More what? More starvation? More death? More humiliation? More horror? What's the matter with you?" I demanded and could barely restrain myself from physically shaking her chair.

Betty just stared down at the bug-infested dirt floor, tears running down her cheeks. My fourteen-year-old sister ground her open-toed, wooden bakia into the dust, and spoke quietly. "I don't want more starvation or humiliation. I just want Daddy and Annie back, and I want to see Mommy really smile again. I want things to go back to the way they were before … before the war. I miss the way things were before."

My sister spoke so quietly that I could hardly hear her, but my fury and disbelief ebbed, as I caught a glimmer of her anguish. I had left that past behind so long ago. Those idyllic days in our San Francisco del Monte villa, with our mosaic tile swimming pool and our tennis courts, and an amah who dressed us girls every morning—even though Betty had been nine and I was already eleven.

I had left that past so far behind, and to tell the truth, that whole life seemed preposterously self-indulgent and trivial to me now. I was embarrassed just thinking about it. I hated prison, but in camp I'd learned about real life, and sacrifice, and survival. I'd watched my mother go from society matron to fudge entrepreneur and single mother par excellence. I'd seen Rosalina go from servant to savior. I'd thrived on Lulu's unconditional friendship and love. I'd relished my studies. I'd learned that not every Jap was the enemy. I still had *Leonore's Suite*, and my poetry and my recipe book. I had the future—wide open before me. But to Betty, our long-ago life in pre-war Manila remained an anchor.

I so loved the unfailingly kind sister I'd never understood. She rose from her chair as if to leave, and I did the only thing I could think of. I sprang up and threw my arms around her and we both just stood there hugging, crying, and shaking, as minutes went by.

Finally, Betty whispered to me, "Remember how beautiful our First Communion was?"

I couldn't believe she had catapulted herself seven years into the past. Since we were late converts to Catholicism, we'd both made our First Communion and got confirmed on the very same day. She was seven and I was nine. We'd worn the most beautiful, full-length white embroidered dresses and long gauzy veils—all made right at Iserson Embroideries. Daddy smiled at us so proudly that day, even though he was Jewish. We'd had a big party at our villa afterwards, and the Davises were there, both Paul and Annie, and so many other friends.

I nodded into Betty's fine brown curls as we hugged. "I remember," I said. "What do you remember about it?"

"I remember how my heart did a little dance when I received communion for the first time," Betty said and snuffled into my ear. "I remember thinking— that day at the party with you and Mommy and Daddy, and all our friends around us, all that good food— that I'd never be that happy again," she sniffed. "And I was right."

I held Betty a minute longer, and let that sink in, but pulled back and whispered urgently. "It's gonna be better than ever, Boops. It really will. Especially with Daddy watching over us from above. It'll be different, but better than ever."

"Maybe…" Betty seemed skeptical, and took a step back from me, the two of us each in our own worlds now. We walked out of the shanty together toward the chow line, and instinctively looked up at the Main Building with its clock striking noon and the stone cross tower still standing undamaged against all odds. Betty's eyes lingered at the top. "Why is it always about the cross?" she said to no one in particular. "Why are we always supposed to suffer?"

We Catholics were in Lent now, the Church's season of penance for our sins, but Lent was so poorly timed this year. It began mere days after our liberation. Father Sheridan decreed that we could all skip Lenten penance this year because we'd been doing it for three years. Well, thank God for that.

"Betty," I tried to keep the impatience out of my voice, but it was as if God or Daddy spoke straight to me, and I said, "This time it's not about the cross and suffering. It's about coming back to life. It's about resurrection, for Pete's sake!" We were still four weeks away from Easter, but I suddenly saw my sister in a new light. "You know, Boops, you are just like Mary Magdalen in the garden Easter morning—weeping. She thinks Jesus has been stolen from the tomb, but instead he's standing right there in front of her—and you!"

Betty looked up at me, her brown eyes swimming, but lit by a reluctant gleam of hope. She gave just a hint of a sheepish smile. "You don't look a lot like Jesus," she dead-panned. I felt my heart lift.

Then we both heard the scratch of the public address system coming to life, and the two of us froze, listening for the commanding voice of Clarence Beliel.

"The following families will be ready to leave for Nielsen Air Field, the island of Leyte, and the United States of America within ninety minutes. Please assemble with your baggage at the front gate for transport to Nielsen."

Betty and I clutched hands, sisters again, bound in ways two friends could never be. We'd been through so much. We'd also been through these recitations before. There would be more than a hundred and fifty family names on the list, and the reading always seemed endless until they got to the "I"s. Mr. Beliel began the roster:

Anderson, T. Maxwell

Adams, Gustav

Ardoin, Artilus and Family

Barngrover, Robert and Family

He droned on in alphabetical order, and Betty and I listened, riveted to the names of the chosen. Then we heard

Cleland, Mary V. and Family

My heart stopped. Lulu! Lulu and her family would be gone in ninety minutes. I wanted to bolt for Room 22, but I had to keep listening. Name after name after name. Letter after letter.

Gross, Morton R.

Hicks, John

An endless string of Hs, then Mr. Beliel began the I's, and in a freeze-frame minute:

Inman, Reginald and Rebecca

Iserson, Agnes and Family

Betty and I shrieked, leapt up and down, hugged each other, and raced across the front lawn, streaking around the back of the Main Building toward the Central Kitchen, while the long recitation of names went on and on and on.

People in the chow line smoked, laughed and talked, apparently oblivious to the life-changing litany over the P.A. I spotted my mother in her pale green shirtwaist about a third of the way back in line. She stood laughing and chatting with Hope, lighting one of Hope's Lucky's. I grabbed Betty's hand and the two of us darted to her side, screaming at the top of our lungs. "We're leaving, Mommy! We're leaving! They called our names! We have to get to the gate. We're leaving!"

My mother broke away from whatever joke she was sharing with Hope, arched both her eyebrows, and leveled her sternest jade green gaze at us. In a voice that brooked no challenge she said, "We are not going anywhere until we've had lunch."

Chapter 45
CALL ME AL

Leyte, Tuesday, March 13, 1945

It had been three days since my first plane ride ever rocketed me from a black and white universe to technicolor. When we flew out of Nielsen Air Field, our rumbling C-47 overflew the gray devastation of Manila, but within minutes soared over turquoise seas and lush green islands. Puffs of white smoke below showed the Japs were still at war with US air forces. They were shooting at us, but unsuccessfully, and by this time we all felt a little invincible. Especially in our big, bulky "gooney-bird," as some of the boys called the C-47.

Our military plane boasted two long rows of bench seats across from each other, with about twenty-five lucky internees on each side. Lulu sat on one side of me and Betty on the other. The windows were to our backs, so we kept turning around to stare below, and drink in the dramatic impact of sky, sea, and islands. I couldn't believe we were out of Manila and up this high. The ferocious rumble of the plane made conversation on the two-hour flight almost impossible. As we started to descend, Betty squeezed my hand and pointed vigorously outside. She had a big grin on her face. Dense forests of palm trees blanketed Leyte and swayed in the breeze; the water swaddling the island gleamed aqua despite its teeming population of olive drab amphibious vehicles. I glanced across the aisle for a second, and saw Hope and my mother with their backs to us, craning out the same way.

A bonanza of good fortune accompanied us on March tenth: the Isersons, the Clelands, the Thomases (Nellie's family) and Hope Miller had all been summoned to the gate that blessed afternoon. Deliriously happy, we'd trucked off to Nielsen with our bags, boarded C-47s, and by dinner time, were in Leyte—amid tens of thousands of GIs.

I do mean *tens* of thousands. Barracks after barracks after barracks—all shaped like Iroquois longhouses, called "Quonset Huts." You could set them up in a hurry anywhere. We descended from the plane to applause, cheers, whistles, and cat-calls from the ground crews, all of whom turned out to see what a God's-honest-American-girl looked like. Four of us teen girls descended the steps of our C-47, and waved enthusiastically to our liberators.

Lulu lost no time zeroing in on the GI of her dreams. While she and I sat in the back of a crowded open truck on the way to the Army Convalescent hospital, a cocky, fresh-faced GI in a Jeep pursued us with determination. The enterprising Private First Class struck up a lively conversation with Lulu over the hood of his car.

"Hey, Sparkly Blue Eyes," he shouted, "how do you like Leyte?"

"It's just like Cebu!" Lulu called back. "Have you seen Cebu yet?"

The two of them jabbered away, laughed, and traded silly jokes for half-an-hour over the ground noise and engine rumble. When we reached the hospital and Lulu leapt out of the truck, PFC Determination was right at her side.

"What's your name, Blue Eyes?"

"Mary Lou," Lulu responded with just a hint of self-importance.

"She's usually Lulu," I told him. "And you're…."

"Al. I'm Al all the time." This sent Lulu into gales of hysterical laughter because he was quoting a line from a song we loved. *Hey, don't you remember, they called me Al. It was 'Al' all the time.* Al smiled a dazzling grin, then grew more serious. "How old are you?" he quizzed Lulu.

"Seventeen," she lied. Lulu wasn't going to be seventeen for another eight months.

"Geez. Just seventeen and the Japs took you prisoner when you were ... what? Fourteen?"

She nodded, and he stared at her as if she were a miracle. Adorable Al was pretty much of a miracle himself —solidly built, five foot ten, sandy hair, rosy cheeks, perfectly symmetrical features, square chin, and eyes as green as the palm trees around us. He glanced over Lulu's shoulder at ex-internees filing into the hospital for the two days of required medical exams and quarantine. "See you in 48 hours?" he asked Lulu hopefully.

"I don't know anything about you, Al-All-The-Time," Lulu played hard to get, and gave him a coy smile.

"Al Burgess," he stuck out his hand, and Lulu took it and held it. "Twenty years old, from San Diego," he rattled it off, as if reporting to a senior officer. "I signed up the day after the Japs bombed Pearl, but I'm going to college when this is over." Maybe Al suspected college would cinch his "good-guy" status with Lulu, which it did. She released his hand reluctantly.

"I'm Mary Louella Cleland from Cebu, now from Los Angeles. Maybe I'll see you at UCLA ... or in 48 hours...." She arched both eyebrows, nicked her chin, and smiled impishly at him.

Lulu was playing the coquette! Where did she learn these tricks?

"You got it. Forty-eight hours." He looked at her like he was the luckiest guy on the planet. When he turned and walked away, Lulu practically swooned in my arms.

***

We'd been sprung from quarantine just yesterday, and Adorable Al had been the first to seek out Lulu. I swear, he was waiting outside the door of the hospital. Now he and a lieutenant buddy—also from San Diego—were off-duty and offered to squire us around Leyte. They gushed over our every move, but tried to impress us with their military knowledge and experience.

"He came ashore right there—back in October." Al was driving, but stopped for a minute, and pointed to Palo Beach, which might have been a beautiful white sand beach if it hadn't been blanketed by naval Landing Craft—LCs—unloading all manner of supplies.

"*I-Shall-Return-MacArthur*. Well, thank God he did," said Lulu with only a trace of sarcasm in her voice. Lulu sat in the front seat of the Jeep, right next to Al.

"Better Leyte Than Never," I piped up from the backseat of the Jeep, recalling the day that coded message floated from our P.A. and fanned the flames of hope. That was the thrilling moment every internee learned American forces had returned to the Philippines.

"Have you seen the photo? Of the invasion?" Al asked us.

He reached under the driver's seat, and whipped out an issue of "Free Philippines," a glossy published by the US Army. From the cover leapt an iron-jawed Douglas MacArthur, striding dramatically through the surf. He was accompanied by fellow army brass and Philippine President-in-Exile, Sergio Osmeña. Arrayed behind MacArthur was the U.S. Seventh Fleet in all its glory, and underneath in bold print: "I have returned!" MacArthur.

It was a dramatic photo. I got goose bumps just looking at it. OK, maybe I'd forgive Dugout Doug for taking so long.

"Bugged the hell out of Mac that he was soaked to the knees for that triumphant return," said Lieutenant Jimmy Henderson, the young officer sitting next to me. He lit an Old Gold, shook out his match, and stared out at the surf. Five years older than Al, Jimmy Henderson had been attached to MacArthur's detail last year.

"He didn't plan it that way?" I asked. The photo of MacArthur conquering the sea was such vintage-MacArthur. It made him look Take-Charge, Larger than Life—Titanic even.

"Nah. Mac jumped the gun by coming ashore too soon. He roared in on a launch after the island was almost secure, but they weren't ready for him yet—or the rest of the brass." Jimmy motioned to the shore, which even now teemed with LCs. One destroyer and a large transport shipped bobbed on the horizon.

"The Leyte invasion was massive, almost as big as D-Day," Jimmy continued. "Two-hundred-thousand troops the first day, three hundred ships. The Beach Master couldn't—or wouldn't—clear a spot for Mac's "pretty-boy" launch. Said they had too many other important vessels docking. He sent word that Mac could walk from where he was. So he did."

"Is that Sergeant in jail now or just a private?" Al quizzed Jimmy, who shrugged.

"The onshore crew had the radio mikes set up for him soon as he got here, though," Jimmy said, as if that made up for everything.

Al went back to his magazine, flipped through the pages till he found what he was looking for. "Here it is—his speech. Listen to this: *People of the Philippines, I have returned! By the grace of Almighty God our forces stand again on Philippine soil—soil consecrated in the blood of our two peoples.... Rally to me!*"

Al was doing a credible imitation of MacArthur's voice, made famous in countless radio interviews before the war. Lulu's suitor delivered Mac's words with power and admiration. *"Rise and strike! For your homes and hearths, strike! For future generations of your sons and daughters, strike! In the name of your sacred dead, strike!"* Then Al's voice lowered and turned flinty as he continued, *"Let no heart be faint...The guidance of divine God points the way. Follow in His Name to the Holy Grail of righteous victory!"*

We all sat in silence for a moment, imagining the impact of those words on the Filipino people, who had endured brutal occupation for three years. Since last October, they had indeed risen and struck. Filipino scouts and guerillas paved the way for American soldiers in Manila. Filipino ground troops struck with US forces at Lingayen Gulf and at Los Baños.

"MacArthur should've been a preacher or a minister," said Al, with something akin to adoration in his voice.

"Oh, spare me!" Lulu shot back, unable to restrain herself. She went on to regale Al with tales of MacArthur playing poker at her home in Cebu before the war, and how pompous and self-righteous he was, and what a "hideous reprobate."

I told them both how even Eisenhower—easygoing Ike—couldn't stand to work with him, and how the man who was now Supreme Commander of Allied Forces in Europe had suffered as Mac's Chief of Staff in Manila, and put in for a transfer so fast it made Mac's head spin. They both looked at us like we'd delivered unwelcome news from another planet.

Lieutenant Jimmy Henderson took one last drag on his cigarette, then exhaled. "Rant at will, ladies, but Mac saved your bacon. General Nimitz wanted him to storm Formosa first, and liberate China before the PI. MacArthur insisted it had to be the Philippines, and talked FDR into it." Jimmy tossed his cigarette into the sand. "Mac insisted on coming back for you—and he pulled it off."

Al leapt to Mac's defense too. "He routed 23,000 Japs from this island alone. Started the invasion of the PI right here, and fought like a hellcat in Leyte Gulf for four days—largest naval battle in history. He bought you your freedom."

The impact of those words struck me like a blow. The war still raged here in the Pacific. If MacArthur had agreed to liberate Formosa, then turn to mainland China, we'd still be starving to death at Santo Tomas. How many more of us would've died? I might never have known the joy of being free and being here on this tropical island paradise, ready to go home. *Douglas MacArthur, thank you.*

"OK. We forgive him for his ego," Lulu spoke my mind, and reverted to her old playful self. "Where do we get to swim, boys?"

Wednesday, March 14, 1945

"Mom, it's just a date to go to the movies." Lulu attempted to cajole her mother into consent. We stood in the makeshift tent that housed nearly a hundred of us, awaiting repatriation.

"Absolutely not. No single dating while we're here. If Al wants to take you to the movies, Mary Lou, you can take your sister and your friends along with you," Mim spoke pre-emptively and sounded exactly like my mother.

Lulu's mother still had her hands full with twelve-year-old Margie and four-year-old Maureen, but Mim, my mother, and Mrs. Thomas had apparently come to some Wise Mothers' Consensus on their daughters' social life here in Leyte. The consensus was: group dates only. Safety in numbers. Their daughters were not going to be alone with any of these hot-to-trot GIs.

I was secretly grateful for this decree. It had taken less than 24 hours for me to see that Leyte was different from Santo Tomas. At Santo Tomas, we civilian internees vastly out-numbered our soldier-saviors. And our liberators, those fine boys from the First Cavalry and the 101st Airborne, were in awe of us and all we'd had been through. They'd seen firsthand the squalor and hunger, the disease and desperation at Santo Tomas. They worked hard to protect us, and "get you back to the Land of the Free, kiddo," as Sergeant Hoy Moffett put it.

Leyte, though, was an army base, pure and simple. This tropical paradise was a way-station for liberated prisoners heading home, but mostly a deployment base for thousands of GIs. We girls couldn't walk outside our Quonset hut without being instantly surrounded by dozens of off-duty soldiers. They were big, eager, handsome, and mostly charming, but the way they looked at us .... like we were the dessert they had given up for Lent. I saw it in their eyes—not just longing, but hunger.

I knew what it was like to be really hungry—what starvation could drive you to. You might fry up weeds in Pond's Cold Cream and declare them delicious. You could wolf down a squash inhabited by a rat. You might gobble up a cloth plug soaked in beef broth and swear it was the tastiest treat you'd ever had. My heart went out to these ravenous American boys, but I didn't plan to be anybody's dessert—or main meal. And I sure wasn't going to let Lulu get herself in trouble and ruin everything by going home pregnant.

"That is ridiculous, Mother." Lulu scowled her disagreement on the group dating policy, but there was nothing she could do about it.

"It's OK, Lulu. We'll be discreet. Al won't even know we're there," I tried to cheer her up.

"He's going to think I'm a baby," she moaned.

"He's going to think you're popular. You've got tons of friends. It'll be fun, and we might be useful too."

"Useful for what?" Lulu harrumphed.

I gave her a look that said *Don't play dumb with me.*

"Oh—that. Don't be ridiculous."

Lulu would've drawn the line with Al, of course, and maybe he wouldn't have pressed it. But "guys are stronger than gals, and you don't know what a sexually aroused young man might do," I could hear my father. I was thirteen when he'd had that conversation with me before an eighth-grade dance at Bordener. His message: Be careful not to give a boy the wrong idea about how "available" I was. I thought he was being alarmist and silly, but his words stayed with me.

In any event, Betty, Nellie, Margie, and I joined Lulu and Private First Class Adorable Al Burgess on a "group date" to the movie tent that night. We Buddies-of-Lulu conspired furiously before the big event. Gary Cooper and Ingrid Bergman were starring in *For Whom the Bell Tolls*. It tolled for Al.

In a particularly romantic moment of the movie, when Ingrid Bergman announced that she was going to kiss Gary Cooper, Al quietly reached his arm over Lulu's shoulder and pulled her close. At my nod, we all did too. I was sitting next to Lulu, so I looped my arm over her other shoulder with my hand clasping Al's arm. Nellie was sitting on the other side of Al, so she reached an arm over his free shoulder, and leaned in. Betty was to my left, and she wrapped her arm around my neck, while Margie embraced Betty and so on. Lulu glared at me at first, then looked both ways and started to giggle. Al was not amused, but the row of GIs behind us just hooted. For the next two days, Al's buddies ribbed him mercilessly about taking all his kids to the show with him.

That didn't stop Al from pursuing Lulu. After the show the two of them attempted to wander off alone to the beach, but we—Lulu's personal destroyer escort—trailed paces behind. We did give the lovebirds five minutes of undisturbed sighing and smooching beneath a grove of palm trees before we all barged in. This time Nellie took the lead.

"Isn't it beautiful, down here?" She brushed past Lulu and Al. "Lulu, did you see our ticket home? Come here!"

Twelve-year-old Mouse raced to her sister, and practically tugged Lulu out of Al's arms, pulling her to the moonlit shore. Betty and I were close on their heels. Al just shook his head, and trailed us to the water's edge.

"There she is: the USS Admiral W.L. Capps—come to take us home," Nellie pointed to the massive military transport ship that bobbed on the horizon. More than six hundred feet long, the Capps was going to carry thirty-five-hundred liberated prisoners and wounded GIs home— we hoped.

"Who's Capps?" Lulu asked, recovering her good spirits and resigning herself to her fate. "Don't we rate a Washington or Lincoln?"

"You got a Washington—kind of. Admiral Washington Lee Capps helped win the Battle of Manila back in the Spanish-American War," Al told her. "That ship's less than a year old. You'll be in good hands."

That sounded like a hint to Lulu, so she reached out to Al, and took his hand. Al squeezed it and stared out at the horizon where dozens of vessels floated, silhouetted in the moonlight. "You'll be traveling in a convoy— the Capps, two destroyer escorts and there'll be some subs with you too, and a couple small vessels. You'll do a zig-zag course, and they'll be on the lookout for mines."

"What do destroyers have that the Capps doesn't?" Nellie asked "The Capps looks a lot bigger."

"The Capps is just a transport ship—no big guns. The destroyers are your protection: they're loaded with anti-aircraft guns, depth charges, anti-submarine detection equipment.... They've even got some small caliber cannon to blast enemy ships."

Enemy ships, submarines, torpedoes, mines… My heart sank and my stomach knotted. I was so tired of danger. Couldn't this war just be over? Did we really have to run another obstacle course against the Japs? A honey-colored sliver of moon gleamed serenely in the blue-black sky. Looking northeast, I saw the brightest star of the Southern Cross wink at me.

"How long will it take us to get home?" Betty asked quietly.

"Three ... four weeks... They'll probably route you through Manus in the Admiralty Islands, then Hawaii, then on to San Francisco." He paused and looked at Lulu's flaxen curls in the moonlight. "Say hi to the Golden Gate Bridge for me, Lulee."

"You're not coming with us?" Lulu asked distraught.

"Nope. Somebody's gotta stay and finish off the Japs. What did your friend's song say—the one you told me about—'Shuffle Off to Tokyo'? I might be shuffling off to Tokyo."

U.S.S. Admiral Capps, Tuesday March 20, 1945

Lulu was pretty close to engaged to Al by the time we boarded the U.S.S. Admiral W.L. Capps, and that meant she didn't notice the icy stares of every Marine who watched us board. It was a balmy ninety-two degree day, but the reception on the Capps could've frozen all of us in our tracks. That's because right up until yesterday, our Marine MPs thought they were off duty, and would be flying back to the United States—a trip that would have taken 72 hours and landed them in the arms of their sweethearts for the weekend. But some high mucky-muck decided at the last minute that this contingent of fighting men was just large enough to serve as military police for our transport ship home. Now it was going to take these 149 boys an extra month to get back to their loved ones. Boy, were they frosted.

We girls were so accustomed to being fawned over wherever we went that this chilly reception stung a bit, but we couldn't blame the boys for being miffed, and it was nice to have a little break from the intense fraternization of Leyte. After going below to stow our bags in berths, Lulu, Nellie, and I set out to explore the marvel that was our ship.

The Capps was a floating city—a brand new troop transport ship making only its second voyage across the Pacific. Everything here was so massive, clean, and modern. "Six hundred nine feet long, five decks deep, cruising radius seventy-five hundred miles or eleven thousand, depending on how fast we're going," a friendly sailor told us. (Not an icy Marine.) "We can transport more than five thousand soldiers—or in your case, about thirty-one hundred soldiers and eight hundred newly freed prisoners of war."

We wandered into places we shouldn't have, and learned that many of the GIs were wounded soldiers heading home. Housed in the ship's modern five-ward hospital, they hooted "Girls!" when we popped our heads in. We were rapidly shooed out, but Lulu shouted "Our heroes! You're our heroes!"

After a wide-eyed perusal of our surroundings, we gathered on the deck along with hundreds of other excited internees. Nellie had brought a blanket, which she spread out, claiming a spot for all of us. Then, as the Capps got underway and sailed east, we leaned back against a cabin wall on the main deck, closed our eyes, and sunned ourselves, basking in our good fortune, and praying no Jap submarine would find us in the next month.

"What do you think it'll be like when we get back?" Nellie asked, her eyes still closed and her face to the sun. "Think we're going to be behind in school?"

"Maybe," Lulu replied absently. "We never had enough books."

I remembered all the nights Lulu and I had huddled in the hall, poring over one of the scarce geometry or history texts by candlelight. We had to share one or two copies among all of us in the class, and take advantage of reading it whenever we got the chance.

"If we're way behind, we're only going to be lost for a couple of months," I said. "We'll be home by the middle of April, and classes go through June. We can catch up in the summer." I closed my eyes and brushed a bothersome curl from my face. The breeze was delightful. "I think we're OK in Latin though. Nobody's better than Mrs. Maynard."

"What I don't get is the music," Lulu changed the subject abruptly. I opened my eyes and stared at her to see if I'd missed something, but Lulu's eyes were still closed and her face tilted skyward.

"We didn't take music," I said, leaning back against the ship wall, and closing my eyes again. "That would've been a good course."

"Not that kind of music, Lee-lung. I mean the singers, the guys American girls are crazy over now. I don't get it. Did you see that *Life Magazine* article at the Officers' Club in Leyte?"

We had been invited to the little Officers' Club on Leyte almost every night to drink cokes, talk, and dance with the young officers. They had some of the newest recordings and latest magazines from the States.

"The article on Frank Sinatra?" I asked. Sinatra, a young singing sensation, had practically caused a riot at New York's Paramount Theater over Columbus Day—girls lined up to get tickets for his performance at midnight of the previous day.

"Yeah. What do girls see in that guy?" Lulu puzzled. "He's emaciated. He could've been an internee at Santo Tomas. It's like swooning over Pablo or Bill or Curtis." Nellie and I both snickered, and I had to agree. I'd wondered about this Sinatra fascination, too. Lulu's eyes were open now, and she was leaning forward, staring intently at the sea, as if trying to puzzle out one of life's great mysteries. "His suit just hangs off him—he looks like he just stepped out of…solitary in Fort Santiago."

"Well, he's got a voice like velvet," Nellie stated the obvious. "Did you hear him sing *Stardust*?"

"But they're going wild for him, Nellie. Thirty thousand girls in Times Square clamoring for 'Frankie Blue Eyes.' They're throwing themselves at a guy whose eyes practically bulge out of their sockets, and they're squealing 'Frankie, Frankie!'" Lulu's flailing hands and high-pitched imitation had us howling with laughter.

"Well, who's your favorite nowadays, Lulee? Does Al sing?" Nellie asked.

Lulu sighed deeply. "He sings to my heart," she said, and lapsed back against the wall, closing her eyes. "I love him. I'm going to marry him."

"You got a ring and a date?" I needled her.

"We've got each other's addresses. True love will find a way." She breathed deeply and basked in the sun. "And I will take Adorable Athletic Al over Featherweight Frankie any day."

Chapter 46
THE ROAD LESS TRAVELED

U.S.S Admiral Capps, Tuesday, March 20, 1945 (continued)

Nothing prepared me for the dining room and our first dinner aboard the U.S.S. Admiral Capps. I'd thought of the Capps only as our ticket home, and I expected the military transport ship to be—well, military. It wouldn't have surprised us to enter a dining hall with rows of rectangular metal tables bolted to a steel floor with countless passengers standing in serving lines for stews ladled from aluminum troughs.

Instead, on the evening of March 20, we entered a graciously lit, carpeted salon that could've been one of the New York clubs that Fred Astaire and Ginger Rogers made famous in their movies. It was the Officers' Mess. But it was not a mess. Tables topped with white linen cloths filled the room, and in the center of each table stood a silver bowl filled with glossy red apples.

Apples! My mouth watered at the sight. Tropical fruits like mangoes, papayas, and bananas had been a mainstay of my diet before the war, but I hadn't eaten an apple since 1937 when we spent that winter in Utica. I was nine-years-old when Grandma Hanagan introduced me to their crunchy sweetness. She baked them into mouthwatering pies, but I didn't see why anyone would bother when you could just eat them fresh. How did the Navy store these treats on Pacific ships and how could they offer them in such profusion? The sight was so heart-breakingly USA, that I felt tears welling. Betty, Mommy, Hope, and I stood agog in the doorway.

"Oh, how beautiful," Betty breathed.

We stared at our seated ex-internee friends laughing and toasting each other with Coca-Cola. The children each had tall glasses of milk. A dark-skinned Navy steward in starched white coat hurried to our side, and escorted us to an open table. Lulu and her family were right behind us. A card at each place setting announced the evening's fare: roast beef, carrots and peas, mashed potatoes, red cabbage, white bread, and ice cream for dessert.

"Heaven!" Lulu rolled her eyes and leaned back in her chair.

Lulu's twelve-year-old sister, eyed the apples longingly. "Can we have one?" she asked Mim.

"*May* we have one?" Mim corrected. "May we have one, please?" Mim corrected herself. "And yes, they wouldn't put them on the table if they were forbidden fruit."

Mim passed the silver bowl around, and we each snatched one perfect apple. I bit into the succulent treat even before passing the bowl to Hope. Red and green skin, perfect white flesh, juice that dribbled down my chin—just the way I remembered.

"An apple for the teacher?" I offered with my mouth full, and she took the last large apple with a knowing smile on her face.

"McIntosh," she nodded her approval. "They're probably from New Hampshire. All the best apples are from New England." She bit in.

"Is that where you'll go, Hope, when we get state-side?" Lulu asked.

Hope nodded, as she savored her bite. Like my mother, Hope was in her early forties and a war widow. She had soldiered through Santo Tomas better than almost anyone I knew—with her teaching, her mint and talinum garden, and her homemade cigarettes, but her husband George's death on the brutal Bataan Death March had scarred her. She carried that knowledge in her eyes like an invisible burden, and she looked older than my mother—her face scored with dozens of fine lines around her eyes and downward slashes near her mouth. As if the loss had been slashed into her.

"I have to go to Pittsburgh first, to see George's father. Then I'll go back to my family —in New Hampshire—White Mountain country." She admired the half-consumed apple in her hand. "Pink apple blossoms in bloom by the time I get back."

"Will you teach fifth graders *The Ballad of William Sycamore?*" I prodded, recalling how Hope had coached Freddy Hopkins through his Thanksgiving Day performance about the pioneer who longed for wide-open spaces.

"And *The Midnight Ride of Paul Revere* and *I Hear America Singing* …" She nodded. Hope was growing misty-eyed, even as the buzz of merry conversation rose around us. "And *The Road not Taken*. I'll teach them all."

I knew all those poems except the last one.

"What's *"The Road Not Taken"*? Who wrote that?" Betty asked the question that was on my mind.

"Robert Frost—a New Hampshire poet." Hope wore her *listen-and-learn* teacher look. "He's finding his way through the woods, and trying to decide between one path—worn and open and another unexplored." Hope closed her eyes and seemed to dredge words from a distant vault:

> *I shall be telling this with a sigh*
> *Somewhere ages and ages hence;*
> *Two roads diverged in a wood, and I —*
> *I took the one less traveled by,*
> *And that has made all the difference.*

We sat thinking for a moment, while the hum of conversation rose around us. My mother raised her glass of coke to the rest of us. "Well, here's to us. We certainly took the road less traveled by, and that has made all the difference." Her jade green eyes smiled even as her face remained serious. "Hopefully, from now on, that difference will be for the better." We each nodded and raised our glasses, lost in our own thoughts.

"I plan to take the road *more* traveled by in the future," Lulu announced, tipping her glass with a jubilant grin. That prompted peals of laughter and "hear-hears" around the table.

Just then a Navy steward arrived balancing an enormous tray of steaming plates, each heaped with delicious roast beef (which bore no resemblance to stringy carabao), creamy mashed potatoes (not watery corn mush), and fresh peas and vegetables from the US—none of which looked even a little bit like talinum. The steward placed the large tray on a stand next to our table and began to serve us—serve us! As if we were guests at the finest restaurant in the United States of America. An unexpected tear rolled down my cheek. Well, we were.

Thursday, March 22, 1945

"Have you seen Lulu, Boops?" The U.S.S. Admiral Capps was practically a city, and keeping track of my best friend was proving to be a bigger challenge than I'd thought.

"She has a new Marine friend. He's showing her the ship. His name's Randy Something."

"Randy? What about Al?"

Betty gave me a broad grin and shrugged her shoulders. "He's not here." My fourteen-year-old sister leaned on the ship rail, tilted her head to the sun, and let the wind lift her fine curls. Betty seemed, for the first time since liberation, content. The squeals of children at play floated through the air.

"Little Dottie's over there. She's so happy," Betty said, turning to the makeshift playground installed on the forward deck. "Isn't this place something?"

"The Navy boys are swell," I agreed.

When Navy crewmen learned they were going to have almost a hundred little kids on board the Capps for a month, its carpenters flew into action. They'd spent the week before the ship's departure from Leyte building sandboxes, play tables, and even cobbling together swings, which they attached to a superstructure on the deck. For the last two days at sea, the little kids had been totally engrossed in play and in freedom.

The crew had not, however, quite solved the problem of our pre-teen boys, who were too old for swing sets and sandboxes. The boys regarded the whole ship as their playground—greasing the rails and marking up the bulkhead with crayons and chalk. They respected no sign, went wherever they pleased, and played pranks on all the crew, whom they generally regarded as their big-brother co-conspirators. Weary mothers just let it happen. They felt safe here among fellow countrymen, and after three years of holding their imprisoned kids in check on pain of death, had decided to relax. Let the kids have some fun seemed to be the new motto.

"Betty, push me!" Dottie—of Comfort Kid fame—called to my sister from her swing.

Betty hurried over to help. I was just about to go below deck to find Lulu, when I saw dozens of young boys and a couple of girls standing stock still by the ship rail. They scanned the sea as if their lives depended on it.

Curiosity got the better of me and as I headed toward them I saw twelve-year-old Freddy Hopkins lean dangerously far over the stern of the ship. A no-nonsense Marine Sergeant whooshed past, knocking my shoulder, and tugged Freddy back by his tee-shirt collar.

"We need your help, buddy, so don't go drowning' on me. No leaning over that rail." The wavy-haired Marine sounded like he was talking to his little brother, and moved quickly from rebuke to conspiratorial plotting. "Did you spot anything?"

"Not yet, Ozzie. Got one yesterday, though." Freddy Hopkins looked up at the broad-shouldered Sarge for the admiring nod that was forthcoming.

I moved closer to both of them. "What did you get, Freddy?"

"I spotted a mine. The Japs planted 'em all over this part of the sea. We gotta zig-zag around 'em and blow 'em up. I'm helping the GIs."

"Freddy here is one of our best spotters." The Sergeant with the rippling chestnut hair put a large hand on Freddy's bony shoulder, then turned to me, his deep-set, brown-gold eyes alight with mischief. Like Ramón, he had impossibly long eyelashes, bushy eyebrows, and a face so perfectly chiseled that Michelangelo could've sculpted it. "It's sure a good thing we've got so many kids on this ship." His eyes told me he was in jest, but Freddy nodded solemnly.

"They put us older kids in charge of spotting for mines," Freddy explained. "Gave us a lesson on what Jap mines looked like, and told us if we want to be Midshipmen when we grow up, our job is to stand right here and study the sea for the enemy. When one of us spots a mine, we report it to the mate up there."

Freddy pointed to the sailor with binoculars perched high on the foretop lookout—a sailor, I thought to myself, who could clearly see every mine for miles around long before the kids.

"Whoever spots the mine first," the Sarge said, "gets a reward. He—or she," he nicked his chin toward the two or three girls at work "can go down to the mess for an ice-cream sundae—no matter what time of day it is. Mess cook's treat."

"I had one at ten in the morning yesterday." The pride in Freddy's voice was unmistakable.

"Well, thanks for keeping us safe, Freddy," I said as the boy turned away and went back to his work.

I waited till Freddy was out of ear-shot. "You are an absolute brainwave," I said to the gorgeous Marine. "Sundaes-for-spotters will keep 'em out of trouble for hours."

"It's our new mission," Ozzie had a conspiratorial gleam in his amber eyes, "not *Take-out-the-Japs*, but *Survive the Kids on the Capps*."

We both laughed.

Ozzie smiled the most disarmingly beautiful grin. "That Freddy reminds me of my fiancée's little brother," he said.

"He's a really great kid." I remembered how Freddy had offered to be last off the roof in the air-raid in order to protect Hope. I stuck out my hand. "I'm Lee Iserson, by the way."

"Ozzie," he replied, giving my hand a brief shake. "Staff Sergeant Edward Farthington Osborne," I knew he was a Staff Sergeant. His green-on-khaki insignia announced his rank. Three stripes on a chevron for a Staff Sergeant—just one for a Private.

"Ozzie! Get the kids below!" a booming voice called from the foretop lookout, where the Navy spotter watched for mines. "We got three mines comin' up here and we're gonna take 'em out!"

Monday, March 26, 1945

Every other day, it seemed, our hearts were in our mouths. When the ear-splitting Battle-Stations alarm sounded, we were jolted from our fantasy world of Capps Resort Cruise to the wartime reality of life on a U.S. military transport in the hotly contested Pacific. We'd been taught what to do when that battle stations siren sounded (go quickly to our staterooms) and the fast-moving crew helped us get there. And we were lucky. So far the terrifying whine had either been a drill or proven a false alarm. No Jap subs yet.

Lulu and I had just scrambled back on deck after the most recent "all-clear." We were supervising a poker game in progress. Five of our favorite men reassembled on the deck, using the well-scrubbed floor for their table. One was Fr. Sheridan. To our great delight, we'd discovered he was on board the Capps yesterday. We hadn't even seen him at Leyte, but came across him saying Mass in the ship chapel on Sunday.

The big Maryknoll priest wasn't wearing his collar now and maybe the four off-duty GIs he was playing with didn't realize he was a priest. He sat in a circle with Lulu's latest heartthrob, Randy and ingenious Sundae-Spotter Ozzie, who were studying their cards. A sergeant they all called "Tubby" and another named "J.D" pored over their hands too, but almost mechanically.

"*Near you it shall not come,*" Father Sheridan muttered, as he settled back into his hand after the battle stations alarm. He smiled up at Lulu and me. "We've been spared."

"Probably because of you, Father," Lulu nodded to him reverentially. Lulu still idolized him, even though she had never followed through on her "Catholic classes" as she called them.

Lulu and I stood and watched, leaning against the boxy generator that flanked their game. I could see down into Ozzie's and J.D.'s hands (they had nothing), but not Fr. Sheridan's, Randy's, or Tubby's. Randy kept stealing meaningful glances at Lulu, who faithfully delivered coy smiles.

"A thousand shall fall at thy side, and ten thousand at thy right hand, but it shall not come nigh thee." Tubby recited, with a very strong southern accent, the fuller text of whatever prayer Fr. Sheridan had been quoting. Tubby seemed to be correcting Fr. Sheridan. "Nigh thee" sounded like "Nahh thee." He continued "because thou hast made the Lord, which is my refuge, even the Most High, thy habitation."

Fr. Sheridan smiled slightly as he decided on his next bet. He looked about a ten thousand times better than he had in February: his shoulders broader, his body sturdier and straighter, and his strawberry blond hair fuller and shinier. The piercing blue light that never went out of his eyes shone like a lighthouse beacon.

"Psalm 91," Fr. Sheridan said, but his eyes didn't leave his hand. "Your father a preacher, son?"

Tubby shook his head. "Nah. In South Carolina, we Christians all know our Bible verses. Just you papists who can't recite 'em." The cocky red-head had a good-natured grin on his face. So they did know he was a priest. Father Sheridan didn't rise to the bait. Maybe he didn't understand him. Tubby had an accent so thick, it was like talking to a foreigner.

"I call." Father Sheridan shoved a pile of money into the center of their circle.

"Too rich for my blood, Padre," said Randy, who winked at Lulu and seemed to be seeking an escape from the game.

"Me too," Ozzie agreed.

J.D. was already out. Tubby laid down three kings, pleased with himself.

The corners of Fr Sheridan's mouth rose slightly, as he fanned five cards on the table. "Strait. Ace High. That beats three of a kind, doesn't it?"

There was something remarkably satisfying about seeing an Ace, King,

Queen, Jack, and Ten march across the table, even though I always liked bridge better than poker. Tubby shook his head with annoyance, and shoved the pile of money toward Fr. Sheridan.

J.D. hooted. "It sure did come nigh thee, didn't it, Tubby?" *Nah-theee…* He was also from South Carolina.

"The Big Guy's protecting us from the Japs, not the Jesuits." Ozzie declared.

"I'm Maryknoll," Fr. Sheridan corrected them. There was no way these boys could keep track of the different religious orders of the Catholic priests and nuns on board. "But we take vows of poverty too, so this is all yours, gentlemen. Just divvy it up." Father Sheridan shoved the pile of bills back to the center and rose to his full six-foot frame. "Besides, we internees all owe you a debt we can never repay." They looked at him in astonishment, silent for a moment, before their faces lit up.

"Well, I'm gonna collect from, Lulu," Randy announced with cocky confidence. The other GIs chortled as they started to divide their winnings.

Father Sheridan's face turned deadly serious. He squatted down and placed a strong hand on Randy's shoulder, lowering his voice. "You watch it, young man. Mary Louella Cleland is the sixteen-year-old daughter of a Navy captain still held prisoner by the Japs." He let that sink in, and Randy stared at him, taken aback. "You treat her like a gentleman and the daughter of an officer. You got that, Sergeant?"

My eyes sought Lulu, who was propped on the other side of the generator. She bit her lower lip, then look away from the game, and out to the sea. Yesterday we'd learned that Lulu's dad was alive, but not in the Philippines. He'd been transferred to a camp in Tokyo. That's all the information the army had, but the transfer was bad news any way you looked at it.

Randy's face cleared as he stared back at Fr. Sheridan. "Yes sir." He answered with conviction.

***

Tuesday, March 27, 1945

"Honest to God, Lulu—aren't you practically engaged to Al?" My best friend never ceased to astonish me. We sat in what Betty referred to as "the Iserson Suite," Lulu on one bed and me a foot across from her on the other. Lulu, who'd hadn't had a date in three years at Santo Tomas, now flitted from one GI to the other like the proverbial bee to the flower.

"Oh Lee, I love Al. I'm going to marry Al, but Randy is a dear friend," she explained with patience. "He's going to be a doctor you know, and practice among the poor in South America."

I couldn't believe this. "How long have you known him? Three days? How can he be a dear friend?"

She gave me an exasperated look. "Well, I knew the minute I made eye contact with you, Lee Iserson, that you were my dear friend. I knew the minute I raced off that truck that brought us to Santo Tomas! I knew it before you even told me your name. And I was right!"

"That's different, Lulee."

"Why?"

"Because we're girls. And because girls know those things about girls," I countered.

But I decided to give up. Lulu was in love with love. Or maybe it was her way of not thinking about what was happening to her dad.

She had been very quiet all afternoon yesterday, ever since Fr. Sheridan put Randy in his place. She knew that her father had been transferred to a labor camp in Tokyo, and the likelihood of him having an NGH guard there—a Nice Guy Haruo—was very low. Was Haruo back in Tokyo, I wondered. When would our boys invade Japan? Ike's forces in Europe crossed the Rhine two days ago, and were now marching to Berlin. How long would it be before MacArthur's forces swarmed Tokyo?

My heart broke thinking about how hard this had to be for Lulu—Lulu's father's life depended on Douglas MacArthur, whom she hardly ever referred to in terms kinder than "reprobate." Would Captain Cleland still be alive when Mac's troops got there? This shipboard romance probably kept Lulu's mind off her troubles—a situation over which she had no control. I decided to ease up on her.

"Well, OK, so he's a dear friend," I conceded. "What are you and your dear friend doing tonight—playing doctor?" I couldn't resist.

"Very funny," Lulu smiled, but she looked at me gratefully. "We're helping rehearse *King Neptune and His Court*"—the ceremony the crew has when we cross the international dateline in a few days. Civilians aren't supposed to be at the rehearsal, but they'll make an exception for us girls. J.D. invited Nellie. You wanna join us? Ozzie's going to be there." Before I could answer, she sped on. "And what about Ozzie? Aren't you just over the moon for him?"

"Nah. He's gorgeous, but he's engaged to a girl in Chicago named Joanie, and he spends all his time talking about what the two of them are going to do when he gets his leave, and how he'll spend half his time with Joanie. And then together they'll go see his family in Minnesota."

"He reminds me of Ramón." So Lulu had seen it too. It was the eyes. "Do you wish he'd notice you instead?" Lulu asked.

"Oh, he notices me fine, and he's a really swell guy," I answered quickly and shrugged it off. "Maybe the fact that he's 'taken' makes everything easy—I can just laugh and joke with him and tell him almost anything. Everything that's been pent up inside me for so long comes out in a rush when I'm with Ozzie." I felt so at home with him. I smiled at Lulu. "He says he never met anyone who talks so fast or has more to say than I do. But I told him that's because you were so busy with Randy that he hadn't talked to you."

"That's true," Lulu conceded as if it were an obvious fact. "And by the way, Randy says he plays the piano really well."

"Ozzie or Randy?"

"Ozzie. Everything from *GI Jive* to *Peer Gynt Suite*."

"You're kidding. Ozzie plays classical music too?"

"That is what Sergeant Randall Dean Eckenrode, the future doctor and healer of South America's poor, has told me. And my dear friend would not lie." Lulu nodded solemnly.

Chapter 47
ROAR LIKE A LION

March 27, 1945

Lulu, Nellie, and I hurried down the corridors of the labyrinthine ship, making our way to the Rec Room, where Randy, Ozzie and J.D. Thanes (the South Carolinian who was sweet on Nellie) were rehearsing. Even as we rushed along, I marveled at the ship's facilities. Down one level, the Mess crew staffed an enormous galley kitchen and a separate bakery to serve more than six thousand meals a day. But now we sped past a barber shop, a library, and even a post office.

Mail delivery from the United States and from the P.I. had awaited us as soon as we'd arrived on ship. I got a letter from my cousin Francis in Utica for the first time in three years, and even one from Hoy Moffett down in Mindanao. My mother got the best letter of all—she learned from her brother, John, that he and Aunt Rachel would meet us at the ship in San Francisco. Uncle John was my mother's youngest brother, and like her, a real maverick. He'd left Utica in 1935 and high-tailed it to California, where he met his motorcycle-riding wife Rachel, and set out to write movie scripts. He hadn't made it big yet, but we all knew it was just a matter of time.

Lulu was not nearly as distracted as I was, and jabbered on about rehearsal for the show, which had something to do with undersea royalty.

"So, what kind of show is King Neptune's Court? I asked her.

"Haven't you been listening? It's not a show. It's an initiation ceremony for 'slimy pollywogs' to become "trusty shellbacks'—loyal subjects of King Neptune's realm." I stopped in my tracks and stared at Lulu. Had she totally gone off her rocker? Neptune? Weren't we on a U.S. naval transport? Lulu and Nellie stopped too.

"It's a Navy tradition. Sailors are called 'slimy pollywogs' if they haven't crossed the equator before. Not us, though. We're 'trusty shellbacks' because we crossed when we came out to the PI."

"But some of the sailors haven't done that," Nellie filled in.

How did everybody know more about this ceremony than I did?

"Right," Lulu agreed. "This'll be the first time for some, so Davy Jones—that's Randy—who is also the servant of King Neptune, puts them through trials to prove their worthiness before they can enter King Neptune's realm."

"At the end, the Pollywogs have to crawl on all fours to the court, and kiss the greased belly of some big fat GI, who's dressed up in a diaper like Neptune's Royal Baby." Nellie parroted what I guessed was J.D.'s description of the show.

"Ugh!"

"It's disgusting," Nellie agreed. "Good thing we're 'trusty shellbacks.' JD is playing Neptune, by the way."

"What's Ozzie's doing?" I asked Lulu.

"Probably some ching-a-lings on the piano for each guy initiated. Did you bring *Leonore's Suite* for later?"

I nodded. I wasn't sure this was such a good idea. That music was special to me, and I hoped Ozzie wouldn't turn it into barroom piano music.

The three of us sped past the laundry, and ducked into the neighboring Rec Room, where we saw Randy, aka "Davy Jones," spouting pronouncements on a makeshift stage. Randy had a bandana tied around his head and a patch over one eye, as he read a silly proclamation about "trials for slimy pollywogs entering King Neptune's realm." Ozzie was at the piano, fingering dramatic chords. J.D. Thanes, draped in a sheet, held a cardboard trident, the three-pronged scepter of King Neptune, in his hand. Thank God it was just practice and there was no fat Marine in a diaper.

Lulu, Nellie, and I glanced around and spotted Father Sheridan sitting in a folding chair in a corner. His poker buddies had apparently invited him to the rehearsal too. We hurried over to the makeshift seats, Lulu scooting in next to our priest friend.

While Davy Jones read, a soiled and bedraggled sailor, who looked like a Filipino, was plopped on stage right next to him. I say "plopped" because his feet were roped together and his hands were tied behind his back, so he had to be lifted into place by two Trusty Shellback sailors behind the stage. What was he covered in? Oatmeal? Lumpy Gravy? It was hard to tell, but they had sure slopped something on this guy. I studied the features of the bound man. Maybe his family was Mexican—who knew—but he was in the U.S. Navy now, and putting up with these ridiculous antics. A very large barrel filled with water rested on the floor below the stage, and a gang plank led from the stage to the mouth of the barrel.

"This Pollywog has crawled through the barrier of slime, befitting his slimy wog origins," Randy intoned with gravity. So that was it: they made him crawl through muck. "And now to cleanse him from his filth and purge him for entry to the royal kingdom, we immerse this Wog in the pool of sea water drawn from Mighty Neptune's Depths." Randy nodded ceremoniously to J.D. Thanes Neptune, who dipped his head at the recognition.

"Let the purge and the cleansing begin!" J.D. thundered.

The two Shellbacks dragged the skinny, slop-covered initiate to the edge of the stage and helped him walk the short plank. Randy actually had to shove him from behind because of his bound arms and legs. Finally, the hapless man plunged feet first into the barrel, his head disappearing beneath the surface, held down by the two Shellbacks who had ascended makeshift steps on either side of the barrel.

I didn't like what was happening. I knew this was some Navy idea of fun, but a ripple of memory ran through me and the knot of fear loosed on

February third, tightened for the first time since our liberation. I wasn't going to watch this. I looked down at the floor, as Ozzie rolled some dark chords on the piano. Then my eyes flew back to the stage of their own accord.

"And now, thrust this slah-mee pollywog deepah into mah salty depths!" shouted J.D. Neptune, roaring an exaggerated laugh.

The two Shellback lackeys shoved the roped man still deeper beneath the water's surface for what seemed to me an eternity. Neptune brandished his trident and chortled, while Davy Jones Randy taunted the submerged initiate.

"Pedro Pollywog, wallow low! Pedro Pollywog, down you go! Hug the depths, you slimy bro!"

The black patch on Randy's eye made his Davy Jones character all the more sinister. I closed my eyes: *Let him up now. Let him up. Let him up now.* Those were my only thoughts, as I waited for the servants of Neptune to yank him out. But they didn't. This was taking too long. It was taking way too long.

"Purge him. Submerge him! Cleanse him thoroughly of his wog birth," bellowed Neptune. The Shellbacks holding him under laughed sadistically and tightened their grip, keeping the flailing boy firmly under water.

This was all wrong. This couldn't be happening again. Tears sprang to my eyes, and my sight blurred as my mind fled to the gate at Santo Tomas. A battered Filipino vendor sat roped to a chair. Abiko's cruel henchman taunted the boy and shoved a funnel down his bruised mouth. Another fiendish ghoul of a guard followed it with a water hose. While Abiko roared in laughter and waved his bayonet in the air, the two thugs unleashed a torrent of water full force to swell the man's belly, and Abiko reached for his bayonet. Now, I heard someone roar with laughter as they held the battered, defenseless Filipino under water. I couldn't stand it.

"You let him go!" I leapt to my feet and shouted at the top of my lungs from the back of the room. "Stop that right now, you bastards! You won't get away with this, Abiko! We'll stop you this time!" I screamed at them with all my might and pointed, like some crazed Old Testament prophet, to the drowning man in the barrel. My arm shook and my extended finger trembled, but I found that I could not race toward them. My feet were glued in place. "You let him go, Abiko!" I added in complete fury.

The submerged seaman suddenly burst gurgling but laughing to the top of the barrel, spouting "That's all you got?" He emerged to total silence though, as Randy, J.D., Ozzie and the other crewmen just stared at me. I was vaguely aware that Nellie had risen beside me, had her arm around my shoulder and tugged me close to her.

"It's OK," she whispered. "We're not there anymore, Lee. It's OK, Lee." Her voice was soothing. "Abiko's dead. The boys were just being silly."

I seemed to come back to myself and realized that Lulu was now staring at me as if I were completely crazy. Well, hadn't she seen what they were doing, for God's sake? How could she be so calm?

"C'mon, let's go out on the deck," Nellie urged me. "Stay here, Lulee. We'll be right back."

Lulu tried to leap up and follow, but I saw Fr. Sheridan grasp her hand, and pull her down. Nellie piloted me out the door, and up a flight of stairs on to the deck. I was still shaking when we reached the rail, but the balmy evening breeze and the moonlight on the water soothed me. There was hardly a ripple on the ocean's surface.

"Lee, you know where we are now— right?" Nels asked in her kindest voice.

"Uh-huh. The Capps." I nodded, tears now running down my cheeks. I felt like the slightest breeze would take me right over this rail. "But Nellie— for a minute, I was right back there again. Abiko and his henchmen were killing that Filipino vendor all over again. Didn't it seem like that to you?"

Nellie had been with me at the gate. She and Fr. Sheridan had watched that water torture too. We'd kept it secret from Lulu though, so my best friend wouldn't worry about her father in a military camp. "You remember it, don't you?" I felt stupid and desperate now.

"Yes," she said quietly. "But I didn't think of their Neptune prank that way."

"Prank?" I was incredulous at Nellie's interpretation. "How can you call that a prank? They held him under way too long. Were they trying to kill him just cuz he was Filipino or Mexican or something? That was no prank." I was sure I was right.

Nellie shook her head. "He's a Navy diver. J.D. told me he can stay under water for up to eight minutes. Even nine sometimes. They're just trying to impress us internees for the show."

"Oh…" Now I felt stupid. It was just a show. I shook my head at how completely I'd lost my senses. And at how much anger and hatred still roiled in me. Fr. Sheridan might say it was righteous anger, but moments ago, I would cheerfully have raced up to that stage and killed Abiko if I could've gotten to him. If I could've moved. If he had even been there. Tears streamed down my face. "They must think I've gone off the deep end or something." I took a ragged breath. "Well, I guess I did go off the deep end."

"Not as much as the Navy diver," Nellie tried to cheer me up, and reached her arm across my shoulders. "Maybe they'll think you were auditioning for a part," she cajoled. "Tell 'em you want to be Queen Amphitrite, who releases prisoners from the deep. Amphitrite was Neptune's wife, right?"

Leave it to Nellie to know who Neptune's wife was. She always was the best student in our Latin class. "I guess so," I muttered.

But I didn't want to be Amphitrite in their Navy show. My breath came slower and more steadily now. Nellie, so calm and understanding, stayed right beside me, her arm still draped around my shoulder. Minutes passed. Another long-ago memory with Nellie came to me, and I let it bubble to the surface.

"Nels, do you remember that paper you wrote … on Ovid? The one you had to erase?"

She looked puzzled, but then nodded.

"Do you remember how you ended it?"

She didn't answer right away. She seemed to be recalling each line from Ovid, the embittered poet who wanted to rain suffering and torture and death on all his enemies. I remembered how Nellie ended that paper.

"I think I just disagreed with Ovid and quoted some line from Cicero. It always pays to memorize Cicero," she teased me.

"What was the line?"

She paused and closed her eyes. *"We were born to unite with our fellow man and to join in community with the human race."*

"Right. Well, do you believe that now?" I asked her. "That we're called to unite with our fellow man? Join in community with the human race? Now? After so much?"

She stared at me wide-eyed and surprised. Suddenly her answer seemed very important to me. Nellie was a full year younger than Lulu and me, but she often seemed decades wiser. She thought before answering.

"Maybe it's not as hard for me as for you—or Paul or the Brooksies or even Lulu. I haven't lost my father or mother. I haven't lost a sib."

"You lost three years," I stared levelly at her, unwilling to let her off the hook.

"Did I?" she challenged in a soft voice. "I don't think so. Did you?" She let that sink in.

Before I could even begin to formulate an answer, Lulu and Ozzie burst on to the deck.

"Oh, Lee-lung, are you OK?" Lulu raced over and hugged me. "Fr. Sheridan told me about that horrible DREAM you keep having. Why didn't you ever tell me about that? I've read about those things." She took both my hands in hers. "*Combat exhaustion.* That's what you have. Did you see that article in the hospital at Leyte? You're just exhausted, Lee. You'll get rested and it'll be all better."

"I'm OK now." I loved Lulu so much. She was convinced she knew the answer to most questions and could solve almost any problem. Over her shoulder, I saw wavy-haired, intense-eyed Ozzie looking at me like he knew my "OK" was just a half-truth.

"Let's go take a walk," he urged me. "Lulu promised Randy that she'd be right back to rehearse the Shellback Installation."

***

That night Ozzie and I walked on every deck of the ship, and we talked for hours. Everything poured out of me. My father's death—so early in the war. The squalor of three years without a shred of privacy. Hunger. The surprise inspections and slappings. The water torture at the gate. Starvation. Then liberation and the shelling. Seeing only blood where Annie's head should have been. Tonight was the first time I'd let myself really think about all the ugliness and horror we'd endured. I wasn't prepared for how much anger and resentment welled inside me. Ozzie—twenty-one-year-old Marine Staff Sergeant Edward Farthington Osborne from Minneapolis, Minnesota, who had been fighting in the Pacific for three years —listened with a face so full of compassion and understanding that I felt completely safe.

I told him about the good stuff too: about making and selling fudge, meeting Lulu for the first time, and how "Climb and Drink" entertained us mightily when we were fourteen. I told him about that English debate, when we had to argue that the "Internment Camp Experience Was Advantageous to our Growth," and how Lulu got booed when she argued that Jap-bowing was a handy skill to know. But that bowing had gotten her out of some scrapes. I told Ozzie about *Leonore's Suite* and the way Haruo played it. I regaled him with stories of my recipe collection, and assured him *The Captive's Kitchen* was going to make me big bucks after the war. I even told him about my neighbor-turned-sweetheart Ramón, and how I'd tried to sneak him into camp for a dance. And how Ramón called me "Leonera" and told me to "roar like a lion."

I wasn't the only one talking that night though. Ozzie jabbered up a storm too—all the places he'd been, the sad and funny things he'd seen. We'd settled next to each other on a bench on deck three. Few people walked the deck now, and those who did cut us a wide berth. Ozzie's voice grew low.

"For me it's Saipan," he confided. "You close your eyes and see the water torture at the gate. I keep going back to Hell's Pocket on Saipan."

"Hell's Pocket?" I didn't know much about the little Pacific island in the Marianas, but I knew the Marines had fought a terrible battle there in June and July of '44. I waited.

"We pulverized that little island before we went ashore—165,000 artillery shells to soften 'em up. The whole damn—sorry—the whole island—looked like the worst stew Mess Chef ever put together— mud, limestone, exploded trees, more mud. And we had 'em so outnumbered. The Japs shoulda just surrendered."

Ozzie took a drag on his cigarette, and shook his head. "But no—not the Japs. We storm those beaches, but they come right back at us. But we fight, and we die. We get a beachhead of about 6 miles secured, and start to move inland. Mountains. Jungles. And they're hiding in this network of caves in the mountain, and firing on us. Our dead and wounded everywhere. We're not making it a picnic for them either. We got 'em outnumbered but they have the high ground."

His low voice gained intensity. Ozzie wasn't really with me any more: he was back on Saipan. I slid closer to hear him better. The GIs never talked about combat with us girls. But I had to know.

"Then some high mucky-muck decides we gotta take the low ground too. We're on the west side of the island now, and there's this gully between some hills. We got so many wounded that we need to set up a medical tent there." He shook his head, staring out at the sea, remembering. "So we storm the Jap positions and take the gully. We clean out the hills—we think. We got a lot of wounded though," he repeated. He put out the stub of his cigarette and lit a new one.

"We set up the tent, get the wounded in on stretchers, and don't the damn Japs come right back at us—launch a banzai charge right into the tent of the wounded."

Into the tent of the wounded! "Hell's Pocket," I whispered. "That gully's Hell's Pocket?" I slid my hand into his.

"Yeah. All of a sudden it's hand to hand. I got a big knife, and some slitty-eyed bastard is coming at me with a bayonet. I got a buddy with no leg on a stretcher next to me, screamin' his guts out." Ozzie's voice grew hoarse and raspy, and he crushed my hand in his, lost in his memories now. "You go crazy in a moment like that. I lunged at that Nip, and knifed him to death. Knifed him over and over again. His blood spurted in my face, and I can still smell it. And I keep on stabbing him. I'd never killed anyone in hand-to-hand before."

Oh, Ozzie. My heart broke for him. He stared grim-faced into the night, jaws clenched and muscles straining, the new cigarette lit but untouched.

"That Jap wasn't any older than me." He brushed at something beneath his eye, and shook his head. "I wasn't thinking about that though. More Japs keep pourin' into the tent, and I'm thinking' *I am not gonna die here.* I'm saying to myself over and over. *I am not gonna die in this God-damn Jap gully.* And we got a hell-fury commander—Captain Salomon, whose practically holding off the Japs single-handed. He comes up with a .50 caliber machine gun, and slices into 'em. He gets those guys on the run."

Ozzie seemed exhausted from the telling, but he kept going. "Anyway, we won that one. Hell's Pocket turned out to be just the first round, but that's the one I keep going back to."

A tear rolled down his cheek, and I gripped his hand tighter. Ozzie took a deep breath, and stared ahead. "I try not to think about it. But sometimes I wake up in the middle of the night screaming and see some Jap hovering over me with a bayonet. And I'm stabbing him all over again. And his blood's in my face."

Ozzie wiped his face with the back of his hand, took a deep breath, and seemed to return to the present. "But here's what kept me going." He reached into his pocket, pulled out a billfold, and extracted a snapshot. "I knew I had to get back to her." He laid a photograph of Joanie in my hands.

She really was adorable—blonde, blue-eyed. Soft waves in her hair. The kind of girl that all tall, dark, and handsome boys go for. I had a flash of jealousy when I realized that my frizzy brown curls and mud brown eyes made me her polar opposite. But I also recognized something alert and intelligent in Joanie's expression—almost vigilant— something that made me admire her. Ozzie said she was studying nursing at the University of Chicago.

"You're one lucky guy. And she's a lucky girl." I handed the photo back to him and smiled my approval.

Ozzie and I talked and cried and laughed till three in the morning. He told me how much he depended on his poker-playing, prank-wielding buddies to keep his fears at bay. He talked about how much he loved his unit. We talked till I was all talked and laughed and cried out. But one last thing gnawed at me.

"Ozzie, do you think tomorrow I should apologize to Randy and J.D. and the other guys for ruining their rehearsal?"

He seemed taken aback. "No." Ozzie reached over and took my hand in his. "What did your Ramón tell you? 'Roar like a lion'?" When I nodded, he said, "That's all you were doing, Lee. Sometimes you gotta roar like a lion." His warm hand squeezed mine. "These guys have been at war for three years—they get it."

A wave of warmth and gratitude welled inside me. "I'll be the model audience during the real show," I whispered, relieved and grateful for the long, slender fingers that enfolded mine.

We sat on the quiet deck, watching the flecks of moonlight dance on the water. We'd left the white sand beaches of the Solomon Islands three days ago, and now our convoy sailed north toward Hawaii. A full moon lit our path. Not a single mine or Jap sub in sight tonight. In six days, we'd be in Pearl Harbor, where the long ordeal of war began. That day, April third, I'd turn seventeen, and return to my very own country, the United States of America. That must have some deep significance, but I was too tired to figure out what it was now.

"Hey—didn't you bring some music for me to play?" Ozzie asked, lightening the mood considerably.

"At three in the morning? Won't we wake everyone up?"

"Nah. The Rec Room's not near the berths. C'mon. Let's go tickle the ivories."

"Well, it's not really a tickle-the-ivories kind of piece," I said. "It's more like a break-your-heart-beautiful kind of piece." He looked at me quizzically, and I continued. "It's more like a 'if you turn this into ragtime or honky-tonk, I'll come at you with a bayonet myself' kind of piece."

Ozzie's deep, rich laugh shook his whole body, and he opened his hand. "Let me see it. Let's go under that light."

The two of us moved near a ship lantern. From my Red Cross satchel I produced a manila envelope and extracted my tattered, dog-eared pages. Ozzie scanned my father's handwritten dedication to me on top, and smiled. "Birthday present, huh?"

"Uh-huh. My thirteenth."

Then he studied the music. In rapid succession, he frowned, raised his eyebrows, looked skeptical, then surprised, then intrigued. "He liked Rachmaninoff?"

"Yeah. You can tell?"

"Yup. Let's go to the Rec Room."

Ozzie, it turned out, was a darned good pianist. He had large hands and those long fingers could span the range required by my father's piece. His soulful rendering touched my heart. He caught something of the color and light that Daddy (and Haruo) had embedded in the music. And I loved seeing him bent over the keyboard, his beautifully sculpted face intent on the intricate notes before him.

The music, as always, transported me. When the piece moved from passionate to melancholy, I closed my eyes remembering my buoyant, brown-eyed father, who had left this testament of his love for me as bright and clear as the most brilliant star on the Southern Cross. It was his work of creation. I thought of Haruo, the kind Japanese guard who played it perfectly, committed it to memory, and added his own gift to me. And now here was Minnesota-born Ozzie, a Marine warrior on Saipan, leaning forward with the same concentration as Haruo, wringing truth from the notes of a Russian Jew and a Jap guard for an American girl who grew up in Manila, came of age in a squalid prison camp, and was bound for Utica.

With my eyes still closed, the music soaring, and my spirit flying, familiar words came back to me. *We were born to unite with our fellow man and to join in community with the human race.* Hours ago I'd asked Nellie if she believed that—not knowing whether I did or not. *Leonore's Suite* reminded me that it was true. When we joined in community with the human race, beautiful things happened. It was only when we turned away that everything withered.

Ozzie played the last rippling notes and let the final chord melt away, his fingers at rest on the keys. A comforting wave of peace washed over me. When I opened my eyes, I was startled to see a tear roll down Ozzie's cheek. For a long time, Ozzie just stared at the keys. And then he looked up at me with intensity, a question in his eyes.

"You played it beautifully," I said.

That couldn't have been the answer to whatever he was asking, because the question lingered in his gaze for a few moments before he snapped back to his polite, self-assured, Mid-western self. He shrugged off the compliment.

"I'd have to practice a lot more to play it beautifully. It's a complicated piece. You should be proud of your father."

"I am."

He smiled back at me ruefully, still seated on the piano bench. Suddenly, the emotional evening, the outpouring of confidences, the flood of insight, and the long night weighed on me. I glanced at a clock on the Rec Room wall—3:20 AM. All I wanted was sleep, but my heart welled with gratitude.

"Edward Farthington Osborne, you are the best friend a liberated internee girl could ever have." I leaned down and kissed him on the cheek. For a second, he put his large hand on the side of my face, and held it there. I liked his warm touch. He stared at me with intense chocolate eyes, before allowing his fingers to brush my jaw line and fall to his lap. He gave me a sad smile.

I knew he was missing Joanie. "Good night, Ozzie."

Chapter 48
MAN OVERBOARD

Tuesday, April 3, 1945

"It's Paradise. I thought it would look like Utica." Betty leaned on the ship rail. In the far distance, white sand beaches, emerald hills, and thousands of swaying palms beckoned. We were still hours away, but we had sighted the Hawaiian Islands.

"You thought Hawaii would look like Utica? Boops, didn't they teach you anything in camp?"

"We didn't get Geography, remember?"

That was true. No maps, no knowledge of the war, they reasoned.

"No, I knew," Betty corrected herself, "but part of me thought—well, Hawaii is the United States of America. It'll probably be cold."

"Never quite got over our winter in Utica, did you?"

My little sister smiled and shook her head, but her eyes were glued to the distant island paradise. That winter of 1937, when we'd returned to the States for a visit, had been one of the snowiest on record in Utica. I loved the sledding and the snow-angels, but seven-year-old Betty, born and raised in Manila, always happiest in the orchid-covered hills of Baguio, was appalled that any place was allowed to have weather like that.

"I hear they have spring and summer in Utica too, Boops."

"Hey, did you get your birthday cupcake?" Ozzie brushed by me, a big smile on his face. "Happy Seventeeth!"

It was good to see Ozzie beam his radiant smile again. For a day or two after we talked, he'd been his cocky, jovial self, then he'd begun to be so quiet around me. I'd been worried about his moodiness lately.

"Scrumptious! Did you order that one for Hope too?" At breakfast, Hope and I, perpetual birthday buddies, had both been greeted with cupcakes studded with candles. Betty, my mother, and the Clelands all sang Happy Birthday to us and showered us with little gifts they had made or poems they had written.

"Nope. Mess cook's got a list of everybody's birthdays. I'm on duty now, but I want to talk to you later, OK? Foredeck—9 PM?"

"Oh, sure." I nodded vigorously. He rushed off.

"He's sweet on you," Betty said with a knowing smile.

"He is not," I said. "He's sweet on Joanie. He just talks to me because he misses her."

"You didn't see the way he was looking at you during the show, did you?"

"I was watching the show. And you were too. We had great seats, didn't we?"

Betty just kept smiling like the Cheshire cat.

Two nights ago—on Easter night itself— King Neptune's Court wowed all the ex-internees and servicemen. The show was topside, on the main deck, and Betty, Lulu, and I were in the second row. The Court consisted of Davy Jones, Neptune, of course, and a hysterically funny sailor dressed up like Queen Amphitrite, along with their royal baby (a fat marine in a diaper with a greased belly) and tons of scribes. First, the "Pollywogs" performed a hilarious talent show for us all with some great singing and tap-dancing, Ozzie providing accompaniment.

At the end, Pollywogs were baptized into the mysteries of Neptune's deep, becoming "Trusty Shellbacks." And this time, I managed to leave all my Abiko imaginings behind, because the Shellbacks didn't hold the pollywogs under water for very long at all. Ozzie, of course, tickled the ivories throughout— rippling mighty ching-a-lings whenever necessary.

Betty hadn't erased her knowing smile, so after a minute I said, "How was he looking at me?"

"Like you were the only girl in the room, and like he was playing that piano just for you."

"Really?"

"Really." Betty was enjoying the fact that she knew something I didn't. Or she thought she knew something that I didn't.

"He's been so quiet lately, Boops. We pal around with Lulu and Randy, and Randy's totally over the moon for Lulu. Lulu, by the way, says she can't figure out who she's more in love with—Al or Randy. But when the four of us are together she talks enough for all of us, so maybe she and Randy don't even notice what's going on with Ozzie." I'd been trying to figure out Ozzie's melancholy for days. "But it's been hard to get two words out of him. And he was always such a conversationalist before."

"But now he wants to talk to you." She arched her eyebrows, as if the meaning were crystal clear.

"And…?" I prompted her.

"And nothing," Betty concluded with an impish smile.

***

My birthday sped along delightfully. In the Rec Room Betty had organized a bridge tournament in my honor. Hope and my mother teamed up against Lulu and me, and we trounced our two elders. I felt a little bad because it was Hope's birthday too, but she didn't seem to mind terribly. A table away Betty and Nellie took on Mim and Margie. When I heard Betty say, "Six Spades" and "No, he's not my boyfriend!" practically in the same breath, I knew that she and Nels were gonna romp over Lulu's mom and little sister. Betty was a conservative bidder, so if she bid Six Spades, they had that slam cold. And nothing irritated and mobilized my little sister more than being accused of being sweet on Martin Rivers, even though we all knew she was.

After lunch, when I stuffed myself with cold ham, white bread, potato salad, and apple pie, Lulu and I (along with almost everyone else) sped back on deck to watch our arrival in the island paradise of Hawaii, where we'd dock for rest of the day. As we sailed into port, it became apparent that

Honolulu's Pearl Harbor wasn't much of a Paradise at all—it was a bustling powerhouse of steel docks, battle ships, aircraft carriers, planes, warehouses, and more American servicemen in one place than I'd ever seen in my life. Pearl Harbor made Leyte look like some two-bit army recruitment office.

We could still see damage from the sneak attack, "the day that would live in infamy," as President Roosevelt called it. The hull of the U.S.S. Arizona, a battleship sunk on December 7, 1941, poked from the sea and testified to the early sucker punch. But around it rose the most thrilling display of military might: hundreds of ships built in California, planes from Seattle, and Jeeps from Detroit. This was how we were going to beat the Japs.

"Nobody's allowed off ship in Honolulu," Lulu complained to me. "What a gyp." We were leaning over the rail, watching the Capps' crew secure the gangplank.

"It's just one more tropical island, Lulee. And we're only five days from San Francisco now. America the Beautiful, here we come!"

"America the Beautiful, here we are!" she said. "See that flag? I want off."

"Not me. I'm waiting for the Golden Gate."

I didn't mind missing Hawaii. I was already visualizing the mighty towers and swooping curves of the world's longest and most beautiful suspension bridge. It wasn't golden at all, but orange-red. I had seen it just once before in my life—in 1937, when it was brand new and we'd sailed home for a visit from Manila. That breath-taking wonder of a bridge spanned the Golden Gate Strait in an almost two-mile expanse. To me it represented everything that was best about America: an enormous, gorgeous, practically impossible feat of engineering accomplished in just four years during the Depression. Its scale and grace thrilled me then, and I couldn't wait to see it again.

"So, tell me what you're doing again after we dock in Frisco," said Lulu.

"Well, Uncle John and Aunt Rachel are going to meet the ship and show us the town. Then Mommy, Betty and I will buy train tickets, and head for Utica."

"I'm gonna miss you, Lee-lung." Lulu's raspy voice faltered, and her hand closed over mine.

I felt a fierce tug at my heart, and turned to her. Lulu seemed to stare right through me—right to the very depths of my soul. Life without Lulu— it was almost unthinkable. She was my second self. We'd shared everything—well, almost everything. Now in her welling blue eyes, I saw all my own sadness, excitement, and hope mirrored in her face. We'd be three-thousand miles apart from each other—on opposite sides of our country, but something important would be starting for both of us. Freedom. Real Life. We both knew it, and longed for it. We were both sad, and we were both happy.

"What are you looking forward to most?" Lulu squeezed my hand, and tried to strike a light-hearted note.

"Maybe the train east," I said. "I'm gonna to watch our big, beautiful, safe country go by from the window of a train. I'm looking forward to that. And no spiders."

Lulu laughed heartily. "I'm pretty sure there are spiders in Utica."

"No tarantulas. No Black Widows," I countered.

My thoughts lingered on Utica. I'd be reunited with a family I hardly knew—with my cousin Francis. I'd enroll in a real American high school, where kids went to dances and listened to music, and probably ate ice cream whenever they wanted. I guess I'd learn to like Sinatra. But I wasn't going to swoon over him. And I needed to think about college. I wanted to study more Spanish. Then I could go to Spain and visit Ramón. Maybe after college, I'd go into the State Department, and that'd give me another chance to return to Hawaii.

Our one-day stop in Pearl was just to refuel and—this really galled us— to be interrogated! At our shipboard briefing last night Captain Haugen told us that FBI agents would board in Pearl Harbor for the day to ask us their questions. *Had we, had any of us, in any way, at any time, aided and abetted the enemy?* Well, of all the nerve! We'd been locked up for three years, starving to death, and now our own government wanted to know if we were traitors?

Lulu and I now stared down at the FBI agents about to board the ship. We were prepared to loathe them, but a finer looking group of interrogators you never saw. We ogled the young agents with their full heads of neatly combed hair in their well-tailored clothes. They wore white and silver-grey suits with wide lapels, broad shoulders, and folded pocket squares poking out of their breast pocket, as they ascended the gangplank.

"Will you look at those suits!" Lulu marveled, just as Randy passed by. "Why don't men in the Philippines wear suits?" she queried me.

"Hey, you're supposed to be impressed with uniforms, not suits!" Randy reminded her.

"Our liberators will always be first in our hearts," Lulu called after him as he raced off.

"The shoulders must be padded, don't you think?" I asked Lulu as we returned to our inspection of the incredibly broad-shouldered FBI men.

"I do not. American men are *HE-Men*. That's what our boys really look like," she insisted.

The afternoon passed without a single FBI agent interviewing the Isersons or Clelands or Thomases about our collaboration with the enemy. The agents seemed to have a list of internees they suspected, and stuck to it. Would I have told them about Haruo and how kind he was to us, if they'd asked me? Would I have told them that I let one nice-guy Japanese guard copy my special music? And that Lulu and I didn't mind bowing to him? Nope. They didn't need to know that.

At my birthday dinner, family and friends toasted Hope and me with iced tea and real lemon slices. Nine PM rolled around before I knew it. The skies had darkened to a deep violet and a waning half-moon shone overhead, as I headed to the foredeck to meet Ozzie.

I hoped Ozzie'd be back to his old self by now, so we could have some last laughs and fun together before docking in San Francisco. I was pretty sure that he would write to me after we got home. Ozzie was a brick, a real stand-up guy, and I was already getting letters from Hoy Moffett and Boyd Davis. I had address slips in my skirt pocket ready for him and others.

Mostly I hoped his gloom had lifted. Had I brought on his moodiness with my outburst at rehearsal and our talk afterwards? That was almost a week ago. It helped me so much to talk about all the things that tormented me, but maybe I'd been inconsiderate. I'd reminded him of all the horrible sufferings he'd endured. Was that it? Could he just not get out from the weight of his memories now?

I spotted Ozzie on the foredeck chatting with Randy and Lulu, and hurried over to join them. Ozzie's face lit up when he saw me. Gosh, he was handsome.

"The Birthday Girl," Ozzie called as I approached.

Lulu's Randy was just putting out a cigarette when I arrived. He had a broad brow, wavy blond hair, and bright blue eyes. When he didn't have a patch over his eye, Randy didn't look sinister at all.

"Congratulations, Lee. Sweet seventeen. I just promised Miss Lulubelle here a stroll around the deck, but I'm sorry about the other night at rehearsal. I went too far with the Davy Jones act and Pedro our diver."

"No, I did. It just triggered some…"

"You don't have to explain," Randy cut me right off. "I felt real bad though. We keep forgetting that you girls fought your own war."

"And now we are triumphant," Lulu looped her arm through Randy's. "Time for a Victory Lap." Lulu winked at me, as they headed off to another part of the moonlit deck, where other lucky couples, liberated husbands and wives, GIs and internee girls, were enjoying the balmy evening.

Ozzie gave me a big grin, lapsed into awkward silence, and then turned to the bustling shore, his arms perched on the rail. I pivoted to watch the activity too. Even at this hour, we could hear the rumble of jeeps and machinery on the docks, but quiet descended between us.

"Randy sure has got it bad for Lulu," Ozzie finally said, glancing sideways at me, but then looking shoreward. The three stripes in his sergeant's chevron rippled as he settled nervously on the rail again.

"She's crazy about him too," I agreed. "But he just might be standing in line behind Al. I'm not sure." I'd told Ozzie all about Al.

As the twilight deepened, thousands of lights twinkled, and I was mesmerized by them. Pearl Harbor should be called Diamond Harbor. The stillness between us lengthened. Ozzie'd said he'd wanted to talk to me, and here we were alone on the foredeck on a beautiful evening on my seventeenth birthday, but so far I had no clue as to why.

"Yup, he's sure got it bad for Lulu," Ozzie repeated and stared out at the glittering shore.

I wondered why the GIs always spoke of love like a disease—"he's got it bad"—like measles or chicken pox or the flu.

"He's got it real bad, all right," he said again. Was that the twenty-fifth time he'd said that? Then a long silence. "I guess Randy and I are in the same boat," Ozzie said softly.

A shiver ran through me even on this balmy night, and I stared at him. Ozzie shifted from the ship rail and looked at me, his brown-gold eyes wide with the same question that I'd seen in them the night he'd played *Leonore's Suite* for me. I remembered what Betty had said that morning, and a wide chasm of uncertainty opened at my feet. Before I could say anything, Ozzie'd found his voice and spoke with conviction.

"Lee, I've never felt about anyone the way I feel about you. You and I—we've walked the same roads. Hacked our way through the same jungles. Sailed the same ships. Literally...." He smiled, turned his beautifully sculpted face toward mine, ran his fingers over my cheekbone, and lifted my chin—holding my face up to his. "I'm overboard for you, Lee, and there's no saving me."

Time stopped. My heart stopped. I met Ozzie's searching amber eyes and leaned up to him, not daring to believe what I'd heard. Ozzie, my standup guy, my understanding, empathetic GI friend and brick, was overboard for me? His large hand on my face warmed every part of me. His caramel eyes, wide with wonder and compassion, enveloped me. Ozzie was gorgeous—perfect even, and when he leaned down to kiss me, and his lips brushed mine, I started to kiss him right back. But an image floated before me, and I blurted out the first thing that leapt to my mind.

"What about Joanie?"

He pulled back slowly and still held my chin. "I'll go to Minnesota and see my family, and then put in for East Coast duty. I'll stop in Chicago to tell Joanie it's over, and then you and I …. Lee, will you marry me?"

I tried to take in what he had just said, but I couldn't. "Will I marry you?" I repeated stupidly. I found myself stepping back as if I'd been struck, and a jumble of confused emotions whirled inside me. Shock, astonishment, wonder.

"It's sudden, I know," he hurried on, "but I've been thinking about it a lot lately. I guess that's why I've been so quiet. I don't have a ring for you yet, but this promise of a new life, it's the best birthday present I could think of for you." He looked at me with such hope and tenderness. "And you'll have a ring, I promise. I'll have it for you before we get married in June. Sooner maybe."

June? Wasn't I going to be finishing my junior year of high school in June? Wasn't I going to be deciding which college to attend? My mind rapidly retraced our talks of the last month. How had I missed this sudden turn of events? There was that night when we'd poured out our hearts to each other, yes. But I kept crashing up against the photo of his beloved Joanie—with the softly bobbed blonde hair and the intelligent blue eyes. Joanie, who was studying nursing at the University of Chicago and waiting for him to come back to her. Gosh, at this point I felt like I knew her!

Now a flood of emotion surged in me, as sympathy and confusion gave way to sudden indignation. "Edward Farthington Osborne, that is the most unfair thing I have ever heard in my life! Joanie's waiting for you! She's been writing and waiting for the last three years in Chicago. While you—you go through jungle warfare and hand-to-hand combat in Saipan by staring at her photo, for Pete's sake! And now you tell me that you're falling for *me*? Lee Iserson? A girl you've known for just three weeks? Of all the unfair things I've ever heard of, that is the most unfair."

I spat out the last words.

Ozzie looked like he'd been hit with a frying pan. "Lee, I … I just don't feel about Joan the way I feel about you." He swallowed hard. Joanie had become Joan. "We have something deep and unbreakable, you and me. Don't you feel it?" He gripped my hand.

"Ozzie," I took a deep breath and paused for a minute, floored, but not wanting to hurt him. "Gosh, I've never been able to talk to a boy the way I've poured out my heart to you." He still wore that dazed look. "I really like you. But I'm the first girl you've gone out with in three years, for Pete's sake, and … you two have been carrying a torch for each other a long time. You've been writing her all through the war. She's got her heart set on you, and you've been holding on for her."

He stared at me confused, eyes full of pain. "Are you turning me down?"

"Well…." I thought about how handsome and compassionate he was, how we'd confided in each other, how well he'd played *Leonore's Suite*. I thought of how kind he'd been to Freddy and the kids on deck, and I knew what a good father he'd make. I saw how much he wanted to kiss me, and part of me wanted to kiss him right back, but I just couldn't make it all work in my mind and heart together.

"Listen, Ozzie. I want your solemn promise tonight that you'll go through with your original plan." He just stared at me. "You promise me that you'll go to Chicago and spend time with Joanie, see if the spark's still there, and afterward, you write me at my address in Utica. OK? If I'm right, and you still love her, and you marry Joanie, well, we are still going to be friends." I reached into my skirt pocket and pulled out the slip of paper with my address on it. "You have to give her—and you— a chance." I stared at him defiantly, and he still seemed confused. "Do the right thing. Then write me about where your heart is. Do I have your solemn promise?"

He searched me with an intensity that scared me, his jaws now clenched, and a muscle on the side of his neck throbbing. Then he pulled away and paced the deck for a minute. Finally, he came back to where I stood, and pointed a determined finger at my face. "All right, Lee. If that's the way you want it. But you'll be hearing from me after Chicago—with a written proposal of marriage." His eyes said: *That Settles That*, and he snatched the slip of paper from my hand. "You will," he repeated and seemed to be regaining some of his quiet confidence and cockiness.

The blast of a ship horn startled both of us, and we turned toward the noise, but so many ships were in the harbor now that we couldn't locate the source. I was inwardly shaking like a leaf, and grateful for the distraction. In the awkward stillness that followed we found ourselves with backs to the shore, staring up at the stars overhead. I wished I could make it all up to Ozzie, and make things better.

"Ozzie, you're the swellest guy. If I were going to marry anyone right now, it would be you. We sure can laugh together, can't we?" He nodded in agreement, smiled slightly, and squeezed my hand, though he didn't turn to look at me. "And I've told you things I couldn't tell anyone else. Not even Lulu."

Ozzie seemed to be searching the sky for something to say or a way forward. "There's your Southern Cross." He pointed to distract me, and released my hand. I had told him, of course, about the constellation that linked me to my father.

"Hawaii's the only place in the U.S. of A," he said, "where you can see both the North Star and the Southern Cross in the same sky." He pointed from one to the other. "It's all North Star from here on. We're gonna lose the Southern Cross tomorrow or the next day."

I knew that. The brilliant kite-like constellation that bound me to my father shone only in the Southern Hemisphere. We were headed to San Francisco. I might be living in the Northern Hemisphere beneath a different set of constellations for the rest of my life, and the familiar cross would be just a childhood memory.

We're gonna lose the Southern Cross...

"You mean we won't be able to see it," I corrected Ozzie.

"Right," he said.

The brightest star in the cross, the one at its base, flickered brilliantly, and seemed to wink twice, as it hovered on the horizon.

"It'll still be there though, Ozzie. We're not gonna lose it. We won't be able to see it, but it'll still be there."

He squeezed my hand again. "Right. Right you are, Birthday Girl. It'll still be there."

My mind flashed back to the scrawl on the first page of "*Leonore's Suite*." *Happy Birthday, dearest Lee, my darling grown-up daughter.*

Chapter 49

THE GOLDEN GATE

April 7, 1945

Before we went topside to celebrate our last night on ship, Lulu, Nellie, and I huddled in the Iserson berth, signing each other's "Forget Me Not" books. We penciled limericks and fond farewells to each other. I had Nellie's green leather volume on my lap. Lulu scribbled furiously in my red autograph book even as she kept up a steady stream of conversation.

"He proposed. The fact remains, he proposed, and you turned him down. So you win, Lee." Lulu kept writing. "You have the most memorable romance of any of us." She looked up and sighed with mock seriousness. "Lee I. and the GI—A Tale of Unrequited Love."

I almost threw my pencil at her. Lulu snickered as she returned to her composition, but it was no laughing matter to me. I'd tried to make everything light and breezy between Ozzie and me for the last four days, as if nothing awkward ever happened, but I knew it was hard for him.

I also knew I had done the right thing. Right now, freedom and the United States of America were the two things that made my heart hammer with excitement. I wasn't ready for any guy to come sweep me off my feet and propose marriage, for Pete's sake. Besides, I was pretty sure I was right: Ozzie'd go home and see Joanie and fall right back in love with her and he should. But if not…

"I didn't actually turn him down, you know. I just deferred him." I paused and looked over at my best friend. "And I think you and Al, or you and Randy, topped Ozzie and me for best romance. Or maybe Nellie and Bill should win. Theirs went on for three years…" I flicked my pencil against Nellie's autograph book, still trying to figure out what to write. "Whereas I didn't even know I was in a romance. I didn't realize Ozzie was 'overboard for me'— till he actually proposed."

"There was just no saving him," Lulu parroted Ozzie's proposal mercilessly, and kept writing. Sometimes I regretted telling my best friend every last thing that occurred in my day.

I ignored her. What could I write to Nellie?

"You definitely win, Lee," Nellie said. "You're the only one with a proposal. Al and Randy didn't pop the question, did they, Lulee?"

Lulu shook her head. "Not yet."

"And the most Bill and I ever did in camp was smooch—maybe twice. I didn't get any proposal—no, siree. "Best War-Time Romance" goes to Lee Agnes Iserson with Edward Farthington Osborne nominated for Best Male Actor." Nellie kept writing, her head bowed in concentration the way it had been when we did our Latin compositions.

Suddenly, I knew exactly what to write to Nellie, and dashed off an inspired summary of our time together. I slipped the little pine-colored book back on to her lap.

"There!" Lulu also finished, but with a flourish, and handed me my autograph book with its black shoelace binding strap.

I snuck a peek at what she had written. "Lee-lung, As you know you are the best friend I have or ever will have…" my eyes started to mist over. Her tribute went on and on, so I closed the book. I couldn't read this now.

Lulu stood, smoothing her jade green shirt-waist dress, its wide belt snugged around her waist. Her eyes sparkled, her cheeks were rosy, and there was no denying that my best friend now had a bosom—and a truly remarkable hourglass figure.

"I win indisputably in a final category," Lulu announced solemnly as Nellie handed me my book, and we prepared to head to dinner. We looked up at her.

"Most weight gained since liberation…."

I burst out laughing.

"Not so fast!" I said. "I'm up 24 pounds." Earlier that day, we had all visited Sick Bay, where the Navy did a final round of weigh-ins for us formerly starving internees. I'd weighed 93 pounds in February before the GIs burst through the iron gates, and I now tipped the scales at 117.

"I'm at 115," Nellie said. "Up eighteen pounds." At five foot six, Nellie was easily an inch taller than me, and she still looked lean and willowy.

"This is hideous," Lulu moaned. "I'm four inches shorter than Nellie, and I'm one-hundred-twenty…." She drew the number "twenty" out in a painful wail. "I have actually gained thirty pounds in thirty days. Hideous. The whole situation is hideous." Lulu's distress was sincere, but she looked absolutely terrific. "I have to start a reducing-diet the minute we dock in San Francisco."

"Ridiculous!" I snorted. "Has Randy said anything? You look fabulous, Lulu. And I think we should dessert our way up and down Lombard Street tomorrow."

"Hear! Hear!" said Nellie. "Let's start sooner. We three are going to sail under that Golden Gate Bridge tomorrow morning chomping on chocolate bars!"

April 8, 1945

Less than twelve hours later, Hope, Mommy, Betty, and I stood in the chilly pre-dawn light with hundreds of other excited internees, hugging the rail of the upper deck and squinting toward land. Fog still blanketed the distant shore, but might be lifting.

Betty fastened the top button of her double-breasted wool coat. We all wore the ugliest matching coats in existence—discarded coats from the Women's

Air Corps delivered to us by the Red Cross the night before we left Manila. The Aid organization had anticipated the forty-eight degree temperatures this morning and our lack of preparedness, but they had mortally sinned against the dictates of fashion. *Hideous,* Lulu had pronounced them, the minute the coats were whisked out of the trunks.

"Warm enough, Boops?" my mother asked.

Betty nodded, and smiled. Her face was hopeful and curious, even though forty-eight degrees was not Betty's preferred temperature. Mommy reached one arm around my shoulder, and another around my sister's and held us close. We were both nearly as tall as she was now. The ship rocked beneath us, as it steamed forward.

For a brief moment, my thoughts fled back to 1942: I'd stood and swayed in a military pick-up truck, clutching the convoy rail, staring at the Santo Tomas cross tower, and feeling my mother's strong hands and arms steady Betty and me, as we'd lurched forward into a vast unknown. The iron gates had clanged shut behind us. My mother had been a steadying force—an anchor and a rudder for Betty and me through it all. My heart welled with gratitude, and I blinked several times, partly holding back tears, as I snuck a peek at Mommy's deeply lined face. Agnes Iserson stared ahead, a slight smile on her face, and my gaze returned to the shore.

We all willed the fog to lift. From Iron Gate to Golden Gate. Where was it? Lulu slipped into place next to me, and snugged her arm through my free arm.

"Are we there yet?" she asked buoyantly.

Lulu wore a blue print scarf tied beneath her chin and the obligatory WAC coat. I couldn't help thinking that she looked like a modern version of Nancy Drew—sleuthing for freedom somewhere in the mist.

"Bluebells are singing horses," I said, staring straight ahead and, using our old code for "things are not what they appear to be."

We both squinted. This was supposed to be San Francisco. Land of the free. Home of the brave. Where was it?

The leaden sky brightened slowly, turning from pewter to pearly pink. A pale white disc gleamed low and feeble through the mist. Then a soft breeze tore at the bottom edge of the sea smoke, and the blanket of fog began to lift like a curtain rising from the steely sea. Hundreds of us on deck fell silent as we held our breath and waited.

Suddenly, gigantic, bold red strokes burst from a blue sky: two soaring flame-red verticals, one endless horizontal dashed with haphazard grace. This mountain-high miracle of a bridge pulsed against the skyline. Its mighty towers, its elegantly draped cables, and its great steel arms reached out to us. Applause and wild cheers broke out all over the deck. Someone intoned, "Oh beautiful for spacious skies…" and a few took up the song. But I couldn't sing a word. I just stood there tears streaming down my face and throat so tight I couldn't swallow.

"We made it…" Lulu whispered, and squeezed my hand. "Home! We're home, Lee," her voice rose giddily. "We're home."

"There's no sawali on that gate," Hope said in her granite voice, and I saw her eyes glisten, as she took a deep drag on her cigarette.

The sky brightened to colors that nearly matched the red of the bridge. Tangerine, apricot, and fiery pink tinged the lifting clouds, and the water turned cobalt, as the sun poked its head over San Francisco Bay. We steamed ever closer to the Golden Gate bridge.

Nellie appeared from nowhere with three chocolate bars in hand, and passed one to me and another to Lulu. We split them to share with Betty, my mother and Hope, and sure enough, we chomped on those chocolate bars just as the ship neared the bridge.

"I like what you wrote me," Nellie leaned her head close to mine as we devoured the Hershey bars, and watched the bridge about to pass overhead.

"It always pays to memorize Cicero," I parroted her wisdom back to her, and thought of his words. *We were born to unite with our fellow man and to join in community with the human race.* "Sort of…"

"What did you write her?" Lulu quizzed me, but her eyes never left the bridge.

"We were born to unite with our fellow girls and dramatically improve the human race." I was speaking mechanically, mesmerized by the specter of the bridge ahead. Lulu didn't take her eyes from the marvel either, but she remained all business.

"You can't say 'fellow girls.' Fellows have to be male. And Cicero didn't say *fellow girls* or *dramatically improve the human race*."

"I know, but I did, and we did," I answered. "I signed it 'Leonorus.'"

Just then the U.S.S. Capps steamed under the bridge and past the massive concrete anchorage of the south tower. Moments before, when we were on the ocean side of the bridge, I marveled at the graceful length and breadth of this steel symphony. Now, under the bridge, I felt its height—and might. The highway linking the north side to the south seemed miles above us, as we steamed past the south anchorage. I couldn't take my eyes off a giant, double-stack of x-shaped girders sweeping skyward, and supporting the tower beneath the road. What an extraordinary feat of engineering to lift this endless skyway so high above the waters.

Just as I turned left to look at the north tower, the crystalline morning air shook. A hot-shot pilot in a P-38 fighter buzzed under the bridge and dipped his wings to us! I glimpsed a big smile on his face. We howled and shouted in glee.

Thirty seconds later, Captain Haugen came over the public address system. "Ladies and gentlemen, that is both a stirring salute from your country and a feat you will never see again. That pilot will be a private before tomorrow morning."

Delighted shouts of protest and laughter filled the air. "Boo! Boo!" "Let him live!" Awestruck internees waved handkerchiefs and watched the daredevil pilot head out to sea. I imagined that fine young man heading straight for Leyte to join the massive air campaign against the Japs. Betty came over and joined me in waving to him.

We had crossed into San Francisco Bay now. Others turned their gaze away from where we had come, and toward the city, but I still stood staring back to the Pacific Ocean and the bridge. The sun had risen slowly and glinted directly on the lower half of the south tower, illuminating the cross-section, where the highway cut the tower in two. For a brief moment, a triumphant white-gold light blazed from the red bridge, and the sun's cruciform image shone right at me. I stood transfixed, and felt for Betty who stood beside me but faced in the opposite direction. I yanked her coat.

"Boops, look!" My sister turned and I pointed.

The happy murmur of voices bubbled behind us, but I heard her quick intake of breath. She leaned into me as we both stared at the dazzling cross.

"Resurrection," she whispered.

One second later the sun moved higher, and the bridge returned to its flame-red expanse. It was an illusion, but maybe one meant just for Betty and me.

Now we both turned toward the city, and moved closer to the rails next to Lulu and Nellie. We tried to make out the approaching docks. People on shore waved furiously to those of us on deck.

"What do Uncle John and Aunt Rachel look like?" Betty asked.

"I have no idea." I replied.

My eyes were glued to the shore. We waved and laughed, not caring who we were waving to. I squinted. Was that Pablo Diablo over there waiting for us? Paul Davis and his mother had gotten back a month before we did.

"Lulu, look over there—is that Paul?"

"Where?" she demanded and I pointed to a stick figure gyrating in the crowd. He waved his index and pinkie like devil's horns toward the ship. Lulu and Nellie both shrieked simultaneously. "Paul! That's Paul!"

Oh—to get off this ship! It was only a matter of moments now. The ship slid alongside the docks and crewmembers started to secure lines.

"Ladies and gentlemen," the booming voice of the Executive Officer came over the public address system. "Welcome home. Welcome to the United States of America. Welcome to San Francisco."

Another round of wild cheers and unrestrained applause kept him from saying what he'd intended. When the jubilation died down, he continued. "The crew of the U.S.S. Admiral Washington Lee Capps, the City of San Francisco, and the Armed Forces of the United States of America welcome you home. When the gangplanks are secured, the U.S. Army Band will play its formal salute. We ask that you wait for their musical tribute to conclude before disembarking. Then you are free to leave the ship at your leisure, and rejoin your loved ones on the mainland. Again, welcome home."

The crew of the Capps seemed to sense our haste, and they tied lines and secured gangplanks as fast as they could. We watched a twenty-five piece Army Band take their places, adjusting their stands and the pages of music—looking expectantly at their conductor.

"Place your bets, ladies," Hope said acidly. 'Star Spangled Banner' or 'My Country Tis of Thee'? I'm sorry, but I could really do without the pomp and circumstance right now." She had crushed her cigarette on deck. "I'm ready for the nearest Clam Shack or Oyster Bar."

Every person there shared Hope's impatience, but after all the U.S. Army had done for us—liberating us, the least we owed them was the courtesy of being a good audience. Weighty silence descended as the Executive Officer's authoritative voice rang out once more over the loudspeaker.

"Ladies and gentlemen, the United States Army Band has the distinct honor of welcoming you to American shores." We applauded politely, but unenthusiastically.

Then a sharp, fast-paced roll on a snare drum split the morning air, and a blare of jazz trumpets caught everyone by surprise. Seven sliding trombones swung into perfectly synchronized motion. "There'll Be Hot Time in the Old Town Tonight" roared from Army horns, saxes, clarinets, and drums in bright major chord precision. The United States Army band had morphed into the most exuberant, rollicking jazz ensemble any of us had ever heard.

Shouts of joy, hoots of delight, and peals of laughter filled the air around me. I turned to see my mother and Hope clapping and laughing like I hadn't seen either of them laugh in three years. Tears streamed down their faces.

My heart leapt into my throat, and a bubble of joy burst in my chest. Betty belted out the familiar lyrics to the tune with child-like glee. Lulu, Nellie, and I joined in. Loudly and lustily, we crooned along with everyone "There'll be a Hot Time in the Old Town Tonight!" We were home. Home at last.

I went off to prison in a Cadillac.

I came home on the U.S.S. Admiral Capps.

EPILOGUE

76 Prospect Street
Utica, New York
May 20, 1946

Dear Lulu,

Today's mail brought—can you guess? —an invitation to Ozzie's wedding! Hurray. No surprise there, of course, because just two weeks after we got back to Utica—I know I wrote you this earlier, but I take such smug satisfaction repeating it—I got a letter from him, and I quote: "All I can say, Lee, is that you were right, very right." Ah-hah! If I live to be an old maid, I'll never regret what I did. Ozzie's a swell guy, but he's sure lucky that girl of his had a guardian angel by the name of Lee. Notice that she made him wait a whole year to tie the knot? Probably planning the Chicago wedding of the season.

I sent regrets because (well, I could never afford to go to Chicago anyway, but) our St. Francis de Sales High School graduation is that same weekend and yours truly will be valedictorian. That's right—STIC girl makes good: valedictorian of her senior class in the USA. And I heard from Nellie (up the road in Amherst, Mass) that she's valedictorian of her class too. (Et tu, Lulee?) Here at St. Francis, I beat out a boy who plans to be a surgeon. You can say a lot of horrible things about Santo Tomas, but we sure got a good education. Who knows where it will lead? "We know what we are, but know not what we may be." (Name that play. Hint: All the best lines are in....)

You know, Lulee, I think often of that "hideous" episode you described, when you started high school in LA last year. I can't believe that without any warning, they trotted you in front of a whole school assembly and asked you to describe your experiences as a prisoner of war. Ugh. How mortifying. But your comeback—*Except for the starving and dying part, we had a really great time*— was classic. A real Lulu. Like you, I'm glad to be able to just blend in now. Nobody asks me much about camp, and I'm happier with it that way.

I was excited for you—getting into UCLA. You might find your Mr. Vanderbilt there—nobody as cute as Al or Randy though. And by the way, have you heard from either of them?

Did you know our Nellie's going to Vassar and wants to study (brace yourself: chemistry). CHEMISTRY? You know the reason she chose Vassar? She's still very athletic, and they've got a really good women's basketball team to go with their academics. The Brooksies, by the way, are out east too, and those two brainwaves are both planning to attend Rensselaer Polytechnic Institute. More STIC scholars make good.

My news about college might surprise you. It's not going to be Cornell. My boyfriend here, Mike McMann (I wrote you about him last time) is going to Notre Dame, and I started to think I might like to go to St. Mary's—the women's college across the street. Not because of Mike really. Do you remember Sister Olivette—first from STIC and then Los Baños? She was the one who introduced us to "Shuffle off to Tokyo" Fr. Reuter? Anyway, Olivette is teaching at St. Mary's, and I'd like to go to a college where somebody understands about the war, and what we went through. My friends at St. Francis de Sales are swell, and I like them plenty, but sometimes they're .... I don't know. Immature? Silly gooses?

Santo Tomas grew us up fast. Maybe too fast. Sometimes I need someone to talk to who understands and remembers. Right now I have my mother and Betty. But in college—well, at St. Mary's, I'd have Sr. Olivette. My plan is to major in Spanish. Then Foreign Service, here I come. Or maybe I'll be an airline stewardess, see the world, while I study for that foreign service exam.

Here's more news from out east: Kay and Harry Hodges are fine. They didn't stay in the PI—they're in North Carolina, and Harry's still working for International Harvester. Hope Miller is teaching fifth grade in Sunapee, New Hampshire, and this summer we're going to drive up and visit her. She's got a beau! His name is Ralph Leone, and he's quite the Granite State farmer and woodsman from what I hear. (Educated farmer and woodsman of course.) Hope's actually talking about getting married again.

Mommy never talks about getting married again. She says Daddy was the great love of her life, and she won't find another like him. And she's too busy to get married anyway. She's working two jobs here in Utica to make sure that we have enough money for me to go off to college next year. But I did get a scholarship at St. Mary's.

Did I tell you Fr. Sheridan came by to visit us on his way to Maryknoll? He said mass for us in our living room here, and Psalm 142 was one of the readings. It says something like: "Deliver me from my persecutors…Bring my soul out of prison, that I may praise thy name…" I got all teary-eyed listening. God did that for us—delivered us from our persecutors, got us out of prison. Another good reason to go to St. Mary's—it's Catholic, and they'll remember God there. I can't believe we went through three years together, and I never got you to convert.

Betty spent a long time talking to Fr. Sheridan, by the way. She's always had a quiet, religious streak, you know. She told me she might become a Maryknoll nun—a missionary and go back to the Philippines someday. Wouldn't that be something? Betty working with the Igarots high up in the hills of Baguio? She'd love that. Mommy wants her to go through college before the convent, but Betty can be very willful. We'll have to see.

You know who asks about Betty all the time is Paul Davis. (He had a crush on her during our summers in Baguio so long ago.) Do you ever see Paul—or Bill? I know LA isn't right next door to San Francisco, but those boys are on your coast. Paul writes me these funny letters that always start: "Lee, old bag, old goat," and end "puddles of purple passion." He complains that you haven't written him, by the way. Pablo Diablo says school is "vile," ("I loathe, hate, despise and abominate school.") and Algebra II may do him in, and he misses the "good old days" of "cooperation" at Santo Tomas. By which he means, how he conned the Brooksies in the back row to sharing their geometry answers with him. And OK, I passed him my paper once when Cuthbert wasn't looking. Paul is definitely not going to be valedictorian, but he says he is "wunnerful." And he's up to 170 pounds. That's OK—he's over six feet. (How much do you weigh?)

Bill is still carrying quite the torch for Nellie—according to Paul. Do you think those two will ever tie the knot? Nellie's writing Bill. Bunny's back in England, but she wants to move to Australia when she's out of college. I'm sure you've probably heard from her. It's killing me that I don't have Ramón Ayala's address. I'm just going to have to see him in person someday when I get stationed in Spain.

I think about Haruo sometimes, don't you? Did he survive the war and those big bombs? I like to think he did, and that he's in some quiet untouched corner of the Japanese countryside, raising a family and maybe he's back to playing piano. Maybe he teaches music. I almost feel sorry for the Japs now that MacArthur's in charge of their country. MacArthur's in charge of Japan! Heaven help them. Is that an example of the "Locust Rule," Lulee? Did you see that photo of Mac standing next to Hirohito, their emperor? They look like Mutt and Jeff. MacArthur dwarfs him.

I miss you more than I can say, Lulu. I didn't know how to write this in your autograph book on the Capps, but I want to say it now: You, Mary Louella Cleland, were the answer to a prayer I never said. My whole life lit up in July of 1942 when I met you, even if we were both in prison. Until then, I had buddies—friends like Bunny, Nellie, Paul and Bill. Great kids. Fun to pal around with—and of course, Betty. But I never had a best friend. I never knew the sunshine each new day brings when someone can finish your sentences, anticipate your questions, share your joys and sorrows, and concoct silly schemes that sometimes make you laugh, and other times prove brilliant solutions to thorny problems. Things I'd never have thought of on my own.

I don't miss STIC or hunger or even Room 4, but I miss you. I miss our nights in the hallways, studying by candlelight and solving the world's problems. I miss our time talking about our fathers.

I wish I could have been with you, Lulu, when you found out about your dad's death. I'm so, so sorry. I pray for his soul and for you. I'm sorry that I never got to meet Captain Morrison E. Cleland, Jr., beloved father of Mary Louella Cleland, my best friend. I'll never understand the Japanese. If they had marked that ship as a transport for Allied prisoners, our Navy never would have torpedoed it. Why didn't they do that? Even just to save themselves? They call those ships "hell ships" but they brought that hell on themselves, and killed hundreds of our boys in the process. It breaks my heart.

You wrote that your dad died off the coast of Mindanao. You know, our fathers are in eternal rest together, Lulee. Remember my father died in Mindanao too? I never get past February 24 without thinking about him dying all alone in Zamboanga. No one to visit his grave. We don't even know where he's buried. And now your dad. They both gave us life and they both died for us and they rest in unmarked graves. I hate war. Thank God, it's over.

I have *Leonore's Suite* tucked safely in my bottom drawer, waiting for the next good pianist to remind me that truth and beauty and love live despite war and death. Maybe one of my children will be able to play it someday, but my future husband better have long fingers, because I didn't get those genes of my father's, and you need hands that can span more than an octave to play that piece.

I have the *Captive's Kitchen* sitting on my desk as a project for this summer. I'm going to organize the whole thing and see if I can get it published. But I have my doubts. When I read the recipes now, I can tell they're not well-balanced. They're all cream and butter and sugar and a lot of eggs. And more cream and butter and sugar. By the way, I've leveled off at 123 pounds. Here's something funny: When I'm really hungry now (which is nothing like as hungry as in 1944), the only thing that satisfies me is a can of Spam. Mommy keeps at least four cans in our pantry just in case.

That's all for now, Lulee. Tell me everything. How much do you weigh? When do you graduate? Do you have a boyfriend? When was the last time you heard from Al or Randy? My mother says that the year I graduate from St. Mary's, she'll drive us across country (we'll need a car), and we'll visit you in California. Let's see—that'll be 1950. Until then, I'll keep writing and wait for your letters. Be guided by the wisdom of Leonorus, my dear. "We were born to unite with our fellow girls and dramatically improve the human race."

>Love from your fellow girl and best friend,
>Lee

P.S. Here is the photo of me from our Utica newspaper last month, when I was named Valedictorian.

THE END

Former Girl Internee Named St. Francis Valedictorian *april 5, 1946*

MISS LEE AGNES ISERSON

AUTHOR'S NOTE

Coming of age under dramatically adverse circumstances, Leonore Agnes Iserson Klee (my mother) never tired of telling stories of Santo Tomas Internment Camp: some funny, some heartbreaking, others inspiring. Many of them were lost on her five unimpressed children. ("Oh that's nice, Mom. You grew up in prison. Can we go to the dance on Friday?") But many stayed with us. Throughout her life, Lee gave talks about her internment camp experience for various civic groups in the Buffalo, New York area. And I remember Mom enthusiastically packing their bags, when she and Dad set off to Las Vegas in 1995 to attend the Santo Tomas reunion—festivities celebrating the fiftieth anniversary of their liberation.

A dedicated children's librarian, Lee always imagined writing a young adult novel about this experience, which had so profoundly shaped her. In 1994 at age 65, when she retired as a librarian, she sat down to her newly purchased Gateway desktop computer and started to plunk away. But Lee didn't cast her first chapters as fiction. Instead she worked on consolidating various talks she'd given over the years into memoir, which she then hoped to translate into fiction.

This she did in fits and starts because even in retirement, Lee kept up a frenetic pace of community involvement, ranging from various charitable activities to bridge groups and lessons (she taught), and St. Mary's College alumnae work. By this time, I had finished my doctorate in American history, and was working in the field. In a letter to me in 1995, Mom wrote, "Honey, if I don't finish this book, you have to." Did Mom have a premonition she wouldn't finish her book? Or even start the novel?

On September 14, 1996, Lee left her family bereft. At age sixty-seven, she died in what was supposed to be straightforward surgery to remove part of her pancreas, but it turned out not to be straightforward. We, her children and our spouses, Lee's ten grandchildren and our dad, were stunned. Lee, Mom,

Grandma was indestructible: She was always energetic and overcommitted. She was the strong, unfailing matriarch par excellence. How could she be dead? We mourned her loss and we were at a loss.

For nearly fifteen years after her death, I was knee-deep in work in the fields of history and education, and consciously put off the task I knew she had entrusted to me. I questioned my ability to write a novel (with good reason). I had taught history at the college level, founded a K-8 school, helped write and edit history text books, and had published on character education. But I hadn't written fiction. I started to ponder ways to cast a coming-of-age story set in Santo Tomas.

The reader should know this: My mother, Lee Iserson Klee, would never have written a novel about herself. She was schooled in a more humble time and her own sense of privacy would not have allowed her to reveal as much as I revealed here. (I'll answer for that later, when I see her.) But Lee died before taking up the pen.

And I liked *her* story. And Agnes's and Betty's. And Hope's. And Lulu's. And Nellie's. And Bill's. And Paul's. I embellished and fortified them, to be sure, but the stories are basically theirs. With unwavering support from my sister Eileen and all those listed in the Acknowledgements, I drew on a lifetime of our mother's stories, writing, and memorabilia to construct this tale. It is historical fiction grounded in a lot of truth.

What's true? Santo Tomas Internment Camp in Manila was very real. I attempted to honor the historical record in many of the particulars recounted here. The way in which internees were picked up and processed (in this case at Villamor Hall), the conditions in camp, the Package Line, the varied camp businesses (including fudge-making), the shows hosted by Dave Harvey first in the patio and then in the "Little Theater Under the Stars," the Hobby Fairs to sell wares made by internees, the vendors in camp, the (un)sanitary conditions, the various choral groups, the young boys' boxing matches in the Starlight Arena, the numerous medical passes of internees to get out of camp, the place of religious life, and of course SCHOOL—those are all based on fact, though specific performances and antics in this book were at times products of the author's imagination. (See the Chapter Notes for specifics.) Life at Santo Tomas was surprisingly eventful and often counter-intuitive.

Lee's family was real. Harold Iserson, American-born descendant of Russian-Jews, went to Manila in the circumstances described here, and ran the family embroidery business until it went bankrupt. He did indeed go into radio, then worked for the Army and died of pneumonia in Mindanao as per the novel. Agnes was the tower of strength recounted in these pages throughout and her biography corresponds with what I've written here (including her stint as "Senga Nagana" on the radio). Lee's little sister, Betty, was just as artistic, sensitive, and earnest as in these pages. She went on to become a Maryknoll missionary sister in the 1950s, served in Chile, and took the name "Sr. Harold Agnes."

Leonore's Suite is real. For Lee's thirteenth birthday Harold Roland Iserson did compose a piece of music (Rachmaninoff-like), which was very meaningful to Lee. It survived the war (thanks to Grandma Naylor) and lived in the piano bench of our home in Buffalo, New York until 1985, when my parents moved to South Bend, Indiana, and it has (tragically) not been found since. My brother Dennis learned to play this piece as a young boy, but he does not remember its intricacies now. So, I embellished based on what is admittedly a faulty memory.

Lee's spiral-bound recipe book (which I dubbed *The Captive's Kitchen*) is real and a special treasure; it contains all the recipes given in this book and a lot more (378 all told, most culled, as per the novel, from the camp's YMCA library). All the poems Lee wrote in this novel are actual poems written at the times indicated here and at those ages.

The characters of Lee and Lulu are as vivid and accurate as I could render them. Lee's close friendship with Mary Louella Cleland (who arrived like a breath of fresh air from Cebu) is much as recounted in the novel, as was their return on the U.S.S. Capps. I sped Lulu into this story prematurely—in July of 1942, because I needed her there for narrative reasons. In fact, Lulu did not arrive until December 1942. But the Cleland family's shipping business, the horrid transport from Cebu, and Lulu's father's story are factual. The conversation in which Lulu is baffled about "what's Jewish?" was based on Mary Lou's own memories, as was the story of extracting a rat from a squash and eating it, and undergoing a tonsillectomy without anesthesia to get more food. Lee, Lulu and Nellie all did return together on the USS Capps, and had the shipboard romances recounted here.

The characters of Hope, Nellie, Bill, Paul, Bunny, and Fr. Sheridan are drawn a bit more sharply for a novel than they were in real life, but they are based on the real-life stories of Hope Miller Leone, Ellen Thomas Phillips and Bill Phillips (who did marry after college), Paul Davis, Bunny Brambles, and missionary priest Fr. Robert Sheridan—not to mention Curtis and Barney Brooks, who did indeed lose both parents one month before liberation. The character of Kay Hodges is a composite of two Kays in camp: Katherine Hodges (whose husband did work for International Harvester) and Catherine Heyda (dear friend of Hope's). Both lived in Room 4, but Lee shared a bed with Kay Hodges.

In this novel, Lee and Lulu and Nellie have many adventures that they shared in captivity (weevil duty, "Climb and Drink," studying in the halls at night, Latin classes with Mrs. Maynard and geometry with Cuthbert, Lulu's recall of the locust incident, planning menus and recipes, playing endless bridge, singing in church choirs with original music by a Dutch priest, playing basketball, not to mention adventures with the GIs, and returning on the Capps together). Enormously amusing letters and even a skit that Lee wrote detail their escapades with the GIs. Bunny Brambles' post-war letters to Lee confirm these. Lee also had the life-long loathing of "creepy-crawlies" that I describe in this book.

The names of the Commandants at Santo Tomas, and of the hated guard Abiko are factual. The spearing of the lemon meringue pie at the gate was too. The horrible water torture I described in this book (witnessed at Santo Tomas) is one that Lee did see in camp, and one that haunted her. She described it to me twice, and it stayed with me much longer and more deeply than I wanted it to. I did not recount this torture in the detail that she did, because I want my teen readers to sleep at night.

I hewed as closely as I could to the actual chronology of events at Santo Tomas, but sometimes, for narrative reasons, I fudged the dates on which events happened. For example, the Package Line opened on January 15, 1942 not January 11, and the Hobby Fair was held on October 12 and November 16 1942, not early December. But for the most part, I honored chronology of events—whether writing about typhoons or "roll out the barrel" antics of the liberating forces.

Sometimes for the sake of the plot and character development, I gave Lee and Lulu adventures which they did not have, but which other interned teens did have. For example, the high school debate topic: "Resolved that the Internment Camp Experience is Advantageous to our Growth" was not a Lee and Lulu adventure, but was in fact debated by high school senior Margo Shiels at Los Baños in 1944, and the Affirmatives carried the day in that camp school too. (God love that teacher.) The incident in which Paul steals a stuffed reptile from the museum and puts it in the bed of a rival in the Gymnasium is based on another internee's story, but it did happen.

Sometimes I invented adventures in order to advance the plot. In real life, Lee got out of camp ten times on various medical passes in the first year and a half, and Grandma Naylor was real, but to my knowledge Lee did not get out with Paul, nor smuggle money in the hem of her skirt on a return trip to Santo Tomas.

The character of Haruo is a composite and fictional, but he is drawn from Lee's own recounting of a Japanese guard, whom internees recognized as consistently kind to them in a discreet way. Lee recounted (in a taped oral interview for the Andersonville Prisoner of War Project) that on the night of their liberation, when GIs liberated the camp and blood lust was in the air, an unusual event occurred. The despised Abiko was shot and dragged through the halls and spat upon. Other Japanese guards were booed and jeered. But one guard, whom internees respected, was not mistreated. When being manhandled by GIs and hustled before the recently freed internee crowd, the internees stopped jeering and grew silent. And some clapped. Then others clapped. And one woman shouted, "He's a fine fellow." And the GIs loosened their grip.

To my knowledge, there was no brilliant pianist guard at Santo Tomas. But the metaphor of human goodness across national divides is true. Lee held no lasting hatred toward her captors. Whenever anyone asked her about whether she hated the Japanese, she said no, and elaborated: "There were good Japs and there were bad Japs. There were good Americans and there were bad Americans." When her husband Dick (my dad) went to Japan on business in the 1960s, Lee very much wanted to go with him. She was eager to see the Land of the Rising Sun. Only finances and five children kept her at home.

And Lee did write in a letter to her cousin Francis (before returning to the US from the camp) exactly what has been recorded here: "Francis, I would not trade this experience and what it has taught me for ten years of my life."

We, her children, think that's exactly what the camp did cost her: ten years of her life. Lee and her sister endured malnutrition and starvation at a critical point in their young lives. Though Agnes lived to be 85, Betty died at age 62 and Lee at age 68.

Finally, one counter-intuitive note about Santo Tomas concerns its spelling. Spanish convention places an accent over the "a" in Tomas (usually rendered Tomás), but the seventeenth century university's incorporation papers lack this, and the university's formal name has remained, as indicated in the novel, Santo Tomas.

Acknowledgements

I owe the deepest debt of gratitude for *Leonore's Suite* to Leonore Agnes Iserson Klee herself, who was twice the woman that she was the girl in this book. As indicated in the Author's Note, many of the incidents recounted in this novel are drawn directly from Lee's stories, letters, and talks. Lee's letters to her cousins in Utica (particularly to her cousin Francis) were invaluable. They vividly described life in camp and post-liberation adventures with the GIs, including the memorable letter, which Lee herself titled "Lee I. and the GIs." Lee also left a first-rate collection of books on Santo Tomas, from which I profited. I hope Mom is looking down and proud of this work, but mostly I'm proud of her. Thanks, Mom.

I am also grateful to my maternal grandmother, the late Agnes Hanagan Iserson, who was every bit the awe-inspiring example of strength and resourcefulness portrayed in these pages (if I did my job). Lee dedicated her own writing about their imprisonment to her mother "whose example of courage and determination made Santo Tomas an asset for our lives instead of a liability." Agnes was one sharp cookie, and if readers would like to know more of her story, it may constitute my next novel.

Thanks too, to my aunt Elizabeth Ann Iserson, who left a lovely essay on Iserson family life in the pre-war Philippines.

Indispensable to me throughout this work—to exhume memorabilia, do research in Manila and California, reflect on chapters, and design the book—was my sister, my best friend: Eileen Klee Sweeney (pictured at age seven on the back cover). I owe her an enormous debt of gratitude. Eileen, a talented photographer and graphic designer, had dug deeply into various aspects of our family's history. She had the Iserson family photo album, a cache of letters from Paul Davis to Lee between 1945 and 1950, which proved treasure troves, and sent me letters from Bunny Brambles to Lee in that same period. Eileen ("Deenie" to her family and close friends) richly documented our trips to Santo Tomas with photographs, helped me tape oral interviews with many of mom's close Santo Tomas friends, still flourishing in California. She gave me feedback on every chapter I wrote. I regarded her highest compliment as: "Oh, that sounded just like Mom." Her help was not simply with writing the book: Eileen brought her substantial graphic design skill and patience to the layout of this book, its cover, and dustjacket. She has been a never-ending source of support. I have some inkling of Lee's love for Betty because of my own love for Deenie, and our mutual love for our mother. I hope the reader sees an echo of the 1941 Iserson Girls Trio (Agnes, Lee, and Betty, who are pictured on the front cover of this book) in the 1961 Klee Girls Trio (Lee, Mary Beth and Eileen, pictured on the back flap of the dust jacket).

Another enormous debt of gratitude—never to be fully paid—is to my mother's best friend at Santo Tomas: Mary Louella Cleland Hedrick. "Lulu" was ever-present in Lee's Santo Tomas stories and adventures, a fact which Mary Lou herself repeatedly confirmed. "We were close. We were *so* close," she told me on more than one occasion. "I remember getting off that truck in front of the Main Building, and Lee just scooped me up, and took me right under her wing, and we did everything together after that." In the last nine years, I have spent many delightful days and hours in Lulu's effervescent company. Thank you for so many gems of stories, Lulu.

I extend heartfelt thanks to other dear friends of Lee's, former internees: Ellen Spencer Thomas Phillips (aka: Nellie) and her now deceased husband of more than sixty years, Bill Phillips, both of whom shared their rich and surprising memories with me. A California resident who has gone from chemist to artist, Ellen was always just an email away when I had more questions. Her stories of Mrs. Maynard's Latin class and Cuthbert's geometry reinforced Lee's, and inspired much of what I've written in that context. Lee began every description of Ellen with the sentence: "Nellie was perfect." And she was right.

Leonore's Suite

I live in New Hampshire and for many years was fortunate enough to be living near Hope Miller Leone, who—as per this novel—settled in Sunapee, New Hampshire after the war. Hope's friendship until her death in 1987 was a great boon to me. Her unpublished manuscript "Nor All Your Tears," is one I drew on frequently in creating many incidents in camp. Hope's gravel voice and acid humor are with me still.

I thank too Liz Lautzenhiser Irvine for her marvelous chronicling of the Santo Tomas experience in her own book, *Surviving the Rising Sun: My Family's Years in a Japanese POW Camp,* and her buoyant reflections. Liz told me the story of a stuffed reptile being smuggled out of the museum and into one of the boys' beds in the Gymnasium. I borrowed it for my scene with Paul Davis.

I have also been fortunate to conduct valuable correspondence over the years with Curtis Brooks, who went on to a distinguished career in Foreign Service. I thank him for numerous thoughtful responses to my queries. His mature reflections on the Santo Tomas experience have served as a rudder for me.

I am grateful to Virginia McKinney Glass and Jody Stapler Norton for valuable oral interviews early on. Ginny gave me insight into the way women of color were treated in camp. (The story about her duty boiling and stirring the menstrual rags is true.) Jody recounted a story of having been released from camp for removal of her braces, and how eager she was to return: all her friends were there, and camp seemed much safer than occupied Manila. That is something I had not considered.

My gratitude goes to former internees Sascha Jansen, Martin Meadows, and George Baker for consistently helpful responses to my queries. Though she has passed away, Sascha (age 9-12 in camp) was a veritable encyclopedia of Santo Tomas reality, legend, and lore. My husband and I were fortunate enough to join a trip she led to Manila in honor of the seventieth anniversary of the camp's liberation. We were richly rewarded for the experience, and I am grateful that she so generously shared her expertise any time I queried.

Martin Meadows (two years younger than Lee) shared surprising memories of his own (for example, being allowed to leave camp to make his Bar Mitzvah at the Jewish synagogue in Manila during the war, but he kept some to himself despite my promptings). An expert on music of the 1930s and '40s, Martin tracked down for me the Abe Lyman-Rose Blane version of "Good Morning, Good Morning," played every day for the camp wake up call. (The Martin Rivers character who appears in these pages is inspired by Martin Meadows.) George Baker (also a young internee) gave many of us a great tour of Santo Tomas when we were in Manila in 2015, and he found an archive of marvelous photos for me. He also told me about his brother Len making sulfa tablets in camp.

Although he has passed on to the next life, I thank too British internee and University of Sussex professor Rupert Wilkinson, whose 2014 volume *Surviving a Japanese Internment Camp: Life and Liberation at Santo Tomas, Manila, in World War II* is the best contemporary overview of Santo Tomas. Rupert and I had a lively email correspondence until his untimely death in 2015. He was consistently open to understanding the Japanese perspective on their experience. Finally, I thank Maurice Francis, a hugely dedicated British researcher, who to this day keeps many Santo Tomas survivors and their descendants in touch with each other through his valuable work.

I incurred many other debts in the writing of this novel. This was my first attempt at fiction, and I needed mentors. I found a very valuable one in Jack Galvin of Newport, Rhode Island. Jack chaired the English Department at Rogers High School in Newport for thirty years, and knows young adult fiction well. After retiring, he taught a course at Salve Regina University (which I was fortunate enough to take) called "Let's Make a Scene." That was eight years ago. Jack and I met regularly after the course ended and was my first coach, always ready with an idea when I was stuck. I consider him both a great mentor and a friend.

I thank my wonderful writer's group in Norwich, Vermont, from whom I have received invaluable feedback for years. Our group, led by novelist

Katharine Fisher Britton was a lively, supportive, and honest one. I have valued the varied perspectives our members brought (from psychological to military). Many thanks to Katharine, as well as Hilary Llewellyn-Thomas, Dan Muchinsky, Rick Eary, Sue Geno, Andrea Harris, Meg Schmidt and Mary Van Buren. I also thank Laura Chasen, of the New York Book Editors group, for her thoughtful and detailed critique of the novel.

Thank you to friends in the Philippines, who came to my assistance with this project over the years: Mary Catherine Budde Chua and her husband Roger Chua, who graciously played host to me twice in Manila, and arranged a very valuable interview with the late Fr. James Reuter, S.J. (who, as per this novel, was interned in Los Baños with Bunny Brambles and Sr. Olivette). Many thanks as well to Maita Oebanda, Collections Management and Documentation Assistant at the University of Santo Tomas Museum. She is a font of information and was a gracious guide for Eileen and me in 2009—even taking us to the top of the cross tower!

I thank my well placed friends, who came up with key details: MIT friend and vintage car collector Bill Hoff, who pointed out to me that 1942 Cadillacs had mohair seats; Dow Jones analyst-turned-high-school-Latin-teacher David Moran, who filled me in on which Latin texts second year students would be translating (Ovid), Father Julian Stead, O.S.B. at Portsmouth Abbey for giving me some pointers on high school boxing (which he coached), and Fr. Damian Kearney, OSB for finding me the St Andrew's missal, which told me what the mass readings would have been at various dates in 1942-1945. I also thank Shira Hoffer, a very astute teen reader of this manuscript, who provided excellent feedback.

I am grateful to to members of my family who gave me helpful feedback on the draft, among them my brother Dennis Klee, but most especially Lee's grandson and my nephew, Richard Francis Klee III (aka Ricky). While a busy doctoral candidate and father of five, Ricky took time to provide helpful and detailed written reflections on each of the three parts, and his enthusiastic feedback has buoyed me.

Boundless and special thanks to my patient, unflappable husband, Javier Alberto Valenzuela, for his confidence, loving support, and great faith in the value of this project. His love and constancy inspire me, and his enthusiasm kept me going. And I thank too my son, Andrés Klee Valenzuela, daughter-in-law and in-love Christina, and my grandchildren Sofía, Emilia, Isaac, and Anna for (in some cases) listening to me ramble on about this project for almost a decade.

Lee's granddaughters and great granddaughters, in a special way, this one's for you: granddaughters Megan, Annie, Katie and Sarah; great granddaughters Sofie, Emmie, and Anna, Marien, Sofía, and Hannah, Ceci and Mia, and maybe a few more, who are yet unborn. This novel, I have been told by editors, is longer than it needs to be and filled with more quotidian detail than necessary. I let this version go to press, though, because I thought the details of Lee's journey and experience would be valued by her grands. Remember: *We were born to unite with our fellow girls and dramatically improve the human race.* I hope your grandmother's courage and spirit inspire you every day.

Finally, I would be remiss if I did not close by thanking God for bringing the Isersons, the Clelands, the Thomases, the Phillipses, the Brambles, the Davises, the Brooks boys, and so many others safely home.

Mary Beth Klee
Hanover, N.H.
September, 2019

Chapter Notes

Leonore's Suite is my attempt to journey with young Leonore Agnes Iserson through her thirty-seven months of captivity, and it is drawn from many sources. Casting the novel as historical fiction allowed me to bring Lee (and the challenges that led to her growth) into sharper focus. But Lee's descendants and friends may want to know: what is true and how do we know? The answer to the first question (what's true?) is "quite a bit." I address that question in general terms in the Author's Note.

In this section, I seek to provide Lee's family/friends with a more specific roadmap to truth versus fiction, and gratify my professional historian instincts. I kept a footnoted version of the manuscript as I wrote and share the fruits of that here. In order to avoid confusion about major characters, I have abandoned my instinct to call Lee "Mom" and to call Agnes "Nana," and instead have used their real names. A select bibliography at the end provides full citation information for the works cited (many of which are unpublished).

Part One: Mañana Came

Lee wrote a nearly identical version of this introductory letter on this date to her first cousin Francis Maher, who lived in Utica. (See Lee Iserson to Francis Maher, 28 October 1941.) She was thirteen-and-a-half, and Francis was a year older (the son of Agnes's sister, Gertrude or "Gert" and her husband, Francis). The first cousins had met and corresponded since 1934, when Agnes, Lee, and Betty made a trip to Utica (first one for the girls) to meet their Hanagan family. My text follows Lee's very closely, but I added the final paragraph on *mañana came*, as a way to introduce the Part One title. When Lee thought about writing her great American novel of Santo Tomas, she chose Mañana Came to be the title of the book. She said the *"mañana, mañana"* mentality of the pre-World War II Philippines was their undoing.

Chapter 1 – I.J.A.

"I went off to prison in a Cadillac." Lee often began her own recounting of the Santo Tomas experience with those words. As to the specifics in the

chapter: The Iserson family at that time lived in a modest apartment at 690 Taft Avenue as per letter to Francis Maher (and it did have slatted shutters). Kay and Harry Hodges were their North Carolina third floor neighbors. Twelve people were packed into a Cadillac limo at pickup (as per text). For details of pick-up, see Leonore Iserson Klee's, *Mañana Came*, unpublished manuscript in author's possession, p. 10. The model year of the Caddie limo is speculative. I chose the 1942 Imperial limousine (Fleetwood); it was their heaviest and most expensive model. (Howard Hughes owned one.) Relatively few were made because the federal government ordered all car companies to switch to wartime production in early 1942. It became the model for Eisenhower's staff car. Civilian driver's seat was leather (cheaper) and back seat, plush white mohair interiors as per collector Bill Hoff's email to me.

Harold Iserson was indeed working for the Army in Zamboanga, Mindanao at this time; at age 39, he was not enlisted in the Army, but worked as a civilian for the Army Corps of Engineers. The "grizzled Brit" Aubrey is my invention and a composite character.

The Japanese conquest of Manila with soldiers riding on bicycles, even horses, is factual, as per Lee's description. Also, see Bruce Johansen, *So Far From Home* (Pine Hill Press, 1996) page 19 for details on Japanese victory parade; Tressa R. Cates, *Drainpipe Diary* (Vantage Press, 1957), for details on cycling army Victory Parade, p. 30. Cates also describes the Japanese typing up receipts for the cars that were appropriated, p. 31. This was their practice in Malaysia initially as well. "Uncle Milton Greenfield" was real, although I don't know if he had his car purloined. He was not an actual uncle, but a family friend; there is a photo of him with the Isersons at a summer gathering in the Iserson photo album.

Betty's bear, called "Cuddles," existed, and there's a photo of Betty with Cuddles (and Lee with her panda, "Max") in the Iserson family photo album. The difficulty of Japanese soldiers driving the car on this trip was my invention, but many Japanese soldiers had just recently learned to drive.

Re: MacArthur: Lee and her family had a longstanding antipathy toward MacArthur as per their comments in the chapter and later in the book.

The references to the Rape of Nanking by Japan accurately reflect the widespread knowledge of it in the PI in 1941. Lee describes the "Looters Parade," in her diary entry of 1 January 1942, and in her *Santo Tomas Talk*. (In her diary she mentions the woman in a racoon coat, but in the *Santo Tomas Talk*, she says "a man.") The dialog about "picking up Americans on Mabini Street, Padre Faura, Taft" comes from the oral history Lee provided to the Andersonville Prison Museum Project (see DVD). The instructions to pack for three days in protective custody are described in many sources, and in Lee's *Mañana Came*, p. 10.

For details of registration at Villamor Hall, see Lee Iserson to Frank Maher, 9 February 1945. The Iserson family was at Villamor for less than four hours. [Aside: Villamor Hall—built in neo-classical style in 1910s—is on Taft Avenue and was the University of the Philippines School of Fine Arts and Music Conservatory at the time; it's now the Supreme Court building. It was part of the original UP campus and located in a district called Ermita (not far from the Iserson apartment) on the large block bounded by Taft Avenue, Isaac Peral (now United Nations Avenue), Herran Street (now Pedro Gil St). It was one of the many imposing neo-classical buildings erected under American governance between 1910-1940.] The conditions at Villamor and Lee's bedraggled English teacher from Bordner (Mrs. Gewald) are factual. See Lee's description in is *Mañana Came*, p. 10. The friendly or leering guard (Haruo) is my invention.

Agnes's position at the Philippine Long Distance Telephone Company was as stated (and may explain why after the war, she sought employment at the telephone company in NYC). Re: the question: "Who will win the war?" That question was on the papers, according to Lee, who recounted her fear of what her feisty mother would write (in an oral interview for Andersonville); Lee did not know what Agnes wrote as her response, so "IJA" is my invention, but is very much in character for Agnes.

Chapter 2 – First Night

In the drive to Santo Tomas, I tried to help the reader visualize "the Pearl of the Orient," the walled and gated city of Manila in 1940. A beautiful city, an exotic blend of traditional Filipino districts (Tondo with fishermen in cascos, canals, caramatas, also fashionable business district of the Escolta), Spanish architecture (Intramuros, the walled city), impressive neoclassical buildings (U.S. inspired 1910-1930s), and art deco stunners such as the Metropolitan Theater (1930s). For a video introducion to Manila made in 1938, see "Manila, Queen of the Pacific." https://www.youtube.com/watch?v=dvpbsyNcI3I

I plotted the Iserson family's route from Villamor to Santo Tomas as down Padre Burgos Avenue, passing the National Assembly (or Legislative Building; built 1926) first and then the Post Office (1936-41) along the Pasig River. They cross Quezon Bridge (not Jones) in my account because it was more direct even though Jones is a more attractive bridge and would've made a better narrative vehicle. Both these neo-classical buildings were stunners built by the Army Corps of Engineers in the 1920s and 30s respectively.

Re: Lee's reflections on "X That Out" in children's magazines. The PI had access to the magazine *Children's Activities*, which was the predecessor to *Highlights* (the latter founded in 1946 by the same husband-wife team Gary Cleveland Myers and Caroline Clark Myers. They founded and edited *Children's Activities* in 1936 and published it for a decade before it became *Highlights. Fun with a Purpose.*)

Harry Hodges' reflections on Santo Tomas as earthquake proof: the dialogue is fictional but the architectural background factual (including Japanese expertise in this field). Dominican friar Roque Ruaño, O.P. was the architect and civil engineer who designed the building. He had a strong interest in quake-proof building, and took pains to procure key materials from Japan (rebars and one article said cement too). The Main Building consists of forty separate small towers on a continuous slab foundation; Fr. Roque made a trip to Japan in 1926 to see effects of 1923 Yokohama quake. Construction of Main Building (referred to as "the Big House" by internees), took place between 1923-1927.

Lee's reference to Cuddles and Max: As per the text, Betty did have Cuddles with her in camp, and Lee did not bring Max. As indicated above, there is a photo of the two girls with their stuffed animals in Baguio in the summer (April-May) of 1941. Lee told stories about longing for Max, and I've captured some in later chapters.

Earl Carroll (insurance executive newly transferred to Manila) was real-life, not fictional. He did look like Clark Kent. He tells the gentlemen to head to the gymnasium; the other major male housing area was the Education Building, but that was not used for housing right away; it became available to the internees later. (See Poster "Organization of the Camp," in the Santo Tomas Liberation anniversary exhibit.) The details about him in this chapter (his business background, red armband and its meaning) come from Earl Carroll's own post-war series of articles for the *Los Angeles Examiner*, "The Secret War of Santo Tomas," beginning Sunday, Aug 19, 1945. Carroll was the only member of the Executive Committee to survive the war.

"Internees ... shall feed themselves." This sign was up on January 6, 1942. See Rupert Wilkinson, *Surviving a Japanese Internment Camp: Life and Liberation at Santo Tomas* (McFarland & Co., Inc., 2014), p. 27.

Room 4 as Lee's home: This is factual. The details about dust, cobwebs, etc. are from Lee Iserson, *Santo Tomas Talk*, p. 2. I invented the sink in the room because I needed it for another incident; it was very like Agnes to get down to business and clean up.

Though Kay and Harry Hodges were real-life Iserson neighbors in the Taft Ave apartment building, the families were not close friends until late

December 1941. When U.S. forces pulled out of Manila, the Hodges invited Agnes and the girls to sleep upstairs in their apartment because there was concern about terrorizing "Sakdalistas" on the street. These were an anti-American guerilla group (Filipino), raiding prior to Japanese invasion. Every night Agnes and girls took their bedding to Hodges and slept upstairs. The couple was originally from North Carolina and Harry worked for International Harvester in Manila.

Number of women in the room: Lee says fifty-six women/children in Room 4 on that first night in her diary entry of Jan 6, 1942; Hope Miller (Leone) says forty-seven in her unpublished manuscript *Nor All Your Tears*. I went with Lee's number.

Lee's aversion to "creepy-crawlies" is factual, and in the PI there were many possible adversaries. The Philippines boasts more than five-thousand species of spiders. Spider fighting was/is a sport among boys.

The bedbug-ridden student bench incident on her first night is factual. Lee told this story many times (and it's her diary entry for January 6, 1942). When the editor I work with in New York told me to delete this incident because it slowed the pace, I decided NOT to in this family version. (Mom would never forgive me.) It might not be put in the commercial version, but I think it shows that Lee was her determined, enterprising self at age thirteen.

Placement of Lee near the window where she could see the Southern Cross: we don't know exactly where Lee and her family slept, but Hope Miller writes of being able to see the Southern Cross at night through the grille of Room 4, so I put Lee there because it gave me narrative opportunities.

Chapter 3 – The Gate

As per the text, a Red Cross Canteen was set up in Santo Tomas almost immediately. Stevens references this in Frederic H. Stevens, *Santo Tomas Internment Camp*, 1942-45. (Stratford House, Ltd. Private Edition, 1946), p. 383. Liz Lautzenhiser Irvine confirms that in her *Surviving the Rising Sun. My Family's Years in a Japanese POW Camp*. (PILiz Publishing, 2010), p. 39. Cholera and typhoid shots are documented in Wilkinson, p. 31. Stevenson puts compulsory vaccinations on February 1, 1942, p. 386.

The Gate and Package Line are documented in many sources. I relied on Lee's memories here (in Andersonville interview and personal stories). There is also a good general description of the long line and loyalty of Filipinos outside the gate, along with "irked" attitude of Japanese toward Filipinos, in A.V.H. Hartendorp, *The Santo Tomas Story*, (McGraw Hill, 1964), p.15. I took liberties with date of the Package Line here. The package line opened on January 15, but for narrative reasons I needed it a few days earlier. Also, note that the package line opened, but the package shed was not built until June 10 (Stevens, 396).

The Iserson housegirl's name was Marina Ramboa (not Rosalina), and I have a receipt for twelve pesos paid to her from camp, but by the Telephone Company, for whom Agnes worked. Re: Lee's patronizing attitude toward servants at this time. Lee, as an adult, looked back with chagrin on the fact that as a child, she was accustomed to "bossing" servants and her "amah" routinely.

Edith Naylor, whom the Iserson girls called "Grandma Naylor," was real; her biography and family life are as per Chapter 3 description. She was a key source for them on the package line.

Lee's and Rosa's conversation about cars: The Isersons owned Studebakers after the war, so I'm speculating they might have owned one pre-war. Those cars were available in the Philippines. The family that owned the Studebaker dealership (the Earl family) was in camp with Lee. I do not know which model the Isersons owned, but Studebaker did make the *President* and *Dictator* models, and this nugget ("The Dictator") was too good to pass up. In 1937, "the Dictator" model disappeared from Studebaker's line and became "the Commander."

Re: Lee's reference to Earl Carroll as a Clark Kent look-alike and a "Man of Steel." Clark Kent (and *Superman*) were introduced in *Action Comics* in 1938 and available in the PI. By 1940, the *Adventures of Superman* were broadcast by radio, and I don't know if Manila's KZRH broadcast them, but let's assume so.

Paul Davis was a dear friend of Lee's into adulthood. His nickname was "Pablo Diablo" and he had a maimed hand, but we don't know why. Lulu speculates that he lost two fingers when they were caught in a closing car door. (Ouch!) Ellen thinks his mother took thalidomide, which was given to pregnant women in the '20s and sometimes caused birth defects; Lee also speculated that. Lee, Lulu, and Ellen all affirmed that he drew attention to it with his story-telling. "It was part of his 'shtick,'" Mary Lou (Cleland) Hedrick said.

Japanese guard who skewers Lemon Meringue Pie in search of smuggled notes: that event is described in Lee's talk, *Mañana Came*, p. 15. (Lee loved telling this story….) I gave the guard the nickname "Bugs Bunny" because I've seen photos of Japanese guards who reminded me of the cartoon character. Bugs Bunny was introduced by name in the 1939 cartoon "Hare-um Scare-um" (and first uses the phrase "what's up, Doc?" in *A Wild Hare* (with Elmer Fudd) in 1940.

CHAPTER 4 - SIDE BY SIDE

Trading Harold's barong-tagalogs (dress shirts) for roast chicken (sent in by Grandma Naylor) is factual and recounted in Lee's, "Santo Tomas Talk," p. 3. The sawali (grass matting) covering on the Espana Street gate went upon January 22, 1942 (Stevens, p. 394). Agnes organizing the girls to get up to clean the bathrooms at 5:30 is factual and recounted in Lee's "Santo Tomas Talk," p. 5.

"Good Morning, Good Morning" as the wake-up music is true. Martin Meadows was able to track down the version used in camp, and it was Abe Lyman and his Californians, vocals by Rose Blane (not the Andrews Sisters as asserted by some. They recorded it after the war.)

Hope Miller was a schoolteacher from Sunapee, New Hampshire, with a mining engineer husband, who at that point was in Bataan, and she had a gravelly voice. I had the privilege of meeting and socializing with Hope numerous times in the 1980s, when she lived in Sunapee and we lived in Grantham. She wrote an unpublished memoir called *Nor All Your Tears*, in my possession.

Bedding and bedroom arrangements are as per Lee's "Santo Tomas Talk," p.3, and also recounted in a letter from Lee to Francis Maher on 13 February 1945 (in author's possession and transcribed digitally); also true was start-up of school early on, and al-fresco arrangement. See Santo Tomas Talk, p3. The incident of boys shooting spitballs from the Ed Building is in Lee's diary, January 27, 1942.

Agnes as Room Monitor: factual; there is reference to this in Lee's talks, and I also have an undated note from Room 4 ladies asking Agnes not to resign as room monitor (comes up later in the story). "First class room" declaration and accolade is factual; recounted in Lee's diary, February 20, 1942.

Radio-Music Committee and nightly music: Lee commented frequently on this; there is a good general description of the set-up in Stevens, pp. 195-200; music began nightly at 7:15 PM. Filipino friends donated mikes and turntables through the package line, Stevens indicates, p. 196-197. A.V.H. Hartendorp confirms it in his *Santo Tomas Story*, p. 29 and indicates it was set up in February 1942, spearheaded by internee A.B. Collette and Earl Hornbostel. Commandant Tomayasu limited broadcast to two hours and allowed no jazz (considered sensuous and lewd by the Japanese). The internees drew from "a library of 3000 records," according to Stevens. P. 197.

Santo Tomas School: the names of principals of Bordner (Roscoe Lautzenhiser) and American School (Lois Croft) are real; characterization of Bordner vs. American School with one (former) accepting of all races and the other exclusively Anglo, "lily-white" and the "horsey set" is how Lee described their differences anecdotally to her children, and also in a letter to Bunny Brambles in a letter after the war. (Bunny was a Bordner student and this was their shared perception. There is a class photo of Bunny and Lee together at Bordner.)

Shanties and "Shanty Towns": Lee's diary indicates that their shanty was complete by March 3, 1942 in the neighborhood of "Glamorville." Other "neighborhoods" were Jungle Town, Froggy Bottom, Hell's Kitchen, Jerkville etc. For a good general overview (with sketches and photos) see Wilkinson, *Surviving a Japanese Internment Camp*, pp. 55-60.

Camp Organization into numerous committees is described in many standard works. McCall, *Santo Tomas Internment Camp: STIC in Verse and Reverse: STIC TOONS and STIC-TISTICS* (Woodruff Printing: Lincoln Nebraska, 1945) lists committees on p. 67, and the "Code of Regulations" on pp. 72-85. "Let's show them how democracy works!" was also an authentic slogan.

Incident of Execution of Escaped Prisoners: details of the execution are taken from Earl Carroll's account published in *Los Angeles Examiner*, August 19, 1945. See also Stevens, pp. 241-245. Lee always insisted that the sailors were picked up in a bar (as per her account here), but I can find no other confirmation of that, so I have Bunny denying that it was true. Nellie's dad did not witness the execution. I put that in for dramatic effect.

The Saturday Night variety show: This show is a composite from the author's imagination. The first shows were held in the patios behind the Main Building, as per text. Liz Lautzenhiser, indicates West Patio, p. 50. Also see Stevens, pp. 187-195, and Wilkinson, p. 32 and also his Chapter 5. Eventually the "Little Theater Under the Stars" was constructed in front of the Main Building, and shanties occupied the two patios. Dave Harvey was the emcee and his real name was David Harvey MacTurk. On the CNAC website there is a video clip of him arranging a microphone for some singers on the stage after the liberation. Stevens (p. 389) indicates that there was a floor show on Mar 14, 1942.

Lee in her oral interview, recalls a fabulous Chinese dance troupe (from Shanghai) swinging from windows, but I don't know if it was this show. See also her *Santo Tomas Talk*, p. 6. Tomayasu did attend the shows (Stevens). The song "Side by Side" (by Harry Woods) was written in 1925 and recorded in 1927; it was a major hit in the 1930s. The performance of it at this time and in this way is from my imagination. Other lyrics for "Side by Side" include the verses as sung (in the 50s) by Martin and Lewis: *Oh the road gets a little bit bumpy/ And our nerves get a little bit jumpy /We beef and complain /But we remain Side by side. /So Please allow us to sum up/ If ever a problem should come up /We'll fight like before /But after the war, we're side by side.*

Chapter 5 – Leonore's Suite

Lee recalling Baguio: Baguio was the summer resort of choice for many American ex-pats in Manila. The details of the Baguio stay are based on Elizabeth Iserson's essay, "Philippines Early Years." The Iserson family summered there annually. The family always had a piano in the apartment, but I invented the piano in their bungalow.

"Honey Bee Cake" - Lee raved about the "Honey Bee Cake" that could be purchased at a local Manila bakery (I don't know the specific bakery; Tasa de Oro was name of one. Eileen Klee Sweeney found the decadent recipe for sugary, buttery, chocolate delight at http://www.foodnetwork.com/recipes/nigella-lawson/honey-bee-cake-recipe.html?oc=linkback); or see her April 11, 2014 email to me.

Facts and Rumors about Bataan: Seventy-six thousand soldiers and twenty-six thousand civilians surrendered in Bataan. See Norman and Norman, *Tears in the Darkness*, 163. They were marched in waves north and not all, but probably 28,000. I have quite a long email exchange trying to document the date that the term "Death March" was first used. Though rumors flew in camp, the term was probably not in use before January 1944. It was at that time that accounts by a survivor (William Dyess) were published in *Life Magazine* and the *Chicago Tribune*. (See my email exchange "The Term Death March" 15 Sep 2016.)

Impregnability of Corregidor: Lee spoke often about her father's confidence in the impregnability of Corregidor. Harold's note to Lee is mostly fictional but one letter from Harold to Lee (November 28, 1941) signs off with "a flock of kisses." I tried to approximate his tone. Lee speaks of news of Bataan's fall (April 3) being followed by an earthquake. The quake was April 8, 1942, five days after the fall of Bataan. See Stevens, p. 392. Stevens also indicates that heavy rains and flooding continued through June, delaying the opening of school, p. 396.

Classrooms on the fourth floor Chemistry Lab is documented in many sources but specifically in Lee's Santo Tomas Talk, p. 4. Lee also recounts the tossing of water bombs. Names of teachers given here (Fr. Monte, Mrs. Maynard, etc.) are actual teachers in the school, but I do not know the physical placement of their classes. "Cuthbert," their math teacher, was beloved by them all and his real name was Carroll Livingston. I do not know the origin of the nickname, and invented this connection, though I might be right about it.

Package shed and arrival of Ghirardelli's cocoa tin sent by Grandma Naylor: these are factual. Package shed construction began on June 10, 1942 (Stevens, 396). The valuable tin of cocoa was indeed the origin of the family fudge business, which was an important cash resource for them, though I don't know the exact date of arrival. Lee recounts it in her *Mañana Came* talk, p. 13. The camp food situation is as per text. The Japanese took over responsibility for feeding the camp over from the Red Cross on July 1, 1942, employing red armband internee buyers; financing as per above at 70 centavos per internee in Japanese occupation pesos, is documented in Stevens, 397. Filipino vendors were allowed in August-Sept 1942. See Teedie Cowie Woodcock, *Behind the Sawali: Santo Tomas in Cartoons, 1942-1945* (Cenografix: Greensboro, NC, 2000). p. 45, but I scooted them in a month earlier here ie July.

Lee's feeling about her formal name "Leonore" is as per the description in this book: "a burden of a name."

Leonore's Suite (the musical composition written by her father) present in camp: This is an instance of dramatic license that I took. The music was real: Harold Iserson did write *Leonore's Suite* for Lee's twelfth or thirteenth birthday; not sure which; and it survived the war, but perhaps not 5020 Glenwood Drive, our childhood home. It used to reside in our family piano bench. We sibs (children of Lee) don't know where it is now. I invented the little note written by Harold for dramatic purposes later in the story. My brother Dennis and I both recall it had Rachmaninoff-like echoes, and Lee told us Rachmaninoff was one of her father's favorite composers. I am not sure whether Lee physically had this piece with her in camp or if Grandma Naylor kept it and gave it back to her after liberation; I assume the former, but use of it in the story is for narrative reasons. Rachmaninoff did play at Carnegie Hall on 12 January 1920, and Harold and Agnes were in New York City at the time. I do not know if Harold attended that concert.

The practice room(s): my own invention; there was at least one piano in camp, and a small orchestra. Hope playing for Lee in the practice room, is of course fictional, but Hope did play the piano.

Chapter 6 – Lulu

Date of Lulu's arrival: The Cleland family did not arrive in Santo Tomas until December 19, 1942 (Lulu was one of 148 new internees from Cebu). This is indicated in Stevens, pp. 309 and 405; also Liberation Bulletin dates Cebu internees arrival at that time), but I needed Lulu in this story sooner.

I also accelerated the dates for opening of the "Little Theater Under the Stars" mentioned later in this chapter. All indications are that the Little

Theater was not set up until late 1942 (Dec). The Japanese gave permission to set up shanties in the Main Building Patios Oct 19, 1942 (Stevens, 402), making it too crowded to present shows in patios. First reference for a movie in Little Theater Under the Stars is December 23, 1942 (Stevens 191), and then permanent establishment for shows from January 29, 1943 forward. (Stevens, 192.) Because Lulu didn't arrive till December, she would have seen these things (upon her actual arrival). The circumstances of her arrival (spotting Lee from the truck) are true to Lulu's memory, who insisted that from the moment their eyes met, they were friends. "She just took me over." "She took me under her wing and showed me around." (See Hedrick, "My Experiences during World War II in Prison Camps," p. 2).

Lulu's housing situation in the early part (at the Annex with her mother, but later moving to the Big House) is as per the text. Bed netting and "fixing the beds:" That was the term used. See photo in Liz Irvine's *Surviving the Rising Sun*, p. 198.

"Braised beef for dinner:" Santo Tomas menu from February 1942 indicated stew, braised beef, boiled beef, or macaroni and cheese.

Lulu's sense that she had entered a country club i.e. Santo Tomas was so far superior to their experience in Cebu was true (as per oral interview) and see Hedrick, "My Experiences During World War II in Prison Camps," p. 2 (she saw Santo Tomas as "the Ritz" upon her arrival, a sense shared by many bedraggled prisoners from other camps who arrived at STIC over the years.

Internees being photographed and turning their backs: The Japanese propaganda arm "Kazamaro Uno" (Press Bureau of the Imperial Japanese Army) sponsored an article on Santo Tomas (implying lovely conditions there) in the *Shanghai Evening Post* probably late July 1942. Author Mervyn Brown reviews the "happy and contented conditions prevailing among the little cluster of allied internees in Santo Tomas." It's clearly a piece of propaganda and is in my article file http://corregidor.org/book_uno/chapter_uno_10.htm

Encountering Haruo: I modeled the physical appearance of this character on a (very nice) former Japanese student of mine named "Haruo," whom I met (and taught) when I was when teaching English as a Foreign Language at Boston University in the 1970s. He was tall, kind, and quite the gentleman. I've learned that the name "Haruo" means "Springtime Man" in Japanese and its numerological meaning is "Helper; Big Brother-Big Sister type."

Chapter 7 – Operation Arigato

Lulu's new residence in the Big House in Room Number 33: is accurate, as was the fact that Lee called Lulu's mom "Mim."

Weevil Duty: for a 1942 sketch of this activity, see Donald Dang's in "Commemorating the Fiftieth Anniversary of STIC," p. 50. The typhoon referenced occurred on September 30, 1942. See Ansie Lee. Sperry, *Running with the Tiger* (2009) for a description, p. 197.

Lee's grade of C in General Science is real: Lee's ninth grade report card from STIC (transcribed and in my files; I have hard copy) shows that she struggled with General Science, taught by W.L. Brooke. She got two Ds in the first two quarters, but pulled off a B and A in third and fourth quarters. (Go, Mom!)

Child internees adopting "sallies" as pets: accurate; See Michael McCoy, ed. *Through My Mother's Eyes*, (Strategic Book Publishing, 2008) p. 35. Jean-Marie Heskett was 7 or 8 when she did this and claims to have had her "Sally" for a year.

Lee calling her friends *Brainwave*: Lee's letters to her friends post-war use this expression a lot; she'll poke fun at herself and say "Brainwave that I am!"

Description of Zamboanga: comes from an Army nurse journal that I read and now cannot find! Sorry...

Arrival of Army Nurses: in early July (either 2 or 3), 1942, sixty-eight army nurses came into camp (Stevens, p. 397) Several were assigned to Room 4 and Lee had great admiration for these "girls," whom she said were the only ones to consistently work 8-12 hours per day in camp. Their story was recently retold (very well) for young adults in Mary Cronk Farrell, *Pure Grit: How American World War II Nurses Survived Battle and Prison Camp in the Pacific* (Abrams, 2014) pp. 80-109 deal with their experience in Santo Tomas.

The "What's Jewish?" conversation about Lee's Dad: Mary Lou Cleland Hedrick told me this story about herself (poking fun at her youthful ignorance) in her May 2010 oral interview in my files DM520019 WMA; text transcript on p. 10.

The story of Agnes Hanagan going to New York in late 1920s and living with her brother Dan is true, but Agnes took the stenography classes in Utica and then went to NYC. The description of how she met Harold (applying for a job; third floor elevator opening) at his father's firm is true and based on an oral interview with Agnes (on CD in the late 1970s). Lee likened her father's physical appearance to the then-famous actor Don Ameche on several occasions. (Don Ameche had the lead in the 1930s film *Happy Landings*, among others. She also listed Don Ameche as her favorite actor in her Autograph book of 1944).

Lee calling her grandfather "A.S." -- is accurate and because of the tension between father and son over business dealings, Lee said they often pronounced it as if with an additional "S." Abraham Samuel (dad) set up the plant in Manila and sent Harold to manage it.

The popular song "Toot Toot Tootsie (Goodbye)" was a 1923 Al Jolson song about a fellow who watches his girl leave on a train – hence the toot-toots.

Lee's description of her parents' honeymoon is accurate and corroborated by photos and a taped (now CD) account from Agnes Iserson.

The threat of maggots/flies in camp: A female fly lives one month, during which time she lays from 500 to 2000 eggs in batches of about 75-150 at a time. A day after the eggs are laid, maggots appear. It takes 3-5 days for them to morph into flies. Mrs. Elsie Harrington was the wife of the British Consul and in charge of at least one of the rooms in the Annex (maybe not the kitchen). See Robin Prising, *Manila Goodbye* (Houghton Mifflin: Boston, 1975) pp. 73-74. Most fly swatters of this time were wire mesh with either wooden or metal handles. The "Got-Ya" flyswatter (mesh and metal) was made in England.)

Lulu's description of her father's "Catholic protection:" and his background are from an oral interview with Mary Louella Cleland Hedrick in May 2010, p. 9 of transcript in which she recounts her dad's renewed connection with his Catholic roots before going off to war.

"Bluebells are Singing Horses" does come from Nancy Drew's *Passport to Larkspur Lane* (published in 1930) and the exact line is "Bluebells are now singing horses." Lee and Lulu were both avid readers, and it's hard to imagine they hadn't read these books, as they were standard pre-war fare for girls.

CHAPTER 8 – SUPER GIRL

"Flossie" Flatland: was Alice Flatland and she was Agnes's faithful assistant in the fudge business (nickname: "Flossie Two-Feathers" for reasons I do not know; Flossie was a fellow roomie in Room 4, and her young daughter Janet occasionally assisted. I had a phone conversation with Janet (Sue Flatland Trigg) at one point. See her video and oral interview at http://memory.loc.gov/diglib/vhp/bib/loc.natlib.afc2001001.21424

The name "Superior Fudge" and the details for the fudge making process come from Lee's *Mañana Came* talk, p. 13-14.

Betty and dysentery: the specific incident here I invented to advance the plot and introduce a complication to "Operation Arigato," but it is not improbable and very much in keeping with the health dangers at the time. Stevens reports generally good health among children (result of preventive campaigns for clean water, food, pest control, and incentives for clean rooms) but two alarms: one for outbreak of amoebic dysentery "traced to kitchen carriers and lack of kitchen cleanliness;" another alarm from dengue fever (mosquitos); Stevens, 117; my choice of November for outbreak is arbitrary. Some of the sense of emergency is gleaned from Grace C. Nash's account of her three-year-old suffering with dysentery (she says bacillary) in April 1942. It's on pp 56-59 in *That We May Live* (Shano Publishers: Scottsdale, AZ, 1984). Lee always indicated that Betty was more prone to bouts of disease in camp than she was. Lee's concern about contracting bacillary dysentery from human excrement is legitimate. The gloves in the closet are my invention, but their preciousness and scarcity at this period is not. Closely fitting latex rubber gloves were expensive, hard to come by, and were not widely used till the 1960s. Still, you do see 1940 advertisements for "latex gloves" by the Seamless Rubber Company in Connecticut – apparently for household use. See http://www.historybyzim.com/2015/08/testing-and-packaging-latex-gloves-1940/

Lulu dubbing Lee "Super Girl" – is her invention. As indicated, Superman comics were published in their recognizable form in 1938. "Superwoman" was first introduced in Action Comics in 1943. In that episode Lois Lane (who actually looked a bit like Lee Iserson) dreams she gained superpowers from a blood transfusion from Superman. The 1943 cartoon image of Lois Lane as Superwoman in Action Comics is on wiki. "Supergirl" didn't arrive till 1959.

The details of getting a medical pass, leaving camp for Philippine General Hospital are based on camp procedures at the time.

The "climb and drink story" is true and recounted in an oral interview with Mary Louella Cleland Hedrick, (May 2010; p. 6 of transcript). I gave it a title ("climb and drink") but Lulu delighted in pointing out silly ways they entertained themselves.

Chapter 9 – Southern Cross

The 1942 Thanksgiving performance of "Ballad of William Sycamore" is based on unpublished memoir by Hope Miller Leone, *Nor All Your Tears*, pp. 35-36. The name "Freddy Hopkins" is fictional.

Our new Commandant Akida Kodaki: Commandant Tomayasu (referenced previously) was succeeded by Tsurumi (Feb 1942 to Aug 1942); Akida Kodaki took over the camp in September 1942; there is some disagreement about how strict he was; Lee's letters describe him as one who liked Americans and wanted to get a job in the US after the war 15 Feb 1945; James Ward indicates he was strict (see his article, p. 170).

Lee's bedtime memories of her family and their pre-war financial straits:

are based on Lee's own stories. The details of the embroidery business, making samples for Bonwit Teller, and plant closing are in Lee Iserson, *Mañana Came*, pp. 2-4. Lee's recollection of feeling deprived because all their clothes (embroidered dresses) were custom-made and she couldn't buy clothes off the rack in a department store is factual and Lee used to laugh at herself for this. Agnes and the girls' radio stint as "Senga Naganah" and for "Jingle Swing" are detailed in the *Mañana Came* text, p. 5. Re: the Nash Program: Grace Nash (an excellent violinist) was interned with them in camp.

Re: newly founded KZRH radio: if a radio station were east of the Mississippi River, the first call letter was W. West of the Mississippi was K. (KZRH radio in Manila has been DZRH since Philippine independence in 1946.) KZRH in Manila began broadcasting on July 15, 1939.

"Jingle Swing" in 1940: lyrics are accurate and from Lee Iserson, *Mañana Came*, p. 4. This program might have been in 1939 and not 1940, but Harold still worked for the radio in 1940 so I put it there. When Eileen and I visited DZRH in Manila in 2009, they could not find records of their 1939-40 programming.

The story of family financial decline (from San Francisco del Monte villa to Taft Avenue apartment) is accurate. Thanks to Curtis Brooks I have the Iserson family phone number, which was listed in the Manila directory under Agnes's name (Mrs. H.R. Iserson) probably because she worked for the phone company and got a price break. Their phone number was 5-70-76.

The name "Warlito" (which I used for their family driver) was the name of the driver Eileen and I had when we visited Manila in 2009.

Thanksgiving Day 1942: The weather was excellent on November 25, 1942; a religious service, as well as Thanksgiving Day performance, took place in the Father's Garden. (Woodcock, 52) The acrostic is mostly factual as well. The letters I and G are accurate couplets (Hope Miller, *Nor All Your Tears*, p, 7); I invented N.

Learning of Harold Iserson's death: Harold died on February 24, 1942 according to Lee's diary – just weeks after Lee and her family's internment. Lee did not find out about her father's death by overhearing. She has recorded two different circumstances: learning of it on January 4, 1943, when Lucie Tohl (pre-war German neighbor in Manila) brought news to camp (this is in Lee's diary), but also indicates Agnes learned of his death from a Maryknoll priest when out of camp on a medical pass (see chronology) in January 1943. In Lee's letter to Frank Maher, 10 February 1945, she indicates that Agnes and Betty found out "on the Outside" when they were out on a pass to see Gramma Naylor. "It was easy for us to see her because we had it put on the records that she was our grandmother. Mommy & Betty were only out of camp the time we found out about Daddy. As you probably know he died of pneumonia in Zamboanga in February of '42. That was 6 days before the Japs got there. We have often thanked God that he went then because the treatment those men received was much worse than ours. He was sent to Zamboanga in Nov of 41, but I will not write any details about that. It would never pass the censor! You see Daddy's friend who was with him came to (*censored; i.e. this word is literally cut out of the letter in a neat rectangle*) from Zam. In a banca (P.I. = canoe) & he lost almost everything. He had the army transcript with the announcement of his death adhesived on him. He came in a terrific storm and it took him 5 weeks! He had to stop at almost all the islands & you know the P.I. is almost all small islands. We didn't find out about Daddy til Jan. of 43 tho." The family later learned of Harold's conversion, when a (newly interned) priest saw the name of Iserson on the prison list. The priest (Fr. Rosario) had been in Mindanao with Harold and came to tell Agnes of Harold's last days and his conversion. The conversion is described by the Jesuit priest Foie Ma. Rosario, S.J. in a letter to Agnes on June 13, 1947. (Copy in author's possession) He administered the sacrament of baptism, but records from the parish of Zamboanga were destroyed in the war. (See my Letter file, "Jesuit to Nana on Harold's death").

Re: Harold's death from pneumonia: respiratory diseases are not uncommon in the PI, and antibiotics were not easily available. Penicillin, the antibiotic most frequently prescribed for pneumonia nowadays was pioneered by Alexander Fleming in the 1930s in London (discovered 1928), but the drug was not mass-produced until after 1945, when its chemical structure was clearly understood. Pneumonia (a bacterial infection) was until that time frequently fatal, and even today there are high rates of mortality from pneumonia in the PI. (38% in a recent study)

Re: Betty longing to go the Rendezvous Café with her father: Elizabeth Iserson described this family ritual of going to Rendezvous café after a movie, in her Creative Writing piece "Philippines, Early Days." The real name of the restaurant was Magnolia Rendezvous; also mentioned in Tiongson article below). Betty describes seeing and loving Sonja Henie, Rogers and Astair, etc.

For a description of the Manila Metropolitan theater of that time see, Nicanor G. Tiongson, *"Manila Metropolitan Theater Reopens Today,"* text of 1978 Manila Metropolitan Theater Reopening Souvenir; this article is in the public domain and is on Wiki; http://en.wikipedia.org/wiki/File:1978METarticle1.jpg

"In the Mood" was 1940 chart topper. Gertrude Lawrence's "Someone to Watch Over Me" was released by Columbia in 1927.

Chapter 10 - Halo-Halo

Banning halter tops and short-shorts for women: accurate; see Johansen, *So Far From Home*, p. 60 and Hartendorp, p. 83. Shorts could be no higher than six inches above the knee according to Lee Iserson Klee, "Santo Tomas Talk," p. 5.

Japanese not employing regular army for administration of Santo Tomas, and instead relying on former consular staff and businessmen: accurate; for example Kodaki the Comandant at this time was in the consular service and continued to serve as Chief of External Affairs in Manila during the period; he came to camp only three times per week. His second in command Kuroda, was a Shanghai businessman engaged in importation of machinery before the war. See Hartendorp, p. 83.

Hobby Fairs in STIC were common; I fudged the date a little here by putting it in December; One occurred on October 12, 1942. See Sperry, *Running with the Tiger*, p. 198. The items for sale in my text are ones that Sperry mentioned or photos of items that I've seen in various other books. (Bill Phillips had a carved bamboo mug in his possession that he got from such a fair.).

Purchasing a license from Internee Executive Committee in order to sell items in camp: this was true for selling fudge as well. See Stevens, pp. 37-38, Hartendorp, p. 115 and Johansen, p. 59.

Prices for Iserson family fudge are recounted by Lee Iserson Klee, *Mañana Came*, p. 14.

The camp's garbage trucks were run by a Brit, and the trucks were named "Rose" and "Any other name." See Iserson, "Santo Tomas Talk," p. 5.

Shakespeare in camp: Lee references a Shakespearean actress who was imprisoned with them and taught history and literature ("Santo Tomas Talk," p. 4 and Andersonville interview). Lee's letters after camp include many quotations from Shakespeare.

Camp population was at 3263 on December 31, 1942: Stevens, p, 406; he writes "serious housing problem exists." The Japanese interned more than a hundred of civilians from the Philippine Sulphur Springs resort in early February 21 (Liberation Bulletin); nearly a hundred nurses from fallen Corregidor and Mindanao (arriving in stages from March to July), and a new group of civilians from Cebu in Dec 19.

Bill Phillips and his shoeshine business: accurate in specifics as per my oral interview with Bill Phillips on May 2, 2010, p. 9 of transcript.

Tagalog slang "halo-halo" comes from oral interview with Lulu, May 1, 2010; p. 6 of transcript and see "The Romantic Affairs of Lulubelle and the Great Eckenboy." (p. 1 "as we say in the PI 'halo-halo' – all mixed up.)

Chapter 11 – O Holy Night

Christmas preparations 1942: concerts were sung by men's and women's choruses on December 22 (see Stevens, p. 405); specific tunes are my speculation. "Santa Claus is Coming to Town" and "Winter Wonderland" were both written in 1934. The Guy Lombardo version of "Winter Wonderland" is 1934.

Lee and family in Utica memories. I put their visit in 1937 (because for dramatic purposes, I wanted Lee to have a memory of seeing the Golden Gate Bridge, which was not completed until April 17, 1937). Their actual visit was in 1934. The memories (her father calling Harold "Earl" and both girls' response to cold) are as per oral interview with Agnes Iserson (on CD, date uncertain, but in the late 1970s). Lulu calling Agnes "Aggie" is true as per oral interview with M.L.Clelan Hedrick, May 2009.

The start of movies at Santo Tomas (December 23, 1942) with *The Feminine Touch* (Don Ameche and Rosalind Russell) is accurate. See Stevens, p. 405.

The version of *Leonore's Suite* played by Haruo resenbles Rachmaninoff's Piano Concerto #2. The description of Christmas activities at Santo Tomas can be found in Cates, *Drainpipe Diary*, p. 141 and Hartendorp, *Santo Tomas Story*, p 204. See also Stevens, p. 405 for Green Bay Packers vs Bears; Bill P. did play for Green Bay as per his oral interview with me.

Chapter 12 – Spread Your Wings

Father Kelley was real, and the gospel for the day (John 21:18) is accurate as per the St. Andrew's Missal. I am grateful to Father Damian Kearney, O.S.B. for lending me this missal.

Lee recalling the hardships of 1943 is from her "Santo Tomas Talk," p. 9. The smuggled note from men in Cabanatuan is as per Cates, *Drainpipe Diary*, p. 172. Japanese flying overhead in formation on New Year's day is also from Cates, p. 145.

Isersons receiving extra financial help from the Philippine Long Distance Telephone Company (Agnes's former employer) is accurate, but I invented the pretext of Agnes sending her oldest daughter into Manila to get it from Grandma Naylor. Lee indicated that she got out of camp various times in the first two years (Lee Iserson to Jane Hanagan, February 14/15, 1945). This foray into Manila was a way of introducing the reader to the dangers of wartime Manila, and to advance Lee's growth as a character.

"They even parade on the Luneta:" The Luneta, an expanse of green park and parade ground was built by the US Army Corps of Engineers in 1900 – filling in a mosquito-ridden moat that flanked the walled old city of Intramuros. Malaria plummeted as a result.

Japanese military picking up STIC "red-armed guys" in Manila: occurred on March 22, 1943, according to Cates, p. 158.

"Clobbered at Guadalcanal" – Gaudalcanal was secured by U.S. forces in February 1943. Major General Kiyotake Kawaguchi, IJA Commander, 35th Infantry Brigade at Guadalcanal described it as "the graveyard of the Japanese army." Robin Prising, *Manila Goodbye*, describes this tightening of security in Manila by angry Japanese in 1943 in retribution, pp. 93ff.

Bill's dad and the shortwave radio: This is factual; see Bill Phillips interview, Folder A, DM520025 – 8:10-19; Bill says his father was a radio engineer; helped design and build the communication towers and transmitting stations; he surrendered as a civilian (Navy gave him that option); they had a hidden radio; see 49:24 in this same recording.

Juergen Goldhagen and Hans Hoeflein: were German Jews in Manila who were not interned. *Manila Memories*, ed. by Juergen R. Goldhagen (Shearsman Books Ltd: United Kingdom, 2008) is the source for these details. I've used names of real people; Juergen was left a train set by one of his American friends and did attend the American School (see p. 24; he was taught by Paul Davis's mother at American School.) The train set was actually given to Juergen by interned American classmate Robert Hinds, p. 45, not Paul Davis.

Incident of Ginny McKinney (housing arrangements and washing menstrual rags) was based on my oral interview with her in May 2010. Ginny was two to three years older than Lee and Lulu; Folder D DM520030; 2:40. Ginny McKinney Glass turned tennis pro after earning degrees in English and then in library science from Columbia. In 1989 she was the number one player in the world in the 60-and-over division. She did not take up tennis until 1951 – inspired by the Hitchcock thriller 'Strangers on a Train,' that had some tennis footage.

Paul's line "What do you think I will do—kill her?": In the thriller *Suspicion*, Cary Grant plays a sinister husband who conspires to kill his wife but denies the intent.

Chapter 13 – Purple Smudge on the Pearl

This specific excursion to Manila is fictional, but Lee recounts that "I was out with some Spanish friends in Sept. '41 for 2 weeks," and "I was out on a day pass about 10 times to visit an old American lady who has become our Foster Grandmother." See Lee Iserson to Francis Maher, 10 February 1945.

The details about charcoal-powered buses and bedbugs in the wooden bus seats are found in Juergen Goldhagen, ed. *Manila Memories*, p. 55. The eerie quiet of the city at this time is commented in that volume too.

The "futuristic" Jai-Alai Club (completed in 1940) was a triumph of art deco, and pre-war Sky Room was as described. This building was used as Kempeitai Headquarters after the Japanese occupation. The white armband Lee describes with red characters can be seen at. http://en.wikipedia.org/wiki/Kempeitai#Uniform. Jai-alai was a passion in the Philippines and the swoop of the cylindrical building was supposed to echo the speed of the game.

Grandma Naylor's Home: location is fictional. I do not know what neighborhood Edith Naylor lived in during the war, but Malate seemed like a good choice because it was distant enough not to be appropriated by the Japanese, but close enough to reach Manila easily by carretela. Many of the details for her garden (avocado, mango, papaya trees) are drawn from Roderick Hall's account of his life in this district during the war. See Juergen Goldhagen, ed., *Manila Memories*, p. 62. Alfonso is fictional; his clothing is drawn from films I've watched of Filipino working men during the war.

Flash Gordon references: The comic book hero, Flash Gordon, was introduced in 1934, and films followed by 1936. The two earlier films Juergen refers to were *Flash Gordon: Spaceship to the Unknown* (1936); *Flash Gordon: The Deadly Ray from Mars* (1938) The film *The Purple Death from Outer Space* was released in 1940. Hans Walser reports that those films continued to show during the war. See Goldhagen, ed., p. 69.

Paul and Lee meeting Juergen and Ramon: the meeting is fictional, but the details about Manila during the war that we learn in the context of their conversation are all accurate. Juergen Goldhagen was, as mentioned, real, but he was four years younger than Paul Davis; these details (about appearance, nationality, Judaism, and background are factual). See his *Manila Memories*. Ramon Ayala is an invention, but the Isersons had Spanish neighbors when they lived in San Francisco del Monte, and they played a nightly concert outdoors, and I wanted a romantic interest for Lee down the road....

"White bread had disappeared from camp." No wheat flour was available in camp after April 1942 according to the Liberation Bulletin. Rice flour was available till May 1944.

The details of theaters operating in Manila during the war (Capitol and Lyric) are from Juergen Goldhagen, ed., *Manila Memories*, p. 67.

Emperor Tojo's visit to Manila and the Gratitude Rallies: Tojo visited Manila on May 4, 1943 with a large parade and forced attendance of students at Gratitude Rally. See Robin Prising, p. 96. Hans Hoeflein also recounts compulsory attendance at gratitude rallies (one on February 8, 1943) in Goldhagen, ed. *Manila Memories*, p.65 and 67. He recounts the kids in his school joking "Nippon-Go, American Come." Ibid., p. 65.

Leonore's Suite 609

The stew Grandma served: the small purple eggplant is known as "talong;" "pechay" is bok choy.

Lee's conversation with Valentina re: "comfort women" and abuse of women: comes from different sources. There was a "comfort house" on Dakota and Herran streets in Manila for Japanese officers. (See Goldhagen, *Manila Memories*, p. 63 – mostly Chinese and Korean women abused.) The story above of the fourteen-year-old Filipina "rewarded" for performance of a Japanese song is the story of Felicidad de los Reyes, "Japanese Comfort Women: One Woman's Story," as told to Anthony Brown. There is a similar account from Maria Rosa Luna Henson who was held for nine months. One academic source (for the 200,000 women abused by the IJA) is Yoshiaki Yoshimi, (Suzanne O'Brien, translator) *Comfort Women* (Columbia University, 2001). I consider it an extraordinary blessing that there were no reported incidents of sexual abuse at Santo Tomas.

Chapter 14 – Return to Oz

Lee's dream of rebuking governess and hearing Rosalina coconut-skating: Lee often poked fun at herself for assuming at age ten that her governess should warm up her hands up before helping her dress; she also described the "coconut skating" to us, but a description can also be found in Bruce Johansen, *So Far From Home*, p. 16

Lee's recollection of her tenth birthday party is based on her own memories and Elizabeth Iserson's description of shooting air rifles at Lucky Strike soda cans in "Philippines: Early Years." There is also a photo of the cake and party in the Iserson album.

Many of the details of the Quiapo market scene are drawn from Robin Prising describing the marketplace at Paco that he and his mother visited during the war. Prising, *Manila Goodbye*, 92-94, and also from Juergen Goldhagen's account of the Quiapo market, *Manila Memories*, pp. 51-52.

Paul's theft of cigarettes and *Time* magazine from a Japanese merchant: fictional event, but the two brands of cigarettes for sale in the PI in 1943 were Akebono and Pirate. Both were much prized. As for the *Time* Magazine theft, see the cover; Feb 15, 1943 of Osami Nagano of Japan (Naval Chief) with menacing "cartoon-ized" tank in background.

Netsuke began life in the 1600s as useful little toggles on cords that cinched the well-dressed Japanese gentleman's silken pouch. By 1700, they had become intricately carved works of art and pricey pieces of male jewelry. Whimsical animals, grimacing monsters and mythological beasts all dangled from the waist of the well-dressed Japanese gent.

Chapter 15 – Starlight Arena

Lee speculating on her mother's "smoothness" and ability to deceive: gives me an opening to tell Agnes's story of sowing youthful wild oats in another novel. The contrast with Mim is invited by Lulu's recounting of Mim's breakdown in Cebu (in her oral interview, May 2010, transcript, p. 7.

The incident of Lee and Lulu leading an April Fool's Day prank, by getting the entire high school to cut class and stand on lawn outside on April 1, 1943 is accurate. See Mary Louella Cleland oral interview DM520019, 31:40. Transcript, p. 11. Roscoe Lautzenhiser's concern about cutting rice ration further is justified. In April 1943, as privation became more acute, the Japanese increasingly used a cut in rice rations as a punishment for infractions.

The gift of a red autograph book: This autograph book exists (and is in author's possession); it was a birthday present to Lee on this date. It was, however, from Lucie Tohl (a German friend on the outside). It's been very valuable to me. Lee filled it with lots of helpful information: names of her teachers for all four years, her classmates, monickers of her friends, and names of her sports (basketball and baseball) teams and their captains.

Boxing-Smoker specifics: the competitions described here were held in July 1943 (See Dang, p.67). An interview with Ellen Thomas Phillips produced a program for the Starlight Arena Boxing Smoker on February 26, 1943. Boys as little as forty-two pounds competed in categories of Atom, Electron, Flea, Gnat, Ant, and Moth weight. Ellen recalled Jimmy Rockwell squaring off against Curtis Brooks.

Men being sent to Los Baños to build new facility: Eight hundred men and twelve camp nurses departed Santo Tomas in May 14, 1943. See Cates, *Drainpipe Diary*, p. 165. Also see Hartendorp, *The Santo Tomas Story*, Chap 9, "The Threat of Los Baños," pp. 147-168. Text for Public Address system announcement is on p 147-148. Bunny's father and brothers were sent there.

The match-up of Tommy McKinney vs Danny MacDonald: is fictional. Tommy existed and was an excellent boxer (brother of Ginny McKinney Glass; described to me in her oral interview), but Danny is fictional. I developed this scene to show the ongoing existence of some racial tensions in the camp. The reflections on why boxing was deemed such an important sport for young men came from Fr. Julian Stead, O.S.B., who coached boxing at Portsmouth Abbey for many years.

Chapter 16 - Lessons from Ovid

Arrival of priests: approximately seventy priests arrived in June and July, and partly as a result of the Japanese occupying the Jesuit-run Ateneo in late June. See Hartendorp, p. 154. Overcrowding loomed large as the greatest camp threat during this time period, and it's one of the reasons that many STIC men even volunteered to help build Los Baños (about 70 kilometers from STIC). Father Robert Sheridan was, as per text, a Maryknoll priest and later a family friend, who visited us in Buffalo after the war. He was a handsome guy! The Maryknoll archives has a good obituary for Fr. Sheridan at http://maryknollmissionarchives.org/index.php/history/1308-sheridanfrroberte?p=2

The teen obsession with bridge: Lee says she played "non-stop" through 1943. Bridge gained new popularity in the 1920s and 30s when Harold S. Vanderbilt (of Newport and America's Cup fame) introduced a new contract bidding system that supplanted the old "auction bridge." He published three eagerly devoured books on the subject – the first in 1929 (*Contract Bridge: Bidding and the Club Convention*) and the next in 1930 (*The New Contract Bridge*), still another in 1933 (*Contract By Hand Analysis: A Synopsis of 1933 Club Convention Bidding*). The popularity of the game expanded worldwide, and Lulu says she knew how to play bridge by the time she was nine. Lulu has told me that she and Lee played the newly popular Blackwood Convention rules, first published in the mid-thirties, and used almost universally by the mid-forties. Incident regarding "Catholic Bridge Group" – fictional, but apparently was so in character that Lulu indicated to me she was glad "your mom was writing down this stuff." She told me she had a very strong curiosity about and attraction to the Catholic faith and almost converted.

Mrs. Maynard and her library work: all true, including the examples (which are far more numerous than the ones listed above). Leila Maynard recorded her experience in a wonderfully informative article called "Dusty Sanctuary," which was reprinted by Santo Tomas Library in 2001 when it reissued its Catalogue of Rare Books. Vol. 1, (1492-1600) as Appendix B. I have this article as a Word Document in my files. She did not, however, regale the girls with her tales. Lulu and Nellie don't recall that she even had this job, though they rave about her as a teacher.

Patron saints of cards: St. Balthasar is actually the patron saint of playing card manufacturers for reasons given, and is sometimes linked with players of card games. The first playing cards (in Europe) came from China (eighth or ninth century Tang dynasty), making their way west through Arabia, entering Europe in the fourteenth century. They entered with the Gypsies, and in the Middle Ages, Europeans believed the gypsies came from Egypt – ergo Balthasar was chosen as the patron. The deck currently used in bridge (52 cards, Ace high) is a nineteenth century refinement of many earlier versions

"Miss Issue Tissue" – Lee references this duty in her "Santo Tomas Talk," p. 5. I gave her the task in this chapter, but don't know if Lee ever did it.

"Lessons from Ovid" essay (the specific one) is my invention but in our oral interview I pressed Ellen Phillips about any one thing that may have bothered her about school in camp (because she loved it all!) and she told me about the practice of having to erase your essays in order to conserve paper. What a heart break! See Oral Interview with Ellen Phillips, May 4, 2010, p. 13 of the transcript. DM520035 WMA

I based many of the specific characteristics of Fr. Sheridan on a poem written by one of the internees (J.E. McCall on Nov 12 1944) titled "The Padre," which describes many different circumstances in which he saw priests pitching in with a cheerful spirit. Among them, priests stoking cooking fires with acacia "green and wet" and stirring the stew. It's in my file "Other Primary Sources." The "picadura" reference is also from the poem, "The Padre." ie "When you've sold your last possessions, and you find that you are broke. And you're out of Picadura and you're dying for a smoke.... See the Padre"

There's lots of factual support for the aging male population in camp post-May 1943, with exodus of young, able men to Los Baños, and influx of sick, elderly from southern islands and Manila (many of whom actually *had* come to the PI during the Spanish-American War.) See Hartendorp, p 154-155.

The Filipino vendor being dragged away to the Southwest Territory. This particular incident is fictional, but Hartendorp reports increased Japanese brutality to Filipinos both in Manila and at the gate of Package Line – increased slappings, beatings, and executions at this time (see pp. 176-177).

Chapter 17 – The Locust Rule

Re: the teen boy discussion of Japanese cruelty: Hans Walser reported the three incidents discussed here: being taken to Rizal Stadium and forced to witness a man having his eyes pried out, beaten about the testicles with clubs, and another man being skinned alive. See Goldhagen, ed., p. 70.

The dark humor of the Jesus joke: in my eighth grade class at Nativity of Mary School, Lawrence Welk told that joke to tremendous hilarity.

Lee mentions repatriation rumors in camp at this point; there were rumors about this as early as July 1943, in Hartendorp, p. 178.

Biographical information on broadcaster Clarence Beliel aka Don Bell, as one sought by the Japanese, but escaped by using his own name is true; he worked with Harold Iserson before the war at KZH; Lee recalls him coming to their Taft Avenue apartment frequently in *Mañana Came*, p. 4. Material on Don Bell's earlier journalism career is found on both Wiki and also his own account in "the Three Lives of Don Bell," a broadcast made in 1976 (Vol. 23, No. 52, Dec 23, 1976). His account makes him sound very established in Shanghai, and the Manila move a natural lateral leap; http://www.kingsbenchletter.com/donbell/db23_52.html, but the wiki site, and Mom's reflections put him in an earlier stage i.e. just breaking into radio. Bell lived through the war and had a distinguished radio career subsequently; recently died in Miami. He did fifteen-minute news segments on the P.A. system. Other folks may have decided which music to play, but I wanted to spotlight his role.

Mary Lou Cleland spoke of their frequent practice of studying in the hall with a candle late at night after lights out; oral interview May 2010; transcript p.10.

The (stunning) story of locusts attacking the Japanese plane in Cebu (while Lulu and other prisoners watched) is factual, and also recounted in her oral interview. See transcript of taped interview, p. 13.

Chapter 18 – Going to Goa

The repatriation rumors proved true. See Hartendorp, pp 178-181.

Discussion of Gaudalcanal: The battle for Guadalcanal raged from October 1942 to January 1943; the island was declared secure by US on Feb 9, 1943. In Battle of the Bismarck Sea (2-4 March 1943) in the South West Pacific theater, Allied airpower pummeled 8 Japanese destroyers and 8 troop carriers with an escort of 100 fighters as they attempted to move almost 7000 troops to strategic positions (Lae) in hotly contested New Guinea. Only 1200 Japanese soldiers made it to Lae.

Discussion of "what did FDR mean by 'soon'?" is in Hartendorp, p. 173.

Hartendorp indicates 350 were repatriated – about 150 Americans and Canadians, equal number of Brits, 30 Dutch and other nationals including officials from Chile. See p. 180. This was announced in the *Manila Tribune* Aug 27, 1943. Hartendorp and Stevens have slightly different national composition indicated in their books. Stevens indicates no Brits were on the ship but I went with Hartendorp because he serves my purposes with the fictional Mrs. Meade. His final composition list was 131 Americans, 15 Canadians and six from other nationalities. (Stevens, pp. 52-53).

The survey to gauge internee opinion about repatriation is factual, as is the wording of the questions. See Hartendorp, p. 181. Fr. Sheridan taking survey is my invention, but not far-fetched. The results of the survey (two-to-one against repatriation) are as per Hartendorp, ibid., p. 181. (Fr. Sheridan was popular in camp; he was elected to fill an office vacated by one of the departing internees.)

Frank Sinatra singing with the Tommy Dorsey orchestra in 1940 is accurate; Tommy Dorsey got top billing; Sinatra was only 25 at the time and "I'll Never Smile Again," was one of his early recordings.

Background on C.C. Grinnell comes from Stevens, pp. 269-271 and on CNAC site; I also have a letter from James Kibbee to Grinnell's widow after the war, describing Grinnell's (excessive by his lights) tendency to try to "find out what the public thought about a proposed plan or measure."

KLIM cans used as footlights for Little Theater Under the Stars is factual. See Rupert Wilkinson, p. 69. The British poster "Keep Calm and Carry On," was printed by the British government in 1939.

The Japanese search for coded messages in internee baggage (sometimes knitting instructions) comes from Cates, 184 and also Hartendorp, 182.

For the speech by Kodaki see Hartendorp, p. 183. To my knowledge there is no extant text of Kodaki's speech, but several accounts confirm that it was conciliatory, apologetic, seemed to be suing for a separate peace, and conspicuously did not exonerate the Executive Comte. (Cates, 184; Stevens, 53, Hartendorp). James Ward article documents the internee suspicion of how decisions were made; p. 173.

Accounts of the performance given that night are numerous. I've drawn from Hope Miller and her *Nor All Your Tears* manuscript. A film was made for this show, which Hope described as: "a very funny cartoon movie, drawings and accompanying patter by two internees, 'The Lost Tribe of the Philippines' … done in the best travel-talk manner and very funny. But nothing could quite cover up the feeling of uneasiness – heartbreak – worry- frustration." (*Nor All Your Tears*, p.45-48) Liz Lautzenhiser Irvine includes the actual script of this "Santomasologue" in her *Surviving the Rising Sun*, pp. 148-154. Hartendorp provides the lyrics for the final song on p. 183. As for the term "travel-talk," James A. FitzPatrick popularized an extensive series of 7-10 minute "Traveltalk" reels in the 1930s, billing himself as "Voice of the Globe." Mostly black and white but intended to introduce his movie audience to the charm of distant regions, these films were shown to movie-goers pre-feature film. FitzPatrick went everywhere. He was Rick Steves before Rick Steves, and you can find many of his films on You Tube. See for example "Siam to Korea" https://www.youtube.com/watch?v=UD-bmrUEdUs.]

Part Two - Our Daily Bread

On an infrequent basis the Japanese allowed internees to send short (censored) messages home. This is a fictional message but typical. The code "Tell it to Sweeney" (explained later in the text) was used to indicate "not!" The Japanese did not recognize its meaning and did not censor it.

Chapter 19 – Bread of Life

Playhouse construction began two days after the repatriation. Kodaki left as Commandant on October 27, 1943 and was replaced by Kato.

Lee's lament about "I ain't got nobody," is based on Judy Garland's portrayal of Mary in *Strike Up the Band* in 1940 (with Micky Rooney).

The poem, "A Friend," by Lee Iserson is authentic. She never did erase it because it is in my possession and dated 1942. It had to have been written early on (February or March maybe) because her handwriting is young and deliberate-looking penciled cursive, and not the slanted forward-march cursive shown even in her recipe book in 1944.

Details on camp food provision in the early stages are based on Lee's memories (boring but they weren't starving), Hartendorp, pp. 12-14, and Johnsen, p. 21. Rupert Wilkinson describes camp buyers and their forays into Manila on p. 38. Hartendorp notes that at first kids and teens got a third light meal from the Annex kitchen, and people who had money could buy meals at a little camp restaurant owned by an American proprietor or buy extra food the Japanese-run camp canteen. (Hartendorp, p. 14)

Lee's fantasy about the "Grand Slam Bridge Dessert" is recipe number five in her spiral-bound recipe book. This recipe book exists and is in the author's possession. Judging by Lee's handwriting (mature and recognizable) I think the earliest she could have assembled it was very late 1943 through to liberation. It holds 374 recipes that Lee copied in pencil and random order from various cookbooks and magazines in the Camp library (the YMCA donated its collection of books, and Santo Tomas had a Home Economics department.) Lee created an index at the back of the notebook, with foods organized by type – appetizer, salad, main, dessert, etc.) and a full bibliography at the end. The nascent librarian in full view!

Re: Dominican sisters: in the tropics they wore all white, rather than black veil and white as in US. Hartendorp (pp. 80-82) and Stevens (p. 115) describe Santa Catalina and how it connected to Santo Tomas.

Lee had very fond memories of singing in this choir and being directed by a pro (former Italian opera director and his wife: probably Mario Bakerini-Booth and his wife Dorothy "Dolly" Baker). They sang original music, some written by a Dutch priest interned with them; also true that Lee and Lulu sang snatches of the Gloria and Credo at bridge. See "Lee Iserson-"Santo Tomas Talk," p. 8. Liz Lautzenhiser identifies the Dutch priest who conducted the "Messiah" choir for Christmas 1943 as Father Visser, who was interned with us." (*Surviving the Rising Sun*, p. 160); He was probably a Mill Hill priest (Congregation of Scheut), and in 1924 Fr Visser seems to have authored a paper on "The Old Portuguese Missions in Dutch India http://archive.

thetablet.co.uk/article/20th-september-1924/11/dutch-university-students-and-foreign-missions. See also the excellent article "War Camp Mass has Aussie Premier" for an overview of Bakerini-Booth and music in camp.

Lee recalls the Christ the King party at Santa Catalina as the last time she ate well at Santo Tomas, and she raved about the generosity of the sisters. Lee Iserson, "Santo Tomas Talk," p. 8. Sr. Ignacia and Sr. Nora are names I remember from Lee's stories.

Re: Ramón Ayala: as indicated before, he is fictional but based on Lee's memories of neighbors: "I remember at one time, we lived next to a Spanish family whose children were all musical, and each night at twilight they would all play a little concert. The beauty of the music and the golden twilight created a poignancy I have never forgotten." (*Mañana Came*, p. 4)

CHAPTER 20 – SHALL WE DANCE?

Possibility of Ramón "breaking into a prison camp:" is not far-fetched. The porous quality of Santo Tomas, particularly before the military takeover in 1944, is well documented. See for example, Rupert Wilkinson, Chapter 3 "A Porous Prison," pp. 35-48.

Re: the high-board partitions forming a corridor between Santa Catalina and the campus, and the guard tower, see Donald Dang's sketch, p. 76.

Details about girls' basketball at Santo Tomas are based on oral interview with Ellen Thomas Phillips (the avid and excellent player described here); also Lee Iserson's red "Autograph Book" lists the names of the girls and boys teams. Those given here are actual team names. Re: court surface: Martin Meadows described it as an "earthen basketball court" in his email of Sep 1, 2014. Lee's comment about the boys' games involving lots of defensive work is meant to document the changing nature of the game. Basketball games in the 1940s were significantly lower scoring because of extended defensive play, a fact that my writing coach/friend Jack Galvin of Newport Rhode Island alerted me too. Lee's self-deprecating attitude toward her own basketball ability is based on fact and was seconded by Lulu in her oral interview to me. She couldn't believe Lee had ever been "captain" of the team (which she was; it's in her autograph book). Lulu said "maybe because she was good at organizing. She and I were terrible." In later years, when asked what [sports] she played, Lee would say: "bridge and the phonograph."

Inspiration for the "Shall We Dance" ditty that Lulu and Lee sing came from the final dance sequence of 1937 *Shall We Dance?* with Astaire singing the bouncy number and then moving into his signature dance moves. (For pure joy, see him in action at :http://www.youtube.com/watch?v=TdoBt-vAX-w; at 8:19.)

Dance lessons at Santo Tomas. Maurice Naftaly was Lee's first dance teacher and the class was at Santo Tomas. (See her blue autograph book and her letter to Jane Hanagan, 15 February 1945, p. 3. Lee said that girls outnumbered boys 3:1). Naftaly had worked in imports for Heaco Trading Company in Manila, and his wife Louise wrote Lee a limerick about looking back in later years on their experience; also found in blue autograph book). Naftaly was born in 1915; making him 28 at this point. I invented his connections to the Jewish musical community because it was a vibrant force in NYC at that time, and he may very well have been part of it.) Lee indicates in several places that he was her first dancing teacher; and after the war, they went to visit him in NYC. (See her letter to Francis Maher, 1946). Re: the Jewish talent in NYC: consider the range of talent: Jerome Kern b. 1885, German-Jewish; Irving Berlin born Israel Isidore Beilin; Russian Jew-1888; Oscar Hammerstein, b. 1895-German Jewish; Ira Gershwin b. 1896-Russian Jew (born: Israel Gershowitz); Richard Rodgers-German Jew, 1902; Rodgers' dad had changed the family name from "Abrahams" to Rodgers; Lorenz Hart – German Jewish b. 1895. This particular dance class is fictional: Maurice taught Lee, but in order to impress Nellie, Bill Phillips took private dancing lessons from their classmate Jane McCleod (oral interview, transcript, p. 5. Bill only uses the name "Jane" but Jane McCleod was the only Jane in their class and she's also mentioned later in the interview.).

Lee's comment about Glen Miller joining the Army and entertaining the troops. Accurate. *Casablanca* was released in 1942, and I don't know if it was shown in camp. This line is Bogart's to Ilsa.

Chapter 21 – The Tempest

The Iserson and Flatland push to make as much fudge as possible for Christmas of 1943 is based on Lee's Manuscript, *Mañana Came*, p.14. The date is not in that talk but comes from Lee's letter Jane Hanagan, 15 February 1945).

Re: the stalled Allied push across the Pacific: November 12, 1943 *Manila Tribune* headline was: "Japanese Land Additional Forces on Bougainville. US Marines Hemmed in at Beachheads." That according to Cates, p. 189. Bougainville was largest island in North Solomons.

K. Kato became Commandant on either Oct 1 or Oct 31 depending on the source. I can't find any indication of what K. stands for in K. Kato so I made up "Konichi". Stevens contradicts himself regarding Kato's tenure - listed as starting on Oct 29, 1943 in his chronology (p. 422) and Oct 1 in the text p. 369. Hartendorp has the info on his Kensington House internment, p. 187.

The November typhoon: was just as memorable as recorded in this chapter and the next. All examples given here were drawn from reputable sources. Hope Miller's, *Nor All Your Tears*, devotes a very graphic chapter to it (pp. 49-50), and the storm is also documented in Stevens, p. 424 and Hartendorp, pp. 189-191. The floating baby python is mentioned in Cates, p. 190.

The exclamation "Jiminy Cricket!" became popular in the 1930s; used in Snow White and Seven Dwarfs (1937); used by Mickey Mouse in 1938 cartoon *The Brave Little Tailor* by Judy Garland as Dorothy in 1939 *Wizard of Oz* and several times in 1930 movie *Anna Christie* starring Greta Garbo; Cartoon Jiminy Cricket made his debut in Pinocchio in 1940.

Lee's comments about dousing the ants with kerosene: Johansen, *So Far From Home* pp. 87-88 notes that even boiling water does not kill ants; kerosene needed to be mixed in with the water to end what turned out to be an infestation of the shanties after the typhoon. The young boy reporting a tree falling on the pavilion: accurate as per Hope Miller, *Nor All Your Tears*, p. 49. Lee's reference to the room environment resembling *Grapes of Wrath*; *Grapes of Wrath* was the most popular movie of 1940. The altercation between roomies is fictional, but not the atmosphere of tension.

Agnes's reaction to the notion of "sneaking Ramon into camp:" the situation Agnes describes (of husbands trying to get their Filipino families into camp, of camp being safer and better-supplied than the city of Manila) was very real and pressing. Her assessment of Japanese response to such a transgression is quite likely, and Agnes's response to Lee (landing on her like a ton of bricks) would have been very much in character. Hartendorp indicates increasing pressure on camp authorities in November and December 1943 to admit Filipino family members, especially after the typhoon. Of the 1500 men in camp, 541 had non-interned families (Filipino wives and children); 170 families desired internment in a letter to the Executive Comte on Nov 24, 1943. Hartendorp, 192.

Chapter 22 – Undanced Dance

Agnes did resign as room monitor, and there is a letter from internees in Room 4, requesting that she not resign (signed by twenty-three ladies including Hope and Alice Flatland; (in author's possession). It is not dated, and I do not know the circumstances that led to her resignation. The details on the new room monitor come from Hope's manuscript "*Nor All Your Tears*," pp. 57-59. Hope refers to her as Mrs. T. and reports "southern gentility" aspect and the detail of "Room 4 Is Your Home." I made up the name "Linda Lee Todd," modeling on Mary Todd Lincoln.

Ramon's letter is fictional, but Lee had a lifetime love of the poet Ruben

Darío, who was born in Nicaragua, but had great influence on Spanish poetry internationally. Here I invent a potential wellspring for Lee's devotion to the poet. This poem is called "Autumnal" or "Poem of Autumn" and was published in 1910. Ramon does not translate poorly because the translation is from Salamon de Selva (also a Nicaraguan poet).

Lulu's little sister Maureen did contract diphtheria and was out of camp for almost a month on medical pass. Phone conversation Lulu, Feb 3, 2014. Mary Lou doesn't remember the exact date. She recalled the hospital had a Catholic name, and an article by Emmet Pearson, MD, indicates that San Lazaro Isolation Hospital is where all highly communicable disease patients from STIC were taken; a shortened version of this 1946 study "Morbidity and Mortality in Santo Tomas," is in January 2014 *Beyond the Wire*. I have a PDF in my "Articles" file.

Re: Lee's disappointment that the Isersons got no mail from home: based on fact and this was a something that rankled as an adult. Agnes mentioned it too in her letter to Ruth Hanagan on 3 March 1945.

Camp food shortages as a result of the typhoon are based on fact. See Stevens, p. 425.

Chapter 23 – Comfort Kids

No more sugar, lard, rice or soap based on Cates, December 4, 1943; p. 192 and Hartendorp p. 200 with specifics on "peanut loaf."

Fudge-making push by Agnes and Flossie as per Iserson, *Mañana Came*, p. 14 when Lee estimates that they "must have made 20 batches of fudge, because she collected nearly P75 ($32.50) that day."

Shakespeare troupe performing "Hamlet" recently: fictional, but I wish it were true! Lee's letters were full of lines from Shakespeare and my suspicion this came from study in camp.

"Comfort Kid/Kit" confusion indicated in Hope Miller's manuscript, *Nor All Your Tears*, p. 53-54. A little girl who assumed they were going to be visited by Comfort Kids.

For details about the (true incident) of the Japanese detaining and slashing the kits, see Hartendorp, 203 and Cates, p. 194. For contents of the comfort kits, see Hartendorp, p. 200-204. Re: Paul's outburst of "we are men, not mice!" John Steinbeck published Of Mice and Men in 1937.

Christmas show: Dave Harvey's spoof (including "Mine Camp") in James Ward, p. 174 (though "Everything's Going to be Lousy" was in an earlier show). Mixed chorus performing Handel's Messiah, movie "Honky Tonk," Cates, 195. Grace Nash actually performed at Thanksgiving not at Christmas (Woodcock, p.50); Santa's arrival in camp, Hartendorp, p. 206.

Agnes rationing the Comfort Kits to last a year: Lee indicated that her mother had been very focused on stewardship of this precious box; I invented the distribution list-by-week to last a year, but when Ellen Thomas read the draft of this manuscript, she wrote in the margin: "My mother did this too!"

Lee hearing the lyrics for Prokofiev's ballet Cinderella in the background: this ballet was performed by the children; it came out in 1940 and was set to music in a 78 RPM that contains this lyric.

Chapter 24 – Prison Camp Number One

Influx of new prisoners from Davao on January 2 as per Stevens, p. 428; camp population comes close to its high (3939 on January 6, Stevens, p. 428 and p. 431); permission for families to live together in shanties outdoors granted on February 1, 1944 (Stevens, p. 430); additional Red Cross medical supplies received in December (Stevens, 427) included sulpha drugs, so STIC doctors were able to save lives that might have been lost in November.

Distribution of identical "playsuits" was on January 29, 1944 according to Hope Miller, *Nor All Your Tears*, p. 60 and confirmed by Lulu. Mary Lou provided the details about color of the print in her oral interview. Mrs. T's expressions ("how perfectly cute" and "I almost dropped my drawers") come from Hope Miller's memories of her *Nor All Your Tears*, pp. 57-59. Reference to Betty Grable: *Million Dollar Legs* was a 1939 comedy starring Betty Grable and Jackie Coogan, and yes, she did wear a playsuit! But hers was a green and orange floral print. Grable was at the height of her career in the war years and got her nickname from her first film.

The Japanese military officially took over the camp as of January 6, but the Executive Committee was not notified until January 10. Changes in administration and procedures took place gradually. (See Stevens, 428 and Liz Irvine, p. 171).

The classic children's book *Ferdinand the Bull* by Munro Leaf was published in 1938 and a faithfully rendered Disney cartoon movie came out that same year. The exchange accurately reflects internee uncertainty about what they could expect under Japanese military rule.

Lee suffering quinsy: I created this scene to show the deteriorating health situation in the camp at this time with many suffering not just from hunger and malnutrition, but from respiratory diseases due to overcrowding. Sulpha drugs had been part of the Red Cross Care packages in 1943. The sulpha came in powder form and was made into pills by teen internee Len Baker at the Santo Tomas pharmacy school. (Email from internee Len Baker, November 4, 2013; "during an outbreak of bacillus dysentery I was trained to make tablets. In the Red Cross shipments of 1943 there was the whole range of Sulpha- drugs, among which sulphathiazole was specific for bacillus dysentery. Unfortunately, this drug arrived in powder form and the pharmacist, Henry Belling, was spending all his time weighing out the doses. The pharmacy manager, Bob Smith, was aware that Santo Tomas had a School of Pharmacy. Did they have a tablet making machine? The question was put to them and the reply was – they had such a machine and we could borrow it. I was taught how to make granules from the powder and we were able to beat the dysentery outbreak. At liberation we still had 2 full bottles of tablets on the shelf! It's amazing how you can enjoy being an internee in Santo Tomas!)"

The permanent closure of the Package Line on February 7, 1944 was a huge blow and is documented in many sources (Stevens, 431 and Cogan, p. 114).

Chapter 25 – Curve Ball

Yoshie is one of the most intriguing and possibly unhinged Commandants that Santo Tomas endured. He did have a well-documented passion for baseball, and according to Cates "our new pint-size Commandant, an ardent baseball fan, and somewhat of an eccentric, was a dynamo of energy. He appeared daily at sundown, armed with gardening tools." (p. 200-201) Re: Lee's comparison of him to *The Great Dictator*; The Chaplin movie was released in October 1940; I do not know for a fact that it was shown in Manila, but I would be surprised if was not. See clip at: https://www.youtube.com/watch?v=yypR80BLEo4. For further description of Yoshie ("wildly gesticulating" "prancing about", see Wilkinson, p. 98.) He did indeed challenge the internees to a baseball game, and the memory of "You play ball with me, I play ball with you," is Lee's. There is a photo of the Japanese playing the internees in my file.

For the closing of Holy Ghost Children's Home and new population sent to STIC, see Stevens, p. 431.

For the changing character of the camp as the Japanese military took over (increased number of army trucks and supplies, erection of pillbox defenses) see Hartendorp, p. 208-229.

"The ladies are here to clean house." The American slang "to clean house" meaning "to administer a beating" appears as early as 1910. The Brits didn't/don't use it (but the citation is in the *Random House Historical Dictionary of American Slang*). Nellie's annoyance that her brother Joe was never asked to do laundry and help is factual, as per her oral interview p. 2 of transcript. Ellen told me that her family did not start doing their own laundry until very late, and I'm assuming 1944, when the gate was closed. Details about the package line staying open for incoming laundry until February 8 are from Hartendorp, p. 222.

"Pistol Packin' Mama" was a 1943 recording, but internees may have had it as they continued to get an influx of records through the gate that year.

The history of baseball in Japan: Horace Wilson, an American teaching at the Kaisei School in Tokyo, introduced the game to his students in 1872. Hiroshi Hiraoka, an engineering student who had studied in the US, also introduced his compatriots to the game in 1878. The first Japanese baseball team was founded in that year (1878, Shimbashi Athletic Club). The sport became very popular in Japan. The Chicago White Sox and NY Giants visited on tour in 1913 (winning all games that they played). A few other matchups ensued in the next few decades. Most famous was the 1934 Major-League All Star tour during which Japan's finest players took on American All-Stars, and did lose all 18 games to the US team, but Eiji Sawamura (1917-1944) became a national hero and baseball legend with his pitching that struck out the four American hall of famers above. The Americans (Connie Mack) tried to sign Sawamura to a major league contract, but he declined. Anti-American feeling was strong in Japan and he said: "My problem is I hate Americans, and I can't make myself like Americans." He joined the IJA and was killed near Ryuku Islands when his ship was torpedoed. (All this from Wiki.)

The baseball card Curtis brandishes is modeled on the 1933 Jimmy Foxx card from the Goudey Gum Co.

The actual game with Yoshie pitching: Lee relates this story in her "*Santo Tomas Talk*," p. 6, and both Hartendorp p. 258 and Rupert Wilkinson, p. 98 confirm Yoshie pitched. I accelerated the date of this match. It took place in May 1944.

Results of the All-Star Series: I have not been able to track down the results. My ending (with Japanese victory) is possible because internees were very conscious of not wanting to incur the wrath of their captors, but I invented it for narrative reasons.

Curtis Brooks as a history buff: totally accurate.

Chapter 26 – Advantageous to Our Growth

For a cartoon image of the "Gangway! Hot Fish Stew" transport (but with two instead of three men), see Woodcock, p. 111.

Radios in camp: Rupert Wilkinson indicates there were at least two radios, p. 72 and that one had a transmitting apparatus that was seldom (if ever) used for fear of detection, see Stevens, p. 265 ff.

Twice-daily roll calls in 1944: Hartendorp and Stevens both indicate twice daily roll call announced on Feb 28 and begun on March 1 (Stevens 434; times are as indicated in text, but switched later to 7 AM to 5:30 PM)

"The Internment Camp Experience is Advantageous to Our Growth" was a topic debated by the senior class at Los Baños Internment camp in 1944; the affirmatives won. Margo Tonkin Shiels (arguing the negative) recounts this in *Bends in the Road* 1999. Their topic was "Resolved: that as a whole, the members of the Class of '47 have benefited more from the experience of internment than if there had been no war in the Pacific." This seemed too good to overlook.

Santo Tomas graduation was held April 10, 1944.

Building the bamboo fence to occlude view from gymnasium to Father's Garden: This activity happened between March 15-30, 1944 – all with objections from the internee Exec Committee, but in the end undertaken, and Yoshie did surprise the men with a food bonus ration. Most documented in Hartendorp, 246-247.

Lulu finding a squash with a dead rat in it and taking it home to roast: is true; as recounted by Mary Lou Hedricks in oral interview: 38:46; p. 11 of my transcript.

Lee's fantasy of Max: Lee did fantasize about Max's miraculous return under these circumstances after the war, particularly when it turned out that her friend Moira Malone's (who didn't make it into the novel, but she was an internment camp friend) dad did not die, but surprised them all by walking in their London apartment one day. Mom (Lee) considered writing this as a short story, but didn't get around to it. I always thought it would make a great short story.

The raid by the Kempeitai is factual, but it was on March 31, 1944 at 12:20 AM. I moved it by four days for narrative reasons. See Hartendorp, 246-247.

Chapter 27 – Unusual Skills

Lee recalls the sketch that Betty made and Agnes references it in a letter to Lee, but we do not have it.

The duck egg birthday cake for Lee's Sweet Sixteenth birthday comes from my imagination, but would be in keeping with Agnes's resourcefulness, and what was available in camp. Factual are the gifts: the poem by Hope to Lee (but was gift for the previous year, written in 4/3/43). I have the original in Lee's autograph book. Stationery is as described. The olive green notebook would be the permanent home for Lee's recipes.

The various "unusual skills" acquired by internees are based on fact (bra woven out of string, for example).

Chapter 28 – Abiko

The opening note to Bunny is fictional, but many notes were exchanged between STIC and Los Baños. Some of the sentences here come right out of Lee's other writing at the time (e.g. her Cicero description). Graduation did take place on April 10, 1944 with ceremony and jokes as described.

Cates indicates that internees knew of the D-Day landing as early as June 9 through disparaging accounts in the *Manila Tribune*. (p. 208)

Abiko's tenure at Santo Tomas: I don't know exact dates of Abiko's reign at STIC, but he was a presence in June 1944, ordering men to build two watchtowers against the outer wall June 4, 1944 (Liz Irvine, p. 180). Wilkinson has the speculation about him being an Olympic swimmer, but it was untrue. (p. 101) My description of Abiko is largely based on Wilkinson, pp. 101-103. The slapping incident was based on the Eileen Faggiano account given in Michael McCoy, *Through My Mother's Eyes* (Strategic Book Publishing, 2008); according to McCoy the slapping took place outside the annex at roll call when a toddler failed to bow. Doubt has been cast on the veracity of several incidents in McCoy's book (doubts which I share), and lots of it is overblown, but this particular slapping is not improbable.

Jimmy Flood and Eric Sollee were actual classmates of Lee's. Mrs. Hildegard Jones was Lee's English teacher in her sophomore year at STIC. (See Autograph book). The "Ham Pancake" recipe is from Lee's recipe book and is number 116. In a letter to Jane Maher on March 1, 1945 Lee says that 65-80% of internees were collecting recipes by July 1, 1944.

The influx of 70 new priests in July 1944 is documented in Stevens, p. 444.

Lee's election as basketball team captain is true (as per her "Autograph Book") and so was her decision to get Nellie to be the coach.

Lee and Ellen did witness one such water torture incident. The water torture that they see here is based on Lee's memories and Ellen's email to me and oral interview. Lee's version was more horrific than this, but I won't inflict it on a teen audience. Lulu did not witness the event. Curiously, though she spoke to us of the event, she never documented it in her talks.

"The Whites" was the actual name of Lee's basketball team, and it evokes the glorified clothing of martyrs. (The phrase: "the white-robed army of martyrs praise you," forms part of the classic Catholic *Te Deum*.)

Chapter 29 – Mass at the Museum

"Cranberry Turkey Mold" is indeed recipe number 217 in Lee's recipe book. Ingredients are as indicated. She lists "The Junket Book" as one of her sources in her bibliography. I don't know if this particular recipe came from Junket Book.

Frying talinum in Pond's Cold Cream is true; see Hope's *Nor All Your Tears*, pp. 88-89. "Frog-Jumping" headline from *Manila Tribune* was on June 9 1944 and is documented in Cates, p. 208.

The Camp's Ten Commandments can be found in many sources, but see Wilkinson, p. 198. The stat about twelve packs of cigarettes for a one pound can of powdered milk comes from Don Holter, "Wings," sent to me by his daughter Heather Holter Ellis (born in Santo Tomas).

Valley Forge reading: Hope recounts that a group of men at Santo Tomas gave a reading of Maxwell Anderson's *Valley Forge* in Spring of 1944. I've fictionalized the date, moving it forward to July. Hope loved American history and literature, and said "a quiet, thoughtful group of men and women left the Father's Garden that evening seeing a parallel between Valley Forge and Santo Tomas, and the significance of the spirit of the common man behind the historical fact." (Miller, *Nor All Your Tears*, p. 7)

The bare wall on way to the landing: In 1940-41, three Filipino artists painted the murals that now hang in the stairwells of the Main Building. One is of Christ Crucified with the spotlight on the Sacred Heart of Jesus and Filipinos kneeling at his feet. I don't know if these paintings hung in the stairwells in 1942, when the University became an internment camp, but I suspect so because they had been so recently painted and belonged in those spaces. No surviving internee I've talked to remembers their presence which makes me think the Dominicans took them down for safekeeping. (See email "Murals in the Main Building" to Lulu and Ellen 12-10-13).

The museum mezzanine location and description are factual; we visited it in Santo Tomas in 2010. The glass cases (transformed to altars) of snakes and iguanas were still on display, but not the large animal heads on the balconies.

Mass at the museum is something Lee both wrote and spoke of as powerful for her; the description of mass at the museum (which she attended more than once) is in "Santo Tomas Talk," p. 7. Lee does not specifically mention a Palawan bearded pig, but it is endemic to the PI is a subspecies of the Bornean bearded pig. I speculated about the specific animals on the walls inspired by Lee's descriptions of "wild beasts" displayed there.

As per the St. Andrew missal, readings for the mass on July 9, 1944 included Mark 8:1-9 (gospel of loaves and fishes). The power of the consecration is indicated in Lee's description, "Santo Tomas Talk," p. 7.

Chapter 30 - Wings

Paris was liberated on August 25, 1944 and internees were aware of this. On September 4, there was even speculation that Germany had surrendered. See Cates, *Drainpipe Diary*, p. 215-216.

"Margaret Whitley" is a fictional teacher name. Lee's third year English teacher was Miss Marguerite Barsot (see her autograph book), who was American, but taught only the girls. Curtis Brooks told me that Fr. McMullen taught the boys and refused to teach girls. Go figure. But I wanted the sexes together in this class for narrative reasons, and it suited my purposes to have a British English teacher.

Liz Lautzenhiser Irvine, p. 185 lists "Columbia the Gem of the Ocean," "Yankee Doodle," and "Dixie" as selections for Sep 13 over the P.A. system. The Japanese canceled the music program on September 14 in retribution.

The students could clear the roof in twenty-five seconds flat: as per Lee Iserson Klee, "Santo Tomas Talk," p. 10.

The iguana theft from the museum: Liz Irvine told me the story of the iguana stolen from the museum as a prank. I invented the involvement of Paul.

"Don't be a complete fool, Lee." The quote (from Paul to Lee) is in a letter from Lee to Bunny Brambles, describing Paul's darkening mood near the end of captivity. See Lee Iserson to Grace Brambles, 3 March 1945.

Hope's student who insisted he be the last off the roof is true. Incident is recorded in *Nor All Your Tears*, pp. 78-79. I made up the name Freddy Hopkins, and his family situation.

Commandant Yoshie replaced by Hayashi: Hayashi came on about this time - either August or September 1944. Hartendorp says he was introduced to the Internee Committee on September 9 (p.314), but Stevens says August 12 (p. 447)

Cates describes Japanese soldiers digging air raid shelters and the thrill it gave the internees knowing that the Japanese perceived imminent danger in *Drainpipe Diary*, August 9, 1944; p. 213.

Roy Bennett was Lee's history teacher, but I have only speculated on her academic whereabouts on September 21, 1944. The reflections on "no maps in history" are true.

The Battle of Saipan had been won in late June 1944.

The air raid: This much celebrated air raid occurred at 9:30 AM on September 21, 1944. See Irvine, p. 185. For extended account see Hartendorp, pp. 318-323. In my story, I have kids emerging with air raid signal and trying to deduce identity of planes (Lee indicated this); her moving account is in "Santo Tomas Talk," p. 10; according to Hartendorp, the air raid sirens sounded only after the first wave of planes came through. See also, Wilkinson, p. 134-35. Curtis Brooks wrote an excellent account of the plane movements (in my primary source non-letters file). This first strike was carried out by the Navy; Army P-38s then took over. For Hope's account of the air raid, see

Nor All Your Tears, p. 78ff. Lee noted that "we were hysterical with joy and it was a full fifteen minutes before they could get us off the roof." ("Santo Tomas Talk," p. 10)

Chapter 31 – Hope Returned

Musical selections on the PA system in wake of raid: Roscoe Lautzenhiser's diary indicated the songs mentioned above were played on the evening of Wed, Sep 21. Liz Lautzenhiser Irvine mentions "Lover Come Back to Me" as played on September 27, 1944. See both references in Irvine, p. 186 and 187. See also Cates, p. 220.

Increasing Japanese military presence in camp: see Liz Irvine, p. 187; children imitating the Japanese drill and goose-stepping behind them, see Cates, p. 218. For Japanese concern about internees watching air raids even from windows, see Stevens, p. 461.

Hope and Agnes planting a new vegetable garden: in Hope's *Nor All Your Tears* (p. 81) she tells of doing exactly this on that date, but she did it with Kay Heyda. I substituted Agnes.

The camp menu listed here was the menu for October 13, 1944 as described in Liz Irvine, p. 189.

"Bicycle Built for Two" came out in 1892 with the title "Daisy Bell" (written by Harry Dacre, an Englishman resident in the U.S.) and then "Daisy, Daisy" or "Bicycle Built for Two."

Ninety-one internees dead by October 1944: this is a ballpark figure based on a manual tally I did of deaths listed in Stevens prior to Thanksgiving. Ninety-one was my count by Thanksgiving.

The poem Lee wrote ("Hope Returned") is in author's possession. It is written on onion skin paper and typed as described above with the blurry "w." I have only speculated on what it made blurry; I also do not know how Lee got access to a typewriter (I made up the Mrs. Maynard possibility), but George Baker told me that his family had a Baby Hermes in camp, so why shouldn't Lee?

"Better Lay-tee than never" closing on the P.A.: is factual and indicated in many sources, among them, Liz Irvine, p. 189.

Chapter 32 – Spot Search

Hunger and not picking up the book: Lee wrote about this as a measure of how malnourished they were—thinking about whether to pick the book up. "Santo Tomas Talk," p. 10. Food rations slashed again in November: the "Liberation Bulletin" reports that happened on November 17, 1944.

The Japanese storing food and cigarettes in full view of internees is documented in Stevens, p. 463 and 467, and see also Liz Irvine, p. 220.

Menu for Thanksgiving Day is factual. See Irvine, p. 192.

"It's a beautiful night for bombing." That line is in one internee's memoirs and I can't remember where I read it, but it really stayed with me.

Ginny McKinney's dad's death: Mr. McKinney died on Dec 14. (Irvine, p. 194)

The doll house project: This dollhouse incident is true and is recounted in detail in Hope, *Nor All Your Tears*, p. 96 ff.

Martin, the woodworker: I modeled this fictional character on internee Martin Meadows, who would have been a year older than Betty and was Jewish (he even got released from camp to attend his own Bar Mitzvah in Manila in 1943).

The spot-search is modeled after frequent spot-searches in camp at this time, but Lee's music and she herself were not taken. The detail of watching wagons cart coffins, where the feet dangled outside is from Lee Iserson, "Santo Tomas Talk," p. 11.

CHAPTER 33 – CHRISTMAS CONCERT

The arrest of members of the Executive Committee: this arrest did take place on December 23, 1944 (see p. Stevens, p. 473 and Liz Irvine, p. 195).

Leaflets dropped on Christmas day: true and the text of the leaflets is as given in the novel.

The little girl lining up her dolls outside the door of the bathroom: true. See Hope Miller, *Nor All Your Tears*, pp. 96-98.

The Christmas menu recounted here is accurate as per Liz Irvine, p. 196. Hope waltzing into the shanty with champagne, and announcing she prefers bourbon: yes; bourbon was Hope's drink of choice. A can of spam selling for $50, see Liz Irvine, p. 221 and the "bomb sticks" as jewelry of choice, see Hope Miller, *Nor All Your Tears*, p. 91. (I invented her fashioning them for Lee and Betty.)

Curfew on Christmas night extended from 7 to 8 PM: accurate; see Liz Irvine, p. 196.

The story of Mrs. Gewald going to Los Baños and losing her daughter to appendicitis for the reasons stated is true. Janet Flatland was related to the Gewalds and she indicated this in her oral interview.

CHAPTER 34 – ROLL OUT THE BARREL

Deaths from November, December (1944), and January (1945) are accurate and as per Liz Irvine, p. 220.

Lee celebrating New Year's with her gang (Lulu, Lizzy Lautzenhiser, etc.)

and singing the songs described is documented in Liz Irvine, p. 199.

Death of Ginny McKinney's dad and of Mr. Brooks (father of the Brooks twins) from starvation documented in Liz Irvine, p. 218 (Mr. Brooks died on January 27, 1945).

Fury at the Japanese storing their supplies and "large fish" in front of internees, see Liz Irvine, p. 220.

Death of Glen Miller: the famous band leader died crossing the English Channel from London to Paris on 15 December 1944.

Lulu having a tonsillectomy (without novacaine) in order to get better food: is a true story! She says it was the most painful experience in her life, and "a ridiculous thing that I did to myself." (oral interview, May 2010, p. 14 of transcript) I changed the timing of her operation though and sped it up. This tonsillectomy actually kept Lulu in the hospital on the night of liberation (something she deeply regrets), so since this is fiction, I decided she and Lee should be together for the liberation!

"Pineapple Raisin Ice Cream" is recipe 361 in Lee's recipe book (as per the text).

B-24 heavy bombers and P-38 lightning dive bombers: these were two of the aircraft seen by internees from December 1944 onward. See Wilkinson, p. 135.

Paul's weight: true; see Lee Iserson to Bunny Brambles, 3 March 1945.

Lulu imitating Snow White's quavering voice: Snow White came out in 1937 and "Someday My Prince Will Come," was written that year by Frank Churchill and Larry Morey. Lulu did have a crush on Jack Aaron.

Lee wearing her "white crepe skirt" is accurate as per her oral interview. (Andersonville Prison Project CD)

Stepping out on to the plaza all dressed up: I fudged the timing a bit. Stevens indicates that curfew Feb 3 was 6:30 PM and lights-out was observed from that time on because of air raids (see p. 362). But it serves my narrative purposes better to have them milling in the plaza and then being ordered in.

Chapter 35 – "Too Damn Big"

The events of the evening of liberation (rumble of tanks, insecurity about whose they were, etc.) are recounted in many sources: see Hartendorp, Chapter 25, "The Deliverance," pp. 403-420, Stevens pp. 361-368, Wilkinson, Chapter 11, "They're Here," pp. 143-156, and Liz Irvine's excellent diary entries, pp. 225-231. The details I recount (re: sharp-shooter from Montana and death of Abiko, etc.) are drawn from those sources.

The Japanese guards taking potshots at internees looking out the windows, and the kids racing about from one part of the building to the next: based on

Lee's recollections in *Santo Tomas Talk*, pp. 11-12; the popularity of *Tom Mix* for boys is factual and many internee boys recall having collections before the war. For example, see Leon Morgan. *Tom Mix in the Fighting Cowboy.* (Racine, WI: Whitman Publishing, 1935).

Bill Phillips' role in showing GIs the front door of the camp: based on May 2010 oral interview with Bill at 47:10-47:50 on tape; on day of liberation, he said he was in his Froggy Bottom shanty when he heard the rumblings, noticed that the Japanese guards had disappeared on the north side, and he climbed the wall to get a better look at what he could hear. Saw US tanks. The GIs actually shouted to him "Where is the Santo Tomas Internment Camp?" (street signs were down at the time), and he yelled "It's around this way," and motioned them down Forbes to Espana. Lee recalled the shout of "he's too damn big to be a Jap!" in her "Santo Tomas Talk," p. 11. The names of the tanks are factual and easily found in many sources (for example, see Stevens, p. 367)

The internee impression of U.S. troops as "giants" was widely shared and attested to in many sources. Mary Lou Cleland stressed this in her oral interview, as did Lee. In addition to U.S. troops being well nourished (and internees emaciated), the average height difference between Japanese males and Americans males in 1945 was approximately five inches (Japanese males 5'2 and American males, 5'7.) Post-war diet changes in Japan made for a significant height increase over 70 years. The average Japanese male is now 5'6. See the May 2019 study at https://livejapan.com/en/in-tokyo/in-pref-tokyo/in-shinjuku/article-a0000962/ So, American boys might indeed have seemed "giants."

"I Surrender" leaflet: true; Liz Irvine shows one on p. 231. These red, white, and blue surrender and safe-conduct leaflets (large, almost 8x11 so that US troops could see them) were dropped by US Forces prior to invasion. Wording in both Japanese and English. Initial wording was "I surrender," (and that was the wording in the PI). The wording "I cease resistance" was a specific later choice in order to avoid the humiliation of "I surrender" and ensure that more Japanese soldiers would indeed "cease resistance." See a good article about this at http://www.psywarrior.com/ICeaseJap.html

The account of Abiko's death is based on Rupert Wilkinson, p. 151 and Liz Irvine, p. 226. Abiko was shot by Major James Gearhart, acting commander for the brigade, who in fact was a taciturn westerner who had spent many boyhood days practicing firing from the hip. Abiko was hit by a second bullet (which I have attributed to Mountain Man for dramatic purposes).

The jubilant welcome provided by the internees and the kids climbing on tanks: Cates, p. 246-247 and Hartendorp, 406. Also see Geoffrey Ward and

Ken Burns, *The War, An Intimate History* (Alfred A. Knopf, 2007) pp. 339-346, which features Sascha Jansen's memories.

Chapter 36 – A Fine Fellow

"Trimm" and Sergeant Hoy Moffett: were real GIs and I've used their actual names, based Lee's letter "Lee I. and the G.I.s" letter to Francis Maher on May 10, 1945.

The GIs cautioning the internees to "get safe" in the Main Building because they had not yet secured Manila: 900 American troops were sent to liberate the camp, but they got separated en route and only 200 were there for the initial liberation, and the others followed through the night. The two-hundred referred to themselves as "the Suicide Squad" because they fully expected their own demise. (Irvine, 232)

The Ed Building hostage situation is described in many sources. Initially, American troops did not realize that internees remained in the Ed. Building (see Hartendorp, p. 408) I have Mrs. Todd informing the soldiers, and that's a fictionalized version of what Rupert Wilkinson recounts on p. 152. He credits two British women with doing it (Joan Meredith and Lorna Wilkinson).

Re: negotiations with the Japanese for hostage release, including the employment of Sergeant Kenji Uyesugi: This is all factual. For details on Uyesugi, see Rupert Wilkinson, p. 155, and see Uyesugi's own account at http://www.discovernikkei.org/en/resources/military/588/. His parents emigrated from Japan (parents opened a restaurant) , but he was born in Colusa, CA and was he one of eight kids, a senior in college when Pearl Harbor was bombed; he immediately enlisted; and had two brothers in the service, while his mother and sisters were in an American internment camp for Japanese.

The joy and horror of the night of February 3 is recounted by many internees; Sascha Jansen was particularly eloquent on the pain of watching fatally wounded GIs die in camp.

Dragging (still-alive) Abiko through the main hall, see Wilkinson, p. 151.

The incident of a Japanese guard being applauded or lauded on that night of bloodlust is true. Lee frequently recounted this story and took time to do so in her Andersonville interview, just at the end. Lee remembered the silence and then some clapping. Rupert Wilkison records the "he's a fine fellow" line (p.151). Wilkinson positions Abiko's abuse after the my "Haruo" incident. Lee always told it in the opposite order, and her feelings about this were pretty much as per the novel. She was very proud of internees in the camp at that moment.

Chapter 37 – Get Strong

Lee often recounted drinking the whole can of evaporated milk (and spending hours in the bathroom) as her first joyful, if counter-productive, return to FOOD.

Details of Abiko's demise are from Wilkinson, p. 151-152.

Details of Japanese exit from camp and resolution of the hostage crisis are from Liz Irvine, p. 233. At 7 AM the Japanese garrison was escorted by one hundred American soldiers to Calle Lepanto and released. A Life Magazine photo exists of this, and Rupert Wilkinson reproduces it on p. 156.

The GIs sitting in Hope's vegetable garden: based on her own recounting in *Nor All Your Tears*, pp. 84-85.

Chopped Ham and Eggs in twist-key can: These were included as breakfast rations in K rations. http://en.wikipedia.org/wiki/K-ration. All the internees commented on the fact that the GIs could not do enough for them, and that they were the recipients of many food gifts (chocolate bars frequently mentioned) and cigarettes.

The boy Lee is describing (Hoy Moffett) is based on her letter to Frank Maher in "Lee I. and the GIs."

Chapter 38 – Smoke on the Waters

Information about internee boy in the Ed Building waking to find a hand cradling a grenade is in Wilkinson, p. 154. Nick Balfour was the unlucky boy, but I made it Barney Brooks so as not to introduce a new character.

Service of Lt. Robert E. Lee (descendant of the Original Robert E. Lee) in the First Cavalry is accurate.

Hope's answer to the young GI about "we knew you'd come back," is in *Nor All Your Tears*, p. 101.

The easy and joyful interaction with the GIs is recorded in many sources and in Lee's letters. As for the nights singing with the GIs, see Lee Iserson, "Lee I. & the G.I.s" p.1. Lee introduces Trimm (with his guitar and "cowboy songs") and recounts all the drama that follows in the text about Lulu dumping Trimm in favor of Andy…. I speculated on the songs from Trimm and chose "San Antonio Rose" (which came out in 1940) and "Smoke on the Water" recorded in early 1944 by Red Foley. The latter was a huge hit with the GIs – thirteen weeks in the Number One spot on the charts, and is mostly about victory over Japan.

Betty calling Lee up to the stone portico to witness hanging of the flag: I don't know the circumstances that brought Lee up there, but there she was – her image captured for Life Magazine probably by Carl Mydans. See the back cover.

"Grand Old Flag," the song, was written in 1906 by George M. Cohan, but used in a movie ("Yankee Doodle Dandy") and popularized in 1942 with James Cagney in the lead.

Chapter 39 – The Second Coming

Lee's father's disparagement of MacArthur is based on fact; as mentioned at outset, she and her family did not hold him in high regard for reasons indicated in the novel; Lulu (and her family) shared Lee's assessment and Lulu's reflections in the novel (about MacArthur and her grandfather) are based on her memories as recounted to me in the oral interview of May 2010 (DM520015. WMA or pp. 2-3 of transcript). She describes most internees' opinion of him as "contemptuous." Ellen too said, "none of us were fond of MacArthur." (her oral interview 24:41, p. 9 of transcript)

MacArthur's visit to the camp on this date is factual. See J.M.Scott, *Rampage*, pp. 216-219. Mary Lou did shake hands with him, as per oral interview. There are also photos of this visit, which used to be online but have since been removed. For a brief account, see Geoffrey Ward and Ken Burns, p 346. MacArthur's assertion: "Manila has fallen!" was made on February 6, 1945 . (see https://en.wikipedia.org/?title=Battle_of_Manila_(1945), but the real battle was just about to begin. The shelling started shortly after his exit.

Agnes writing Hoy Moffett's mother about what a fine young man she had raised: true; see excerpt from her letter published in *Abilene (Texas) Reporter* May 24, 1945 and in my files.

The incident here with soldiers Hoy, Trimm, and Andy is true and based on Lee's letters to Frank Maher (Lee I and the GIs; May 10, 1945). I made up physical description for Andy (who is Sergeant Anderson) and I also don't know what his first name was; I put Andrew Anderson, to make the nickname doubly appropriate, but might not be right. Lee just refers to him "Andy and "Sergeant Anderson." Lots of the wording of Trimm's speech is taken directly from Lee's letter, as is her description of Hoy Moffett as a red-headed Texas Errol Flynn look alike and Andy as a lady-killer. The timing of this incident may have happened after the shelling, but I think I've actually got it in the right place based on Lee's letter. Some of Lulu's speech here is modeled after a silly romantic play that mom wrote about her on the ship when they were homeward bound. (in author's possession).

The Shelling (beginning February 7): by far the deadliest and most tragic day for the internees and a horror that Lee often recounted. Their movements that night and the death of Annie are recounted in a letter to Bunny Brambles, March 3, 1945. Also watch Lee's interview (with Lulu) for the Andersonville Project. Lee had lasting and vivid memories of Annie

Davis's death. I have no evidence that Betty and Annie were planning a play at the time; that was for narrative effect, and to stress the proximity of their rooms (3 & 4) – how close the Isersons came to this danger. Lulu's confusion about whether she had seen her mother during the shelling (because of the identical playsuits) is as recounted in her oral interview. Ellen's (Nellie's) location given in oral interview with Ellen. Ellen also told the story of her mother walking alongside Mrs. Brooks, and she (Ellen) not being able to figure out who was on the stretcher. (Oral interview transcript, May 2010, p. 2). Curtis and Barney Brooks lost both parents in a single month and just prior to complete freedom in liberation.

Chapter 40 – Choose Life

The setting of this first scene (on the stairs of the Main Building during the shelling) was indeed the safest place, and has been photographed. It is reprinted in Liz Irvine, p. 234.

Lee writing her letter of February 9, 1945 to Francis Maher: that letter exists and is as described i.e. on Red Cross stationery form 539A (in author's possession). The quotes are as per the letter, i.e. the powerful "I wouldn't give up this experience for ten years of my life."

The letter Lulu wrote her grandmother is real. February 8, 1945; she read it to me in her oral interview; here's part of the text (written just after the shelling): "Mommy was knocked out from artillery. But she is not injured. Only some scratches. A piece of shrapnel grazed Maureen's stomach, but so far we are in one piece. We have been going to school the whole time and I am almost graduated from third year. Since the Americans came, the Japs have been bombing us, and we have to sleep on the floor of the bathroom for protection. We applied for repatriation and expect to be with you soon. The soldiers are so nice to us; they give us all their own rations, and we girls are having the time of our lives." Incident involving death of Dr. Walter Foley is in Lee's Andersonville interview and verified by Stevens, p. 490.

Chapter 41 – Birdseye View

The slain bodies of the four Executive Committee members (Johnson and Larsen were the others) were discovered by American forces on 21 February 1945, according to Stevens, p. 483. They had been tortured and beheaded. Their bodies were returned to camp and they were buried there on February 23, 1945. (Hartendorp, 424-425.).Agnes's attack of pneumonia is documented in her letter to Ruth Hanagan on 3 March 1945. This letter also reveals Agnes's frustration at the lack of communication from her family, indicating that other internees received lots of letters but Isersons did not.

Leonore's Suite 635

Climbing the tower: Bill Phillips indicated that they were not supposed to do this, but that he occasionally was able to get the key and sneak up (see his oral interview, p. 3). This visit on this date is fictional, and a way of helping the reader see what became of Manila and how this affected the teens. I have Paul in here for narrative reasons, but Paul Davis had left five days earlier with Curtis and Barney Brooks on the first repatriation ship. See Lee to Bunny Brambles, March 3, 1945. The specific buildings and their demise are as accurate as I could make them. Many of my details came from Richard Connaughton, et al, The Battle for Manila, Chap 7 "The Unwanted Battle" as well as from You Tube interviews with American servicemen who fought in it. But the recent and definitive work on Manila's ruin in this horrible battle is James M. Scott's, *Rampage: MacArthur, Yamashita, and the Battle for Manila*. (W.W. Norton & Co., 2018). This is an outstanding book; see Chapters 14-18 for a riveting and horrifying account.

The MacArthur quotation that Bill reads ("my country kept the faith") was in a speech at Malacañang Palace on February 27, 1945, restoring the Commonwealth Government. The Tacitus is classic.

Lee lists "Deep Purple" as her favorite song in 1945. See her autograph book. (It was recorded by Guy Lombardo's orchestra in 1939).

Chapter 42 – Keepsakes

I'm having fictional fun in this chapter based on some facts. The facts: Lee and Lulu did take this wild and crazy ride to Muntinglupa with two GIs to see their liberated Los Baños friends. One of the GIs was Boyd Davis (as per the text) from New York state. See Lee Iserson to Bunny Brambles on 1 March 1945. "Dick Church" from New York is fictional, and he is there as a Richard F. Klee Sr. (Dick Klee aka Dad) stand-in. Dick's mother's maiden name was Church. The origin of this: maybe a year before his death, I was reading Dad a chapter from the (unfinished) book aloud, and he was enjoying it, and after I finished he said: "Am I in the book?" I thought he was having a Senior Moment, and I said: "Dad, you weren't at Santo Tomas." He said with a small smile: "I could be." And after he died, I decided: "Of course, you can be, Dad!" The Dick Church character is modeled on the young Dick Klee, except that the young Dick Klee wasn't married, wasn't old enough to be a soldier, and wasn't in Santo Tomas. But Lee often compared Dick's looks and dancing to Danny Kaye. So, Dad, you're in the book.

The details of the wild ride come from Lee's "Lee I and the G.I.s" letter, p. 4. If the reader would like a sense of the joy Lee and Lulu must have felt as they set off, check out the photo of jubilant Liz Lautzenhiser on her way to Muntinglupa in the army jeep, in Liz Irvine, p. 264.

Chapter 43 – Victory Rolls

The specific interview with Bunny is fictional, but I have watched other filmed interviews of Los Baños internees (including Fr. Reuter) and approximated the stage and setting. Many of the details for the extraordinary Los Baños rescue came from Bruce Henderson, *Rescue at Los Baños* (William Morrow, 2015), pp. 226-266. Paratroopers usually jump from between 1000 and 2000 feet; the extraordinarily bold decision to drop from 400 feet in order to preserve surprise and have success was very gutsy, and many internees commented on how amazed they were to be able to boys' faces as they jumped. (Henderson, p. 234.)

The Shakespeare quote is Henry VI, Part II, Act 1, Scene 1.

Sr. Olivette is a bit-player in this novel, but was a great friend of Lee's in later life. She was a Holy Cross sister, who spent one or two days at Santo Tomas, then was transferred to Los Baños where most of the religious were sent. Lee's decision to attend St. Mary's stemmed in part from knowing that Sr. Olivette would be there (as she explains later in the book). The songs cited here are factual, and I have a CD from St. Mary's archives with Sr. Olivette and a young CSC sister performing them in 1995. Fr. Reuter, S.J. was a young Jesuit and a frequent performer of these routines. He went on to be a major champion for social justice in the Philippines during the Marcos years. It was my great honor to meet and interview him one or two years before he died. There is a film clip of him being interviewed at Muntinglupa. (He was gorgeous.)

Dick sings "By the Light of the Silvery Moon;" that tune was published in 1909, and popular in Tin Pan Alley venues in the '30s and '40s; Doris Day made it popular in 1953 in a film of the same title.

Lee often reflected on how astonishing it was that Agnes had let her (and Lulu) go off with these two young GIs whom they didn't know and who probably hadn't seen American girls years. She also said that they were perfect gentlemen. It gives you a sense of the trust between the internees and the GIs.

Chapter 44 – Not Before Lunch

The thirty-six day Battle of Iwo Jima raged from Feb 19-Mar 27, 1945 and resulted in 6800 American dead and 26,000 US casualties. 19,000 Japanese died and 1083 were taken prisoner.

The girls' (sisters') conversation and Betty's reservations about going home are fictional, but accord with Betty's character and there are many recorded instances of the children of Santo Tomas having known nothing but STIC, being worried about going home. Betty's are not juvenile reservations; they accord with her sense of loss; she loved the PI and their family life there from an early age, and Lee did not.

Betty's reflections on their First Communion and Confirmation and the party afterward are based on actual events, documented in their photo album.

The story of Lee and Betty racing to the chow line to tell Agnes and her response are as per Lee Iserson, "Santo Tomas Talk," p. 13. It was their great good fortune that the Clelands (Lulu's family), Thomases (Nellie's) and Hope Miller were evacuated on the same ship as the Isersons.

Chapter 45 – Call Me Al

Most of the events in these final chapters are drawn from two main sources: (1) a long letter that Lee wrote to Francis Maher on 10 May 1945 after their return to the States, and probably from Utica (Francis at that point was in the Army), and it is composed almost like a book. (She may have imagined sending it to other friends as well.) The header is "Lee I and the G.I.s" and beneath that Chapter I – Manila (followed by three-and-a-half pages of now-typewritten text; I transcribed it and have it in digital form) and then Chapter II – Adventures on Leyte & Adm. Capps (followed by an equally long section). The typewritten text (original was in fountain pen) runs seven pages, single-spaced. (2) a charming and very silly three-page and three-act play called "The Romantic Affairs of Lulubelle and the Great Eckenboy" that Lee wrote for Lulu upon returning to the U.S. It is typewritten and mentions Lulu's return to Los Angeles. It focuses on her friend's "halo-halo" feelings about Al and Randy (both introduced in the final chapters) and based on REAL Al and Randy Eckenboy.

Lee introduces Al in her letter as "Prince Charming in the guise of Pfc. Al Burgess [who] rode up on a not quite white charger (a jeep) … and followed our truck all the way across Leyte talking to Lulu." See "Lee I and the G.I.s" p. 4. I've substituted "Jimmy Henderson" (who gives the reader the scoop on MacArthur's Leyte invasion) for Lee's "Jimmy Anderson," a 24-year-old Texan, who didn't necessarily serve with MacArthur's invading force.

The information on MacArthur is drawn from Mark Perry, *The Most Dangerous Man in America: The Making of Douglas MacArthur* (Basic Books, 2014); see p. 288 for the beach incident. An abridged version of Mac's speech is on p. 289.

Lee's letter "Lee I and the GIs" conveys their awareness of their new situation (being surrounded by sex-starved GIs, who hadn't seen a "God's honest American girl" in two years, p.5), and their decision not to do single-dating. The movie incident is part truth-part fiction. In "Lee I and the GIs"

Lee recounts making Al's life miserable when he took Lulu to the movies, but I've invented the manner of misery (linking arms around each other). I don't what movie they saw but *For Whom the Bell Tolls* (Ingrid Bergman and Gary Cooper) came out in 1943.

The initial frigid reception of internees by G.I.s on the Admiral Capps and the stats given (149 Marines re-assigned) are in "Lee I and the G.I.s" p. 5.

Information and stats on the Admiral Capps itself come from a real treasure trove of a book: the official *U.S.S. Admiral W.L. Capps –A.P.121- Cruise Book* (leather-bound, private printing for crew, in author's possession). The great flaw with the *Cruise Book* is that it has no page numbers! So I can only cite the work itself. There's some disagreement between stats (about the ship) in this book and the wiki article on the Capps re: crew size; so I did not include that number. *Cruise Book* indicates full complement of 435 (400 enlisted and 35 officers); Wiki says 619 and doesn't explain the different figure. The *Cruise Book* has a fold-out page, cut-away diagram of the ship (location of Mess Deck, laundry, bakery, infirmary, troop berthing, rec room, butcher shop, etc.) It was a floating city, and most details about the ship come directly from the book.

Lulu discussing Frank Sinatra: internee girls were puzzled over his success, which they'd learned about in Leyte. (Lee particularly thought Sinatra was a strange string-bean of an idol.) October 12, 1944, however, was known as the "Columbus Day Riot," as America's first pop star drew bobby-soxers out in force. For photo and article, see http://www.theguardian.com/music/2011/jun/11/frank-sinatra-pop-star.

Chapter 46 – The Road Less Traveled

Specific details on the Capps dining room and meals are confirmed by Sascha Weinzheimer Jansen, who returned on the same ship. See Ward and Burns, The War, pp. 382-383. In his TV special *"The War,"* Ken Burns featured Sascha as his representative and her memories are featured in the book. I had phone conversations with Sascha about the Capps years before her death, and she radiated the joy of that return.

Hope affirming New Hampshire as source of the best McIntosh apples: Hope was a Granite-Stater and was on her way back home to Sunapee, N.H. Her reflections on Robert Frost: Frost was a descendant of Granite-staters and a graduate of Dartmouth College, who made New Hampshire his focus in his 1924 Pulitzer Prize collection "New Hampshire." "Road Not Taken" was first published in 1916, but in a largely unnoticed work ("Mountain Interval"). Its republication in 1951 made it famous.

The Capps *Cruise Book* has all the details about building swings attached to a superstructure on the deck, and a photo of the playground, as well as the Captain with two little girls from Santo Tomas.

Ozzie, Mom's pal-turned-heart-throb, is described in detail in "Lee I. and the G.I.s" p. 6. The story is inspired by Lee's shipboard romance with Emmet Wellington Osborne. I don't know what his rank was – or whether he was Navy or Marine. I made him a Marine because the MPs were in charge of ship order, and he would've been leading this "sundaes for spotters" scheme. Sascha told me about the Sundae-for-Spotter scheme. There is also a funny poem written by a GI and published in the ship newspaper ("The Bull Sheet") called "A Soldier's Plea," and it's about trying to get the kids to behave on the Capps. It ends with: Now don't get me wrong, Pal, we're friends, you and me. You remind me of my boy whom I'm longing to see. But hold it, Lad, hold it! You're one up on the Japs. You're raising all HELL with the Admiral Capps!" (also reprinted in Ward and Burns, p. 382).

G.I. preparation for "King Neptune and his Court" is based on fact; it was performed on the Capps, and the *Cruise Book* has a photo of internees watching it, all smiles, with a wonderful photo of Lee and Betty together in the second row. (Upper left corner of un-numbered page).

The banter between Lee and Lulu about Al versus Randy was inspired by Lee Iserson, "The Romantic Affairs of Lulubelle." The first line of the play is "Enter Lulubelle and her conscience, otherwise known as Lee."

CHAPTER 47 - ROAR LIKE A LION

Re: ship layout -- The Capps *Cruise Book* has photos of the two-chair barber shop (located in retail store and services area on board), but the ship map does not indicate where that was, so I'm just guessing here.

King Neptune's Court and crossing the equator: this performance/ceremony was typical and is described at https://www.veteransunited.com/network/the-navys-line-crossing-ceremony-revealed. I also have a recording of a 1962 ceremony that seemed similar in the Capps CD.

Location of the rehearsal: The ship map in the *Cruise Book* shows Laundry and Rec Room in same area, hence my choices. (See left panel.) Lee's experience of the rehearsal and response are fictional. They were a way for me to help her resolve some of the horrors she's dealt with, embrace freedom, and develop the relationship with Ozzie.

"Slimy bro" - The shorthand of "bro" for brother is found in 17th and 18th century literature; the contemporary slang of "bro" was introduced in 1926 by African-American vaudeville singer Frankie "Half-Pint" Jaxon in his song "Hannah Fell in Love with My Piano," (piano pronounced "pee-anna") which contains the line "You gonna put it in my stocking, the money, bro?"

Re: the Navy diver who could stay under water for up to 8 minutes: The record for free-dive breath holding ("static apnea") is 11 minutes and 35 seconds. If divers are allowed to breathe pure oxygen before diving, the record is 20 minutes and 21 seconds.

Lulu worried about Lee's "combat exhaustion." "Combat exhaustion" was the 1940s wartime term for PTSD.

Walking the deck with Ozzie and talking about "everything" is in Lee's "Lee I and the G.I.s" letter, pp. 5-6. "We had more fun together. I didn't realize until after I started going with Ozzie how pent-up everything inside me was because then it was that I really went nuts. He told me all about the girl he was engaged to in Chicago & how he'd met her & how he was going to spend ½ his furlough in Chicago with her and ½ in Minn, with his family. In fact he'd talk so much about his Joan that I felt I'd known her all my life. And laugh. Lord, I don't know what we laughed about but we never stopped laughing. It did me an awful lot of good to be with Ozzie on that ship." His background on Saipan and participation in the battle of Hell's Pocket (which was as horrific as described) were my invention.

CHAPTER 48 – MAN OVERBOARD

Lee celebrated her seventeenth birthday on the ship, but I don't know if it was at Pearl Harbor. (The *Cruise Book* has a map of their route.)

Conversation with Betty about Utica: the last visit to Utica would have been 1934 (based on reality), not 1937. As indicated above I changed the date because I wanted Lee to have seen the Golden Gate bridge before. Betty's feelings about "cold" versus the tropics are based on fact. See Lee and Betty together for the performance of "King Neptune and his court" in the *Cruise Book* photo.

F.B.I. agents boarding the ship in Pearl and interviewing internees about possibly traitorous collaboration with the Japanese is true. See *Cruise Book* for FBI boarding. (in the paragraph to the right of the photo of Lee and Betty watching King Neptune). There is another source for this regarding their intent (finding collaborators) that I cannot come up with at this writing, and it bugs me because it's out there! (The *Cruise Book* indicates the date of the boarding as April 8, but that can't be right because the ship docked in San Francisco on April 8.)

Ozzie's quiet and melancholy referred to in Lee's letter. Her conversation with Ozzie did occur on her seventeenth birthday (complete with "he's got it bad" metaphors), as did his proposal, and her "deferral." See "Lee I and the G.I.s" letter, pp. 5-6.

Chapter 49 – The Golden Gate

Signing "Forget Me Not" books: Many of the girls had autograph and forget-me-not books, which they got the GIs and each other to sign. Lee's (red, tied with shoe-lace binding) is as described and is in author's possession. This is indeed the first line of Lulu's farewell to mom, but it's not as long as I indicated here. I invented Lee's to Nellie.

Lulu's lament about her weight and gaining a pound a day since liberation is true and as per her oral interview, p. 2.

The information on the coats they had been given by the Red Cross came from Sascha Jansen in a phone conversation.

This instance of a hotshot pilot who flew under the Golden Gate bridge is fictional, but it is based on a true incident involving Medal of Honor recipient US Army (Air Corps) pilot Maj. Richard Ira Bong in his Lockheed P-38 Lightning fighter in 1942. He and three fellow pilots looped the Golden Gate Bridge. Bong was reprimanded for such insolence and show-boating. But he was a brilliant pilot, returned to duty in Pacific, and became highest scoring air ace of World War II, shooting down at least 40 Japanese aircraft. He flew from Leyte during the Philippines campaign. Bong was known as "Ace of Aces," and one of his early flight instructors was Captain Barry Goldwater (late Senator from Arizona). He died in August 1945, when as test pilot for Lockheed (Burbank CA) the plane's fuel pump malfunctioned, the plane exploded and though he parachuted out, the chute was too low to deploy.

The Capps sailed under the Golden Gate bridge at 7:30 AM on April 8, 1945. The musical salute from the United States Army band ("Hot Time in the Old Town Tonight") is factual, and recounted by Hope Miller (along with internee impatience to get off the ship) in *Nor All Your Tears*, pp. 103-104.

Epilogue

Lee and Lulu exchanged many letters after the war, but this one is a fictional device to provide denouement and fill the reader in on what happened to whom. The details (of whereabouts of friends, etc.) are accurate to the best of my knowledge and come from sources/conversations too numerous to list.

Lee being named valedictorian at St. Francis de Sales high school is true, as well as details about the salutatorian. (Ellen Thomas was also valedictorian of her class in the U.S.) Ozzie's letter to Lee ("you were so right") is recounted in her "Lee I and the GIs" letter. I invented the date of Ozzie's wedding. Lulu recounted the episode of being dragged onto the stage of her new High School (without warning) to describe her prison experience in her oral interview. "Except for the starving and dying part, we had a really great time," was an exact quote from her in the interview, summarizing their years at STIC. (Way to go, Lulu!)

Re: Lee deciding to go to St. Mary's: Sr. Olivette was a factor, but the germ of the idea of St. Mary's College came from internment camp friend Kay Heyda. I combined two "Kays" (Kay Hodges and Kay Heyda) into a single character (Kay Hodges) for the purpose of this book. Both Kays were Room 4 residents. Kay Heyda had attended St. Mary's in the 1930s, and filled Lee's imagination with the beauty of the campus (its arcade of trees, its serenity, the loftiness of ideas taught there, Sr. Madeleva's poetry. This imagery had strong appeal for Lee in the crowded squalor of Santo Tomas. I couldn't squeeze this into the novel because Kay Heyda was not a character. AND, as late as the spring of 1945 (after the Iserson return to Utica), Lee writes about having nearly decided on Cornell for college (where Nellie went), and doesn't mention St. Mary's. She did not decide upon SMC until Spring of 1946, as per this letter.

Lee corresponded for years with the Hodges, who did return to North Carolina. She and her family stayed in touch with Hope Miller Leone, and visited Hope (and Ralph) in Sunapee in the late 1940s. Fr. Sheridan remained a life-long family friend (as did Fr. Richard McSorley, who didn't make into the novel as more than a bit player) and visited us (Klees) in Buffalo when we were growing up. Betty's decision to enter Maryknoll was very much inspired by the Maryknoll example she had in camp.

Re: Paul Davis: Lee had a stash of letters from Paul Davis (post-war) that allowed me to follow his journey, and the quotes (about school being vile, missing "cooperation" of STIC, etc; in author's posession) and weight figures are based on his very entertaining letters. Information about Ellen Thomas's college plans and the Brooks' twins are from conversations with them. Paul filled Lee in about Bill still carrying the torch for Nellie.

Lulu's father's death: Mary Lou did not learn what happened to her father, Captain Morison Cleland, Jr. until after the war. The details of his death (in a "hell ship") are as per the account from Mary Lou Cleland Hedricks. It is both true and touching that both girls' dads were lost in/near Mindanao and lie in unmarked graves.

"The Captive's Kitchen," my name for Lee's recipe book, never got published, but maybe in these days of self-publishing, I'll get it out there! It's very hard to transcribe as it was written completely in pencil (which is fading after seventy-five years) and in really, really tiny script.

The report on her weight: many of Lee's letters to Lulu and friends post-war reference her weight! Curtis Brooks is the one who told me once that when he was really hungry even now, only a can of Spam can satisfy him, and heaven knows, we Klee kids grew up with Spam at 5020 Glenwood Drive in Williamsville New York through the 1960s and early 70s.

The photo of Lee is snipped from the Utica newspaper announcing her graduation and naming her Valedictorian. Another mention is in Syracuse Herald Journal, April 21, 1946.

SELECT ANNOTATED BIBLIOGRAPHY

This is a modest bibliography of sources used in the writing of this novel. Many of my sources (letters, poems, essays) are unpublished and in the author's possession, but I will happily share digital files if contacted at klee.mb@gmail.com. For ease of use, I have divided the bibliography into published and unpublished sources.

Published

Carroll, Earl. "The Secret War of Santo Tomas," *Los Angeles Examiner,* August 18-29, 1945.
  A series of ten articles authored by Earl Carroll, summarizing internee experience with high drama.

Cates, Tressa R. *The Drainpipe Diary.* New York: Vantage Press, 1957.
  Daily diary of a nurse, who was engaged to be married in January 1942. Tressa and her fiancé were both interned at Santo Tomas. A detailed diary (hidden in a drainpipe to avoid discovery by the Japanese). There are some discrepancies in her dates compared to the Stevens' volume (for example, arrival of commandant Yoshie), and I favor Stevens. Cates edited this work post-facto, and apparently mis-dated some items. Immensely informative though.

Cogan, Frances B. *Captured. The Japanese Internment of American Civilians in the Philippines, 1941-1945.* Athens, GA: University of Georgia Press, 2000.
  A carefully researched and comprehensive look at all ten civilian internment camps in the Philippines.

Connaughton, Richard, John Pimlott, and Duncan Anderson. *The Battle for Manila.* Novat, CA: Presidio Press, 1995.
  I relied on this for Chapters 39-41 and wrote most of this novel before 2018, when James M. Scott's excellent book, *Rampage,* came out. Scott's is now the definitive work.

Dang, Donald, *Survival in Santo Tomas: A Portfolio of Sketches and Commentaries. Commemorating the 50th Anniversary, 1942-1945.* Private Edition, 1991.
  An excellent spiral-bound collection of the camp cartoonist's collection.

Farrell, Mary Cronk. *Pure Grit: How American World War II Nurses Survived Battle and Prison Camp in the Pacific.* New York: Abrams, 2014.
   Written for young adults; an outstanding overview of interned Pacific nurses.

Goldhagen, Juergen R., ed. *Manila Memories.* United Kingdom: Old Guard Press, Shearsman Books Ltd., 2008.
   Enormously useful collection of four narratives about Manila during the war by German Jewish civilian boys in Manila who were not interned because they were German. Many had been students at the American School and had friends in Santo Tomas.

Hartendorp, A.V.H. *The Santo Tomas Story.* New York: McGraw Hill, 1964.
   One of two indispensable primary sources (see Stevens for the other), this work is by journalist and designated camp historian, A.V.H. Hartendorp, who hid much of this manuscript from captors during his three years of imprisonment. The chapters are organized chronologically, but also topically: Organization of the Camp, Opening Months, Will to Democracy, Supplying the Camp, Rainy Season 1943, etc. Published nearly thirty years after liberation, this volume is drawn from a larger work by Hartendorp.

Irvine, Liz Lautzenhiser and Debbie Irvine Hammack. *Surviving the Rising Sun. My Family's Years in a Japanese POW Camp.* PILiz Publishing, 2010.
   Outstanding compendium of family war memorabilia, diary entries, chow line coupons, photos, academic "degrees" awarded, and much else, with helpful narrative thread linking them. Liz Lautzenhiser ("Lizzie" to Lee) and her family were interned at Santo Tomas, and Liz was two years older than Lee. Her father (Roscoe Lautzenhiser) was Principal of H.A. Bordner School before the war and co-principal of STIC school (with Lois Croft).

Jansen, Sascha and Angus Lorenzen, eds. *We Were There Too, Uncle.* BACEPOW, 2018.
   A rich compendium of articles that have appeared in BACEPOW newsletters over the years. "Historical Background," "Prison Camp Proiles," "Camp Life," "Health," "Fine Dining," are among the topics. Most written by internees reflecting on aspects of their experience at Santo Tomas.

Johansen, Bruce E. *So Far From Home: Manila's Santo Tomas Internment*

Camp, 1942-1945. Omaha, NE: Pine Hill Press, 1996.
A helpful, main lines overview and an easy-read.

Lorenzen, Angus. *A Lovely Little War.* Palisades, NY: History Publishing Company, 2008. Subtitled *"Life in a Japanese Prison Camp Through the Eyes of a Child,"* this vivid memoir recounts life in Santo Tomas from the perspective of an active young boy.

Maynard, Leila. "Dusty Sanctuary," in Catalogue of Rare Books, Vol. 1 (1492-1600), Appendix B. Manila: Santo Tomas University Press, 2001. Copy in author's possession.

McCall, James E. *Santo Tomas Internment Camp: STIC in Verse and Reverse: STIC-TOONS and STIC-TISTICS.* Lincoln, Nebraska: Woodruff Printing, 1945.
Lots of excellent stats in here.

Mitchell, Alex. "War Camp Mass Has Aussie Premier," in online site "Come The Revolution," on April 26, 2013. http://cometherevolution.com.au/war-camp-mass-has-aussie-premiere/
Excellent information on Mario Bakerini-Booth, Dave Harvey and original music at Santo Tomas. He does not mention Fr. Visser.

Nash, Grace C. *That We May Live.* Scottsdale, AZ: Shano Publishers, 1984.

Norman, Michael and Elizabeth Norman. *Tears in the Darkness: The Story of the Bataan Death March and its Aftermath.* New York: Farrar, Straus and Giroux, 2009.

Prising, Robin. *Manila Goodbye.* Boston: Houghton Mifflin, 1975.
The author's (heart-wrenching) account of his childhood and captivity in Santo Tomas at Holy Ghost home and in camp. Outstanding details of life in Manila during the war, as Prising's parents were outside camp.

Scott, James M. *Rampage: MacArthur, Yamashita, and the Battle of Manila.* New York: W.W. Norton, 2018.
This outstanding recent book will be the go-to for the Battle of Manila for years to come. Meticulously researched, compellingly told, and unflinchingly honest portrayal of the horrors of that battle.

Shiels, Margo Tonkin. *Bends in the Road.* Queensland, Australia: Self-Published, 1999.

Stevens, Frederic H. *Santo Tomas Internment Camp, 1942-1945.* Limited Private Edition. Stratford House, 1946.
The indispensable work by the man who initially chaired the "American Emergency Committee" before the war (to consider what to do if the Japanese conquered the Philippines), endured all three years of captivity at Santo Tomas, kept copious records, and managed to hide his work from the Japanese during camp. Stevens' detailed chronology at the end makes it invaluable.

U.S.S. Admiral W.L. Capps – A.P. 121—Cruise Book.
> A slender, leather-bound pictorial history of the Capps (Lee's repatriation ship) from 1944-1946, written and produced for crew members with great photos, wonderful details, and astonishingly little publication information (and no page numbers).

Ward, Geoffrey and Ken Burns. *The War. An Intimate History. 1941-1945.* New York: Knopf, 2007.
> The companion book for the Ken Burns television special by the same name about civilians in World War II. Several sections pertain to Santo Tomas and Burns chose Sascha Weinzheimer Jansen as his lens into the experience. Sascha led a return trip to Santo Tomas that Javier and I participated in in 2015. She was a fountain of information.

Ward, James Mace. "Legitimate Cooperation: The Administration of Santo Tomas Internment Camp and Its Histories, 1942-2003," *Pacific Historical Review,* Vol. 77, No. 2 (May 2008), pp. 159-201.
> One of the few contemporary professional historians to devote efforts to Santo Tomas. A very informative and interesting take on the interaction between internee administration and Japanese captors. (Ward was then a doctoral candidate at Stanford)

Wilkinson, Rupert. *Surviving a Japanese Internment Camp: Life and Liberation at Santo Tomas, Manila, in World War II.* Jefferson, NC: McFarland and Co., 2014.
> A recently published, highly useful overview of camp life. British scholar and ex-internee, Rupert Wilkinson (age eight at liberation, and later Professor of American Studies at the University of Sussex, UK) incorporates recent historical scholarship and internee testimony. The book is organized topically and chronologically ("War Clouds Over Eden," "Internment," "Porous Prison" "Dorms, Shanties, Sex," "Cheer Up: Everything's Going to be Lousy," "Hunger," to "They're Here" at liberation.) The appendices include a handy chronology, as well as a review of Santo Tomas literature. Some internees have questioned the accuracy of specific incidents, and some reject Wilkinson's larger interpretation, which they regard as excessively charitable to the Japanese, but this is a fine general overview for the modern reader.

Woodcock, Teedie Cowie. *Behind the Sawali: Santo Tomas in Cartoons, 1942-1945.* Greensboro, NC: Cenografix, 2000.
> A wonderful compendium of images.

Unpublished

Works written by Lee, upon which I relied, are listed under "Iserson, Leonore" if they were written prior to her marriage, and "Klee, Leonore Iserson," if written after her marriage. The reader interested in finding words and works attributable to Lulu (Mary Louella Cleland in the novel) should seek them under Hedrick, Mary Lou Cleland, and those attributable to Nellie (Ellen Thomas) can be found under Phillips, Ellen Thomas, and a manuscript by Hope Miller is under Leone, Hope Miller. All works (and many more of Lee's letters) are in the author's possession.

Brooks, Curtis. "September 21, 1944" email to Maurice Francis on 21 September 2015, and copied to STIC email group. In my files as "Curtis Brooks-Air Raid-9-21-15"
Excellent description of the first American air raid.

Davis, Paul to Lee Iserson. Sixteen letters from, 9 May 1945 to October 1, 1946, in my file, "Paul Davis to Leonore Iserson, 45-46"
Reveal Paul's cocky Cary Grant style and absolute irreverence. "School bores me to tears. After one has been accustomed to waterbombs and banana peels – spit balls & erasers seem so common place and dull." Many end "Well, old Sack, do write again soon" "Honestly, the way Bill drools over Nellie. I keep writing her & telling her to start dropping him easy, but she won't."

Hedrick, Mary Lou Cleland. "My Experiences during World War II in Prison Camps."
A three-page type-written overview of her family's experience from Cebu to Santo Tomas.

Hedrick, Mary Lou Cleland. Oral Interviews with Mary Beth Klee at her family home in Calabasas, CA. 1-4 May 2010.
Recordings and transcript in author's possession.

Iserson, Agnes. Oral interview with Mary Beth Klee at 5020 Glenwood Drive, Williamsville, NY, late 1970s. Taped and turned to CD.

Iserson, Elizabeth. "Early Years: The Philippines."
A two-page, single-spaced essay that Betty wrote in the 1970s for a creative writing class. She wrote: "When reviewing my life as a whole, I think maybe the happiest years were the early ones. My memories of growing up in the Philippine Islands are full of remembrances of happy shared family experiences, success and companionship in school, tropical beauty and lots of satisfying, imaginative playtime."

Iserson, Harold. Letter to Lee, 28 November 1941.
> Scan of a type-written letter to Lee written on this date from Zamboanga. In my digital files "Harold to Lee, 1941." Very few letters exist from Harold to the girls and Agnes.

Iserson, Leonore. "A Friend" (poem)
> Handwritten poem composed by Lee in 1942 at Santo Tomas.

_____. *Autographs.*
> A red, leather-bound volume tied with a black shoelace. A treasure-trove of information in which Lee lists all her classmates, teachers, and monikers for her friends. This was a birthday present from Lucie Tohl on April 3, 1943 (through the Package Line, I imagine).

_____. *Diary, 1942-1947.*
> A black, leather-bound diary set up to allow one page for each day of the year but multiple years on each page. Many pages are empty. I suspect that Lee did not have this in camp with her, but acquired it and filled it in upon returning to Utica. We see the same ink and penmanship for 1942 entries as for 1947, and the most closely documented year is 1946, when she graduated from high school and started at St. Mary's. Nonetheless, she has quite a few entries regarding Santo Tomas. (I digitized these.)

_____. Letter to Jane Hanagan, 14/15 February 1945. In my digital file "Leonore Iserson to Jane Hanagan from Manila, 45."

_____. Letter to Francis Maher, 28 October 1941. In my digital file "Leonore Iserson to Francis Maher from Manila, 1941-45."

_____. Letter to Francis Maher, 9 February 1945. In my digital file "Leonore Iserson to Francis Maher from Manila, 1941-45."

_____. Letter to Francis Maher, 10 February 1945. In my digital file "Leonore Iserson to Francis Maher from Manila, 1941-45."

_____. "Romantic Affairs of Lulubelle and the Great Eckenboy."
> A three-page, three act play (spoof) that Lee wrote about Lulu being torn between Al and Randy. Delightfully silly.

_____. *Recipe Book.*
> Olive green, spiral-bound notebook into which Lee copied 374 recipes, titled "The Captive's Kitchen" in novel.

Iserson Photograph Album, Manila Years, 1927-1941. In Eileen Klee Sweeney's possession.

Klee, Leonore Iserson. *Mañana Came. Memories of Growing Up as a Japanese Prisoner of War.*
> A fifteen-page manuscript that Lee began in the 1980s, and

intended as the beginning of a book, but did not finish. This manuscript is more detailed on the pre-war part of her life than her "Santo Tomas Talk," but the latter takes the reader up to liberation, whereas this concludes with the first two years of Santo Tomas.

_____. "Santo Tomas Talk."

A six-page, single-spaced text recounting of the Iserson family's time at Santo Tomas, and the basic text Lee used for speaking to community groups – which she did from 1960s to her death in 1996. This version was probably composed in the late 1980s, because it is on a computer printer print-out of that vintage (perforated edges to be torn off).

_____. and Mary Louella Cleland Hedricks. Video/DVD Interview on February 3, 1995 for Andersonville National Prisoner of War Museum. Oral Interview conducted at fiftieth anniversary of liberation reunion in Las Vegas, Nevada. (The only video of Lee and Lulu together and after fifty years!)

Leone, Hope Miller. *Nor All Your Tears.*

A typewritten, unbound manuscript that Hope produced in February 1946 upon her return to Sunapee, but typed in its present form in 1955. It is 112 pages double-spaced. Hope recorded many day-to-day incidents.

"Liberation Bulletin," a flyer printed shortly after Liberation and containing a summary of events deemed important in February 1945.

Olivette, Sr M.(Whalen), C.S.C. "Reflections on the Experience of Being a Japanese Prisoner of War in Los Banos During WWII," July 19,1993. Text and CD from the St. Mary's College Archives. In the 1990s, Sr. Olivette partnered with a younger CSC sister to do a presentation of songs and music that had kept prisoner spirits high in Los Banos. This is a treasure and all the songs in the novel come from this presentation.

Phillips, Bill. Oral Interview with Mary Beth Klee at family home in San Diego. 2 May 2010.
Recordings and transcript in author's possession.

Phillips, Ellen Thomas. Oral Interview with Mary Beth Klee at family home in San Diego. 2 May 2010. Recordings and transcript in author's possession.